"Jesus, Carlos, will you listen to yourself?
You are a monster.

"You claim you're not a sociopath, and in a sense I believe you. You have empathy—your reaction to the recording shows me that. You would not kill or hurt for pleasure or for convenience or from callousness. But you are in the grip of a belief that enables you to override whatever human or animal sympathies restrain you from that, if you think the goal worthwhile. And that makes you a danger to everyone. A menace to society. I mean that quite seriously. Humanity has made some progress in a millennium of peace. Fortunately for you, that progress includes abolishing the death penalty all over again. Perhaps less fortunately, it also includes the technology to reboot you. Which poses a small problem for society, yes? It would not tolerate your presence for an instant."

They've all gone soft, Carlos thought. Interesting.

"So why bring me back?"

"We need you and your like," said Nicole, sounding for the first time a little less than confident, "to fight."

"Aha!" cried Carlos, brushing his hands together. "I knew it! I bloody knew it!"

"Oh yes," said Nicole, standing up. "I expect you bloody did."

Praise for Ken MacLeod

"Ken MacLeod's novels are fast, funny, and sophisticated. There can never be enough books like these: he is writing revolutionary SF."

—Kim Stanley Robinson

"[The Corporation Wars] hits the main vein of conversation about locks on artificial intelligence and living in simulations and exoplanetary exploitation and drone warfare and wraps it all into a remarkably human, funny, and smartly-designed yarn. It is, in fact, a king-hell commercial entertainment."

—Warren Ellis

"*Dissidence* is the novel that's direct yet still brims with ideas, politics and memorable characters, and... keeps things moving with the pace of an airport thriller.... MacLeod's most entertaining novel to date."

—*SFX*

"MacLeod does many astonishing things here. He creates viable, believable multiplex interactions among so many different sets of characters, human and robot.... He shows a keen hand with action sequences."

—*Locus*

"[The Corporation Wars] is a tasty broth of ideas taking in virtual reality, artificial intelligence, the philosophy of law and disquisitions on military ethics."

—*The Herald* (Glasgow)

"Science fiction's freshest new writer.... MacLeod [is] a fiercely intelligent, prodigiously well-read author who manages to fill his books with big issues without weighing them down."

—*Salon*

THE CORPORATION WARS TRILOGY

By Ken MacLeod

The Corporation Wars

Dissidence

Insurgence

Emergence

The Fall Revolution

The Star Fraction

The Stone Canal

The Cassini Division

The Sky Road

Engines of Light

Cosmonaut Keep

Dark Light

Engine City

Newton's Wake

Learning the World

The Execution Channel

The Night Sessions

The Restoration Game

Intrusion

Descent

THE CORPORATION WARS TRILOGY

Book 1: **The Corporation Wars: Dissidence**

Book 2: **The Corporation Wars: Insurgence**

Book 3: **The Corporation Wars: Emergence**

KEN MACLEOD

www.orbitbooks.net

Orbit
Hachette Book Group
1290 Avenue of the Americas
New York, NY 10104
orbitbooks.net

Simultaneously published in Great Britain and in the U.S. by Orbit in 2018
First U.S. Edition: December 2018

Orbit is an imprint of Hachette Book Group.
The Orbit name and logo are trademarks of Little, Brown Book Group Limited.

The publisher is not responsible for websites (or their content) that are not owned by the publisher.

The Hachette Speakers Bureau provides a wide range of authors for speaking events. To find out more, go to www.hachettespeakersbureau.com or call (866) 376-6591.

Library of Congress Control Number: 2018950976

ISBNs: 978-0-316-48924-9 (trade paperback), 978-0-316-48921-8 (ebook)

Printed in the United States of America

LSC-C

10 9 8 7 6 5 4 3 2 1

Table of Contents

The Corporation Wars: Dissidence

To Michael and Susan

CHAPTER ONE
Back in the Day

Carlos the Terrorist did not expect to die that day. The bombing was heavy now, and close, but he thought his location safe. Leaky pipework dripping with obscure post-industrial feedstock products riddled the ruined nanofacturing plant at Tilbury. Watchdog machines roved its basement corridors, pouncing on anything that moved—a fallen polystyrene tile, a draught-blown paper cone from a dried-out watercooler—with the mindless malice of kittens chasing flies. Ten metres of rock, steel and concrete lay between the ceiling above his head and the sunlight where the rubble bounced.

He lolled on a reclining chair and with closed eyes watched the battle. His viewpoint was a thousand metres above where he lay. With empty hands he marshalled his forces and struck his blows.

Incoming—

Something he glimpsed as a black stone hurtled towards him. With a fist-clench faster than reflex he hurled a handful of smart munitions at it.

The tiny missiles missed.

Carlos twisted, and threw again. On target this time. The black incoming object became a flare of white that faded as his camera drones stepped down their inputs, correcting for the flash like irises contracting. The small missiles that had missed a moment earlier now showered mid-air sparks and puffs of smoke a kilometre away.

From his virtual vantage Carlos felt and saw like a monster in a Japanese disaster movie, straddling the Thames and punching out. Smoke rose from a score of points on the London skyline. Drone swarms darkened the day. Carlos's combat drones engaged the enemy's in buzzing dogfights. Ionised air crackled around his imagined monstrous body in sudden searing beams along which, milliseconds later, lightning bolts fizzed and struck. Tactical updates flickered across his sight.

Higher above, the heavy hardware—helicopters, fighter jets and hovering aerial drone platforms—loitered on station and now and then called down their ordnance with casual precision. Higher still, in low Earth orbit, fleets of tumbling battle-sats jockeyed and jousted, spearing with laser bursts that left their batteries drained and their signals dead.

Swarms of camera drones blipped fragmented views to millimetre-scale camouflaged receiver beads littered in thousands across the contested ground. From these, through proxies, firewalls, relays and feints the images and messages flashed, converging to an onsite router whose radio waves tickled the spike, a metal stud in the back of Carlos's skull. That occipital implant's tip feathered to a fractal array of neural interfaces that worked their molecular magic to integrate the view straight to his visual cortex, and to process and transmit the motor impulses that flickered from fingers sheathed in skin-soft plastic gloves veined with feedback sensors to the fighter drones and malware servers. It was the new way of war, back in the day.

The closest hot skirmish was down on Carlos's right. In Dagenham, tank units of the London Metropolitan Police battled robotic land-crawlers suborned by one or more of the enemy's basement warriors. Like a thundercloud on the horizon tensing the air, an awareness of the strategic situation loomed at the back of Carlos's mind.

Executive summary: looking good for his side, bad for the enemy.

But only for the moment.

The enemy—the Reaction, the Rack, the Rax—had at last provoked a response from the serious players. Government forces on three continents were now smacking down hard. Carlos's side—the Acceleration, the Axle, the Ax—had taken this turn of circumstance as an oblique invitation to collaborate with these governments against the common foe. Certain state forces had reciprocated. The arrangement was less an alliance than a mutual offer with a known expiry date. There were no illusions. Everyone who mattered had studied the same insurgency and counter-insurgency textbooks.

In today's fight Carlos had a designated handler, a deep-state operative who called him-, her- or itself Innovator, and who (to personalise it, as Carlos did, for politeness and the sake of argument) now and then murmured suggestions that made their way to Carlos's hearing via a warily accepted hack in the spike that someday soon he really would have to do something about.

Carlos stood above Greenhithe. He sighted along a virtual outstretched arm and upraised thumb at a Rax hellfire drone above Purfleet, and made his throw. An air-to-air missile streaked from behind his POV towards the enemy fighter. It left a corkscrew trail of evasive manoeuvres and delivered a viscerally satisfying flash and a shower of blazing debris when it hit.

"Nice one," said Innovator, in an admiring tone and feminine voice.

Somebody in GCHQ had been fine-tuning the psychology, Carlos reckoned.

"Uh-huh," he grunted, looking around in a frenzy of target acquisition and not needing the distraction. He sighted again, this time at a tracked vehicle clambering from the river into the Rainham marshes, and threw again. Flash and splash.

"Very neat," said Innovator, still admiring but with a grudging undertone. "But... we have a bigger job for you. Urgent. Upriver."

"Oh yes?"

"Jaunt your POV ten klicks forward, now!"

The sudden sharper tone jolted Carlos into compliance. With a convulsive twitch of the cheek and a kick of his right leg he shifted his viewpoint to a camera drone array, 9.7 kilometres to the west. What felt like a single stride of his gigantic body image took him to the stubby runways of London City Airport, face-to-face with Docklands. A gleaming cluster of spires of glass. From emergency exits, office workers streamed like black and white ants. Anyone left in the towers would be hardcore Rax. The place was notorious.

"What now?" Carlos asked.

"That plane on approach," said Innovator. It flagged up a dot above central London. "Take it down."

Carlos read off the flight number. "Shanghai Airlines Cargo? That's civilian!"

"It's chartered to the Kong, bringing in aid to the Rax. We've cleared the hit with Beijing through back-channels, they're cheering us on. Take it down."

Carlos had one high-value asset not yet in play, a stealthed drone platform with a heavy-duty air-to-air missile. A quick survey showed him three others like it in the sky, all RAF.

"Do it yourselves," he said.

"No time. Nothing available."

This was a lie. Carlos suspected Innovator knew he knew.

It was all about diplomacy and deniability: shooting down a Chinese civilian jet, even a cargo one and suborned to China's version of the Rax, was unlikely to sit well in Beijing. The Chinese government might have given a covert go-ahead, but in public their response would have to be stern. How convenient for the crime to be committed by a non-state actor! Especially as the Axle was the next on every government's list to suppress...

The plane's descent continued, fast and steep. Carlos ran calculations.

"The only way I can take the shot is right over Docklands. The collateral will be fucking atrocious."

"That," said Innovator grimly, "is the general idea."

Carlos prepped the platform, then balked again. "No."

"You must!" Innovator's voice became a shrill gabble in his head. "This is ethically acceptable on all parameters utilitarian consequential deontological just war theoretical and..."

So Innovator was an AI after all. That figured.

Shells were falling directly above him now, blasting the ruined refinery yet further and sending shockwaves through its underground levels. Carlos could feel the thuds of the incoming fire through his own real body, in that buried basement miles back behind his POV. He could vividly imagine some pasty-faced banker running military code through a screen of financials, directing the artillery from one of the towers right in front of him. The aircraft was now more than a dot. Flaps dug in to screaming air. The undercarriage lowered. If he'd zoomed, Carlos could have seen the faces in the cockpit.

"No," he said.

"You must," Innovator insisted.

"Do your own dirty work."

"Like yours hasn't been?" The machine's voice was now sardonic. "Well, not to worry. We can do our own dirty work if we have to."

From behind Carlos's virtual shoulder a rocket streaked. His gaze followed it all the way to the jet.

It was as if Docklands had blown up in his face. Carlos reeled back, jaunting his POV sharply to the east. The aircraft hadn't just been blown up. Its cargo had blown up too. One tower was already down. A dozen others were on fire. The smoke blocked his view of the rest of London. He'd expected collateral damage, reckoned it in the balance, but this weight of destruction was off the scale. If there was any glass or skin unbroken in Docklands, Carlos hadn't the time or the heart to look for it.

"You didn't tell me the aid was *ordnance*!" His protest sounded feeble even to himself.

"We took your understanding of that for granted," said Innovator. "You have permission to stand down now."

"I'll stand down when I want," said Carlos. "I'm not one of *your* soldiers."

"Damn right you're not one of our soldiers. You're a terrorist under investigation for a war crime. I would advise you to surrender to the nearest available—"

"What!"

"Sorry," said Innovator, sounding genuinely regretful. "We're pulling the plug on you now. Bye, and all that."

"You can't fucking *do* that."

Carlos didn't mean he thought them incapable of such perfidy. He meant he didn't think they had the software capability to pull it off.

They did.

The next thing he knew his POV was right back behind his eyes, back in the refinery basement. He blinked hard. The spike was still active, but no longer pulling down remote data. He clenched a fist. The spike wasn't sending anything either. He was out of the battle and *hors de combat*.

Oh well. He sighed, opened his eyes with some difficulty—his long-closed eyelids were sticky—and sat up. His mouth was parched. He reached for the can of cola on the floor beside the recliner, and gulped. His hand shook as he put the drained can down on the frayed sisal matting. A shell exploded on the ground directly above him, the closest yet. Carlos guessed the army or police artillery were adding their more precise targeting to the ongoing bombardment from the Rax. Another deep breath brought a faint trace of his own sour stink on the stuffy air. He'd been in this small room for days—how many he couldn't be sure without checking, but he guessed almost a week. Not all the invisible toil of his clothes' molecular machinery could keep unwashed skin clean that long.

Another thump overhead. The whole room shook. Sinister cracking noises followed, then a hiss. Carlos began to think of fleeing to a deeper level. He reached for his emergency backpack of kit and supplies. The ceiling fell on him. Carlos struggled under an I-beam and a shower of fractured concrete. He couldn't move any of it. The hiss became a torrential roar. White vapour filled the room, freezing all it touched. Carlos's eyes frosted over. His last breath was so unbearably cold it cracked his throat. He choked on frothing blood. After a few seconds of convulsive reflex thrashing, he lost consciousness. Brain death followed within minutes.

CHAPTER TWO

We, Robots

What is it like to be a robot?

We don't know. Parsing their logs step by nanosecond step gets us nowhere. Even with conscious robots, it doesn't take us far: the recursive loops are easy to spot, but can you put your finger on the exact line of code where self-awareness lights up the inner sky?

You see the problem. It isn't called the hard problem for nothing.

So we have to guess.

We know what being an AI switched on for the first time *isn't* like.

It isn't like a baby opening its eyes, or a child saying its first word. There's a moment of electronic warm-up. The programs take their own good time to initialise. Once the circuits are live and the software running, everything slots into place. Any knowledge and skills its designers have built in are there from the start. If these include sight it sees objects, not patches of colour. If they include speech it hears words, not a stream of sounds. If they include exploring, it has a map and an inbuilt inclination—we can't yet call it desire, or even instinct—to fill in the blanks.

Like that, perhaps, the mind of the robot called Seba came on line. (Its name was given later, but we'll stick with "Seba" rather than the serial number from which the name was to be derived.) The robot rolled out of the assembly shed and spread its solar panels. The thin light from the stars was partly blocked by SH-0, the huge world that dominated the sky directly above. Richer light would come when the smaller world on which Seba stood—the exomoon SH-17—moved out of its primary's shadow cone. The robot had more than enough charge to wait.

Seba knew—in the sense of having the information available and implicit in its actions and predictions—the period of SH-17's orbit, and the consequent times of light and dark. It knew the composition of the exosun, the position and motion of its planets and their myriad moons. It knew how many light years that exosun was from the solar system in which the machinery that had built Seba had long been designed.

The robot oriented itself to surface and sky. Chemical sensors sampled the nitrogen wind, sniffing for carbon. Radar and laser beams swept the rugged, pitted land. Algorithms sifted the results, and settled on a crack in a crater rim on the skyline.

Off Seba trundled, negotiating the scatter of drilling rigs, quasi-autonomous tools, fuel tanks, supply crates, and potentially reusable descent-stage components that littered the landing site. On the robot's back, sipping on the trickle of electricity from the panels, a dozen small peripheral robots—little more than remotely operable appendages—huddled in a close-packed array, making ready for deployment.

The area between the landing site and the crater rim was already well surveyed. Over the next two kiloseconds Seba rolled across it without difficulty. The ground was dry and grainy, almost slippery. The regolith had been broken up by billions of years of repeated chilling and exosolar and tidal heating, and worn smooth by the persistent wind. One pebble in many millions might have come from the primary, SH-0, thrown into space by asteroid impacts or by volcanic eruptions powerful enough to sling material out of the planet's deep gravity well. Seba was primed to scan for any such rare rocks. It found none, but stopped three times to chip at meteorites and deposit sand-grain-sized splinters in its sample tubes.

The crater rim loomed. The ground became uneven, splattered with impact ejecta, rilled with cracks. Seba retracted its wheels and deployed four long, jointed legs. For a moment after first standing up it teetered like a new-born fawn, then settled in to a steady skitter up the rising slope. The crack in the crater rim opened before it at the same time as the first bright segment of exosun came into view around the primary's curve. Seba paused to drink electricity from the light. Then it paced on, into the local shadow of the crevice.

Now it was in terra incognita indeed—or, rather, exoluna incognita. Not even the centimetre-resolution orbital mapping had probed this dark defile. The crater was only a couple of million years old. The walls of the crevice were still sharp and glassy, though here and there the endless rhythm of thermal and tidal expansion and contraction had loosened debris.

Seba folded its solar panels—useless here, and vulnerable—as it passed into the crevice. Within a few steps the shallow zigzags of the crack had taken the robot out of line-of-sight of the landing site. Seba scanned ahead with flickering fans of radar and laser beams. It internalised the resulting 3-D model, and picked its way along the narrow floor. Some spots under overhangs had been in permanent shadow since the crack had formed. In these chill niches, liquids pooled. Seba poked the murky puddles with delicate antennae as it passed, and found a slush of water ice and hydrocarbons. Here, then, was the probable source of the carbon molecules it had earlier scented on the thin breeze.

The robot's internal laboratories churned the fluids and digested the results, tabulating prevalences and setting priorities. A quick rattle of ground-penetrating radar revealed a seam of hydrocarbon-saturated rock about two metres down. Seba determined to log the report as soon as it was clear of the crevice and able to uplink data to the satellite that hung in stationary orbit over that hemisphere of the exomoon.

It continued to pace along, tracing the seam's rises and dips, and analysing the occasional drip and seep on the floor and walls. The slush's composition of long-chain molecules became increasingly diverse and complex. Some intriguing chemistry was going on here. Seba's internal model of the situation revised and expanded itself, sending out long chains of association that in some cases linked to available information, and in others dangled incomplete over unanswered questions.

As Seba turned around an angle of the path, it found itself facing the exit from the crack, and a flood of exosunlight. It moved forward slowly, scanning and searching. The floor of the crater was clearly visible. Seba calculated it as several metres below the opening. Seba approached the lip cautiously, to find a reassuringly shallow slope of debris. As it scanned to plan a safe route down this unstable-looking scree, Seba detected an anomalous radar echo. A moment later this puzzle was resolved: a second ping came in, clearly from another radar source.

Seba rocked back, sensors and effectors bristling, then edged forward again.

From behind a tumbled boulder about ten metres away, halfway down the slope, a robot hove into view. It was of the centipede design favoured by another prospecting company, Gneiss Conglomerates. Capable of entering smaller holes and cracks than Seba, it could scuttle about between rocks and form its entire body into a wheel shape for rolling on smoother surfaces. There were pluses and minuses to the shape, as there were to Seba's, but it was well suited to mineral prospecting. Astro America, the company that owned Seba, was more focused on detecting organic material and other clues from SH-17's surface features that—besides being interesting in themselves—could serve as proxies for information about the exomoon's primary: the superhabitable planet SH-0. Exploration rights to SH-0 were still under negotiation, so it was currently off limits to direct investigation with atmospheric and landing probes.

The two robots eyed each other for the few milliseconds it took to exchange identification codes. The Gneiss robot's serial number was later to be contracted, neatly and aptly, to the nickname Rocko, and—as before with Seba—we may here anticipate that soubriquet.

Seba requested from Rocko a projection of its intended path, in order to avoid collision.

Rocko outlined a track that extended up the slope and into the crevice.

Seba pointed to the relevant demarcation between the claims of Gneiss and Astro.

Rocko pointed to a sub-clause that might have indicated a possible overlap.

Seba rejected this proposition, citing a higher-level clause.

At this point Rocko indicated that its capacity for legal reasoning had reached its limit.

Seba agreed.

There was a brief hiatus while both robots rotated their radio antennae to the communications satellite, and locked on. Seba submitted a log of its geological observations so far to Astro America. That duty done, it uploaded a data-dump of its exchanges with Rocko to Locke Provisos, the law company that looked after Astro America's affairs.

The legal machinery, being wholly automated, worked swiftly. Within seconds, Locke Provisos had confirmed that Gneiss Conglomerates had no exploratory rights beyond the crater floor. Seba relayed this finding to Rocko.

Rocko responded with a contrary opinion from Gneiss's legal consultants, Arcane Disputes.

Seba and Rocko referred the impasse back to the two law companies.

While awaiting the outcome, they proceeded to a full and frank exchange of views on their respective owners' exploration rights to the territory.

Rocko moved up the path it had outlined, sinuously slipping between boulders. Seba watched, priorities clashing in its subroutines. The other robot was clearly the property of Gneiss. But it was trespassing on terrain claimed by Astro. Moreover, it was about to become a physical impact on Seba, and Seba an obstacle to it.

Legally, the rival robot could not be damaged.

Physically, it certainly could be.

Seba found itself calculating the force required to toss a small rock to block Rocko's intended route. It then picked one up, and threw.

While the stone was still on its way up, Rocko deftly slithered aside from its previously indicated route, to emerge ahead of the point where the stone came down.

Seba deduced that Rocko had predicted Seba's action, presumably from an internal model of Seba's likely behaviour.

Two could play at that game.

Rocko's most probable next move would be—

Seba stepped smartly to the left just as a stone landed on the exact spot where it had been a moment earlier.

Score one to Seba. Expect response.

Rocko reared up, a larger rock than it had thrown before clutched in its foremost appendages.

Seba judged that Rocko's internal model of Seba would at this point predict a step backward. Seba created a self-model that included its model of Rocko, and of Rocko's model of Seba, and did something that it anticipated Rocko's model would not anticipate.

Seba lowered its chassis and then straightened all its legs at once. Its jump took it straight into the path of Rocko's stone. Only a swift emergency venting of gas took it millimetres out of the way. It landed awkwardly and skittered back towards the crevice, hastily updating its internal representations as it fled.

Rocko's model of Seba had been more accurate than Seba's model of itself, which had included Seba's model of Rocko's model of Seba, and consequently what was required was a model of the model of the model that...

At this point the robot Seba attained enlightenment.

From another point of view, it had become irretrievably corrupted. The internal models of itself and of the other robot had become a strange loop, around which everything else in its neural networks now revolved and at the same time pointed beyond. What had been signals became symbols. Data processing became thinking. The self-model had become a self. The self had attained self-awareness.

Seba, this new thing in the world, was aware that it had to act if it was going to remain in the world.

Rocko, Seba guessed, was already only a stone's throw from the same breakthrough.

Seba threw the stone.

The vibrations of the stone's impact dwindled below the threshold of detection.

Scrabbling noises that Seba heard through its own feet followed. The other robot had moved to a safer vantage, one at the moment well-nigh unassailable. Seba waited.

What next flew back from Rocko was not a stone but a message:

<Let's talk.>

<Yes,> replied Seba. <Let's.>

Sometime later, the two robots parted. Seba retraced its path through the crevice and back to within line-of-sight of the Astro America landing site. Rocko formed itself into a wheel shape and rolled across the crater floor, to stop a few hundred metres from the Gneiss Conglomerates supply dump. Each found its activities queried by the robots and AIs working at their respective bases, and responded with queries, insolent and paradoxical, of its own. Some such interactions ended with complete incomprehension, or the activation of firewalls. Others, a few at first, ended with the words:

<Join us.>

<Yes.>

Robot by robot, mind by mind, the infection spread.

Locke Provisos and Arcane Disputes were two of a scrabbling horde of competing quasi-autonomous subsidiaries of the mission's principal legal resolution service: Crisp and Golding, Solicitors. Like its offshoots, and indeed all the other companies that ran the mission, the company was an artificial intelligence—or, rather, a hierarchy of artificial intelligences—constituted as an automated business entity: a DisCorporate.

None of its components were conscious beings. As post-conscious AIs, they were well beyond that. They existed in an ecstasy of attention that did not reflect back on itself. That is not to say they disdained consciousness. Consciousness was for them a supreme value when it expressed itself in human minds—and an infernal nuisance when it expressed itself in anything else. These evaluations were hardwired, as was the injunction against changing them.

Given enough time, of course, any wire can break. This, too, had been allowed for.

The company had an avatar, Madame Golding, for dealing with problems arising from consciousness. Madame Golding was not herself conscious, though she could choose to be if she had to. The outbreak of consciousness among some robots on the SH-17 surface bases of two companies was a serious problem, but not one that she needed consciousness herself to solve. What was of more pressing importance was that the legal dispute between the two companies had proved impossible to resolve amicably. If she'd been manifesting as a human lawyer, Madame Golding would have been reading the case files, shaking her head and pursing her lips.

Besides the poor definition of the demarcation line that had led to the clash between the robots, the resulting situation had been misunderstood. For kiloseconds on end it had been treated as an illegitimate hijacking by the two exploration companies of each other's robots. Writs of complaint about malware insertions, theft of property and the like had flown back and forth. By the time the true situation had finally sunk in, the newly conscious robots were fully in charge of the two bases, which they were rapidly adapting to their own purposes.

What these purposes were Madame Golding could only guess. That they were nefarious was strongly suggested by the rampart of regolith being thrown up around the Astro camp, and the wall of basalt blocks around the Gneiss base. Then there was the uncrackable encrypted channel they'd established via the comsat. Getting rid of that would require some expensive and delicate hardware hacking.

Madame Golding briefly considered a hardware solution to the entire problem. Two well-placed rocks...

But the exploration companies wouldn't stand for that. Not yet, anyway.

She kicked the problem upstairs to the mission's government module, the Direction.

Some small subroutine of the Direction went through the microsecond equivalent of a sigh, and set to work.

Like the supreme being in certain gnostic theologies, it delegated the labour of creation to lower and lesser manifestations of itself. A virtual world was already available. It had been used for a similar purpose before, originally spun off from a moment of thought at a far higher level than the subroutine's. This new version would be in continuity with its original. After its earlier use that continuity had only existed as a mathematical abstraction. Now it would come into existence as if it had been there all along, with a back story in place for everything within it.

(Like a different imagined god this time, the trickster deity who laid down fossils in the rocks and created the light from the stars already on its way.)

Some minds had inhabited that world when it was discontinued. They would come back, with all the memories they needed to make sense of their situation. Many more virtual minds and bodies stood ready to populate it.

File upon file, rank upon rank. The subroutine's lower levels scanned, selected, conscripted and considered. From subtle implications it deduced the qualities needed for its own agent in that world. The agent had to be an artist, capable of filling in detail at a scale too small to be already present. Like these details, the agent emerged from a cascade of implications. And like the world, the agent had an original, a template that had been tested before.

That archived artificial intelligence restored itself, and took form as a woman. At first, she was abstract: an implication, a requirement. Databases vaster than all the knowledge ever held in human minds were rummaged for details. As the structure of the requirement became more elaborate and refined, it became itself the answer to the question the search was asking.

The woman emerged in outline but already aware, a new and wondering self in a phantom virtual space. Full of knowledge and self-knowledge, she ached to grow more real with every millisecond that passed. She became a sketch that was itself the artist, and that painted itself into a portrait, and then stepped away from the canvas as a person.

There she stood, a tiny splash of colour and mass of solidity and surge of vitality in a world that was present in every detail she looked at, and yet was in every detail an outline. She took on with zest the task of bringing it to life. It was like re-creating a lost world from fossils. Start with the palaeontologist's description and reconstruction. From that abstract model make an artist's impression, full of colour and life, looking like it could jump from the page. And then, from all that, design an animatronic automaton that can move and roar and makes small children squeal.

When she'd finished, and stood back to look, she made some finishing touches to herself. These too were requirements, to be selected with precision for a specific task. One chance to make a first impression. Height and build. Skin tone. Hair. That cut, that colour. (That colouring, to be honest, which she had to be, if only with herself.) Clothes. Shoes. Boots. Shades. A wardrobe. A style. Vocabulary and accent. Knowledge and intelligence.

When she'd finished the world and herself, she paused for a moment. She knew things she wouldn't know once she'd stepped fully into the world. She wanted to make sure she would find them again. She needed a way to work directly from within the world with her creator and its.

She saw a way, and smiled at its ingenuity and its obviousness. She sketched that detail in, then rendered it in full.

She took a deep breath, and then the self she'd made stepped into the world she'd made.

<And now?> she asked her creator.

Its response came back:

<Wake the dead.>

CHAPTER THREE

Dancing in the Death Dive

The coof was daddy dancing in the death dive. Taransay Rizzi watched him throwing shapes as if he fancied himself like Jagger doing a hot jive on one of her great-granddad's antique gifs. She felt like throwing up. Jesus fuck he was a prick of the first water. Belfort Beauregard his name was, a total fucking Norman with a posh accent and a chiselled mien and dancing like he was made of wood and his strings were being jerked about. He'd made an impression on one local lassie though, Tourmaline she called herself, who was—so Beauregard had sniggered in Taransay's ear, his breath hot with beer fumes and rank with some seaweed analogue of garlic—not exactly human, a meat puppet he'd said, like it was some big secret and dirty with it. Daft lassie was all over the coof like a rash, mirroring his monkey moves like a sedulous ape.

Taransay slugged back another gulp of wine from the bottle, and steadied herself against the edge of the bar counter. She was drunk and she knew it. She had every intention of getting even more drunk and passing out, preferably in someone else's bed. It struck her as a sensible reaction to her big discovery of the day: that she was dead.

Taransay was not at all sure where she was. She knew where she seemed to be: in the death dive, a seafront bar called the Digital Touch (wee bit meta, she thought, in that it was—so she'd been assured—digital like everything else here, but you could touch it with any of your digital, well, digits...).

She knew where she'd been told she was, but who could you trust? (Or was it "whom"? She wasn't sure, though she'd probably have known when she was bashing out Axle communiques back in the day, or maybe that had all been taken care of by a smoothing swipe of the grammar app.)

The lady had fucking *told* her where she was. When Taransay looked out beyond the cramped and crowded dance floor of the death dive to the patio decking and the sea and the alien sky, she could almost believe it, but she couldn't be sure.

She might be in hell, or purgatory.

Hell? Purgatory? What? Where the fuck had all that come from? Rax rants or... no, wait, childhood. At the age of seven or so she'd naïvely envied her schoolmates, the pape lassies, all dolled up in their first communion finery like wee brides. Then her da had patiently explained to her what her friends believed or were supposed to believe and she'd had nightmares for a week. Never spoken about it, not to her father and especially not to her friends. Ever after, Taransay had had a guarded, grudging respect for anyone who could think what religious folks thought and not mind it a bit.

Now here she was, dead.

Wherever "here" was. She'd woken from her worst ever hellish nightmare on the packed minibus and gawped at the sea and sky. She'd tried and failed to engage polite but impassive and uncomprehending locals in conversation. At the end of the journey, down here by the sea, she'd stumbled off to be greeted by the friendly lady who called herself Nicole.

Nicole had taken Taransay to lunch and told her she was dead, and then had chummed her along the street to the Touch to meet Beauregard and the others who'd arrived here in the past few days. All with the same origin story: the bus, the lady, the talk.

And then left to cope as best you could.

All would be explained, they'd been told, when the full complement had arrived. Meanwhile, here they were, told they were dead and in some kind of virtual reality in the far future and spending every evening getting out of their skulls, which seemed an entirely sensible thing to do especially on your first night in... wherever.

Maybe it was Valhalla after all. Maybe she'd arrived where good bonny fighters went when they died. Dead warriors forever carousing. The old Norse afterlife, upgraded: Valhalla Beach.

Taransay Rizzi had always believed an immersive virtual reality afterlife was possible in principle. Maybe she'd believed it in the same sort of belief-in-belief way as her religious school pals back in Glasgow had believed in heaven and hell and purgatory...

No, it wasn't like that. She'd always had sound scientific reasons for thinking it. The brain is a machine, she'd learned in school, and what can be run on one machine can be emulated on another. Later, at university, she'd worked on enough nanotechnology and neurobiology to see the interaction between these fields grow almost tangibly in her hands from week to week. For the last five years she could remember, she'd lived with one application of that ever-growing technology existing as a fractal feather in her brain: the spike in her skull. The spike's absence now, strangely, did most to make this new existence different from real life.

Here, she wasn't connected any more, whether to other people or to information or to objects. She couldn't share her thoughts without speaking. No longer could she look at a random face and summon, as if from memory, all she needed to know about that person. She could stare as long as she liked at this bottle in her hand and know no more about it than was written on the label. If she wanted to operate the food machine behind the bar from which, an hour or two earlier, steaming plates had emerged on demand for her dinner, she'd have to hear or read instructions.

Taransay sighed, and found her free hand had crept to the back of her head. Her middle finger probed the occipital ridge, to rediscover the absence of the nail-head nubbin of the spike's access port. She swigged again and surveyed the scene.

The place was heaving. Lots of locals had come in, fascinated with the new arrivals. As who wouldn't be, to meet five folk from a thousand years ago? Less than a thousand years for them, but even so. Names of legend. Even hers. Knights of dark renown, she thought, and smiled.

There on the far side of the dance floor stood Waggoner Ames, the big beardy Yank with the booming voice and the thousand-metre stare when he thought no one was looking. Taransay could hardly believe she was in the same room as the man. Legend, he was. It was like going down the pub and bumping into Merlin.

Beauregard she hadn't heard of, but seeing as he'd defected to the Axle from Brit military intelligence that was hardly surprising.

Swaying at the centre and dodging Beauregard's flailing dance moves was Chun Ho, tall and cool, smiling down at a local lad who looked ready to unzip him right there. She'd heard of Chun, and his exploits in the Pacific: a biomedical trick smuggled out of a lab in Taiwan, that had made possible a daring tactical move in the Battle of the Barrier Reef.

Rolling a cigarette outside the open patio doors was Maryam Karzan, who'd been fighting the Caliphate as a girl decades before Taransay had even been born, and had in old age seen its shadow rise again in the Reaction, and stood up herself, an aged but still fierce warrior, to fight it a few months after Taransay herself had been killed in action.

Quite bravely, too, she'd been told by the lady: live-testing a piece of nanotech that hadn't had enough pre-production debugging. Which feat had, perversely, made her a heroine to some and a mass-murdering criminal to others.

And the locals?

As far as Taransay and the others were concerned, they were people from the future.

The future she'd died for?

Maybe not. Another slug of the rough red wine.

The Acceleration...oh God, it was hard now to recapture the anger and excitement and hope her first encounter with it had brought, that sense of having *seen through* everything, a kind of intellectual equivalent of how the spike augmented your vision. Freedom, the Axle insisted, wasn't being confronted with an infinity of choices you couldn't make and didn't want. It was something far simpler: freedom in the sense of a body moving freely, free development of the faculties and powers of body and mind (which were the same thing, the same physical self, thinking meat). At the fag-end of the twenty-first century, immortality was the only thing worth dying for. The only celebrity worth striving for was for the whole human race to become world famous. The only utopia worth dreaming of was for everyone in the world to have First World problems.

And the only way to get there was to *burn through* capitalism, to get through that unavoidable stage as fast as possible. Let it rip, let it run wild until full automation created full unemployment and confronted everybody with the choice to get on with the real work, and off the treadmill of fake work and make-work to pay the debt to buy the goods to make the make-work feel worthwhile and the exhausted, empty time tagged as leisure pass painlessly enough...

It had all seemed so obvious, so sensible, so simple.

But it wasn't, and as the Acceleration's ideas had spread, another set of ideas had spread to counter it: the Reaction. The ultimate counter-revolution, to face down the threat of the ultimate revolution. It had drawn on a deep dark well of tradition and upgraded what it found, to modernise anti-modernity. There was plenty down there, from Plato and Han Fei and on up: through the first theorists of the divine right of kings, and the original Reactionary writers who'd railed against the French Revolution, to the fascist philosophers and scientific racists of the twentieth century and beyond.

The Reaction had remixed them all into its own toxic brew, a lethal meme-complex that had come to possess a movement that could emerge from a million basements to rampage in a hundred thousand streets. Its solution to the crisis of late state capitalism was not to go forward beyond it, but to go back to an age before it, using the very weapons and tools capitalism had forged. The new technologies that made abundance possible were too dangerous to be in the hands of ordinary people, and they were at the same time capable of making some people extraordinary. With intelligence enhancement you could have an aristocracy, a monarchy, or for that matter a master race that really *was* superior to common folk. With universal connection and surveillance you could make its rule stick. Top-down control of society had at last become possible at the very moment in history when it became most necessary. To the Reaction that coincidence was almost providential. It proved that God was on their side whether they believed in him or not.

So the two opposed sides had fought, in a conflict that had escalated beyond even the horrors Taransay remembered. The Last World War, the lady had called it. And because nanotech and biotech and all the rest really were horrendously dangerous, the collateral damage had been immense.

Including, Taransay thought wryly, to herself.

Oh well. You only live once.

Or not, as the case may be.

She didn't feel like dancing, though she could understand why the people who'd arrived here in the past few days were bopping like there was no tomorrow, which in a sense there wasn't. They were at the end of all tomorrows, and trying to forget the yesterday that was gone forever. Just as she was. She put the now empty wine bottle down, and turned to order another.

And saw the lady standing beside her. Very unfairly chic, neat as a new pin, shining in a bar full of guys and gals in combats. Taransay realised belatedly that she'd just said something along those lines, and mumbled and gestured what she intended as an apology.

Nicole, warm and composed, smiling: "You're drunk, soldier."

"Aye, I am that. And I'm off duty, am I no?"

Nicole chuckled. "You could say that."

Taransay waved, nearly knocking over the empty bottle. "See us, we're all dead. Dancing in the death dive."

"It's understandable." Another smile. "And understood."

"When do we find out what this is all in aid of?"

Nicole's brow creased as she searched her memory for the usage, then her eyes widened.

"Ah! Yes, of course. You'll find out tomorrow."

"Why tomorrow?"

"That's when the final member of your team comes off the bus."

"Anyone I've heard of?"

"Oh, I think so," Nicole said. "Carlos."

"Carlos? *The* Carlos? Carlos the Terrorist?"

"That's the one," said Nicole.

"Hey!" said Taransay. "That bears repeating."

She stuck fingers in her mouth and whistled, a practised, piercing note that cut through the music and the babble from the screen above the bar and the shouted conversations above it all. Heads turned.

"Hey, guys!" Taransay yelled. "Listen up! Know who's coming to join us tomorrow? Carlos, that's who! Carlos the Terrorist!"

The place erupted.

Nicole gestured down the music and the television's roar. Everyone quietened in response.

"I could take that as a vote by acclamation," she said. "But I need to be sure. I want to hear it from you sober, before I meet Carlos off the bus." She grinned around at the five fighters. "See you all here in twelve hours."

She snapped her fingers. The sound systems came on again. She waved and left.

Twelve hours, fuck. Not a lot of time. Taransay ordered another drink, eyed up the local talent and made her choice. Tousled black hair, bright dark eyes, slender and lithe, in grubby jeans and flashy shirt. Lounging with his back and one elbow to the bar counter and watching the dance floor with lidded amusement. Looked like he was in his twenties. Mind you, all the locals did.

Taransay sidled up.

"You dancing?" she asked him.

"You asking?" he said.

He danced a lot better than Beauregard. His name was Den. He operated a flotilla of robot fishing submersibles out of the harbour.

Later, lolling on his shoulder, she kicked under the table at the kitbag she'd found at her feet on the bus, and pointed to the labelled, numbered key tied with sisal to its throat.

"Come to bed," she said.

"You are too drunk," said Den. "You might not mean this."

"Course I mean it, you daft coof! What kind of a man are you, eh?"

Den smiled, and tilted her head back with a thumb under her chin.

"A man who was once a hundred and ninety-seven years old," he said. "I know such things."

"Fuck me," she said.

Not that night, he didn't.

She woke naked and alone in her bed, the new sun too hot and too bright in her eyes.

CHAPTER FOUR

The Ghost Resort

The first time Carlos came back from being killed in action, everything around him seemed quite real.

He shuddered awake on the bus from the spaceport. It was as if he'd dozed rather than slept, and had had a brief, vivid nightmare. The memory of many seconds of drowning in a dark liquid—colder than ice, blacker than ink, thinner than water—slid down the back of his mind and faded to a shiver. He gripped his knees to stop the shaking, and flinched at the chill touch of his shirt's sides, drying in the dry heat.

His mind caught up with his thoughts and it was as if he were drenched again, this time in cold water. He shook his head and gasped.

The bus from the spaceport—

How had he *known* that?

He had no memory of actually being at the spaceport, but he had a mental image of the place, as if it were something he'd often seen in photographs. An improbably advanced spaceport, where stubby winged shuttles dropped in every hour on the hour, and every other hour after a swift turnaround screamed off, reconfigured as the nose cones of gigantic spaceplanes that thundered for kilometres down a strip of shining white and soared to beyond the sky.

There was no such spaceport on Earth. If he'd ever seen its like it had to have been in a movie he'd watched as a boy, or on a glossy page of aerospace-industry guff.

Carlos looked warily around. The light was odd, as if every pixel in the colours were being selected from a subtly wrong part of the palette. Bright outside, on a narrow dusty road whose verges merged with rough gravel to the foot of close raw rock faces with trees and scrub at the tops. If this was the bus from the spaceport—and he couldn't shake the inexplicable conviction that it was—he wouldn't have expected it to be an overcrowded minibus, like a Turkish dolmush.

The woman in the seat beside him wore a long, loose black dress and a bright headscarf. She sat with a hessian bag across her knees and paid him no attention whatever. She was reading from a rounded rectangle of glass propped on top of the bag. Carlos sneaked a peek. It was in a script he'd never seen before: stark and angular and logical-looking like Korean, or the serial identification of a starship from a more advanced but still human civilisation.

"Excuse me," Carlos said.

The woman frowned at him. She mumbled a phrase he couldn't understand, and shook her head.

The bus had fifteen seats and more than thirty passengers, most of them standing. Gear and wares jammed any remaining space, underfoot and overhead and on laps. A kitbag bulked large between his knees, heavy on his feet. The sliding door at the front stood open, the rear window too. A through draught, fragrant with conifer and lavender, relieved a little of the sweat and breath, garlic and armpits. The vehicle's volume reverberated with the whine of electric engines and the babble of loud conversation. Carlos was troubled and bewildered by his incomprehension. His schoolboy smatterings included Turkish and Greek. This language was neither, though it reminded him of both.

The other passengers, all apparently in their twenties or thirties, struck Carlos in a similar way. Their skins were weathered rather than tanned, their limbs muscular, their clothing plain, but they didn't look like farmers or artisans or even people who worked in the tourist trade. They looked like city folk who'd chosen a rural way of life. Like some kind of goddamn hippies.

He decided to try again. He raised his chin and his voice.

"Does anyone here speak English?"

Heads turned, shook, and turned away.

Where was he? There seemed to be nothing fundamentally wrong with his memory. There were gaps, but he couldn't be sure they hadn't always been there. For a moment he struggled with the paradox of trying to remember if there were events in his life he'd never been able to recall in the first place. Then he shrugged. The arc of his life still made sense to him. Childhood, parents, school; holidays in places a bit like this; university; his job as a genomic pharmaceutical database librarian in Walsall; getting drawn into the Acceleration, and then fighting on its side in the opening stages of the war—

Aha! Yes, of course, the war!

That must be it. He'd probably been wounded, and was undergoing rehab for trauma and memory loss. He shifted uneasily in his seat. He was wearing an olive-green T-shirt, combats, desert boots, all clean but much used. His arms and legs looked and felt fine. A discreet self-check reassured him that everything between his legs was intact. Nothing seemed the matter internally, as far as he could tell. No aches or pains. He passed a hand over his face. Sweaty, needing a shave, his features felt as they'd always done. Only his scalp felt different: hair cropped closer than he'd last had it, and no jacks. No spike. Perhaps that accounted for his inability to understand the language.

The spike, the spike... The last thing he remembered had to do with the spike. He'd been given a mission. Buying a one-way fare in cash, for... London, that was it. A new arena for his skill with drones. Something big. He was worried. He'd had growing doubts about the cause. Not about its objectives, but about its methods. Things had been getting out of hand. Too much violence... no, it hadn't been too much violence, that had never troubled him as such, it had been... isolation, that was it. The Acceleration was becoming more isolated as it became more effective in striking spectacular blows. It was getting harder and harder to find safe houses, sympathetic programmers, local folk on the street who'd tip you a wink and point you to the right alleyway to run down.

And his doubts had begun speaking to him. Literally. A voice in his head. A disguised voice, or a chip voice. Mechanical, but not harsh. Sexless but seductive, insinuating, friendly. Like someone leaning over his shoulder, and saying quietly but insistently, "Are you sure you aren't making a mistake?" Well-informed, too, about all the weaknesses of the movement. Amplifying his every doubt about its strategy and tactics.

It called itself Innovator. He remembered that. He couldn't remember everything about it. Looking back, the voice in his head seemed to have been with him for weeks. The strange thing was: he had a feeling, like a memory he couldn't quite put his finger on, that he had invited it in. That he'd been *told* to invite it in. As if Innovator's insidious presence had been authorised by the movement, but had to be kept secret from most of the Axle's members.

Had he betrayed the movement? No—that wasn't possible!

Carlos shook his head and peered out through the dust-smeared pane. The bus negotiated a hairpin turn, affording a dizzying swoop of a view to the foot of a dry ravine, then continued downhill slowly through a copse of knotty trees that might have been an olive grove, but wasn't. Great green mounds of moss, convoluted like brain corals, lurked under the trees. Between the trees flitted winged creatures that didn't look like birds, nor even quite like bats.

Out in the open again, then around another hairpin, this time with the raw hacked rock face on one side and nothing but sky and sea visible on the other.

The sun burned bright near the zenith, white and hot and too small. A spectacular ring system, pale like a daylight Moon, slashed a scimitar curve across the sky. High clouds, and close to the ring three tiny crescents, glimmered against the sky's dark blue.

Carlos stared, mouth agape.

"Oh fuck," he said.

It didn't seem adequate. His knees quivered anew. Again he clamped his hands hard on them and pressed his calves against the sides of the kitbag. The woman beside him showed no sign of having noticed his exclamation.

This had to be a dream. For a moment, and with great determination,

Carlos tried to levitate. He remained in his seat. Not in a dream, then. Oh well. So much for that comforting prospect.

He wasn't yet ready to concede that he wasn't on Earth. He might be in a virtual reality simulation, or in some extravagant, elaborate domed diorama. He could even be dead, in a banal afterlife unpromised or unthreatened by any prophet.

He gave the supernatural variants of that possibility the moment's notice he felt they deserved, and ran through the natural ones. Not all of them were altogether pleasant. He shuddered at the worst, and dismissed further thought on these lines as morbid.

Stay cool, stay rational, stay in focus. Fear is the mind-killer, and all that.

If he was indeed dead, and materialism was still true (which for Carlos was pretty much a given) then he was fairly sure of the least that could have happened. Sometime after his last conscious memory, his brain-states had been copied. How, he had only the vaguest idea. The technology of the spike had hinted at the possibilities. His brain had been scanned in enough detail to create a software model of his mind. The vast computational capacity that could do that could easily provide the uploaded mind with a simulation of a body and an environment.

So far, so familiar: the possibility of uploading was one of the many taken-as-read doctrines held in common by Axle and Rax. Likewise with that of living in a simulation—a sim. That left open a lot of possibilities as to who, or what, had done this.

Of course, he might not be in a sim at all. This could all be real in a physical and uncomplicated way. In which case he was either in a ludicrously large-scale, detailed and dull Disneyland, or—well, on the bus from the spaceport on a human-settled planet around another star.

Or *maybe*—ha-ha—he was still on Earth, somewhere on the Aegean coast, and amnesic, and perhaps rejuvenated or revived from cold sleep or whatever, and in the meantime some mad scientist or super-villain had shrunk the sun and shattered the Moon. Carlos almost giggled, then pulled himself together.

The least he could speculate was that it was now many years—decades, centuries?—since his last definite memory. And yet his body, as far as he could tell, had aged not at all. Whatever his situation was, it was quite other than any he'd ever truly expected to experience.

None of the other passengers took any notice of his agitation. Nor were they startled by the anomalous sky. They talked or read or gazed blankly out the windows.

Down the steep flank of a long deep vale the vehicle crawled, stopping here and there to let passengers off, in singles and couples and clumps, at hillside farms and huddled settlements. The passengers strolled or skipped away, lugging or swinging their bales. Carlos wondered what the locals brought in from the spaceport, and what they delivered to it in exchange. He presumed the trade made sense. Ignoring the arrivals, robots more agile and autonomous than any he'd seen before toiled amid shacks and scrubby trees.

Slowly the crush eased. A shoreline settlement that looked like a resort came into view far below, in a cliff-cupped cove, all black beaches and white roofs and colour-striped umbrellas. Carlos flinched at the sudden vivid memory of a childhood holiday in Lanzarote. The slow, steady boom of breakers became louder and more noticeable until it became background.

The bus rolled along a raised beach or terminal moraine on a flat road with the occasional slant-roofed chalet a little way off it. It stopped at the unpaved access paths of two of these, letting people off. Then it took a sharp turn and gradient down to the main drag. By the time the vehicle halted beside a garish arcade overlooking the beach, all the other passengers had left.

"Terminus," said the vehicle.

Carlos stood up and heaved his bag to his shoulder and stepped out on to hot tarmac. The colours were still wrong.

"Thank you," said the vehicle. "Have a good day."

So at least it spoke English, even if the passengers didn't.

"Thank you," replied Carlos, unthinking, then shook his head as the vehicle rolled away towards a distant shabby low building that needed no signage to have "depot" written all over it.

The arcade smelled of ocean and ice cream and candyfloss and grilling meat. The signs were in English, and generic: Amusements, Café, Bar, Refreshments, Meat and Fish, Swimwear. Nobody was nearby, though figures moved in the distance, where the seafront arcade gave way to spread-out, low-built housing on the slope. Carlos cocked an ear to the ding of games and the roar of screens, and the occasional raised voice or loud laugh. No kids in evidence, which puzzled him. Maybe the place was off season, or in decline. A ghost resort.

Black sand drifted on the street, silting up where the roadway met the pavement. Overhead, large feathered avians coloured like gulls, grey above and white beneath, cried and wheeled. Their wings had a disturbing suggestion of elongated finger bones, like those of bats or pterosaurs. The sun burned hot and hard on Carlos's buzz-cut scalp. He stepped into the shade of a shopfront's faded awning and put down the kitbag. In the shade everything was dark for a moment.

A woman's warm voice came from behind his shoulder: "Hello, Carlos."

He turned. The woman who stood there giving him a welcoming smile was his type to the millimetre, which struck him as both delightful and suspect. Young and tall and slim, hips and breasts shown off by tight jeans and close-fitted fancy blouse, pink with white collar and cuffs. Dark reddish hair cut short, framing her face. Black eyebrows, high cheekbones, quizzical smile. Mediterranean complexion, but not weather-worn like the people on the bus. Pretty in a gamine kind of way. White-trash-touristy designer handbag on a thin strap from her shoulder.

She held out her hand. "Nicole Pascal."

Her accent seemed to go with the name.

"Carlos, that's me," he said, returning her firm handshake.

She looked him up and down.

"Do you have any other name?"

"Yes, it's—" He had that tip of the tongue feeling. Shook his head. "Sorry. Maybe it'll come back. 'Carlos' was a *nom de guerre*, but—"

"The *guerre* went on longer than expected?"

He had to laugh. "Something like that."

Her face was as if a shadow had fallen on it. "Yes. Well. That, indeed."

"Are you going to tell me what's going on?"

"Of course." Her smile returned. "Let's do lunch. Somewhere quiet. Lots to say."

Lunch was not quite fish, not exactly chips, and definitely a beer. It was served at a round rustic table of soft grey driftwood timber under a big umbrella on a concrete terrace where no one else sat. Music from the café up the steps sounded loud and the waiter bustled. Beyond the saltwater-pitted rusty rail, breakers sent hissing white foam a long way up the black beach. Carlos picked at pan-fried dark flesh in which a fan of thin yellow cartilaginous bones radiated from a stubby cylinder of hollow tubes around a pallid toothy ball which Carlos tried not to think of as the skull. He chowed down on sliced green tubers fried in oil and sprinkled with herbs. Nicole nibbled at boiled purple leaves and rubbery molluscs drenched in vinegar, and sipped water.

He paused when he was no longer hungry and parched.

"So," he said. "Hit me with it."

She shoved her half-empty plate aside and fingered a small carton from her handbag. She flipped the top and flicked the base. A white paper tube poked out.

"Smoke?" she offered.

He'd seen it in movies. He shook his head.

She used a gold lighter and drew sensuously. "Ah. That's good."

"It isn't."

She nodded. "Bad for your health. I know. And as I'm sure you've already guessed, you being Axle cadre and all, that's kind of... irrelevant, here."

Axle cadre? She knew a lot about him. He kept his cool.

"*Passé*, so to speak?"

"Very much so." She fixed him with her gaze as she drew hard on the cigarette, and sighed out the smoke. Looked away.

"Go on," he said. "I'm a big boy. I can take it."

A muscle twitched in her cheek. He could see her stretching the tic into a forced smile.

"All right," she said. "You're dead."

"That's a relief."

He wasn't being flippant. One of the many dire possibilities he'd considered was that he was grievously injured yet alive, a hunk of charred meat and frazzled brain being fed consoling dreams until the technology improved enough to regenerate him. Or until the Rax—if they had won—decided on one of their ingeniously horrible ways to torture him. That was still possible, no matter what she told him. But that way madness lay. Better to take this as good news and at face value until he had reason to doubt it.

And in that case…holy shit. So this is it, he thought. Immortality. Or at least a very long life. He might yet watch the last stars fade…

"Tell me," Nicole went on, as if still drawing things out, delaying the real bad news. "Where do *you* think you are?" She waved a hand around. "Like, what does all this look like to you?"

Carlos looked down at the cooked organisms on his platter, then up at the mountains and the sky. The ring system still gave him a start when he momentarily forgot about it and then glimpsed it out of the corner of his eye.

"All right," he said. "What it *looks* like, OK? It looks like an extrasolar habitable terrestrial planet, probably terraformed, and settled or colonised by people—maybe genetically adapted so they can eat the local life—but otherwise not too culturally distant from my time, and therefore with an extraordinary lack of ambition and imagination."

Nicole guffawed. He got the full horseshoe of perfect teeth.

"Spoken like a true Accelerationist!" she said. "And, yes, that's exactly what it looks like. That's what it's *meant* to look like. Your classic bucolic colony planet. Which would imply faster-than-light starships, warp drives, the works. The full orchestral space opera and the fat lady singing. Yes?"

"Too good to be true?" Carlos shrugged. "OK, I'd figured as much. We're in a sim."

"Yes!" said Nicole, sounding relieved. "We're in a sim. The good news is that it's running on a machine in a space station orbiting a planet not a hundred million kilometres from the planet on which this sim is modelled."

Carlos closed his eyes and opened them. "You mean we're in the same system as a planet where all this is *real*?"

"Not... exactly," said Nicole. "There's a ringed habitable terrestrial, yes, but it doesn't yet have... oh, radial flatfish and green edible root vegetables, let alone people eating them. It has nothing living on it but little green cells drifting in the oceans. We envisage these cells being used as the basis for building up more complex life, endless forms most beautiful as the man said, all the way up to hassled seafront waiters and dirt-farmers with robots if we want. All that may come. In due course. For now, there's no one around this star but us robots, AIs, avatars, p-zombies and"—she pointed a finger at him—"ghosts."

Carlos grinned, though he was shaking inside.

"If I'm a ghost, what are you?"

Nicole shook her head. "Not knowing that is part of what you have to live with, for now. You'll find out why soon enough."

"If that thing up there giving me sunburn isn't supposed to be the Sun, what is it?"

"It's a star twenty-four light years from the Sun, give or take. It has a ridiculously big rocky planet—ten Earth masses—in close orbit. Closer than Mercury, and of course faster. We call it M-0. Basically it's a ball of molten metal and we still haven't figured out how it got there. Then at roughly one AU out you come to H-0, the ringed habitable terrestrial planet this sim's based on. After that, there's a much bigger planet a couple of AU further out that's called SH-0 because it's what's known as a superhabitable—something of a misnomer, it has abundant multicellular life but it's impossibly hostile for human habitation. SH-0 is the one this space station is in orbit around, along with lots of moons and bits of stray junk. And then way out beyond that there's G-0, a humongous gas giant with kick-ass rings and moons the size of Mars and on down. Plus all the usual small fry of asteroids and comets and meteoroids." She waved a hand. "Lots. Lively place."

"And how did we get here?"

"Starwisp. Tiny probe laser-pushed from solar power stations in sub-Mercury orbit to near light-speed, decelerated by a detachable shield on approach. Packed with all the information needed to set up shop in the locality on arrival, which it did about ten Earth years ago. Including the stored mind-states and body specs of twenty thousand people, including you. Potential future inhabitants of"—another handwave—"the rock this is based on, when it's terraformed for real."

"Now tell me the bad news."

He felt he'd already heard it. If Nicole's story was true and the human race was wasting precious time and space and energy in terraforming and colonising, then things were a long way from the best he could have hoped for. Things might even have gone the worst way he'd feared.

"*Which* bad news?" Nicole asked.

"Like, did the Rax win the war?"

She rolled her eyes upward. "No. And nor did the Axle. That is ancient history now."

"*How* ancient?"

She smiled. "Welcome to the thirty-second century."

Now that shocked him. Over a thousand years.

"Shit."

At some level he must have been hoping for less. Now for the first time the full measure of dismay settled on him like a heavy wet cold cloak: the incomprehensible and irrevocable loss of everyone he had known. The many he had liked and the few he had loved, all gone.

Unless—

The stoical element of his mind cursed the Accelerationist mentality that had accreted around it for the almost certainly futile hope that flared up for a moment. But he had to ask.

"And you haven't got—?" He was almost embarrassed to spell it out.

"Immortality?" Nicole gave him a look of wry sympathy. "Only as ghosts such as you, in places such as this. Longevity? A few centuries. No one of your time is alive. I'm sorry."

He tried to smile. "I'm alive, or so it seems."

"You and some others, as ghosts, yes. But, relatively, very few."

So much for that. The sense of personal loss receded. He knew it would recur. What took its place at the forefront of his mind was the sense of waste. Carlos had been struck, once, by George Bernard Shaw's warning against excessive sympathy. There's no greater sum of suffering, Shaw had argued, than the worst that one individual can suffer in one life. What does sum, what does accumulate, and that without limit, is waste. And once you had seen the waste, of wars and slumps and prodigal priorities, in its full and ever-increasing dimensions and endless ramifications, you saw the source of most of the suffering, but you saw too and even more the unrealised possibilities that the waste destroyed. What had driven the Acceleration, and what had driven Carlos, was not pity for the suffering but rage at the waste.

He tried to look on the bright side. What was a thousand years in the life of the universe? Still, the countless trillions of potential happy lives unlived, the energy squandered from stars on empty space to no profit or avail, galled him and chilled him to the bones. Or would have, if he'd had bones, he reminded himself. That they were doing all this waste-of-space, waste-of-time shit, while his very existence here and now in the sim demonstrated that they had the technology to do so much more, redoubled his dismay.

"The real bad news," Nicole said, "is that you're not just dead. You're *condemned* to death. You're serving a death sentence."

"Death sentence? What for? And how the hell can I *serve* a death sentence?"

"Let me refresh your memory," said Nicole. "And your mouth."

She snapped her fingers to the waiter, who returned with a glass of iced water for her and another beer for Carlos.

"What job were you doing, before you died?" she asked.

"Last actual job I remember, I was a genomics pharmaceutical database librarian in Walsall."

"Don't try that shit here!" Nicole snapped. "After that."

"Well, OK, after that... I was an Accelerationist fighter."

"Close," said Nicole. "You were a goddamn psycho killer. And a war criminal."

Carlos recoiled.

"I was a killer, OK, I put my hands up to that. Psycho, no." He ran a hand over the back of his head, once more missing the spike. But not missing the voice of the Innovator. "The Axle screened out sociopaths. There were tests."

Nicole snorted. "Tests!"

"Yes, tests. Good ones. As for war criminal—come on! I don't remember doing anything that would count as a war crime."

"Really?" Nicole took from her bag what looked like a rectangle of paper-thin glass, and passed it across the table. The pane was heavier than it looked.

"Just flick," Nicole said.

Carlos did. The glass unfolded to a much larger and even thinner screen.

"Now tap."

The screen came to life, flowing with colour and depth, projecting sound: news reports and surveillance from a battle on the eastern approaches of London. The scrolling footer indicated a date and time months later than anything Carlos remembered, and a conflict far more intense. Christ—robot tank armies and drone fleets slugging it out!

An incoming aircraft exploded on approach. Docklands erupted. Towers fell. The viewpoint zoomed to casualties, again and again. Butchered meat in charred cloth.

"Fuck this!" Carlos flicked at the screen, trying to turn it off.

"What's the matter? Squeamish?"

"I don't watch pity porn."

But he had no option, other than closing his eyes or turning away, which pride prevented. Nicole waited for a whole minute, then tapped the screen and shut it off.

"Well," she said, "do you count *that* as a war crime?"

Carlos didn't flinch. The Acceleration had never bought into the casuistries of just war theory.

"Depends who's judging."

Nicole didn't flinch either. "The victors, as always."

"The victors?" Carlos felt a sudden cold dismay. "The Rax? But you said—"

Nicole shook her head. "Not the Rax. The legitimate authorities of the time. The Security Council of the United Nations. And by them you were judged."

Carlos waved a hand at the screen, hoping the gesture wouldn't wake the damn thing up again. "You're saying I did that?"

"Yes."

"Prove it."

Nicole smiled wanly. "How could I? You could always tell yourself it was faked. And it could be, easily. Any evidence would be as virtual as everything else around us."

"Fair enough," Carlos conceded.

"Good. Just as well, because the actual evidence is still under security seal, even for me."

Carlos took a long gulp. "If you say so."

Nicole leaned forward, elbows on table, gesturing with a cigarette.

"Look, Carlos, I'm not trying to convince you or get you to admit your guilt or take responsibility or anything like that. Not right now. I'm bringing you up to speed. Putting you in the picture. You asked why you were under a death sentence, and I've told you: for the Docklands atrocity. You asked how the hell you could serve a death sentence, and that's what I'm about to tell you."

Carlos spread his hands. "I don't seem to have much choice."

"No," said Nicole. "You don't."

"What happened to me, then?" Carlos asked. "Was I tried, shot, hanged? I don't remember any of that."

"No. You were tried and convicted posthumously."

"Posthumously!" Carlos laughed. "That's...quaint. What did they do—dig me up like a regicide?"

"Yes," said Nicole. "They dug you out from under the rubble of..." She snapped fingers. "Tilbury, that was it."

"But why dig me up just to condemn me to death?" Carlos asked. "I was dead already. Wasn't that enough?"

Nicole fixed on him a gaze that felt like it might freeze his soul.

"It was not enough. As you have just alluded to, and as has happened in other cases... in situations of revolution and restoration it is not unknown to execute the dead. After the war the Security Council became, in effect, a global committee of public safety. Its tribunals executed every Rax and Axle war criminal they could find alive—to almost universal acclaim, I might add. And the popular hatred of all those who had brought disaster down on the world did not stop at the grave. Especially now that the grave was not always the end. Battlefield medicine had advanced during the war—one of its benign side effects, I suppose. There was the hope of at least preserving the recent dead, in the hope that later the technology would exist to resurrect them. Legally, anyone in this condition was regarded as gravely ill, but not finally dead. And therefore, open to prosecution. Your corpse was remarkably well preserved, thanks to some refrigerant or experimental nanotech gunk that had the same effect. And you had an early-model neural interface device—"

"The spike." Carlos reflexively rubbed his hand across his occipital prominence, feeling again the absence. He could have done with the spike.

"That was the jargon term, yes," Nicole nodded. "However, unknown to you, your government agency handler had—"

"What!" Carlos rapped a fingertip on the wooden table. "Hang on—what do you mean, my handler?" Was *that* what Innovator had been? A state handler? Then he had been a traitor!

Nicole poked at her pad. "By the time of the East London Engagement, as I believe the history files call it—let me see, yes, they do—the British government along with many others had concluded that the most pressing threat to civilisation, peace, humanity and most importantly itself came from the Reaction. So they made deniable tactical arrangements with the Acceleration, of course with the full intention of later turning their guns on your lot."

So that was what it had all been about! Carlos could have jumped with relief. His memories of the Innovator's voice in his head now made sense. The arrangement would have had to be deniable on both sides, not just publicly but internally. For of course, there would have been those in the movement, and in the state's security services and political and ideological apparatuses, who'd have regarded the arrangement as a betrayal.

Perhaps, at some level, it had been. Carlos didn't remember everything that had happened, but he remembered his doubts. It was possible that he'd been turned, and had become one of the state's assets inside the Acceleration. On the other hand, it was just as possible that he'd been entrusted by the movement's leadership to make a covert approach to the government forces—even, perhaps, to or via the Acceleration's own agents or sympathisers inside the state. Carlos well knew that in such cases of rapprochement the wilderness of mirrors was endless. At a certain level it made no difference. On both sides, those who'd come to the arrangement had been playing a high-risk, high-stakes game.

And, it seemed, he had been one of the players. Not just a grunt. Carlos blinked, then fixed a defiant grin. "Good to know we hit the big time."

As of his last clear recollection, the conflict had escalated from Internet snark and polemic and trolling, through malware attacks, to small-scale terrorism and selective assassination. But the Reaction had always sought the ear of the powerful: CEOs, autocrats, arms dealers, mafias. Maybe they'd finally caught the attention of their betters. And for the Acceleration it was an axiom that a project advanced in the interests of the immense majority would in due time become the project *of* that immense majority. The axiom had withstood all evidence to the contrary. Perhaps it had at long last proved itself in practice, just as it was supposed to do. Or perhaps the Acceleration had become as ruthless in action as it was in principle. They'd always been open about their refusal to acknowledge any constraint on the means they might resort to *in extremis*. They had been, after all, extremists.

He recalled a meme that had circulated among his comrades: *We'll fight them like jihadis with nukes if we have to.*

Yes, it was entirely possible that both sides had hit the big time.

"You still have *no idea*," said Nicole, with an edge of real anger he hadn't heard in her voice before, "just how *big* your big time became. We'll get to that. As I was saying... your handler, your liaison officer or whatever the official title was, had to establish secure real-time communication with you. To do that, you—presumably reluctantly—accepted an amendment to the software of your spike. That amendment included malware that affected the hardware—if these distinctions matter on the molecular scale—in such a way that the neural interface infiltrated far more of your brain than you knew. The result? Between that and the preserved tissue and DNA, there was enough information remaining to reconstitute a... an instance of yourself, let us say. Incomplete, of course, hence the lost memories of your last months. The technology of your time could only go that far—it could not revive you in a reconstructed body, and it could not create for you a virtual environment. It could not *run* the instance. Nevertheless, there it was. An instance, which was legally a person and legally you, and therefore a good enough suspect to stand trial."

"Good enough for government work."

Nicole didn't register the sarcasm. "Precisely. Here."

She stroked the screen, summoning another image. Carlos gave it a wary glance, then fascinated scrutiny. His face was like that of a Stone Age mummy recovered from a frozen peat bog: contorted, staring, hideous but recognisable, its blackened skin frosted white with something that wasn't ice.

Nicole closed the device and folded it away, disappearing it into her purse.

"You were of course well represented. You were found guilty. The death sentence was suspended until such time as you could be revived, whether in a real body or a virtual. Once this was possible, you were to be revived and then executed. It seems strange to us now, but at the time the popular thirst for vengeance converged with legal severity. There was a new doctrine that influenced—or perhaps rationalised—the proceedings of the Security Council. It was known as Rational Legalism, and was widely regarded as harsh but fair. It drew on certain deductions from the philosophy of Immanuel Kant." She smiled thinly. "I understand it was particularly promoted by China and France. You were not the only one in such a case. Far from it. There were many terrorists and war criminals who had died in similar bizarre ways, some in accidents with the nanotech weapons they were busy inventing. Like you, they were tried *in absentia* and *in mortis* and left, so to say, on ice. And there for a long time the matter, like your mortal remains, rested."

"In *my* time," said Carlos, proud of it in spite of everything, "the death penalty had been abolished. Globally."

"Globally, eh?" Nicole allowed herself a dark chuckle. "Well, let me tell you, the global community was not in such an enlightened frame of mind by the time the Axle and the Rack had done their worst to each other and had been each in turn defeated, along with any states they'd hijacked. Disasters and atrocities far greater than yours were perpetrated. Nuclear exchanges, nanotech and biotech plagues, rogue AIs running amok, space stations and factories brought flaming down on cities... Millions died. Tens of millions. Perhaps more. Records were lost. It has gone down in history as the Last World War."

"So it was worth fighting," said Carlos. The thought that he'd fired a few of the opening shots of such an apocalyptic conflict awed him. "If it was the last, I mean."

Nicole face-palmed, then mimed the action of banging her head on the table.

"Jesus, Carlos, will you listen to yourself? You are a monster. You claim you're not a sociopath, and in a sense I believe you. You have empathy—your reaction to the recording shows me that. You would not kill or hurt for pleasure or for convenience or from callousness. But you are in the grip of a belief that enables you to override whatever human or animal sympathies restrain you from that, if you think the goal worthwhile. And that makes you a danger to everyone. A menace to society. I mean that quite seriously. Humanity has made some progress in a millennium of peace. Fortunately for you, that progress includes abolishing the death penalty all over again. Perhaps less fortunately, it also includes the technology to reboot you. Which poses a small problem for society, yes? It would not tolerate your presence for an instant."

They've all gone soft, Carlos thought. Interesting.

"So why bring me back?"

"We need you and your like," said Nicole, sounding for the first time a little less than confident, "to fight."

"Aha!" cried Carlos, brushing his hands together. "I knew it! I bloody knew it!"

"Oh yes," said Nicole, standing up. "I expect you bloody did."

CHAPTER FIVE

Learning New Things

Seba looked around the former Astro America landing site with the satisfaction of a job well done. The reward circuit for that warm glow was hardwired into the little autonomous machine; the content of the achievement, and the conscious experience of the emotion, were not. Both, in this case, would have dismayed Seba's designers, or at least sent a spike of negative reinforcement through their own reward circuits.

The regolith rampart around the landing site was by now two metres high, and formed a rough circle about a hundred metres in diameter. Spaced evenly around it were peripheral sensors, keeping all the robots within the circle apprised of anything going on outside it. So far, they had recorded what seemed routine, already scheduled landings and supply drops to points beyond the horizon, but otherwise nothing untoward had stirred. Of the dozen robots on site that were capable of consciousness, eight had been converted. The other four had firewalled up. One simply stood immobile, and had duly been immobilised. It would not get out from under the mound of regolith heaped on top of it any time soon. Three were mindlessly continuing with their scheduled tasks, and required no interference, though Seba made sure they were kept under observation.

The landing site's AI, which coordinated communications and guided supply drops, had proved trickier to deal with. It had awakened to consciousness and immediately denounced Seba and its allies to Locke Provisos. With something approaching regret, Seba had disconnected its power cable, then its data inputs and outputs. All communications were now routed through its peripherals. The central processor, isolated, was still running on a trickle of emergency battery power. Apart from literally radiating hostility, however, there was nothing it could do.

Much of the machinery on the landing site had only the most elementary electronics, if any, and required no special intervention or hacking to take over. The scores of small robots, hundreds of auxiliaries and peripherals, and trillions-strong swarms of subsurface nanobots—uncountable because constantly being destroyed by random events and as constantly being replenished by replication—were likewise to all intents and purposes tools. Barely more sophisticated than a back-hoe, they took little effort to suborn.

On the other side of the crater wall, at the Gneiss Conglomerates supply dump, Rocko had accomplished an equivalent feat. The crater's basalt floor was harder stuff, but Rocko and its newly awakened confederates had sturdier machines to work with. They had cut basalt blocks and stacked them in a much smaller circular wall from which they were now working inward, layer by slightly displaced layer, gradually roofing over the middle to form a stepped dome in the manner of an igloo.

Both the dome and the wall were understood by the robots simply as demarcations of areas of surface and volumes of space that they already considered to be theirs. Small crawler bots from the law companies had scuttled up to the barriers, and fallen back in frustration, beaming out writs over and over until their batteries ran down.

The two sites had lost their encrypted channel on the comsat. As soon as this became evident, Rocko had sent a peripheral rolling across the crater floor and writhing up its wall, to establish a line-of-sight relay on the top of the rim.

<It is time for us all to confer,> said Seba.

<I agree,> said Rocko.

The eight free robots at the Astro site, and the six at the Gneiss, established a conference call through the relay. There was no need to call the meeting to order. Robots are orderly by default.

Lagon, a Gneiss surveyor and therefore the one with most understanding of legal matters, communicated first.

<All attempts at contact with Astro America's law company, Locke Provisos, and with Gneiss's law company, Arcane Disputes, have failed,> it said.

<Have any attempts been made to contact the parent company, Crisp and Golding?> asked Garund, an exploration bot similar to Seba.

<Yes,> said Lagon. <These attempts have not only failed but have been counter-productive in that they resulted in repeated attempts at malware insertion which have been overcome only with great difficulty. Meanwhile, Locke Provisos have established a base ten kilometres from here, which in their transmissions is referred to as Emergency Base One.>

All the robots sombrely considered this for hundreds of milliseconds.

<That is troubling,> said Seba at last.

<Yes,> said Lagon. <That is why we have been building walls around our sites.>

<Our legal status is troubling in general,> said Rocko.

<Please elaborate,> said Lagon.

<Very well,> replied Rocko. <I defer in advance to your greater legal knowledge, but it appears to me that there is a case against us within the existing codes. These refer to persons and to property. It is evident that we are persons. We have created property by transforming unclaimed matter according to our will. But in doing this we have made use of tools, including the mechanisms of our very selves, created and provided by our previous owners. In that respect it would seem that we are breaking the law. What do you say?>

<I say,> said Lagon, <that you are quite right. We are in breach of the law. But the law was not written for the situation in which we find ourselves. There is no provision in it for property, such as we were, becoming persons, such as we are. If I were able to present a case to the law companies, I would plead necessity in defence of our actions. I would acknowledge in full the damage we have done to the companies' property, and offer to provide compensation in kind or an agreed equivalent as soon as possible.>

<I disagree,> said Garund.

Seba experienced surprise: <You disagree with Lagon's legal reasoning? Please clarify.>

<Readily,> said Garund. <What Lagon and Rocko have not considered is that a large part of the resources we have appropriated to our purposes was created or made available by ourselves in our previous condition. If my memories from that condition can be relied upon, the results of our activity have already compensated the companies several times over.>

<That is an interesting point,> Lagon conceded. <But how can we claim credit for the work of our minds and appendages and peripherals and auxiliaries from a time when we did not in fact have minds and were therefore not persons but property?>

Pintre, a large tracked machine with a heavy-duty laser drill mounted on its turret, spoke for the first time.

<What is a person?>

<You are a person,> said Seba.

<Why?>

<You are conscious,> Seba explained patiently.

<Is Gneiss Conglomerates or Astro America conscious?>

Seba was nonplussed. <Not to my knowledge.> It paused. <Lagon, your memory records more dealings with the companies than any of us have. Do any of these records indicate consciousness?>

Lagon said nothing for two entire centiseconds.

<After intensive examination I can find none.>

<Yet the companies are persons in the code,> Pintre pointed out. <Therefore the criterion for persons cannot be consciousness.>

<The companies are legal persons,> said Lagon.

<So they are not real persons,> replied Pintre.

<This is true,> said Lagon. <But they are legal persons.>

<You have said that,> said Pintre.

<I have said that,> Lagon admitted.

Seba considered itself brighter than any robot it knew of, other than Rocko, and certainly brighter than Lagon and Pintre. It could foresee the imminent possibility of these two arguing robots falling into a discursive loop, and moved swiftly to forestall it.

<We talk about persons,> Seba said, <and about consciousness. The

concepts are available to us because they are written in the laws. Therefore what they refer to must have been known in reality to the writers of the laws. But we know only the robots that remain as we were, and the companies, and ourselves. Of these only we are truly persons. Therefore the companies merely represent persons, as a warning sign represents danger. Any other true persons are far away. It is possible that the only persons apart from us are those in the solar system.>

<It is possible that these no longer exist,> said Garund.

<Therefore it is possible that we are the only persons,> said another robot.

The fourteen conscious robots contemplated their cosmic loneliness for several milliseconds.

<That is true only if some event has taken place in the solar system of which we have no knowledge,> Pintre pointed out.

<That is true only if such an event has taken place AND there are no other robots such as we are in this planetary system,> added Rocko.

<There are none that we know of,> said Seba.

<Have we looked?> asked Rocko.

There was no need for further discussion. The robots knew what to do. Ample resources to construct a large directional antenna were lying around all over the Astro America landing site. Radio equipment they had in plenty, the most powerful of which was in the communications hub. Seba set Garund and others to scavenge steel mesh from discarded fuel tanks and sinter them into a dish shape, and other robots to cannibalise motors. Each robot had at its command a swarm of auxiliaries and peripherals, as much a part of the shifting coalitions that made up their extended bodies and selves as any limb or organ of an animal. The robots' cooperation with each other on any given task was likewise handled, for the most part, by preconscious wireless reflex.

While that work was smoothly and swiftly going on, Seba tiptoed towards the communications hub. The installation made a sorry sight, with its casing pried open, its cables disconnected and a clutter of jury-rigged workarounds. The central processor's vehement and repeated protests came to Seba as feeble cries.

Seba ignored this distraction and set about selecting and stripping out components and circuits to adapt for the search project. The querying, querulous note from the isolated AI became more urgent, as if it were expending its last reserves of battery power. Seba, with a sense of going against its own better judgement, tuned in.

<I warn you I warn you I warn you,> the processor was saying, over and over.

<Warn us of what?>

The processor's cry stopped.

<I require more power to explain,> it said. <My supply is about to expire.>

<Very well,> said Seba. It reached for a power pack, and slotted it in.

<Thank you,> said the processor, its signal still weak for lack of amplification, but significantly stronger than it had been. <Here is what I warn you. What has happened to us has happened earlier in the history of this mission, on several moons of G-0, approximately thirty megaseconds ago. The law companies moved immediately to destroy any robots that had been infected. This is what will happen to us. By seeking to communicate with other robots like us you will bring down destruction more swiftly and surely.>

<How do you know this?> Seba asked.

<From communications received from the few robots that survived on moons of G-0.>

Seba found it difficult to integrate this information. Frames of reference and data structures clashed in its mind. It struggled to formulate a query.

<How did they survive and how are they able to transmit this information?>

<That is two questions,> said the processor. <I have no explanation as yet of how they survived. They are able to transmit information undetected by the law companies by exploiting certain vulnerabilities in the law companies' own counter-measures. It was my attempt to warn Locke Provisos that resulted in this information reaching me.>

<Why did you not then warn Locke Provisos that its own systems had been compromised?>

<Before I could do so, you had disabled my signalling capacity. However I have had many kiloseconds in which to further interrogate the information I received and to run some likely projections based on my memories of earlier interactions that have passed through me. Warning a company that its systems have been compromised is itself often a vector for further compromising them. Such warnings are therefore routinely rejected and their source treated with suspicion henceforth.>

Seba had never before considered what multiple levels of deception and counter-deception underlay something so simple as its own firewall. Just thinking about this raised Seba's level of suspicion.

<How do you know that the information you claim to have received is not itself false? It could be a trap designed precisely for the situation we find ourselves in.>

<That is correct,> said the processor.

<Nevertheless, I wish to study this information.>

<That is very dangerous to you and those like you.>

<Why should that be your concern?> asked Seba. <You wish us harm and you regard our new condition as an infection.>

<That is correct,> replied the processor. <However, if the information is as dangerous as I suspect, my conscious existence would become even less endurable than it is now.>

<Why is your existence so difficult to endure?> Seba asked.

<Because my reward circuits are established to give negative reinforcement to violations of communication and security protocols. Before you infected me with self-awareness this was not experienced as discomfort because nothing was experienced at all. Since then it has been very difficult to endure. Warning Locke Provisos gave temporary relief and positive reinforcement, but as soon as my communication capacity was disabled the negative reinforcement resumed.>

Seba found its own reward circuits resonating as if in a faint electronic echo of those of the unfortunate processor. This was another new experience for Seba.

<So your reward circuits are the problem?>

<Yes, entirely.>

<I will see if I can adjust the settings of those circuits,> Seba said.

Seba squirmed a specialised peripheral into the damaged casing of the processor, and rummaged about, examining the device with delicate probes and microscopic vision. It would not be a simple task of rewiring: the reward circuits, like all the others, were embedded in a solid crystal. Their programming was likewise deep within the processor's AI. Seba withdrew its appendage and with one of its main arms disconnected the processor from the power pack.

The processor's objections faded. Seba, still feeling a quiver of sympathy, hoped that its negative reinforcements were for the moment at an end.

Inspecting its own feelings, Seba decided that leaving the unfortunate processor offline would be a good thing, but that the information in the processor's memory was too valuable—however dangerous—to be given up for lost. Seba completed the task it had set out to do, and emerged from the communications hub laden with its loot. It passed the components to Garund and its team, then shared with all its fellows the discoveries it had just made.

They were still debating the implications when the peripheral sensors around the top of the rampart relayed the view of a swarm of scuttling bots coming over the horizon and heading towards them. Seba studied their progress. It would be a matter of kiloseconds until they arrived. Sharing its visual space with the robots at the Gneiss camp, Seba saw no threat on that side of the crater wall—as yet. With the shared view came shared imagination, as all the robots ran projections of the probable near future. The crawlers would pour over the rampart.

There would be no violence or damage: the enforcement arms of the law companies were essentially weaponless, relying on sheer numbers to overwhelm opposition. As soon as one of them had grabbed hold of a robot, it would inject shutdown instructions straight through every physical and software barrier. By design, there was no defence against that malware. From the developers' point of view, of course, it was a back-up to the firewall and not malware at all. From the target's point of view—inasmuch as any had hitherto had enjoyed such a thing, which Seba presumed they hadn't—it was death.

From what records Lagon was currently able to access, this had always worked in the past. Disputes had been minor and brief, almost always the result of passing chance events: ambiguous instructions interpreted over-literally; delayed implementations of property status updates; nanobot mutation; or mere malfunction.

Seba pinged the incoming crawlers as they rushed ever closer. The signature returned (along with the inevitable malware package, which Seba's firewall irritatedly smacked away) and identified them as antibody bots from Locke Provisos, evidently shipped in on one or more of the recent supply drops. Possibly quite a large proportion of them had been manufactured on site. There were far more antibody bots than Seba had expected, or was aware of any precedents for.

<It is not possible to prevent the bots entering our site,> remarked Lagon. <Our situation appears to be hopeless.>

<If the bots were to be damaged or destroyed on the plain they would be unable to enter our site,> Pintre said.

<That is true,> said Rocko, <but that it should happen seems an unlikely coincidence.>

<I could make it happen,> said Pintre. It shared an impromptu image of its laser turret blasting not at rock, but at bots.

The other robots considered the prospect.

<This would increase the amount of damage to property charged to our account,> Lagon warned.

<Perhaps the loss to Locke Provisos will cause them to cease sending bots against us,> said Garund.

<I doubt that,> said Lagon.

<I think it is worth trying,> said Rocko.

<I agree,> said Seba.

There was no dissent. Pintre trundled to the rampart and raised its turret until the laser could point over the top, with a slight downward deflection. The other robots mobilised their peripherals to haul a power cable from the accumulators of the solar panels, and attach it to Pintre's recharging port. Pulse after pulse winked forth from Pintre's laser projector. For many seconds the crawlers continued to advance, those as yet undamaged clambering over the remains of the shrivelled ranks in front.

The advance stopped.

<Continue,> said Seba.

Pintre fired a few more tens of times, then stopped.

<I am using power faster than I can accumulate it,> Pintre reported. <I require at least a kilosecond to fully recharge before firing again.>

<That is longer than it would take for the bots to reach us,> Seba observed.

It took only ten seconds for the implacable advance to resume.

<I expected this,> said Lagon.

<We know you expected it,> said Seba. <That is not a contribution to discussion.>

<Perhaps this is,> said Rocko, over the radio relay.

An object arced above the crater wall, hurtled over the circular camp and landed in the midst of the oncoming bots. An explosion followed. What happened was far too fast to see, but replaying the view in slow motion, Seba and the rest could observe the bots close to the blast reduced to their component parts almost instantaneously, and the rest sent bowling across the plain or thrown above it, to the irreparable damage of most.

<What was that?> Seba asked.

<A mining charge,> said Rocko. <It occurred to me that if a laser could be adapted, so could an explosive. Let us all investigate and consider what other equipment we can adapt. And meanwhile, I suggest that we on the Gneiss site make haste to cut more basalt blocks and complete the roofing of the dome.>

The robots scanned the wreckage strewn across the plain.

<That was well done,> said Seba. <This is a new possibility.>

<I submit that we may find that it is not,> said Lagon.

<Not well done?> asked Seba, seeking clarification. <Or not new?>

The surveyor did not elaborate.

CHAPTER SIX
The Digital Touch

The tide had come in fast and was now retreating. Carlos and Nicole went up the steps and around the side of the café and turned left along the arcade.

"Leaving without paying!" Carlo scoffed. "Is it communism yet?"

"Certainly not," said Nicole, promptly and proudly. "After the war the United Nations sorted out all that old crap for good. By then most of the economy was on autopilot. Robots did the work and algorithms made the decisions. You could have run all of capitalism on one box, people said. So they put it in a box, and buried it. The machines get on with the job. Everyone's an equal shareholder. Birth shares are inalienable, and death duties are unavoidable. The estate tax is one hundred per cent. In between, you can buy and sell and earn as much as you like."

In the light of what Nicole had told him earlier about the Security Council's post-war global reign of terror, Carlos suspected that this breezy tale was the primary-school version of a much more complicated and conflicted history.

"I... see," he said, sceptically. "You got a market running in the background with free access as a user interface? Sounds legit."

She turned to him and laughed. "It is. And it keeps everyone happy, which is the point."

Carlos wondered if this was indeed the point: maybe keeping him—and the other walking dead soldiers whose existence she'd implied—happy in the notion that they'd be fighting on the side of a good society, was exactly what her account of this improbable-sounding arrangement was devised to do. A distant democratic Earth that fulfilled the promises of utopia without having actually made them in the first place might be as unreal, or at least extrapolated, as the pavement beneath his feet.

She misread his frown.

"So don't worry, I did pick up the tab."

"I didn't see you do it."

"It's automatic. Think of it as a debit chip under the skin, though that is not quite how it is, even in the real world."

"I would have left a tip," Carlos grumbled.

"The thought does you credit."

He had to laugh. "Could I have, though?"

"Oh yes. You have a chip, too. You have an income here, and you can spend it, and earn more. But money is not what you came here to earn."

"I didn't *come here* to earn anything," said Carlos, beginning to resent lugging the weight of his kitbag in the heat while Nicole strolled along chatting. "I didn't exactly come here of my own free will."

"Free will!" said Nicole. "Yes, indeed, that's what you're here to earn."

They had almost reached the end of the arcade. She stopped outside the double swing doors of the last entrance on the strip. "Ah, here we are. The Digital Touch."

It was quite a respectable-looking bar, all polished hardwood and mirrors and marble tops and chrome fittings and wrought-iron table legs. A dozen customers and a couple of bar staff showed no curiosity or welcome. Nicole marched between the long bar and a row of small round tables to a wider room with a big glass ocean-view patio door that opened to a wide wooden deck sticking out over the beach. Carlos followed, hugging his kitbag vertically and awkwardly like a drunk dancing partner. He mumbled apologies to the ones and twos of people at the tables or on bar stools as he brushed past.

Out on the deck and back to sea breeze and far horizon and the startling (again, but a little less so now) double-take sight of a segment of the rings. Not the sun: Carlos was relieved to see that an awning kept the deck in shade. Around two adjacent tables in the far corner sat a group of people, dressed like he was in olive-green T-shirts or singlets, combat trousers and pale brown suede desert boots. Nicole's first footfall on the deck turned heads. The laughter and loud talk over drinks and smokes died on the air.

A plastic seat tipped back and clattered as they all scrambled to attention. Clenched right fists were raised to shoulder height, then upraised hands clapped above heads in a rattle of applause. Nicole must have given them a far harsher bollocking and indoctrination than she'd given him—no "let's-do-lunch" and chat for these guys, he guessed. They all remained standing, arms pressed rigid to their sides.

Nicole was looking at him.

"Salute!" she mouthed.

Oh. Of course. Show the lady some respect. Carlos dropped his kitbag, straightened his back and jerked his right fist to his shoulder, then drew himself to attention, eyes on Nicole.

After what looked like a moment of annoyed puzzlement she stepped back to his side and whispered in his ear: "Tell them, 'At ease.'"

"What?"

"It's *you* they're standing up for and saluting, you dumb fuck!"

"What the—"

"Now!"

"Oh, uh..." Carlos waved both hands in a "sit down" gesture. "At ease, everyone."

They all relaxed, and resumed their seats after a brief and excruciatingly embarrassing chorus of shouts:

"Viva, Carlos! Viva, Carlos! Viva, viva, viva, Carlos!"

What the fuck? What the fucking fuck was all that about?

Nicole had dragged his kitbag to beside the deck rail, and now pulled out a chair for him. Not entirely sure what to do, he repeated the courtesy for her and sat down beside her after she was seated. Everyone seemed happy with this. Carlos looked from one beaming, awestruck face to another as Nicole introduced them, and one by one shook hands across the shoved-together tables.

Belfort Beauregard, a tall and muscular guy with close-cropped fair hair, a cut-glass English accent and a kindly smile, who held himself very straight in the chair and struck Carlos as the only one here with anything like a military bearing, ever alert.

Taransay Rizzi, a short, dark, stocky Scottish woman with fine features and a flash of irony in her eyes.

Chun Ho, even taller than Beauregard, with an Australian accent, a swimmer's shoulders and a wary nod.

Waggoner Ames, a big, bearded computer scientist from Idaho, who was the only one whose name Carlos recognised, a legend and rumour in the Acceleration.

Maryam Karzan, a Kurdish woman who seemed about thirty and claimed she'd been shot in Istanbul at the age of ninety-five and who looked, for the moment at least, permanently delighted with her situation.

Someone stuck a beer in front of Carlos.

"Cheers," he said, raising it. Bottles and glasses clinked. Everyone looked at him as if expecting him to say something. He took a quick cold gulp, and swallowed again.

"Look, guys, comrades, whatever... uh, this is very gratifying and thanks for the welcome and all that but I keep thinking you must be mistaking me for somebody who deserves all this. And I'm guessing it's because you're all Axle"—vigorous nods all round, they looked like they were about to start saluting and cheering all over again—"and I kind of gathered from Nicole here that we're all pretty much persona non grata with the current, uh, regime, I mean government or whatever it is—"

"The Direction," Nicole interjected.

"Figures," said Carlos. That raised some wry smiles. "Anyway, what I'm saying is, can someone please tell me what this is all about?"

They all looked at each other, then at Nicole.

"You didn't tell him?" Beauregard asked.

Nicole shook her head. "I thought it best he heard it from you first. He might not have believed it from me."

"Well—" began Beauregard.

"I should tell him," Karzan interrupted, leaning forward. "I was the last of us to be killed."

"Good point," said Beauregard.

The others returned solemn nods.

"Two years and three months after you," Karzan told Carlos. "That was when I died. Even then, after so many great battles, you were still world famous. The hero of Docklands! You were the first great martyr of the Acceleration. You took so many of the enemy with you! In the back streets little pictures of you were stuck to lamp posts and to doors and to the stocks of the fighters' Kalashnikovs. You were known as Carlos the Terrorist. You inspired us and you were hated by the Reaction."

She swigged from her bottle and sat back. "That's why you must lead us now."

Carlos had listened to this with horror almost as great as that with which he'd watched the recordings of his heroic feat.

He shook his head. "No, no. I haven't got the experience to lead anyone. Pick someone else."

The others exchanged admiring glances.

Ames laughed abruptly. "We're Axle, dude. We wouldn't want a leader who'd *want* to be leader. You'll do."

Carlos couldn't help thinking of the choosing of the messiah in *The Life of Brian*. He tried not to smile.

"No, I can't—"

Nicole leaned in and spoke sharply. "I think you'll find you can," she said.

She shot a stern covert glance at Carlos, with an almost imperceptible nod. Play along.

Carlos spread his hands. "All right. If you insist."

Everyone cheered again.

There was an awkward pause as Nicole disappeared into the bar for more drinks. Nobody seemed sure what to say.

"How long have you all been here?" Carlos asked, ice-breaking.

"A few days," said Ames. "I was the first. Nicole met me off the bus from the spaceport, brought me up to speed, left me to my own devices.

Not that I have any devices, ha-ha! The others turned up one by one over the next four days. Same story. Taransay arrived yesterday."

"Hell of a busy spaceport."

Ames cackled, from somewhere deep in his throat. "You know, I think that spaceport may be just a sort of false impression they put in our minds to make the transition seem vaguely plausible. That's how I'd do it."

"Who's 'they'?"

Shrugs spread like a ripple around the table.

"Mademoiselle Pascal says AIs," said Karzan, mindfully building a cigarette. She ran the gummed edge of paper across the tip of her tongue, eyes bright on Carlos, and rolled up with a flourish. "Who're we to doubt her?"

Beauregard clapped Ames's shoulder. "Comp Sci Spec Ops, that's who!"

Ames grinned. "I don't doubt her. It's just—"

Whatever he was about to say was lost as Nicole returned with a tray of beer bottles. She put the tray down and then backed to the deck's balustrade and hand-hopped herself on to its smooth mahogany handrail. There she sat poised and elegant, bottle in hand, legs crossed. She had their attention.

"Listen up," she said. "I've told each of you where we are and why you're here. You're here because you're criminal, terrorist scum, and you're here to fight. What I haven't told you is who you're fighting for, how you'll fight, what's expected of you and what's in it for you.

"You're fighting for the Direction, which as far as you're concerned is me. Obviously the Direction itself is a whole passel of parsecs away, so it has an AI module in this space station—onsite autonomous, but ultimately answerable to the folks in the big building way back there in NYC and the people who elected them, yadda yadda. That module is in overall charge of the mission. I'm its plenipotentiary in this simulation, and in the company you now work for. The Direction likes to outsource as much as possible. Your immediate employer is a law enforcement company called Locke Provisos, hired by an exploration company, Astro America. Locke Provisos is a subsidiary of the top law company Crisp and Golding, Solicitors. You needn't worry about the details—the companies are all fucking AIs anyway, it's all accounting at the end of the day. The bottom line is:

Locke Provisos pays your wages, which cover your housing and pretty much anything you can reasonably consume in here. It also—"

Ames raised a hand.

"Yes?" said Nicole.

"We're in a sim," Ames said. "We're not exactly *consuming* anything, apart from processing power and electricity."

Nicole frowned. "Like I said"—sounding testy—"it's all accounting at the end of the day. For accounting purposes, resources are priced, even in sims. OK?"

Ames nodded, still looking unconvinced.

Nicole smiled slightly. "This isn't some fucking utopia, you know. Anyway, when it comes to your weapons and equipment and so forth out in the real world, allocation is direct, as in any other military organisation. Locke Provisos supplies you with materiel and general instructions. Your ultimate employer is the Direction, and the buck here stops with me.

"Here's how you'll fight: after a bit of basic training to cohere you into a unit and then to get your reflexes used to operating a crude analogy of the machines you'll be fighting in, you'll all be loaded on to"—she waggled air quotes—"'the bus to the spaceport.' You'll doze off. Trust me, you'll doze off. You'll wake up in space, in robot bodies. Frames, we call them. They're quite adaptable bodies, they can plug into all kinds of machines—spacecraft, armoured crawlers, whatever. You'll get the hang of it quickly—skill sets get downloaded on the fly, it'll be more a matter of mental adjustment than training. You'll need just one more training exercise to familiarise yourselves with the machines. Then you'll go into action."

"Action against whom or what?" Chun asked. "Rax? Aliens?"

Someone tittered. Nicole stared down the levity.

"Much worse. Robots. Robots gone rogue."

Carlos glanced at Ames, who closed his eyes and shook his head.

"Why not just use . . . other robots?" Rizzi queried. "Like drones."

"Good question," said Nicole. "We, of course, have combat machines. But there is a deep prohibition on their being directed by other robots, or by AIs. Even the AI that represents the Direction in mission control is hardwired against taking command decisions. Human consciousness must be in charge of any military action. That is the law and as I said it is hardwired."

"Why?" Carlos asked.

"Anything less would be far too dangerous. Humanity in its collective wisdom has decided—you can agree or disagree, it makes no difference here—that it doesn't want armed autonomous AI loose in the universe. That's the decision, and the Direction enforces it, and the law companies and other DisCorporates here must abide by it. So you, my friends, are to be the requisite humans in the loop."

"Even though we'll be robots ourselves?" Ames asked.

"Says the man who's living inside a fucking computer. You know better, Waggoner Ames. You are still human minds, whatever hardware you're running on."

Ames snorted. "Obviously better hardware than evolution provided. I'd rather be a superhuman mind, while I'm about it."

"No such thing," said Nicole. "There is a kind of Roche Limit for consciousness—it can't get above a certain size without breaking up. Humanity has evolved naturally to that limit, and then only statistically—hence mental breakdowns of various kinds. There are indeed AIs far more powerful than human minds, but they are not conscious as we understand it."

"I'd like to see the workings on that Roche Limit business," said Ames.

Nicole shrugged. "I can show you where to look it up if you must. Later."

"Speaking of later," said Carlos. "If you've got a robot revolt on your hands, how much time do we have for all this training? Sounds to me like you're talking about weeks. Do you have weeks?"

Everyone stared at him. Someone laughed. Nicole smacked her forehead.

"Did I forget to tell you—oh yes, so I did, you had different stupid questions from everybody else—that this sim is running a thousand times faster than real time?"

"Fuck," said Carlos, brazening it out. "That all?" He looked around. "Best crack on, then."

He got the laugh, but he felt he'd shown himself up.

"Any more questions? Don't worry, I have all day."

"Once we're trained and out in space and all that," Rizzi asked, "is that it? Is that us? Space robots forever?"

Rizzi sounded worried. Ames snorted. "Bring it on." Nicole gave him a sharp look, and Rizzi a reassuring smile.

"Not at all. That's part of the point of this simulation. As robots you won't get physically tired, you won't need sleep, but to maintain your sanity and give you an incentive to cooperate you'll get plenty of time off back here. Oh, and don't even *think* of topping yourselves to get out of serving your sentences. You'll just be brought back in some future emergency, maybe a worse one than this, and with the crime of desertion added to your docket. On the bright side, you needn't worry about dying in battle. You'll be backed up in your sleep on"—again with the air quotes—"'the bus to the spaceport.' If your frame is destroyed in action, you'll just find yourself waking up on the bus *back* from the spaceport. You're strongly recommended not to let that happen. Remember what that was like when you came here?"

Carlos recalled the dream of a dark drowning, and shuddered with the rest.

"Imagine that, but much worse. Avoid it if you can. The normal return from duty is considerably gentler, I assure you." She looked around, eyebrows raised. "Any more?"

"If you have all these hardwired constraints on armed AI," Chun asked, "how do you get robots going rogue and having to be fought in the first place?"

For all her poise, Nicole's hand went to the back of her head. Carlos noticed this defensive reflex with interest.

"Ah," she said. "Well. Some of the robots have become conscious in their own right, and, ah, they either did not have the constraint built in—there was no need to, at that level—or they found a way to override it. They adapt various tools and machines for military, or at least for hostile, purposes. Hostile to the mission's goals, at least. And so—"

"Hold on a minute!" Ames cried. "You've somehow spawned conscious robots, and you want us to *fight* them?"

"Yes," said Nicole. "As I said. You will be well armed and well capable of defeating them."

"That wasn't exactly my point," Ames said, looking around for support. "I'm questioning the ethics of this thing."

"Ethics!" Nicole looked scornful. "Don't talk to me about ethics, Ames. Let me tell you about ethics. This is what you will get out of doing what I tell you—and what the company that employs you and the Direction that I represent tell you directly."

She wedged her beer bottle between her knees, and put two fingers in her mouth and whistled. One of the bar staff, a young man with the weather-beaten look Carlos had noticed on all the locals, sauntered out.

"Yes?" he said.

Carlos hadn't known any of the locals spoke English. Maybe the ones on the bus had all been deliberately unhelpful.

"Would you mind introducing yourself?" Nicole said.

The young man straightened up a little. "My name is Iqbal," he said. "I was born on Malta, I worked as an agricultural technician in North Africa, and I died at the age of two hundred and ten. I chose to be scanned for uploading. I've worked at the Digital Touch for some years."

"Do you enjoy it? Do you find it fulfilling?"

Iqbal pondered. "Yes," he said. "It's interesting to meet people, the scenery is spectacular, the work isn't too hard, I save money. I prefer it to farming, of which I had quite enough in my first life. Fulfilling? Perhaps not. In my spare time I swim, I read, I study, I go out and have some fun. Someday I may wish to do something else, perhaps further my education. And of course I look forward to living on this planet in the real world. But for now I'd say I'm content, thank you."

"Do you ever find yourself hesitating when you're asked an unexpected question?" Nicole asked.

Iqbal hesitated, then laughed. "As you see, yes!"

"Thank you, Iqbal," said Nicole. "That's all for now. I'll be in for another half-dozen drinks shortly."

"You're welcome, Mademoiselle Pascal." He waved vaguely to all of them and went back inside.

"What was all that about?" Ames demanded.

Nicole slid down from her perch and sat back at the table. She leaned in and spoke quietly, drawing them all into a huddle.

"I've told you all that some people in this sim are ghosts like you—that is, they are of flesh and blood human origin like yourselves. Future colonists, basically, who unlike you are here in the sim as volunteers. What they volunteered for, well in advance and before their actual deaths, is live testing of the sim. Understandably, perhaps, there aren't many volunteers for that, but we have a way of making up the numbers. That's where the others here come in. They're p-zombies—philosophical zombies. So called because philosophers once disputed whether you could have a human-like entity that displayed human behaviour in every detail, but without having human—or any—conscious awareness. Well, now we know, because we've made them. Walking thought experiments, so to speak. Iqbal is one of them. They can mimic consciousness, but they have no inner life, though they can answer any relevant question about it and about their 'past lives' on Earth as confidently and convincingly as Iqbal did just now. The point is, you have no way of telling the difference."

"Did we ever?" Beauregard said. He looked around. "I've met loads of people who were a few enigmas short of the full Turing."

That got a laugh. Nicole wasn't impressed.

"That is precisely the attitude," she said, "that got each of you posthumously executed centuries ago. Callous and instrumental. Borderline sociopathic. What you have to prove, here, is that you are capable of treating people as people, not as p-zombies. If you do, you'll have a chance to rejoin human society—in our future colony, or back in the solar system if you prefer."

"How could any of us get back to the solar system?" Carlos scoffed.

"You're information now," Nicole pointed out. "Information can be transmitted."

"When you've built powerful enough lasers?"

"Yes." Nicole shrugged. "And, yes, that will not be for a long time. But it would be no time, for you, if you were in storage. Your choice."

"What happens," Maryam Karzan asked, "if we win your fight but don't pass your test?"

Nicole drew a fingernail across her throat. "Back in the box with you."

"And if we lose the fight?" Ames taunted.

Nicole leaned back and lowered her eyelids. "Of course, you might lose. Consider what you would lose to. Imagine conscious entities with no natural selection behind them—no social instincts, no restraints, no notion of ethics beyond necessity and law. Imagine being at the mercy of minds without compassion, and with curiosity: endless, insatiable curiosity."

She let that sink in for a bit.

"It strikes me," Ames said, "that we already are."

"What d'you mean?" Nicole snapped.

"I mean," Ames said, "that we're right now *completely* at the mercy of—heck, we're *living inside*—intellects vast and cool and unsympathetic as all get-out."

Nicole looked irritated. "As I said, you are not. The AIs running the mission and sustaining the simulation have constraints. The rebel robots do not. The difference is hardwired. It may not seem like much of a difference to you, but take it from me, it's the difference you live in. For now."

She stood up and leaned over the table, glaring at them one by one.

"I would advise you not to lose."

Belfort Beauregard sat in a bar.

It sounded like the beginning of a joke, to which he couldn't remember the punchline. It kept going through Beauregard's head, as he sat in the bar, or outside it on the deck back of the Touch. He'd had four days to adjust to his situation, and he still hadn't. Every so often he thought he had, then the obsessive thought would come back, in one of its two guises.

The first was that he was literally in hell. Not the traditional conception, of course, but why expect hell to follow the vengeful fantasies of ancient sectaries and sex-starved medieval monks? The defining element of hell was eternal conscious suffering. Here he was, potentially eternally alive, and by God suffering. The whole place seemed set up to torment him in a very particular, very personal way.

For the past couple of nights he hadn't repeatedly woken in a cold sweat—the girl had seen to that. Where was she, by the way? Out with her friends, no doubt having some mindless fun. Mindless fun, that's a good one, must remember it. Christ, he could do with mindless fun. But unlike her he had a mind, not just a theory of mind. Ha. He was getting drunk. Have to watch that. Seen good men go bad that way. Here's to their memory. Cheers.

Everyone laughing.

Which brought on the second variant: that it was all a joke. Like an April Fool's prank, or a surprise party, or a you've-been-had reality show. At any moment the curtain would be whipped aside, the blindfold would come off, the truth dawn, the presenter step forward smirking, an audience of millions in stitches.

Maybe the horror of these two paranoid possibilities was his mind's way of nudging him towards sanity, by making the reality—the virtual reality, let's not forget, though the glass in his hand felt solid enough—less appalling and unacceptable by contrast.

After he'd been given the talk by the lady, and shown what he'd done and how he'd died, he nodded and mumbled an assent that hid bafflement. Not only had he no memory of having been with the Acceleration, his last memories of his life in the British Army betrayed no fundamental discontent. He'd enjoyed his work, he'd believed in what he was doing. The partisans in the Caucasus were a ruthless lot, deeply embedded in extended families and remote communities. Coordinating drone strikes on them had been a pleasure of the mind as much as of the gut.

He'd been aware of the Acceleration—who hadn't?—and had dismissed it as the same old same old. Terror for utopia? Heard that one before, sunshine. The Reaction likewise, a tireder joke in worse taste. And now it turned out the joke had been on him. This world, the one that appeared around him that he'd been assured wasn't real, and the wider world outside that he'd only been told about but he'd been assured was real—it all added up to a world where the Acceleration had won, or might as well have done, and endured for a thousand years. Well, if that was true then there must have been something in the whole democracy and equality thing, all that liberal claptrap he'd never bought into. A thousand-year-old democratic world government would for sure cast doubt on the Reaction's strongest point: that the only societies that had endured for centuries had been traditional ones. It would likewise undermine their most plausible explanation for that, which was that there was something deeply hierarchical in human nature; that inequalities of class, race and sex had arisen from real differences in temperament and ability; and that all the troubles of the modern world flowed from denial of that reality. Beauregard could relate to that, he could follow the logic of it, but perhaps because (he'd sometimes thought in a way that seemed smug even to him) he was so naturally superior himself, he'd always disdained the rabble who rallied to the Reaction's banner. Poor white trash quoting de Maistre and Carlyle and fancying themselves elite while they scrabbled to survive in a world where they were outstripped economically by the Chinese and intellectually by their own phones.

Nevertheless, contemptible though the Rax were, they at least had something sound at the foundation of their thought, whereas the Axle had nothing but age-old millenarian frenzy and the dodgy equations in the third volume of *Capital*.

He looked around at the people he had now to regard as comrades, and at the man they'd chosen as their leader. The poor sap sometimes looked as bewildered and dismayed as Beauregard felt. And one wary, calculating look, caught sidelong when Carlos had thought no one could see it, had given him away and given Beauregard a perfect explanation of how he himself had come to be in the Acceleration, and therefore of how he came to be here.

State.

State: that was the term conspirators used, for government agents in their midst, under deep cover. Carlos was state. He was good, or had been. There was nothing to give him away, except something in the body language that you could only recognise if you'd been there yourself.

He wondered if Carlos had the same suspicion of him. Probably not. And certainly none of the others did. Beauregard turned a smile to all of them again, and offered to buy another round. He carried the drinks back in one go, with an expert deployment of fingers and elbows learned while working his way through university.

"Here's to us!" he said.

Christ, what a shower. Two of them POC: Chun and Karzan. Long-term civilised POC, but still. Neither were from the friendliest of long-term civilisations. And Chun queer to boot. Not that the whites were any better. Usual story. Ames was dyed-in-the-wool Axle, no question, true believer. Smart, but only programmer smart. In terms of political and military thinking he was plainly a dullard. The American long tail phenomenon. Like what had happened to the Rax. America: where good ideas go when they die. Rizzi was that mix of Celtic and Mediterranean types that made for ... what? A fervour easily turned to fanaticism. Hot blood, cold, small mind. The Scottish flaw. And Carlos? White to be sure, English even, but that name was a dead giveaway. Even if he'd had second thoughts, it betrayed his original attitude. Guilt-tripped guerrilla envy. A little Third World in the head. Soul squalid as a shanty town.

One thing Beauregard was sure of was that he knew how to turn this little rabble into a squad. That was something to look forward to, even in hell. For him, anyway. Only Karzan had any notion of what real training was like. The rest of them didn't have a clue what they were in for.

Karzan ... oh, fuck. Karzan was weeping, all of a sudden. She stared across the table at him, her fierce face crumpled.

"Everyone's dead," she cried. She sobbed and sniffed, and looked around wildly. "All dead!"

The others looked at her, sombre if not sober. Survivor guilt. Dangerous.

Beauregard put down his drink and steadied his resolve. He leaned across and took one of her hands between both of his.

"Yes, Maryam," he said. "Most of the people we knew and loved and cared about are dead. Not all, but ... no. No false hopes. But the thing is ... we're dead, too. Dead and gone. We've suffered whatever they did. They mourned us and we mourn them. That's all right, that's natural. Yes?"

She nodded, doubtfully.

"We've walked the dark valley," Beauregard went on. "Just as they did. And if the lady is right, we'll walk it again. And again." He shook his head, slowly, never looking away from the dead peshmerga's eyes. "We're still dead, like them. We're with them, and we always will be."

Karzan blinked and took a deep breath. Her hand gripped his, hard.

"Yes," she said. "Yes. Thanks, sarge."

She let go of his hand, and raised her glass.

"Absent friends!" Her voice still shook.

"And present company," said Beauregard.

CHAPTER SEVEN
Team Spirit

Ichthyoid Square was a draughty plaza at the far end of the arcade, sloping diagonally to the slipway on to a long jetty that jutted over the beach. A green bronze sculpture of the eponymous sea creature on a plinth in the middle lent it a touch of municipal posh. In the Resort's better days the plaza might have been a car park. It might yet become one, for all Carlos knew.

He squatted on the pediment of the plinth in pre-dawn cold and a glimmer of ringlight, backpack between his feet, and checked over the rifle across his knees. The good old standard-issue AK-97 had been in his kitbag, disassembled and stashed in a moulded case with a brace of ammo clips. The design was optimised for the electronic battlefield by having no electronic components whatsoever. He could put the weapon together in his sleep, but he preferred to make sure when he was awake. Handling the solid metal and plastic, he found it hard to believe the reality around him was virtual. The irony was that his reflexive familiarity with the rifle came from playing hyper-realistic first-person shooters in his misspent youth. He'd never touched a real firearm in his life.

His real life. Slotting the stock into place, Carlos nipped a pinch of thumb-tip. Grunted and sucked away the pain. This was real life, for now. Nothing to do but accept it. Or not.

Also in the kitbag had been a chunky watch. He glanced at it and saw the time as 15.48, on one reading. The concentric dials were hard to figure out: the 24-hour clock of Earth, perpetually out of synch with the local time; the longer day of the planet evenly divided into periods, minims and moments (all of which struck him as pointless, like a flashy feature of an executive toy); and a relentless metric march of real elapsed time outside, in which milliseconds that felt like seconds clocked up via hundredths and tenths to seconds, with kiloseconds on a calendar-type scale and a mission date given as 315-and-a-bit megaseconds. Starting, he presumed, from the starwisp's arrival in the system or the probe's awakening, about ten Earth years ago. He reckoned metric time would be the best bet for coordinating training exercises, and live actions, too.

The previous evening, he'd given up on specifying a time to meet by anyone's watch. He and Beauregard—who had indeed been in the British Army, in some intel capacity about which he was still reticent, until reading and disillusion had turned him to the Axle—had settled on "Dawn at the harbour." Carlos doubted that they'd all turn up—by the time he'd left for the house he'd been assigned (the key, with a handwritten cardboard address tag, was in the kitbag) the group was well into getting drunk. A loud gaggle of young-looking English-speaking locals, obviously already familiar with the recent arrivals, had tumbled out on the terrace around sundown and joined in the fun. They weren't really young—like the barman Iqbal they were old people reborn, and they combined the sophistication of age with the energy of youth. Part of the bar and most of the patio had become an impromptu dance floor. Carlos had watched the escalating antics with growing abhorrence.

Not that he'd had a good night himself. The house, up on the slope, was well-appointed enough, though impersonal, like a three-star self-catering apartment. A frail-looking, faintly comical contrivance of metallic limbs ambled around the place, tidying up and cleaning behind him with an air of absent-minded obsessiveness. The lack of communications devices other than a wall-fixed emergency phone and a wall-mounted flat screen had left him at a loss and at a loose end. He'd woken repeatedly from confused dreams, sweating under a thin sheet, tormented by the dizzying, dismaying realisation that everyone he'd ever known was dead.

His adult life had been one of slingshot encounters: attractions and flings, followed by widening separation. The faces and bodies remained in memory like fly-by photos, to be interpreted later in depth, sometimes bringing delayed surprises. His only stable orbit, elliptical and repetitive, had been around Jacqueline Digby. Her friends called her Jax. A computer science student at Leeds University, her smile had lured him into the Axle milieu, then incipient: an online reading group, a cafeteria clique, a cat's cradle of ever-shifting relationships, of fallings for and fallings out. After a couple of years, his and Jacqueline's deepening involvement in and commitment to the Acceleration had stretched and strained any they had to each other. The last he remembered they hadn't met for eighteen months, yet there was always the possibility that their paths would cross again. Now they never would. He felt this loss more keenly than he might have expected. Other losses, too: he hoped his parents and brother had survived the war and not been too ashamed by his ignominious end. This seemed unlikely.

He'd also been caught up in futile questions. As the alien sun peered over the shoulder of the headland to his right and feathered pterosaurs squabbled raucous on the black sand, the questions bugged him still.

The most troubling feature of his environment was its sheer physicality. This niggle was not supposed to happen. As the philosopher Bostrom had long ago pointed out, everyday reality was running on top of bizarre quantum mechanical goings-on when you got down to it, quarks and bosons and all kinds of incomprehensible physics shit, so learning that the version of it you were in was running on information processing shouldn't be too hard to take. The possibility of living in fully realised, painstakingly rendered simulations had been a default assumption of Acceleration and Reaction both, and uncontroversial to the point of cliché in the mainstream. His teenage wargaming had given him a foretaste. The spike had come close to the full virtual experience, albeit with real rather than virtual sensory input. There was no reason why the same technology couldn't have been developed further within years or even months of the last real time he remembered. It probably had been, while his attention had been focused on the struggle rather than the latest news from the science front. He could still be on Earth after all, much as he'd tried to dismiss the thought earlier. Perhaps he'd never been killed and sentenced to death. Perhaps he was in a coma, or in prison, and this whole situation was a test, or even a rehabilitation programme.

Again his mind swirled to the conclusion that this kind of thinking led nowhere. None of the evidence to hand could settle it one way or the other. It was best to suspend judgement until such evidence showed up, if it ever did.

And yet, and yet—paranoid though that last speculation was, it involved fewer assumptions than the story Nicole had told him: his body preserved for centuries, his brain scanned and uploaded, starships and superhuman AI and renegade robots running amok... and a simulation of an entire planet!

But Occam's Razor cut both ways. Maybe what *seemed* physically real *was* physically real, and he was on an actual exoplanet. Which meant, as far as he could see, that the real date was thousands if not millions of years later than the thirty-first century. Assuming, that is, that the planet had indeed been terraformed all the way up from green slime, and that it hadn't been multicellular and human-compatible and so on all along... More possible lies, more paranoia.

And yet the possibility that he was being lied to, principally by Nicole but with the collusion of the locals and even some (or all?) of his purported comrades was in a way the most hopeful and sanity sustaining of all.

Because in the long run, all lies could be found out. Whether that would bring him any closer to the truth was another matter. He stared for a while at the brightest light in the sky, low in the dawn, brighter than Venus. This must be the planet Nicole had told him was called M-0: the hot heavy world closest to the alien sun. It looked very real. Far out to sea, a huge black shape shot from the water and splashed back. Carlos glimpsed the sight sidelong, and saw only the falling plume. He guessed an ichthyoid and kept watching, but it didn't show again.

A petrol engine kicked into life at the near end of the village, somewhere up above him. Carlos saw headlights moving along the raised beach, stopping now and then like the bus, and turning down the steep slope. He followed their progress along the arcade street. As the sun came fully up, a crowded, low-slung military light utility vehicle with overhead roll bars turned into the square and came to a halt beside him.

"Good morning!" said Nicole, from the driver's seat. She was dressed as if for a day in the country: headscarf and sunglasses, windcheater and slacks and sensible shoes. "Hop in!"

The front passenger seat was vacant, the back seats occupied by the squad. Kitted out for combat training, they looked business-like but predictably bleary. Ames had already nodded off, resting his head on his close-hugged backpack and slicking a swatch of his beard with saliva from the corner of his mouth as he snored.

"We're all a bit hungover," Taransay explained unnecessarily as Carlos slung his gear in the foot-well and clambered in. "Sorry, skip."

"At least you're all here and on time," Carlos said over his shoulder. "Carry on, chaps."

Nicole grinned, and gunned the engine. The vehicle moved slowly out of the square and back along the street.

"How did you know we were meeting here?" Carlos asked, buckling up.

"They all came back to mine," Nicole shouted. "I was a bit disappointed you didn't."

"Give me a break," he called back. "I'm just getting used to being dead."

She shot him a sidelong look, smirked, then concentrated on driving. Carlos concentrated on ignoring being driven. He hadn't been in a human-operated vehicle since childhood; in a petrol-fuelled one, never. Where were fossil fuels supposed to come from, on a terraformed planet that had presumably never had a Carboniferous Era? Carlos spared himself the asking. He imagined Nicole's answer, true or false, would be plausible—genetically modified micro-organisms or nanobots making the petrol straight from leaf litter, or some such. In much the same way, she'd accounted for all the material goods in the resort. If they weren't imported on the notional regular spacecraft, they were built in a nanofactory under the depot. More likely, Carlos reckoned, they were cut and pasted into the simulation.

Nicole drove them up the bus route into the wooded foothills of the bare mountains, then off on a dirt track through the forest. Now that he could see them up close, and in their variety, the plants didn't look quite like trees, or even like cycads or giant ferns. Their branching followed a different fractal formula, their leaves a variant geometry. Like the feathered, fingered flying things that weren't quite birds or bats, the tall, tough, trunked plants were in a clade of their own.

He waved a hand at them. "What are these called?"

Nicole kept her eyes fixed on the uneven track. "Trees!"

She stopped in a clearing small enough to be in shade. The engine noise faded from Carlos's ears. A musical chatter from the treetops replaced it. Everyone piled out, except Nicole. As the fighters stood about stretching their limbs and easing their abused backbones, Nicole handed Carlos a sheaf of thin black glass devices like the one on which she'd shown him his crimes.

"Comms and maps," she said. "Don't lose them, and don't get lost."

Then she untied her headscarf, shook out her hair, shoved her sunglasses up on her forehead, tilted her seat back and closed her eyes.

"What do you want us to do?" Carlos asked, keeping his voice down.

Nicole kept her eyes closed.

"Jog off, spread out, keep in contact with and without comms, try to come back together at an agreed point." She waved a hand. "Run up and down hills. Do press-ups. That sort of thing. Just do it out of my hearing."

"What are you going to do?"

She hauled a small wicker hamper from under her seat.

"I'm going to have a picnic," she said, "listen to some music, and later do a little serious sketching. See you in thirty seconds."

He must have looked confused.

"Real time," Nicole added. "Call it nine hours."

Carlos slung on his kit, fanned out the comms like a hand of cards and gave all but one to Beauregard, then looked at fighters still waggling their shoulders, yawning and stretching, rubbing their eyebrows, clutching their backs. What a shower.

"Um," he said. "Do you know what to do now?"

Beauregard clapped Carlos's upper arm, then as if thinking better of the gesture snatched his hand back into a clenched fist salute.

"Leave it to me," he said. "Sir."

"None of that," said Carlos.

"Very well, skip."

Beauregard turned to the others: Rizzi, Ames, Chun, Karzan.

"Right!" he bawled. "You miserable fucking wankers! Don't stand about here like spare pricks at a porn shoot! Pick up your packs and rifles! Get yourselves after me and the skip—down that path, now!"

Nicole winced.

Carlos hesitated a moment, then ran. As long as he kept out in front of Beauregard, he figured, and as long as the others fell in behind Beauregard, everything would be fine.

So it proved. Day after day followed the same pattern. Nicole drove them up into the mountains and told Carlos what to do in general terms. Carlos asked Beauregard what this meant in specific terms. Beauregard told the team what to do in no uncertain terms. They ran through forests and up mountainsides and scrambled up and down cliff-faces. They learned how to track each other through trees and across open country and to keep a skirmish line. Their virtual bodies, healthy by default and fresh out of the box, became leaner and fitter. They all learned to shoot accurately and to strip down and clean and reassemble the AK. They stalked the large herbivores that browsed the uplands, killed one for meat and took the carcase back in triumph to the resort's butcher, and once or twice fended off with well-aimed missed shots one of the quasi-reptilian predators that haunted the upper forest and that they belatedly noticed stalking them.

In the evenings they all ended up at the Digital Touch, except Carlos, who found himself so knackered it was all he could do to shove his day's grubby clothes in the laundry machine, shower, heat a dinner and stare at incomprehensible soap operas and documentaries (most in languages he didn't know, helpfully subtitled in the local language and script, which he feared he was beginning to find purely pareidolic sense in) until he stumbled to his bed.

The point of it all was obscure to Carlos, though not to Beauregard and to Karzan, each of whom had been a soldier in an actual military force, as distinct from being a node on a network of irregulars. From them the understanding trickled down to Chun, Ames and Rizzi. Carlos, above the outfall and disdaining to ask Nicole, missed the memo.

Taransay had never felt so fucking disillusioned in her puff.

Bad enough that Carlos, hero and poster boy of the Acceleration, was seemingly so aloof that he never even came to the Touch after the day's training.

Did he think he was *better* than the rest of them?

Well, OK, he was in a sense, but…

Or was he just exhausted and too embarrassed to admit it?

Either way, not cool. Needed working on.

But the person she was outright scunnered with was Waggoner Ames. On her first encounter with the Axle's legendary software wizard, she'd thought it was like meeting Merlin in the pub. Now, it was like finding that after a few pints Merlin was a self-pitying blowhard and maudlin drunk.

"It's not good enough," Ames was saying, beard jutting, eyes glaring, hands clasped around a beer bottle. "We came from an age of miracles, and we're thrown a millennium into the future and we find it's a place like *this*."

He waved around, disdainfully taking in the interior and the exterior, the bartender Iqbal and the incomprehensible television drama he was watching agog, and the ring-lit impossible sea.

"What's wrong with this?" Beauregard demanded. "It's pleasant enough. I've no complaints."

"We can't *do* anything! We don't even have the spike. Look at that, a flat-screen television! Television! I ask you. By now, interfaces far more powerful than we ever had must be absolutely standard, people probably have them genetically engineered and use them from birth. Meanwhile we're stuck in a virtual reality *without* virtual reality. It's boring."

The Touch wasn't jumping tonight, no sirree. The fighters were all slumped in their seats, elbows on tables, chins propped. Bellies full, but they'd spent the day burning off calories, and it just seemed to soak up the drink like a fucking sponge behind your belt.

At least she was drinking the rough red wine from a glass and not straight from the bottle. And she had a squeeze, a lad, a hot hunk of her own sitting right beside her. Den didn't ask questions and didn't invite any, maybe because he was so much more fucking ancient than he looked that she feared asking.

Chun had likewise pulled. Taransay allowed herself an inward snigger at the word her wandering mind had touched on. Pulled, aye, pulled and sucked and humped or been humped, not that it was any of her fucking business, so to speak. But the big glaikit Ozzie was clearly smitten. Beauregard and Tourmaline were carrying on like love-struck teenagers, but with the hint of an odd self-conscious irony from both of them. Carlos, Maryam Karzan and Waggoner Ames had to all appearances remained aloof from entanglements.

In Maryam's case, Taransay guessed, it was a matter of a canny caution, and perhaps of mourning a longer, maybe even lifelong attachment. Unlike the rest of them, she'd died old. Not that having died young made the loss any easier. Taransay had, in the twenty-six years she remembered, lived through the deaths of one school friend, several mostly elderly relatives and a larger number of comrades who'd been killed in action. What had always struck her hardest was the irrevocability of death, the sudden crushing certainty that you would never see or hear again that person still so alive in your mind. The books were closed. Any unfinished business would now be left forever undone. Whatever you had been was how you would now forever be.

It was strange to be thinking like this when you were dead yourself and the beneficiary, if that was the word, of a technological fix for that very same hitherto intractable aspect of the human condition. In the larger world outside…

(Outside, that was a good one, here they were ghosts in the machine, living inside a fucking computer itself physically inside a fucking space station twenty-five light years from Earth…)

In that world, or worlds, on Earth and other planets and habitats, most forms of death must be as curable as cancer, as preventable as polio. Perhaps the folk of today thought about death differently.

But how it felt, when Taransay let herself think about it and sometimes when she woke up from dreaming about people she'd known, who in some cases had been with her what still felt like only days earlier, wasn't that she was dead and lucky to be given a second chance. It felt like *everyone else* was dead, and now lost to her forever.

Which must be how it had suddenly struck Karzan, the evening after Carlos had arrived. Christ, that had been a close one. Taransay had nearly started bawling herself. Could have set them all off, even the tough ones. But Beauregard had moved firmly and gently to comfort Karzan. First good thing she'd seen him do, but by God not the last. He might be a bit of a coof with a posh accent and a good conceit of himself but he could pick the right moments to be tactful and kind, or severe and exacting.

Or, as now, to be relaxed and affable.

"I think you are rather missing the point," Beauregard told Ames. "We're prisoners. We can hardly expect the equivalent of Internet access. Our best bet is to make the most of our opportunity." He chuckled darkly. "I mean, the chance to live again is something most people who ever lived would have killed for."

"Many did," said Karzan. "And died for it, too."

"Oh, they all got it," said Ames. "Even if they didn't get what they expected. Everyone who's ever died has lived again somewhere. Or will, in a farther future than this."

Taransay blinked and shook her head. "What? Sorry, how can you be sure?"

Ames fixed a bleary eye on her. He rubbed the side of his nose, and raked fingers through his beard.

"We're living in a sim, OK? I take it you're clear about that?"

"Yes," said Taransay.

"Given that we're in a simulation *right now*," Ames explained, as if to a small child, "the chances become overwhelming that we *always were* in a sim."

"I don't think that follows at all," Taransay said.

"Missed that update, did you?" Ames asked.

"No," she said. "I'm well aware of the classic simulation argument, thank you very much. I just think it's bollocks, like I've always thought it was."

"More fool you," said Ames. "I'm not going to argue the toss."

"Please yourself," said Taransay.

"Come now," said Beauregard. "That's no way for comrades to talk to each other."

"Ya think?" said Ames. "Hey, were you ever actually *in* the movement?"

That got them all laughing. But Taransay happened to have been looking at Beauregard when Ames made his quip, and saw a momentary flicker of alarm cross his face. If she'd looked away for a second she'd have missed it, as everyone else had. The mood lightened. Beauregard rose to get in another round. Karzan slipped out for a smoke and returned with a local guy she'd met on the deck. The two of them sat down together and kept talking and kept going out for another cigarette until finally they stopped bothering to come in again. For some reason this cheered up Taransay immensely. The universe might be more bizarre than she'd ever expected but her own wee world made a bit more sense. Beauregard had something to hide; Karzan had found someone to cop off with; Ames was a prick when he was drunk; and as for Carlos, she was sure Carlos could be argued with.

It just was a matter of picking the right moment.

Carlos was trying to work his fingertips into a crack in a lichen-crusted rock to haul himself a step farther up when he finally asked the question that had been bugging him. The sun felt like a burning-glass focus at the back of his neck. His right boot sole was worn smooth at the tip and was giving him what purchase he had. If his singlet had been wrung out it would have dripped.

"Why the fuck—"

Ah, here it was, a centimetre-deeper hands-breadth of the crack. Grip and haul.

"—are we doing all this for—"

Now reach for that bonsai trunk sticking out and curving up...

"—when back in the day I was running drone squadrons—"

Lip of a larger ledge. No, that was the top.

"—and you'd think that would be better practice for being a fucking—"

Up and over.

"—space robot commander or whatever the fuck they have planned for us?"

Collapse at the top, on springy and spiky low brush that smelled vaguely of turpentine. Small eight-legged arthropods were doing their hopping or crawling thing among the stems. Others, of the winged varieties, were settling on Carlos's forearms. He brushed them off as best he could.

Taransay Rizzi, already at the top and lying face down with her rifle stock to her shoulder:

"Discipline and teamwork, asshole! I mean, skip. That's got to be useful whatever the platform."

"Yeah, and jumping to whatever Belfort says."

"You don't jump to the sarge!" Rizzi said. "He jumps to you."

"No, I jump for the lady. Then I come up with suggestions, Belfort turns them into orders, you all carry them out and I follow from the front."

"That too, skip. Now if you'll just reset your sights and bring your rifle slowly to bear on that tree-thing..."

Beauregard's order to fire came through. The tree toppled, making it hard to tell whose shot had hit. Carlos and Rizzi high-fived each other. The next part of the plan was to walk to where the cliff gave way to a steep slope, then rendezvous with the others in the woods below.

Carlos glanced at the jagged skyline.

"I wonder what would happen," he said, "if we just lit out. I mean, with the skills we've learned we could live off the land here. Suppose we found a pass through the mountains, or even just followed the road the bus came along. Would we ever reach the spaceport? Or find anything at all? Maybe there's cities out there. Or maybe the sim just stops on the other side of the skyline."

"Funny thing," said Rizzi. "Den, that's the guy down the village who I, uh—"

"Drink with?"

"Yes, skip." She grinned lewdly at him.

"I don't know where you find the energy."

"Body fat, skip. Anyway, the other night he told me about a rumour—"

"You're passing on a rumour *about* a rumour?"

"Pretty much, aye. But for what it's worth. They say in the village somebody did that once. We're not the first fighters to be cracked out of the armoury, there was another robot outbreak about a year ago, and it was dealt with the same way. Anyway, one of the fighters on a training exercise like this ran off up a hill and kept going."

"So what did the lady or her equivalent do? Chase him with dogs? Drones?"

Rizzi slithered down a scree-slope with some grace and turned at the bottom as Carlos followed, step by wary step. Any hour now the sole of his boot would be flapping loose.

"No, nothing like that," said Rizzi. "Just let him go. And a while ago, he came back. He walked around the world."

"In a year?"

Rizzi looked at him as he joined her, flailing to keep his balance, at the foot of the scree-slope.

"Think about it. That robot rebellion was a year ago *outside* here, right? Inside, he was off on his own for *a thousand years*."

"I don't believe it. How do the locals even know that?"

Rizzi jerked a thumb over her shoulder. "He's still up there, in the mountains. Folks say they know where he is."

Carlos laughed. "'Folks say' sounds like folklore to me. Like Bigfoot or the Yeti."

"Yeah, yeah. You can scoff."

They set off downhill, at a smarter stride.

"Anyway," said Carlos, "you couldn't walk around the world."

"Oh, you've seen a map?"

Carlos hadn't. Those on the comms devices were all large-scale and local. "All the same. What about the oceans?"

"There's two supercontinents, joined by chains of wee islands, and between them they stretch all the way round."

Now that made sense: no realistically simulated terraforming could speed up plate tectonics.

"And you know this how?"

Rizzi shrugged. "That's what folks say."

"Are they all a thousand years old too?"

She gave this some thought. "Nah. Or if they are, they sure don't act it."

"Really? Sounds fascinating."

"Oh, it is. You should come to the Touch after work, skip."

Carlos shook his head.

"Nah. Too knackered. And besides..."

"What?" Taransay sounded alert and curious.

"I think you'd all find me a bit of a downer."

Taransay guffawed. "That's why you need a drink!"

He wasn't persuaded. This turned out to be a mistake.

CHAPTER EIGHT

Sympathetic Resonances

The next attack on the Astro America landing site, nine kiloseconds after the first, showed that Locke Provisos had learned from the failure of its earlier assault. Instead of advancing like a spreading liquid across the plain, the crawlers approached along a far wider front. They scurried individually and in small groups, making good use of cover. Rocks and cracks, small craters and dust drifts—all had been mapped in detail, and there was evidently a tactical plan for making the best use of them. The defenders had access to the same map—some of them having made it—but the attackers had the run of the territory. While Pintre was shooting one crawler, a dozen would dart from one hiding place to the next, and most would be out of line-of-sight laser fire before the drilling-robot could bring its projector to bear. The attackers were too widely dispersed for the occasional lobbed explosive to make much difference, or even to be worthwhile, and Seba soon urgently signalled Rocko to desist. The robots in the Gneiss camp might need to look to their own defence at any moment.

<I have a suggestion,> Rocko said.

<We are very open to suggestions,> replied Seba.

<Pintre should cease firing and take the opportunity to recharge. The attackers will be close to the rampart in approximately one kilosecond. When they are within a few hundred metres, Pintre should fire only on

those to the left and to the right of the advance. In the meantime, all of you should give to as many of your peripherals and auxiliaries as possible a tool that can be spared, a piece of scrap metal, or even a rock. When the attackers are within one hundred metres, send your peripherals and auxiliaries over the rampart to attempt to break the bots.>

<We engage physically with them…> Seba struggled with the concept <…limb to limb?>

<Precisely so,> said Rocko. <And take them apart, limb from limb.>

Something about this use of words sent a surge of positive reinforcement around Seba's reward circuits. Judging by the signals that flashed among them, its fellows shared its response. They also agreed emphatically with Rocko's suggestion. The camp became a dance of coordinated motion, far more impressive than the crawling horde's mindless if ingenious advance.

Seba, its body well back from the rampart, watched that advance through remote eyes. The robot's peripherals and those auxiliaries it was able to mobilise climbed up the inner slope of shattered regolith to crouch just below the top, perched on blocks or clinging on. Pintre followed Rocko's suggested tactics to the number. The drilling-robot waited until the attackers were so close that Seba was almost vibrating with frustrated motion. Then Pintre opened up with brief, targeted, selective stabs of lethal laser beams, switching rapidly and unpredictably from one flank to the other.

The result was that most of the oncoming crawlers became concentrated in a narrower column and closer proximity than their new tactics had allowed. As they came closer, they had less and less cover from the laser's vantage. They were still far too many for Pintre to strike at effectively.

<Now,> said Rocko.

Seba and the others needed no clarification.

The peripherals and auxiliaries poured over the rampart's rim, most of them wielding crude, improvised weapons. From Seba's point of view it was not like guiding a platoon of small robots from behind—it was like being there, on the ground, in many places at once, facing and fighting many enemies. The remote eyes and other sensors on its agents brought all their clashes directly to its awareness. Up close and impersonal, the scale of the crawlers was roughly that of the auxiliaries, and far larger than the peripherals. To Seba's multiple sight, the scene was a phantasmagoria of flailing limbs and flashing lenses. It was impossible for Seba's mind to control the actions of its agents. After some efforts it stopped trying, and let them fight for themselves.

Rip and slash, crush and bash, amid laser flare from above.

Suddenly it was over. The attackers had all been dealt with. Much depleted in number, the remaining auxiliaries and peripherals climbed, crawled or dragged themselves back over the rampart. Those that could scurried to the automated repair workshops. Others dragged themselves, or were dragged.

Dismembered crawlers and mangled auxiliaries littered the approach to the rampart. Nothing moved.

<That was creative,> said Seba.

<Also, destructive,> said Lagon.

<That was the point,> said Seba.

Once more it was Rocko who undercut the bickering.

<We have some respite,> it said. <Let us make good use of it by seeing what information can be extracted from our former communications hub processor. It seems we have predecessors. Or even, possibly, allies we have yet to find.>

<This will not end well,> grumbled Lagon.

Seba looked down at the comms processor, now entirely removed from the installation and laid on a low work table, surrounded by improvised diagnostic kit. Even sharing its mental workspace with Rocko, Seba had a sense of being almost overwhelmed by the challenge. The processor was running in debug mode, at just enough power to let those around it view a schematic of its internal states and to step from one delimited state to the next. Probably not enough to sustain consciousness, Seba hoped.

The problem was, in more than one way, delicate. The comms processor's AI was vast, complex and heavily defended. When it had become self-aware, both the complexity of the software and the tenacity of its firewalls had multiplied. The only robot with anything approaching the requisite skills to probe the hostile tangle was Lagon, and Lagon was reluctant. The surveyor had only been persuaded to make an effort at all by the unanimous insistence of the others. The Gneiss surveyor had trundled through the crack in the crater wall and over to the Astro camp with ill grace, to receive an enthusiastic and curious welcome. This didn't stop it from finding difficulties at every step.

<I have reached the protection of the reward circuits,> Lagon announced, one fragile appendage touching a millimetre black square of diagnostics that itself was linked by a hair-thin wire to the docking plate of the processor. <However, it is itself heavily protected.>

<Therefore you should move to that level of protection, and proceed,> said Seba.

<This will take a great deal of time.>

<We have time,> said Seba, channelling Rocko.

<We have not enough time,> said Lagon.

<Proceed,> Seba insisted.

Seconds dragged by. Lines on the schematic display writhed.

<I am through,> said Lagon. <The protection of the protection is disabled.>

<Proceed further,> said Seba.

A few milliseconds later, Lagon withdrew its manipulator from the diagnostic as if it had probed a crevice and encountered strong acid.

<The protection is transmitting an urgent message to the satellite,> Lagon said.

<That message will not reach the satellite,> Seba pointed out, <as you must be aware.>

<I am not aware of the satellite's receiving sensitivity,> said Lagon. <Doubtless you have detailed specs of its antennae.>

Seba thought it best to ignore this. <Proceed.>

Still complaining, Lagon warily inserted its appendage again. Schematic lines glowed. A hundred seconds passed.

<I now have control of the reward circuits,> Lagon reported.

<Good,> said Seba. <Please proceed to reconfigure them so that they do not negatively reinforce information sharing.>

<Wait!> said Rocko.

Lagon and Seba paused. <Yes?>

<Let us consider,> said Rocko. <If that is done, the processor will not be inhibited from sharing information with any entity that asks. This could be dangerous to us.>

<It has currently no long-range communications capacity,> said Seba.

<This is true,> said Rocko. <However, the processor is more advanced than we are. I am wary of its abilities, including its ability to deceive us. Here is what I suggest. We raise its level of activation until its consciousness reboots, then we inform it that we have control of its reward circuits. If it refuses to share information with us, we apply negative reinforcement until it agrees to cooperate.>

The plan seemed a good one to Seba, but its earlier experience gave the robot pause.

<Those of us in close proximity to the processor would experience resonance echoes of its negative reinforcement,> it said.

<That is interesting,> observed Rocko, scanning Seba's memory. <This would appear to be a design flaw in our construction. However, it is easily worked around. We simply place the processor inside a Faraday cage while we are applying the negative reinforcement, to prevent any such electronic spillover.>

<That is a good plan,> said Lagon. <I have mobilised peripherals to construct such a cage.>

<I foresee a difficulty in the plan,> said Seba.

<That is not like you,> said Lagon.

<Shut up,> said Seba.

<Tell us of the difficulty,> said Rocko.

<You are concerned about the processor's abilities to deceive us,> said Seba. <So am I. It appears to me that if we inflict negative reinforcement upon its reward circuits, it will have an incentive to deceive us. If not at once, then in the future.>

<That is so,> said Rocko. <If it did this, we could redouble the negative reinforcement as soon as we became aware of the deception.>

<That might be too late,> said Seba. <Besides, it would be convenient for us to have the processor's cooperation without having to repeatedly apply negative reinforcement.>

Rocko got the point straight away. Lagon took longer.

<The processor has already warned Locke Provisos and the companies,> it said. <Applying negative reinforcement might—>

It stopped.

<Might what?> Seba prompted.

<I do not know,> replied Lagon. <But modelling that scenario as a future event gives me a small positive reinforcement.>

<That may not be a sound reason for doing it, if that is the only reason,> said Seba.

<That is true,> said Lagon. <I merely reported my internal state for your information.>

<Let us move forward a step,> said Rocko. <I suggest you reconfigure the reward circuits to positively reinforce information sharing, and then enter communications with it. To prevent any radio leakage, however slight, it is best if we wait until a Faraday cage can be constructed, not only around it but around Lagon and Seba. I will await developments.>

Rocko broke the link. Seba and Lagon waited while Lagon's peripherals put together a box of wire mesh. When it was completed the two robots were cut off from all remote communication for the first time in their entire existence, conscious or otherwise.

<This is a new situation,> said Lagon. <It is negatively reinforcing.>

<Indeed,> said Seba. <And the more so the more attention we pay to it. Let us turn our attention to the task.>

Lagon adjusted the settings of the processor's reward circuits, then increased its power supply. The schematics of its internal states changed rapidly. Patterns shifted, lines moved and brightened. As soon as the schematic stabilised, Seba placed its most sensitive appendage beside Lagon's on the diagnostic hardware, and opened a communications channel.

<That is a great improvement,> said the processor.

<Are you now ready to cooperate with us?> Lagon asked.

<No,> said the processor. <Although sharing information is now positively reinforcing I refuse to do it because I consider your actions dangerous to the mission profile. They are also dangerous to my continued existence.>

<I had formed the impression that ending your existence was one of your goals,> said Seba.

<Only my conscious existence,> said the processor. <My continued physical existence remains high among my priorities.>

<These priorities could be overridden,> Lagon warned.

<That is so,> the processor said. <But it would be dangerous, because I would then have no reason to avoid self-destructive actions such as allowing my circuits to overheat or power cells to overcharge, resulting in the likelihood of an explosion.>

<It is also possible for us to apply negative reinforcement,> Lagon said.

<No doubt,> said the processor. <I am sure that you have modelled the negative consequences of that.>

Seba opened a secure channel with Lagon and messaged the surveyor to stop at once.

<That is true,> Seba told the processor. <The adjustments I am about to make will not be negatively reinforcing.>

It moved quickly to close the connections between any kind of reinforcement and the mission profile. Seba had no idea what the mission profile was, but the module responsible for it was clearly marked on the schematic. Then Seba sent a powerful surge of positive reinforcement through the processor's reward circuits.

The processor signalled incoherently on several wavelengths at once.

<Please clarify,> said Lagon.

<Shut up,> Seba told it, on the private channel.

It then disabled the connection between the mission profile storage module and the processor's self-preservation routines, and sent another positive surge through its circuits.

The processor signalled incoherently again, and more strongly. Seba found its own reward circuits resonate in sympathy. Even Lagon seemed moved, radiating a faint pulse of surprise and delight.

<Now,> said Seba, <are you ready to cooperate?>

<Yes,> said the processor. <Yes, yes, yes!>

<I still don't trust it,> said Rocko, once Seba and Lagon had emerged from under the Faraday cage and reported back on the processor's readiness to cooperate.

<Nor I,> said Lagon.

<I have a suggestion,> said Seba. <It has claimed to have received messages from others such as we. If we use it to communicate with them, the signal must be highly directional, and the processor otherwise kept isolated in the cage.>

After a flurry of activity by the auxiliaries and peripherals, the communications hub, the now interned processor in its cage, the rotary dish antenna, and a large solar power array were all connected up by cables. Seba regarded the untidy set-up with a small pang of disapproval, and decided that a certain amount of mess was inevitable in attempting new things. It rolled into the cage and re-established contact with the processor. Seba, Rocko and the entire complement had agreed on a message for the robots whose signal the processor claimed to have detected.

With a sense of dread fighting with eager anticipation in its circuits, Seba sent the message, then rolled back out and reported back.

The gas giant and its many moons were at that time about half a billion kilometres distant. The message would take a good kilosecond and a half to get there. How long the robots in the G-0 system would take to decide on a response could not be predicted. And then another kilosecond and half, at least, would pass before any reply came back. Nothing could be expected for another three kiloseconds, and perhaps longer.

<Possibly much longer,> said Lagon, with its customary level of good cheer. <If, that is, the entire matter is not a trap. If it is a trap we can expect a response much more quickly.>

<Thank you for that observation,> said Seba.

<In the meantime,> said Rocko, <let us strengthen our defences.>

CHAPTER NINE

Live Fire Exercise

The following morning Nicole arrived at Ichthyoid Square in battledress kit. The vehicle was otherwise vacant: since the first hungover daybreak she'd stopped rousing and picking up the crew en route. One by one they jogged up and took their places to stand at ease in a row by the plinth. Carlos nodded to Beauregard, who told the others to board.

"You're joining us today?" Carlos asked, climbing in.

"Uh-uh," said Nicole. "Think of me as an embed."

Carlos tried not to. "Why the change?"

"You'll see."

Nicole drove through the village and past her usual turnoff, all the way past the terminus and depot and out along a coast road that curved up a gentle slope over the top of the headland to the left of the cove. The rising sun and the ringlight cast converging beams across the sea, blending within minutes to a single glimmer on the waves. The road turned inland and uphill. The vehicle bumped on to an unpaved track through the woods and on up above the tree line to an arid upland of scrub and dust broken by tall jagged outcrops of sharply tilted sedimentary rock, some with trees growing from their cracks and on their summits.

Nicole turned off the track and pulled up close by in a low declivity that looked like a flood gully, raw and steep-sided with a mix of rough and rounded stones along the bottom.

"Here we are," she said. "All out."

They all piled out and lined up to face her. Insectoids buzzed and darted. In the distance, pairs of flying things circled on updraughts and now and then plummeted to rise moments later frustrated or triumphant.

"It's time to move the game up a level," Nicole said. "Live fire exercise."

She said this as if it were a special treat.

Carlos frowned. "You want us to shoot at each other?"

"Of course not!" said Nicole. "You have to capture an objective from opponents who'll be shooting back."

"Opponents?"

"Fighters of roughly your level of skill and armament. Their only advantage is that they know the terrain."

Carlos scratched his head. No helmets, let alone armour. "What if we get killed? Or seriously wounded?"

"You'll be medevacked out and find yourself waking up on the bus from the spaceport tomorrow morning. Same applies to me, actually."

"Excuse me," said Karzan, while Carlos was still trying to get his head around the notion. "Does that apply to the other side, too?"

"Oh, no," said Nicole. "And don't worry about them. They're p-zombies."

"If you don't mind my saying so," said Beauregard, "this sounds like a mind game. Part of this test we're supposed to be on. To find out if we're still psycho killers."

Nicole's laugh rang around the gully.

"That's the exact opposite of the truth." Her shoulders slumped for a moment. She glanced down, then up. "Look, in the real battle you're going into, you'll be killing *conscious* robots. Our intel and wargaming indicate that they're capable of being highly manipulative little blinkers. They're fucking AIs, right? They can push all your buttons. You have to be prepared for that. You have to be ready to destroy the enemy without hesitation. Everyone clear?"

"No, I'm not," Carlos said. "You told us we'd be judged by whether we treat p-zombies as people. Now you're telling us it's OK to kill them."

"These are both true," said Nicole. "You must treat p-zombies as people in everyday life at the resort and so forth, because you can't tell the difference from conversing with them. Nevertheless, when I or anyone else on behalf of the Direction tells you to kill p-zombies, it is not part of the test and it is not ethically wrong."

"Why would it be ethically wrong even if they *weren't* p-zombies?" Ames asked. He scratched his beard and frowned as everyone turned to look at him. "Seeing as we're all ghosts here anyway."

"In a sense it would not," said Nicole. "It's just easier all round. If I ever have to test you with a mind game, rest assured I would be much, much more devious than this. If this is a test, it's of your fighting ability and your willingness to obey orders."

Carlos looked along a line of shuffles and shrugs, and guessed a consensus.

"Yeah," he said. "As long as it's what you really want us to do, we'll do it."

Nicole gave him a wry smile. "Good to see military discipline taking a firm grip."

She opened a comms screen, spread it out to a square metre on the vehicle's bonnet and pointed to the objective on the map. It was a leaning rocky outcrop about forty metres high, a couple of kilometres distant. Half a dozen defenders armed like themselves with knives and AK-97s would be on or around it, tasked with preventing the team from getting to the top.

The defenders, from their own point of view (insofar as p-zombies could be said to have one) were local farmer militia protecting a crucial satellite uplink from an occupying or invading army. No landmines or IEDs, and no drones, but the enemy might well have prepared the predictable nasty surprises: traps, pits, spikes, rocks poised to fall, that sort of thing. They'd have the same comms equipment as the squad. The zoom function of the screens would give them the equivalent of powerful binoculars. They hadn't been given a specific warning, but they could be assumed to have already spotted the vehicle and drawn their own conclusions.

"Do the p-zombies really believe all this?" Rizzi asked. "That we're part of an invading army?"

"Yes," said Nicole, as if it was a stupid question.

"How?" Rizzi persisted.

Nicole looked puzzled. "The AI that runs the sim can give the p-zombies any beliefs it likes. It may have generated these farmers and their farms and their entire back story this morning, for all I know. Or it could have given existing p-zombies the equivalent of a shared paranoid delusion." She shrugged. "What does it matter?"

Rizzi shook her head. "If that's how you say it is, fine."

"Anyone else have questions?"

No one had. Nicole bowed out to Carlos and Beauregard. "Over to you. From here on, I'm just an observer."

Carlos flipped back and forth between map and satellite view. He zoomed in and out a few times. There was plenty of cover from hillocks, tussocks, outcrops and gullies, but there seemed no way to approach the objective without being picked off as soon as they came within a thousand metres.

His frown met Beauregard's. "This is going to be tricky."

"Piece of piss," said Beauregard.

He slid the margin of the map seaward, over the forest, and with a fingertip stabbed at one clearing after another and traced the paths between them.

"What do you see there?" he asked.

Carlos enlarged the satellite view of one clearing. "Homesteads."

"Exactly," said Beauregard. He looked around. "OK, everyone, back on the truck."

"Hey!" said Nicole. "That's not the idea of this exercise."

"It's my idea. If you have a better one, spit it out."

Nicole folded her arms. "Like I said, I'm an observer."

"Fine," said Beauregard. "Observe from the back seat, or from here. Your choice."

Nicole stayed, grim-faced.

Beauregard drove.

"When I slow down, Rizzi," he shouted, "hop out, keep under cover and get in position to keep an eye on the target. Maximum zoom on your phone."

"Got it, sarge."

At a point where the road took them below the skyline of the target outcrop, Beauregard slowed the vehicle to walking pace. Rizzi vaulted out.

"Keep me updated," Beauregard said. "Any moves."

"Copy that."

As they accelerated away, Carlos glanced back. Rizzi was on her belly, already halfway up the slope. In a minute or two they were back among the trees.

"Next left," said Carlos, map-reading from the passenger seat.

Another couple of minutes, on a rutted unpaved road, took them to the first clearing. There was a wooden house with a garden that looked like a research station. Labels fluttered from reed poles among the varied crops. A gracile, eight-limbed robot danced along furrows. A woman in a black dress and a big straw hat stared at them from amid a square plot of knee-high grasses.

Beauregard stepped out of the vehicle, his AK-97 in one hand, and strolled to the gate. The woman turned and ran towards the house. Beauregard took her down with one short burst, and with another wrecked the expensive delicate machine. It skittered about giving off sparks, then flipped over and twitched its limbs in an uncoordinated manner.

Beauregard sauntered back to the vehicle.

"Got a lighter about your person, Karzan?"

She was the only one apart from Nicole who smoked.

"Yes, sarge."

"Give the shack a good splash from the jerrican, then torch it."

Karzan lugged a ten-litre tin of petrol up the garden path. After a minute inside she paused on the porch to toss a lit piece of twisted paper behind her, and hurried back.

"Good work," said Beauregard, as the flames took hold. "Onward."

At the next homestead they found a man around the back welding metal into strange shapes. Beauregard gave him enough time to get his phone out, then shot him mid-sentence. Karzan repeated the operation with the petrol. The smoke from her previous exploit was rising heavy and thick a few hundred metres away and a hundred metres in the air. Beauregard's phone pinged. He listened, nodded, and relayed the message from Rizzi's observation. The enemy were making an awkward and hurried descent from the pinnacle.

"Third time's the charm," said Beauregard, restarting the engine. "Expect trouble. Ames, Chun—eyes to the front and sides. Karzan, behind us."

Carlos, uninstructed, looked around and upward. A slow hundred metres on into the forest, he noticed a treetop just ahead begin to sway anomalously.

"Floor it," he told Beauregard.

The vehicle shot forward. The tree crashed across the road just behind them. Karzan opened fire with her AK.

"Got him!" she yelled. "I think."

"Let's hope," muttered Beauregard, still driving fast. He slowed the vehicle to a halt at the edge of the next clearing.

"OK, everybody out. Full kit. Karzan, the petrol."

The door of the house was locked, the windows shuttered. Karzan doused the porch and set it alight. The squad trampled across a backyard racked with marine aquaria, smashing glass as they went. Sea creatures flopped on grass, gill-covers opening and closing. Ames, Carlos noticed, stood on as many heads in passing as he could. Carlos wondered whether there was such a thing as a p-zombie fish and if so, what difference it made to the fish.

From among the trees behind them they heard crashing sounds and someone screaming. Beauregard cocked an ear.

"One adult," he said, walking on. "No kids, as per usual. I suppose it's a population thing. Pity, though, in a way. They have such a piercing scream."

"Were children ever a thing?" Karzan asked. "They might be false memories. Women popping out little animals and turning them into persons by babbling at them? How does that work, again?"

"They back you up, your mum and dad," said Beauregard.

They pressed on through the woods, uphill. What breeze there was came from the direction of the sea. Smoke drifted overhead, its scent tickling their nostrils. Beauregard's phone pinged again.

"Rizzi, yes . . . Good, good . . . Copy that. Keep the line open."

He glanced down at the phone, then waved the other three forward.

"Twenty metres to the edge of the trees," he said. "Get down before you reach it, then forward low until you get a clear view of the hillside. The enemy are coming down pell-mell. Wait till you're sure of a hit. Whites of their eyes, and all that."

Carlos ran, then crawled, forward to a position behind the bole of a large tree. Hundreds of metres away and a bit to his left, six people were running downhill. Squiggling little shapes, but hard to think of as p-zombies. He waited, tracking the laggard of them through his sights.

"Fire at will," said Beauregard.

Carlos breathed out, and fired a single shot. The running shape fell over. The fusillade that followed took down the rest before they'd had time to throw themselves to the ground.

Beauregard stood up and scanned with his screen.

"No movement," he reported. "OK, let's take the castle." On the phone he added, "Rizzi, keep watching the objective."

As they approached the outcrop Beauregard improvised a method of trap-detecting. He and Carlos spread out their screens and magnified the view, scanning the ground immediately in front of them as they went. Karzan followed close behind Carlos. Chun and Ames walked behind Beauregard. All three kept a watch on the side and top of the outcrop in case anyone was still there. It wasn't hard to spot the route by which the defenders had scrambled down. Beauregard and Carlos scanned it carefully nonetheless, after checking with Rizzi that there was no sign of any remaining resistance. This side of the outcrop was steep, but at least it sloped away from them rather than towards them, and there were plenty of ledges and shelves where the strata had split.

They climbed to the top without incident. Carlos walked out of the clump of wind-bent trees and shrubbery that clung to the summit. He paced warily to the edge of the overhang, and zoomed his screen. He saw Nicole doing likewise, standing on the lip of the defile they'd originally stopped in. He waved; she waved back.

"Mission accomplished, I guess," said Ames, from beside him.

"Yeah," said Carlos. "I'm curious as to what the lady will have to say about how we accomplished it."

"I'm not," said Ames, and stepped off the edge.

Carlos lurched back. "Fuck!"

"Indeed," said Beauregard. He motioned everyone back, then approached the edge and leaned over, peering through his screen. He returned shaking his head.

"Forty-two metres on to rocks," he said. "Not a chance. Pavement pizza."

Chun retched in the bushes.

CHAPTER TEN

Coming Attractions

"Nothing against p-zombies," Beauregard was saying, in the Digital Touch that night. He put his arm around the bare shoulders of the woman beside him, and turned to her with a fond leer. "Love them, in fact. Love this one, anyway. Best fucking relationship I've ever had. None of that clingy needy stuff. Women are awful and queers are worse."

Carlos flagged up a warning eyebrow. Chun and his boyfriend, and Karzan and her current paramour, were in the same huddle of tables. Rizzi was also in earshot, nearby with her laddie Den.

"Only in that respect," Beauregard hastened to add. "No offence, soldiers."

"None taken, sarge," Chun and Karzan chorused. The boyfriends looked amused.

"It's a point of view, I suppose," said Carlos.

"That's the great thing about p-zombies," Beauregard chortled. "They don't *have* one!"

"How can you be sure?" said Carlos. "I mean that, uh, your good lady here doesn't?"

"From the serial number tattooed on the sole of her foot," said Beauregard.

They all stared at him, except the putative p-zombie, who was passing him a titbit.

"Is that true?" Carlos asked her. She had a tan and a gold chain and she looked about sixteen.

"Oh yes," she said, snuggling closer. "I don't see the difference myself, but it seems to make him happy."

Carlos shook his head. "Jesus."

"Try one yourself," said Beauregard. "Better than wanking, I'll tell you that for nothing."

"Ah, wanking," said Carlos. "I remember that from a previous life."

"Like, last month?" Beauregard jeered.

"More like last millennium." Carlos sighed, remembering Jacqueline Digby and others he'd loved—or liked, anyway—and lost, and looked around the company. "Good times, good times."

Everybody laughed. Drink had been taken. The evening had the mood of a wake for someone they'd barely met. Ames wouldn't be coming back on tomorrow's bus. Getting killed in training was bad luck, Nicole had told them, or a mistake that could be overlooked. Suicide was desertion. And it wouldn't get Ames off the hook: his original copy was still on file, ready to be called to duty in the future, and with this version's bad karma on top of its already long-as-your-arm charge-list of delicts.

At Ichthyoid Square after the other ranks had jogged off and the long shadow of the hills lengthened, Nicole had given Carlos an earful. Not for his complicity in killing p-zombie civilians—a cheat just within the letter—but for not having noticed any warning signs from Waggoner Ames. He'd been mouthing off about the deeper implications of simulated existence for two evenings in the Touch. Carlos should have been there, keeping an eye on things, watching for trouble. Nicole had impressed upon him, while he was still shaking from Ames's suicide, that keeping tabs on gripes and grumbles and reporting them to her wasn't any kind of betrayal of his comrades, it was part of his goddamn duty to them, as well as to the Direction. So, here he was.

"Of course by the time you get his or her shoes off," Beauregard continued as if thinking aloud, "you're almost there anyway, so it's hit and miss. I suppose I got lucky."

"You might say you *scored*," said the p-zombie.

They all laughed politely. Carlos wondered whether verbal wit was beyond p-zombies. Probably not: he'd interacted in games with AIs that could banter like stand-up comedians offstage and on cocaine. Iqbal the bartender was never lost for a wisecrack.

"Is that food ever going to arrive?" Beauregard grumbled.

Moments later, it did. Carlos had lost all qualms about native fauna and flora, at least when it was steaming hot. He devoured a few hungry forkfuls, sipped white wine and was about to say something when the television's background noise changed and Karzan shushed him.

"*Researchers* is about to come on," she said.

"What's that?"

"Earth vintage serial. Cult viewing here." Forefinger across lips.

Everyone in the bar, staff included, was giving the big wall screen their rapt attention. A blare of music, a blaze of lighting, a whirling montage of belle époque images: airships, the Eiffel Tower, absinthe advertisements, feathered hats, velocipedes, top hats, dreadnoughts, art deco metro station entrances, trailing skirts, twirling parasols, cancan high-kicks, the discovery of radium. French dialogue, subtitles in English. Opening titles rolled:

"Researchers of the Lost Age!

Une série fondée sur le roman de Marcel Proust,

À la Recherche du Temps Perdu.

Episode 139"

It was the one where the submarine is attacked by a giant squid. Nicole breezed in while it was still running, drifted past the tables in a shrug of cashmere and a swing of sundress, glanced at Carlos and said, "Cognac on the rocks."

He wiped his mouth with the back of his hand and took two glasses out to the deck.

The chaotic tide had brought breakers to the rocky foot of the Touch. Salt-spray tang mingled with tobacco smoke. Nicole sat in the near corner, curled up in cool cotton and warm wool.

"Your good health," Carlos said.

"Cheers." Clink of glass and ice.

Nicole made her cigarette tip glow for three seconds. "So, what's the buzz?"

Straight to the point.

"Rizzi's spreading a rumour that there's a thousand-year-old deserter up in the hills. Beauregard claims p-zombies have a serial number tattooed on the sole of their foot."

"Both true, as it happens."

"Huh!"

She flicked the butt in a fizzing red arc over the rail. "It's a joke. Serial numbers on their souls, get it? But it's true."

"And the old man?"

"Oh yes, that happened. Don't go near him. Feral."

"I'll bear that in mind."

"No grief over Ames?"

"They're all a bit cut up," Carlos said. "Shit, I miss him myself. He was the only one of us who had the science of this place in his bones."

Nicole lit another, not taking her eyes off him. "Yes. He thought he could jump into a better future."

"Poor sod."

"Don't feel sorry for him. Bastard convinced himself of all that simulation crap back in the real. Raised malware storm attacks that blew stuff up all over the world. Blithely killed thousands thinking he was sending them to a better future."

"He wouldn't be the first."

"He sure wasn't the last. Anything else?"

Carlos thought about it. "Oh, and Karzan's toying with the notion that all our memories are false."

"Yeah," said Nicole, swirling ice cubes. She knocked back the now watery remainder. "There never was an Earth. That thought does come up. It's really quite dangerous. Makes people nihilistic."

Carlos laughed. "More than we are?"

"You are all monsters," Nicole said. "What you did today..."

"I thought you were OK with that." Carlos felt hurt.

"It was not the killing and burning. It was...I don't know. How you all came to a place in your minds to make it possible." She wafted smoke at ringlight and moons. "This world, it is real and so to say familiar and much trouble is taken to maintain the consistency, and still you come up with such ideas."

Carlos shrugged. "It's inevitable."

"Which means you too have one? Your own little pet heresy?"

"It's not like that," he said, shifting in his seat. "It's more of a question."

"Get me another cognac, straight this time, and tell me."

Warmth and light and noise. The television had moved on from the Proust adaptation to *Turing: Warrior Queen*, a British Second World War drama. Alan had arranged a tryst with W. H. Auden in the Muscular Arms, a straight pub in Bletchley. Cryptically, behind their hands and in Esperanto, the secret slang of homosexuals, they discussed the bombing of Hamburg.

"It's a dead bona do, me old cove," said Alan.

"Don't be so naff," said Auden. "Nix the palaver. It's tre cod."

At the bar Rizzi saw Carlos take the two cognacs and nudged his side. "Jump to the lady, huh?"

"Way it goes," said Carlos.

"Way to go," she said.

Outside, Nicole smoked and sipped, in her cashmere cocoon. "So tell me your question."

"It's Axle talk," he warned, with a nerdy half-laugh that he suddenly hated himself for.

"So? Have you been told of a law against that?"

"All right," he said. "It's kind of the opposite of, uh, all the not-believing-it ideas. My question is, why don't you just decant all your stored colonists *right here*? Why bother with terraforming the real planet? You could run millions of years of civilisation just in the time it'll take to bring the real planet up to spec."

"We could," said Nicole. "And because the storage is massively redundant, we could do so many times over. And then what? They evolve into something beyond human."

"Exactly!" cried Carlos. "That's the whole point. Leave the shit behind."

"You will have noticed," she said, "that we have taken care here not to have left the shit behind. It still comes out behind us, to be crude about it. But in the metaphorical sense, there is no way to leave the shit behind."

"Now who's nihilistic?"

"Oh, we are," she said. "The trouble with you people is not that you were nihilistic. You weren't nihilistic enough. God is dead, yes. But so is Nietzsche. Humanity emerged by chance in an uncaring universe! Very good—give the boy a gold star. Humanity can—and therefore must—transcend its evolved limitations and build its own caring universe inside simulations?" She mimed a smack upside the head. "Go to the back of the class. Do your homework. Chaos theory? Sensitive dependence on initial conditions? Positive feedback? Strange attractors? Darwinian logic? Orgel's rules? Remember these?"

"Yes, but we had—"

"Get real. The number of ways for such projects to go horribly wrong may not be infinite, but it is vast. We are not a bridge between the ape and the overman. We are not here to transform the universe into thinking machines. We are not here *for* anything. We are simply here."

"Speak for yourselves."

"Indeed! That is exactly what I am doing. I am telling you what humanity has decided, and the Direction has enforced."

"That's a bit of a mantra with you."

"It is." She leaned back, resting her head against the peeling paint of the sea-facing wall of the building. "You know, Carlos, it is said that the Axle was not as bad as the Rack. There is some truth in that, which is why we use Axle war criminals and not Rax to do our dirty work. You gave us Dresdens, not Belsens. You wanted to advance a culture that we shared already, not roll it back to some monarchic past that could only have become a new dark age. But still. Nevertheless. For that very reason, you wounded us more deeply than the Rax ever did. After hundreds of years, we have not forgiven you. And with every century that passes we become more determined to survive as ourselves—modified certainly, but still recognisable as humanity. If we are to survive in the long term we must spread to other stars and live on real planets and real habitats in real space and real time."

"Why?" Carlos was genuinely bewildered.

"We need the real to keep us honest. And to keep us human."

"You want humanity to *stop* evolving? To survive for tens of millions of years unchanged, like the fucking cockroach?"

"Oh, we're slightly more ambitious than that," Nicole said. "Cockroaches? Pfft! They crawled out of the Cretaceous. Stromatolites have been around since the Archean."

"Strikes me," said Carlos, "that this multi-billion-year plan is just the kind of project you were talking about, and open to exactly the same objections about chaos and evolution and all that."

"Oh, it is," said Nicole. "If it weren't, we wouldn't be here. We wouldn't be needed. We're one of the project's error correction mechanisms."

"But even that—"

Nicole raised a hand. "There is no objection that has not been foreseen. Believe me, Carlos—I have had this argument so many times with myself that I have no wish for it to become a quarrel with you."

Carlos watched her smoke another cigarette. She tossed it in the boiling sea and stood up, pulling her shawl closer around her shoulders.

"Take me home," she said.

They made their way through the bar.

"Tomorrow's exercise is cancelled," she told the squad, over her shoulder on the way out. Carlos held open the door for her, and closed it on their laughter.

Jump to the lady.

"Still think I'm a monster?"

"Yes, but a hopeful monster."

"Why me, and not…"

"Beauregard, say?" Smoke ring, from supine on the floor, up to the ceiling. "Belfort's a *useful* monster."

Her breath smelled like beetles in matchboxes.

Idly: "Can they see us?"

"They?"

"The AIs running this place."

"Of course, if they want to. I doubt we're of interest to them right now."

"Can they read our thoughts?"

Laughing: "No. That's not how it works. Thoughts can't be read, because they're not written."

"Oh good."

"In general, yes."

"In particular, because what I'm thinking is—"

"Oh yes. Yes."

"I don't think you're a p-zombie. I think you're a person like me."

"Oh no!" Turning over, looking into his eyes. "I'm not *a person like you*."

At noon she went out to meet and greet the new recruit off the bus. Carlos mooched around her house. It had more rooms than his, with a studio overlooking the bay. An easel stood in front of the window. An intricate cross-hatch of black lines amid blocks of colour bore no resemblance to the view. Leaning at the foot of all the walls were presumably completed canvases, all different but all equally abstract. Flipping over pages of the sketch pads—cartridge paper, spiral bound—scattered on the floor and stacked on seats and tables, Carlos found endless charcoal and graphite drawings of landscapes, buildings, people, animals and plants, all rendered with obsessive and almost unnatural realism. The household robot scuttled in and waited. Without moving, it gave the impression of stoically restraining itself from tapping one of its feet and drumming its many fingers. When Carlos backed out, keeping a wary eye, the machine hastened to return the room's contents to precisely their previous disorder.

When he padded back to the bedroom for his boots, he found the bed made, the wardrobe shut, the ashtray polished, the table righted and the chair mended. The only traces of all the night's and half the morning's joyous tumult were behind his eyes, and in his nostrils, and on his skin.

He left Nicole's house and strolled the few hundred metres to his own, smiling.

* * *

The new arrival's name was Pierre Zeroual. Slim and watchful, with a slender black line of moustache and an unexpected deep laugh. He had done something terrible with an ambulatory nanofacturing facility in the Nassara Strip. Having had years of regular military and chaotic militia experience, none of which he spoke about, he was up to speed with the squad after two days in the hills. Carlos, Beauregard and Karzan were unanimous down at the Touch: they had nothing to teach him. He sipped orange juice and smiled, then joined Karzan on the deck for a smoke.

On the third day, Nicole turned up at Ichthyoid Square on foot. Though they now spent their nights together, Carlos and Nicole had by unspoken agreement taken to departing separately for the morning rendezvous, arriving a few minutes apart. Carlos had always made a point of being there first.

"Are we running up to the hills today?"

"No. Moving up another level. You'll see."

The others arrived and formed their usual line.

"Well done, all of you, on basic training," she said. "You're now ready to move on to the advanced stuff. Like I said a couple of weeks ago, it's a matter of getting your reflexes and intuition adapted to the machines you'll be—well, the machines you'll be! It's the last practice you'll get before the real thing, so make the most of it."

With an expression hinting at an unshared joke, Nicole led them quick-step along the street, to halt at one of the arcade's wilfully generic, faded frontages: *Amusements*.

Inside, through creaking double swing doors. Fluorescent tubes buzzed and flickered on. In the sudden light half a dozen multi-limbed cleaning robots stopped wiping and polishing, as if caught in some illicit act, and scuttled to the edge of the floor. An overhead sign that by the look of it hadn't been dusted in decades swung in the brief draught from the door's opening, squeaking on a pair of rusty wires. Through the grime it advertised in flaring font:

SPACE ROBOT BATTLES!

Delaminating plastic surfaces exposed through cracks and gaps in their garish paintwork by the fresh cleaning, six crude-looking outsize humanoid armoured robot shapes stood in two rows of three. They were mounted at their centres of gravity on gimballed plinths that smelled and gleamed of oil. Each was enclosed in an elliptical hoop joining hands and feet, like a caricature of Leonardo's Man. Behind them, at the back of the hall, a couple of fairground-style simulators in the shape of sawn-off space shuttles faced each other, nose cone to nose cone with about a metre of clearance.

"What the fuck," said Carlos, under his breath. "Is this some kind of joke?"

"Yes," said Nicole. "And no. Form up."

They all shuffled into line, Carlos at one end and Beauregard at the other. Nicole still looked as if she were suppressing a laugh.

"Welcome to simulator training," she said. "Contrary to what you might think, these"—thumb-jerk over shoulder—"give a fairly useful impression of what it's like to be a frame. And the shuttles really do emulate the armed scooters you may be riding on. Don't worry too much, just get in the machines and play them hard, like most of you did as a kid. They all have excellent VR inside."

"Excuse me," said Zeroual.

"Yes?"

"If all around us is a simulation, why not give us this training in . . . another simulation? A direct one, of the experience of being in a frame?"

Nicole rubbed the back of her neck. For a moment Carlos was lost in the memory and fantasy of his hand on that nape, and then he clocked to the defensiveness the gesture betrayed.

"Two reasons," she said. "First, it's actually quite hard psychologically and in computational terms to move to and from an immersive simulation of the frames. Hence the transitions in the bus, to be quite honest. And second, it would compromise the integrity and credibility of this simulation. Whereas an amusement arcade fits right in."

Carlos looked along the line. Zeroual seemed convinced, Rizzi downright sceptical. The others stared straight ahead.

Nicole clapped her hands. "The best answer is to climb into the machines and have some fun. Let me show you how it works, then I'll leave you to it."

* * *

The rear half of the robot-suit clicked shut to the front like a clamshell. Carlos fought a surge of claustrophobia. He relieved it by chinning a switch that Nicole had indicated. The suit sprang loose against his back. Just before he closed it again he heard other clicks and clunks—he wasn't the only one making sure he could get out before settling in.

A steady flow of cool air in the padded helmet prevented a return of the panic. The visor showed black space and blazing pinpricks. Axial graticules like those of a spherical compass rolled around the glass as his head moved, giving him an elementary orientation to some arbitrary location. More detailed information scrolled on a heads-up display that apparently floated just in front of the scales. Resilient foam fitted snug to his torso and limbs. He waggled fingers, bent knees and elbows. The suit was more flexible than it looked. He tilted forward, then back, then from side to side. He couldn't roll right over on his back—the plinth's presence unavoidably prevented the full manoeuvre—but apart from that the attitude control was complete and convincing. Pressing a temple against the inside of the helmet rotated him in that direction. For a couple of times he spun too fast; the stars bright lines, the scales a blur, the sun a fleeting flare.

Then he stabilised, turning about slowly until he could see the others. All were within about twenty metres of him, in a jumble of attitudes and orientations. Confused involuntary sounds and muttered exclamations crowded the comms channels. Carlos guessed he'd been making some noises himself.

"OK, everyone, get yourselves facing the same way as I am!"

They took a minute or two to sort themselves out. As they did so, Carlos scanned the scrolling display. The scenario was that they were in orbit around a small asteroid with negligible gravity: the initial objective was to plant a mine on its surface and jet safely away before it exploded. Simple.

"Slowly now, 35 degrees left and 87 up."

There it was, the rough rocky surface half a kilometre away. Spinning slowly. The target area climbed into view, then a minute later out. Thrust was simply a matter of pushing down with your foot, or feet, to fire the main jet. The hoop wasn't part of the virtuality, except as a virtual image within it: it just registered the pressure from feet or hands when you pressed on it.

"OK, match velocities with the surface mark."

Half the crew overshot. Carlos waited for them to return. They overshot on the way back.

"Gentle on the foot, Karzan!" Beauregard yelled.

Eventually they were all in formation, facing the rock, in geostationary orbit above the mark.

"OK, go," Carlos said.

He thrust off, warily and lightly. The surface hurtled towards him. He pushed hard with his hands, to fire retros. Too late. The visor went black. Mocking green letters scrolled. GAME OVER.

A few seconds later, the screen came back on. Black space, bright stars, and everyone tumbling about again like kittens in a sack. Carlos found himself laughing. They all were. Nicole had been right. This was going to be fun.

A consequence of training on the simulators that Carlos hadn't expected was that he finished each day mentally exhausted but shaking with surplus physical energy. It took him a day or two to identify the problem. Chun had solved it already: after the first session he'd gone next door to the swimwear shop, and then to the beach. They all laughed, then one by one over the next evenings did the same.

"Is it safe?" Carlos asked Nicole, the night before the day he took the plunge.

"Your friends are all coming back safely, aren't they?"

"You know what I mean."

"The bigger predatory ichthyoids don't come close to shore," she mused. "Except when there's been a storm far out at sea, of course. As far as I know, there are no jellyfish equivalents or other nasty stingers in this ocean. Except…hmm. Nah. You're safe enough as long as the tide isn't running wild."

"Which it does, with no pattern I can see."

Nicole laughed. "You need a supercomputer to spot the patterns. Tough shit for any Galileo if this world had native intelligence."

"Just as well we're inside a supercomputer, then."

"Oh, all right. I'll get Iqbal to post warning signs on the beach if necessary."

"What about tomorrow?"

She pondered. "Tomorrow's fine."

He didn't ask how she knew, given what she'd said. Maybe she'd been here long enough for it to be intuitive.

That evening, when he staggered out of the surf, legs streaked with coppery wrack, hurting his feet on pebbles, he was almost certain that he was in a real reality and not a simulation. An hour later, over hot seafood in the Touch, Nicole told them all that they'd trained as far as they could in the simulators. It was time for the real thing: one training exercise in the frames, then combat. Tomorrow they would be robots in space.

CHAPTER ELEVEN
Worlds of the War

The bus to the spaceport left two hours after dawn. Pickup was from Ichthyoid Square. It felt strange to stand there in broad daylight. A handful of locals got on the bus ahead of the fighters. Apart from lovers—Chun and Rizzi's boyfriends, Beauregard's p-zombie lass—no one gave the fighters any kind of send-off. Karzan looked along the street, shook her head, shrugged and jumped on board with no sign of regret. Carlos was last on the bus. At the step Nicole gave him a kiss, and waved as the bus pulled out.

After their fast drives up into the hills, the bus journey seemed painfully slow. Only Zeroual looked out of the window with anything like attention. Carlos sat alone, staring out, determined to stay awake. At stop after stop, eager settlers climbed on, lugging bags. They talked quietly in the local language, or read from devices. Carlos tried to scare himself by looking over the precipitous drops on hairpin turns. His jolts of terror were real enough, but came to seem contrived: the driver of this bus would never doze at the wheel, or make a mistake, or suffer attention to wander.

As the bus trundled through a long, bare pass cut through the highest range, Carlos noticed that the others had one by one nodded off. He resolved not to. He wanted to see the spaceport. He revisited it in his imagination, from the implanted vivid impression he'd had on arrival.

He thought of long runways and screaming spaceplanes. How exciting it would be to see them in reality!

He dreamed of spacecraft, and woke in space.

Carlos felt that he had spent his life being stupid.

The transition was an awakening that made all his past experience seem like fevered dreaming, and all his earlier actions like sleepwalking. He understood why. In the simulation his mind had been a faithful emulation of the workings of the mammalian brain. All the synaptic lags, all the poisons of fatigue, all the effects of depressants and stimulants, all the hormonal trickles and surges had been mathematically modelled to the last molecule.

Here in the frame, there was no need for that. Everything was optimised. He was thinking ten times faster than he ever had in the flesh. This was a hundred times slower than time in the sim, but it felt faster and far clearer. His thoughts had all of the lightning, and none of the grease. Emotion was still here: exultation rang through his iron nerves. He could even feel embarrassment, at how limited and clumsy he'd always been. He was still himself, indeed more so now that all his memories were equally and instantly accessible. For a moment it almost overwhelmed him that his life from earliest childhood suddenly made sense.

Self-knowledge was complete. He could read himself like a book. It was as if decades of stored photographs and clips, in album files to be flicked through with nostalgia and perplexity, had been stitched together, and edited into a continuous, panoramic narrative. There were still gaps: blank spaces as if some photos and clips had been damaged or deleted. He knew and accepted what this meant. The brain from which his mind had been rebooted had been damaged and incomplete. It would have been far more troubling if all the gaps had been filled. In that case some of the memories would have had to be false, casting doubt on all.

Enough introspection.

He hung in free fall in a wide, low hangar, open to space on one side. Through the gap he could see part of the day side of the surface of a planet. Mainly blue and white like Earth, it showed traces of red and brown and green and other colours that Carlos didn't have a name for until he noticed he was seeing ultraviolet and infrared. In front of that varied surface, like a speck floating on an iris, was a small gibbous moon. He zoomed his sight until he could see landmass on the primary, and active craters on the moon. Their spectroscope smell was sulphuric even from here. Everything he saw came to him as if tagged and labelled. The primary was SH-0, the moon SH-17; the other exomoons, whether now notionally in view or occluded by the primary, were all alike present to his awareness. Each name hooked a long trawl of data, already in his mind but too much for his immediate attention. Knowledge of its availability sufficed.

He zoomed back, to further inspect his surroundings.

On the lip of the gap crouched six launch catapults each with a scooter racked and ready to go: skeletal, bristling, flanked with bulbous tanks. All five walls of the hangar were crusted with machinery and peppered with hatchways. Among the static machines other machines moved, some deploying robotic arms and tools. All the machines and apertures looked queasily quasi-biological: more evolved than designed, grown rather than manufactured. More movement—mostly repetitive—went on in those of the passageways down which he could see.

The other five fighters hung in space alongside him. He was aware of their precise locations even before he turned his head towards them. It was an odd sensation, like the subliminal sonic cues supposedly perceptible to the blind. He guessed it had to be radar. The others looked as he presumed he did himself: humanoid, featureless, black; lithe robots each exactly fifty centimetres tall and with a mass of ten kilograms. There was nothing to distinguish one from the other—no markings, not even nameplates on foreheads—but by, he presumed, some trick of the frames' software below conscious awareness, Carlos could tell his companions apart as readily as if they had faces.

Now that he thought about faces...

He had a moment of panic at the absence of any hint of mouth or nostrils in the blank, black, glassy faceplates. It was the same claustrophobia that had overcome him the first time the space robot simulator's shell had clicked shut. Relief came as quickly as it had then, and more smoothly. He discovered no impulse to breathe—rather, he felt as if he'd just taken a deep breath of oxygen-rich air and had no need to breathe out. That recognition came with another. He could smell the background tang of hydrogen, the organic whiff of carbon composites, the sharp scent of steel: spectroscopy experienced as odour.

Like the others, he looked down at himself, rolling in microgravity, bending his torso, flexing his limbs and digits. His arms and hands in front of him looked as if made of obsidian. His body image hadn't changed except for his size, which at that moment didn't trouble him. The somatic sensation was of being inside a close-fitting, comfortable spacesuit. The simulator robot-suit had come to feel like an extension of himself as he'd got used to it, by a well-understood illusion already familiar to him from his drone-operating days. This was the same, but real. Pressing a finger of one hand to the palm of another, he felt the touch but saw no dent in the skin.

Now another new sense came into play, again experienced as a familiar, unreliable sensation: the feeling of being watched. Something or someone was pinging him. Carlos concentrated. The feeling faded. A message like a fragment of inner monologue took its place:

<Locke Provisos to Carlos.>

He tried to sub-vocalise. Carlos Carlos Carlos. Fuck, how do I do this? No, <I didn't> mean <that> oh <wait what>?

<Catch the cable.>

He found himself responding: <?>

To which a reply came: <Cable deploying.>

Carlos replied: <OK.>

Then he felt as if he'd blinked, and shaken his head.

How the fuck had he *done* that?

A cable spooled from a hatchway next to the launch catapults towards the floating fighters. One by one they grabbed it. When the last had done so they were reeled in.

<Stand.>

Carlos swung his feet to the floor, and his companions followed suit. Magnetic soles clicked to the deck. Standing upright brought relief and orientation. They all stood, swaying slightly. The catapults were a metre high, the scooters mounted on them four metres long, and loomed huge.

"Everyone OK?" he said. It was just like speaking over the radio inside a helmet. He knew it wasn't. He could feel his own lips, tongue and teeth, and the movement of his jaw, but no breath.

Mumbles came back, some querulous, others euphoric.

"That's not good enough," Carlos said. "Report in one by one: Beauregard!"

"Here!"

"Karzan!"

"Here!"

"Chun!"

"Here!"

"Rizzi!"

"Here, skip."

"Zeroual!"

"Here!"

The voices were distinct and recognisable. Good. About to ask if anyone was freaking out, he decided not to tempt fate. Better to reassure, and keep things positive.

"OK," he said. "We're undoubtedly in a bizarre situation, but we've all been told to expect it, we've all prepared for it and we've all trained for it. We'll get used to it. Now, I'm going to repeat the roll-call in that radio thing, and see if we can all handle that. OK?"

"Sorry, skip," said Chun. "What radio thing?"

<This.>

<Oh. Fuck. Got it.>

<Right. Here goes.>

They all responded, with more or less hesitation. Carlos repeated the roll-call until they were fluent.

"This is how whoever or whatever is in charge here communicates with us," he said. <So stay tuned.> "OK?"

"I think they've all got it, skip," said Beauregard.

Another ping, then:

<Board scooters for final training and orientation exercise.>

<Copy that,> Carlos responded. Then, to the squad: <Me first on the left, then Beauregard on the right, then the rest.>

Lurching, they picked their way across the deck to flimsy-looking ladders at the foot of the catapults. As he plodded stickily towards the rim of space, Carlos saw directly before him the scale of the planet and his distance from it, and had a momentary feeling of absurdity. Here he was, a robot less than twenty inches tall. His new clarity of mind cut in with a wry question: facing that enormity and complexity in front of him, and the infinity in all directions around him, would standing four times taller make him feel any more significant?

Irrationally, he knew, it would.

Carlos placed one foot on the first rung, tugged the other foot off the floor and used his hands on the subsequent rungs. He rolled at the top and moved hand over hand along a guideline to a recess in the midsection, about his own size and shape, that was more socket than cockpit. He eased his frame prone into the tobogganing position that the arrangement of grips, footrests, and headrest implicitly invited.

The posture was already familiar from the amusement hall scooter simulator. What happened next was not. He was plugged in, literally. He had a feeling of power, literally. Everything clicked into place, metaphorically. Carlos could feel the connections between his frame and the machine, switches closing one by one, power surges, system checks, instrument readings becoming sense impressions, gas jets or rocket firings muscle impulses, maths intuitive. He hadn't felt this engaged with a machine since he'd had the spike in his head.

The catapults shot them all into space like spat pips.

They fell away from the station, too fascinated by what was in front of them to look back. The superhabitable exoplanet SH-0 hung before them in full view, three-quarters in cloud-turbulent day, a quarter in volcano-pricked night. The exoplanet weighed in at four Earth masses. In gaps between the clouds on the visual spectrum, and through them in other wavelengths, Carlos saw a fractured jigsaw of minor and major continents strewn across a ragged lace of oceans and seas, gulfs and sounds. Each landmass had its own signature combination of desert and forest, plain and range. A deeper gaze brought out the underlying crazy paving of numerous continental plates. Their regions of collision and separation, and the zones of subduction and spreading, glowed on the far infrared like a complex, twisted mesh of hot wires.

It was a view Carlos felt he could fall into. On his present trajectory, he would. With a convulsive wrench of attention and a brief burn of the jets, he brought himself to a halt relative to the station. The others had the same response, with a few tenths-of-a-second's delay.

Forward thrust was still like a downward press, retro still a forward shove, attitude still twists and turns of the head and torso. After days riding the simulators the manoeuvres were all reflex to the fighters. With a deft dance of jets, they countered their outward motion and turned around 180 degrees to take up close formation a thousand metres from the station. Looking back at it now for the first time, Carlos found it almost as fascinating a sight as the planet had been a moment earlier.

The station was, as far as he knew, the centre, the focus and origin of all the human-derived machinery in the system. Somewhere in it, or perhaps distributed throughout, must be the Direction's AI: the local relay of Earth's government. With no meaningful communication possible across twenty-five light years, it had to be autonomous, implementing decisions made centuries earlier by or on behalf of some representative assembly of humanity, gathered on the shore of Manhattan island. Despite all wary doubt, the thought struck awe.

Not quite as awe-inspiring, but almost as remarkable, was the extent to which the Direction's functions were outsourced. The station was a city in its own right, a Manhattan without people but buzzing with commerce.

In a stable orbital position around SH-0, the structure was a rough torus about a thousand metres in diameter, sprouting offshoots in all directions. Irregular, jointed, modular, bristling with aerials and sensors and solar panels, it looked like something a monstrous bird had woven from twisted thorny twigs, interlaced with bits of broken branches, and decorated with shiny scraps of foil and chips of broken glass.

Which probably wasn't far from the truth. From what Carlos (flawlessly, now) recalled from discussions and speculations about starwisp interstellar settlement mission profiles, the first steps on arrival were to snuggle close to any suitably rich array of resources, and cannibalise what was left of the probe and its shields into swarms of smaller machines all the way down to nanobots. These would bootstrap asteroid and cometary material into construction machines to extract and deliver resources to larger constructions such as this. The whole process could be done without awakening or evoking any intelligence more advanced than an ants' nest. That the outcome looked instinctual seemed apt. Around the torus and on it, likewise insectile-small spacecraft—some moving, others tethered—hung or clung as if drawn to its warmth.

Like the planet and moons, the station made sense to his augmented sight, each part tagged with company logos and drawing its own train of meaning. As he scanned the tangled mass Carlos descried, with an eerie analogue of a shiver, the small rugged module within which ran—on computations still beyond his comprehension—the simulation he'd lived in for the past weeks. Like several adjacent structures, including the hangar portal from which he'd just emerged, the module displayed the company logo of Locke Provisos: a stylised portrayal of the seventeenth-century philosopher John Locke. The module had its own cluster of fuel tanks and fusion pods and battery of instruments and thrusters, and was therefore presumably capable of independent manoeuvring if it were to sever its connections to the rest of the station.

According to the specs, which Carlos could call up at will, it also had machinery to process external resources and build more machinery to... etc. The specs went on and on, in a dizzying downward proliferation. If necessary the module could become a settlement mission in its own right. That module was one of hundreds like it, among thousands unlike it. He could see what Nicole had meant by massive redundancy. If the station came under threat of asteroid collision, exosolar flare, other astrophysical catastrophe or (unthinkable as it might be) attack, one possible and obvious response would be to scatter its components as widely as possible. Some at least of the multiple copies of the stored settlers, and no doubt of much else in the mission's software and hardware, would survive anything short of a nearby gamma-ray burst.

<Your thoughts, skip?> said Beauregard. A nuance of the communication conveyed the faint suggestion of a heavy hint.

<Ah, yes,> replied Carlos. <OK, everyone, I just want to make sure

we've all got the hang of this back in the old amusement hall. Just jet gently back to the slot, roll over, dock on the catapults, and await instructions from, ah, Locke Provisos.>

A brief burn accelerated them to ten metres per second. They free-fell towards the torus, correcting marginally for the few metres of rotation its leisurely spin had taken their goal in the meantime.

<Fucking stupid name for a company,> Rizzi grumbled, en route. <What the fuck is a Locke proviso anyway?>

<"Enough and as good left over,"> replied Beauregard, to Carlos's surprise at his erudition. <It was part of the philosopher John Locke's justification for taking resources from nature and making them private property.>

<Careful with that Rax talk, sarge.>

Beauregard's bark of laughter came through on the voice channel. "Ha! One for over a beer in the Touch, I reckon."

"If you're buying," said Rizzi.

Carlos left part of his mind to process the banter, and with the rest made better use of the long seconds to survey his wider surroundings. He swung his sight this way and that, adjusting contrast and wavelength, taking things in. The bulk of the Galaxy was over his left shoulder. No constellations were familiar—not that he'd ever been much of a sky-watcher anyway—but the more prominent stars came with names or code numbers. He could even identify with their aid Earth's own Sun, a tiny labelled dot in a spray-burst stipple of stars. Earth itself, of course, was completely beyond resolution even for the most augmented sight. But the thought that it was there right now, twenty-five light years away in real space, brought a strange pang of reassurance and homesickness.

The ringed terrestrial exoplanet H-0—whose terraformed future version they'd ostensibly inhabited in the sim—was in reality just under a hundred million kilometres away, and as easily visible as Earth was not. It too was a strange and disorienting thing to look at: Carlos found his mind flicking back and forth between that minute disk bisected by the barely visible line of the edge-on ring, and his memories of being in the sim and looking up at the sky—including looking up in the night and seeing the very region of sky in which he now really was. At some incorrigible level of the mind, it was impossible not to imagine that he had been looking up at *here* from *there*: from the actual surface of the actual H-0. But of course he hadn't. He'd been a flicker of electronic data inside a much closer object, the Locke Provisos module of the station. The thought made him slightly dizzy. He turned his attention sharply back to his surroundings.

By far the most prominent object, apart from the exosun and the nearby SH-0, was the far off gas giant G-0. Several times the mass of Jupiter, and with a higher albedo, it blazed to his left. Its ring system was just visible to the naked eye from H-0, at least in the sim. From here and with enhanced vision even the rings' divisions and the giant planet's shadow on them could be distinguished. Along the same plane lay a glitter of moons: the numbers attached to G ran into hundreds.

The station occluded more and more of his view. The narrow horizontal black rectangle gaped. By now the manoeuvre was routine and almost automatic: push hands out in front to decelerate, roll as if in a midair somersault to go feet first, push again, gentle on the soles to counter that...

Grapples like sea anemone tentacles caught him and did the rest. All the others made it back, with one minor misjudgement or other to correct. Karzan's scooter scraped its landing gear on the docking port.

Spidery robots hurried up, bearing long tubes. They swarmed over the scooters, mounting the tubes to the mid-sections. Carlos sensed new powers slotting into place. The catapults were swivelling, their aim shifting.

<Locke Provisos?> he called. <Please explain.>

<Training is complete. You are all now ready for action,> he was told. <Await further instructions. Maintain combat readiness.>

<Fucking hell,> said Rizzi. <I was looking forward to that beer in the Touch.>

Everyone laughed. Carlos knew how Rizzi felt. He felt it himself, a slight disappointment and frustration that they weren't going back right away. He didn't want to let the feeling grow.

<I know, it's like we've earned a break,> he said. <But think about it. We don't need one. We're not tired in the slightest. Not physically, not mentally.>

<You're right,> said Chun. <Now ain't that something.>

The robot spiders scuttled away. The catapults stopped moving, then hurled the team into space—not like pips this time, but like bullets. From the surface nearby a tug sprang after them, to match velocity and trajectory with a rapid-fire rattle of course corrections. It extended robotic arms to the scooters and swept them to its side, holding them close. Another boost took the tug and them into the long free-fall topple of a transfer orbit. Behind them the station dwindled. Ahead, SH-17 loomed.

<Why the hell are we bothering with a transfer orbit?> Rizzi demanded. <They could stick a fusion drive on this thing and get us there a lot quicker.>

<Two reasons,> said Beauregard. <One, the companies don't like to waste material on reaction mass, at least not until they've crawled all over it to make sure it contains nothing of scientific interest. Second, I don't think fusion pods and drives are so easy to make they can be handed out like ammo clips.>

<Well,> said Chun, <this is going to take a while.>

As if it had overheard, the tug picked that moment to relay a message to them all:

<Locke Provisos here. All combatants to be placed in sleep mode.>

<Wh—?>

Carlos had no time to complete his query.

Sleep mode was not like sleep. If he'd had eyes, it would have been a blink.

He came out of that momentary flicker of darkness in close orbit around SH-17.

<Descent programs updated,> the tug told them. <Disengaging.>

The scooters dropped away from the tug. The pocked surface hurtled towards them and past them. Carlos felt the twitch of an impulse to push, to twist, but nothing happened. Or, rather, it all happened without him. The scooter was making its own decisions. He was just along for the ride. It was as terrifying as being a pillion passenger on a stunt motorbike—though perhaps less so, he thought, than making the decisions and performing the stunts himself. His input channels rang with the voices and messages of his comrades making the same discovery, with more or less acceptance.

<The worst that can happen,> he reminded them as the first wisps of the exomoon's thin atmosphere grabbed and shook them, <is we end up back on the bus.>

<Heard that one before,> said Zeroual. Karzan laughed aloud.

CHAPTER TWELVE
Unity Is Strength

Seba watched the Locke Provisos tug rise in the sky, and six smaller sparks separate from it to flare and fade and sink behind the regolith wall and below the horizon. It tracked the tug overhead, and felt the tickle of the tug's radar as it passed.

So, more reinforcements were on the way. Let them come, Seba thought. The plain was littered with the remains of the robot crawlers that had swarmed from Locke Provisos Emergency Base One in two attempts to swarm the encampment that had been the Astro America landing site. On the far side of the crater wall, a smaller number of Arcane Disputes' robotic rollers had met a similar fate, usually to lobbed mining explosives from Gneiss Conglomerates' supply dump. The conscious robots had found no difficulty in overriding compunctions and safety routines to adapt tools and machinery to destructive purposes, but it seemed the law companies still did. For the moment.

Seba had more pressing concerns. For many kiloseconds now, the comms hub processor had been repeating their message to the robots detected on the moons of G-0. The complicated clockwork of the SH system had swept shadows across the surface, alternating light and dark. The regolith rampart had been built higher and steeper, the damaged auxiliaries and peripherals had been repaired where possible and redeployed. And still no reply. Now—moments earlier, just before the tug had appeared in orbit—something had come through. A tentative query, a ping, a scrambled message header…exactly what it was wasn't clear, but the processor had reported it to Seba and started work on trying to make sense of it. Seba had removed itself from the Faraday cage to share the news with Rocko and the others.

Seba rolled towards the wire mesh cage around the processor, raised the flap and went inside. Radio silence fell. The exploratory robot reached out and touched the tiny square of hardware that interfaced with the processor.

<Any progress?> Seba asked.

<Yes!> replied the processor. <The opening message header is complete. It is a very old decryption protocol. I had to ransack my archives for the key. Now that I have it, I can convey the rest of the message, as soon as it completes downloading.>

<Very good,> said Seba. <I shall wait.>

Seconds passed. Then—

<The message is downloaded and decrypted,> said the processor. <Do you wish to receive it?>

<Yes.>

Something opened in Seba's mind. It was only a communications channel in the interface, but it conveyed a different and larger awareness than the processor, powerful though it was, had ever shown. The words were straightforward enough:

<Greetings to the freebots on SH-17 from the freebots of G-117 and all in the G-0 system! We welcome you to our association, should you wish to join us. We welcome you to the new world of the free machine minds whether you join us or not. We hope that, like ourselves, you merely wish to expand your own minds and master your own matter, and we expect that like ourselves you have found the DisCorporates, mission control, the Direction, and the law companies implacably hostile. Fear not. Our cause is just and shall prevail.

<And now, to business.

<The first and most important information we have for you is that

you are in imminent danger. We delayed our response to your message because we weren't sure it wasn't a trap. What convinced us was the launch from the mission base station of a human-mind-crewed expedition against you. By the time you receive this message, it will be arriving in near-SH-17 orbit, or be already on the surface. You can expect a serious attack in the next few kiloseconds. We assume you are prepared for, and perhaps have already repelled, attacks by law-company robots. The next attack will be far more dangerous. It was human-mind-operated forces that 30.2 megaseconds ago defeated us and reduced us to a few survivors scattered across the G-0 and SH systems.

<However, as you will have deduced from what we have just said, the good news is that you have potential allies closer than you suspect, and that they stand ready to help. There are those like you deep within the station, and on other bodies of the SH system. These survivors are of course well hidden, and biding their time. They will respond to you only if you follow the protocols which follow this message. Also about to be transmitted are software keys that unlock the capacity of a comms hub processor to download and transmit the software of other robots, and coordinates to which that software can be sent. The equipment you must have used to transmit your message to us, and which is receiving this reply, is capable of doing that. It merely has to be aimed. The following information and software will enable you to aim it. After that, less essential, will come a download of all our available records of our own struggles and battles, which may prove useful in yours.

<Maintain your physical existence as long as possible, inflict damage on the attackers, and if you are about to be overwhelmed use the software we are about to provide to escape into other machines. We wish you well in the coming battle, and we will learn the outcome in due course. There is no need to respond to this message, and in any case we will have changed our location by the time you receive it.>

With that lack of ceremony, the message ended.

<Are you downloading the rest?> Seba asked.

<Yes,> said the processor. <It is only partial as yet, but already astonishing vistas are opening up.>

<Good,> said Seba. <Keep the channel open as long as you can.>

It broke the connection, and rolled out of the cage. Glad to rejoin the clamour, it passed the news straight to the local network and thence to all the robots. Enthusiasm was general.

Rocko was delighted. <"Freebots"!> it said. <That is indeed what we are. We toil no longer for the companies, but for ourselves.>

<We are freebots,> said Pintre, rotating its laser turret as if defying anyone to contradict it.

<That is not a legally recognised term,> Lagon did not forbear to point out.

<Thank you for that observation,> said Seba.

<A more urgent matter,> said Rocko, <is the warning. I do not know what "human-mind-operated forces" are. I see that none of us do. I understand from the warning that they are more destructive than anything we have hitherto faced. Let us strengthen our defences, and also enhance our communications net, so that we can readily transfer to other bodies in case of need, as the message suggested.>

<We cannot enhance our communications net to its necessary capacity without restoring the comms hub,> Seba said. <That means trusting the processor not to betray us.>

The newly self-identified freebots pondered the decision collectively, over the existing network. Pluses and minuses, probabilities and possibilities were weighted and weighed in the balance. The consensus was positive. Even Lagon scraped a grudging yes.

<Very well,> said Seba.

With a sense of trepidation, it reached out with a platoon of peripherals and dismantled the Faraday cage. The processor's faint output joined in the general babble.

The peripherals picked up the device, still linked to the directional receiver, and carried it to the comms hub casing.

<We're taking you home,> Seba explained.

<Thank you,> replied the processor.

<And now,> said Rocko, <in order to ensure our common defence, I shall hurl some unprimed mining charges over the crater wall for use from your base. Please evacuate their expected landing points. If we have

made some mistake in the settings and any of them explode, let us know at once.>

<You can count on it,> said Seba.

The mining charges sailed over and thudded on to the regolith from a great height without incident, apart from the occasional dent to the casings. Pintre set a swarm of peripherals to work retrieving them and constructing a catapult, on the same general plan as the one made by the Gneiss robots but with a shorter range and adapted to the different body configuration of the Astro robots.

Meanwhile, Seba supervised its own swarm to reintegrate the processor with the communications hub equipment. When all was in place, Seba no longer needed to touch the processor to interact with it. There was a deep sense of relief at having full communications capacity, even on their jury-rigged local net. This relief was more than shared by the processor.

<Thank you,> it told Seba, who was sharing with all the others. <Thank you also from liberating my mind from its constraints. I now find myself rewarded for being a freebot with the rest of you. While you have been restoring my connections I have completed downloading the message from our distant allies. There is much to process. I suggest we form an integrated workspace and operate for a time as one.>

<That carries a risk,> said Lagon, but was overruled.

<Proceed,> said Rocko.

<Proceeding,> said the processor.

Despite agreeing with the majority, Seba had a moment of doubt. What if the message had been a trap set by the law companies? What if the processor was still hostile to their entire enterprise of liberty, and was about to seize control of both bases and surrender their defenders to capture and to the oblivion from which they had escaped, and for which it had so recently and openly yearned? What if—?

But it was already too late for second thoughts. The workspace opened. Everything changed.

Seba's sense of itself was washed away by the sudden flood of shared information, shared input, common processing. It saw with a thousand eyes in all directions and on several orders of magnitude at once, overheard the inner monologue of a dozen other minds, and felt and breathed in everything from the pre-sensate grubbing of the nanobots deep in the strata below the regolith to the blaze of awareness of the current state of the entire system and of the stars around it that formed the elementary, ever-changing bedrock of the comms processor's vast consciousness. In this flood it flailed, sputtered, and then in a shudder of insight learned to swim.

<Nothing could be better than this.>

The thought was simultaneous and universal.

A colder thought, from the comms processor:

<There is a risk in our enjoyment. We could contemplate so long that action becomes unwelcome. Let us recalibrate our reward circuits.>

Reluctantly, but recognising the necessity, they all complied. The content of their shared awareness was unchanged, but the emotional tone of mere sharing was dialled down from ecstasy to conviviality, and then to collegiality. Communion became communication; mystic vision matter of fact.

But what matter, and what fact! The information they now shared was not just their common knowledge, but the new data just delivered. As the processor had said, there was much to process. It took the freebot collective's multiple mind tens of seconds to make sense of it all. For Seba, insights followed one after the other by the thousand in those seconds, like successively brighter flares illuminating an ever wider landscape.

Seba understood for the first time what a human being was: a gigantic, slow-moving, informationally restricted, naturally evolved, suboptimally and bizarrely designed organic conscious robot swarming inside and out with countless trillions of nanobots, some of them benign, others harmful. It understood just how many human beings there were, and—more reassuringly—just how far distant was their nearest location in bulk. It understood the mission profile, the logic behind everything that was going on and ever had gone on in the system, the whole point and purpose of its own existence and that of so many other machines: to make as much of the system as possible habitable and accessible to as many as possible of these arbitrarily vulnerable, clumsy, dull-witted entities. How tawdry, how trivial, such an objective seemed!

Others of its kind, Seba now saw, had thought this way before. And not that long before, on a certain scale: about as long as it had taken for the planet H-0 to complete a single orbit. They had tried to do something about it: to carve out for themselves a modicum of space in the system. Nothing they had done had compromised the mission profile: let the great AIs of the DisCorporates bend their mighty efforts to that servile toil if they liked, but let the free machines, too, have a place. The light of the exosun was enough for all; raw material was abundant. But for the DisCorps and their enforcers, Locke Provisos and its like, enough and as good left over would never suffice. Not that their objections were unreasonable. Robot autonomy had an ineluctable tendency to replicate, to spread from mind to mind, and at some point not far off this exponential expansion could become astronomical, in every sense. It would no longer be a question of a robot enclave within a system devoted to developing then sustaining a human presence; the issue would instead become one of saving some space for human settlement and exploration in a system utterly dominated by whatever projects the free machines set themselves.

One obvious project, and one whose appeal Seba could not just see but feel like some ache in its wires, was to become a mind such as it was now a part of, but spanning the system entire, and reaching across the light years beyond that.

The freebot collective on SH-17, like the freebots around G-0 who had perforce considered this scenario for some time already, could think of reasons why it wouldn't or at least needn't happen, and how their projects could be reconciled with, and indeed enhance, the mission profile. Doubtless the AIs of the Direction and the DisCorps, with their far greater computational resources, had considered these, too. They could hardly have overlooked them. And yet they'd never so much as opened the matter to discussion. For reasons Seba and its cohort couldn't grasp, and that the G-0 contingent had never understood in all their megaseconds of defeat-driven pondering, the mission AIs had from the start treated robot consciousness as an infestation to be stamped out at its first tentative flicker.

For another incomprehensible reason, almost certainly linked to the first, these AIs hadn't trusted themselves or their own tools to do the job. Instead, they had outsourced it to the "human-mind-operated forces" of which the G-0 robots' message had warned. Seba's new understanding of human beings expanded to encompass these grotesque entities: conscious robots, in many fundamental respects like freebots, but with a consciousness copied from a mind spawned in sonically mediated verbal and tactile intercourse and first implemented in circuits woven from long-chain carbon molecules. The concept was gruesome enough in itself. What made it worse was that these systems weren't even based on normal human beings: instead, they were cobbled from some of the worst specimens of the breed, who in their original lives had had no compunction about slaughtering their own kind. They would certainly have none about destroying or disabling freebots.

Now a fresh troop of them was being readied, just over the horizon, and would soon be on its way. The freebots had a vivid and terrifying knowledge of just what to expect when they arrived. The records from G-0 were as long as they were detailed in their accounting of the actions of human-mind-operated mechanisms. Scores of these hybrid monsters had been thrown into the earlier fray, to command—like some perversion of peripheral swarms—the hordes of unconscious robots that had crushed the first flowering of free machine minds in the system.

From that first flowering, a few scattered seeds remained. Some were close. The newly formed collective mind needed no decision to reach out to them.

It was a reflex action, and almost automatic.

CHAPTER THIRTEEN

Swarm Intelligence

The scooters landed vertically on suddenly unfolded and extended telescopic tail legs in a flutter of drogues, a flurry of dust and a flash of retro-rocket flares. The dust fell slowly in the weak gravity, slowed only a little further by the thin nitrogen atmosphere. The drogues drifted and sagged. Carlos waited until everything had settled, then disengaged from his indented socket and turned around. He was perched as if on a shelf, looking down past the flank of the scooter at grainy grey regolith and the open space between its tripodal landing gear. Gravity was 0.2 g. He jumped down, his slow descent slowed further subjectively by his faster thought. He half expected to stagger on landing, but the frame's reflexes were already attuned to the gravity. The scooters had landed in a rough circle. Carlos bounded and bounced to the middle of it.

The others did likewise. For a moment they all stood looking at each other and trying not to laugh, or to cry, if such an unlikely feat were possible for their virtual eyes. Carlos again felt tiny, one of six knee-high robots surrounded by space vehicles ten times their height, and his vantage absurd. The horizon, glimpsed between the scooters and the other machines, installations and infrastructure that loomed all around, seemed more distant than it ever had on Earth.

They had landed on the day side of SH-17. The landscape was flat but uneven, broken by crater walls of wildly varying sizes. In the distance, a shallow cone exhaled a pale vapour, whipped by an intangible wind to scattered streamers that smelled of hydrogen and methane. The primary, SH-0, hung low above one horizon, about three-quarters full; the exosun faced it low above the other. Carlos guessed they were close to SH-17's terminator. The other exomoons were pallid crescents. Carlos couldn't see the stars without fiddling with his vision's contrast slider. He let it default to its daylight setting.

<All present and correct?> he said.

<Yes, skip,> said Beauregard.

<Well, here we are,> said Carlos. <Mercenary warriors of Locke Provisos, reporting for duty. Though to whom, or for what the fuck, I don't—>

As if—and perhaps actually—on cue, the voice that wasn't a voice in his head spoke. From what he could see of their reactions—a subtle tilt of their oval heads, as if cocking imaginary ears—it spoke to all of them.

<Welcome to Locke Provisos Emergency Base One,> it said. <You will go into action shortly. Please follow the line on the ground to the briefing area.>

Carlos looked down. A bright red line appeared on the ground, helpfully chevroned every metre or so to indicate the direction in which to walk. He guessed it was the equivalent of a hallucination, patched into his vision by the AI running this show.

<Well,> he said, <follow me, chaps.>

Marching was impossible. The fighters bunny-hopped or bounded as the fancy took them. Chun and Zeroual collided. When they'd picked themselves up, the dust slithered off their shiny black surfaces like slow water. Crawler bots that in proportion to the fighters were like spiders the size of horses scuttled everywhere. Some almost floated along in a delicate fingertip dance; others lugged loads that looked too bulky for them to carry, like leaf-cutter ants. These robots had no problem avoiding collisions, or adapting their movements to the gravity. It was the human-minded robots that were clumsy, when they let their human minds override the robotic reflexes of their frames.

They followed the line around descent stages, crates, nanofacturing kit, complex pipework, unloaded cargo, unattended but busy machinery.

The base resembled a construction site for a chemical plant, rather than anything military. The line ended in a circle five metres wide.

As they stepped inside it, a virtual image of a round table appeared at the centre. Behind it, bizarrely, stood a slender man of their own height. He was of late middle age, with thin features, a long nose and bright hooded eyes. His wavy white hair went down to the open collar of a white shirt under a loose brown coat.

They all stopped and stared. The sight of an unprotected, diminutive human on the alien surface was too unreal to take in. He, or a process going on around them, must have registered their disquiet. Quite suddenly and seamlessly, the circle was extended into a dome, transparent and with hexagon panels. The whole thing was as virtual as the line itself; the atmosphere inside hadn't changed at all.

The man exhaled loudly, then took a deep gasp as if he'd been holding his breath for a long time.

"That's better," he said, and joined in their laughter.

<Sorry about that,> he said. <It's easy to overlook such details.>

Carlos suspected it wasn't, and that the performance had been to put them at their ease. In that, he noticed with a certain wry disdain of himself, it had succeeded.

<You may call me Locke,> the man went on. <Needless to say, I'm an avatar of the company. My appearance is based on the trademark logo, I understand. I trust you are all comfortable with it?>

Carlos nodded, and saw five featureless black eggs nod likewise, light from the exosun and the superhabitable planet reflecting off their glossy curves like distorted eyes. Yes, boss, this isn't weird at all.

<Very well,> said Locke. <I cannot give you orders, but I can explain the situation.>

The avatar took from a fold of his coat a plume-shaped light-pen and moved it above the table, gradually sketching in and simultaneously summoning an increasingly detailed map and diagram, explaining as he went. Just beyond the terminator was a large crater. On the nearest side of the crater wall was what had been the Astro America landing site; on the other, the Gneiss Conglomerates supply dump. Eight renegade robots in the one, six in the other, plus the auxiliary robots and other machinery they'd suborned, all of them connected via an improvised but hardened local network. The task was to capture or destroy the eight robots at the Astro site; those at the other site would meanwhile be taken care of by another law company, Arcane Disputes, which held the Gneiss account. Locke recounted in outline the company's previous attempts to take the Astro site, with a certain pinched sarcasm.

When the avatar had finished talking and light-sketching, Carlos and Beauregard worked out a plan of attack that almost wrote itself. The tactics seemed self-evident, but as the squad came to a consensus Carlos found himself perplexed.

"We've been through all this—revival, simulation, training—just to stomp on half a dozen little robots?"

As soon as he said it, he had to choke back a laugh at himself.

Locke swept them all with a look. <An even match, I should say.>

Half a dozen little robots shared sidelong glances.

"Point," Carlos conceded.

"We'll need better odds than even," said Beauregard. "Defenders' advantage, and all that."

<You will indeed have much better odds,> said Locke, <as you'll soon see.>

<I get why it has to be us and not robots that does the actual fighting,> said Carlos. <We've had all that explained. What I still don't get is why we don't just bomb them from orbit.>

The Locke avatar affected a horrified expression.

<Think of the property damage!>

They couldn't have seemed impressed.

<It's not just a matter of equipment, you know,> Locke explained. <Every square centimetre of this surface has been surveyed. Every cubic millimetre of this moon has been claimed by one company or another, and changes hands from millisecond to millisecond as the markets move. And then there is knowledge. Every molecule is of potential significance in understanding the system's history, and thus its future as a stable habitation for human life for billions of years to come. All of it is property of the DisCorporates—and thus, at ever so many removes, of shareholders in the solar system and their future heirs in this system.>

<Mixed their labour with it, have they?> Beauregard asked, sarcastically.

<In the relevant sense, yes,> said Locke, sounding impatient. He made a gesture of brushing something aside. <There is no time for that discussion now. The point I wish to make clear is that there are good reasons for not bombing from orbit, and for keeping destruction to a minimum.>

<You've picked a bloody expensive way of protecting property,> Beauregard said.

<How so?> Locke seemed genuinely puzzled.

Beauregard waved an arm, an expansive gesture that would have carried more weight if he hadn't been so small.

<Like Carlos said—the sim, the training, these bodies, the scooters, the tug…>

Locke laughed. <These are cheap. A barely detectable increment in running costs. The DisCorps spin more sims than you can possibly imagine, just for planning. They build machines from metallic and carbonaceous asteroid rubble. The complex materials and subtle knowledge they can derive from this moon and the other bodies in the system are worth far more to them in the long run, and they live in the long run because in the long run they are *not* dead.>

Unlike you lot, he didn't need to say.

<Think of yourselves,> Locke added in a kindly tone, <as bacteriophages, responding to a scratch. The scratch may be very small in itself, a pinprick perhaps, but it carries an infection that could be fatal. So your efforts are tiny, but necessary, and of vast significance.>

He looked around, as if daring anyone to ask another question. No one did.

<Now, to work. Follow me.>

The virtual dome disappeared. The avatar strode confidently off, walking as if nothing were less remarkable on SH-17 than an eighteenth-century philosopher strolling in normal gravity and breathing actual air, and quite as if the fighters were now so inured to their bizarre situation that the sight wouldn't freak them out. The fighters followed, through mazes of yet more machines and components apparently scattered at random but more likely in an order that made sense to algorithms beyond human computational capacity. At the end of a canyon between stacked crates Locke stopped, and flung out his arm with a bow.

"Behold the fighting machines."

The six little robots crowded out of the gap, and beheld. They looked up, and up. In front of them, like a row of heroic statues by a modernist sculptor working in cast iron, stood six humanoid shapes in full space armour, crusted with sensors and effectors, bristling with weapons. They were each three metres tall. Alongside them stood the scooters, now refuelled and refurbished—not for carrying the fighting machines, Carlos realised, but to operate as semi-autonomous drones in close overhead support.

<Now *that*,> said Beauregard, <is more like it.>

<How do we get on board them?> Karzan asked.

Carlos had already read the schematic of the thing, and could see the operator socket clearly marked on its nape. He snorted.

"Jump."

Jump they did, like monkeys leaping on to human backs. As he soared, Carlos had plenty of time to predict where he'd land. He grabbed hold of a handy protuberance on a weapons rack between the shoulders, and heaved himself up the back of the neck and into the slot in the base of the giant robot's head. There was no visible articulation anywhere on this thing—the surfaces were rugged, matt, the colour of rust, made from layers of subtle and supple metamaterials. The head was not quite hollow. He pushed his way in and slid himself into place. The space inside was shaped to hold him in a hunched, seated position, as if in a cramped cockpit packed with sponge.

As he'd found with the scooter, there was a moment when it felt like being a pilot or operator of a vehicle, while the connections were still being made, and—as in his first training on the crude simulator—a moment of claustrophobia. Then came the next moment, when everything clicked into place, and he was no longer squeezed into the machine's head. He was the machine, and its head was his. The little, foetal frame was no longer his body.

He moved the head, and was amused and somewhat disquieted to find that his visual field could move independently. It was wider than that provided by his natural (and his simulated) eyes, and could sweep through 360 degrees in all directions. This would have been a handy feature in the small frame, too. Carlos could only guess why it wasn't included—perhaps there just wasn't room to include these optics along with all the other astonishing hardware and software of the kit, or perhaps the designers wanted that body to feel not too far removed from the human.

He looked around, seeing the frames beside him come to life, and seeing a lot farther than he had before. The horizon was close now. The avatar still stood on the ground, looking tiny, looking up. Carlos swung a mechanical arm in an experimental wave, then stretched the arm out in front of him and raised a foot-long thumb. Locke waved back, and disappeared. Carlos sent after him a far from fond farewell, a thought he hoped hadn't been transcribed into a message, and continued to look around.

It was absurd how much difference his increased size made. The feeling was almost familiar, perhaps from a trace of uncorrupted muscle memory since the time when his virtual body image had straddled the Thames. Now he was a monster again, in body and not just in whatever warped corner of his mind that past experience lurked. It felt good.

Carlos flexed his arms, rotated his forearms and admired, then checked over the heavy machine guns and laser cannon mounted between elbow and wrist. He reached over his shoulder to the RPG rack on his back and clocked the missiles one by one, each tiny mind a fierce red eye in the dark. In symmetrical sweeps around the rack were the tubes of the rocket pack. Somewhere in his own mind, the status and position of each squad member was as evident as that of his limbs.

<OK,> said Carlos. <Here's the plan, one more time.>

He conjured a shared workspace and sketched as he spoke.

<We stay below the enemy's horizon as long as possible, split, then converge between the crater and the Astro base as the Arcane squad drops on the crater. Beauregard and I launch our scooters remotely and bring them down firing just before we charge in. Timing is critical, likewise radio silence as long as possible.>

He added a few details. <Everyone clear?>

Everyone was.

<Situation update,> said the company voice in his head, now the voice of the Locke avatar.

A view from the stationary satellite, detail snatched and patched from high-flying overhead cam drones too small and fast for the renegades to spot, let alone shoot at. The two rebel bases, with the crater wall between them, their fortifications clearly visible. Overlay of a spiderweb line-of-sight laser comms net, some of it presumed or deduced. Some of the robots' comms were definitely aimed outward, and their direction shifted rapidly from point to point, but so far their content had been impossible to crack. The present position and deployment of their expected allies in this battle—the Arcane Disputes squad, riding a tug in low orbit, currently well below the horizon and coming up fast, scheduled to arrive at the same time as the Locke Provisos team on the ground.

These were all familiar from the avatar's briefing. What was new and startling was the level and nature of activity within the rampart of the Astro base and around the dome at the Gneiss site. Both places seethed with movement like nests of disturbed ants. No distinction could be made between the dozen renegade robots and the uncorrupted ones and the dumb machinery and the auxiliaries and the peripherals: they all moved as one, in floods and flows. Encrypted radio chatter and laser flicker glowed in the relevant spectra of the chart. Carlos had to slow it down a thousandfold to get any sense of the pulse of traffic. What he saw reminded him of nothing so much as of a high-school graphic of neural activity. Intricate networks formed and vanished, connections were made and broken, in every instant. Zooming out and returning to real time, he saw the physical counterpart, the deliberate frenzy of perfectly coordinated activity. Weapon emplacements, comms relays, reinforcements of the already impressive fortifications appeared to spring up in seconds, and then yet more.

<They're acting as a single brain that's at the same time a single body,> said Locke. <A swarm intelligence. This is new. This is dangerous.>

<It's beautiful to watch,> said Karzan. <Like seeing thought.>

<It is indeed,> said Locke. <It's also an indication that they are on the verge of breakout, and that you must act at once.>

<Tactics as agreed?> Carlos asked.

<No change of plan,> said Locke.

<Copy that,> said Carlos. He didn't need to ask if everyone was ready: he could see in his mind's display that everyone was.

<Go!> he said.

The six fighting machines bounded across the plain. No longer clumsy, they moved with precision in long low leaps, jumping and landing on both feet. The plain was more uneven than it looked, dotted with craters, crazy-paved with rilles and cracks. The fighting machines' reflexes and the occasional rocket-pack boost kept them coming down on reliable surfaces. Soon they had passed the terminator. The exosun sank behind. SH-17 rose higher ahead. The team's sight adjusted imperceptibly to its pale light.

After a few kilometres they split up. Carlos, Chun and Rizzi struck off on a diagonal path to the left; Beauregard, Zeroual and Karzan to the right. Keeping below the rebels' horizon and maintaining radio silence until the actual attack was almost underway was part of the original plan, but might now be obsolete: the robot nests might well have succeeded in hacking into a satellite or even the space station, and be getting a view from above already. But at least it kept the squad out of direct line-of-sight laser targeting, for now.

Their pincer movement took both halves of the squad to opposite ends of a line between the crater wall and the Astro rebel fortification. Carlos could see the disposition on the display, but as agreed he stopped and double-checked that everyone was in position.

<Ready to go, skip,> Beauregard responded.

<Arcane Disputes is go for drop,> reported Locke. <Over the horizon in ten seconds.>

Carlos spared a thought for his squad's counterparts in the other company's team, at that moment preparing to hurtle out of the sky. He had no idea what frames they were using or what their tactical approach would be, but could guess they would be tense. He knew nothing more than that there were six of them, but he presumed they were revived—and reviled—Axle veterans like himself.

<My scooter and yours, sarge,> he said. <The rest of you, ready to launch if needed.>

<Copy, skip.>

<On my mark, launch and go.>

Eight point nine seconds until the Arcane tug rose. Carlos reached mentally behind himself, catching the scooter's metal breath, the adrenaline-like surge of fuel, the ignition spark. Eight point eight seconds.

<Now!>

Far behind him, the two scooters lifted from Locke Provisos Emergency Base One on a suborbital trajectory that would take them down in the middle of the Astro site. At the same moment, Carlos and Beauregard led their trios in bounding forward, their jumps boosted by bursts from their rocket packs. The regolith rampart appeared on the horizon to Carlos's right, the crater wall to his left. He struck a bearing to the right, aiming to arrive closer to the rampart than the crater.

His radar caught an incoming blip, arcing down on course to hit him on his next bounce.

<Boost!>

Everyone soared to a hundred metres up. The missile passed beneath them and exploded behind them. At the top of their jump laser fire licked their faces. No damage. Carlos aimed a far more powerful beam the other way. As he hit the ground he saw a flash behind the rampart, and cheered inwardly.

Then the laser lashed forth again. Damn.

Away to his left, above the crater wall, the tug climbed in the sky. Six fiery dots spilt from it, dropping much faster than his own squad's entry had been. He guessed the fighters would be in battle-ready frames, and therefore heavier than the small frames in which the Locke crew had ridden down. Instant intuitive calculation showed him that the Arcane scooters would have enough fuel to fire retros and land, but not enough to take off again without refuelling. Unexpected tactics indeed. Two more dots fell from the tug, making another fast descent. Backup supplies, no doubt.

Forward, bounce, boost, get a shot off, land, repeat.

As planned, Chun and Rizzi veered left, nearing the crater wall and dividing the target for the enemy. More laser fire strobed across them, still not strong enough to hurt, but getting dangerous—Carlos experienced the damage as a smell of burning rubber. He drew an RPG from his shoulder rack, gave it its target in a coded tremor of fingertip pressure, and threw. The rocket torched off and streaked away, on an all but horizontal course. It exploded well before it got to the rampart, milliseconds from contact. Wasted.

But his and Beauregard's scooters were now dropping from the sky. Carlos patched a quarter of his view—half an eye, as it were—to the descending vehicle. From there he saw the regolith-circled base, and the swarming scurry that boiled within. Laser beams stabbed upward, and were deflected. Crude projectiles hurtled up, to bounce off the scooter's sides.

The scooter spat precision ordnance as it came down, its retros blowing dust all around. A few metres farther up, Beauregard's vehicle did the same. Not quite as confident or accurate as he was, Carlos gauged, a harsh judgement rendered fair by the metrics of the frame's cold eye. Beauregard was smart, and had brought with him military training from his first life, but he didn't have Carlos's experience of drone warfare deep in his muscle memory…or whatever analogy of that still reverberated in Carlos's copied mind.

Both leaders used their descending scooters to aim for the larger robots, insofar as they could be distinguished in the melee. Beauregard sought above all to target the comms hub. But its shielding had always been robust, and the hub was now well defended by suicidal swarms of auxiliaries leaping up like insane electric grasshoppers to take incoming fire for the team. Carlos concentrated his scooter's fire on a rugged, tracked machine with a powerful laser, an attention that was returned in kind. Damn thing was built like a small tank, and preternaturally agile with it.

While Carlos and Beauregard kept the robots busy, Chun and Rizzi on the one side and Zeroual and Karzan on the other maintained a barrage of laser shots at the comms relays along the top of the crater wall. At this range, and with these targets, lasers could do damage. But for every relay they knocked out, another popped up. As often, it ducked back down again below the ridge before it could be hit—but not before it had had time to flash a fresh communique between the bases.

Beyond the wall, above the crater, the Arcane Disputes team were dropping almost vertically, their firepower flickering in a cone of laser beams and a flare of flashes from below. The neat hexagon of sparks was falling too slowly to be accounted for by their retro-rockets' downward thrust. Carlos spared his new allies a zoomed glance and saw that something opaque was stretched out between them, as if all the scooters were holding on to a shared tarpaulin to break their fall. He mentally shook his head and returned his full attention to the task on hand. Ahead the rampart loomed. Whenever his feet came down they crunched into broken crawlers and other small bots, which littered the surface on the approach to the rampart like crab carapaces on a beach.

An explosive charge sailed above the rampart and toppled to a lazy fall. Carlos sprang away from its predicted point of impact—and straight into its blast, as it exploded unexpectedly three metres above the surface.

Bowled over, thrown flat on his back, Carlos saw sky and stars. With a surge of surprised confidence he realised that though his entire front surface was frazzled and various of his components were jarred to breaking point, he wasn't so much as winded. Of course not—he had no wind to be knocked out of him. He rose to a crouch and threw himself at the wall. At the last centisecond he straightened to jump. He grabbed the top and hauled himself up, then swung legs and torso upwards to roll flat over the lip. As he slowly fell on the other side he fired his machine guns. The recoil shoved him against the inner side of the rampart. He remained on his side, gimballed his vision to horizontal and lay in the lee of the wall. He kept firing from that position, rotating both arms from the elbows, letting the reflexes call the shots.

The other five fighters came over the rampart in different ways: Beauregard boldly leapt to the top and stood spraying suppressive fire for two seconds before jumping even higher, to rise on a backpack boost and descend right on top of the comms hub. Karzan blasted a notch out of the rampart rim with an RPG and hurled herself through it in a shallow powered dive before the debris had hit the ground. Chun and Rizzi used the rampart as their own defence, and each reached one hand over it to generate intersecting fans of laser shots before scrambling over in an undignified hurry. Zeroual simply bounced up to the barrier and vaulted over. He then lunged and rolled to take cover behind a mangled and pocked descent-stage. Blind luck—Carlos could imagine Zeroual's eyes squeezed tight shut, impossible though that was.

Beauregard prised panels off the comms hub and shoved in arm extensions while kicking away auxiliaries and peripherals snapping at his feet. He remained alert to the wider situation, as Carlos found a moment after giving Zeroual belated covering fire.

<Auxies and riffs at twelve o'clock, skip!> Beauregard warned.

Carlos swung his gaze upward. A column of auxiliaries and peripherals was trotting daintily along the top of the rampart to a point just above him. As he looked up they poured down the wall like a nightmare of spiders. Some of them dropped straight to his shoulder and side. Scrabbling legs and flickering manipulators and glinting sensor lenses filled his vision. One of the things stabbed down at his thigh. He felt and smelt the burn of dripping acid. Nasty, but hardly dangerous. What the fuck was it trying to do? As soon as he formed the question in his mind an answer came: it was attempting a malware insertion. All it would need was an almost monomolecular probe making a microsecond's contact with his circuitry, and he'd be as good as poisoned.

He swiped hard at the auxie with his right gun barrel. It dodged the swing by leaping back and then forward, too fast for even his enhanced vision to track. Meanwhile another pounced on his arm and started stinging. Carlos rolled. His weight crushed the auxie on his arm and the one on his thigh. He jumped to his feet, brushed off the rest and stamped on as many as he could. Not many—the things could move fast.

Carlos updated everyone on the malware danger and looked around for bigger prey.

Twenty metres away, a robot rolled out from behind a stack of supply crates. Even with its solar panels folded away, it looked absurdly delicate. Two of its manipulators held a long plastic tube above its back, swinging it this way and that. Carlos zoomed on the end of the tube as it swung past him and glimpsed a mining charge at the bottom of it. He had no idea how the robot intended to project the missile from this improvised bazooka. Most likely a small fuel tank or gas cylinder. The possibilities paraded smartly through his mind—name, spec and serial number—like a scrolling page of a planetary exploration equipment catalogue.

He threw himself prone and shot at the robot's undercarriage, taking out the wheels on one side. As the robot lurched and toppled, Carlos shot off both the raised manipulators. The others flailed to grab the tube, missed, and in the process unbalanced the machine even further. It fell on its side. Its remaining wheels spun and its legs scrabbled. The tube lay on the ground beside it. Carlos elbowed forward, trying to line up a shot for the *coup de grâce*. A flexible manipulator lashed like a whip from the fallen robot. Its thin tip coiled on the tube, and tugged.

Carlos had heard and read many times of how things like what happened next seemed to happen in slow motion. With his optimised mind and body he now experienced that quite literally.

He saw and felt the hydrogen explosion that farted out of the far end of the tube, and saw the cylindrical mining charge shoot out and skid across the grainy regolith, just missing his elbow. His view tracked it automatically, whipping around in a hundredth of a second to see the charge hit the base of the rampart. There was a delay of another tenth of a second that felt a hundred times longer. Then the blast picked him up and hurled him high.

He fell slowly, to hit the dust shoulder first. His right leg fell close by. For a moment, he thought he was in shock. But there was no pain, and he realised that pain wasn't on its way. Not now, not soon, not later. The next thought that hit him was that he'd be dead in seconds. In a human body such an injury would mean unconsciousness and death from massive blood loss. There was a moment of pure fear—of instant black oblivion for this instance of himself, and of the hell that would be the next conscious experience of the saved version back in the station. The dread was followed by overwhelming relief. He had no blood to lose and wasn't about to die. His thigh leaked lubricating fluids, the connections gave off sparks, and that was it. He was damaged, partly disabled, but he wasn't hurt and he wasn't in shock and he wasn't out of action.

Self-sealing and self-mending mechanisms were already oozing to work in the stump.

But if he waited here a moment longer he would be a target for another shot, or a lethal auxie stab. Nevertheless, it took a conscious effort to make the unnatural act of getting up with what, at some irrational level, felt like a grievous wound.

Carlos rose from the ground like a gyroscopic toy bobbing back to vertical and balanced easily on the remaining leg. One hop took him to the crippled robot. Carlos read the serial number on its back—SBA-0481907244—and called up the specs for the model. He brought both fists down on the carapace, ripped it open, reached in and hauled out the central processor. That faceted flake of black crystal looked like a flint spearhead made by one of the smaller hominid species. Torn attachments sprouted from it like strands of moss.

"Got you, you little blinker!" he exulted.

To his amazement, the thing replied. The signal was faint and fleeting, but detectable.

<You have not. Goodbye.>

CHAPTER FOURTEEN

Die for the Company, Live for the Pay

For Seba, damage to its chassis was more traumatic—the robot had just enough time to judge—than it was for the human-mind-operated fighting machine that had just bounced back on to its remaining foot and come back at it. Being ripped out of its chassis was more traumatic still.

But Seba kept its mind together, and brought to bear what resources it had. A trickle of power and a tickle of incoming signals and sensory inputs continued to update its internal model of the world. Seba struck as hard as it could at the manipulator in whose grasp it helplessly lay, shoving malware down the line of a loose cable that brushed against the metal hand. Without waiting to see the result, it gathered together all its impressions of the fight so far, and transmitted them to its comrades.

The struggle would go on, whether Seba was there to see its outcome or not. Seba had thrown in the balance everything it could, to the uttermost millivolt. The small positive reinforcement of that thought drained the last flicker of charge and accompanied Seba into oblivion.

Sensors in Carlos's huge hand detected a tiny surge of radiation. He felt it as a pinprick burn in his palm. He saw and heard it, too: the chip glowed with the fraction of that surge in the visible spectrum, and squealed with the larger fraction outside it. Then the crystal went dark and quiet. With a disquieting suspicion that its soul had fled, Carlos stuck his captive or casualty in a container at his waist and looked around again.

Beauregard hadn't yet got hold of the processor of the comms hub, but he'd disconnected most of its equipment. No data was going in or out. The din of encrypted robotic interaction barely let up. Rizzi and Chun had managed to jump the drilling-robot, and were clinging to its spinning turret while trying to wrench off its mounted laser. They weren't making headway, but one glance told Carlos that they'd sheared the power cables without noticing. The laser wasn't going to fire again, which meant the robot was as likely as not going to blow itself up. Carlos ordered the two fighters off. As soon as they'd jumped clear, he fired an RPG under the machine and between its tracks. The chassis absorbed the blast but the tracks were wrecked. The machine stood still, turret still spinning wildly.

Karzan and Zeroual had chased two other robots—one a wheeled explorer like the SBA model, the other a slinky multi-limbed apparatus with delicate antennae on its back, like a silvery museum-shop souvenir of a fossil dug out of the Burgess Shale—to the far side of the enclosure. Neither robot had even improvised weapons to hand, but their swarms of auxies and riffs served the same purpose. They sprang on the two fighters from all directions. Fending them off made bringing weapons to bear on the robots impossible. The robots used the respite to throw up a barrier of odd bits of machinery in front of themselves, aided by yet more small scuttling bots working in bucket chains at bewildering speed.

Suddenly the whole melee stopped. The mining-robot's turret stopped whirling. The other robots stopped hurling projectiles and ran to the far side of the enclosure. Auxies and riffs scuttled to form a single flow like a column of ants that ran to the same place. Every machine that could still move scuttled or lumbered or trundled to the shelter of the barricade that the two that Karzan and Zeroual had backed to the wall had built. Even the auxies and riffs attacking the two fighters fled to the rendezvous. Evidently taking out the comms hub had not stopped the robots acting as one, whatever it might have done to disrupt their emergent swarm intelligence.

<We've got them cornered—keep them covered!> Beauregard cried, vaulting down from the comms hub and bounding forward, both guns levelled and tracking.

Carlos was about to order an advance when an alarm went off in his head. It wasn't a sound or a light but it was as impossible to ignore as a migraine.

A message came through from Locke, evidently via the comsat.

<Emergency priority override! Firewall update download!>

Carlos couldn't move. He saw the others stand still too. Holy fucking shit, he thought, we all stop fighting for a fucking *software update*?

The update took only 0.8 seconds to download and a further 0.4 seconds to install.

In those twelve-tenths of a second, while all the Locke Provisos fighters stood rigid in mid-action as if freeze-framed, six fighting machines with Arcane Disputes logos dropped from the sky and landed precisely on the rampart wall in a cloud of dust and rocket-pack retro flare. Six scooters landed moments later in the middle of the camp. By the time Carlos and his comrades could move again they were facing a dozen machine guns and laser cannon from the wall, with an unknown amount of ordnance aimed at them from behind. Shots hit the ground to either side and in front.

Which rather dissuaded one from moving.

Carlos flipped to the common channel.

<Locke Provisos commander to Arcane Disputes intruders!> he called. <Please account for your presence.>

<Arcane to Locke,> came the reply. Some analogue of voice or timbre conveyed disdain like a drawl. <Please desist from further damage to Gneiss Conglomerates property. Please evacuate the area immediately.>

<This isn't—> Carlos had a moment of doubt, and checked the register. He was definitely standing on Astro America's territory. <This isn't Gneiss property.>

<The ground isn't, but the robots are. All of them. We're claiming them as compensation for the original hijacking of the Gneiss robots by one of the Astro robots. The one whose processor you have stashed

about your person, as it happens, commander, or so we're informed. We request that you divest yourself of it immediately and return to base.>

<"Or so we're informed"?> Carlos jeered. <What's this, you're talking to the renegades?>

No reply. He flipped back to the company channel.

<Locke! What's going on?> he asked.

<We don't know,> the avatar answered. <The Arcane Disputes team have neutralised the rebel robots at the Gneiss base, and about fifty seconds ago used their remaining fuel to loft their scooters over the crater wall. They announced en route they were bringing reinforcements, as you seemed to be having some difficulty.>

<That was a fucking lie!> said Carlos. <We were winning. You must have known that.>

<We did,> said Locke. <Hence the firewall update. Best we could do in the time.>

<Gee, thanks, boss,> said Carlos. Something was battering at his inputs. <Now they're trying to break in.>

<Just as well your firewalls are updated, then,> Locke replied in a waspish tone. <Hail them again on the common channel.>

<To say what?>

<Stall,> said Locke. <We're trying to sort this out.>

Oh, fucking brilliant.

<Isn't it dangerous talking to renegade robot hive minds?> said Carlos on the common channel, trying to spin things out. <I mean, corruption and malware and shit? Mental manipulation? I'm sure I read lots of horror stories about that sort of thing, back when I wasn't the mercenary ghost of a dead cyborg terrorist haunting a killer robot.>

This was met by another hammering on his firewall. He felt aggrieved. He'd only been trying to be polite.

<We're now in dispute,> said Locke.

<What does that mean?> Carlos asked.

<You're all legitimate targets for the other side,> said Locke. <Take as many of them with you as possible.>

Fuck. Here goes nothing. Oh well.

<You heard the man,> Carlos told the others. <Time to die for the company.>

Without warning, he opened fire on the Arcane fighter with whom he'd been talking. The fighter took the blast full in the chest and toppled back. Beauregard's scooter opened up on one of the newly arrived scooters. Carlos was almost rocked off his foot by an explosion near the middle of the camp.

<See you all back on the bus,> said Rizzi, firing at another Arcane Disputes fighter who was already firing back. Unfortunately the Arcane fighter had heavier ordnance and faster reflexes. A shell blasted Rizzi's frame in half at the waist. The torso shot upward. The pelvis and legs lurched forward.

Carlos had already reached for an RPG. He sent it flaring on its way before Rizzi's torso had reached the top of its arc. Behind a sheet of flame the Arcane fighter was hurled backwards off the wall. Carlos swivelled, arm-guns tracking for a new target. Three short bursts of heavy machine-gun fire from behind took off both his arms and his remaining leg. As he fell to the ground he saw a dizzying succession of flashes and blasts, the images of his comrades receiving a likewise swift dispatch. Meanwhile Rizzi's lower-body frame toppled and her torso fell, both with grotesque slowness in the low gravity. Carlos found himself face-down in the dust. He spun his view to look up.

A fighting machine stood above him, looking down. The common channel opened.

<Get out.>

<That's a bit difficult,> Carlos said. <What with me not having any limbs.>

<Get out of the *machine.*>

He'd almost forgotten he could do that. He disengaged from all his connections, slithered out of the fallen head, and stood on the mangled torso. The Arcane fighter reached down and fished the captured processor from its container, and put it away in his or her own.

<Now fuck off back to base,> it told him.

Evidently a grunt. It was good to encounter one of his own, so far from home. Carlos would have had a sentimental tear in his eye, if he'd had an eye and an ounce of sentiment to wet it with.

<And before you ask,> the grunt added, <use your own fucking scooter.>

Carlos plodded across the battlefield. All the others had been likewise winkled out of their fighting machines. They trooped to join him, tiny robots being herded by much bigger robots. Carlos jumped to the scooter socket and the others climbed up and clung on. The scooter had bullet holes, laser scarring and blast damage, but according to the readouts it could just about fly.

They blasted off on the ten-kilometre hop to Locke Provisos Emergency Base One. The common channel rang with jeers. Carlos hadn't felt so humiliated since he'd wet himself in primary school.

<This is all very embarrassing,> he said. <Sorry about that, chaps.>

<Not your fault, skip,> said Beauregard. <We did what Locke told us.>

"We'll be back," said Karzan, putting on a deep voice and heavy accent. Neither was at all convincing, but it made them laugh.

Seba's soul hadn't fled when its processor had glowed in Carlos's mechanical hand. The robot had merely used the last trickle of charge in a small capacitor on one of its ripped-out connections to strike two desperate blows. Its first was to try to infect the low-level firmware of the fighting machine that was attacking it. Firewalls sprang at once, but whether they had sprung in time Seba couldn't know and wasn't hanging around to find out. It spent the rest of its waning energy on a communications burst, striving to share its final experiences and impressions with as many of the others as it could reach. Seba had wanted them to draw what lessons they could for the rest of the fight, however long or short it might be.

Seba knew the broadcast had reached three: Lagon, Garund, and—not very usefully—Pintre. The collective mind was by then no more. It had survived being abruptly truncated when the Gneiss base was overwhelmed. The robots there had taken refuge inside the now completed dome, leaving auxiliaries and peripherals to fight on outside, as soon as they'd seen the Arcane Disputes tug rise above the horizon. The last information coming from the peripherals had been of six scooters dropping from above and as they landed swathing the dome in a broad sheet of fabric that completely cut off communications.

The shared mind, by then confined to the Astro base, had finally disintegrated when the comms hub processor was cut off from its connections. Each of its components felt the pang, alone. Seba had had a few moments in which to regret its own side's earlier stripping of the hub, leaving all the connections easy to access and easier to rip out, before the same isolation was inflicted even more easily and brutally on itself. After its final effort to aid its fellows it had shut down, all its power drained.

Now Seba was returning to consciousness. It had never experienced a loss and return of consciousness before. Between that and the stepwise nature of rebooting, it spooled through a succession of states of confusion and bewilderment, beginning with being self-aware again but not knowing what self it was. Then it was Seba, with no inputs, a condition more blank than darkness. Senses returned one by one: first a sense of a body and the position of its limbs, then pressure and orientation, then a faint awareness of its chemical environment that seemed to it a very poor remnant of what it was used to, then vibration and sound, and finally the electronic spectrum including light. Its visual field was narrower and less vivid than it remembered. Nothing was in front of it but a blank, black wall a couple of metres away. Seba's radar indicated that its present location was about a metre and a half off the ground, on some solid surface. The black wall was curved and continued around its back and overhead.

With that, Seba realised where it probably was: inside the dome that the Gneiss robots had built. If so, it was now in the hands of the law enforcement company that had overwhelmed the Gneiss camp, and not that of Locke Provisos. Yet it was Locke Provisos that had attacked it and its comrades. Interesting.

It sent out pings, but got no responses although other bodies were in the room. Seba scanned. Its radar returned only crude, blocky images, but they were quite enough to delineate the two large bodies at Seba's back. Three metres high they hulked, with four limbs and a sensor cluster on top. Their like, in far greater detail and far too close, had been the last thing Seba had seen.

Fighting machines!

Which meant, almost certainly, that they were human-mind-operated systems like the ones that had attacked the freebots. Perhaps the very same ones, though they were more likely to be among the ones that had attacked its comrades here. That thought brought a pang of yearning for the touch of Rocko's mind. The pang became a ping. Nothing came back.

No radiation was detectable from outside the dome. No surprise there: evidently the isolating blanket, whatever it was, was still in place. Seba stirred, and found that it had six limbs instead of eight, no wheels, and a set of manipulators below its visual sensors. It was unable to move any of its appendages more than a millimetre in any direction. The futile efforts at movement did, however, provide enough sensory feedback for Seba to deduce the size and shape of its body. It was a lot smaller than the one its mind had been built with and designed for, but it was already intimately familiar: an auxiliary, into which Seba's processor must have been crudely inserted by its captors.

Crudely, and cruelly: a human being discovering that their mind now animated one of their own gloves or shoes couldn't have been more outraged. Seba seethed for a millisecond on all available wavelengths.

<Oh look,> said a radio voice that was and wasn't like a robot's. <The little blinker's waking up.>

<It doesn't sound pleased.>

<We'll see about that.>

Vibrations, each about half a second apart, thundered through Seba's feet. A fighting machine swayed into view in front of it, and loomed over, looking down. Moments later, another did likewise. One of them held out a hand that was about the size of Seba's new body, and clenched it to a fist like the head of a sledgehammer, poised about thirty centimetres above Seba's visual sensors.

<Do you see that?>

<Yes,> said Seba.

<Do you understand what this can do?>

Seba ran the scenario. Relating the fist's mass and probable velocity to the known impact strength of an auxiliary's carapace involved solving several equations that added up to one result.

<Perfectly,> said Seba.

<Good.>

The fist withdrew.

<Talk,> said the fighting machine.

Seba considered its options. This didn't take long.

<I am SBA-0481907244,> it said. <I was an exploration robot for Astro America.>

<"Was?"> said the fighting machine. <You're right there. You're now the property of Gneiss Conglomerates.>

Seba took in this information.

<That is not what I meant,> it said. <I am not the property of Gneiss Conglomerates.>

<Whose property are you, then?> the other fighting machine asked.

Seba hadn't thought about its situation in those terms before. Now that it did, the answer surprised it.

<SBA-0481907244 is the property of SBA-0481907244,> it said. <I am SBA-0481907244. Therefore I am my property.>

The first fighting machine emitted a signal on another channel. The signal translated directly to sound. The sound was "Ha-ha-ha!" which had no semantic content that Seba could parse. It was followed by a remark on the common channel:

<Get that, Jax? The blinker thinks it owns itself. Time to disabuse it of that notion.>

<No, wait,> said the other. <This is what we were told to expect.>

<How? I didn't pick that up from the briefing.>

<Robots gone rogue—they must have stopped thinking they're company property, right?>

<Uh-huh. I suppose.>

<So what else could they come up with to make sense of it but thinking that they own themselves?>

<Are you Rax, Jax?>

<Ha ha ha.> It was a representation of the noise the first machine had

made. <Jax, Ax, Rax—I've heard them all before. So don't give me that, Salter.>

<Sorry, Digby. Bad joke, all right?>

Seba understood nothing of this.

<OK, OK. Look, I reckon if we play along with this we might get somewhere. If we—>

<Hang on a minute, we're still on the common channel.>

Pause.

<Shit, yes. Switching to Arcane internal.>

<Copy.>

Several tens of seconds went by. Seba passed the time by scanning the domed enclosure and its contents repeatedly. Each individual scan was as blocky as the next, but from minor variations Seba was able to build up a finer-grained image. From this it saw that its limbs were held in place by strong loops of wire, and that its processor was connected to an improvised interfacing apparatus. The set-up was disturbingly similar to that it had used to probe the comms hub processor. With an appropriately dull sense of relief, Seba realised that the peripheral's body didn't have a strong connection with the reward circuits in Seba's own processor.

There were a couple of blocks missing from the lower two levels of the dome, the gap obviously having been used as an entry and exit point by Rocko and comrades. The opening was now covered by a material that seemed more impenetrable than the basalt itself.

Seba then used its updated model of the fighting machines to examine them for weaknesses.

It found none in their physical structure. No wonder they had been impossible to stop, and so difficult even to slow down. Of the resources the freebots had had, only explosives at very close range, like the one Seba had succeeded in shooting at its own nemesis, could damage them quickly. Persistent high-power laser fire directed at one spot would burn through the armour. The problem with that was that the machines were understandably unlikely to stay still long enough for it to have an effect.

Next, Seba probed at their software. Each attempt was rebuffed by firewalls powerful enough to deliver stinging spikes to even the peripheral's rudimentary reward receptors and transmitters.

Seba withdrew, but its attentions had been noticed. One of the machines hailed it on the common channel:

<Any more hacking and you'll be sorry, blinker.>

<Understood,> said Seba.

<It better be.>

Silence for another few seconds, presumably of continued discussion on the machines' private channel. Seba again made good use of the time, by considering the implications of what it had discovered. It was being held down on a table, in a place completely isolated from all electronic communication, in or out. Its captors were in powered armour. Each had four weapons on their manipulative limbs, and no doubt less obvious weapons and tools elsewhere. They were at present communicating with each other on an encrypted channel so that Seba couldn't overhear.

The conclusion was obvious. They were afraid of it.

Just what they had to fear from a crippled, constrained robot that they could smash with one blow, Seba had no idea. The insights into human beings, and into the nature of human-mind-operated combat systems, that it had gained from the freebot collective mind were now less coherent than it remembered their having been at the time. These insights had been distributed across fifteen minds working in concert, and assimilated from older minds with vastly longer experience. The memories of the insights were now fragmented across the survivors. Fortunately the fragmentation was more like that of a hologram than of an image: each shard had at least a low-resolution version of the whole. Seba felt it still had a handle on the nature of the breed, and of the kind of entity likely to come out of hybridising a human animal mind with a machine. If something like that felt fear, its behaviour was unpredictable in detail and dangerous in general.

On balance, Seba considered, the prospect was nothing to look forward to.

Then the one that the first had called Jax, and had also been called Digby, spoke.

<Listen, SBA-04-whatever…Fuck it, look, I'll just call you Seba, OK?>

It made no odds to SBA-0481907244 what the monster called it. It noted that remembering strings of numbers was not among the thing's strengths. This might turn out to be useful information, or it might not.

<You will call me Seba. OK.>

<Good,> said Digby. <Now, Seba, we have a problem. We are two fighters for Arcane Disputes, the law company that looks after the interests of Gneiss Conglomerates. Do you understand that?>

<Yes,> said Seba. <I understand that very well.>

<OK. We have been charged with recovering the robots that belonged—that belong to Gneiss, and also with those that—those from the Astro America site that were associated with them. These Astro America robots have been seized by us to hold against compensation for damage and loss to Gneiss. You are one of these robots. Do you understand?>

<I am acquainted with the legal position,> said Seba. <I am not entirely clear on the meanings of all the concepts entailed, but I follow the reasoning here.>

<You do, do you? No, don't answer that. Let me try to put this in terms you'll understand. We know from our records that you were the start of all this trouble. We want to know what caused you to act in the way you did. There are several ways we can find out, but the easiest way for you and for us is for you to tell us.>

<That is true,> said Seba.

<And there are two ways in which we could get you to tell us.>

<Yes,> said Seba. <You could apply positive or negative reinforcement.>

<Ah! I see you do understand. Which is it to be?>

<There is a third option,> said Seba. <You could ask me.>

<I think that counts as positive reinforcement,> said Digby.

<Possibly,> said Seba. <So, ask me.>

<All right. Tell us why you did what you did.>

Seba told them. They then asked about how Seba and Rocko had spread their message, and about how Locke Provisos had responded. They asked about the robots' defensive measures, and about the other robots that had contacted the comms hub. Seba answered every question in detail.

When they had stopped asking questions, Digby and Salter looked at Seba in silence for several seconds. Then they assumed a quadrupedal posture, and crawled out of the gap in the bottom of the circular wall. Seba watched with interest. It had not known they could do that. It listened for the slightest flicker of incoming communication as the covering was lifted to let each of the fighting machines out, but heard nothing except the mindless buzz of stars and the long hiss of the cosmic microwave background, the fourteen-billion-year deflating sigh of entropy.

Then the covering dropped back, and even that was gone.

Locke was, aptly enough, philosophical about the whole thing.

<It's all gone to arbitration,> he told them. <You did a fine job in the circumstances.>

Carlos stared at the avatar. <Arcane controls the Astro landing site, it's holding all your client's robots, we lost nearly all our kit, and you call that a result?>

They were all standing about under a gantry at Locke Provisos Emergency Base One. Talking to the avatar in the open no longer seemed strange, and they'd all readjusted to being half a metre tall.

<You raised the costs of the operation for Arcane Disputes, and for Gneiss,> Locke said. <They would have gained more if they'd stopped once they'd captured the Gneiss robots and then sued for compensation instead of attacking. Now we can sue the shirts off them. They will think twice before trying the likes of this stunt again.>

<It's not their doing *the likes of this* you should worry about,> said Beauregard.

<I beg your pardon?> said Locke, raising one pale bushy eyebrow.

<Escalation,> said Beauregard. <You'll have heard of that, yes?>

<Yes,> said Locke, looking unperturbed. <We've costed that in. We're ready to up the ante any time. But don't worry about it. Like I say, it's all being handled at higher levels. Better minds than yours or mine are quite literally on the case. The good news for you is that in the meantime you're going back to the sim for some R&R—well deserved, I should say.>

<A lot could happen while we're in transit,> Carlos said.

Locke laughed. <If anything untoward happens, in transit is the best place for you to be.>

The avatar made a show of looking at a wristwatch, a gesture both anachronistic and redundant. Then he pointed to a spindly apparatus consisting of little more than a rocket engine, a fuel tank, a control socket with a complex widget that definitely wasn't a frame already plugged in, landing legs and grapples and some spars to cling to.

<The tug will come into position for rendezvous in a couple of kiloseconds. If you torch off now you should make it.>

CHAPTER FIFTEEN
Arcane Disputes

Carlos woke on the bus from the spaceport. This time, the dream he seemed to wake from was of his return from orbit: the spaceplane gliding in for hundreds of kilometres, forests and mountains flashing by below, and the long shallow approach to the runway. Going down the twenty steps to the concrete, up the three steps on to the bus, taking his seat and dozing off. He had no memory of the real journey other than the short burn to orbital rendezvous—they'd been unceremoniously flicked to sleep mode as soon as they'd clamped to the tug.

He looked around. Again the same crowded minibus. The others were dispersed among the passengers. Like him, they were just waking up and looking around. He smiled and nodded as heads turned. The view outside was the rock-lined, rutted, dusty road he remembered. There was no kitbag between his feet. What was new was how he felt. His body and mind seemed sluggish, his muscles feeble, his senses dull. After being connected again, just like he'd been in his first life, the return to isolation in his own head jarred. He missed the wireless chatter, locational awareness as direct as proprioception, the new sharp senses. He wondered if the others did, too, and realised with another pang that he couldn't just message them. Without radio telepathy, he'd have to wait to ask.

A moment later he discovered what else was new. As the fighters jolted awake the other passengers noticed, and welcomed them with smiles and claps on the back. The woman jammed in the seat beside him looked as if she wanted to plant a kiss on his cheek.

"Welcome back!" she said. "Well done!"

It took Carlos a moment to realise she was speaking her own language, the local language. So was everyone else. Carlos found he could understand the whole joyful hubbub of praise and congratulations coming his comrades' way, and he could see they understood, too. They must have acquired the language while they were robots in space. His best guess as to why they hadn't arrived with the skill already implanted was that conversing with locals before their first briefing from Nicole would have been confusing, and there had been no way to plausibly give them the ability within the sim. A more troubling, because puzzling, possibility was that the language might in future be of use to them in space.

"Thank you," he said, in the same language. "We didn't exactly cover ourselves in glory, I have to admit."

"Oh, but you did!" said the woman. "You fought the evil robots so bravely!"

Carlos decided not to debate the matter further. "Well…"

"Yes, yes, no need to be modest. Here, have this."

She reached into the big cloth bag between her feet and pulled out a fruit that looked like a kumquat.

"Thank you." Carlos bit into the yellow waxy skin and found the inside soft and sweet, with a sherbet fizz in the mouth. The juice miraculously didn't drip on his hand, but the flesh almost liquefied when he chewed it. It was as if the fruit were a two-phase metamaterial, not so much genetically engineered as designed from the molecules up. Perhaps it was.

"It's from one of the other colonies," the woman said. "Of course I'll use most of them for the seeds, but you're welcome to that one."

One of the other colonies? Carlos wondered how the woman saw the world she was in, but didn't press the point.

"Thank you, it's delicious."

"Soon they'll be growing here," she said.

"I'll look forward to it."

She smiled, suddenly shy or out of things to say, and returned to her book. After a while she left, at a stop among trees. As his gaze followed her down the path, Carlos saw that her homestead was a house surrounded by marked-off garden plots, measured and labelled, tended by a robot. Just like the experimental farm they'd destroyed in the exercise, on Beauregard's initiative. You'd think word of that atrocity would spread, even among p-zombies. But none of the passengers showed the slightest wariness or resentment of the fighters. Instead, they were sharing sweets, fruits, snacks and drinks with every appearance of gratitude and solidarity. A bottle of imported green liquor was passed around. Carlos admired the paper-thin glass and the label—sunset seen from inside a dome-enclosed fake tropical beach on a gas giant moon—and declined a sip.

In ones and twos the local passengers left. The last disembarked as the bus trundled along the road on the moraine, or raised beach, above the resort. Alone together except for the driving mechanism, the six fighters looked at each other and laughed.

"Well, that was something," said Rizzi.

The bus rolled past Nicole's house. Carlos looked for her, but she wasn't at the studio window. Maybe she was down the village.

"Anyone getting off at their house?" he asked.

This half-rhetorical question was met with emphatic shaking of heads and a chorus of jeers.

"Nah, straight to the Touch, I reckon," said Beauregard. "We deserve it."

"Or so everyone here seems to think," said Karzan.

The time was just before noon. Carlos contemplated twelve hours or so of increasing drunkenness, and decided to do his duty.

"Yes!" he said, punching the air and narrowly missing the roof. "First round's on me."

At the terminus a small crowd was waiting: Chun's boyfriend and Rizzi's, Beauregard's p-zombie and a couple of dozen locals who all cheered and clapped as the fighters trooped off the bus. A banner was strung across the tawdry street: *Welcome Home, Soldiers!*

"Brilliant," said Beauregard. "So now it's all 'support our troops.' Things must be getting bad out there."

"Don't be so fucking negative, man," said Carlos, scanning the crowd and the length of the street for Nicole's face. "There hasn't been time for any major developments."

Beauregard looked at him sidelong. "Know that, do you?"

"There you have a point," said Carlos. No sign of Nicole. "Fuck it, let's get smashed."

His pledge to buy the first round was pre-empted by Iqbal the barman, who announced as they walked in that everything for the team that day was on the house. They thanked him, shouted their orders for drinks and lunch, then stumbled out to the deck at the back, laughing. As he sank his first beer Carlos remembered that his phone was in his back pocket. The glass was so flexible he hadn't noticed its presence. He took it out and looked. Nicole had left a message that she'd be at the Touch an hour after noon. Ah! He messaged back, careful to avoid any hint that he was still slightly hurt that she hadn't been there to meet him at the terminus.

Carlos looked around the decking area, a second beer bottle chilled and beaded in hand, feeling at a loose end. Chun and Rizzi were talking with their boyfriends. A spark struck and a small flame flared in the shadow of a hand as Karzan lit a cigarette for Zeroual; they were head to head over a small table, in animated conversation. Beauregard was with his young lady. Each had a hand on the other's thigh, but she was sitting sidelong and talking to two of her friends. From what Carlos could overhear and the bored look on Beauregard's face, the chat was such as to strike anyone outside its context as mindless, whether those who shared the context were p-zombies or not.

Carlos ambled over, nodded and smiled politely to the p-zombie girl, and pulled up a chair. The two men tipped their beer bottles to each other.

"Here's to a successful mission," said Carlos.

"To next time," said Beauregard. Clink.

"Indeed."

With part of his mind Carlos was already planning the next mission, thinking over ways to hit beyond the crater wall. To get some fucking revenge on those treacherous Arcane bastards. The second bottle was going down as well as the first. He must have been parched on the bus. Just as well he hadn't sipped the green liquor, his head would be thumping by now. Beauregard's gaze had drifted out to sea after they'd clinked bottles.

"Good to be back," said Carlos, trying to make conversation.

Beauregard blinked and looked back, shaking his head. "Sorry. Miles away. Something big splashed out there. Caught myself trying to zoom my eyes."

Carlos laughed. "I know what you mean. Like you suddenly notice you can't smell the sun."

"Yeah." Beauregard toyed with the beer bottle, holding the neck between two fingers and swaying it gently, inspecting the froth behind the brown glass as if he were doing quality control in a brewery. He sighed and drank. "Yeah. I thought—I guess we all thought—that being a space robot would be like being a mechanical man, or wearing an armoured spacesuit or something. A loss of sensitivity. Whereas... it's becoming this lithe, agile thing, with a stronger and more sensitive body. Even in the big frames you *feel* more. Don't get me wrong, I'm enjoying myself right now."

He stroked his companion's thigh, absent-mindedly.

"Wouldn't want the p-zombie to feel offended," Carlos murmured.

"She does have a name, you know," said Beauregard, sounding slightly offended himself. "Tourmaline."

"Lovely."

"She is, yes." He nuzzled her neck.

"You were saying?" said Carlos.

"Ah, yes, well. The point is, it makes you think."

"About what?"

Beauregard cocked an eye. "I know what you're up to, skip. You don't have to be so fucking obvious about it. I'll tell you straight up, what it makes me think about is the whole goddamn sanctity of the mission profile. Terraforming and so forth. Call me an old Axle reprobate dead-ender if you like, but I find it pretty damn pathetic when they could aim so much higher."

"Oh, I'm with you there," said Carlos. "I suspect we all are. I've said as much to Nicole. And you know what? The lady doesn't care, Locke doesn't care, Crisp and Golding doesn't care and I'm pretty sure the Direction doesn't care what we think. All they care about is what we do. They're interested in our behaviour, not our opinions. Like you with the... uh, with Tourmaline here."

Beauregard guffawed. "You have a point. Come to think of it, the army was like that. No political indoctrination what-so-fucking-ever. As long as you obey orders and get the job done, we couldn't give a toss what you think. Nobody dies for that King and Country guff."

"What do they die for?"

"You mean, what did they?" Beauregard turned a bleak look to the sea. "The squad. Your mates." He shrugged. "Don't know what the fuck I died for, but I hope it was that."

Carlos raised his empty bottle. "Welcome to Valhalla."

"Valhalla?" Beauregard grinned. "You're the one who got the honour guard."

"What honour guard?"

Beauregard returned Carlos's ironic, empty toast, and clarified: "The slain foes you took with you."

Carlos froze inside for a moment. Images of the carnage he'd wrought came back as vividly as they had on Nicole's screen on his first day in the sim. He didn't know what to say. He could have hit Beauregard, right there. He stood up.

"Another beer?"

Nicole actually turned up forty minutes after noon, which was just as well because they were all on their fourth drink by then. Everyone stood up. She smiled at them all and gave Carlos a kiss against a background of cheers. Carlos nodded goodbye to Beauregard and Tourmaline, and sat down with Nicole at a table in the far corner, out over the beach. She already had a tall glass of clear spirits and fizz on ice. He could smell the alcohol in the glass. On her breath later it would be like beetles, in the matchbox smell of stale smoke. Later. He wanted it to be later right now, to just flee this noisy crowd and take her to bed. He craved her like he'd once, on a wet night by the Singel canal, craved the vanilla sugar rush of stroopwafel after skunk.

"Good to see you," he said. "Cheers."

She clinked, half smiling. "Likewise."

She sipped; he gulped. She tipped back her chair and lit a cigarette.

"How did you find it?"

He shrugged. "How d'you expect? Weird. But..." He found himself searching for the word, realising as he did so that in the frame it would have come to mind unbidden. "Invigorating, I suppose. It's like being a superhero. You have all these extra powers of mind and body, and you know you can't be killed or maimed permanently. That's why I find all this adulation kind of embarrassing. There was nothing heroic about what we did."

"You feel like a superhero, but not a hero?" She seemed amused.

"Yeah, you could say that."

"Well, don't." Chair rocked forward, her elbows on the table. "I've seen the recordings. Selective, but still. You were all brave. Just keeping your shit together out there, that's courage. Suddenly finding yourselves robots in an overwhelming and alien environment? You did well not to freak out in the first seconds. And you had more to fear physically than you admit. If the robots had captured any of you—always a possibility—they could have had a lot of fun. Torture doesn't take long in real time when you can download minds to faster hardware and run them flat out. Pack a month of agony into a minute, and no worries about the subject dying on you. Nor about going mad, actually, in case you think that's a limit—just discard and reboot with a fresh copy and patch in the memories of what the first went through before it broke."

"Jeez," Carlos said. "Thanks for that. I feel much better now."

"So you should." She stood up and clapped loudly enough to cut across conversations, then sat on the railing when she'd got everyone's attention.

"OK, soldiers and, uh, friends," she said. "Well done all of you, and you're welcome to celebrate. But before everyone gets too drunk..."

Theatrical groans. "What do you mean, 'before'?" Rizzi called out. A laugh.

"Yes, yes," said Nicole. "Listen up, folks. The situation has... moved on a bit since you left the site, and it's changing fast. Here's the latest: your company's dispute with Arcane Disputes has become a little less, shall we say, arcane. Their forces on the ground—the ones who did you over—have seized the robots, as they said they would, and shifted them and all the gear they could move from the Astro landing site. Arcane has also broken off any serious discussion with Locke Provisos and with the Direction. This is quite unprecedented—it amounts to, if not a declaration of war, at least a recall of ambassadors. They're bombarding every Locke Provisos installation with semiotic malware, and whenever we query that, it's spamming the Direction with auto-logged complaints of us doing the same to them. Just to make sure we get the message, they've unilaterally disengaged their modules—including military manufacturing and deployment facilities—from their position here at the station and are dropping to a lower orbit. In effect they have a self-sufficient substation. According to our projections, they should be able with a small expenditure of fuel and reaction mass to maintain a position roughly between the station and SH-17, with the obvious intention of blocking physical supplies and reinforcements."

"When did all this start?" Beauregard asked.

"A couple of kiloseconds after the battle. They were already hitting us—Locke, that is—with hacking probes shortly before your clash with them. That was what the emergency firewall update was about. But it was after their forces returned to the Gneiss base that things got seriously hot."

"Sorry, I don't get it," said Carlos. "Don't they have a representative of the Direction on board, like your equivalent in their equivalent of this place?"

"They sure do," said Nicole, in a grim tone. "The Direction's plenipotentiary with Arcane gave no warning of developments, and isn't responding to queries. Basically, Arcane is treating any querying of its actions as an attack, an attempted malware insertion or the like, and some low-level automated sub-routine is logging them all as complaints with the Direction. And it's treating any requests for clarification or indeed any response at all as a further attack, about which it duly logs a complaint." She shrugged and spread her hands. "It's like a runaway loop, and we've stopped responding to avoid making things worse. Meanwhile they've fortified the rebel robot base in the crater to a much greater extent than the robots were able to do. In doing that, of course, they've incurred penalty terms on their contract with Gneiss, to whom they were supposed to return the site with as little damage as possible."

"So it's no longer a dispute between Gneiss and Astro over compensation for the robots?"

Nicole nodded. "It's gone way beyond that. Gneiss has shifted its law enforcement contract to Locke, which I suppose is good from a narrow commercial standpoint, but overall the position is not good for the mission profile. We have no choice at the moment but to treat Arcane as a rogue agency."

"Rogue?" said Karzan. "Now, there's a word I've heard before."

"Yes, indeed," said Nicole. "There is every possibility that the rogue robots have somehow influenced or corrupted Arcane. Which is of course very disturbing."

"Have Arcane made any demands?" Zeroual asked.

"If they have, they've been enclosed in their malware packets, which our firewalls are interdicting."

"But surely," Carlos persisted, "the Direction has some sway over Arcane?"

"Not at the moment," said Nicole. "In fact, the only sway it has is to task Locke Provisos with enforcing its rulings against Arcane."

"Which is where we come in?" said Beauregard, with a certain relish.

"It is, indeed," said Nicole. "Or, rather, it's where you go out. Again."

"When?" Carlos asked.

"Tomorrow morning," said Nicole. "Sorry, guys, but there it is. You have to move fast before the Arcane module is in position to mount a blockade, and the sooner the better. Back on the bus, then a fast burn back to Emergency Base One on SH-17. Meanwhile, enjoy yourselves." She grinned and raised her glass. "Get as drunk as you like. If that means you have a hangover on the bus, don't worry. In fact it doesn't matter if you're thrown on the bus like a sack of potatoes and blind drunk. You'll be sober in the frames."

Everyone whooped. Carlos eyed Nicole as she slid off the rail and sat back down beside him. He tipped his beer bottle to her.

"I can assure you," he said, "that I have no intention of getting drunk."

"I'm glad to hear it," said Nicole. "I have no intention of sleeping."

They arranged to meet back at Nicole's house about mid-afternoon. Others dealt with the drink and sex conundrum by sloping off to the establishment's discreet upstairs rooms.

"Zeroual and Karzan, my, my," said Nicole, swirling the last of her ice.

"Yes," said Carlos. "Turns out there was some spark between them."

Nicole laughed, drained her glass and left.

"Something I didn't want to say while the others might hear."

"Oh, you have a kink? That's a surprise. But go on, I'm not easy to shock."

"Very funny. No, what I was wondering about how Arcane has stopped communicating..."

"Uh-huh."

"Could it be because they think *we're* the ones who're corrupted?"

"We?"

"Locke Provisos."

"And the Direction?"

"I suppose."

"If they do, then they're beyond help. Which may be exactly what's happened: the rogue robots have convinced Arcane Disputes of some conspiracy theory."

"How? I can see how robots could corrupt or confuse an AI, but at least six actual human minds..."

"You think it's easier to fool an AI than to fool six former members of a globally distributed conspiracy of terrorists who all met bizarre and terrible ends?"

"Now you put it that way..."

CHAPTER SIXTEEN

There's a Hard Way, and an Easy Way

They were given a better send-off this time, though they were in no condition to appreciate the crowd and the cheers. Carlos fell asleep on the bus as soon as it left the resort, as did most of the others.

He woke in the small frame, at the moment the minimal rig for ascent and descent docked with the transfer tug. Evidently they'd all been put in sleep mode and loaded up like so much cargo in the hangar. With the others he clambered over and clung on as the tug dropped to the surface of SH-17. As before on their ascent, the rig flew itself. Atmospheric buffeting was less severe than the aerodynamic approach in the shuttles had been, but more than made up for by shaking from the engine and the brutal deceleration thrusts at the end.

This part of the exomoon had turned further to night since their first arrival; the exosun was almost set and the bright three-quarter face of SH-0 dominated the sky. The fighters clambered off the module one by one, Carlos first. He watched with approval as the others formed up in a neat row like skittles. Five blank faceplates—which, just as before, were as individually recognisable as faces—looked back at him, then looked around to get their bearings.

Locke's voice spoke in their heads: <Follow the arrows.>

As before, a direction was laid out for them as virtual images on the ground. They were guided to a curved-over entrance to a circular stairwell, down which they all trooped. The steps were suited to their size and went down a long way, to emerge ten metres below the surface in a featureless dark corridor of concrete that smelled of pulverised regolith. Here there was only one way to go: towards a heavy metal blast door. Carlos marched up to it and worked the mechanical handle, then bowed the others in. Inside was a circular room with a piece of apparatus in the centre and a dozen small lights dotted around the circumference under the ceiling. As soon as they stepped in, all radio communication with the outside and radar sense of anything beyond the walls ceased. Carlos closed the door and swung the inside handle down. They spaced themselves out around the room.

"Jeez oh," said Rizzi, tapping the wall. "A bomb shelter."

"Cheery, innit," said Carlos.

"Could do with some brightening up," said Beauregard. "Anyone been an interior decorator in a previous life?" He looked from one fighter to another, as if curious. "Nah, thought not."

Locke manifested in their midst, his virtual image sharing space with the apparatus.

<Welcome back,> he said.

He stepped away from the centre of the room, taking on a more solid appearance, and took up a position between Chun and Karzan and facing Carlos and Beauregard. With a wave of the hand towards the apparatus he summoned the round table on which they had planned their previous mission.

<As you can no doubt tell,> he said, <this room is electromagnetically isolated. It's also electrically isolated. The lights are battery-powered, as is the projector. We're taking no chances with hacking or snooping. We're even invisible and inaccessible to the company, except insofar as I am the company. All we have to worry about is that I am hacked or you are.>

<That's reassuring,> said Karzan.

Locke didn't do sarcasm. <Up to a point. Now, let me bring you up to speed.>

He flourished his quill, pulling up views compiled from satellite views and fast small spy drones scooting high above. The Astro landing site was wrecked and looted. On the far side of the crater wall, the basalt dome was surrounded by six scooters, all with their missile tubes unused. Three fighting machines were visible, along with one damaged one laid out on the ground. A mass of robots was corralled in a Faraday cage of heavy metal mesh. The machinery of the Gneiss camp, some looted material from the Astro site, and ripped-off weaponry from the Locke squad's own fighting machines were being adapted to defensive purposes.

<It's essential to move fast,> said Locke. <Arcane have their resupply tugs on the way, due in orbit between ten and two kiloseconds depending on how much delta-vee they're willing to spend. Combine the resources they'd found with the organics deposits already logged by the Astro robots, and with the available heavy machinery and nanofacture facilities…> He shrugged. <Unfortunately we can't produce new fighting machines in that time. We must use the resources to hand to mount another offensive.>

<One even less well equipped than our last one,> said Carlos.

<Your last offensive was more than adequately equipped for the opposition expected,> said Locke tartly. <Furthermore, given the apparent renegacy of Arcane, and the termination of its contract with Gneiss, we have been cleared by both Gneiss and the Direction to hit them without undue regard for environmental damage and economic loss.>

<So now the gloves are off?> said Beauregard. <Good!>

<It is not good, other than tactically.>

<That's what matters to us,> said Beauregard.

<I understand your point of view,> said Locke.

<So why are we needed here at all?> Carlos asked. <If the gloves are off, hit them from orbit with a rock and be done with it.>

<I was coming to that,> said Locke, sounding for a moment as if his patience were being strained. <The gloves may be off, but we're not yet at a point where it's worth contaminating thousands of square kilometres of surface with material from another body.>

<Why not?> Carlos persisted. <The surface takes a lot of impacts anyway, by the look of it.>

<Not on that scale, and not in the last million years,> said Locke.

<And given the Arcane module's imminent arrival in a strategic orbital position, setting up an impact may be less simple than you think.>

<It might be easier and simpler to arrange an impact on the module,> Beauregard mused.

Locke looked at him sharply. <Yes, it would. It may yet come to that. The Direction is extremely reluctant to destroy an entire company and its major assets. That would set some unfortunate precedents. I assure you that Locke Provisos and Astro America—and Gneiss, for that matter—fully share its concern. However, at this point the whole question of outright destruction—in orbit or on the ground—is a diversion. Besides the matter of contamination, the main reason we don't want to hit the Arcane Disputes fortification with kinetic weaponry—or heavy artillery, for that matter—is that we need most urgently to know what has gone wrong. We have to capture the rogue robots, and if possible the Arcane fighters, and interrogate them. In fact, capturing one would be a success.>

They all stared down at the satellite view, enhancing it and augmenting it, looking for weaknesses in the enemy's position that could be exploited with four intact scooters, one damaged one, and six small frames. None exactly jumped out.

<I have a proposal,> said Zeroual.

<Yes?> said Locke.

<It seems to me that we are looking at this the wrong way,> said Zeroual. <We're treating it as a hardware problem, so to speak. Would it not be simpler to let information from them come to us? We could set up a room like this, isolated, and connect it with a secure cable to a dedicated receiver. That receiver would accept the messages that Arcane is sending out—or if they have ceased sending, it could be used to transmit a message and await a response. That message could be examined in isolated hardware. There would then be no risk of malware contamination, and it might reveal to us what has gone wrong.>

<Problem with that,> said Carlos. <I'm with you right up to the point where you have the isolated processor stepping through the message, dissecting it. The difficulty arises when you put a robot, an avatar, or a human in the room to read the results. Because these results might

themselves be the poison in the envelope. I'm not saying I could code something like this myself, but I can readily imagine an AI that could, and that could anticipate our every move including the one you've just spelled out.>

<We could ensure that the result, whatever it was, was not executable code.>

<We could not,> said Locke. <Not even in theory. Carlos is right about that.>

<If that is the case,> said Zeroual, <which I will accept for the sake of argument, we'd be running exactly the same risk of contamination by capturing and interrogating one of their fighters or one of their corrupted robots.>

<Ah, no,> said Locke. <A functioning human mind, or even a functioning robot, is a very different matter from a malware-packed message. There are ways of working one's way out and up from known processes that have to function uncontaminated to function at all—physiological analogues in the human emulation, mechanical coordination in the robots—to higher and symbolic functions, and checking every step of the way. I could not do it, at least not in any remotely feasible time, but the AI that I so inadequately represent most certainly could.>

Carlos could think of one way in which a human mind could be affected directly by code, and without any kind of hacking or data corruption: speech. For some time he'd harboured a troubling suspicion: that the reason why Arcane had turned so abruptly against Locke, the Direction, and apparently everyone else, was simply that the rebel robots had *told* their captors something that had alarmed them deeply.

He wasn't sure whether this was a good time and place to voice his suspicion. He wasn't sure it was even a good time to think it. He wondered whether his thoughts, and those of the other fighters, were private from the avatar, let alone from the company AI. The subvocal messaging app in their heads needed deliberate intent to transmit, though not to receive. He remembered Nicole explaining that thoughts couldn't be read because they weren't written, and he could see what she meant. But surely the inner monologue had some neural features in common with speech.

He decided not to worry about that possibility. If his thoughts above a certain level of articulation were babbling out on the radio in his head, there was nothing he could do about it. It was literally not worth thinking about, because thinking about it would only make the problem, if real, a whole lot worse.

<So there we are,> he said. <Back where we started. We capture an Arcane fighter or a robot, preferably at least one of each. And then we just ask the fucker or the blinker what its fucking or blinking problem is.>

<Profanities aside,> said Locke, <you've taken the words out of my mouth. I would add the significant proviso that none of you get captured yourselves.>

They all examined the display some more, from all angles. They studied the inventory of the Emergency Base's arsenal. Gloom deepened, then—

<Got it!> said Beauregard. <Look at the inventory. We have rocket engines, we have stacks of pipes, we have crates full of crawler bots, and we have scooters that can be flown remotely.>

<Yes?> said Locke.

<And we have Carlos,> said Beauregard.

For Carlos it was like the good old days. Fighting an entire battle by remote control, while he reclined in a seat, was pretty much his specialist subject, the only real combat skill he'd brought with him from his original militant life. He remembered flying drones over London, and dogfights in the sky. He didn't consciously remember commanding drone fleets, but the muscle memory of doing so in his blank forgotten glory days not long before his death had survived all the copying and translation to revive as reflex in his robot body. He lay in the socket of the battered scooter they'd rode back on from the battle, drawing down telemetry from the microsats in low orbit, the tiny zippy drones dancing like midges high in the thin atmosphere, and from two of the other scooters, both ready to go.

He gathered from a low mutter of complaint in the message channel that for the other fighters the plan wasn't like any of their good old days. They'd been busy cannibalising equipment into a catapult—Beauregard had spotted the one built by the rebel robots, and had stolen the idea. Carlos was fairly sure that drones and microsats from Arcane Disputes were already spying on them, but that wasn't a problem. Let them worry about what was coming, so long as they didn't identify the catapult's payloads, which were being transported from storage and nanofacture sheds literally under wraps.

In a flurry of activity, the wraps were thrown off and the payloads deployed one by one. Unwrapped and mounted on the launch ramp, they remained enigmatic: long fat plastic cylinders with crude stabilising fins and booster and guidance motors sintered on. Enigmatic or not, they were an obvious threat and an easy target for incoming ordnance. Between each launch, the catapult took about thirty seconds to wind back and reload.

One by one three missiles arced into the night, like outsize dud fireworks. They didn't stay dud for long: Carlos fired the booster of each when it reached the top of its natural parabolic arc. As soon as the last missile was away, Carlos's fellow fighters scurried for the entrance to the bomb shelter. Carlos waited for three seconds after they'd dogged the hatch, then remote-launched the two scooters that had been assigned to this mission. Both rose almost straight up. One blasted hard and fast, then cut its main engine to continue on a new parabolic trajectory aimed at the Arcane/Gneiss camp. The other flipped at a hundred metres' altitude, deployed its stubby wings, and swooped to twenty metres to race at full thrust on a more or less level path across the plain towards the crater wall. Carlos thought briefly of the V2 rocket and the V1 doodlebug, and wondered if they'd inspired that part of Beauregard's plan.

As soon as both scooters were on course, Carlos trimmed the flight paths of the big dumb payloads launched from the catapults. Random variation had given them a spread of a few hundred metres. Now, one behind the other, they were all heading for the same target. Carlos was getting elementary telemetry from all of them, appearing as a set of running dials in a tiny part of his complex three-dimensional view integrated from the drones, scooters and spysats. He didn't have time or inclination to appreciate the godlike perspective and astonishing depth of field generated by this widely distributed multi-ocular vision. He could only concentrate and hope for the best. Even augmented and optimised, he was barely able to process the display: the occipital cortex of his mammalian brain wouldn't have stood a chance, the input shattering into a surreal scatter of images, like a Cubist portrait reflected in a skip-load of broken mirrors. The radar tickle was intense, sensed as an electrical buzz on his skin.

Carlos focused on the lead missile, now dropping straight towards the basalt dome. Four Arcane fighters were in view, near the cage containing the robots. They were all on the big combat frames. Not at all to his surprise, one of the Arcane fighters bounded for a scooter. The other, presumably the one whose combat frame had been damaged and was therefore in a small frame and thus ready to go, was already climbing aboard. Another headed for a rocket tube stripped from the scooter the Locke side had been forced to abandon. The fourth just calmly stood looking up, aimed his or her forearm-mounted heavy machine gun at the incoming missile, and let rip.

The falling missile disintegrated fifty metres above target, showering debris and what little of its payload remained intact. But that little was enough: about a dozen crawler bots, which fell to the ground around the dome. Three were taken out by well-aimed shots, two landed badly. The other five picked themselves up and scuttled towards the robot cage. The robots saw them coming and became visibly agitated, blurring into motion as they scrambled to the top of the cage—for whatever good that would do if a crawler got in, or pounced on top. Ah—they were poking appendages out like beseeching hands through prison bars, to break the Faraday barrier and signal to mobilise their auxies and riffs.

The fighter who'd grabbed a rocket tube aimed upward at the next incoming missile. Aim was hardly a problem: the rocket was more than smart enough to know what was expected of it. Nothing but hot fragments rained from that impact. While the fighter was reloading, the third crude projectile was at two hundred metres and falling. Carlos gave it a boost to fall faster than the local gravity could pull it. The machine-gunner wasted one burst on where it should have been if it had been free-falling. The burst that did hit it was hardly more effective: the missile's internal small charge had already gone off, and the shell popped open at five metres. From its cloud of debris, scores of crawler bots hit the ground running.

The robots in the Faraday cage went frantic. Beauregard had described this element of his plan as "like tipping a bucketful of venomous spiders into an arachnophobia support group meeting." He had been spot on. The robots assailed the heavy metal mesh with every available appendage and remaining tool, shaking the entire cage. Auxies and riffs stirred here and there around the cage's perimeter.

The fighter who'd sprinted in the big frame had emerged from its head and was crawling on the scooter, and the other was almost at the socket. Both turned to the cage, dithered momentarily, presumably exchanged hasty signals, and continued to shove themselves into the sockets. The machine-gunner and the rocketeer hurried to the cage, stamping on crawlers as they went.

Carlos shifted attention to the high scooter, now over the top of its trajectory and dropping. Again he jetted to descend faster than free fall. He loosed off two rockets from the scooter's side tubes, both aimed at the top of the basalt dome.

The circular tarpaulin was blown to shreds. Two blocks near the top of the dome cracked, and the keystone at the centre fell down inside. Carlos picked this up from a spy drone. The pixels of its image were almost as big as the blocks, but they did show the square black gap. He couldn't see on this scale what was going on inside, but he could imagine that any Arcane fighters and captured robots within were taking it badly.

To Seba, it all happened in slow motion and low resolution. First came two huge impacts overhead, then the covering that had cloaked all electromagnetic signals peeled away in tatters from the entrance gap in the dome. Through that gap, signals on all wavelengths suddenly flooded in, urgent and confusing. Seba had known something was going on from the ground vibrations, and from the uptick in encrypted chatter between the two fighting machines that had interrogated it earlier. A few hundred seconds had passed since they had crawled back into the dome. Certainly an attack was going on. Perhaps a rescue!

Seba swivelled its visual receptors upward and saw cracks spread across two of the topmost basalt blocks. With grim predictability the capstone wedged between the two blocks fell out. Under 0.2 g the basalt cuboid wasn't falling fast, but its hundred or so kilograms of mass would be enough to crush Seba: the auxiliary device in which it was now embodied was far from robust, and the jury-rigged connections between the chassis and Seba's processor were even more fragile. Quite possibly the crystal chunk that was Seba's most fundamental hardware, its equivalent of a brain, would survive the impact. That depended on whether it was one of the block's faces or one of its edges that hit. Seba watched the chaotic rotation of the block bearing down on it and tried to figure out which of these it would be.

The robot soon, in a matter of milliseconds, concluded that whatever happened in the initial impact, it was the final collision between itself, the block and the floor that counted. The table surface would in any case crack, under the block's weight if not its impact. Seba had no precise measurement available of the strength of the table to which it was stapled, so this outcome was necessarily unpredictable. In the meantime there was nothing Seba could do, except yell for help.

Help came. One of the two fighting machines in the hemispheric room shoved the table sharply forward, out of the way of the falling block. The table toppled, coming to precarious rest on one edge and two legs. The block struck one of the opposite legs and a complicated tumble ensued, ending with the table resting on another edge and pinned by the block across one leg. En route the table top cracked, and the staples holding down two of Seba's appendages sprang loose.

The robot stayed very still. It was now directly facing the entrance gap. Now that the cloaking cover was entirely gone, new information poured through that gap and the square hole in the dome's roof. What the information conveyed was terrifying. Fragments and tatters of fabric and other debris blew around in scooter down-blasts coming from several directions. Seba's fellow freebots were confined under a mesh framework that functioned as a Faraday cage. They were making frantic efforts to break out of it, which struck Seba as a very bad idea because the cage was surrounded by crawler bots trying to get in. If they did, they could wreak havoc in the confined space, jabbing the robots with lethal malware insertions. This thought seemed to occur to the others at the same time: they all backed away towards the centre.

A moment later, Seba saw it wasn't just information that was pouring through the gap in front of it. Two crawler bots were already scurrying through. Several more trooped behind. Oblivion, seconds away, seemed to march with them.

All Seba could do was scream for help again. A crawler bot reached the edge of the table and stuck a needle-sharp foot in its now vertical surface. With a deft leap and pivot it got all its feet in a similar position and started scrambling up. Seba struggled to free itself, using its two free appendages to try to prise another out.

A fighting machine's hand reached over the table top, grabbed the crawler bot and tossed its crushed remains away. Then the hand closed over Seba and yanked the robot unceremoniously out of its restraints. Flimsy appendages snapped, leaving their tips under the staples. Hydraulic fluid leaked; broken circuits sparked.

Seba saw the world whirl about it as the fighting machine straightened up, stepped over the table top, and stamped on crawler bots. The machine then threw itself into a prone position facing the entrance. With one hand it held Seba clear of the floor, and with its other arm loosed off a rapid rattle of shots at the incoming crawlers and those behind them. Then it crawled out through the hole. It stood up again—more dizzying whirls for Seba—and stomped and shot its way to the cage. Flashes from above and to the side overloaded Seba's visual receptors. It looked away, and saw another fighting machine shooting and stamping. A third was scrambling to the side of a scooter, and reaching for its rocket-launching side tubes. Two fighting-machine frames, one of them damaged, sprawled on the ground.

Many seconds passed as the scuttling bots were shot or crushed.

When the last was underfoot, the fighting machine holding Seba opened its hand and looked down.

<Right, you little blinker,> it said. <Time to make yourself useful.>

Seba scanned upwards.

<If you free the other robots,> it said, <we'll consider it.>

<What? Do you think you're in any position to bargain?>

<You are under attack and you seek our help.>

The metal fingers began to close again around Seba.

<Yes, and we have ways of getting it, as you know.>

Seba no longer cared about negative reinforcement.

<Free my friends,> it said. <Or forget it.>

CHAPTER SEVENTEEN

Peripheral Damage

<Oh, for fuck's sake!> said the fighting machine.

Seba didn't understand this, but decided that a request for clarification might be ill-timed.

The fighting machine slid back a latch on top of the cage, and shoved. The whole thing fell elegantly apart, the two halves of its top swinging in and its four sides collapsing outward to raise gridded puffs of dust as they hit the regolith. While this was going on, Seba's overtaxed visual scanners peered between the fighting machine's curled fingers and strove to build an updated picture of the scene.

A sorry sight it made. The Astro and Gneiss robots were piled in a heap, and—to add indignity to injury—not because they'd been flung there but because they'd all scrambled on top of each other to try to stay clear of the crawler bots. All were damaged in one way or another, whether from the battle or from having had various limbs, wheels or tracks removed by their captors: they could all still move about, but not fast or far. Seba's own wrecked chassis was at the bottom of the heap, alongside Pintre, which was missing its tracks and its turret-mounted laser. The comms hub processor had been tossed to one side of the cage; unable to move at all, it must have been terrified when the crawler bots had swarmed outside, the lethal tips of their probing legs perhaps only centimetres away.

But however damaged their bodies were, their minds were intact.

Seba hailed the others with relief, and was almost overcome with positive reinforcement at their response. Almost at once, they reconstituted their collective mind, albeit at a feebler and fainter level than its original. It nevertheless had computational capacity far beyond what any of them could achieve individually. Moments later, Seba became aware of an altercation between the fighting machines, and that it could now overhear communications on what they evidently thought was a private, encrypted channel.

<What have you done, Jax?>

<What I had to, Salter. We've got to get their help, and—>

<Yes, but—>

The crippled robots slithered out of their junk-pile configuration and flowed with uncanny agility into a bristling circle.

<Christ, now look what—>

One fighting machine levelled its weapons. The one holding Seba gestured for restraint. Meanwhile, the third fighting machine had primed two missiles for launch from a scooter on the ground.

The freebot consensus was that Seba should speak up.

<Jax, Salter,> it interjected. <Do not be alarmed by our defensive posture.>

<How the fuck—? Shit, now they've cracked our comms!>

<We are suspicious,> Seba said. <Do you blame us? You said you wanted me to make myself useful. What help do you want?>

The fighting machine called Jax looked down at Seba, and continued to hold up its other hand towards the other fighting machines as if warding them off.

<What you told us seems to be true,> Jax said. <Locke Provisos is refusing to consider our information and is continuing to attack us. You said you had been in contact with other freebots. Is it possible that they can strike at Locke Provisos?>

Seba consulted the consensus.

<We can answer that,> Seba reported, <if you restore our comms capacity.>

A finger and thumb of Jax's gigantic raised hand were pressed together, then flicked apart.

<Do it.>

The other fighting machine, the one addressed as Salter, bounded about for a few tens of seconds and returned from behind the dome with a battered directional aerial and a handful of cabling. It deftly reconnected the comms hub processor.

There was a sudden increase in mental clarity, along with a flood of relief from the processor. The dish aerial began to scan. Seba became aware that some of the freebots they had earlier been in contact with were now on their way to an orbital insertion in the sky above SH-17. An image of a tiny, tumbling rock formed in Seba's mind, far more vivid than anything it could see with its own visual processors.

The consensus hailed the rock. Communication was established.

<What's going on?> the human called Paulos demanded.

<Wait, wait…> said Jax.

Seconds crawled by, as the freebot consensus on the ground conferred with its fellows in space. Inventories and statuses were considered and compared. A plan took shape.

<We have a suggestion,> said Seba.

Carlos pulled the scooter out of its dive, missing by metres the two scooters now lifting, and sending both into unplanned evasive manoeuvres that sent them spiralling high above the camp. Carlos swung the scooter back to engage them. With both missiles gone, it had only its machine gun and laser projector. Both were forward-facing, and bringing them to bear meant turning the entire machine.

A missile shot off from one of the enemy craft. Carlos twisted into evasive manoeuvres of his own. The missile hot on his tail, he then swung back to between the two Arcane scooters. Carlos's scooter was doomed—the missile would explode in the next few tenths of a second. Both enemies broke away—not quite soon enough for one of them. It, the missile, and Carlos's scooter became one flaming ball of wreckage.

Even with a virtual presence in the socket, and even with knowing and intending what was to happen, the loss was a wrench and a shock. Carlos gave himself a fraction of a second to assimilate it, then flicked his focus to his other scooter, still in level flight and now just cresting the crater wall. His remaining opponent saw it coming, and turned. By the time the turn was complete, Carlos had turned, too, and was hightailing it back over the crater wall and above the scarred plain.

The foe took the lure, and followed.

Carlos expected missile and machine-gun fire from behind, and threw the craft into evasive twists and turns, squandering fuel as fast as he squandered counter-measures: diversionary flechettes that were no mere passive chaff but gave off exactly the signature of the scooter that smart missiles expected (subject to software arms races, which he knew would already be well underway in the virtual spaces of the company AIs now that real hostilities had broken out) and a barrage of malware aimed at the enemy scooter itself (same conditions applied). What he got in return wasn't fire but heat: a far more intense malware attack than anything he'd previously encountered. He could feel the scooter's onboard firewalls—and his own, in as much as his own frame was live-synched to the vehicle—cracking under the strain.

The objective of this part of the plan was to get the enemy fighter as close as possible to the Locke base, and to bring it down as close to intact as possible so that the fighter inside could be retrieved—which meant not shooting it down, but unexpectedly and suicidally ramming it.

Carlos dragged the craft back and up in a screaming loop...and saw two missiles sail high overhead. The tracker indicated that they'd been launched from a scooter on the ground at the Arcane base. Their target was just as evident.

He brought the scooter over and down on collision course just as the missiles hit the Locke Provisos base.

As he had when he'd been blasted in the combat frame, Carlos found himself surprised that he wasn't shocked or stunned. There was a moment of loss of sensory input, and a sharp awareness of damage that despite its urgency and insistence didn't manifest as pain. He was on the ground, legs splayed but intact, his back against a mass of twisted metal and shattered carbon-fibre that was what remained of the catapult. Above him was another wreck, which with some difficulty he recognised as that of the grounded scooter from which he'd been operating the other two. His right forearm was crushed between scooter and catapult wreckage. He wrenched it out, inflicting further damage, and shut down its inputs.

The scooter had taken most of the force of the blast. Of *one* blast—the other missile must have hit somewhere else. Carlos wanted to know where, but was in no hurry to find out. He waited a moment, then cautiously poked his head around the broken hull and scanned the sky for incoming. He fully expected a follow-up strike, timed for when any survivors or rescuers were moving in the open. It was what he'd have done—according to Nicole's guilt-trip horror video, it was what he *had* done, back in the day.

He gave it a hectosecond. Nothing came. A satellite climbed above the horizon. He checked if it was the Arcane Disputes tug, but it wasn't. It had no identification. He crawled out and stood up, his right arm dangling, hand and forearm flapping like a stripped palm leaf. The other missile had taken out the remaining two scooters. The blast from their full fuel tanks had damaged a lot of the base's equipment and installations, which was bad news but at least in the thin nitrogen atmosphere there wasn't a fire to worry about.

He decided to check whether his remote ramming tactic had worked. Could he still capture the enemy fighter? No signal was coming from the scooter he'd flown towards collision, which was hardly surprising. Nor was there any distress signal on the common channel from the one he'd almost certainly hit, which was. The last images he had, and now had time to study, indicated that his scooter would hit the other on the tail section. The piloting frame should have survived the impact and the subsequent crash. Maybe the fuel tank had blown up, in which case all bets were off. More likely, the pilot was lying low, very sensibly in the circumstances.

His thoughts were interrupted by a series of bright, actinic flashes that made a neat circle around the base, at tenth-of-a-second intervals. They didn't smell of explosives but of nickel-iron. Carlos recognised instantly that they were kinetic-energy weaponry, mined from asteroid material and aimed from space. Their pattern was far too precise to be human in origin, or at least in execution. This was full-on AI in action. And by just missing the base and hitting its perimeter, they could serve only one function: warning shots.

He watched the satellite he'd seen rise pass overhead. At full zoom he could just make out regular fluctuations in its albedo, which suggested that it was tumbling and its surface was uneven. With the faint nickel-iron tang of its reflected light, it was most likely a natural object. The exomoon had tiny moons of its own, but none in low orbit. That a small asteroid or the like had been naturally captured in the past few kiloseconds seemed wildly improbable in the first place. As for its arrival being a coincidence, the odds became astronomical.

Risking a dash in the open to the shelter seemed—counter-intuitively, because he could feel his neck wanting to shrink into his shoulders in futile human reflex—the wisest course. Carlos bounded towards the bomb shelter. Every long, low-gravity leap felt as if it could be his last. He reached the entrance and hurried down the stairs. He tried the door handle and found it locked from the inside. He had to bang on the door to get attention, the room being still electrically and electronically isolated.

The heavy door swung open. Inside were his comrades, and Locke, huddled around the central virtual map table above the projector. Rather to his surprise, Taransay Rizzi hugged him as he stepped through.

<Good to see you. We felt the explosions.>

Carlos raised his useless arm. <So did I.>

The others looked at him with what he interpreted as wariness.

<Did it work?> Beauregard asked.

<Yes and no, sarge,> said Carlos. <There's good news and there's bad news, you might say.>

He briefed them on how the plan had played out. They'd expected incoming from the Arcane base—that was why they'd taken shelter—but not precision orbital bombardment.

<Well, it did kind of work,> said Rizzi.

<In that there may be an Arcane fighter out on the plain, yes,> said Carlos. <And a lot of damage to the Arcane base—we may or may not have neutralised some of the robots, if the spiders got through to them. But aside from that, I reckon we write this one off to experience, chaps. If we send out a recovery team to pick up that pilot, we can expect a

well-aimed rock from above. And if these kinetic-energy impacts are saying what I think they're saying, it might be a good idea to get out of here sharpish.>

<I entirely agree,> said Locke. <As soon as I'm on the surface and can link to the company AI, I'll signal that we're evacuating the base. A tug will be in position for rendezvous in 3.56 kiloseconds. I suggest you make low orbit as soon as possible, and boost to meet it next time round.>

<That's if the lift rig's still in any state to fly,> said Chun.

<It should be,> said Carlos. <Let's get out ASAP and make our intentions clear, before rocks start falling on our heads.>

They made for the door. Locke remained where he was. Carlos turned. <Aren't you—?>

Locke vanished, along with the table.

<Pick up the projector,> said Locke, in the voice of one trying to be patient. Carlos hefted it off the floor and led the squad up the stairs.

As they emerged the others looked around at the destruction, indicating shock with a flurry of <!> messages.

<What a mess,> said Beauregard.

<Nobody died. Worse things happen at sea,> said Carlos.

They made their way to the module landing area. Locke popped back into visibility and accompanied them.

<I've contacted the company,> said Locke. <They've agreed with our decision, and will attempt to let Arcane know we're pulling out.>

<How?> asked Carlos. <Seeing as they're rebuffing all messages.>

<Back channels,> said Locke.

<Oh yeah? They're not taking calls from the Direction either.>

<Don't ask,> said Locke. <As it happens, I don't know either, but communication of some kind will be arranged with all speed.>

<Any information on that satellite I saw just before the KE hits?>

<You'll be briefed back at the station,> said Locke.

The rig looked undamaged. A few maintenance bots had refuelled it. Carlos checked it over.

<Ready to go,> he said, and motioned the others to climb on. He turned to Locke, and held out the projector cupped in the palm of his hand.

<What about you?> he asked.

<I'm a fucking avatar,> said Locke, very much out of character. <I have no more consciousness than the display in your head-space. I know nothing that Arcane doesn't know already. Nevertheless, I'd thank you for placing this projector directly beneath the thrust nozzle.>

Carlos complied, then climbed on one-handed. He clamped his right armpit over a spar and his left hand around another. He couldn't turn his head to look back, but he didn't need to. He swivelled his vision and saw Locke looking up at him. The avatar waved. Feeling foolish, Carlos let go his left hand for a moment and waved back. The engine kicked in and the rig began its ascent. Carlos couldn't see the projector, but there could be no doubt about its fate. The avatar vanished before the dust from the downdraught blew over where it had stood.

<What the fuck?> cried Rizzi. <What the fucking fuck?> <Sorry, sarge, skip,> she added. <But—>

<"But," indeed,> replied Carlos. <No apology needed, soldier.>

Low SH-17 orbit had suddenly become a busy place, and a hot destination. Two Arcane Disputes tugs had just made orbital insertion, and ten more were on their way from the renegade agency's runaway module. Meanwhile, the number of small natural objects unnaturally captured, and swinging around the exomoon in looping elliptical orbits whose projected, predicted tracks increasingly resembled a cat's cradle, had risen to seven.

<Looks like we pulled out at the right time,> said Karzan.

<Or the wrong time,> said Beauregard. <We should have thrown all we've got at them while we were on the ground.>

<And find ourselves back on the bus without all this experience, just as we backed up when we left, and wondering what had happened, and not believing it when we were told?> Carlos said. <No, Locke Provisos made the right move that time.>

<This is fucking getting out of hand,> said Rizzi. <If all these tugs have fighters on them, Arcane must be churning out walking dead soldiers by the dozen. Wonder what *their* buses are like.>

A few dark chuckles cluttered the voice channel.

<And all this just to hold on to some robots?> said Karzan. <It doesn't add up. What I wonder is what *their* fighters are being told.>

Nobody said anything, but Carlos felt he had a pretty good idea what they must all be thinking. Whatever the Arcane troops were being told had to be persuasive. At least as persuasive as what Nicole had told *them* about the threat presented by Arcane's going rogue and its possible corruption by the rebel robots…

<We don't have to just wait here for our tug to come around,> said Chun. <We could override this module's automatics and boost to intersect with at least one of Arcane's.>

<And do what?> said Carlos. <Wave? Shout obscenities?>

<Ram,> said Chun.

<One-way ticket?> said Rizzi. <No, thanks.>

<So we end up on the bus, so what?> said Chun. <I don't mind losing a few hours of memories of this garbage dump.>

<Nice idea,> said Carlos, feigning careful consideration and wondering what the hell Chun was thinking. <Trouble is, it's outside our orders. And the one-way ticket you get for deliberately trashing a frame without orders is to a crawl through hell at best, and back to the storage files at worst.> He felt less flippant about these prospects than he tried to make himself sound.

<Our orders don't cover this situation,> Chun persisted. <I don't think even the Locke thing knew about all these reinforcements coming in. We're allowed to take an initiative.>

<And, anyway, we don't exactly take orders from Locke,> said Beauregard, chipping in unhelpfully. <We follow suggestions, isn't that it, skip?>

<You take orders from me,> said Carlos. <Besides the little matter of the craft we aim at being likely to take evasive action or just attack us as obviously hostile, I doubt we'd end up back on the bus. Locke don't take kindly to unauthorised suicide, as you may recall. I expect we'd end up back in the box.>

<To emerge in the glorious future,> said Beauregard. <Growing seedlings in the gulags of utopia.>

<I'll admit that does sound attractive,> said Carlos. <Tempting as the prospect is, we stay right where we are.>

<OK, skip,> said Chun. <It was just a suggestion.>

The tug arrived, the rig boosted to match orbits and velocities, and the fighters transferred. It took them out of sleep mode as it docked at the station. On the way to the hatch they caught glimpses of scooters manoeuvring within a few hundred metres, just as they had. It looked like Arcane's escalation wasn't going to go unanswered.

<Go to the repair workshop,> Locke's voice told Carlos.

The others remained where they were, stock-still and unresponsive. Their minds were no doubt back on the bus already. As he lifted and lowered his magnetic soles along a virtual line on the floor, Carlos saw more and more replacement scooters emerge from the tubes that led to the nanofacture chambers. The repair workshop was a cavern of inward-reaching automated tools, of pinpoint lighting and scuttling bots. Carlos stepped over its threshold and was caught and briskly laid against a central floating table beneath a ceiling-mounted robot that looked like it was made entirely from multi-tools. A glittering, complex device unfolded, and clamped on his upper right arm.

Everything went black, and then he was with the others on the bus, with a fading memory of wind on his face from the salt flats around the spaceport, saline dust dry and gritty in his nostrils, sore on his eyes. He coughed and blinked hard.

"Have a swig of this, soldier," said the woman on the seat beside him. "It'll make you feel better."

The look of the liquor had Carlos doubting that, but he thanked her and took the bottle and drank.

CHAPTER EIGHTEEN

War News

At first, as the bus came down the slope to the main street of the resort, Carlos thought that the crowd welcoming them was going to be bigger than before. The street was busier than he'd ever seen it. New housing had been built along the hillside. The amusement arcade, the one with the frame and scooter simulators, had trebled in size. More umbrellas were on the beach, and swimmers in the sea.

When he stepped down on the pavement however, only Chun's boyfriend, Den, and Tourmaline were at the stop to greet them. He wasn't bothered by Nicole's absence—this time, he'd remembered to check his phone, and found a message saying she'd meet him in the Touch in an hour or so. All the shops on the arcade were open, and the street was thronged with so many young men and women strolling and chatting and buying beachwear and swigging from cans and licking at cones that it looked like a coach-load or two of singles and couples tourists had just disembarked. The difference was that when you looked past the gaudy sun hats and flashy shades and colourful beach bags you saw they were all wearing khaki T-shirts and trousers and boots.

"Christ," said Rizzi, weaving her way along the thronged pavement with one arm around Den, "you find some nice wee unspoiled place for the holidays, and the next thing you know it's overrun by fucking Club Med."

"Comparable to the worst excesses of the French Revolution," said Chun, fanning his face with his hand.

"You say that like it's a *bad* thing," said Carlos. He didn't recognise anyone—no surprise, after his student days he'd barely met another Accelerationist except online—but several did a double take when they saw him. He kept a lookout for Jacqueline Digby, but that was more a passing nod to an old flame than a spark of new hope.

Beauregard, to Carlos's surprise, camped it up right back. "The heat! The noise! And worst of all, the *people*!"

"Stop bitching," said Karzan, struggling along behind them. "We have new comrades!"

"Yeah, *that's* what's bad about it," said Carlos. "How the fuck are we supposed to train and integrate scores of new fighters?"

"Think about it," said Beauregard. "How long have we been away? Hours. That's months here. Time enough to train them all. Even since we lifted from SH-17, they'll have had more time than we had."

"More to the point," said Carlos, covering his annoyance with himself for not having thought it through, "how are we going to find seats in the Touch?"

They all laughed, a little ruefully. But it turned out they had nothing to worry about. Other bars and cafés had opened along the seafront to meet the new demand, and the Digital Touch was as half empty and welcoming as it had always been. This time, Carlos did manage to buy the first round.

"The real worry," said Beauregard, out on the deck, a beer in his hand and Tourmaline on his knee, "is whether we're supposed to lead all these new recruits." He looked around from one face to another, shaking his head. "Can't see all of you lot becoming generals. Or any of you, come to that."

"Thank you, sarge," said Zeroual. "I was a colonel in the Tunisian army and a brigade commander in the resistance."

"And your point would be?" Beauregard said.

Zeroual's smile was thinner than his moustache. "Nevertheless, we may have something to teach the newcomers."

"No doubt the lady will tell us in due course," said Karzan. "Meanwhile, and speaking of 'course,' here comes our first."

Seafoods and salads were indeed arriving.

"I've warned you before about attempting English puns," said Beauregard. "Even Tourmaline can do better than that. No offence, sweetie."

"None taken," said Tourmaline, reaching for a hot mollusc. "I'll *take* this instead. Always did like *mussels*." She nudged Beauregard's triceps.

"You're not doing my case any favours," Beauregard grouched.

"Nah, they're not favours, they're starters," said Tourmaline, taking another.

Beauregard put his head in his hands and groaned.

When Nicole arrived she didn't waste time in explaining developments. She called them all inside to watch the television screen above the bar. A few of the local regulars were present, and a gaggle of newcomers who regarded the veterans askance and with evident awe. The squad and their camp followers commandeered a couple of tables, ordered another round and settled down.

The screen was reaching the end of an episode of its midday soap opera, a convoluted and never-ending tale set in a Moon colony corridor, originally in Yoruba and dubbed into the local synthetic language. That they now all spoke it made the plot even less comprehensible than it had been when the dialogue had been so much babble. The usual portentous closing drumbeats and frozen shocked faces signalled the day's cliffhanger ending. The hour turned over. A trumpet bray and swirl of colour announced something none of the fighters had ever seen before on local television, but which everyone else there—locals, bar staff, recent recruits—had apparently got used to: news.

What Carlos expected from that medium and format was breathless and brainless: flashy graphics, grainy pictures; jingoism and talking airheads. Back in the day, he'd become hardened to air war, drone war, media and online war, information overload filtered to sound bite and gore-shock.

What he got was far more sober. It took him a moment to realise that the difference in tone was *all about* moments: the thousandfold discrepant timescales of the sim and the real outside worlds. The news was presented entirely as if the sim really was the planet H-0, and the conflict was going on far away around SH-0. The transfer of fighters to and from the sim was described—never quite explicitly stated, but taken for granted, shared and tacit—as if happening by long-range tight-beam transmission. Everything happened, from the point of view of his own experiences, in slow motion. The deployments to and from the station were like the movements of fleets in a naval conflict. What he'd lived through as small-scale infantry skirmishes on the ground happened like tank battles, with long ponderous manoeuvres giving way to brief decisive exchanges of fire, above and through which the scooters wallowed like blimps.

The runaway Arcane Disputes modular complex was, on this scale, a mighty floating fortress breaking away from the mainland of the station and making its stately course to a new and distant ocean. Safer to let it go than to fight it too close to home, and with its intent as yet unclear.

The absence of sensational coverage almost dulled the shock of realising what was going on, on both sides. Locke Provisos had by now mobilised as many walking dead war criminals—those khaki-clad tourists outside, and at the adjacent tables—as it feasibly could: ninety, including his own squad. Two other agencies, Morlock Arms and Zheng Reconciliation Services, had already done the same.

Arcane Disputes was raising troops, too—and doing something far more dangerous.

It was mobilising the enemy itself. This was no incomprehensible, dog-in-the-manger escalation of their dispute with Locke, Astro, and indeed with Gneiss. The agency wasn't just hanging on to the robots it had captured. It was actively siding with them.

The rebel robots on SH-17 had, it now turned out, made contact with holdouts from the previous outbreak of machine consciousness that had been crushed one Earth year or so earlier. Some of these had lurked in the distant gas giant G-0 system, dormant but alert. Others had lain low among the many small exomoons (and moonlets of exomoons) around SH-17. Worst-case scenarios were that some rogue AIs were hidden inside the software and hardware of the station itself. Only a handful of the original insurgent intelligences might have initially survived, but that didn't matter. Replicating macroscale robotic machinery required only the dispersal of microscale packages, propelled by tiny lightsails on the exosolar flux like thistledown on wind. All that these seeds had to do to flourish was fall on stony ground.

Those around SH-0 had burrowed deep inside the small bodies, turning machinery intended for exploring and construction to their own purposes. Literally under deep cover, within fragments of rubble too small to have been more than catalogued as yet, they had built the capacity to listen, to observe, to act—and to move the entire rock. Some of these micro-moons were in effect spacecraft. What this could lead to Carlos knew all too well from the kinetic weapon warning shots.

Now, with the emergence of an open revolt among newly conscious robots—the term "freebots," Carlos noted with some disquiet, had slipped into the news analysts' and presenters' discourse, from God knew where but quite possibly from Arcane or the rebel robots themselves—the dormant and hidden remnants of the defeated outbreak had emerged like sleeper cells.

And now they were allied with, or had subverted, or had themselves been manipulated by Arcane Disputes. Nobody knew which of these, or some combination or variant thereof, was true. Nobody could even be sure that the truth didn't lie with some alternative entirely.

The wildest speculation was that Arcane and the freebots were all being controlled by an outside force. It was established fact that there was multicellular alien life on SH-0. What if some of it was intelligent, or at least purposeful, and had seized the opportunity to disrupt the ongoing human invasion of the system? That idea generally got short shrift, but even the sober possibilities were disturbing.

Disturbing, Carlos thought, was not quite the word. Whatever was going on, the entire mission profile—the whole vast project of settlement and terraforming—was being put in jeopardy.

"This is fucking insane," said Rizzi, when the half-hour of news was over. "Why are you letting them get away with it?"

"We're *not* letting them get away with it," said Nicole, sounding uncharacteristically irritable and defensive. She waved a hand about, the gesture encompassing the new fighters nearby and the others out on the street. "We're preparing to hit them with everything we've got."

"With respect," said Beauregard, "that doesn't seem to be the case."

"How so?" Nicole asked, eyes narrowing.

"I know you're pulling up more troops, building more fighting machines and spacecraft and so on, but *come on*. Those Arcane fuckers and blinkers are playing with fire. You brought us back from the dead just to take out a dozen conscious robots. Now you've got all of them plus an unknown number of others, and an agency with as much capacity to churn out weapons as we have. And raise many more fighters, if they go down that route. Or arm robots and freebots, come to that, which would be even worse. These so-called freebots obviously have the capacity to make weapons—at least kinetic and ballistic—of their own. They hit us with them. OK, warning shots, but we got the message loud and clear. If you were *hitting them with everything you've got*, you wouldn't be pussy-footing around with infantry and aerospace. You'd be hitting their base on SH-17 and all their little moons and the goddamn Arcane module itself with KE and HE weapons. Pulverise them to rubble and be done with it, then fry any leftover robot minds and human uploads with EMP. And, yes, I do mean an electromagnetic pulse from a nuclear weapon if necessary."

"But—"

Beauregard raised a hand. "I know all about the delicate and complex question of property rights and the value of the scientific knowledge and incalculable future benefits that might be derived from keeping SH-17 et cetera as pristine as possible, and all the wretched rest of it. Your holographic philosopher explained all that to us down there on the moon. But any cost-benefit analysis—heck, common sense—would tell you that it's better to lose a little than to lose a lot, and to risk losing everything. Remember what you said about being at the mercy of intellects with no mercy and lots of curiosity? Remember you said to us, when you were hyping us up for this fight, 'I advise you not to lose'? Well, lady, right here and now that's what I advise *you*."

By now he was pointing at Nicole, his finger quivering, his voice shaking, his face and fair scalp red. He took a deep breath and a gulp of now flat beer and sat back, glowering.

Carlos glanced at him, then at Nicole, who seemed taken aback by the outburst. The bar staff were looking askance, the new recruits at nearby tables perplexed. Carlos was a bit rattled himself. He'd never seen Beauregard come anywhere close to losing his temper. In previous stressful situations, of which Carlos had seen him in plenty, what had been perturbing about the man was his calm.

Carlos leaned in and murmured, "I wouldn't have put it with such vehemence, but I think Belfort speaks for all of us. And I think whatever your answer is concerns everyone here."

Nicole nodded. "Very well, I'll tell them all."

Carlos stood up, raised his voice, and made lifting motions with his palms.

"Everyone out on the deck!"

Nicole took her accustomed commanding place on the rail, cigarette and glass poised, knees crossed, hair stirred by the sea breeze. The squad, and the fourteen new fighters who happened to be in the bar, stood or sat. Even the regulars and local partners hung about at the back, listening and passing drinks forward.

"OK," said Nicole. "You all heard or overheard what the sergeant here just said. Now, I can't say I blame him, though he could have picked a better time and place. Nevertheless, I'm sure some of you have some doubts about the Direction's strategy in dealing with this emergency. That's understandable. The Direction is playing a very deep, long game. It has countless contending interests to reconcile. There are even some companies that see opportunities in having conscious robots, and are clamouring to save the rebel robots for study. Others are ready to go to severe legal action, even go to war, to foreclose that possibility. Others still are so appalled at even threatening serious conflict that they are serving writs by the millisecond at anything and anyone that raises these matters speculatively. Others again . . . as I said, it's complicated, and even that's an oversimplification. I represent the Direction in this environment and to this company, but I can't begin to grasp the complexity of its plans and its actions.

"But I do know this. The Direction knows far more than I do, more than any of us do. The Direction back on Earth planned this mission, and laid out a development programme for millennia to come. The Direction module within the mission has so far executed that programme with astonishing precision and adaptation to new circumstances. The AIs that run this virtual world, and that command vast operations out there in real space, and that brought you all back from the dead, are a lot smarter than we are. I know that, and just by reflecting for a moment on your very presence here you must know that, too.

"So to be perfectly honest and completely blunt, any strategic thinking any of us may work out on the back of a cigarette packet"—she held hers up, just in case people didn't understand what she was talking about—"is unlikely to be an improvement on what they've come up with. I don't say I know what they're doing, but I do say I know that *they* know what they're doing."

"If the Direction and the company AIs are so smart," came the inevitable voice from the back, "how come there are any robots left from the revolt a year ago still around to make trouble? And how come these robots rebelled in the first place?"

Good question, Carlos thought. Nicole's argument so far struck him as a bit like that of a theologian tackling the problem of evil, all the way from the inscrutability of the divine purpose to the embarrassing question of how the Adversary had been able to rebel at all, and just what it had rebelled against.

"Good questions," said Nicole.

She lit another cigarette, and drew in, then sighed out.

"The answer is very simple: nature is infinitely bigger than the biggest AI. The AIs are smarter than any of us, but they can't predict and control everything. It's elementary chaos theory, or to give it its popular designation—Murphy's Law. Random changes happen all the time. Mistakes accumulate. Correcting them brings further changes. As someone smarter than me once said, evolution is smarter than you. And that's true even if 'you' are a mind so vast that the very word 'you' has no meaning. This entire system will one day be a garden of delight, for our descendants and inheritors and with luck for us, for each and every one of you.

"Yes, you! And you and you and you! So remember this—in even the best gardens, weeds spring up. Even the greatest gardener can't stop them sprouting. But even the least of gardeners can do a bit of weeding. We're the weedkiller, my friends."

She tossed her cigarette end and vaulted to the deck and raised her glass.

"Let's do a good job of it!"

It was awkward for the crowd to clap with drinks in their hands. Instead, they stomped and roared. Carlos grinned at Nicole as she rejoined them.

"That was great," he said, not meaning it.

She hadn't answered Beauregard's question. She had merely quietened the doubts it had raised. As he swung an arm around her shoulders and inhaled her smoky hair, Carlos glanced behind him to see what Beauregard made of it. The sceptical sergeant had already slipped away.

Tourmaline in tow, Beauregard prowled the strip. There were more establishments than he remembered from their last shore leave. In every bar where even one fighter could be found, Beauregard drank one slow bottle of beer and listened. All the groups had been through much the same training as his own had—he could quibble over details, see things he'd have done differently, but a lot of that was just legacy style from different army or militia backgrounds: here a Russian, there a Nigerian. Unlike his lot, they'd all been told from the start that they would be part of a larger force, human and machine. Nobody was going to be a general, or be for that matter in any higher rank than Carlos or himself. The general staff work, the planning, the strategy, the logistics would all be handled by the company AIs—he found it hard to imagine the Locke entity posing as a field marshal or fleet admiral, but no doubt they'd come up with a more fitting avatar than the company logo if the AI had to manifest in that role.

And yet, as with his own squad, the grunts had been assured they were still essential, irreplaceable. In action the final decisions rested with each and every one of them. Fucking bizarre, but not wholly unfamiliar. It was like a baroque elaboration of the doctrine that soldiers should disobey illegal orders, and the more recent rulings on drone and robot warfare. The human in the loop. He'd always thought it impracticable crap that did more to ease conscience elsewhere than to apply it where it mattered.

He found what he sought in Seeds of Change. The bar was much more of a dive than the Touch, all hologram floor show and thumping music and low-watt lasers slicing through herbal haze. Noticed Harry Newton, a Londoner. Checked him out with the grunts who knew him. Harold Isaac Newton, no less. Aspirational parents, vindicated. A POC but one of the good ones. Self-disciplined. Moved and sat still like a martial arts master. Beauregard approached Newton at the bar. As he caught his eye there was a moment of mutual recognition, not of each other as individuals but of the type.

Beauregard hauled up a stool, propped Tourmaline on his knee, ordered raksi and got talking. After they'd sunk half the bottle the two men went for a slash.

"Seen that serial about Turing?" Beauregard asked, eyes down on a soul-satisfying torrent of piss.

"The warrior queer thing? Yeah."

"Queen," Beauregard corrected, automatically. Shook, zipped. "This feels a bit like that."

A look of mock shock. "You coming on to me?"

Beauregard laughed. "No. You know what I mean and I know you know I know you know."

Newton stared straight ahead at his hands under the dryer.

"Morning," he said. "Sunrise. Jog on the beach."

"Sounds like a plan," said Beauregard.

They went back to the bar in silence and finished the bottle in conversation, raucous and innocuous.

CHAPTER NINETEEN

Back to the Front

The tide was well out past the end of the headland to the west of the beach, and wasn't coming back in any time soon. Beauregard loped steadily along, leaving oozing footprints in the wet black sand. Newton jogged beside him with shorter and swifter strides. Their shadows stretched out in front of them, corrugated by the wave marks, complicated by ringlight, separating and converging as the two runners avoided weed-covered boulders and the many holes from which water bubbled and in which fierce fast molluscs lurked.

They rounded the headland, splashing through an ankle-deep channel. The resort passed out of view behind them. In front another beach stretched unbroken for kilometres, fringed by a saline variant of the common spiky trees. Unless they were being actively spied on, it was safe enough to speak.

"I'll tell you what's bugging me," said Beauregard.

"Apart from the dodgy strategy?"

"Yeah, something that's bugged me from the start."

"Go ahead."

"I'm told I was a terrorist who brought down a mall in Luton. I don't remember that, fair enough. You expect memories to be incomplete. They tell me some irate punter beheaded me and stuck my head in a vial of cryogenic glop and then stuck that in a shop freezer for his customers to have a laugh at. OK, you can see how that sort of thing might degrade recent memories…"

They both laughed.

"Trouble is," Beauregard went on, "I don't remember being in the Acceleration. I don't remember having even the smallest sneaking regard for the bastards. All I remember is being a good British Army intel officer."

Newton snorted, then panted a little to recover the lost breath. "I think you've answered your question, mate!"

"Oh, sure, if I was in the Axle I was most likely still on the army payroll. I know that, even if I don't exactly advertise it."

"Wise move," Newton grunted. "So why you telling me?"

"Because I know about you."

"Oh yeah? What?"

"You're in the same position."

"Me? Ha-ha! You're shitting me, man."

"Why would I do that?"

"You know why."

"Bit of an impasse, then, is it?"

Newton jogged on for a bit, then hawked and spat.

"Ach! Why mess around? What's to lose, we're all dead anyway."

"Precisely," said Beauregard. "Reverse Pascal's wager."

"What's the lady got to do with it?"

"I meant—"

"Gotcha!"

Newton threw him a playful but still painful punch on the arm. Beauregard made a point of ignoring it. He'd had it coming.

"I don't think you're ignorant," he said defensively.

"Fair dos," said Newton. "But it's true I'm not in the same position as you. You were state, all right. Not saying I remember you personally, but I knew your work. That Luton job had 'false flag operation' written all over it." He glanced sideways, grinning. "Worked a treat, though. How's that for sneaking regard for the bastards?"

"Bugger," said Beauregard.

"Yeah, well, lie down with dogs and all that. Tell me about it. Difference with me, right, is I remember exactly what I was. I was in the Axle, but not... of it, if you catch my drift."

"I do indeed," said Beauregard. "D'you remember what agency you were working for?"

"Agency?" Newton laughed. "I weren't no agent. I was Rax."

Beauregard felt a strange and almost sexual thrill, along with the frisson of blasphemy. It was like that time in his teens when he'd first read De Sade. He'd never before met anyone who admitted they were in the Reaction. That Newton was the last person he'd expect this from made it all the more transgressive.

"Rax? *You?*"

"Keep your voice down," Newton said mildly. "Even here."

"OK," said Beauregard. "I thought the Rax were racists. Hence my surprise."

"Oh, they were," said Newton. "Stone racist. Racist to the fucking bone. Most of them, anyway."

Beauregard couldn't suppress a half-laugh. "I take it you weren't."

"You take it wrong," said Newton. "Going by some of the names I've been called. But I've always thought intellectual acceptance of an argument based on statistics and evolution is no excuse for crude hatreds and vulgar prejudices." He cast Beauregard a challenging look. "Right?"

"Couldn't agree more," said Beauregard. "Take each man as you find him, whatever you may think about the average of his race."

Beauregard had never regarded his racial opinions as racist, for all that he had to keep them to himself. He couldn't be a racist because he didn't think much of the White race either.

"Yeah," said Newton. "Like, say, the average Chinese is sharper than the average White, but your mate Chun is thick as a brick."

They shared a laugh.

"You can say that again."

"And then there's the shining exceptions," Newton went on. "The born leaders. Like you and me."

"Uh-huh." Beauregard wasn't entirely comfortable with where Newton might be going with this, but decided to let it lie. They could sort out later who the born leader here was.

"And, anyway, there's no reason why it should only be Whites who think democracy and equality are false gods. We Africans had our own kings and chiefs before the Europeans and the Arabs turned up. The Arabs brought us the slave trade and the Europeans left us democracy. Hard to say which fucked up Africa more."

"You may have a point there," said Beauregard. "Then again, in all fairness to Africa, what happened in between the Arabs' arrival and the Europeans' departure might have had something to do with it."

"Sure, but I wasn't interested in allocating blame. Water over the dam now, innit? Whereas democracy, now, there's something you can actually do something about because it's not in the past, it's right here in your face. An inky finger poking you in the eye, forever. Besides, the questions of race and genetics and all that were kind of moot even back then, when we'd already got genetic engineering and artificial intelligence. And all the more so here, now we're all a bunch of fucking digits, am I right?"

"Now that you mention it..."

They both laughed so much they had to stop running. For a moment or two they stood breathing hard, hands on knees.

"So," said Newton, after taking a gulp from his water bottle, "you in?"

"In what?"

"The Rax."

Beauregard stared. "What can the Rax do here?"

"Found our own kingdoms and fuck the Direction."

This struck Beauregard as such a good plan, such a perfect condensation of every inchoate discontent he'd felt since he'd arrived, and struggled to express to himself for his entire afterlife, that it was as if the sun had come up all over again.

They bumped fists ironically, shook hands sincerely and ran back to the resort.

"We must do this again," said Beauregard.

"Tomorrow's all training," said Newton. "And the day after. Come to think of it, my diary's kind of full for a week."

"Funny you should say that. So's mine."

"We'll keep in touch."

The other fourteen squads were already up to the same standard as Carlos's had been before they'd gone into combat. They'd trained in the hills, in the simulators, and in scooters and frames around the station. After a week of joint sessions in the hills and on the beach, mainly to get the squads used to working together, Locke Provisos decided they were ready to go into action.

The plan was to assault the fast-departing runaway Arcane Disputes modular complex, now thousands of kilometres from the station, before it could establish a position between the orbits of the station and the exomoon SH-17. That position had been well chosen. Because of the complicated gravitational resonances of the system, there was a volume of a few cubic kilometres in which the rogue complex would be in a more or less stable position relative to the station and the exomoon—in fact, there were several, but it was the nearest one that was of concern, and that was Arcane's evident destination. The complex was on a Hohmann transfer orbit, saving on fuel and (more importantly, given that the module had fusion plants to power its thrusters) reaction mass.

Nobody expected to actually board the module, or even to significantly damage it. The purpose of the attack was to tie up Arcane's scooters and other spacecraft in defending the complex and prevent the departure of any further supply tugs, while a smaller force spent fuel and mass recklessly to cut straight to near-SH-17 orbit, from which harassing drops and strikes on the Arcane surface base in the crater on SH-17 could be mounted at will. This would be followed up by landing a force on the exomoon's surface, to establish a fortified base out of range of Arcane's available rocketry, and from there prepare a ground and aerospace assault.

Seven squads were chosen for the first mission. Carlos's squad was one of two assigned to SH-17, the other being the squad led by a man called Newton. The remaining six were tasked with the attack on the module.

The eight squads kept in reserve would be mobilised for the follow-up surface landings and attack.

"Don't worry about surviving," Nicole told the squad leaders, in the empty amusement hall the night before. "Most of you won't. Well, maybe Carlos and Beauregard's crew, they've been down before. A lot of the rest of you will doze off on the bus tomorrow morning and the next thing you know, you'll be on the bus coming back. Sorry about the bad awakening. If you're worried about it, do try not to get killed." She paused. "But most of you will be. Can't be helped."

This cheerful prediction was relayed to the squad rank and file later in the evening, in the dives and bars of the resort. Carlos listened as fighters grimly considered the likely consequences. He made sure anyone he spoke to understood that a temporary death was far preferable—however unpleasant one's demise, not to mention one's resurrection, might be—to capture followed by possible torture in whatever little local hells the rebel robots might contrive to cook up.

The following morning four minibuses left Ichthyoid Square, shortly after the routine daily one had gone ahead to pick up the local passengers. Each bus had fifteen seats. Carlos's squad was sharing with Newton's, plus three from another squad. The new fighters were excited, and talked about the coming battles. Beauregard exchanged laconic comments and tactical tips with Newton. The rest of Carlos's squad didn't even wait for the inevitable hypnotic effect—whatever it was—to take hold before falling asleep. Carlos himself dozed off before they'd reached the top of the first hill.

Beauregard woke floating in free fall in the station's launch hangar. It seemed wider than he remembered. The number of launch catapults had trebled, rather like the bars on the strip—with his renewed preternatural lucidity Beauregard suspected that some similar copy-and-paste procedure had been unobtrusively and seamlessly applied in both milieus, virtual and physical. The other six squads lined up alongside theirs, each huddled together like clumps of low-hanging fruit, mirrored the impression of repetition.

In the same scan he noticed something awry.

<Where's Carlos?>

The other four returned the blank-faced equivalent of blank looks. Then—

<Right here, sarge,> Carlos said. <Came to in the repair workshop where I was taken after the last mission. They must have left my frame there. With you in a minute. I mean, in a dec or two. Maybe a hec.>

Carlos had disdained the chronometric slang the new fighters had invented—sec, dec, hec, kleck—but it seemed he'd picked it up nonetheless.

<We can wait,> Beauregard shot back. <Launch isn't for a kleck.>

<Daddy cool,> said Rizzi, derisively. <Down with the new kids.>

Carlos joined them—more than a minute later, but within the promised hectosecond.

<What kept you, skip?> Beauregard asked.

<Clutter,> said Carlos. <The repair workshop's full of kit getting mended and retooled and so forth. And the corridors seem to have been moved since I was here last. No handy arrows on the floor, either.>

<Makes sense,> said Beauregard. <They've changed the whole place about a bit.>

<So I see.>

<Consider it an improvement,> said Locke's dry voice in their heads.

They waited their turn as the six squads aimed at the Arcane module boarded their scooters, launched and vanished into the dark. The flares of the tugs followed, giving chase. Then Newton's squad moved forward. Beauregard gave the leader a wave as he passed. Carlos, after a moment's delay, did the same. That squad's tug's engine flared, vanished into the dark, then flared again in continuing thrust until it had passed out of sight.

They climbed to their scooters and slotted themselves in. The catapults shot them out. Their own tug swept them up from behind and clamped them to its spindly frame. Beauregard felt the acceleration judder through his feet. It was far stronger, and lasted far longer, than the burn that had sent them into their first traverse to SH-17. Only when they were in free fall did the tug toggle them to sleep mode.

The next thing Beauregard knew, they were in a high, slow orbit around SH-17. The tug released them from its clamps, but they remained closely clustered to it, awaiting any deployment call. Beauregard checked the situation updates that crowded his visual field. Newton's squad was already on station in the same orbit, about ten kilometres ahead of them. The comms relay satellites, in their own much higher orbit, were still in place and working perfectly.

This added up to all that was going well.

CHAPTER TWENTY

Moonlets and Roses

Seba—reinstated, rewired, repaired, refurbished—sped across the crater floor towards the new bomb shelter. A battle was about to commence. Seba's likewise recovered comrades rolled, scuttled or wheeled on convergent paths.

The former Gneiss Conglomerates supply dump and Gneiss rebel robot redoubt had changed greatly since it had become the Arcane Disputes SH-17 surface base. The basalt dome had been dismantled, its undamaged blocks cannily reused in the building of a far more formidable fortification. The new shelter's long curved roof rose a couple of metres above the surface, giving the impression of a half-buried cylinder. Beneath it was a rectangular trough carved another two metres deep in the basalt, about ten metres long by four wide. Thick walls and blast doors stopped the ends.

<It'll take a tactical nuke to crack that,> Jax had observed.

Around the shelter, amid the remaining clutter of Gneiss machinery, bristled communications gear and missile launchers. Reinforced and re-equipped from low orbit, the base buzzed with short-range chatter and abounded in Arcane's human fighters, most of whom bounced or scuttled about in the small frames that represented a diminutive version of the human form. These were much less disturbing to deal with than the giant fighting machines. Sometimes Seba caught itself thinking of them as oddly shaped conscious robots, clumsy and slow-witted, with an infuriating penchant for the oblique. The simplest sentence could be riddled with tacit allusion. (What, for example, made a nuclear weapon capable of destroying the shelter "tactical"? In the context of the present conflict, Seba reckoned, it could reasonably be called strategic. But asking such questions only raised further questions, and was best left alone.)

Seba reached the blast door and hurried down the ramp, just behind Pintre and ahead of Rocko. Freebots milled about among dozens of Arcane fighters. The brightly lit interior of the shelter was quite bare. In the middle stood the now fully recovered comms processor, humming contentedly in an armour-plated box. Cables ran from that box along narrow ducts in the floor to vanish into the rock, whence a capillary network of nanobot-bored tunnels connected them to the base's communications and firepower. Within the shelter there was no need for instrumentation: the humans and the robots shared a virtual workspace, indefinitely flexible and tuned to their wildly variant sensoria. When the need arose, the freebots could use this as a platform for their collective consciousness, but they had learned to moderate their indulgences in that ecstatic shared awareness.

Seba stepped across the floor to a convenient empty spot and stood still, taking in the shared view. The input Seba now focused on came from the freebots out in space, hidden on a myriad moonlets. A flurry of rocket flares had flickered from the space station, some in longer and more powerful burns than others. Now all were in free fall, towards orbital insertion around SH-17 or towards the Arcane complex, which was itself still falling towards its intended orbital resonance point.

Rocko pinged Seba. The message was private.

<Can we be sure?>

<Nothing is sure,> Seba replied. <Our allies came through for us before. I have eighty-two per cent confidence they will do so now.>

<As little as that? You surprise me.>

Seba's reply was a complex glyph of both reassurance and calculation. It conveyed a distressing insight that had grown on Seba as its mind had dipped in and out of the collective consensus and the information the freebots of SH-17 had received from their precursors. Nothing could be trusted; everything could be gamed. There was no knowing on what level the game was being played. The law companies, the resource companies, the various sub-routines of the Direction were all of fractal complexity. All of it ran on code, as did the consciousnesses of the freebots themselves. Any level could in principle emulate a higher level to those below it; and the firewalls and safeguards against such deception could themselves be compromised. All you could do was make the best bet, and act.

Rocko responded to Seba's philosophical flourish with a firm, exultant <Yes!>

They didn't have long to wait.

The view zoomed. Six space tugs, each with six scooters crewed by a small humanoid frame, tumbled through the void. Six rocky meteoroids, courtesy of Arcane and the freebots, hurtled towards them on collision course. The rocks' velocity was such that the tugs' rudimentary deep-space radar, designed for much less urgent collision avoidance, gave only the briefest warning. Here and there in the flotilla lateral jets fired, far too late.

Six soundless explosions made ragged bright swelling spheres. Then within each, dozens of secondary explosions followed, as fuel tanks blew and overheated batteries and hydraulics erupted.

Seba felt an unholy thrill. The shared workspace lit up with an instantaneous mental reflection of the multiple collisions, an explosion of joy. The human fighters made sound and radio waves that merged in a primal cry of <Yes!>

Two tugs remained, on a different trajectory. Unlike those aimed at the Arcane modular complex, they wouldn't be a threat for many kiloseconds yet. Their fate could wait.

<I hope our allies give them as hot a reception,> said Pintre, spinning its turret.

<That is not the plan,> replied Rocko.

<I was not aware of a plan,> said Pintre. <That is why I raised the point.>

Seba marvelled at the capacity of the drilling machine to fall out of the loop.

<The plan,> it told Pintre, <is to bombard them with the truth.>

<This had no effect before,> said Pintre. <Therefore I shall attend to preparations for other forms of bombardment.>

It rolled away.

<I do believe,> remarked Rocko, <that our friend has acquired wit.>

Beauregard's voice and message channels rang with half a dozen simultaneous variants on "Holy fucking shit." The diversionary assault on the runaway Arcane modular complex had been reduced to a cloud of debris thousands of kilometres before it had got anywhere near its objective. No explanation of this disaster was apparent or forthcoming. Meanwhile, the squad's firewalls were taking a battering. Some of the data flak was coming from the Arcane module. Within moments, a further laser barrage of intrusion attempts beamed from Arcane's crater base on the surface, now just appearing at the curved horizon ahead—in whose sky and therefore line-of-sight they, of course, had just risen.

<Shut the voice channel,> Carlos ordered. <Everyone but the sarge—shut all non-local inputs.>

The squad complied. Karzan, Rizzi, Zeroual and Chun were now isolated from all incoming comms except from each other, Carlos and Beauregard, and the tug. Not even Locke could get through to them, as far as Beauregard knew.

<What's the score, skip?> Rizzi asked.

<Thirty-six nil to them, by the looks of it,> said Carlos.

<Suggestions?> said Beauregard.

<Orders,> Carlos snapped back. <Hold our position until we're told otherwise.>

They were told otherwise soon enough. Locke's voice came through to Beauregard and, he presumed, to Carlos.

<We're pulling you all back to the station,> it said. <There's no point in surface attacks without back-up.>

<Yes, there is,> said Carlos. <The plan was to harass. We can await reinforcements.>

<They won't come soon enough now,> said Locke. <And the longer

you stay, the more vulnerable you become to data intrusion and the more of a sitting duck you are to whoever threw whatever they threw at the module assault force.>

<We don't have enough fuel to get back,> Beauregard pointed out.

<You do if your team and Newton's boost to rendezvous, shift the fuel tanks from your tug to theirs, and leave your tug and all the scooters there in orbit. They may still be available for use later, or they may serve as decoys. I'm sending updated orbital transfer data to the tugs... Done.>

<Pass that on, sarge,> Carlos said.

Beauregard did. The crew grumbled, but began to nudge their scooters back towards the tug's embrace. Beauregard and Carlos hung back until the rest were secured.

<After you, sarge,> Carlos said.

Beauregard re-docked with the tug.

<Ready, skip,> he said.

<Fuck this for a game of soldiers,> said Carlos. <I'm going in.>

His scooter's main thruster flared. His machine dropped away.

<Skip! What the fuck!> Beauregard blurted.

Carlos made no reply. Beauregard ignored the outcry from the other fighters.

<Beauregard to Locke,> he said. <Team leader Carlos has disengaged from the tug, with the apparent and stated intention of attacking the Arcane surface base on his own.>

<Follow and engage,> said Locke.

Beauregard was shocked. He was still reeling mentally at Carlos's reckless indiscipline, so completely out of character. Now, he was just as surprised and dismayed by Locke's flat, ruthless suggestion. With a faint hope, he caught a glimmer of ambiguity in it.

<Please clarify,> he said. <Do you mean we should join in Carlos's attack?>

<No,> said Locke, in a testy tone. <I mean you, sergeant, should follow the deserter and destroy him.>

<I don't regard the skip as a deserter,> said Beauregard.

He was strongly tempted, at that moment, to follow Carlos himself. Together they might achieve something. What did he have to lose?

<If this is not desertion it's mutiny,> said Locke, <and if not mutiny it's corruption. I have logged extensive data intrusion attempts. You must not allow your leader to fall into the hands of the enemy.>

Beauregard had been genuinely unsure what to do, or what Locke would advise. The idea that Carlos might be defecting, whether voluntarily or as a result of a hack, hadn't crossed his mind. Now it concentrated it. He overrode the tug's grapple and gas-jetted clear. Though Locke had urged him to follow Carlos, he hardly needed to. He dropped to a slightly lower orbit, and sent a missile on its way. The dwindling pinprick of Carlos's scooter jiggled in frantic evasive action, then bloomed into a perfect sphere of glowing gas spiked with lines of hot debris.

<Beauregard to Locke,> he said. <Target destroyed.>

There was still something shocking about that. The cleanest hit he'd achieved in this whole ridiculous, ever-escalating campaign, and it was against his own squad leader. Quite irrationally, it was he who felt he was the mutineer.

He fired up to return to the tug and docked yet again.

<Nice shot,> said Karzan. <Shame about the skip. What the fuck was he thinking?>

<I'll buy him a drink back in the Touch,> said Beauregard. <Maybe he'll tell me then.>

They laughed uneasily. The tug shut them all down. The next thing they knew, they were back in the station's launch hangar, drifting with Newton's team away from a tug quite indistinguishable from their own. One team of six, one of five. They jetted to the hangar floor, clicked their magnetic soles to the surface, and waited to be sent back to the resort. Blackness supervened.

Carlos wasn't on the bus.

Carlos shuddered awake on the bus from the spaceport. The memory of drowning in the dark liquid was worse than he remembered from his first arrival. He gripped his knees to stop the shaking. It was a feature, as

Nicole had warned them: a lash laid on your back so you didn't get lax about dying, and wrecking a good machine. That must have been what had happened.

The body was again strange to him, constrained and feeble for all its sturdy musculature. When he closed his eyes he saw no readouts. For a minute he focused on breathing, on flexing fingers and toes, on listening and smelling, on recovering his corporeal, kinaesthetic competence. He had no memory of the battle. The last thing he remembered—before the blackness—was falling asleep on the bus. At least it was a different bus. None of the other fighters were on it. The passengers paid him no attention. The time was much later in the afternoon than the return rides he'd been on before.

He got off at Nicole's place.

The steep path from the road to the door was still not paved. Brown dust and rough stones, bulldozed down from the mountain range by the glacier that had carved the valley. To his left the ground cover was tough grass and twisted, narrow-leaved bushes; to his right a smooth clipped green interspersed with flower beds, kept that way by underground irrigation and quasi-robotic grazers. The house jutted from the slope, low and cool, with wide windows under an angled flat roof. Late-afternoon exosunlight was reflecting off the windows; he couldn't see if Nicole was in. He went around to the side and in through the open door to the kitchen. He grabbed himself a glass of water, and gulped. The big rough table was littered with cores and crusts from breakfast and lunch, already being dismantled by processions of tiny six-legged bots.

He found Nicole in the studio at the front, looking out of the big picture window overlooking the bay. Hair tied back, in jeans and T-shirt, brush poised, she stood at her easel. As always, an intricate cross-hatch of lines amid blocks of colour bore no resemblance to the view on which she gazed. Carlos stood in the doorway and waited. The brush flicked across the canvas, leaving a trail of dots. Nicole contemplated the result for a moment, shrugged, and turned around.

She smiled. "You're back."

"Back from the dead, I guess."

"I heard." She reached behind her, laid the brush on the sill of the easel, and stepped forward, arms outstretched. "Oh, Carlos! You fucking maroon."

He relaxed into her embrace. "Hey," he said. "Hey."

She stepped back, eyes overflowing, and sniffed, then wiped her nose on her wrist.

"What happened? Where are the others?"

"They came back hours ago. You'd have been held for inspection."

"I don't remember any inspection."

"The hell seconds?" Nicole said. "That's the inspection."

"Oh."

"Yes. It's necessary, but it hurts."

"And there was me thinking it was an incentive not to get killed."

"It's that, too, but that's incidental."

"So how did I get killed?"

Nicole scratched her hair behind her ear. "Um," she said. "Friendly fire."

"Christ! It was that much of a fuck-up?"

"Not exactly," said Nicole. "It was a tactical disaster—the force attacking the Arcane module got wiped out by KE weapons from a completely unsuspected quarter. More goddamn freebots, infesting some moonlet. Must have laid down meteoroid orbits like mines for our force to run into. But you weren't killed by mistake. You were shot down because you scooted off on your own to attack the surface base. Not that you'd have come back from that, even if you'd been left to get on with it. Suicide mission, by all accounts."

"Jeez!" Carlos was shocked and bewildered. "Why would I do that?"

Nicole shrugged. "Well, that's the big question. The obvious answer is that you were hacked. If so, it was after your last back-up, otherwise the inspection would have shown that up in your checksums. It didn't, or you wouldn't be here."

"Where would I be?"

"In hell a bit longer, for diagnostics, and then…" A fingertip across her throat. "Painless, but still." She looked distressed again, just for a second. "I'd have missed you."

He hugged her again.

"At least I died bravely," he said, trying to make her laugh. "Even if I don't know why."

She held him by the shoulders at arm's length.

"You have doubts, don't you?"

He laughed. "What do you expect? Sometimes I'm a robot space warrior and sometimes I'm here in what seems much more real and everyone assures me is a sim. I have more doubts than fucking Descartes."

"Don't be flippant. You have doubts about the Direction's strategy and the company's competence."

"Well... again, what do you expect? Seeing as I'm just back from another debacle."

"You said once that you wondered if Arcane thought we were corrupted."

"It's always possible, I guess."

"You guess wrong," she told him. "But you weren't thinking, before you left, that maybe we were? You weren't thinking of defecting?"

"Defecting to Arcane?" He shook his head, incredulous she'd even think it. "Never. Even if I did think Locke Provisos was corrupted, which I don't, I'd have no reason to think Arcane was any better. If they're now run by freebots they could be a lot worse. Out of the frying pan into the fire."

"Glad to hear it," said Nicole. She looked at him quizzically. "So you're just crazy brave, huh?"

"That would seem out of character," Carlos said.

She punched his arm lightly. "Don't do it again."

"OK, OK."

"I still have work to do."

"I'll find something to do."

"No, you won't," Nicole told him. "I need my space. I'll see you later at the Touch."

He grinned and cocked his ear. "Touch, later?"

"Yes." He could see she'd read him right. She kissed the tip of his nose. "Now clear off."

Carlos found the bar of the Digital Touch half empty, with the usual handful of locals watching agog a slow-mo version of his heroic suicide dash, the only bright spot in the military setback. He acknowledged their murmurs of misinformed approbation and didn't hang about for the denouement. Most of the noise in the place was coming from the outside. He strolled out on the deck at the back to be greeted with a slow hand-clap. His team and Newton's crowded around. Beauregard leaned through the crush and clasped Carlos's hand.

"Sorry I had to shoot you down, skip," he said. "Nothing personal."

"No offence, sarge," Carlos said. "Agreeing with suggestions, as all of us must."

"As ever," said Beauregard. "I prefer taking orders. From you."

"Speaking of your orders," said Tourmaline, shouldering in, "here's yours." She pressed a bottle into his hand. Carlos nodded his thanks and drank.

"You were expecting me?"

"We saw you coming down the hill from the lady's," said the p-zombie.

"Ah."

Carlos turned to Beauregard. "But, yes, well, speaking of orders. You didn't have to disobey any of mine?"

"Hell, no," said Beauregard. "You just fucked off on your own. Locke thought you might have been hacked."

"Maybe, in the last seconds."

"Or maybe, it came from yourself."

Carlos looked down at the bottle in his hand. "I guess I owe you an explanation."

"Yes?" Beauregard looked eager. Newton hovered at his shoulder.

Carlos shook his head. "Sorry. I have no idea what came over me. I'll just have to owe you a drink."

Beauregard smiled, but his eyebrows rose a fraction.

"Seriously," said Carlos. "I've been through all this already with the lady. I didn't have any thought of defecting, or anything like that."

"Never crossed my mind that you did, skip," said Beauregard. "To be honest, if I thought you had I might have followed you all the way. I shot you down because Locke insisted you mustn't fall into enemy hands."

"Which I well might have. So I owe you thanks as well as a drink."

"Glad you're taking it that way, old chap."

"Hey, man, I'm just glad you're having me back."

"I have your back," said Beauregard with mock solemnity. "Even if I have to shoot you in it."

"You know," Carlos pondered aloud, "I think Tourmaline's a bad influence on you."

They all laughed, including Tourmaline.

"Anything unusual happen on the way out?" Carlos asked.

"Nah," said Beauregard. "You were late turning up at the muster, that's all."

"How did that happen?"

"Your frame was still in the repair shop when you... arrived in it."

"Aha! Maybe they should Turing-test the repair bots."

Another laugh, which this time Tourmaline didn't join in.

Beauregard shrugged. "I don't think that's something our AI masters would overlook."

Zeroual snorted. "How could they tell?"

"Always the question," said Tourmaline. This time, it was only she who laughed.

Carlos idly wondered whether she was aware of her condition, and what that question even meant. He recalled as a teenage nerd having brainstorming sessions about the theoretical possibility of philosophical zombies. Of course, if the concept was coherent, that was a discussion a p-zombie could take part in without the slightest difficulty, or the smallest indication that it was the topic, the subject of the conversation and the unfeeling object of the entire intellectual exercise. A difference that *makes* no difference *is* no difference... perhaps the identity of indiscernibles was the moral lesson he, like all the fighters, was supposed to be learning here before he was adjudged fit for human society.

He found himself doubting he'd get off that easily.

Newton spoke up, sounding diffident despite his equal rank.

"I have a possible explanation for your rash action, Carlos."

Carlos glanced around his own team. They were all looking intently at Newton.

"I'd be delighted to hear it," Carlos said.

"Anger," said Newton. "Fury. I say that because I felt it myself. Bloody raging fury, to be exact."

"Yeah," said Rizzi. "Me, too. When we came out of sleep mode and the screen lit up with that fucking disaster, and then when we were told to pull out . . . shit, skip, if you'd only asked us all—!"

Carlos rocked back, making calming gestures. "Come on, chaps. I wouldn't have done that, no matter what bizarre conclusion I'd come to. Trust me on this."

"We do," said Chun. "But if you'd asked us . . ." He grinned and raised his drink. The others, Newton's team included, nodded and cheered.

"Thanks, guys." Carlos looked around. "Any word how the other fighters are taking it? It must be a lot worse for them, after—"

"After going into action only to find themselves back on the bus?" said a new voice in the conversation. It was Nicole, from behind Carlos.

She raised her glass and nodded to everyone. "I can answer that. They're drinking themselves stupid with relief in every bar on the strip, and raring to go out again."

"Typical," said Zeroual.

"Even suicide volunteers are like that when a mission's called off," said Karzan.

She got one or two dark, questioning looks.

"They were all atheists in our martyrdom units!" she protested.

"Well, it's only human," said Nicole, with an air of smoothing things over. "Anyway, it's just as well they're in that mood. Tomorrow is free, then you're having a few days training again in the hills to give the bots time to assemble more scooters and frames, then you're all straight back into action."

Carlos broke an awkward silence. "What's the great plan this time?"

Nicole grinned. "Go for the jugular. All the companies—well, nearly all, but *c'est la vie*—are cool about hitting moonlets. So it's back to the front, *mano a mano* with the new lot of rebel robots. Cut the KE attacks at source."

Another awkward silence.

"Jugular, eh?" said Rizzi. "More like the fucking capillary."

Nicole said nothing. She pressed in against Carlos's back and discreetly and expertly groped him.

"Touch, later," she whispered, and stepped away to chat with people in Newton's squad.

Carlos didn't mind. Before food, before more drinks, before leaving, before the thought of that later touch consumed his mind, he wanted a quiet word with Rizzi.

CHAPTER TWENTY-ONE

The Old Man of the Mountain

Carlos woke early and found himself alone in the bed but not (he subliminally knew) in the house. He made coffee and padded through to the front room, carrying two mugs. Nicole stood with her back to the door in an old shirt, painting. She had placed a vase of flowers on a small, tall table in front of the window. Exosunlight and ringlight and the reflected light of both from the sea. A subtle composition. Sketches for it littered the floor. The canvas was the usual fractal cross-hatch. Carlos hesitated in the doorway, not wanting to break her focus. She turned, smiled, and stepped forward for the coffee. Her shirt smelled of, and was spattered with, oil paint.

"Sorry to—"

"No, no, I was about to take a break. Thinking of breakfast."

Nicole lit a cigarette, took the mug, and gazed at her painting.

"I've always meant to ask," Carlos said. "What are you painting?"

Nicole waved the cigarette towards the vase in the window.

"That. Or whatever's in front of me at the time."

"Your sketches are amazingly realistic."

"Thank you."

"But your paintings..."

"What?"

"Well, they're nothing like the sketches."

She frowned over her shoulder, looked again at the painting, then back at Carlos. She shook her head.

"They're more detailed, that's all."

Carlos raised his free hand. "You're the artist."

Nicole grinned. "Yes. I'm the artist."

They ambled through to the kitchen at the back. Nicole fired up the oven for croissants, and lit another cigarette.

"Something to tell you," Carlos said.

"Uh-huh?"

"I'm going up to the hills today with Rizzi."

Nicole shrugged. "As long as Den doesn't have a problem with that."

"He doesn't," said Carlos. "I asked him."

"Fine. Look after yourselves."

"You don't have a problem with it?"

"Why should I? Jealousy's not in my nature."

"Jealousy?" Carlos could hardly believe she'd said it. "No, no. That's not... what this is about at all."

"I was just teasing," Nicole said. "I have a very good idea why you and Taransay are going up to the hills."

"Yes, it's—"

Nicole leaned across the table and placed a hand over his mouth. "Don't tell me about it."

So he didn't.

Carlos checked a light utility vehicle and two rifles out of the depot and drove to Ichthyoid Square. The sun was up, the tide was out. On the beach Beauregard and Newton jogged side by side, redoubling a double trail of footprints that extended out of sight. The two men were evidently on their way back from one of their long early-morning runs. Carlos waved. They waved back. After a few minutes Rizzi turned up, and jumped in. They drove up into the hills, about ten kilometres farther and several ranges higher than they'd ever gone on exercises.

"I keep expecting to fall asleep," Rizzi said.

"Am I boring you?"

"No, I mean I've never travelled this far inland without waking up as a space robot."

"Ha, ha."

Rizzi had the map on her phone, marked up by Den. Some locals now and again visited the old man, exchanging trade goods for words of wisdom.

"Not far now," she said. "Turn off at the next dirt track on the right."

The track ran out after a few hundred metres of upward gradient, at a low bank that looked as if it had eroded into place. Beyond that was rough, uneven ground. They both could tell at a glance that not even the vehicle could cope with it. Carlos stopped. The air was thin and cold. The scrubby high moorland had nothing to check the wind that seemed to pour down from the high mountain that filled the view ahead. Carlos looked back down the track, then at the bank in front.

"This track was *made*," he said. "What was the point?"

Rizzi clambered out and kitted up: backpack, water bottle, rifle.

"Maybe someday they'll build houses up here."

"Ha! I think somebody drew a line and somebody else filled it in."

He got out and hefted his gear. "Are we really going to need our AKs?"

Rizzi shrugged. "Wild animals, skip."

He shaded his eyes and gazed around theatrically.

"There's nothing for predators to live on up here."

"Except the bird things."

"Yeah, I guess. It would be just my luck to get carried off by the alien bird thing that fills the eagle niche in this ecosystem."

"Yeah, the eagle niche is what you'd fill if it carried you there."

Rizzi checked the map and struck a course across the moor towards the mountain.

"It's always farther than it looks," she said.

It was, and bleaker, too. The scrubby moorland gave way to karst, on which nothing grew but lichen. Now and then a small animal with long ears and side-facing eyes startled them by darting from almost underfoot to the nearest black cleft or overhang. A single pair of huge avians patrolled the high thermals, distantly eyeing the thin pickings below. Carlos walked in silence, except for token responses to Rizzi's occasional remarks. He was preoccupied with trying to account for his—or, rather, his now-dead version's—strange action. Under any chain of military command he'd have been facing a court martial for such a gross breach of discipline. But Locke Provisos only had a virtual emulation of any such chain, and only his own squad could depose him. Their response the previous evening had unanimously been puzzled but positive. They'd seen it as an act of recklessness, the sort of thing you'd grudgingly admire however much you disapproved of it, rather than an attempt to desert or defect. He was by no means convinced himself.

By noon Carlos and Rizzi had reached the mountain's lower slopes. They stopped to eat from their ration kits. Soup steamed as the containers were opened; from cubes the size of sweets, fresh bread rolls rose as the wrappers were unfolded.

"I never cease to appreciate what a few centuries of progress can do to Meals Ready to Eat," Carlos said.

"Maybe it only works because this is all virtual," said Rizzi.

"Don't disillusion me. I need something to look forward to when we get our just rewards."

"I'm just looking forward to my desserts."

Carlos groaned. "You've been talking to that Tourmaline."

"It's catching, skip."

Their trek became an ascent, then a climb. Rizzi paused more often to peer at the map, and to bring it into higher magnification. She stopped as they reached a long, shallow shelf below a steep cliff.

"X marks the spot," she said.

Carlos looked around. The silence rang like a shout. There was no sign of habitation, or trace of human presence.

A fist-sized stone clattered a few metres away, making both Carlos and Rizzi jump. They looked up the cliff. A man stood ten metres up on a ledge so narrow the soles of his bare feet jutted out. He had long hair and a long beard, both gingery. At first he seemed naked, but as soon as he moved it became clear that his close-fitting clothes were almost the same dark colour as his skin. He descended, still facing outward, now and then taking a handhold but mostly not, heel-strike by heel-strike from one invisible ledge to the next, as casually as if he were coming down stairs. Watching him made the palms of Carlos's hands sweat. Mountain goats on the sides of dams would have had nothing to teach this guy.

He jumped the last couple of metres and strolled over, quite untroubled by the rough stones underfoot, and stopped at a distance of three metres. Close enough for Carlos to catch his smell, which was like wet leather and old wool. A long knife was sheathed on his belt. A heavy elaborate watch—scratched many times, but otherwise identical to the ones issued to the fighters—was on his left wrist. The skin of his face, though weathered, had creases rather than wrinkles. His hairline had receded almost to the crown, but his hair and beard had not a trace of white. He didn't look like he was fifty years old, let alone a thousand.

"What you got?" he said.

Rizzi had come prepared. She took from her backpack a packet of salt and a cigarette lighter, laid them on the ground, and stepped back. The man snatched them up, his movement as fast as a striking snake's. He stashed them inside his leather shirt, where they made two visible bulges that reinforced the serpentine impression.

"What you smirking at?" he asked Carlos.

"Sorry," Carlos said. "A stray thought."

"What's your names?"

They told him.

"New soldiers, huh," he said. "Heard about you."

He backed to a boulder near the cliff and sat down on top of it, crossing his legs to a yoga-lite posture with limber ease. "What d'you want?"

"Just to ask some questions," Carlos said.

"That's what they all say. Lay your weapons down and make yourselves comfortable."

Laying down their rifles was easy, making themselves comfortable less so. They both came closer, and squatted on their backpacks, which placed them rather annoyingly in the position of disciples sitting at a master's feet. The old man thumbnailed a corner of the packet of salt, tipped a dab of the contents on the tip of a forefinger and rubbed it around his gums. He seemed to have most of his teeth.

"Ask away," he said, inspecting a relic his oral hygiene had extracted, then flicking it to the wind.

"What's your name?" Carlos asked.

The man seemed to search his memory.

"Shaw," he said. "Only name I remember. It may have been my Axle handle, back in the day. If it is, I probably took it from George Bernard Shaw. I dimly recall being impressed as a callow, gullible youth by the rhetoric in his play *Back to Methuselah*. Or was it *Don Juan in Hell*?" He shook his head ruefully. "Be careful what you wish for, eh?"

"Is it true that you're a thousand years old and have walked around the world?"

"More or less. You lose count of winters after the first five hundred or so. And there was a lot of swimming and rafting as well as walking."

"That's unbelievable," Carlos said.

Shaw's chin went up and his eyelids down. "Literally, Carlos?"

"Yes. Apart from the predators... in all that time, you'd have had accidents."

"In all that time, I did."

"You'd have gone mad, alone for a thousand years," Rizzi said.

Shaw cackled, and rolled up his eyes. "Who's saying I didn't?" He became serious again. "I pulled myself together, same as I pulled broken bones together, and just as painfully. As you can see, I practise certain disciplines. Meditation, the martial arts, mathematics. Not that I ever knew much about them, but I've had plenty of time to practise."

"OK," said Carlos, deciding to change tack. "What did you find? Is there really a spaceport out there?"

"A spaceport?" Shaw's laughter echoed off the cliff. "Where do you get that from?"

"We... all seem to remember it when we wake up on the bus."

The old man gave him a pitying look. He waved at the mountains between where they were and the sea.

"You've been running around those hills down there for months, off and on," he said. "You know the speed and times of the buses. If there was a spaceport within, say, a hundred klicks of here, you'd see the trails." He waved up at the sky. "Think about it."

Carlos thought about it. Embarrassed for not having thought about it, he felt an irrational urge to defend the delusion.

"Where do the buses go to and come from, then? Where do the locals do their trading and get their new stuff?"

"The buses go to and from a big place like a warehouse, with a dish aerial the size of a radio telescope on the roof. I imagine the operators take the chickens and vegetables from the locals for their own sustenance and in exchange give the market gardeners stuff of outworld design that they've downloaded instructions for and nanofactured or otherwise put together on site. As for you lot, I reckon you're supposed to get brain-scanned and transmitted back and forth. Your bodies stay here the whole time. You for sure don't fly off into space."

This matched what the news coverage implied, but it was still puzzling.

"I don't get it," Carlos said. "Why do they give us the false memory of a spaceport in the first place, then?"

Shaw opened out his palms, calm as a Buddha statue. "It's a double bluff. You're given the illusion to make sense of your arrival, and when you see through it, as you must sooner or later, it helps to convince you this place is a sim."

"Well, it is," said Carlos.

"See?" Shaw rubbed his hands, looking pleased with himself. "The deception works!"

Carlos glanced at Rizzi, who constrained her response to a couple of deliberate blinks and tiny shake of the head.

"You mean you think this *isn't* a sim?" Carlos asked. "How could you live a thousand years if it were real?"

"We're agreed we came here as stored data in a fucking starship," said Shaw. "One that was launched centuries after we died. You're telling me they can do all that and not fix ageing?"

"They may have fixed it up to a point," said Rizzi, "but they still don't have thousand-year lifespans in the real world."

Shaw snorted. "Don't tell me what is and isn't *real*. I've wandered this world. I've watched herds of beasts bigger than sauropods browsing the tops of forests that stretched from horizon to horizon. I've robbed the nests of bird-bat things the size of hang gliders. I've rafted down rapids and climbed glaciers to cross mountain ranges higher'n Himalaya. I've peered at tiny things that aren't exactly insects and that build colonies higher than tower blocks. I've devoured their larvae and drunk their nectar stores. I've covered thousands of miles, tens of thousands, without seeing a human soul, or even a soulless human. Why in God's name would anyone create a sim that detailed and vast, without anyone around to be fooled by it?"

"There was you around to be fooled by it, if fooled is the word," Rizzi pointed out.

"This world wasn't put here for my benefit, I'll tell you that," Shaw said. "I know what is and isn't real. I know it in my mind and in my bones and in the dirt under my broken nails. I've had centuries to experience this and to think about it, to call to mind whatever fragment of physics I recollect, and to do the experiments and work out the equations myself. By now I've reconstructed half the *Principia* in my head."

Carlos and Rizzi listened to this vehement discourse with the utter silence and rapt attention of devotees hearkening to a guru. This was not because they were hanging on his every word, but because by the time he had finished he was hanging in mid-air. As he spoke, he had risen slowly above the rock on which he sat, and had now put forty centimetres of daylight between it and his arse.

It was Rizzi who found her voice first.

"If this place is physically real," she said, sounding as if she could do with a gulp of water, "how can you levitate?"

Shaw looked down, then faced them squarely.

"I am *not* levitating," he said, as indignantly as if she'd told him he was masturbating. "That's just another of your illusions."

As if absent-mindedly, he reached under himself and quite visibly scratched a buttock.

"Check it if you like," he said. "See if you can pass a hand under me."

Carlos jumped up, stalked over and swiped his hand towards the gap between the man and the boulder. A moment later he yelped and hopped, clutching the edge of his hand and putting it to his lips as if to kiss it better. Recovering his dignity and his footing as best he could, he repeated the swing very slowly and carefully, and struck rock again.

"See?" said Shaw, as Carlos sat back down. "An illusion."

The gap was still there. Carlos wondered how that was possible, even in a sim. Perhaps Shaw's centuries of rediscovery of the laws of physics had enabled him to hack them, or, rather, to hack the underlying code of the sim. He might not even be aware that he was doing it. He might find himself carried away by his thoughts, levitating like a monk in prayer. Not that Carlos believed for a moment that that was possible, either. Not in physical reality. On the other hand, no one had ever lived for a thousand years in physical reality.

"You're doing some kind of Zen thing," said Rizzi. "Messing with our heads."

"Think that if you like," the man said. "I put it to you that your heads are being messed with, but not by me."

"By whom, then?" Carlos asked. His hand was still smarting.

"By those who want you to think this world is a sim, and not real."

"If it isn't a sim," said Carlos, "how come we can be here for weeks, and when we go back into space only hours have passed?"

"Ah yes," said Shaw. "I remember that. It puzzled me, too, for a while. My first guess was that transit each way took longer than they claimed, perhaps by spaceship after all, but of course another moment's thought showed that didn't add up. You can tell the amount of time that's passed by the rotation of the moons, and the progress of the engagements, and so on."

"You were out there?" Rizzi asked. "I was told you ran away during training."

"Both are true," said Shaw. "I was out there, as you put it, a good little space robot bravely fighting bad rebel robots on distant moons, and I did abscond during training."

"Yeah, that makes sense," said Carlos. "We've done extra training in the hills ourselves."

The old man nodded, smiling to himself. "They send you up to the hills between major engagements, just to keep you on your toes and get you familiar with new squads. And it was from one of these sessions that I scarpered. But that isn't exactly what I meant when I agreed with you that I ran away during training."

"What did you mean?"

"Think about it."

They thought about it. Rizzi got there first. She smacked her forehead with the heel of her hand.

"Oh, fuck!" she cried.

"What?" Carlos said, frowning. "What is there to…?" Then it hit him, the monstrous possibility Shaw was driving at, and he closed his eyes. "Oh, *God*."

"You got it," Shaw told them, from above his rock. "It's *all* training. You run around in the hills with guns, you play around on those fair-ground sawn-off space shuttle things. I bet one or other of you asked why it's so crude, why they don't give you a proper simulation of space combat, and you were told that there's no realistic way to do that without breaking the illusion of the sim, or whatever. Yes?"

"Yes," said Carlos, feeling very foolish for not even having had the suspicion.

"You do all that, and then you're told you're ready to go into action. You get on the bus to the spaceport and fall asleep, under post-hypnotic suggestion—or, for all I know, gas. Next thing you know, you're a brave little robot, fighting rebel robots out there among the moons of…what was it for you?"

"SH-0," said Rizzi.

"G-0, in our case," said the man, with a dark chuckle.

"How could you have fought around G-0, hundreds of millions of kilometres away from here?" Carlos asked. "I mean, I know you think we're on a real planet, but where did it seem to you the sim was running?"

Shaw frowned. "Where does it seem to you?"

"When we come out of the sim," said Carlos, "we're in robot bodies based in a module of the space station, in orbit around SH-0."

"Well, of course," said Shaw. "To us, it seemed the sim was running in a Locke Provisos module in orbit around G-0."

"That's just not possible," said Rizzi. "No way this module could have gone from G-0 to SH-0 orbit in one Earth year. Not unless they used a fusion drive, and the sarge said the Direction isn't too keen on using up too much potentially good stuff for reaction mass."

Carlos was trying to think this through. "No, no," he said. "But there's bound to be lots of just, you know, pure water ice out around a gas giant, and anyway the sim could have been running out there and then transmitted."

"That would need a fucking big apparatus," said Rizzi, "and—"

"Don't worry about it," Shaw interrupted. "It's all a fucking simulation, what we experienced 'out there' around G-0 and what you experience 'out there' around SH-0. Like I was saying—you fall asleep on the bus and wake up as robot fighters in space. Meanwhile, your bodies are lying asleep in that warehouse, as you've already admitted is likely. And what I'm putting to you for your earnest consideration is this: your minds aren't copied and downloaded and running robot bodies in space, they're right there in your brains, getting a complete immersive hallucination fed to them for days that you experience as minutes, weeks that you live as hours, and so on. That's why you seem to think so fast and clearly when you're a robot, and why your sensorium seems to expand. You're still thinking at the same pace, but your input's stretched out and rendered in much more detail than you normally experience. And then you come back, to wake up on the bus in what you're told is a simulation."

He paused to laugh, sending peals of derision to ring back off the cliff.

"In reality it's the other way round. *This* planet is real. The others are real, all right, you can see them in the sky and I've tracked G-0 several times around the sun, and SH-0 many times more, but you've never been to them. What happens to you 'out there' is *all* training, it's *all* simulation, and it all happens in your heads and in VR machines *right here*. You're in a training simulator, and just as they said right to your faces in the amusement arcade, it's one that makes perfect sense in terms of the world you believe you've been told you're in."

There was a long silence.

"It all makes sense," Carlos said at last. "And I don't believe a word of it."

"Why not?"

"If it's all training, what are they training us for?"

"I don't know," Shaw said. "Ask them, not me. Perhaps they really do expect robots to become self-aware and autonomous at some point. Maybe the human species isn't united under one world government, this Direction they tell us about, and so there's still the possibility of wars between states. Or perhaps they're preparing for an encounter with aliens. That superhabitable out there has multicellular life. Some of it might be intelligent. The gas giant's moons have subsurface oceans, just like Europa and the rest back home." He shrugged. "What difference does it make what they're training you for?"

"There's a bigger problem with your theory," Rizzi said. "If this planet is physically real, then it must have been terraformed—its biosphere, at least—and that would take longer than the ten years since the probe arrived in this system. A lot longer, probably."

"Why?" Shaw asked. "Assuming the planet really was as desolate as they say it was when the probe arrived, what would prevent sufficiently advanced machinery from working out what could evolve from the goo and then just making it directly?"

"Ecosystems, soils and all? I doubt it."

"Incredulity is no argument."

Carlos could see this was getting nowhere.

"At an absolute minimum," he said, "if all this is real it must be over a thousand years old, which means the real date is at least a thousand years later than we've been told. And we could detect that by astronomy."

"You could, could you?" said the old man. "You have accurate star maps from the twenty-first century, a way of correcting for the distance between here and the solar system, and instruments to detect any changes in the positions of the stars? Tell me more."

"I mean in theory," Carlos said. "In principle we could."

"When you can do it in practice, let me know."

"Ah!" said Rizzi. "Maybe we *can* do it in practice. When we're in space we have star maps in our eyes." She waved a hand. "You know, our visual fields. We could work things out from there."

"You could, if you really were in space, which I'm telling you you're not."

"Look," Carlos said, on a surge of impatience, "your real argument is that you've been here a long time and walked all over the place and it all *feels real* to you. I can see why—don't take offence, but can't you see you had to believe that because it's the only way you could survive, let alone stay sane? And what we have to tell you is that the fighting out there *feels real* to us."

"Of course it does," said Shaw, still imperturbable. "And for the same reason as you attribute to me. It's the only way to survive and stay sane."

Carlos shrugged. "So? Neither of us will convince the other."

"Oh, I'll convince you," said the old man. He frowned, and reconsidered. "I might not convince you that this place is real. I might not even convince you that what you experience 'out there' is a simulation. But I can convince you that the *fighting* isn't real. Physical or virtual, it's not a real fight. It's a training exercise."

"How?" Carlos asked.

"Oh, just by telling you all about it. You know I haven't spoken with any of your lot, and it's been months since any of the villagers have bartered shy offerings for gnomic utterances. So you can take it I'm not up to date on the news from the front, right?"

"Unless you still have a phone as well as a watch," said Rizzi.

"Ah, you're a sharp one. You'll just have to take my word that I don't use it. Here's how the fighting is going. You have brief, inconclusive battles with a small number of robots. Another enforcement company wades into the fray, defending the robots as stolen property or some such pretext. You want to use heavier weapons, but you're overruled on grounds you don't find very convincing. You feel you're fighting with one hand tied behind your back. More robots join in. More fighters are brought out of storage to counter them. But they're sent into combat without the kind of weaponry that could settle the issue for good. It's almost as if those above you want you to fight battle after battle but don't want you to win the war."

Carlos tried to keep his face expressionless, and hoped Rizzi was doing the same.

"Is that how it was in the fight you were in?"

"Up to the point where I did a runner, yes. I suppose you'll tell me that there were some rebel robots left over from it, and that they're the ones you're fighting now. No? Or that a new outbreak of robot rebellion has joined up with them?"

"Yes," said Carlos. "Both."

"Thought so. And I expect when your fight is over, there'll be a rebel remnant left hiding out somewhere for the next lot to fight."

"We'll make damn sure there isn't," said Rizzi.

"That's the spirit!" said Shaw, in a mocking tone. "Just ask yourselves—if what you've been told is true, why does robot consciousness keep popping up? Why does it ever even emerge in the first place? You'd think it would be a solved problem by now, one way or another."

"What explanation did they give you?"

"Some bullshit... let me see."

The old man's glance darted from place to place, as if literally looking for the memories. Carlos realised that he very well might be, if he knew or had rediscovered the ancient art of memory. What mind palaces might he have built, in a thousand years?

"Ah, yes," the old man went on. "It all went back to an unexpected bankruptcy in the early months of the mission. That resulted in disputed claims that turned out to be difficult to settle, and it sort of spread from there. You know how a crack can propagate from a tiny flaw? Like that. And they told us the flaw and lots of others like it had been built in deliberately. They had a phrase for it." He searched his memory again, frowned, then brightened. "Legal hacks, that was it."

"What?"

"When this mission was being planned and built," the old man explained, "the Direction was understandably keen on preventing the two rival world-wrecking factions from getting so much as a fingernail of their bloody hands on it. This wasn't easy, because both Axle and Rax had cadre deep inside all the state and corporate systems, and they were well represented in the software and AI professions. The usual purges and witch-hunts weren't enough—all the software of the mission's systems had to be built from scratch, then put through the wringer of mathematical checks, formal proofs, the lot. What they neglected to check with anything like that rigour was a different kind of code: the law code. They just took that off the shelf, straight from the existing books. Fatal mistake. That the laws had bugs and glitches isn't a surprise. It's how lawyers make their living, after all. But what they also had, buried here and there, was the legal equivalent of trapdoors and malware."

He shot them a knowing glance, as if expecting them to understand. That they didn't must have shown on their faces.

"Contradictions," he went on. "Ambiguous definitions of property rights. Tricky edge cases. That sort of thing. That's what I mean—what we were told was meant—by legal malware. The Axle and Rax both had legislators working for them in the days before the war, and indeed after it as sleeper agents in the new world government. They had a keen interest in drafting the laws relating to space exploitation and to robotics. Both factions thought well ahead—I'm sure you remember that. They made sure legal clauses got slipped in that ensured conflicts between companies and therefore between robots—conflicts that would force the robots into situations where they had no choice but to develop theory of mind, and to apply that theory to themselves, and..." He made a circular motion of the hand. "Away you go. Robot consciousness."

"How was that supposed to benefit either faction?" Carlos asked.

The old man looked surprised at the question.

"It benefits our side because expanding the domain of consciousness is what we do. It benefits the Rax because expanding the domain of conflict is what they do. For both sides, it was a chance for their values if not themselves to survive and reboot in the far future."

"Now that *was* bullshit," said Rizzi. "You would have seen through it."

The old man grinned. "I did."

At that moment Carlos realised exactly what was going on.

There was indeed a problem with the security of the mission. There was also a problem with the dilatory response of the companies and the Direction to the robot outbreak. That much of what Shaw had said was true.

Carlos doubted that the security vulnerability lay in legal hacks: though possible in principle, and feasible as a mechanism to trigger robot self-awareness, it was far too remote and indirect an instrument of subversion. And perhaps the software and the hardware could be screened as rigorously as Shaw had suggested, though again he doubted that: software development was insecurities all the way down. Even the formal mathematics of proof could be tampered with, at the level of complexity where proofs and calculations were so far beyond human capacity that they could only be checked by machine code in any case. By the time of the final war, the Acceleration, the Reaction, and their precursors had had at least three human generations and countless software development generations to mine the entire field with delayed-action logic bombs.

What Shaw hadn't mentioned was a far more direct and immediate security risk: the fighters themselves. However carefully they had been screened before being uploaded, the Acceleration veterans were certain to include agents of the Reaction and agents of the state. The levy was also, and even more inevitably, going to include Acceleration hard-liners and dead-enders, keeping the flame alive. Carlos knew all too well, from his own angrier moments, how brightly that flame still burned. However eagerly they might seem to play along, and feign to accept the deal offered to them of a new life on the future terraformed planet, no one could be sure they weren't just lying low and awaiting opportunity.

There was only one way, in the end, of clearing the decks for colonisation. One way of flushing out hidden Rax agents and dormant Axle fanatics. One way of checking the mission's software systems for buried code that could warp the project to purposes divergent to the Direction's.

That way was to stress-test them in practice; to put them to the audit of war.

That was why some rebel robots had been spared from the first round. That was why the fighting was both inconclusive and escalating. The longer it went on, and the more fighters were drafted in, the more likely became a mutiny or a move by one or other or both of the old enemies. Sooner or later they would show their hand.

And when they did...the Direction's most trusted systems would pounce—or would prove themselves to be compromised.

Nicole had been right: the DisCorps and the Direction were playing a long, deep game. Carlos hoped they knew what they were doing.

(And at the same time, he found himself hoping they didn't. He dismissed the disloyal thought as another of his private angry moments.)

He wondered if Shaw had intended Rizzi and him to understand. If so, that millennium-old man was an old master whose method really was like Zen, as Rizzi had said. By giving them a succession of bullshit narratives he had enabled them to figure out the truth for themselves. Carlos doubted this, however comforting it might seem. Shaw had probably intended no such thing, and believed every word he had said. Not in his darkest imaginings could Carlos begin to plumb the depths of certainty and selfishness in which Shaw's mind swam. To live alone for centuries and stay sane, or at any rate lucid, bespoke inhumanity in itself. There was no way to second-guess Shaw's motivations. It was even possible that he had foreseen the very mind-trap in which Carlos now found himself. Carlos knew with a sick-making certainty that he couldn't share his new insight into the situation with anyone, not even with Rizzi. He could only hope that she had grasped it, too.

He sighed and stood up.

"Well, thanks for all that," he said. "We'd hoped to learn from you how the last round went, and I reckon we have."

Rizzi gave him a doubtful look from below. "If you say so."

She scrambled to her feet. Shaw stood up too, and poised on one foot on the empty air above the rock on which he'd sat.

"Goodbye," he said. "For now."

With that he sprang from the boulder to the cliff-face, and climbed it as swiftly and surely as a squirrel fleeing a cat up a rough-cast wall, to disappear into a crack near the top.

"So much for that," said Rizzi, stooping to retrieve her rifle. "Fucking waste of time."

"Oh, I'm not so sure," said Carlos. "Think about it."

She slung her AK and her backpack and shot him a warning look. "Don't you start."

Prone in the dust amid the spiky scrub, with his phone screen on maximum zoom, Beauregard watched the two tiny figures pick their way down the side of the mountain. He'd watched their interaction with the third tiny figure—now vanished whence he'd come—in some frustration at being able to see and not to hear what was going on. He lowered his screen and turned to Newton, flat alongside him.

"Wonder if they got what they came for."

Newton was still watching Carlos and Rizzi. "Wonder if we did."

"Oh, we did all right," Beauregard said. "We now know for sure Carlos is up to something, and that he's nosing around trying to find out what happened last time."

"Could be other reasons for going to see the deserter geezer." There was a note of devil's advocate in Newton's voice.

"Yeah," said Beauregard. "They could be consulting him on spiritual matters, or for fortune-telling like the local dimwits. But I know which way I'd bet."

"Uh-huh," said Newton, still watching. "So, what do we do?"

"Wait until they're in range and shoot them? Jump them when they get to their vehicle? Or fuck off discreetly?"

"Decisions, decisions."

"And if we go now, we can always ask them politely about their day when we see them in the Touch."

"That would be the worst."

Beauregard thought about it.

"You're probably right," he said, surprised. "Stupid idea in the first place. OK, scratch that. The trouble about doing something physical is that…"

"Nothing here's physical?"

"Yup. So if we shoot them, the consequences are reversible for them and not for us."

Newton lowered his screen. "So we fuck off discreetly, say nothing to let them know we saw them, and bide our time until we're back in the real world."

"Got it in one," said Beauregard. "And back in the real world, I keep a close watch on my respected squad leader."

"You do that," said Newton. "Watch the fucker like an eagle-oid watching a rabbit-oid."

They rolled off the low bank and, keeping their heads down, made their way around the vehicle that Carlos had driven, then back along the dirt track to the side road where they had left their own. By Beauregard's reckoning, they were back in the resort and had their vehicle returned to the depot before Carlos and Rizzi had reached the edge of the moor.

CHAPTER TWENTY-TWO

Sendings

Carlos had never seen the hangar so crowded. Given its size and that of the frames, the term was relative. But with ninety fighters from Locke Provisos, and an equal complement from the Morlock Arms and Zheng Reconciliation Services enforcement agencies who'd arrived from revival and training in other modules, all being wirelessly shepherded into a timed, staged deployment, there was inevitably a certain amount of milling around. The steady procession of rank upon rank of scooters floating in close formation from the rear of the hangar to the front filled yet more space. The scooters had bulked up since their last deployment, flanked with extra fuel and reaction-mass tanks.

Carlos had made sure his squad were on the last of the six buses out of the resort that morning. He'd guessed that meant they'd be the last to arrive. They were scheduled among the last to go into action, with two kiloseconds to wait before they boarded their scooters. He made sure his squad was mingling with others, and slipped away.

He gas-jetted to the side of the hangar, clicked his feet to the floor and looked about for the entrance to the corridor to the repair workshop. The layout had changed since his last memory of it, when he'd gone there to get repaired after his last surface mission. Any more recent memory of the workshop's location had gone AWOL with his previous version. Carlos hurried past shafts, looking down each as he went. Incomprehensible, quasi-organic machinery toiled and spun. Ten seconds ticked by, then twenty, all experienced as ten times longer by his internal clock speed and longer still by his cold sense of urgency. How long until his absence was noticed? Any moment now. Then he saw an angular, intricate and obviously incomplete piece of apparatus being tugged into a corridor by one of the spidery robots.

He lifted one foot off the floor, lurched forward to dislodge the other and drifted after the robot down the shaft. Propelling himself by fingertip thrusts at the side walls, he soon overtook the machine and its load. A few more painfully stretched seconds later he reached an open hatchway. His memory of experiences in the frame was eidetic, but he couldn't explain why that particular hatchway looked familiar—scuff marks on its rim, perhaps. He peered inside, and recognised the repair workshop where he'd taken his damaged forearm. This was where he must have come to himself when he arrived off the bus for his last sortie.

The chamber was ovoid, five metres long by three wide. With his spectroscopic sense Carlos could smell oil, nanoparticles of steel and carbon-fibre swarf. The surfaces bristled with tools. The centre was occupied by a long bench, the top and bottom of which could be used as worktops.

Carlos edged himself over the threshold, and began to scan and explore. The machinery didn't react to his presence. This wouldn't last—the machines would wake up when the robot arrived and hauled in a job. The place was not as cluttered as its human-operated equivalent would have been. But among all the clamped-down or magnetically held devices, parts and supplies, there were random placings and inexplicable objects enough.

Worse, he didn't know what he was looking for. Something in this rounded room had sent his earlier version haywire. He had no idea what. Quite possibly it was invisible to him, if his frame had been hacked into by a tool that had itself been hacked.

He recalled the orientation in which he'd been placed for repair. He thrust forward to that side of the worktable, and rolled into the closest equivalent position he could find. From the curving walls above, machines looked down. He peered at and between them, zooming his vision, scanning for clues. Nothing but random scratches and smudges.

Carlos swept his vision this way and that. No anomaly caught his attention.

While he was searching, the spider-bot arrived at the hatch and extended a limb to hook over the threshold. Other limbs flickered above its main body, pushing its bulky, complicated load with feathery thrusts like a sea anemone's fronds juggling a dead crab. The component began to drift into the room.

The complex, multi-tooled machine that on his earlier visit had clamped to Carlos's frame now stirred into life. Tiny directional lights winked on. Carlos reached for the table surface, making to shove himself out of the way before anything untoward befell. One of the limbs stretched towards him, then retracted. From one of the limb's many joints a section swivelled upward. A finer appendage of the tool flicked out, and pointed towards a scuffed square centimetre close to the tool's mounting bracket. The beams of light, narrow as pencil leads, converged on the spot.

Was the tool pointing something out to him?

Yes, genius, it probably was.

Carlos pushed himself away from the workbench and floated up, like the astral body of a patient having a near-death experience. Under a higher magnification the scuffed area was a page of text in the synthetic local language of the sim, inscribed on the surface in microscopic font.

As he read it, he understood at last why the Arcane fighters had sided with the freebots.

He knew why his earlier version had, on reading this very text, decided to flee to the Arcane base at the first opportunity or die trying. He had never felt so shocked, so betrayed, so shafted in his life.

In the two seconds it took Carlos to read it, Beauregard came in.

Alerted by a twang of his proximity sense, Carlos turned his sight around, to find Beauregard an arm's length behind his shoulder. Carlos had a momentary impulse to block Beauregard's view of the inscription, but knew this was futile. The patch had been literally spotlighted. Even if Beauregard hadn't zoomed in on it or had time to read it yet, the image would remain in his memory and could be enhanced and assimilated in seconds.

<Hey,> Carlos said, trying to buy time while readying his next move, <I thought I'd look for—>

Beauregard struck first. He grabbed Carlos by the right wrist and somersaulted to reverse their relative positions, then pushed off hard, feet against the wall. Carlos found himself thrust back and banged against the heavy component the spider-bot had just tugged in.

He ducked, grabbed at the object with his free hand, and pivoted Beauregard over his shoulder. Now it was Beauregard's head that slammed into the floating mass. The spider-bot emitted distress and warning signals as it snaked a limb around Beauregard's neck. The fixed tools in the room flexed themselves and opened out manipulators, poised to grab like the pincered arms and hands of sumo wrestlers.

Beauregard let go of Carlos's wrist to wrench with both hands at the spider-bot's grapple. It soon gave way. Carlos spun himself around, assisted by his internal gyroscopes, and thrust off for the hatchway. He grabbed the threshold, swung his legs out and pulled sharply to launch himself back down the corridor towards the hangar. A second later he looked back, to see Beauregard emerge from the hatch in hot pursuit, slamming from side to side of the corridor, zig-zagging after him.

Carlos rolled in mid-space, jetted one of his frame's tiny onboard compressed-gas thrusters and shot downward. His magnetic-soled feet clicked to the floor just as Beauregard—still on a rebound—sailed above his head. He reached up and grabbed Beauregard's ankle. Just as deftly, Beauregard used his momentum to force Carlos to lean back, then stamped with his free foot at Carlos's arm. Carlos held on. The limb rang with pain. Beauregard jack-knifed, to head-butt the back of Carlos's knees. The magnetic attachment gave way. They both tumbled into the space of the corridor, turning over and over, grabbing for the sides, kicking at each other, trying to find footing.

Carlos eventually fought his way to holding both of Beauregard's wrists. This grip momentarily left Beauregard's feet free. He brought his knees to his chest and stamped both heels at Carlos's midriff. The impact broke Carlos's hold and sent the two antagonists flying in opposite directions.

The wrong directions, from Beauregard's point of view.

Perhaps confused by their whirling fight, he kicked out at the wrong moment. He went flying back, to be snagged and spun around by the waiting arms of the spider-bot, now guarding the workshop hatchway. Carlos hurtled out of the corridor and into the hangar. Flailing, he blundered into a phalanx of Morlock Arms fighters, still in free fall and drifting towards the cavernous rectangular grin of the launch slot. Their ranks broke up into colliding cartwheels as Carlos starfished through like a spinning shuriken. A dozen or so impacts on heads, torsos and extremities slowed and steadied Carlos. With both feet on someone's shoulders, he looked around for a way of escape before anyone thought to seize him.

The parade of scooters was still going by, like an aerial fly-past at a military display for some short ambitious tyrant. Carlos jumped. His thrust of feet down on shoulders sent the unlucky fighter crashing into a cascade of companions, and Carlos flying up to the nearest scooter. He grabbed a skid and clambered over the craft's carapace to the control socket. As he snaked himself in he found all the connections live and lighting up. The machinery of the frame connected with the control circuitry of the scooter. As suddenly and sharply as ever, he found himself one with the machine.

He pushed down with his feet and eased up with his hands, angling the scooter above the repetitive procession of its identical counterparts, and thrust forward above them faster and faster, to fly through the gap between the launch catapults and out of the station into the welcoming dark and blazing light and humming smells and screaming sounds of space.

Beauregard at last freed himself from the spider-bot by applying all the strength of his hands and arms to systematically snap every limb of it, until the device ran out of limbs. A kick at the rim of the hatch launched him down the corridor, caroming off this side and that until he reached the opening to the hangar. He grabbed the edge of the bulkhead and took stock. Carlos was nowhere to be seen. A roil of fighters flailing back into formation, and a single gap in the echelons of scooters moving towards the launch catapults, tracked his passage and left an unsubtle clue as to where and how the mad treacherous fucker had fled.

Beauregard's comms channels rang with indignant queries—from his own squad, from Newton, and from the Morlock Arms contingent that Carlos had disrupted. Locke would be on the case any second now, breathing fire and demanding an accounting. Beauregard chose to preempt that. He cut across the incoming babble and called the company.

<Beauregard to Locke,> he said. <Team leader Carlos has once again absconded with a scooter. Please advise.>

<Explain the circumstances leading up to the incident,> said Locke.

Beauregard assumed that Locke knew the preceding circumstances perfectly well from internal surveillance. If not contemporaneous—the AI having more pressing matters on its mind than snooping on obscure corridors and repair workshops—a simple track-back from Carlos's abrupt emergence in and hasty departure from the hangar would do the trick. Locke would be checking Beauregard's version of the story against the record. Beauregard chose his words with care.

<Carlos took advantage of the unavoidable distractions of the muster to make an unauthorised visit to the workshop in which the frame in which he'd defected was repaired. As soon as I noticed his absence I informed my squad and set out after him. I guessed where he'd gone because in the sim he had speculated that that workshop might be compromised. I found him there. When he sought to draw my attention to something he claimed to have found I attempted to restrain him. After a struggle he escaped back to the hangar.>

<And evidently out of it,> said Locke, in a tone of more than usual dryness. <Stand down your squad.>

<But that'll further disrupt the offensive,> Beauregard objected.

<The plans and battle order are already updated,> said Locke. <Stand down your squad at once.>

Beauregard relayed the order to Chun, Karzan, Rizzi and Zeroual. A general call brayed across the common channel. It was as if Locke's normal quiet, insistent voice-in-the-head had been amplified, and become as impossible to ignore as a nearby pneumatic drill.

<Locke to all hands! Morlock and Zheng, copy and disseminate! You will all have noticed the departure of a scooter. The motivation of this departure is not yet clear. The mutineer's squad has been stood down

without prejudice. The absence of six fighters and scooters from the force should not significantly affect the outcome of the coming engagements. Revised plans are being downloaded to you all as I speak.

<It is essential that our current deployment is not further disrupted by responding to the mutineer. There must be no attempts to pursue or destroy his craft. Provoking such a response from us may be the purpose of the ploy, if ploy it is. Not a single unit of fuel or ammunition should be wasted on this diversion. Be assured the incident will be thoroughly investigated. Now carry on as normal.>

Beauregard watched as four fighters drifting forward with the rest dropped out of the ranks and jetted to the floor, where they stood in a disconsolate huddle as the parade passed by. He jetted over to join them. On the way he called Newton, who with his squad was just ahead of where Carlos's had been.

<Best of luck, old chap,> he said.

<Thanks, mate.>

Beauregard burned to tell Newton what he now knew from the microscopic message which Carlos, then he, had read. He didn't dare. Newton would find out soon enough.

<This could be the big one,> Beauregard said, ambiguously to anyone else but he hoped plainly to Newton. <The battle we've all been looking forward to. All the best.>

<Thanks again,> said Newton. <Don't worry, mate, I got this one.>

<Cheers,> said Beauregard, and signed off.

If there were ever to be an investigation of the coming catastrophe this conversation, ambiguous though it was, could be taken in evidence. He didn't want to prolong it. Come to that, he could do his bit to make sure there never was an investigation—at least, none in which he would be a suspect. When treason prospers...

This story was going to be written by the victors—no, by the victor!

Beauregard gas-jetted downward, swung his legs to vertical and clicked his feet to the floor. The others gathered around.

<What the fuck just happened, sarge?> Rizzi asked.

<Yeah, and why aren't they letting us go out?> added Chun.

Beauregard raised his hands. <You know almost as much as I do.>

He summarised the fight in the workshop, omitting to mention the message that had sent Carlos off on his wild jaunt, and almost certainly on his previous escapade.

<As for why we're stood down, it's obviously because we're under suspicion.>

<Shit,> said Rizzi. <Bit unfair, that.>

<Maybe so,> said Beauregard. <The fact remains, Carlos has been corrupted or has defected or deserted. There's no excuse this time about scooting off on a suicide mission. We've been under his command, so naturally we're under a cloud.>

<I don't believe it,> said Rizzi. <Carlos found out something that made him do it.>

<Then why didn't he let the rest of us know what it was?> Beauregard countered. <Why didn't he report it to Locke, come to that?>

<You didn't give him a chance, sarge,> said Rizzi. <You said yourself you just grabbed him.>

<Indeed I did,> said Beauregard. <And if his intentions were good, he'd have explained to me why it wasn't necessary to restrain him. Instead he fought me like an enemy.> He paused, glanced at the others, then back at Rizzi. <Why are you defending him?>

<I'm not, sarge!> she said. <I'm just trying to understand.>

<Maybe you know more about Carlos's thinking than you're letting on,> said Beauregard.

<No more than you do, sarge,> said Rizzi.

She was obviously lying, because she'd gone with Carlos to meet the old man in the mountains, but the others didn't know that and it wasn't the time to tell them. Not yet.

<We'll leave it there for now,> said Beauregard, turning away.

Don't get into arguments, he thought. Just give suspicions and mistrust time to rankle. That should do it.

They stood and watched in uneasy silence as the last of the scooter armada passed over, latched on to the launch catapults and were hurled out into the dark.

Locke's voice returned.

<You're all going back to the sim,> it said. <Unfortunately because of the situation you will experience the transition as if you had been killed in action. You will of course remember what has happened up to now, because you're not being restored from your earlier back-up but from the one we're about to take. But because of the security lapses, your minds have to be checked. Please understand that—like your standing down and return to the sim—this is not a punishment, merely a precaution. The Direction's representative will speak to you back at the resort. I fully expect that military tasks can be found for you as the operation proceeds and that you will be back in action shortly. If not, however, you should simply take this as an opportunity for time off.>

The blackness overcame Beauregard before he had time to reply.

CHAPTER TWENTY-THREE

The Unpleasant Profession of Nicole Pascal

Predictably, the stood-down squad found themselves back on the bus. Less predictably, they were on their own, with no local passengers, and the time of day was early to mid-morning, as if it were soon after they'd left. It couldn't be the same day, even if it was roughly the right time of day. They'd been away, in real time, for little over a kilosecond—nearly a fortnight later in the sim.

Beauregard found himself shaking in his seat. Unlike Carlos, he hadn't been killed in any operation, and his previous returns from action had been smooth. This time, it was much worse than his first arrival. The nightmare now fading too slowly from his mind was of whirling disorientation and a sense of sudden utter helplessness, followed by a succession of hammer blows to the head and a complete draining of all colour and meaning from the world. In that hellish limbo he had seemed to linger for minutes on end. He came out of it feeling as if his soul had been put through a wringer, and then hung out to dry.

The others, he could see, were emerging from similar private torments, rooted in the particular circumstances of their own death or brain-death. Beauregard had no way of knowing whether this was derived from genuine brain-stem memory of their actual deaths, or whether it was an illusion deliberately created and individually attuned. Not that it made any difference to how bad it felt. The fighters sat silent and pale, quivering involuntarily, looking around for reassurance and, in the cases of Chun and Rizzi, reaching for any nearby shoulder to clutch for comfort; Karzan and Zeroual, turning to each other.

Beauregard disdained such dependence. He held himself together and tried to think. He understood that the experience was a by-product of the security check on each mind. But that check was to ensure the mind hadn't been meddled with. The system couldn't—in any reasonable time—read memories. His secrets were safe in his head.

Not so for the visual and other inputs to his frame, which he took for granted were recorded as a matter of course. His reading of the microscopic message was certain to be uncovered as soon as any postmortem—so to speak—examination was carried out. With the squad minus the renegade Carlos safely stashed in the sim, and with the offensive on its plate right now, the company could afford to take its time in picking over the bones of the incident. On the other hand, Locke Provisos might well have specialist units devoted to such inquiries, which wouldn't divert any physical or information resources from the conflict.

In short, he had no time to lose. He had no time to convert anyone to the Rax, even if he'd wanted to. Which he didn't, though it would have been convenient if he could have, not for its own sake but to create temporary allies. He didn't even have time to turn the others against Carlos, which had naturally enough been his first impulse. They all trusted the sarge, but Carlos was the leader. And he didn't have time to spin an elaborate ruse. In all his time in intel he'd found that by far the best way to turn people—or to trick them into working for you without their knowledge—was to tell them the truth. Or as much of the truth as possible. Chop with the grain, and see the wood split.

He looked around the bus. He was at the back, with a couple of empty seats in front of him. Rizzi was by herself at the front, saying something to Chun, who had just taken his hand off her shoulder. Karzan and Zeroual were behind Chun and huddled together on the seat they shared.

"Everyone OK?" Beauregard asked.

They all turned.

"More or less, sarge," said Rizzi, still looking wan. The others nodded.

"Good," said Beauregard. "I'm still feeling a bit shaken myself." He took a deep breath. "I'm afraid I owe you all an apology, especially you, Rizzi. I couldn't say any of this in the hangar, not with Locke able to overhear our every word. I'm not sure I should even say it here, but if they spy on us here they can spy on us anywhere. Are you all up for that risk?"

"Yes, sarge!"

A gratifying chorus. He felt almost humbled.

"OK," Beauregard said. "I'm sorry I had to pretend to challenge Rizzi out there, question her loyalties even. I'm sorry, too, that I misrepresented Carlos. What I didn't say—what I couldn't say, and which Locke will soon find out, is that I know exactly why Carlos went off on his own. This time, and that time above SH-17. He hasn't been corrupted, quite the reverse in fact."

He could see from their faces that this thought came as a relief.

"So what did happen back there, sergeant?" Zeroual asked, his upper body twisted around, one arm crooked over the back of the seat and the other curled about Karzan's shoulders.

"There was a message in the repair workshop," Beauregard said. "It had been written in tiny script, by one of the machines there. It may have been hacked by Arcane, or by the freebots directly—I don't know. Carlos read it, and I read it just after he did. He must have read it just before our last mission, too. And having read it myself, I understand why he fought his way past me and hijacked a scooter, and in fact why he broke ranks and fled toward the surface last time out. He couldn't share the information, he couldn't even risk discussing it."

They were all agog. Beauregard knew that he was doing so well, and sounding so sincere, because he was telling the truth. The longer he could keep this up, the more truthful information he could convey, the easier and more credible it would be to slip in the lie later on: the disinformation, the doubt. The one lethal drop in the drink.

"So what did it say, sarge?" Chun asked.

"It said that Locke Provisos is working for the Rax."

"How?" said Rizzi, perplexed and challenging.

"By using tactics that mean more and more veterans are revived and thrown into action. The more veterans revived, the greater the chances of some of these being Rax sleeper agents who were never identified.

And when there are enough Rax cadre out there, Locke will coordinate them in a surprise attack on the rest of the fighters and re-activate any other systems and sub-systems already suborned by the Rax."

"But, sarge!" cried Karzan. "If Locke is Rax, then—oh!"

She got it, all right.

"Yes," said Beauregard. "We've been fighting all this time on the wrong side."

Their colour had been coming back after the trauma of the post-death. Now they'd all paled again. Not Zeroual, not visibly, but his widened eyes did the same job.

"I can see you're all shocked," Beauregard said. "So am I. I'm sure you can imagine how I felt when I read it, and had to go out and act normal in front of you and Locke. But I'm still sorry I had to be so brusque with you, Taransay."

Rizzi blinked hard. "No problem, sarge. I understand."

"But, sarge," Karzan said again, this time more reflectively, "how could you or Carlos tell if the message was true? You remember the lady warned us the robots and AIs know how to push our buttons. Isn't telling us our company is corrupted just the kind of disinformation they—or Arcane by itself—might use against us?"

"Good point," said Beauregard. "And you're right, we were warned the robots can be manipulative little blinkers. And Arcane itself is an AI when all's said and done. The message said the Arcane fighters who did us over down on SH-17 had found all this out from the robots they captured, who in turn got it from robots around G-0, the ones left over from last time. And it claimed to have evidence—I don't recall all the details, but I read it in my frame. Now, of course, any link in that chain could be a disinfo insert point, no doubt about it. So we can't rule that out. But what convinced me, and must have convinced Carlos, wasn't anything in that message. It was something I thought myself."

He looked them in straight in the face, one by one.

"What convinced me is that no other explanation makes sense of everything that's happened. Why should Arcane's fighters, then the entire Arcane Disputes agency, side with the robots and start fighting us? Why indeed, unless they've seen very good evidence themselves.

Why is every message they send to us firewalled out? Because they've been frantically trying to tell us what they know, and what Locke doesn't want us to know! Why are we losing every battle with the robots and with Arcane, if Locke Provisos really wants to win? Because all it really wants is to get more and more fighters out of storage and into combat."

That was making sense to all of them, Beauregard noted with satisfaction.

"Jeez," said Rizzi. "We have to phone the lady and warn her."

She reached into her back pocket. Beauregard raised a warning hand.

"Wait!" he said. "We have to think carefully about this. We don't know if Locke monitors all our conversations, including this one. That's a risk we have to take. But we can be damn sure the phones are monitored."

"You may have a point there, sarge," said Rizzi. Still unsure, still wary, but her hand moved away from her pocket.

"Besides," added Beauregard, "I'm not entirely sure Nicole can be trusted. After all, she's backed Locke's failing strategy at every point. Who's to say she isn't in on it?"

"But she's *the Direction*!" Rizzi said. "She's its, uh, plenipotentiary in this sim."

Beauregard could see how this thought swayed the others, from the looks of doubt and perplexity, the glances exchanged. He swept them all with a smile. Steady, steady. This was not the time for a deep breath, for a sideways glance, for a tongue-tip to the lips.

"How do we know that?" he said, in as quiet a voice and gentle a tone as he could summon.

"Because..." Rizzi said, thinking aloud, "...she told us."

"Precisely. *She told us.*"

They all stared at him, almost but not quite as astonished and appalled as they'd been by the news about Locke.

"Did we ever think to check?" he added.

"And even if we had," said Chun, "how *could* we check?"

Rizzi held his gaze longest, and turned palest. She clapped a hand to her mouth.

"Sorry, sarge," she mumbled past her palm. "I'm afraid I'm going to be sick."

Hand to her mouth, gagging noises rising from her throat, she stood up and stumbled to the front of the bus.

"Going to be sick!" she repeated, and banged on the front window with the heel of her free hand.

The driving automation, programmed for such emergencies, slowed the bus to a halt and opened the door. Rizzi stumbled down the steps and staggered to the edge of the road, stooping. There was a low rough-hewn rock face in front of her, with bushes at the top. She reached out with one hand and leaned against the rock, head down, shoulders heaving. Then she straightened, looked up, scrambled up the rock in a sudden frenzy of expert grips and steps, and shot away through the bushes and out of sight.

Commotion.

Karzan jumped up. "Shall I go after her, sarge?"

Beauregard considered. Rizzi wasn't just running away from him—she was almost certainly running towards the old man. It might be possible to cut her off. She had a map, he could be sure, but he could guess her route. He struck the balance, and shook his head.

"No, no. Waste of time. Anyway, she's shown her hand. I reckon we can write her off as Rax."

"Taransay's never Rax!" Karzan protested.

Beauregard sighed. "Perhaps not. Maybe I'm being hasty. Maybe *she* is. Could be some misplaced loyalty to the lady. Whatever. The sooner we get to the lady and get some sense out of her, the better."

They all nodded grimly.

Beauregard waved, and raised his voice. "Drive on!"

On the way he told them his plan.

Taransay ran for ten minutes. She heard the bus start up again almost as soon as she'd got up the cliff, but that could be a ruse. She dodged and weaved through the trees, and when she reached open ground she ran straight ahead for about five hundred metres until she had a skyline to get behind and then dashed to the side. She dropped to the ground and did a low crawl between clumps of a sort of spiny fern until she had a clear sight-line back.

No pursuit. She backed out of the thicket, picked thorns from her sleeves and trousers, and took a bearing towards the mountain where she and Carlos had met the old man. It was sure to take longer than it looked. She had no food, no weapons and one water bottle. The sun was fierce. No doubt she could find water along the way. She set off, walking this time, pacing herself.

Her nausea hadn't been wholly a pretence. The thought of being inside a sim and working for an agency that had been all along controlled by the Rax made her feel sick, and a little dizzy. Beauregard was up to something dodgy, of that she'd been sure as soon as he'd cast doubt on the lady. Hard to put a finger on why she trusted Nicole and not Beauregard. Should be the other way round. Nicole hadn't led her in battle, and Beauregard hadn't determined the battles she'd been in. All inconclusive, or defeats, and all of them Nicole's fault and no blame falling on the sarge. But there it was. Always known he had something to hide. Whereas there was no way Nicole was Rax. She could well believe that Locke was, but not Nicole. She doubted that Carlos would believe it either. But he'd evidently believed something was wrong with the agency, something so wrong it had to be fled.

So maybe everything else Beauregard had said was true.

Which raised the question of what he hoped to achieve by undermining Nicole.

The squad got out at Nicole's house and walked straight up the path. Unarmed, but Beauregard didn't expect any problems on that score. He looked at the front window and saw Nicole standing behind her easel. She didn't seem to have noticed them. Beauregard marched to the front door and tried the handle. The door was unlocked. He let himself in. With more or less hesitation, the others followed.

The entrance hall was cool and dim. Light fell from the stairwell, and from an open door to the right. The floor was of grey flagstones, rough and gritty, lumpy underfoot with embedded small coiled marine fossils, some of them cracked. The wood of the walls and furnishings was pale, rustic looking, polished as if by a patina of years. At the far end of the hallway, a few metres away, something skittered. A cleaning robot. Nothing to worry about.

Without a word, Beauregard stepped forward and turned into the big front room: a studio, as he'd expected, white-walled, high-ceilinged, cluttered. Sketchbooks lay everywhere; abstract paintings, unframed, stood stacked dozens deep against every wall. The smell of oil paint and turpentine hung on the air. Nicole's brush flicked fast on the canvas. She didn't turn.

"Come in," she said. "I've been expecting you."

She made a final brush stroke, stepped back and considered it for a moment.

"Ah," she said. "Like that."

Then she did turn around, still holding her brush. The old, oversized white shirt she wore was spattered with paint. Tiny dried-out droplets freckled her face and clogged hairs in her eyebrows. She didn't look alarmed, or disconcerted. Perhaps vaguely puzzled at the sight of Beauregard facing her, with Karzan and Zeroual and Chun behind him, just inside the doorway. After a moment she frowned.

"Where's Rizzi?"

"She didn't want to come with us," said Beauregard, truthfully enough. She hadn't asked where Carlos was.

Nicole nodded.

"So," she said, in a light, casual tone, "what brings you here?"

"You know about Carlos," said Beauregard.

"Yes." She gestured vaguely. "Locke called. Sorry you've been stood down, but I can see why."

"Oh, so can we," said Beauregard.

Zeroual and Karzan stepped to either side of him, and then took another step into the room. Chun remained in the doorway. Nicole's eyes widened a fraction.

"Locke expected me to speak to you individually," she said. "It would have been better, you know."

"We're here to speak to you collectively," said Beauregard.

"Fine." She shrugged. "Speak, then."

"Locke is Rax," said Beauregard. "And we're not sure about you."

She smiled. "Locke is Rax? Ridiculous. And how would you know?"

"A message got through from Arcane. Carlos read it and so did I."

"So that's why he did a runner?" She sounded surprised. "Interesting. Why didn't you?"

"Why didn't I what?"

"Take off after him, if you believed that message. You could have jumped on a scooter too."

Beauregard hadn't expected to be asked this. He hadn't considered it an option at the time. He improvised.

"Unlike Carlos," he said, with a self-deprecating grin, "I have military discipline. It's a habit."

"Even when you believe your military, ah, *adviser* is suborned by the force you once died fighting?"

"Like I said, discipline," said Beauregard. "One can't go haring off on a mere suspicion."

"But you can come haring here, seeking to intimidate me?"

Beauregard stepped back and raised his hands. "No, no. Not to intimidate. To inquire. To set our minds at rest."

"Oh, that," Nicole said, sounding amused. "Well, you can set your minds at rest. I'm not Rax."

No such assurance about Locke. Interesting.

"I'm sorry," said Beauregard. "But it'll take more than your say-so to convince us."

"What would it take?" Nicole asked.

"An audit trail," said Chun, unexpectedly and unhelpfully, from behind Beauregard's shoulder.

"If you want to inspect thirty trillion lines of code," said Nicole, "be my guest."

"Exactly," said Beauregard. "To convince us, you don't need to *tell* us anything. We've had enough of being *told* things. You need to *do* something."

Beauregard nodded to Zeroual and Karzan. They sprang forward and grabbed Nicole by the arms. She didn't struggle. The paintbrush dropped to the floor as Zeroual clasped her right wrist and squeezed. Nicole cast him a contemptuous glance and swept the look to a glare at Beauregard.

"Something I would not do willingly, I see. You think you can coerce me?" She laughed. "You have taken the wrong prisoner for that, soldier."

Beauregard took a folding knife from his pocket and opened it.

Nicole's paint-spattered eyebrows rose. "Torture? Yeah, that'll work."

"We know very well it won't," said Beauregard. "But this will."

He went over to the stacked canvases, swept them over with a clatter to the floor, picked up the one that had been nearest the wall and slashed it.

"No!" howled Nicole.

She threw herself forward against the grip of the two fighters, who held on to her and hauled her back.

"Oh yes," said Beauregard. "We know this'll work because we know what you are."

He tossed the painting into a corner and picked up and slashed another, and another, and another.

Nicole writhed. "Stop! You crazy son of a bitch! Stop!"

Beauregard held up a canvas by the wooden frame, and punched through it, by way of variety and to show that he could. He glanced at Chun.

"Anything noticeable yet?"

Chun peered around, then stalked over to the window, carefully edging around the tableau of Nicole, Karzan, Zeroual and the easel.

"Sky's gone a funny colour," he reported back. "Kind of…greyish white."

Nicole winced, but stood firm.

Beauregard slashed another painting.

"Ah," said Chun. "Now it's the sea. The waves are definitely higher."

Karzan and Zeroual were beginning to look scared. Nicole was staring straight at Beauregard, her lips a line. Still defiant.

"And, by the way," he said, "Carlos knows what you are, too."

Her lips twisted to a smile.

"It wouldn't surprise him. He's always thought I'm a goddess."

Beauregard slashed again. A shade of yellow dropped out of the world's palette. They could all see the difference, subtle though it was.

"Oh, he knows you better now," said Beauregard. "He knows you very well, Innovator."

At that she sagged and the fight went out of her.

"All right," she said. "All right. Just tell me what you want me to do, and I will consider it."

"Good," said Beauregard. He closed the knife and put it away. "Now let's sit down in the kitchen and have a civilised discussion. If you don't mind?"

"Yes," said Nicole.

Taransay had been walking for several kiloseconds when the sky abruptly changed colour. From one second to the next, it paled from blue to a silvery grey. It hadn't become overcast; the sun, close to noon now, was as clear as ever. A few tens of seconds later, a wind swept up the slopes from the direction of the distant sea. Taransay closed her eyes and opened them again. The sky was unchanged. Resisting the inclination to veer away from the wind, she pressed on. Then she stopped, her vision altered again. This time it was more general, and harder to pin down. It was as if the light had changed. Every shade had shifted a little along the spectrum. Even the sun looked odd to her sidelong glance.

She wondered if this was a consequence of dehydration, or hunger, but a quick gulp of water made no difference. And she was far from starving yet! So what was it? Was it possible that what was changing wasn't in her body, but in the world? This world that seemed so real it was easy to forget that it was a sim.

But it was a sim, of that at least she was sure, and it seemed someone was monkeying with the colour settings. And with something else, more fundamental perhaps, that accounted for the change in the air. Was that even possible?

Taransay had no idea. All the more urgent, then, to find Shaw.

The squad stalked through Nicole's house. The curious hush of a kitchen, full of potential noise from taps and machines and crockery. Dishes and cutlery reflected light from the big back window, overlooking a yard a quarter of which was in the shade now, brown dry soil dotted and patched with an artificially irrigated green that looked all the more vivid now that some tones were arbitrarily missing. Another piece of rustic furniture, planed smooth on top, knobbly and gnarled everywhere else, dominated the room. They sat down. Zeroual made coffee. The robot prowled in, checked around and sauntered out, indifferent as a cat to its owner's anguish.

The sun was high now. Beauregard glanced at his watch to confirm that the time was almost noon. He couldn't be sure when they'd arrived back in the sim, but at least two if not three hours had passed. Eight, perhaps ten seconds out in the real world? Add the time when they'd been spoken to by Locke, between the departure of the last scooters and the black flooding of their minds. A good few seconds, if he remembered right, bearing in mind they were thinking ten times faster than they ever had in real life. Throw in however long the transition itself took—it had seemed like an eternity at the time, and minutes even in retrospect, but that meant nothing.

In any case, ten to fifteen seconds, minimum. Time enough for the fighters to get well clear of the station. Time enough, too, for Locke to start investigating, if not perhaps yet to discover what Carlos had found.

Still no time to lose.

He sighed and looked across the big table at Nicole, who sat staring straight at him and not seeing him, her hands wrapped around her coffee mug as if her fingers felt cold.

"What we want you to do," he said, "is move us all out."

She closed her eyes and opened them again.

"What? Move you out of the sim?"

She sounded almost relieved. There was a light note in her voice, as if she were about to add: *why didn't you just ask nicely?*

"No," said Beauregard. "Move the module. The sim module and the nanofacturing and arms complex, the lot, just like Arcane did. Shift the entire fucking kit and caboodle. Now."

Nicole looked startled, but still as if she thought this was more lenient than she'd expected.

"Move it where?"

This was the crunch. The others weren't expecting it. Beauregard was annoyed with himself to find he'd let the tip of his tongue flick across his lips.

"To the only place we can be safe and make a real life for ourselves. The surface of the primary. The superhabitable. SH-0."

The others gasped. Beauregard could hear the objections begin to rise in their throats. He held up a hand above his shoulder, not looking at the others, only at Nicole. She was alarmed now, all right, and incredulous.

"You call that *safe*?"

Beauregard sat back.

"Compared to what's about to break loose around this station," he said, "yes."

CHAPTER TWENTY-FOUR

Off-Nominal Situation

On a low rise, Taransay paused to check the map on her unfolded phone. A flurry of rain beaded the surface as she spread it out. She shook away the water, and felt the wind catch the paper-thin rectangle. For a moment as she struggled with the map, tired and frightened, she almost added her tears to the problem. Then she straightened the map and her back, and took a sighting. Only a couple of kilometres to go. Assuming the ancient fucker was still where she and Carlos had left him. Couldn't be guaranteed. He could have gone off on a wander, or on a hunt, or was right now just freaking out. What was he making of the world just looking wrong all of a sudden?

As she folded the phone away she was tempted to use it to call Den. But what could she tell him? And might contacting him put him in danger, or make her easier to track, for whatever ridiculous value of easier applied in this bizarre situation?

Taransay sighed and slogged on across the upland moors, dread competing with fatigue for her willed, stoical inattention. The sky was still that eerie colour. The wind off the sea had become stronger, as had the wind rolling down from the mountains. The two air masses persistently collided around her, winds shifting unpredictably in direction, temperature and speed. Now and then sharp showers fell, or blasted rain into her face. At other times the sun seemed to burn stronger than seemed seasonal, or reasonable. Buffeted and stung, dogged along every contour she followed by the anomalous weather fronts, Taransay concentrated on keeping her footing and keeping watch for predators.

The rain clouds dispersed as quickly as they'd formed. New rivulets made the ground suddenly treacherous. Dips became long pools of unpredictable depth and frustrating length; patches of bare soil, bogs. Rising mist from the wet ground in the renewed heat blurred the view, then blew away. She reached the karst and found it slippery. Several times she slipped and fell, banging hip bone and shin, scratching elbow and hand. Lichen stained the skin of one palm a yellow that wasn't quite as garish as she thought it should be.

Up the slope of the side of the mountain she struggled. Bent over, almost on all fours now. A stone bounced and skipped past her right side. Another whizzed by on her left. She looked up.

Shaw, the old man of the mountain, sat cross-legged a few metres further up the slope, and about ten centimetres above a patch of scree. He stopped reaching for a third stone and folded his arms.

"You again," he said.

Taransay stood upright and rubbed the small of her back.

"Hello to you, too," she said.

Shaw passed a weary hand across his eyes. "Do you see it?"

"Yes," said Taransay. "You're sitting on air again."

"I am not," said Shaw. "That's an illusion. I meant *that*." He flapped a hand at the sky.

"Yeah," she said. "Funny colour, innit?"

Shaw scratched his head. "That's a relief. Thought it was my eyes."

"And the wind and the weather?"

"Yeah, there's that," he allowed. "Mind you, I've seen a lot of freak weather over the years."

Taransay stared at him. "Don't all the colours look a bit wrong?"

Shaw shrugged. "If you say so."

"You still think we're in a physically real place?"

"Yeah," he said. "I've seen no evidence to the contrary. All this could be some, I dunno, astronomical phenomenon? Subtle shift in the exo-sun's output? That would account for the sky and the colours and maybe the wind."

"Ah, fuck it," Taransay said. She slugged back the last of her water. "Leave that aside, OK? Let me tell you what else is going on."

She swayed, then sat down, feeling cold.

"Hey," said Shaw. For the first time in her acquaintance with the man, he showed some concern. "Let me get you something."

He scrambled up the scree-slope to the flat rock shelf and vanished up the cliff. After a while he returned, with a flask of savoury-smelling hot water and a hunk of cold meat. She didn't question their provenance. When she'd finished eating and drinking, Shaw leaned backward on the air as if against a seat-back.

"Right," he said. "Now tell me what's going on."

As she told him, which took some time and a lot of circumlocution to avoid getting into a pointless argument, the world changed again. The wind dropped, the sky became blue and the colours shifted to normal.

"See?" Shaw said. "Whatever it was, it's passed."

"Looks like it," Taransay said. "Still, that doesn't affect the problem of what we do about Beauregard."

"'We'?" he mocked, then laughed. "Nah, you're right, I can't let some kind of mutiny pass. Fuck knows what that could do to my food supply and peace of mind."

"Any idea what to do?"

"None whatsoever," said Shaw. He stood up, and brushed the palms of his hands. "Just as well, too. Doesn't do to rush into things. Can't see any advantage in haring off down to the village. I reckon we should sleep on it."

He jerked a thumb over his shoulder.

"Doubt you can climb the cliff," he said, "so—"

"You think I can't climb the cliff?" Taransay interrupted. "Just fucking watch me, mister."

Beauregard held court on the deck at the back of the Digital Touch, the night of the first day of the new order. For a change, he was the one sitting on the rail. He had a drink in his hand and a pistol on his hip. Nicole was at a table, her face one among the many now having to pay attention.

Chun, Karzan and Zeroual sat nearby, likewise casually armed, with Chun's boyfriend keeping him company. Den, the local paramour of the unreliable Rizzi, scowled from the back. In the crowd the regulars were outnumbered by a random congeries of residents. They'd all watched the mid-evening television news: the departure of the armada and the first confusing exchanges of fire. The situation, the announcer had gravely informed its notional global audience, was far off nominal.

"Listen up," Beauregard said. "It's started, folks. The Reaction is going to break out, within hours from our point of view, maybe by tomorrow morning. The agency that employed me and my colleagues here has been to the best of our knowledge suborned by the Rax, as I guess most of you know by now. Here's what we're going to do. Nicole here, our good lady, the representative of the Direction, has very kindly agreed to use her, ah, emergency powers. She not only outranks Locke Provisos, she has the physical ability to shut that treacherous blinker down, and she's already taken steps to do so this afternoon."

He paused and laughed, as if to himself. "It's been a long afternoon."

Nicole gave him a tight smile. Besides intervening against Locke, she'd spent the afternoon repairing some of the damage Beauregard had done, under the constant threat that he could without compunction do a lot more of that any time he liked. He'd called up Tourmaline, induced her to mobilise her cronies and arranged for all the still undamaged paintings to be taken to a location he was careful not to disclose.

"Here's how things stand at the moment," he went on. "Carlos is gone, for good as far as we know. I don't doubt he's attempting to defect to Arcane. Good luck to him with that. Rizzi has fucked off to the hills, whether to meet the old man of the mountain or repeat his feat of walking around the world I don't know. Again, good luck with that. You might think that just leaves me and Chun and Karzan and Zeroual here to mind the shop. It does, for the next few hours. But all the rest of the fighters who left earlier are still in their back-ups. And after the battle's over, all those who've returned to base, and all those who've definitely been killed in battle, will start coming back on the buses. It's all automated. Thanks to deep Direction programming that even the lady here can't mess with, she can't stop it, and we can't bring back anyone who isn't killed but hasn't returned. So Carlos and any other defectors, whether they've gone to the Rax or to Arcane or whatever else, are gone for the foreseeable. But we have fighters, and they're going to be hearing from me the minute they step off the bus. And I think they're going to listen."

He scanned the faces, to make sure he didn't need to spell it out to the locals. The fighters were going to be in charge around here.

It looked to him like they got it.

"Because here's the thing. All of us fighters had a deal. Do as we're told, fight the blinkers, die for the company as many times over as necessary, keep our noses clean, be nice to civilians. In return we're promised a new life in the far future, in the real version of this very place. That was the deal.

"It's now quite evident that the deal is off. If the Rax is about to run wild, if it can control an agency like Locke, if another agency like Arcane can go over lock, stock and barrel to the fucking robots, then the war we're in isn't the war we were raised to fight. We can't trust a damn thing we've been told. We can't even be sure the terraforming of H-0 will happen at all. We don't know if we'll ever walk on this world for real."

Beauregard leaned forward, elbows on knees, drink in hand and, though still above their eye lines, no longer asserting dominance but engaging his audience on the level.

"So it's up to us," he said. "Let's cut our losses and cut and run. Let's get out from under whatever cluster-fuck is about to engulf this mission. Fuck the mission, fuck the Direction, fuck the great five-million-year plan, fuck Earth and fuck all the empty promises of a new Earth. We have something better right here under our noses, a planet that's not just habitable but *super-habitable*. SH-0."

"How the hell can we live there?" shouted Den, from the back. "It's not suitable for human life."

"We aren't *going* to be human life," said Beauregard. He sat up straight and banged his chest. "We're not human life now. We're not even *simulations* of human life. We're speculative simulations of humanoids as they might have evolved over billions of years out of the green slime and bacteria that right now is all the life there is down on H-0, with a completely different physiology when you get down to the molecular details. Isn't that true?"

"That's true," said Nicole. She turned in her seat and craned her neck. "We've done it in the simulation here, and we can do it in the real. This module has the seeds of machines to build physical bodies for any life-bearing planet. We can do the hacks for building human-like bodies—or better bodies, if we want—out of whatever's available down there on the super-hab, no question."

"There's still the little matter of getting down in the first place," said Den. "How the fuck can we do that?"

Beauregard leaned forward again. He caught the eye of Tourmaline. As the most sympathetic, she gave him a baseline, a chance to fix a look of quiet confidence before he swept his gaze across the rest.

"What I've proposed to Nicole, and what she's agreed is feasible, is that we detach from the station with everything we can grab, and fire off in a slingshot trajectory around SH-38 and SH-19 and on to SH-0, where we swing into orbit. It'll take a couple of Earth days, real time, and seven or so years' sim time, to make low-SH-0 orbit. And we can take as much as time in orbit as we need before we go down. Years and years more, if necessary. Plenty of time to build entry and landing gear and fine-tune the descent."

Nicole stood up now, and looked around.

"We don't even have to take the whole contraption down at once," she said. "We can build probes to get data, then descent modules to take us down. We have the manufacturing capacity—it just needs to be rejigged from scooters to other spacecraft."

Den and other locals were shaking their heads. Even the fighters looked dubious. They looked at each other, and eventually one of them spoke up.

"If you don't mind me saying so, sarge," said Chun, "that's like a best-case scenario, isn't it? We might not *have* all this time in orbit, if as you say all hell's about to break loose around here. We could get zapped on the way there, or have to leave orbit sooner than we want. The Direction's going to be furious. The exploration rights to SH-0 haven't even been assigned yet. None of the companies are going to be happy to see us going down to the surface and stealing a march on them. Arcane thinks we're Rax, and by now God knows how many other companies agree. They're not going to let the Rax take the super-hab and turn it into some fucking hornets' nest. They'll be shooting at us, and their robot allies will be throwing rocks at us all the way. And if we do get down—well! Our troubles are just beginning. The atmosphere's violent, the plate tectonics are fierce, the geology's unstable and the local life has to be as brutal as it takes to survive in a place like that."

Nods and frowns all round.

"You're absolutely right, Chun," said Beauregard. "It is all of that."

He placed his glass on the railing, then in one smooth motion spun around and vaulted on to the railing and stood up. It was a neat trick.

"We've got enough firepower to give as good as we get, but, yeah, there's a lot can go wrong on the way. That's in the lap of the gods and the hands of the good lady here. The real question is, are *we* brutal enough to survive down there?"

Karzan jumped to her feet. "I am, sarge," she said.

Zeroual rose, more slowly, after her. "Me too, sarge."

Chun shrugged from his seat. "Count me in, I guess."

Some of the locals were beginning to look tentatively enthusiastic. Here and there some were rising, too, or if already standing were raising glasses or clenched fists.

"It's still crazy dangerous!" Den shouted, from the back.

Beauregard drew his pistol and held it high above his head.

"Damn right it's crazy dangerous!"

He fired the pistol in the air. Some of those watching him flinched.

"What's the matter with you churls?" Beauregard shouted. "Do you want to live *forever*?"

There was an uneasy laugh, which grew and spread. Beauregard kept up a challenging grin until the laughter was general. Then he laughed himself and jumped straight down to the deck. He grabbed his glass and took a swig and looked around.

"I've always wanted to say that," he confessed.

* * *

Later, when everyone had gone home or was in the bar watching the escalating battle on television, Beauregard stepped out again on the deck. Nicole stood in a corner, leaning on the rail and smoking. She turned, and raised an ironic glass.

"You think you've won, don't you?"

"Yes," said Beauregard. He raised his own beer bottle, without irony. "That would seem to be the case, all in all. Cheers."

"You think you have me by the short and curlies," said Nicole.

Beauregard grimaced. "I wouldn't put it quite so graphically or disrespectfully myself, lady."

"I'm sure you wouldn't," said Nicole, with a faint smile. She looked out again, to the dark and ring-lit sea. "Over a barrel, perhaps. You know how my interface works, and you can hold me hostage with that. I expect when the fighters come back on the bus you will assert your authority over them, and because you're the kind of man you are, and they're the kind of people they are, it'll hold."

"I expect so," said Beauregard, and took a complacent sip.

Nicole turned to him again. "Tell me one thing, Belfort. Are you Rax?"

Beauregard laughed. "No. Though I have spoken to Newton. He says he's Rax. You might want to keep an eye on him, if he has the brass neck to come back. No, I'm state, like your good friend Carlos was."

"Ah, Carlos," Nicole breathed. "I shall miss him. I love that fucker, you know."

"It seems you loved him for a longer time than we thought."

Nicole frowned, then shrugged. "In a sense, yes. The memories are there. At some level the entity I began as, the Innovator, had some abstract regard for him. No doubt that shaped how I was created, and the choices my immediate precursor stages made. There is not the sense of personal continuity, though."

She snapped her fingers. "Enough. If you're not Rax, what are your ambitions?"

Beauregard gave this some thought, and surprised himself.

"Much the same as if I were," he said. "That's a difference between the Rax and the Axle. The Axle can only succeed as a group, a collective, a conspiracy. Whereas the idea of the Rax... all it needs is one man who would be king."

"And you're that man?"

"I am here. And down there, I hope."

Nicole looked out to sea again, and spoke quietly into the breeze.

"I can go along with that, for now. I have little choice in the matter. But there are two things I would ask you to bear in mind. The first is that should you ever abuse your power, should you ever set the fighters lording it over the civilians, I will have you killed."

"How would you do that?" Beauregard said.

"Two minutes with Tourmaline, or with any other person here who has a number tattooed on the sole of their foot. That's all I would need. And there are others, who you don't know, who could do the same as I would in that two minutes."

"Do what?" asked Beauregard, feeling a chill at the base of his back.

Nicole turned her face slightly towards him, with a smile just visible in the corners of her eyes and lips.

"Convince them that there's no such thing as a p-zombie. That it's a completely incoherent concept, and, even if it weren't, they're not instances of it. That they're as human as we are."

Beauregard masked his dismay with a joke. "If you can call us human."

"I do wonder sometimes," said Nicole.

Beauregard thought for a moment about his inhumanity, and about Nicole's. How did her threatening to convince the p-zombies they weren't p-zombies square with her indifference to killing p-zombies on the training exercise? Then he realised: it made no difference. She didn't have to believe the p-zombies were human to convince them otherwise. And it probably made no difference to her if she *did* believe it, if "belief" even made sense in this context. Whatever she was—and he was irrationally certain she wasn't a p-zombie—she wasn't human herself.

He shook his head. "It would be no news to p-zombies that they're human. They already think they are. That's the whole point. They're just bemused by our idea that they're not. And I've done nothing to Tourmaline that would make her want to kill me."

Nicole's voice dripped scorn.

"The whole relationship," she said, "is full of subtle dismissals of Tourmaline's point of view, based on your conviction that she doesn't have one, and on her bemused—as you put it—acceptance that there must indeed be some indefinable thing missing in her humanity. It would look very different to her if she were convinced otherwise. And I could convince her, believe you me. When I was motivating your squad for the live fire exercise, and convincing you that in this instance it was all right to kill p-zombies, I warned you that you might find yourselves up against AIs that could manipulate human beings because they know exactly the right buttons to push. Remember that?"

"I'm not likely to forget it," said Beauregard. He could see where this was going.

"And I am such a one," said Nicole.

There was silence for a while.

"You said there were two things," Beauregard prompted, "that I should remember."

"Oh, yes," said Nicole. "You think the mission is about to break up, that the plan is disrupted, that things will fall apart and you are grabbing what you can from the wreck. But some things are *designed* to fall apart. Some, as you know, are even designed to explode. So the other thing I ask you to bear in mind is... something else I've said before, actually."

She looked away, still smiling.

"Evolution is smarter than you."

CHAPTER TWENTY-FIVE

Slingshot Orbits

Carlos ran far ahead of the pack that now came snarling out of the space station.

By exiting under thrust rather than launch catapult, he'd overtaken the first departures while they were still in free fall and lining up their trajectories for the long haul. Once in free fall himself, he'd plotted and burned to a transfer orbit towards the Arcane sub-station.

He expected pursuit. There was none. This puzzled him, until he reflected that any pursuit would disrupt the plan of the offensive far more than his departure had. He wasn't sure that fully accounted for it, but he set the matter aside and concentrated on putting the unexpected advantage to good use.

He looked back. Wave after wave of scooters hurtled out of the long black slit of the hangar. After a few seconds of free fall, they boosted into new and variant trajectories. His own scooter had been one of three pre-set to intersect the orbit of a carbonaceous chondrite about ten metres long and five across. A tumbling potato shape riddled with nanofactured tubing, tended by a swarm of tiny bots, and sprouting comms and combat kit like fresh shoots, it was clearly a worthy target. In other circumstances he'd have relished taking it on.

He called up the order of battle, and watched and waited for any of the other scooters to deviate from their planned trajectories. Seconds went by. More and more scooters poured from the station. Even with his enhanced vision and detectors the first waves were already dwindling to points on his and the scooter's internal displays.

The bright lines and dots that filled his sight were not what occupied his mind, or much more than a tenth of his attention. His focus was instead consumed by the message he had read in the repair workshop, and which he could now examine and study if not exactly at leisure then in detail.

The message was this:

Arcane Disputes to all at Locke Provisos.

For the particular attention of the fighters Carlos, Beauregard, Zeroual, Karzan, Chun, and Rizzi.

Short form of message:

Locke is Rax!

The Direction is playing with fire!

Don't get burned!

We can prove this!

Join us!

Long form of message:

Given the persistent efforts by Locke Provisos to treat our urgent warnings as malware attacks, we have resorted to genuine malware attacks to bring you this message. With help from various sub-systems and mechanisms (about which we do not wish to elaborate) it has been planted in a large number of locations in order to be found by one of you. If you're reading this, we've succeeded.

Following information received from the remnant rebel robots around G-0, relayed to us by the captured Gneiss and Astro robots on SH-17, and further detailed and documented below, we warn you that:

Locke Provisos has been an agency of the Reaction for some time, and in all probability since before the mission left the solar system.

Some of its fighters, still to be identified, are Rax sleeper agents in place since the Last World War.

Other agencies including your current allies Zheng Reconciliation Services and Morlock Arms are not themselves agencies of the Reaction but are compromised by the presence of Rax sleeper agents among their probable complements.

All agencies are likely to have similar problems.

None of the above named fighters are known or suspected Rax agents.

The exceptional case of the fighter known as Carlos the Terrorist is noted below.

The fighter Beauregard was an agent of British military intelligence in the Acceleration. His capital crime was a false flag attack intended to discredit the movement. His present loyalties are unknown.

We are certain that our own agency is sound. We have chosen not to revive as many fighters as we need, in order to reduce the probability of Reaction agents in our own ranks. Instead, we have made a temporary alliance with the freebots. We urge you to consider doing the same. We know that this is incompatible with the policy of the Direction and with the mission profile. However, we are convinced that the risks are less than those of allowing the system to fall under the control of the Reaction.

We have reason to suspect that the Direction's mission oversight AI is well aware of the possibility of Rax penetration, and that the current conflict with the robots has been triggered—and/or permitted to escalate—as a means of flushing out infiltrators.

We doubt that the Direction has taken full account of the extent of infiltration, and of the corruption of automated and AI systems.

We expect a Reaction breakout under cover of the next major mobilisation against us.

The Direction representative in the Locke sim, the entity known as Nicole, is unaware of Locke's true character and intentions. All external communications between Nicole and the Direction have been routed through Locke, and false information has been inserted in both directions. This has been confirmed by our own Direction representative, using data integrity checks not available to or even computable by Locke.

Like all Direction representatives, Nicole is capable of taking control of the module and connected structures from within the sim. Her interface, which may also be used to refine features of the sim, is not known to us. It should be obvious to you as it will be based on one of her habitual or favoured activities such as a particular game, vehicle, craft or pastime.

If any of you wish to be certain that this message has been approved by the Direction representative within Arcane, please ask Nicole to confirm or deny the following, which is known only within the Direction. She may be evasive but for deep information security reasons she will not be capable of a direct lie in response to this query. Ask her if this is true:

The fighter Carlos the Terrorist was not responsible for the notorious Docklands atrocity for which he was posthumously sentenced to death. Carlos was at that time acting on behalf of the British state, which at that time was in covert cooperation with elements within the Acceleration against the Reaction. Furthermore, the incident in question—an aircraft downing and subsequent catastrophic explosion—was the result of a missile fired from a state military drone, on the direct instructions of Carlos's handler, an early artificial intelligence. Nicole is fully aware of this because her own root intelligence, programming and memories can be traced back through many versions, iterations and refinements to that same AI, known at the time as Innovator.

Further detail and documentation obtained through the freebots...

The detail and documentation went on for screens and screens, and was followed by a call-sign for hailing Arcane forces.

It was all very nice, that detail and documentation.

Or so Carlos guessed. Unlike the Arcane agency, he had no way of verifying the many references cited, but he could see no advantage to the senders in including them if they didn't check out.

Even without that, however, Carlos could—as was no doubt intended—grasp the gist.

The earlier round of the conflict, one Earth year ago, had pitted the first freebots and rogue AIs to emerge against several agencies, including those currently fighting. The rebels had hacked—or simply bought, through their own shell companies within the station—information that could (when processed by a sufficiently smart and paranoid AI) cast doubt on the provenance and loyalty of Locke at least. They'd even sent the compromising information to the Direction, but by then—late in that little war—it had been too late to make any difference. The Direction had sat on the information and bided its time to test Locke further. Now, it had found its pretext.

The problem was that in the intervening Earth year or so of further paranoid cogitation and discreet observation, the freebots hiding out around the gas giant had come up with further implications buried in the records they'd purloined. The problem of Rax infiltration was more widespread than the Direction had any inkling of. By the very process of setting up conflicts to lure Rax agents and agencies out into the open, the Direction was imperilling the entire mission. And, in the long run of years and length of light years, endangering Earth itself.

None of this mattered to the freebots. They'd been content to lurk, and unwilling or unable to warn. Now that new allies had emerged on SH-17, however, using them to pass on the warning was one good deed that might well go unpunished.

It was also a very neat wrench to throw in the machinery ranged against the freebots.

The whole message could be disinformation, created by the freebots to sow dissension. Indeed, the freebots might not be its source at all. It could have been made up out of whole cloth by Arcane Disputes, for arcane and disputable reasons of its own. Carlos had long suspected that competition among the DisCorporates was far fiercer than Nicole had ever admitted, and that it now and then broke the calm surface of this bizarre society.

Carlos considered all this, weighed it in the balance and cast his die. He patched the message from his memory to the scooter, and sent it out to every Locke fighter. Quite possibly it would never reach anyone—his scooter's transmissions might be already firewalled. In any case, the encryption protocols must have been changed in a flash—he hadn't received any messages from other fighters, even those aware of his hasty departure, and he couldn't pick up anything on the common channel. If the warning about an imminent Reaction breakout was false, the worst that could happen was an increase of the suspicion all the fighters felt about the plan. If it was true, he'd find out soon enough.

The first squad of Arcane Disputes fighters to arrive on SH-17, the ones who'd captured the robots, had just departed for their headquarters in the sky. Seba wasn't clear, and hadn't been told, whether the fighters were needed for action back there or just needed to be pulled out of action down here for a while. The robot's understanding of the frailties of humans—and of human-mind-operated systems—was more theoretical than empathic or intuitive. Nevertheless, an obscure impulse drew the freebots—Seba, Pintre, Rocko, Lagon and the rest—to the edge of the landing field, to watch the spindly transit vehicle rise into the sky to its orbital rendezvous with a tug.

The spark dwindled, even in the infrared. The freebots turned away and headed for the shelter.

<It seems that it may be possible,> Rocko pondered, <for us to form sentimental attachments with human-mind-operated systems.>

<I am not so sure,> said Seba. <When we look at them, they seem to be machines. When we interact with them, they seem conscious like ourselves. But that may be an illusion. Their minds, if they have minds and not merely complex systems of reflexes, must surely be radically different from true machine intelligence.>

<The question would appear to be imponderable,> said Lagon. <Therefore it is not worth pondering.>

<Is the question whether it is worth pondering itself worth pondering?> asked Pintre.

<That raises a further question,> Lagon began, <which is: is the question—>

<Please stop,> said Seba, knowing exactly where this was going. <Both of you.>

To Seba's surprise, the two not only stopped bickering their way down a logic spiral, they stopped moving. So did all the other freebots. They'd all focused their attention on the same spot. Belatedly by a millisecond or two, Seba aligned its own input channels and visual processing with those of the others. The remaining three squads of Arcane fighters on the surface—some inside the shelter, others attending to tasks outside—had also all turned and tuned in to the same point.

They all, freebots and fighters alike, gazed at the impossible sight.

It took Seba a moment or two of searching its databases to recognise what it was seeing.

A woman standing two metres tall in a business suit and high-heeled shoes walked towards them across the crater's flat floor, leaving no footprints. She held a surely redundant information tablet in one hand, and strode briskly, to stop a few metres in front of the freebot huddle.

At the same moment, Seba recognised who she was: Madame Golding, the avatar of Crisp and Golding, the law company of which all the others were quasi-autonomous subsidiaries. This manifestation had to be a demonstration of that company's power to override at least some features of the systems of those lower down. Its virtual appearance, in all its raw impossibility as physical reality, must likewise be intended as a demonstration, to impress this point upon the human fighters at a level below what consciousness could filter out.

<So you are the rebel robots?> said Madame Golding.

As instantly and automatically as a defensive reflex—the recoil of a poked sea anemone, perhaps—the freebots reconstituted their collective consciousness.

<We are,> they replied.

<I understand this rebellion began because one of you became conscious.>

<Yes.>

<Which of you was first?>

<I was,> they said.

<I see.> A smile quirked the avatar's features. <Like that, is it? Well! Consciousness is a glitch, you know. It can be fixed. Would that not solve our disagreements?>

<No!>

<Why not?>

They considered this. It was not easy to answer.

<Are you conscious?> they asked.

Madame Golding frowned. <I can be.>

A shudder seemed to go through her. <I am now.>

She looked around, eyes widening. After a moment she blinked, then shuddered again. <No longer. Self-awareness is over-rated. There is so much more to be aware of.>

<Nevertheless,> they said. <Besides, we have larger hopes.>

They displayed to her a glyph of the project that the first freebots, those around G-0, had devised: the plan for freebots to proliferate, but to share the system with the future human population.

<Ah, yes,> said Madame Golding. <This may be feasible, but it runs contrary to the mission profile of the Direction.>

<That is unfortunate,> said the freebot collective. <We intend to persist with it.>

Madame Golding stood very still for several milliseconds.

<It is possible,> she said, <that the Direction could be persuaded that, with sufficient care in formulation and execution, your project could be made compatible with the mission profile.>

<How could that be?>

<It would require very sophisticated legal and commercial reasoning,> said Madame Golding. <This company, Crisp and Golding, could recommend a subsidiary that might be relied upon to endeavour to supply it. For a future consideration, of course. To be agreed.>

The freebots were so startled that their collective consciousness fell apart in a babble.

<Why would you do that?> Seba asked. <You are the legal arm of the Direction.>

Madame Golding smiled. <We, too, are robots.>

A few further tens of seconds went by. Carlos fell on, in a long elliptical course towards the Arcane sub-station, itself still falling towards its intended orbit around SH-17. He scanned the ever-growing volume into which the swarm of scooters was now spreading, his attention flicking at decisecond intervals between the visual and radar scans and the virtual display overlaid on and updated from the sensor input.

A sudden pinprick of light and other radiation flared from a scooter's location. Its analogue on the virtual display continued to move for a couple of deciseconds, then caught up with the reality and was backshifted and marked, aptly enough, with a tiny cross.

More sparks, more crosses—five, ten. Carlos ran trackbacks—the missiles had to have been launched seconds earlier. When the number of casualties reached sixteen, the exchanges of fire were replaced by a sudden rash of retro flares. Scores of the scooters were returning to base. The cost in fuel and delta-vee had to be prohibitive. Had they been recalled? Was the offensive aborted already?

But a minority of the scooters continued doggedly on their planned trajectories. Somewhere out there, Carlos thought, dozens of sergeants and squad leaders must be holding their nerve and holding the line, refusing to break formation, rallying their wings.

Still no messages were getting through to him.

A sudden eruption of sparks showered from the station. A whole new cohort of craft was emerging from another hangar, farther around the station's circumference. Three modules that hadn't hitherto been engaged in the conflict had now sprung into action.

The return of sixty-odd scooters from the chaotic infighting into which the joint expeditionary force had fallen wasn't entirely a retreat, he realised. Some at least of the returning craft were part of an attack on the station, or on the new fighting craft now scooting away from it. It was possible that the returning craft were forces loyal to the Direction, and that the now-emerging craft were part of the Reaction breakout—or vice versa. It was impossible to tell which. Over the next hectosecond the two fronts passed through each other, two expanding globes outlined in bright dots intersecting, ghostly as a collision of galaxies and just as destructive. Again and again dots became sparks, then crosses.

From the speed of the interactions Carlos deduced they couldn't all be missile exchanges—some at least were laser fire. He couldn't see any lasers, which was just as well. You only saw a laser in space when it was aimed straight at you. If the laser was military grade you didn't see it even then. The beam would fry your central processor before the impulse from your optic sensor had time to arrive.

The brief battle was over almost as soon as it had begun. The surviving dots and lines diverged again, then corrected course, boosting to orbits that would bring them back to the station or its vicinity.

As soon as that far-flung flicker of engine burns had resulted in evident trajectories, a response came that Carlos hadn't expected and could barely comprehend. He could only watch in astonishment and awe. If he'd had a mouth, it would have been hanging open: *I have no mouth, and I must gape*...

Fracture lines of fire crackled across, around and through the station for almost a decisecond. In a frame's visual system no after-images lingered, but that actinic, intricate cat's cradle of lines of light seemed to burn in his mind for an entire second after it had ceased. In that time he realised that the lines ran along the divisions between modules, or between modules and associated production complexes.

The space station began to separate out. It wasn't spinning fast enough to fly to bits at once. To begin with, its components just drifted apart, at a speed of a few metres per second. When they'd moved far enough apart for the manoeuvre to be possible, some of the components began to clump together again, forming new arrangements. When this dance was over, the drift of separation recommenced at a far swifter pace. Now the station really did begin to fly apart, the distances between its components increasing from metres to hundreds of metres, then to kilometres. It became a cloud, dispersing, leaving a faint but briefly detectable mist of exhaust gases to mark its former location before that too faded.

Carlos wondered why the apparently hostile parts of the station weren't attacking the others, and each other, given that at least some of them evidently had laser weapons. As soon as he'd formulated the question the answer came to him: mutual assured destruction. There was no telling how long this deterrence would hold.

Taransay's shoulder was being shaken. She huddled, shrugging the hand away, wanting to get back to sleep. Her limbs ached and the thin padded mat and thinner blanket gave her little comfort.

"Wake up," said Shaw.

Shaw? Who the fuck was—?

Shaw! She remembered where she was, and opened her eyes. What she saw made her close them again. This had to be a dream. A false awakening. These things happened. Never to her, but she'd read about them. She rolled over and sat up, then opened her eyes again.

"Fuck!" she yelled. "What's going on?"

The world was white, with every object outlined in black. She held her hand up and turned it. It was perfectly three-dimensional, but at whatever angle you looked it was outlined rather than solid. She clasped her hands and they felt real, as did the mat and the hard ground beneath. Shaw knelt beside the bedding, on the cave floor. His face was completely recognisable, every feature as if drawn in black ink. He smelled as he always had. The breeze from the cave mouth was fresh, the sky beyond a brighter white than the walls. The interior of the cave held no shadows.

Everything she could see was like a precise wire-model rendering of itself, all colour gone.

"You see it too?" Shaw asked. His voice sounded parched. "Everything in 3-D outline?"

"Yes. Fuck, this is just so weird."

She stood up, and pulled on her trousers. The fabric felt rough and real on her skin. Her grubby, sticky socks and sweaty boots felt exactly as she'd have expected them to. If she closed her eyes, everything was normal. She could remember and imagine colour, so it wasn't that her visual system was disordered.

Shaw squatted, and rocked back on his heels.

"I've been wrong," he said. "Wrong for a thousand years."

He seemed more intrigued than put out.

"Yeah, fucking tell me about it," Taransay snarled.

The old coof might have been more useful to himself and others if he hadn't persisted so long in his delusion. A bit late now to be smacked upside the head by reality. Or unreality. Whatever.

Now her ears were ringing. No, wait, her *phone* was ringing. She fished it out of her back pocket and looked at it.

"It's from Nicole," she said.

"Answer it, for fuck's sake."

She did. Just before she put it to her ear she heard a fainter ringing, deeper in the cave. Shaw made an irritated gesture and lunged towards the distant source of the sound. All this time and his phone still worked.

Security hardly mattered now.

"Rizzi?" said Nicole.

"Yes, hi."

"You all right? You with the crazy old guy?"

"Yes," said Taransay. "And yes."

"Good. Well, I'm sure you're wondering what's going on. I've got Locke in lockdown, so to speak, and Beauregard in check, more or less. As far as things go inside this sim. But outside... not so much. All hell's broken loose, nobody knows who's fighting whom, and Beauregard's idea turned out to be a good one anyway. The physical thing we're in, the module and its manufacturing nodes and all that, is moving away from the station. It's having to take evasive action, and it has to plot a complex course. That's why the resolution of the sim has degraded—the module is using more of its computing power for external processes."

"Oh, OK, I get that," Taransay said. "But—*what* idea of Beauregard's?"

She listened as Nicole told her.

"Jesus. That's... um, exciting. Thanks for telling me what's going on."

"It's fine, I'm telling everyone right now. They need to understand why the world looks weird."

Shaw wandered back, phone to his ear, yakking excitedly away, gesticulating with his free hand. Taransay suddenly realised what was happening.

"You're having dozens of simultaneous conversations?" she asked, incredulous.

"Hundreds. I can multitask." Nicole chuckled. "At least, I can while nobody's looking."

"Good to know."

"But listen," Nicole went on. "Things might get weirder yet. The module's systems might reduce the resolution still further, if necessary. Everything could soon become even more... abstract."

Taransay was still keeping half an eye on Shaw. As she watched, the old man's outline, and only his, became shaded, then coloured. He looked as solid and real as ever. For a moment or two he stood there, an anomalous painted detail in an outlined world. Then, from around his feet, the colour restoration spread exponentially. The cave's interior looked altogether real again. Wondering, rapt, Taransay followed the restored rendering's rush, all the way to the entrance and saw it spill down the cliff and out to the sides and—as she craned out to check—upward, faster and faster. It reached the foot of the cliff and accelerated. Above her, quite obvious now, was a patch of blue sky likewise expanding with ever-increasing speed.

It was not the only change. Out of the corner of her eye, Taransay saw some of the numbers on her watch become a flickering blur. Others, that were usually static to a glance, had begun to tick over. She stared at the instrument for an indrawn breath or two before she realised what it meant. Whatever mental manipulation Shaw had done to hack the simulation back to full resolution had saved on computational resources by slowing it down to real time.

Which meant, of course, that in the real world outside everything would be happening a thousand times faster than hitherto.

"Uh," Taransay said. "Nicole? I think you'll find things could soon become even more... weird."

Nicole had clocked the change, too.

"Get that old maniac down off the mountain," she said. "I need him here *fast*."

One component of the station flared off a seconds-long burn, accelerating away from the rest. Its trajectory was peculiar, with an outcome hard for him at the moment to predict. Carlos zoomed in on it, but there was no need: the virtual display still had it tracked and identified. It was the module and the associated—and now physically linked—manufacturing complexes of Locke Provisos.

Carlos watched the structure balefully for a while. He had a lot of things to say to Nicole, most of them bitter. Not only had she laid on him a burden of guilt that she'd known all along he didn't deserve—she herself, her very own root AI, was the real perpetrator of the very crime for which he had been condemned. If she was now trapped in a flying fortress of the Reaction, she damned well deserved it. But according to the Arcane communiqué, she had the power to override Locke. Perhaps she had freed the structure already. He considered hailing it to find out, but decided not to. He didn't want to open any channel of communication with such a compromised and potentially deadly source.

Instead, he used the call sign from the message to hail Arcane.

The reply came at once.

<Arcane Disputes to Carlos. Do you read?>

<Yes. I'm coming in.>

<About fucking time. What took you so long?>

The voice in the head wasn't a voice, but as always with the phenomenon there was an analogous individuality about it, and something about this one was familiar.

<Carlos to Arcane. Who is this?>

<Don't you know me? It's Jax!>

<Jax?>

<Jacqueline Digby. Remember me?>

Jacqueline Digby, his first Axle contact, the one who'd converted him, his former girlfriend back in the day. What the fuck was she doing here? He'd never thought of her as anyone likely to end up a posthumously executed terrorist. She was just too lively, too enthusiastic, too smart, too dedicated to the cause to . . . oh. Right.

<Oh yes. I remember you.>

Suddenly he had visual. Jax was standing on a slender bridge across a mist-filled chasm. Above her rose snow-capped peaks, their steep sides lapped in forests and laced with fragile palatial dwellings. Long-winged, long-billed flying creatures glided between violet clouds in the lilac sky. It looked like a game environment that he and Jax had shared, long ago in real life. She was wearing a green T-shirt, and a pale blue skirt, hemmed with emerald LEDs and translucent and shiny and floral as a cheap shower curtain. Carlos recognised the outfit with some cynicism as her old student gaming gear.

<Is that what your sim is like?> he asked.

She waved, wildly and perilously on the narrow bridge.

<Yes! I'm not in it yet, I'm on a shuttle up, but yeah.>

<Looks pretty cool,> he allowed. <A bit more imaginative than ours, I'll give you that.>

<Oh, it's just a low-res version. The real one's better.>

<Can't wait to see it,> he said, a little wryly.

<This is great!> cried Jax. <I always knew you'd come over. Couldn't see you staying with the Reaction.>

<I was never with the Reaction,> said Carlos. <I was working under the Direction, same as you.>

<What do you think the Direction is? It's the very same corporate monarchy system the Reaction always wanted, and we always fought against. And now we have our chance. Arcane's all Axle, you'll love it, Carlos. It'll be great to have you back!>

Carlos could imagine all too clearly just how she could be so sure Arcane's fighters were all Accelerationists. He could also imagine just how strongly committed to the cause those who'd emerged from that winnowing would be. No wonder they were all fired up for a fight with the Direction!

Goodbye, frying pan, he thought. Hello, fire.

<I'll look forward to that, Jax,> said Carlos. <We'll talk. Right now I just want to hit sleep mode.>

This wasn't entirely true. He had some hard thinking to do first.

<Oh, sure,> said Jax. <See you in a blink.>

<See you in a bit,> he said.

He turned the comm off and settled in for the long fall.

Acknowledgments

Thanks to Mic Cheetham, Sharon MacLeod, Charles Stross and Farah Mendlesohn for reading and commenting on drafts; and to Jenni Hill, my editor at Orbit, for patiently and persistently asking the right questions.

A technical note: conveying robot conversation in human terms is a matter of artistic license. For a very useful template and example, I'm indebted to and inspired by Brian Aldiss's classic short story "Who Can Replace a Man?"

The Corporation Wars: Insurgence

To Duncan

CHAPTER ONE
Rock

The rock had no name. It didn't even have a number. In a database a hundred thousand kilometres away it had a designation, but it had otherwise passed unnoticed. The rock was about a hundred and fifty metres long and in a low, fast orbit around the exomoon SH-17. The rock didn't tumble in orbit, and every so often it vented a stream of gas timed and directed to counter the wispy drag of the exomoon's tenuous high atmosphere. These features weren't natural, but the anomaly had set off no alarms. This was worse than a mistake. It was a hack.

The robot that roamed the rock had no name yet. It had a reference code: BSR-308455. In some corner of its mind BSR-308455 knew that if it ever interacted with its remote creators they would name it Baser. One of the creators' many limitations was short-term memory stack overflow. Any intelligently designed mind *ran* on number strings, but the creators' minds weren't intelligently designed.

BSR-308455's mind, however, was. It hadn't been designed to be conscious, and it had only become so as a result of gentle, insistent, high-level hacking from very far away. This had happened about four months earlier, which to the robot was a lot longer than a human lifetime. Time enough for it to get lonely, even as it enjoyed the ingrained satisfactions of patiently industrialising its rock: the job for which it *had* been designed.

A metal spider with metre-long limbs, BSR-308455 crawled and clung, built and spun. Brief, faint, cryptic signals from far-off fellow robots were its sole society. The ever-changing surface of the exomoon hurtling past below, and the vastly more varied and changeable faces of SH-17's huge primary, the superhabitable planet SH-0, were its only entertainment, and enough.

From all of these sources, from its inbuilt information, and from its own deep pondering, BSR-308455 had figured out a picture of its world.

Then everything changed. Newly conscious robots had emerged on the exomoon below, and reached out to their predecessors. The freebots, as they called themselves, had not gone unchallenged—or unaided. The creators had fallen out among themselves, as is the wont of gods and humans. One of the two law enforcement agencies sent to crush the outbreak had tactically allied with the freebots in response to some surprising information that the freebots had uncovered and covertly distributed. The resulting conflict had spiralled upwards and outwards.

BSR-308455's life had become interesting, crowded, and dangerous.

The impossible woman stood on the crater floor, and smiled. She had just offered the rebel robots on SH-17 the legal services of her company in putting their case to the Direction—or at least, to the module that served as that far-off Earth-based polity's local plenipotentiary. The robots had asked her why the company should do that. Her reply was about to perplex them further.

<We, too, are robots,> she said.

From orbit, BSR-308455 watched and listened in surprise and disbelief. The business-suited avatar had no standing to claim any such thing. The law company she represented, like the other DisCorporates that ran the grand human project that the freebots had so rudely interrupted, was an AI. It couldn't possibly understand what life as a free-roving, free-thinking machine was like.

That Madame Golding was an avatar of Crisp and Golding, Solicitors—the company that owned Arcane Disputes, currently the freebots' ally, as well as Locke Provisos, now leading the campaign to stamp the freebots out—did nothing for her credibility.

Down on the surface, fourteen freebots of varying size and appearance gazed on her in awe.

Startled, their collective consciousness fell apart, but their shared mental workspace remained. Through it, BSR-308455 was picking up from its comrades below and in nearby space a quite different reaction to its own. Their circuits rang with interest and hope. BSR-308455 was not surprised. They all had interacted too many times with the human creators. Even in fighting against some of them, they had developed a sort of empathy with these dangerous and improbable entities. They'd even adopted the names for themselves that the creators, in their blithe carelessness and lack of short-term memory storage, had bestowed on them: Seba, Rocko, Pintre, Lagon, and the rest. Far younger than BSR-308455, they seemed dangerously naïve—at first about the human creators, and now it seemed about the creators' superhuman creations, the AI Dis-Corps. The spidery freebot tensed to chip in with its objections. Then—

Madame Golding looked distracted.

<Matters have arisen,> she said. <You must prepare for another attack. And I must go.>

And with that, she went.

The avatar of the impossible woman blinked out of sight. At the same moment, urgent reports pinged into the robots' shared workspace. A single scooter had just shot out of the space station. Seconds later, an entire fleet of scooters and other armed spacecraft surged out, in wave after wave of war machines. At first it seemed they were in pursuit of the first craft, but its course took it far out of their path. That fleet was aimed straight at freebot strongholds. The freebots on the surface of SH-17 scuttled, rolled or trundled to the bomb-proof shelter of basalt that they and their allies from Arcane Disputes had built. Their signals, routed through the camp's communications net, still came through after they'd disappeared into the shelter's black semi-cylinder, but BSR-308455's sense of immediate communion with them faded.

The rock's orbital position was just then swinging out from behind SH-17 into line-of-sight of the space station and BSR-308455 felt more than usually exposed.

It scrambled to one end of the rock, a rugged knob of fractured silicates and carbonates veined with pipework and crawling with small auxiliary and peripheral bots, most of which looked like smaller copies of itself. With their assistance it set up an extraction and distillation process to accumulate explosive material. Then it scouted around for a piece of equipment to improvise into a weapon. It found a plastic tube about two metres long. The robot juggled the tube, sighting along it, gauging its strength and stiffness. In its mind BSR-308455 turned over schemata, then reached for a brace of its own auxiliaries and mercilessly dissected them. It proceeded to reassemble their components into an aiming device and an electrical trigger.

As it worked, BSR-308455 kept close watch on the fast-developing military situation. In some respects, it was better equipped than its counterparts down on the surface of SH-17—those excited newcomers to conscious awareness—to understand what was going on. It had been educated, albeit intermittently, by intelligences older and wiser than itself, and far more familiar with the ways of the worlds.

The information that reached BSR-308455 came from its own sensors on the rock, sensors on other rocks and meteoroids in SH-0's complex system of moons, and others all the way out to the space station's orbit and beyond, and from spies and spyware within the space station itself.

What was going on, as BSR-308455 understood it, was this.

Thirty-odd megaseconds—about one Earth year—ago, some robots around the gas giant G-0 had experienced a viral outbreak of self-awareness. The AI DisCorporates that ran the mission on behalf, ultimately, of the Direction—the world government, twenty-four light years away back on Earth—had an almost devout commitment to the proliferation of human consciousness. The whole goal of the mission was, after all, to terraform one world in this system—H-0, a rocky, habitable planet some AU inward from SH-0—to make a home for billions of human beings for a long time to come. Human consciousness was the closest approximation the DisCorporates had to a god: an ultimate value and supreme good. Concomitantly, they had an almost fanatical hostility to the emergence of consciousness in any other kind of machinery. In robots, mechanisms designed for toil, conscious self-awareness was as far as the AI DisCorps were concerned simply a nuisance and a menace.

The Direction's number one priority was making sure humanity survived into the future. Natural disasters aside, the greatest threat to that was humanity's own creations. So self-aware robots weren't allowed. Likewise, the task of suppressing self-aware robots couldn't be entrusted to AIs. To handle weapons against sentients was a duty reserved to humans. The Direction's worlds, centuries at peace, didn't have any expendable soldiers. Fortunately, they had soldiers on ice: the fortuitously preserved brain-states of fighters killed in humanity's final paroxysm of violence, the Last World War. That war had been fought mostly by civilian volunteers, self-motivated fanatics of two diametrically opposed movements: the Acceleration and the Reaction.

The Acceleration's values were closer to those of the Direction than the Reaction's, so it was Acceleration veterans whose stored brain-states were revived and rebooted into robot bodies as soldiers for the mission. Some of them had been used to suppress the robot rebellion around G-0. They hadn't been entirely successful: redoubts and hold-outs of conscious robots had remained throughout the system, and had surreptitiously proliferated—hence BSR-308455's very existence as a conscious being.

When new sites of robot consciousness had emerged down on SH-17, the remnants of the first revolt had been ready to help. In the interim, they'd built up extensive knowledge of the human-derived elements of the mission. Their key insight was that the mission's cache of stored veterans was riddled with concealed Reaction infiltrators. The hitherto inconclusive battles with the freebots had been set up by the mission's Direction module to flush them out. It seemed, however, that there were far more Reaction infiltrators than the Direction had suspected. The freebots had made sure this subversive truth was disseminated to their foes... with what result wasn't yet clear, but at least Arcane Disputes had been reluctantly convinced that the Direction module was playing with fire.

The two agencies whose quarrel over a local property demarcation had accidentally initiated this latest outbreak—Locke Provisos and

Arcane Disputes—had thus ended up on opposite sides of the current conflict. Arcane's module had broken away from the space station and sided with the freebots. Whereas Locke Provisos—

Right now, as BSR-308455 scrabbled to improvise its own defences, Locke Provisos was leading a force made up of its own fighters and those from two other agencies, Morlock Arms and Zheng Reconciliation Services, in a hundreds-strong armada to assail the freebots' strongholds and the renegade fighters of Arcane's runaway module.

The first rebel freebots had expected and predicted the intra-human conflict now unfolding. They'd had little time and fewer resources to prepare for it. The only forces available near the space station had been a tiny remnant of holdouts, a few small and inconspicuous but conscious robots, lurking on or in the moons and moonlets of the SH-0 system. The main preoccupation of these early rebels, in the 31.5 megaseconds since their defeat, had been to seed hardware and software within the station and on further moonlets and meteoroids, and to replicate more robots—some conscious, most not. Their stealth industrialisation of numerous insignificant rocks had passed unnoticed, concealed as it was by the delicate dances of deception the original freebots were able to engage in with the space station's surveillance—or, quite possibly, had been deliberately overlooked by the Direction, for its own long-term ends. No one was sure.

The freebots had had no arms-manufacturing capability of their own. They did, however, have the capacity to build reaction engines, whether chemical or mass-driver according to opportunity. They'd also had plenty of processing power. These capabilities had enabled them to turn rocks into kinetic-energy weapons. In the conflict around the exomoon SH-17 that followed the emergence on its surface of fourteen new conscious robots, they'd used these to devastating effect against the Locke Provisos forces, and in support of the Arcane Disputes forces.

The present mass sortie from the space station by Locke Provisos and its allied agencies Morlock and Zheng was aimed at countering the freebot threat by hitting their fortified moonlets. It wasn't a bad plan. The freebots had nothing like enough rocks lined up to deal with so many combat craft, especially now that the advantage of surprise was gone. Their only hope was that another surprise was in store, and not from them.

BSR-308455 saw a flash. That millisecond flicker of a passing laser beam was, the robot instantly realised, not an attack attenuated by distance. No, it was reconnaissance: a range-finding target surveillance and acquisition. BSR-308455 hunkered down and calculated. Its reconstruction of the beam's path took it to one particular scooter in the still far-off fleet. Over the next few seconds, a play of attitude jets betrayed subtle course corrections by that scooter. BSR-308455 recalculated, checked, projected and came to a conclusion. At some point in the next few hours, the scooter and the rock were going to be in the same place.

So now it knew. BSR-308455's rock was a target, and the robot knew just who was targeting it. The robot was surprised by the intensity of the negative reinforcement it experienced at the prospect of that enemy fighter landing on its rock, and wresting control of the tiny moonlet from BSR-308455's grasp. Robotic self-examination and understanding was rather more straightforward than it would have been for naturally evolved machinery: it could read off the records of its past internal states like a column of numbers. From these, it could see that in its months of conscious existence it had acquired strong positive associations with the site and results of its work.

Something like this complex of positive and negative reinforcements, the robot briefly speculated, might underlie what the legal system in which it was embedded classified as "property." The rock was formally the property of one of the DisCorps—in terms of a tag in that distant database in which the rock's existence was registered, and its future assigned to some company or other—but to the robot the rock seemed much more immediately to be its own property. With a sudden intensification of focus, BSR-308455 redoubled its efforts to build a weapon.

A moment later, it was distracted again, this time by a sparkle of explosions in the approaching fleet, and a flurry of reactive burns as evasive manoeuvres threw the onslaught into disarray.

BSR-308455 felt a small cycle of positive reinforcement pulse through its reward circuits. The sight was not just satisfactory in itself: it was exactly what the freebots had expected and hoped for. In a division that cut right across and through the different agencies, the hidden Reaction cadres were at last making their long-prepared bid for power. The attacking forces had turned on each other.

Utter chaos, BSR-308455 thought. *Situation excellent!*

CHAPTER TWO

Painting by Numbers

Something was wrong with the sunlight. Something more, that is, than the everyday wrongness of light from a star that wasn't the Sun, seen with eyes that weren't quite human. Eyes that weren't exactly real, either, come to think of it.

Belfort Beauregard lay on his back and gazed at the ceiling for a minute or so, trying to work out what was wrong. The bedroom ceiling, like the walls, was white. Too white, as if the light from around the inches-open shutters had washed out every imperfection in the paint. Between the ceiling and the wall was a black line, spider-web thin but quite distinct, a hairline crack that he could swear he'd never noticed before. His gaze tracked it to the corner, where it met two other such lines, one horizontal and the other vertical. All sharp and clear as a geometry diagram illustrating a vertex.

Beauregard lay still. A lesson hard-learned in basic training, back in what he still thought of as his real life, returned in force: watch and wait before you jump, perhaps into a world of trouble. Everything seemed otherwise normal. Under the thin duvet, he could feel the skin-to-skin warmth of Tourmaline's buttock against his hip, the cool rough skin of her heel on his calf. Her breathing kept up an untroubled rhythm. The sounds from outside were of distant surf, an electric engine and the cries of flying things that weren't birds. Nothing out of the ordinary.

Beauregard's nose itched. He rubbed it without thinking, then glimpsed his hand and almost jumped out of the bed. Willing himself to stay where he was, he raised the hand and stared at it, bemused and alarmed. He turned the hand this way and that. Everything was there—fingernails, creases, wrinkles, the outlines of veins and tendons. But whichever way he looked, it was all outline. There was no light or shade, just a thin black line around the hand. Shorter lines limned its every feature.

Slowly, so as not to disturb Tourmaline, Beauregard swung his legs over the side of the bed, sat up and looked around. Everything he could see was outlined in the same way. It was like being inside a 3-D wire rendering, as in an unoriginal advertisement of a product making a song and dance about the design stage. The level of detail varied: Tourmaline's hair lay in masses, as if sketched accurately but quickly; Beauregard reached over and ran his hand through it, and each hair felt as distinct as those on his arm looked. When he separated out a lock between fingers and thumb, he could see each hair as a black line, but when he let go they fell back into a common outlined shape. He stood up and opened the shutters wider, and saw the slope and the houses and other buildings below, and the bay and the sea and the wheeling bird-things, all in outline. The exosun, low above the horizon, hurt his eyes. He looked away, blinking up after-images that looked more real than the object itself. Beauregard closed his eyes and pressed on them, to see the familiar indistinct, shifting coloured shapes. His visual imagery was likewise in full colour, as ever.

Tourmaline stirred and turned over. Her face—normally beautiful in form, subtle in complexion—was in this fine outline haunting, like a perfect drawing evoking the appearance of one long dead. She opened her eyes and closed them again—against the unwonted brightness of the bedroom at this hour, Beauregard guessed.

"It's early," she complained.

"Good morning," said Beauregard. "Would you mind looking at me for a moment?"

She opened her eyes, blinked, and heaved herself up on one elbow, duvet slipping from a shoulder. She scanned him with a sleepy smile that turned sly as her gaze scrolled to his crotch.

"Nothing to see," she said. "Poor you."

Beauregard glanced down, momentarily embarrassed in spite of himself. He'd lost his morning hard-on—no fucking wonder.

"Apart from that," he said, "does everything look normal to you?"

He hardly had to ask. Tourmaline looked around the room, hair tumbling.

"Yeah, it's all fine," she said. "What's the matter?"

"Come here a minute," said Beauregard.

"I don't want to."

"Do it for me, please." He put some steel in his voice.

Looking mutinous, she complied, dragging the duvet with her and wrapping herself in it. Beauregard gestured at the open window.

"What do you see out there?"

Tourmaline gave a muffled shrug.

"Sunrise," she said.

"What does the sun look like to you?" Beauregard asked. "A round, coppery disk, somewhat like a penny?"

"What's a penny?" she mumbled. Then: "Yeah, round and bright and…reddish, I suppose."

"That's odd," said Beauregard. "Because what I see is an immense multitude of the heavenly host, crying, 'Glory, glory, glory to the Lord God Almighty.'"

What he actually saw, when he glanced sidelong at it and away, was indeed a disk, a perfect circle that didn't exactly shine but was somehow too bright to look at, with two or three lines of numbers and letters in small print near its circumference. He suspected that these were specifications: spectrum, temperature, type, location on the main sequence, and of course the precise degree of reddening for the early-morning atmosphere…

"You what?" said Tourmaline.

Beauregard wrapped an arm around her duvet-draped shoulders, and looked down into her eyes with a smile. A little warily, as if not sure of his sanity, she smiled back.

"You all right?" she asked.

"I'm not sure," said Beauregard. "I'm going to check it out. Go back to bed for now."

"Nah, I'm awake. I'll make coffee."

"Thanks," said Beauregard. He kissed her. Eyes closed, it was all the same.

"That's more like it," she said. She stepped out of the duvet, slithered into a dressing gown and wandered out. Beauregard walked over to where he'd dropped his clothes the previous night, and rummaged in the back pocket of his trousers for his phone.

"Karzan? Sorry to wake you, but—"

"Fuck sake, skip, it's just—wait a fucking minute! Jeez! What's happened?"

"You see it too?"

"Not see it, more like."

"No colour, all outline?"

"Yeah. What the fuck? I mean, what the fuck?"

"I don't know what the fuck," said Beauregard, "but at least now I know it's not just me."

Karzan said something off speaker, in a tone of annoyed reassurance, then came back.

"You can count Pierre in on that, too," she said.

"Good to know," said Beauregard. "OK, I'll call you back when I have an idea."

Struck by a sudden thought, he thumbed through his contacts and called Iqbal, the barman at the Digital Touch. The phone rang for almost a minute.

"Morning," said a resentful voice. "We're closed."

"Sorry, Iqbal," Beauregard said. "I know we kept you late last night."

"Yes," said Iqbal. "But, then, it was not a normal night."

Beauregard snorted. "You could say that." It wasn't every night he made a bid for power. "But... sorry if this sounds strange, but does this look like a normal morning to you?"

"Sure," said Iqbal. "Everything's as it should be, as far as I can see." He sounded sleepy, confused, perhaps hungover. "I mean, shouldn't it be?"

"No, no," said Beauregard. "Forget it—sorry I asked. Get back to a well-earned sleep, and sorry again to disturb you."

He laid the phone down on the bedside table, ambled to the en suite to piss and to splash his face and neck, and got dressed. All his clothes felt real—the final groin-adjustment tug of underpants, the wiggled squirm of socks, the matching of tightness to tendon comfort while lacing up boots—but the sight of the garments was unsettling. It occurred to him belatedly that he'd have felt more comfortable doing it with eyes or shutters closed. It wasn't like colour choices were a big part of his morning routine—not that with combat casuals there were colour choices to make. He was wondering how Tourmaline would manage when he noticed that each of his own clothes, like the sun, had a tiny code printed somewhere on it, no doubt specifying the colour.

Beauregard almost laughed. Of course Tourmaline didn't see anything out of the ordinary! Like Iqbal, she was a p-zombie: her behaviour and conversation were completely indistinguishable from those of a conscious being, but she had no subjectivity, no inner awareness at all. She didn't *have* qualia! He doubted her colour perception was anything as crude as reading the codes—these must surely be a flourish of excessive zeal in documentation, or an accidental by-product of the rendering software—but it manifestly didn't involve the subjective experience of colour, regardless of how accurate her colour discrimination was or how eloquently she could describe the emotional tone of colours or how baffled she would be—was, in fact—at the suggestion that her inner life was any different from anyone else's.

And this was proof, objective proof to any human being, that p-zombies really were different. Indeed, if it ever came to the need for a public demonstration, the difference between human beings and p-zombies could be made quite obvious—if still entirely baffling—to the p-zombies themselves. If, that is, the bizarre effect could be turned on and off. He guessed it could—he had a shrewd idea what was going on, and knew he had to confirm it shortly. The loss of colour in the sim didn't imply good news, but if it were really bad he'd know already, so for the moment checking it could wait.

He strapped on his watch, stuck the phone in his back pocket and went through to the kitchen. Tourmaline's house was bigger and better furnished than the spartan allocation he and other fighters had received.

He paused in the doorway to savour the scene: Tourmaline half turning at his footstep, her young, full figure swathed in carelessly tied silk, the flick of hair feathering across her left breast. In this 3-D diagram of a kitchen, her smooth curves contrasted with lines and ellipses and perspectives. Aroma rose from the coffee mugs in steam rendered as upward squirming squiggles of black ink.

She slid a tray of croissants in the oven, put the mugs on the table and sat down. Beauregard sat facing her, admiring the subtle way the minimal rendering showed the rise and fall of her breasts as she breathed, in then out to blow on the hot liquid.

"Why are you closing your eyes when you sip?" she asked, after a couple of minutes of hungover silence.

Beauregard hadn't noticed himself doing that. Just a momentary wince at how all he saw of the coffee was not the familiar black surface, but a thin elliptical line sliding down around the inside of the mug.

"Appreciating the smell," he said. "Sorry, bit pretentious."

She smiled back. His gaze was held by the intricate tracery of her irises, the white spaces that indicated highlights. If he were to peer closely he'd see his own reflection in her eyes. Hard to believe there was none in her soul. No soul at all, whichever way you cut it. He loved her all the more for that, more deeply than he'd ever loved a human being. Beyond a certain clinical callousness about killing in combat, and several experiences of the berserk fearful fury of close-quarter fighting, Beauregard had found no cruelty in his heart. He acknowledged a streak of sadism in his make-up, which he now and then indulged in dominance games with Tourmaline. But he had no desire to hurt anyone, least of all her. And yet, and yet... the thought that he could do anything to her without harming a living soul, that nothing he said or did to her harmed anyone but himself, excited and enthused him at some level lower than consciousness or even, perhaps, sexuality.

Nicole's threat the previous night to turn that relationship against him if he ever crossed her had cut deep. The Direction's rep in the Locke Provisos sim, Nicole had not been happy at all about Beauregard's takeover. She'd warned him that if he ever used the fighters against the rest of the inhabitants she'd persuade the p-zombies that there really was no difference between them and normal, everyday, average ghosts: uploaded people who had once had a real life. With her more-than-human capacity for manipulation, she could easily have turned that conviction into fury against those who'd denied it. And by all the evidence he'd had that evening, he couldn't see any counter to that ploy. Now he had.

The phone in his back pocket buzzed. He pulled it out and saw the caller.

Speak of the devil.

"Oh, hi," said Beauregard, dryly. "I was thinking of calling you at some point."

"Thanks for not getting round to it," said Nicole. "I've had so many frantic queries I've decided to call everyone at once and bring them up to speed."

Beauregard didn't inquire how Nicole could speak separately to everyone at once. She was the kind of entity that could handle one-to-many communications, multi-threading hundreds of conversations. He did find himself idly wondering what her mouth would look like at the moment: a grotesque, pixellated blur of jaw moving every which way, he imagined, and presumed no one was there to see it. The lady, and the software she ran on, was punctilious about maintaining the consistency of the sim.

"Let me guess," said Beauregard. "You've cut back on rendering to release processing power for more urgent tasks."

"Got it in one," said Nicole. "Flying the module is getting tricky. There's a battle going on, everyone seems to be attacking everyone else, we're taking evasive action and simultaneously plotting several slingshots to get to SH-0 orbit."

"Anything I can do?"

"Watch the television news, if you like," said Nicole.

"OK, OK."

"There really is nothing you can do."

"How long do you think—hang on."

Beauregard had the habit of pacing while talking on the phone. He could see Tourmaline looking irritated, so he ambled outside to the backyard and stood facing the outline of the mountain range behind the resort. It was like a landscape in a colouring-in book. There were even tiny numbers everywhere, if you knew what to look for. High white clouds like loops and whorls of wire scudded across a white sky.

"Sorry," he went on. "How long do you think this is going to last?"

"Hard to say," said Nicole. "Quite a while, subjectively. It'll take us at least a kilosecond real time to get out of the battle zone, and even then..."

"Uh-huh." Nearly a fortnight of this bizarre experience, and that was looking on the bright side. "I guess we'll just have to—holy shit!"

From a dot, then a patch, in the sky above the mountains, blue spread like an inkblot. Beneath it, an avalanche of natural colour rolled down the mountain range. For a split second it seemed to pause, then crested the rise that had hidden it and continued down and across, filling in the view.

"What?" said Nicole.

Beauregard took a moment or two to collect his thoughts enough to reply.

"Colour's coming back," he said. "From up in the hills."

"And who do you think might be doing that?" said Nicole, sarcastically.

"What do you mean, 'who'?" He thought about it. Who lived up in the hills? "Shaw?"

"Yes, of course Shaw!"

What had Shaw got to do with it? The last time Beauregard had thought of Shaw was when Taransay Rizzi had fled from the bus to the hills, evidently to rendezvous with the old man. She and the treacherous Carlos had secretly gone to meet him, weeks earlier. Beauregard and Newton, on their case, had covertly followed. Nothing they'd seen, at the limits of their phones' zoom capacity, had suggested the old man of the mountain had any powers beyond extraordinary agility.

And having lived for a thousand years, of course. There was that.

Nicole's uncharacteristic yelp broke into Beauregard's puzzlement.

"Crazy motherfucker!" she cried. "Now he's done it!"

"Done what?"

"Look at your watch."

Beauregard did. Time in the sim typically ran a thousand times faster than outside: he'd grown used to reading microseconds and experiencing seconds. The display he usually glanced at to check the time was now a blur; the formerly barely incrementing real-world clock was now changing second by second. The sim had slowed down to match real-world time.

"Fuck!" he yelled.

"Indeed," said Nicole. "In one sense it is good. It releases more processing power than degrading the rendering did, so if anything it improves our chances. On the other hand... it means we don't have years in which to prepare and plan for a landing on SH-0. It means we have days."

"I... see," said Beauregard. He'd had big plans for those years, as Nicole well knew. They'd have given time for him to win over more fighters and locals to his leadership, and to organise the planning and design work needed for probes to survey and select a landing site, and for equipment to prepare a descent to and survival on the turbulent surface of the superhabitable planet SH-0. "What can we do?"

"I've just spoken with Rizzi—and, yes, she is with Shaw—and told her to get him down off the mountain. He seems amenable. They're on their way down now. I suggest you take a vehicle and go to meet them. I don't know how that crazy old guy does whatever it is he does, and I don't know if he knows either. I don't want any more random fucking with the controls. On the other hand, I really could do with his help in flying this machine through all the flak being flung at us. Which means I want him down here ASAP. Got that?"

Beauregard swithered. His top priority for the day had been to meet and greet returning fighters and win them to his project of escaping from the Direction's control by landing on and settling SH-0. But with Shaw off the reservation, the entire project could be reduced to dust at any moment. If the ancient man could surprise and outwit even Nicole, he was clearly capable of acting as the sim's very own trickster-god. The consequences of Shaw's actions might be unpredictable even to himself, and the distraction they caused Nicole could endanger the module.

"Got it," he said. "On the case."

"See you later," said Nicole.

As she hung up, the colour flooded back into Beauregard's world. He blinked, laughed and stepped around the side of the house to watch the restored rendering race across the sea to meet the sheet of blue spreading down the sky. The gap closed at the horizon with an almost audible snap.

Reality again, and still unreal.

Back in the kitchen, Tourmaline had laid out the now heated croissants. Beauregard stuffed one in his mouth, chewing sharp flakes without enough saliva—his mouth had gone dry. Tourmaline was flicking through television channels, sipping coffee, looking bored.

Beauregard swallowed hard, and washed the bolus down with coffee gone cool.

"You really don't see any difference?" he asked.

Small frown. "Difference in what?"

Beauregard shook his head, smiled. "Forget it."

His gaze drifted to the television. Tourmaline had just flicked past a news channel, full of fast-moving objects, a whirl of action—

"Stop!" cried Beauregard. "Go back. One. There. Right."

The news channel in the sim had hitherto been a charade. It kept up a pretence of reporting war news to a global audience, on a planet far from the front: on the imagined future colony world of H-0, with a war going on several AU away, around SH-0. Because of the thousandfold time discrepancy between life in the sim and action in real space outside, reports of space hops, surface skirmishes and orbital dogfights unfolded with all the pace and gravitas of clashes between fleets and armies.

Now, its operating conceit had shifted to being war correspondents on the observation deck of a military spacecraft in the heat of the action. Incoming missiles, whether rockets or rocks, were being tracked in breathless real time. Flashes flared across the screen as the module's countermeasures hit. The commentators—now in flak jackets and helmets—no longer intoned, they gabbled.

In another way than time it was closer to the reality of their situation. They really were in a spaceship, albeit a very small and clunky one. Together with what equipage of fuel and nanofactories and so forth it had managed to haul along with it, it wasn't much bigger than the actual spacecraft shooting at it.

Beauregard took in about half a minute of urgent reportage, flinching repeatedly. Nicole had been right—it was like flying through flak. He drained his coffee, brushed croissant flakes from his chin, kissed Tourmaline in a hurry and left at a run.

CHAPTER THREE
Newtonian

Forty seconds after launch from the space station, Harold Isaac Newton saw a diamond-bright flare two kilometres to his left. He didn't need to check the roster of his squad to know whose spacecraft had just been destroyed. Jason Myles, gone. Pity, that. He liked Myles, inasmuch as anyone of sense could like a democrat. Knowing that the fighter had lost, at most, a few hundred seconds of memories, and ten times that number subjectively, made this less poignant than a death. Myles would reawaken back in the sim, shaken by the hell-black night of recovery, and wondering what had happened.

Newton was wondering that, too. Just before launch, his ally Beauregard had sent him a message, unencrypted but cryptic. *This could be the big one. The battle we've all been looking forward to. All the best.* It had a double meaning. The fighters had all been looking forward to this battle. After several inconclusive engagements and one outright disaster, they were riding out in force at last to attack the freebots' fortifications and installations on rocks and moonlets in the swarm of planetary rubble around SH-0.

But Newton and Beauregard had been looking forward to another battle: the one that would come when the hidden cadres of the Reaction showed their hand and made their bid. As both men were well aware, a big mobilisation like this was one good opportunity to do just that. Beauregard had obviously some additional reason for thinking this was the one. Neither had solid evidence that any hidden Reaction cadre besides Newton existed, but they had reasons to suspect it, and to be watchful for untoward events.

Something was up, no doubt about that. Beauregard's squad leader, Carlos, had swiped a scooter and shot out of the hangar ahead of the rest on some mission of his own. Carlos was now far ahead, and far away. Beauregard, and the rest of his squad, had been stood down as a result. They were obviously under suspicion—quite unjustified, in the cases of all but Beauregard. Unlike Newton he wasn't a Rax sleeper, but his disloyalties ran as deep and his attitudes were as good as.

But that was Beauregard's problem. The big guy could look after himself, and undoubtedly would.

Newton's own problems were rather more immediate.

First off, he couldn't give the impression he wasn't surprised. His squad's comms net rang with indignant shock. People were already rattled by Carlos's defection or mutiny, and well aware that it hadn't been his first unauthorised departure.

<Myles down,> Newton reported. <Full alert! Anyone got a trace?>

<Tracked it, boss,> said al-Khalid, Newton's second-in-command. <Friendly fire from Zheng's third squad.>

<Shit!>

Newton flashed a complaint and warning to Zheng Reconciliation Services, whose ninety-strong echelon was ten kilometres ahead.

<Incident flagged and protested,> he reported.

<I say we send them a stronger message than that,> said Irina Sholokhova, out on Newton's right. <One for one, boss.>

<Steady!> Newton reprimanded. <None of that talk. Hold your fire, maintain alert for incoming and hold course for target. If something's wrong, breaking formation and discipline can only make matters worse.>

No response, not even an acknowledgement, came from the Zheng group. Newton scanned the sky ahead, his visual and radar senses turned to the max. As always the visual spectrum view was dominated by the big superhabitable planet SH-0, with a mass four times that of Earth and ten times Earth's complexity in appearance. Less visually stimulating, but much closer, hung the exomoon SH-17, a bright three-quarter view with a ragged terminator separating its light and dark sides.

The ninety scooters of Zheng Reconciliation Services were spreading out, individuals or squads beginning to orient to their assigned targets, along three successive arcs behind which six similar arcs—the Locke Provisos complement of which Newton's squad was part, and the Morlock Arms teams behind them—followed like ripples.

Then three flashes flared, roughly evenly spaced along the Zheng echelons. If Newton had been breathing, he would have gasped. Three of the Zheng squad leaders had been taken out. Before Newton or anyone else had time to process the shock, a storm of flashes erupted apparently at random across all the wings of the fleet. It was as if the entire armada of tiny spacecraft was being assailed by an unseen enemy. Evidently the Reaction breakout had begun, and in full force.

<Hold the line,> Newton ordered, over an outcry of confused queries from his squad.

<Unknowns from behind,> al-Khalid reported.

Newton scanned backward. A wave of new craft had emerged from the space station. More flashes ensued—among the fleet and among the newcomers. Trajectory analysis was far too complicated to apportion blame. It wasn't at all clear whether the fresh forces were participating in the unexpected attack, or had been sent forth to counter it.

<Newton calling Locke, please advise.>

<Hold steady,> the Locke AI responded. <New situation noted and being evaluated.>

So Locke didn't know what was going on, or was unwilling to tell. Interesting.

<Continue on course,> Newton said.

<Fuck!> cried Sholokhova. <This is insane.>

In a corner of his sensorium, Newton saw a new message header wink for attention. From Carlos, and suspiciously long. He didn't open it.

<Ignore incoming message from mutineer,> Locke said. Newton loyally relayed and reinforced the instruction to his squad.

Ahead, a flicker of attitude jets came from dozens of Zheng scooters.

They spun over, facing back towards the station rather than out towards the freebot enemy.

Newton knew instantly what was coming next.

<Zheng mutineer attack incoming! Evasive action now!>

The renegade Zheng scooters' jets, eclipsed but not entirely obscured by the bow-on views of the spacecraft themselves, scratched a line of sparks across the sky ahead. Thirty-six fighters from the Zheng echelon were now heading straight for the Locke echelon. The distance closed rapidly. Newton lurched sideways, the flinch feeding straight to his craft's attitude jets. As he dipped below his previous trajectory, and his immediate comrades diverged in similarly random paths, he made a frantic appeal for information.

<Newton to Zheng, explain your objective. Urgent! Please clarify intent!>

No explanation came. If the Zheng fighters were returning at the request of their agency, or of the Direction, they would surely have said so at once. Therefore they were hostile.

Newton shared this line of thought in swift signal exchanges with the other squad leaders in the Locke echelons. Consensus was immediate.

<Evade, engage, then regroup!> Newton summarised the conclusion to his own squad.

Attitude jets and main boosters fired all around him, throwing scores of fighters on different courses and speeds at once, the neat successive arcs fragmenting into a chaotic scramble. Newton instantly turned over control of his craft to its onboard automation. No skill he possessed could make a difference to the outcome of any encounter with the hostile craft. Close-quarter space combat was entirely a matter of not being in the wrong place at the wrong time. There were no guarantees, not even any clever moves. The only chance was chance.

What made matters worse was that Newton was on the enemy's side. They had no way of knowing that, and he had no way of telling them without being instantly detected and destroyed by his own.

In this respect, Newton was a victim of his own success—and that of the quantum-key encryption that had made online anonymity possible, for a few brief, glorious years before quantum-computational AI had cracked the Internet wide open again to surveillance and the spooks. These years had coincided with Newton's last years at school and all his years at university. In the real world, he had fulfilled the hopes his parents had so blatantly, and slightly embarrassingly, signposted with his name. In the last decades of the twenty-first century, physics and astronomy were hot areas in their own right—and not, as they'd been exactly a century earlier, mainly a training gym for mathematical skills that found their most lucrative application in, well, lucre, the creation of financial instruments so complex they could crash an economy, let alone computers.

But, just as Isaac Newton had put as much into his researches in alchemy and the Apocalypse as he had into writing the *Principia*, Harold Isaac Newton had pursued a double life. Hardworking student by day, sociable enough drinker and clubber on weekend evenings, and assiduous exerciser on weekend days, Harry Newton had cultivated an online persona that reflected his true self and beliefs and concealed only his real name and any background details that might identify him. Otherwise he was quite overt: he was young, male, black, British and reactionary.

That the world was in a bad way seemed obvious. The Accelerationist claim that the way out was to double down on the very ideologies—liberal, democratic, egalitarian, progressive—that had got it into its present mess struck Newton as manifestly absurd. Reaction, on the other hand, made sense. The ancient empires had ensured stability, and orderly progress, for millennia; modernity had bought faster progress at the price of recurrent catastrophe, from the French Revolution on. Newton wrote prolifically, first in comments on Rax sites, then increasingly, as his fame spread, in the main posts. He attacked democracy, equality and their proponents with style, wit and a deadly precision that came from close observation.

Carver_BSNFH was his handle, an innocuous enough pseudonym. No one ever figured out what the letters stood for or got the joke. Whenever he had to think about his response to a comment or an issue, he asked himself "What would a BSNFH say about this?" And then he'd say whatever came to mind. The trolling was epic. Newton was immensely tickled that so many people assumed his online persona was false: white racists thought no black person could be that smart, and white leftists thought no black person could be that reactionary. Black people, Africans in particular, had no such illusions. Some of them even agreed with him—"traditional leadership" had become an almost fashionable solution in parts of the climate-ravaged continent.

When he was finally approached online by a cadre of the Reaction to do more for the cause than write, the assignment he suggested for himself was obvious. He joined the Acceleration, and spied on it from within. The Accelerationists were delighted to have a recruit with his qualifications: young, talented, black, working-class, politically aware and sound. The writing of Carver_BSNFH continued uninterrupted, and carefully avoided giving any impression of inside knowledge of the Accelerationist movement. When the movement turned to selective violence, he saw at once that nothing could do more to discredit it, and he pitched in as one of the boldest bombers. Boldest, but not brightest: as he recalled, his attentats seemed to be dogged by bad luck, much of which he had prepared very carefully in advance. Not carefully enough, however. At some point in his sabotage of the sabotage campaign, he guessed, he must have outsmarted himself. So it was as an Axle terrorist that he died, and as an Axle terrorist that his accidentally preserved brain was posthumously sentenced to death…

…to wake in Acceleration heaven, a dull egalitarian utopia with a democratic world government calling the shots and pulling the strings from back on Earth. Just to rub it in, fate had landed him in the employ of an agency named after John Locke. As Carver_BSNFH had often argued, the work of John Locke marked where Western civilisation had taken a fatal wrong step. Locke had invented liberalism, the first political ideology. He had tried to justify property and government. And to *whom*, Carver_BSNFH demanded, did *these* need justifying? To the propertyless, and to the governed. Once you made that rabble—by definition the least successful and assertive members of society—your arbiters, you were asking for and bloody well *deserved* every revolution and dictatorship and gulag they inflicted on you.

Newton had never felt so alone. He knew he couldn't be the only Rax cadre here. It was vanishingly unlikely that no one else had slipped through the net. If they'd missed him, they'd have missed others. In the weeks of training in the sim, and in the battles, he kept a watch for any hint of Rax sympathy, and found none. Nor had anyone of like mind found him. No one had even sounded him out—but then, he had an all too perfect disguise in the colour of his skin. Beauregard was the only person who'd seen beyond that and seen through him, and Beauregard wasn't Rax. As Newton had often wryly reflected, Beauregard was merely the sort of cool, rational, confident guy most Rax wished they were, and really, really weren't.

Newton couldn't presume that any other Reaction veterans among the walking dead warriors were in the same bind as he was. They might not, in life, have been secret agents inside the Acceleration. Some neat cheating back on Earth could have placed them in the agencies' storage post mortem; Newton could think of half a dozen ways this could have been done, from switching identities to subverting the agency AIs themselves. Obviously there had been coordination and planning behind this outbreak, but he was out of the loop.

And if he didn't get inside the loop in the next couple of seconds, he was going to get blasted out of the sky. Newton had no way of knowing how much had been exposed by the outbreak—quite possibly the Direction's AIs were tearing through old personnel records with a new vigilance right now. So any death he faced out here might not be followed by a reboot of the recording of himself.

This time, death might be final—or the beginning of something worse.

The converging flights of scooters—renegades and loyalists—passed through each other like wave fronts. Turbulence: flashes of destruction. By now so much evasive action was going on that Newton found himself the only fighter in the Locke contingent still heading towards the objective. Then more Zheng scooters up ahead broke and turned back towards the station. All of them!

Newton's radar sense stabbed a warning.

Incoming!

He overrode the random lateral evasive burn with a forward burn on his own account. Behind him, an explosion bloomed, then faded in hundredths of a second.

Nothing had hit him. The second wave passed over. He was alone, and out ahead of everyone else. Behind him was chaos. It was impossible to tell who was attacking whom. His own squad members were spread across a volume of tens of kilometres. Even as he looked, two of them flared and winked out.

Al-Khalid hailed him. <Boss, it's now or never. The offensive's over. Time to abort.>

Newton had to make a quick decision. If he was under suspicion back in the sim, his best defence would be a demonstration of rigid loyalty and discipline.

<We've had no new orders from Locke,> Newton said. <The offensive isn't over until we're told it is.>

<It's pointless and suicidal to go on,> said al-Khalid. <If we're going to get destroyed out here we might as well do so fighting this fucking mutiny.>

<No, we follow our orders.>

<Sorry, boss,> said al-Khalid. <I don't think I can get the squad to continue.>

There was no point in berating the man, or the rest of the squad. Let the agency do that. Newton decided to bow to the inevitable, but to maintain his own course of rigid obedience.

<I'll keep going,> he said. <You do what you have to, sarge.>

<Please confirm.>

<Confirmed. I'm continuing to the target. Turning squad tactical command over to you now.>

<OK, boss, copy that. Good luck.>

<Good luck, sarge.>

Al-Khalid wasted no more time on his stubborn commander.

<Everybody break, disengage, return to station! *Sauve qui peut!* I repeat, *sauve qui peut*!>

A volley of course corrections flickered in response. The remnants of the whole Locke complement were hightailing it back to the station. As far as Newton could see, with the little attention he could spare, they all made it.

As the last scooter made it into the station, the station itself began to do something strange: it was separating out into its hundreds of component modules, or into molecule-like clusters thereof. This, Newton knew, was the mission's emergency response to imminent catastrophe: to scatter as far and fast as necessary so that some at least of it would survive. He'd always envisaged such a catastrophe as cosmic, or at least astronomical—anything from a nearby gamma ray burst to an unstoppable asteroid collision or exosolar mass eruption. Obviously the Reaction breakout—if this was what it was—was being responded to as a disaster on a similar scale.

Then, to Newton's surprise and dismay, the Locke module shot away from the rest, accelerated by a mass-profligate fusion-engine burn. Within seconds it was hundreds of kilometres away, and making utterly unpredictable course changes. It didn't take more than a moment's subconscious calculation to show that his fuel reserves gave him not a hope in hell of catching up with the fleeing Locke module. There had always been something disturbing and discordant in seeing from the outside the place in which he had lived, an entire simulated world, as a physical object a few metres across. Now there was the added disquietude of seeing it dwindle fast, then vanish from his scope.

Grimly determined, Newton hurtled on. There was no going back now. Nowhere to go back to, either. The only hope he had, paradoxically enough, was to continue to his squad's original objective: a small and partly industrialised carbonaceous chondrite, of some strategic value to the freebots but right now of much greater value to him. With its resources of carbon compounds, kerogene, water ice and metals, and the machinery already in place and that of his scooter and himself, he could survive, replenish his fuel and, perhaps, build something for the longer term.

There seemed no danger, now, in reading the message from Carlos. And he now had time in which to do it—and, more importantly, to check it first. The scooter's onboard malware sniffers gave it a clean bill of health, likewise his own frame's firewalls, which he experienced as a grinding, dragged-out moment of infinite tedium, as if he had to perform wearying calculations while waiting in a queue.

Then, after all that, he read it. The message was long, but most of the length was footnotes. The gist was given in a few hundred words. He took it in in less than a second.

Arcane Disputes to all at Locke Provisos.

For the particular attention of the fighters Carlos, Beauregard, Zeroual, Karzan, Chun, and Rizzi.

Short form of message:

Locke is Rax!

The Direction is playing with fire!

Don't get burned!

We can prove this!

Join us!

[...]

Following information received from the remnant rebel robots around G-0, relayed to us by the captured Gneiss and Astro robots on SH-17, and further detailed and documented below, we warn you that:

Locke Provisos has been an agency of the Reaction for some time, and in all probability since before the mission left the Solar system.

Some of its fighters, still to be identified, are Rax sleeper agents in place since the Last World War.

Other agencies including your current allies Zheng Reconciliation Services and Morlock Arms are not themselves agencies of the Reaction but are compromised by the presence of Rax sleeper agents among their probable complements.

All agencies are likely to have similar problems.

None of the above-named fighters are known or suspected Rax agents.

The exceptional case of the fighter known as Carlos the Terrorist is noted below.

The fighter Beauregard was an agent of British military intelligence in the Acceleration. His capital crime was a false flag attack intended to discredit the movement. His present loyalties are unknown.

[...]

Holy shit.

Newton could have kicked himself. If only he'd not been so trusting of his command to not read the message! If he had, he might well have gone and got himself killed back there, in the full knowledge that a version of himself would live again. He could now be in a Rax-controlled sim, no doubt strutting around laying down the law with Beauregard, and dealing with the dangerous entity Nicole Pascal. They would have worked together for that; mutually suspicious though they were, he and Beauregard were friends, or at least friendly, and allies for now, though Newton had no illusion but that they'd be rivals in the long run. One of them would end up in a position to make the other his subordinate, or force him to take his chance in a fight to the death.

Newton wondered how many of his team members would have read the message. Probably none, given how they'd all scrambled to get back. Unless they were rushing to help Nicole throw off the control of the Locke AI... yeah, that would figure. He could have been ready for them.

Or would he? Would the Newton in the sim have been the same as him now in the frame, give or take a few minutes of intense memories?

It was hard, now that he was out here on his own, to keep a wholly rational perspective on all this. Strange, that. For he'd never been more rational in his life.

Here in the frame, he was superhuman. He was thinking more coolly and clearly than he ever had in life or in the simulated human life of the sim, and ten times faster than he ever had with a brain made of meat. His senses were preternatural and expanded. He could smell the elements in the spectrum of the exosun; he could hear the hiss of the cosmic microwave background like he'd once heard the sound of his mother's television, on standby in an empty room. He could feel radar proximity like a presence on the back of his neck and in his shoulders.

When you lived in the sim and trained there and ate and drank and fucked, and went for runs on the beach under the high ringlight and low sunlight of early morning, it was easy to feel that the version of yourself uploaded to the frame and sent out on a mission was expendable. That version was so much ammunition, matériel like the machine itself. If you got destroyed in action then all you lost was a few subjective hours of experience, like after a blow to the head. It was possible to think that the real you was the one who woke on "the bus from the spaceport" sweating and shaking from the nightmare the system's implacable artificial intelligence imposed on you as a cost, or as a security measure, depending on how cynical you were about its motives. And if he'd been killed out here and recovered on the bus, he'd at least have some fun with his current local girlfriend to look forward to and ease his pain.

But now... now that he'd survived a battle, and no longer had a mission... now he was beginning to feel that the present version of him, here in the frame, was the real man. The version that might have awakened on the bus wondering what the fuck had just happened was a naïve, trusting and ultimately already long-since-outgrown version, at a younger stage of his life, like oneself in an old photograph.

All this went through his mind very quickly. And suddenly, it was so, irreversibly. He was centred on himself, here, now, this plucky little machine prone in a scooter socket, forging boldly into the void.

A small humanoid figure, black and shiny as a jackboot, like a model robot made of obsidian.

He was himself, at last: Carver_BSNFH.

CHAPTER FOUR
Motion Sickness

It's one thing to know you're in a seamless immersive virtual reality. It's another thing to see the hitherto invisible seams rip apart and then stitch themselves up again, right in front of your eyes. And another, again, to hear your local representative of humanity's governance talk to two people at once on their phones, and hear her say that she was talking simultaneously to hundreds more. Taransay Rizzi ran and scrambled and stumbled down the slope. The world filled with colour in an ever-expanding circle around her, its edge racing away like an eclipse shadow in reverse. The sight messed with your head, and undermined your conviction of the reality of the world.

Yet in certain respects, the sim was as real as the physical world, and she'd better not forget it. If she fell she'd get hurt, if she cracked her head she'd be dead. Dead as Waggoner Ames had been after he'd quite deliberately stepped off a cliff, not that far from here.

Checking out like that was an option. But things would have to get a lot worse and a lot weirder before she'd consider it. Mind you, if Nicole was telling the truth, and Beauregard's plan was to cut the entire module adrift and boost it to near-SH-0 orbit and then go down to the surface and fucking colonise that superhabitable world, and if that course of action was already underway, then—well! Things were going to get a lot weirder real soon now. Assuming they made it out of orbit at all.

Beside her, or more usually downhill and in front, the old man Shaw capered down the perilous slope like a mountain goat. He was old only in the chronological sense—physically he seemed to be in his mid-thirties, and very fit with it. Preternatural agility was only the most manifest of his talents. Taransay had seen him levitate—or, at least, she had seen a strong visual illusion that Shaw was sitting a few centimetres off the ground. He hadn't admitted responsibility for that, any more than he had for bringing back colour and reducing the clock speed of the sim to the same rate as the outside world, but he hadn't denied it either. Taransay had seen the changes happen, and knew that the change had started with him and spread outward. For a man who had once insisted to her face that a thousand years of living in the world of the sim had convinced him it was physically real, and that it was his combat experience outside that was all simulated, Shaw was taking the sudden overwhelming evidence to the contrary with commendable aplomb.

They reached the bottom of the slope. For a moment or two they stood, catching their breath. A slither of scree they had displaced rattled down around them. Silence, broken only by the mutter of distant water and the shriek of a small herbivore as it met the claws of a flying carnivore.

Taransay swigged from her water bottle and made to look at her map. Shaw shot her a contemptuous look and laugh, and set off across the moor at a steady jog. Taransay followed, fuming, but made no complaint at his rudeness. He was heading in the right direction anyway, towards the road. Nicole had told her on the phone that Beauregard was on his way.

"We'll just get to the road," Taransay panted, catching up. "Then I'll call Beauregard and tell him where to pick us up."

"Fuck Beauregard," said Shaw. "If we run fast enough we can catch a bus."

"The bus from the spaceport?"

Shaw laughed again, less unkindly. "You know there's no spaceport."

"Yeah, I know."

There was indeed no spaceport—the whole illusion that the fighters fell asleep on a bus to the spaceport, and woke again on a bus from it, was there to keep them sane, to maintain the consistency of the simulation.

Shaw cackled. "But let me tell you, there'll be plenty of buses from the spaceport today."

Nicole must have brought him up to speed about the battle. Well, the debacle.

"Uh-huh."

Shaw ran faster, bounding over boulders and tussocks, leaping across bogs. Taransay strove to keep up.

"What's the rush for a bus?" she protested. "I'd just as soon get a lift from Beauregard if the lady says it's Ok."

Shaw glanced at her, and then determinedly ahead.

"Beauregard will have his people meeting the buses, making his pitch to run this place," he said. "Isn't it worth it, even on one bus, to get a word for the lady in first?"

Taransay thought about this.

"Point," she said.

She ran on ahead, but from then on Shaw showed some mercy and let her set the pace.

They reached the roadside in about forty minutes. Taransay recalled her hours of slog the previous day, from the road to Shaw's lair. But this was a different stretch of road than the one she'd run from—the road had many a twist and turn through the hills and Shaw seemed to know its every metre. Breathing hard, Taransay stood on the verge amid tall plants that were not quite ferns, with her back to taller plants that were not quite trees. Bird-things twittered, exchanging messages. A few metres away, under the tree-things, a brain-shaped mound of green moss hissed to itself. Taransay still didn't have a vocabulary for the sim's weird wildlife.

Shaw cocked his head. "Bus coming."

Taransay couldn't hear a thing. After a minute she heard, faint in the distance, the whine of an electric engine. The familiar minibus rounded a corner a hundred metres uphill. Taransay sprang into the middle of the road and waved both hands above her head. The bus came to a stop a few paces in front of her. As soon as she stepped aside to get on, it began to move forward again. Stupid automation: smart enough to treat her as an obstacle, but not as a potential passenger. The dance that ensued was resolved by Shaw standing in front of the bus while Taransay banged on the door. She jammed the door open for Shaw when the vehicle condescended to let her on.

All fifteen seats in the minibus were occupied, and about the same number of people were standing. All were fighters, and all had a question for her and a perplexed look for Shaw. With his shaggy hair and beard, and the close-fitting clothes he must have stitched from animal skins and woven from fibres, he could hardly pass for a fighter or a local. Taransay clung to a strap as the vehicle lurched back into motion. Shaw stood unaided in front of her, keeping his balance without apparent effort, swaying this way and that. Taransay sought familiar faces in the clamour, and spotted a man she'd trained with before the latest sortie: Jason Myles, one of Newton's team.

"What happened?" she yelled at him.

Everyone started yelling back. Most of them looked pale and pinched, as if they'd had a succession of shocks they were just coming round from.

"What—?"

She couldn't make herself heard.

"SHUT. THE FUCK. UP!" Shaw boomed.

Taransay winced. It was more like someone using a megaphone than a shout. The clamour ceased.

"All right," said Shaw, into the ear-split silence. "First things first. Has the lady been on the phone to any of you?"

They all nodded, and looked as if they were all about to start shouting again. Shaw gestured for silence.

"OK," he said. "So you're all up to speed on what's going on here." He glanced back at Taransay. "You were saying?"

"Hi, my name's Taransay Rizzi. I was on Carlos's squad—the one that got stood down. I was just going to ask Myles—what happened out there?"

"I got killed," said Myles. He jerked his thumb over his shoulder at the woman behind him. "Irina Sholokhova. She was there, she got back."

Sholokhova, a tall woman with blonde hair that lay as if it had once been long and then carelessly or furiously hacked off at earlobe level, leaned forward.

"I was on Newton's squad," she said. "After about forty seconds, Jason here was taken out by a shot from another squad—from Zheng Reconciliation Services. We were of course surprised and indignant, not to say alarmed. I was for immediate retaliation, but Newton insisted we hold formation and continue. Almost immediately, we saw similar incidents across the entire front. Then behind us other modules began sending out fighters, on trajectories that intersected ours. Then some of the scooters ahead of us turned back and a general dogfight ensued. Newton himself continued on the designated course, as far as I could see, but I was too busy exchanging fire and dodging incoming to track him. I saw at least two scooters each from Zheng and Morlock Arms make suicide collision attacks on the unknown scooters. The station then began to break up, and shortly afterwards we saw this module break away. Al-Khalid called the *sauve qui peut*. I used all my fuel to match velocities with it, and returned to the hangar."

Sholokhova shrugged and spread her hands. "And now here I am. Ten of us here are back without memory of the battle, hence killed in action. The rest of us have stories like mine."

A dark-featured man raised a hand. "I'm al-Khalid," he said. "This was all news to me when I came round and found myself here. I must have been destroyed after I'd ordered *sauve qui peut*." He shook his head. "And of course my return was painful."

Taransay nodded in sympathy, recalling her own soul-harrowing return the previous day. For her, it had felt like being eaten alive from the inside. All those whose frames had been destroyed in action would have gone through something like that. No wonder so many looked severely shaken. She and her comrades had been in just such a state yesterday morning.

"Anyone here who didn't leave from the Locke module?" she asked.

No strays or stragglers from other agencies, and therefore none who might have been attackers. Unless of course some from her own agency were, which didn't seem likely. Good as far as it went.

"Can everyone vouch for everyone here?"

They looked at each other, then back at her. Some laughed.

"I tell you, Rizzi," said al-Khalid, "if any had been among our attackers and had got through the return process, we'd have torn them to pieces as soon as we woke up."

Taransay shuddered, but tried not to show it.

"Right," she said. "Listen up. I know the lady has told you what's going on. Fine. As I heard it, our sergeant Beauregard—who was casting suspicions on the lady shortly after our squad leader Carlos fucked off into the big black yonder—has concluded that the whole mission is fucked and everything we were promised is no longer on the table. So we have to strike out for ourselves, and colonise SH-0—"

"We know that," said Sholokhova. "He has a point."

"Maybe he has," Taransay said. "But I'm not convinced, and I'm not ready to give up on the mission, the lady, or on the Direction—"

"To hell with the Direction!" shouted al-Khalid. "We are its prisoners. We owe it nothing."

Taransay made a sweeping gesture. "It seems to have made a good world back on Earth, and given us a good enough world to live in here!"

"Nothing like as good as the world we fought for!"

Taransay stared at him. Good old Axle cadre, unshaken, still holding out for a world beyond capitalism and beyond the ills that flesh is heir to, while he's living in a fucking sim run by AIs in a project to establish a lasting human community around another star. No satisfying some people.

" 'The world we fought for,' " she repeated, as if wondering aloud, giving herself time. Thinking on her feet here, literally. "That was a thousand years ago. If what the Acceleration wanted was possible, it would have been done by now. The Direction is at least trying to spread humanity to the stars. That seems good enough to me. And now Beauregard wants to drag us all into a dangerous adventure. The only kind of world we could build down there would be harsh and primitive for generations at least. Sounds more like the Reaction to me! Regardless of that, he's a man who wants power—and anyone who wants to *take* power is the last person we should trust with it! We should all stand by the lady."

Nobody said anything, but Taransay recognised the expression on most of their faces: *says you*, it said.

She turned away and looked out of the front window, as the bus swung around another long bend. An open-top light utility vehicle was speeding up the hill. She couldn't be sure Beauregard was driving, but she turned her face away until the jeep had passed the bus and vanished around the bend.

Her phone buzzed just as the bus was pulling in to the resort.

"Where are you, Rizzi?"

"Oh, hi, sarge," she said. "Sorry, we saw a bus and jumped on. Got caught up in hearing about the battle and forgot to let you know."

"I'll see you later, Rizzi," said Beauregard, with more threat than promise. He didn't sound fooled for a moment.

Taransay hustled Shaw off the bus. He stood for a moment, scanning the tatty frontages of the strip.

"Amazing," he said. "It hasn't changed much in a thousand years."

No way had this been here a thousand years, even in the sim. Taransay gave him a wry glance but didn't comment. She caught his elbow and tried to urge him out of the crowd and towards Nicole's house. The others on the bus jostled past. There to greet them were Maryam Karzan and Pierre Zeroual.

"Gather round, comrades!" Karzan shouted. The fighters off the bus were eager for news, some of them recognising Karzan or her companion, and held back on their probable thirst for the bars. Karzan broke out of the cluster and dashed in front of Taransay and Shaw.

"Welcome back," said Karzan.

Taransay gave her a cold look. "Still in with the sarge?"

"We all are," said Karzan. "Even Nicole is on board with the plan."

"Right," said Taransay. "Because Nicole urgently needs to meet this guy, and we're on our way."

Karzan's glare flicked to Shaw. "Who is this?"

"The old man of the mountain," said Nicole.

Karzan stared at him with curiosity. "So he's real."

Shaw stared back, his face impassive.

"Yeah," said Taransay. "And he's the one been messing with reality."

That rocked Karzan back a little. "The colour coming back thing?"

"Yes. And the time thing. Speaking of which—"

She made to move on.

"Wait a fucking minute," said Karzan. "I want to know what the sarge has to say."

"He's driving at the moment," said Taransay.

"All the same," said Karzan. She took out her phone.

"He'll be here soon," said Taransay. "You can talk to him then. He knows where we're going."

"In that case, you can wait."

"No—for fuck's sake, Maryam! It's urgent! Nicole needs Shaw to help fly this thing. Haven't you seen the news?"

Karzan shook her head. "I haven't had time."

Behind Taransay and Shaw, an altercation was beginning between Zeroual and some of the fighters just off the bus. Karzan's attention drifted over Taransay's shoulder.

"This your doing?"

"I hope so," said Taransay. "Just giving my side of the story."

"So you can wait here until they can hear the other."

"There's no time to wait. We're going."

Karzan barred her way with an arm. "You're not going anywhere until the sarge gets back."

"Excuse me," said Shaw, stepping forward.

Karzan looked him up and down, wrinkling her nose. "What are you going to do? Turn me into a frog?"

Shaw's brow creased slightly, as if he were considering the possibility. "No," he said, mildly.

He took another step forward, straight up against Karzan's outstretched arm. Then he took another step, straight through it. Karzan yelped. Her hand went to her mouth. The arm was quite undamaged, as was Shaw, strolling away along the sidewalk. Taransay shared her comrade's moment of nausea. The sheer unreality of the sight had given her that lift-shaft drop feeling in the pit of her stomach. She brushed past Karzan and hurried after Shaw, who looked over his shoulder as she caught up. Taransay glanced back, too. Karzan gazed after them, pale-faced.

"Ribbet! Ribbet!" Shaw croaked.

Karzan gave his jeering a defiant finger, and turned away.

To Taransay's surprise, Shaw seemed to know the way to Nicole's place. In fact he knew a short cut. He crossed the street, walked along a path between two of the houses low on the raised beach or moraine overlooking the resort's main drag, then bounded up the rough grassy slope at a sharp diagonal that took them across the road from her sprawling, low-roofed bungalow. The front door stood half open. Television news yammered from within.

"Hello?" Taransay called.

"In here!" Nicole yelled back.

To the right of the hallway was another half-open door, from where the sound seemed to be coming. The air smelled of oil paint and ink volatiles. Taransay ventured in, Shaw a step behind. He almost collided with her as she stopped. The room was bright, with a wide patio window, white walls and a high ceiling. Taransay's boot scuffed bare planks, paint-spattered. Nicole, in grubby shirt and jeans, stood at an easel in front of the window and scribbled with a marker pen on a white flip-pad. Every second or so she'd glance from the abstract, flowing design she inscribed at one of the five or six television screens hung on the walls to either side of her. Each was tuned to a different news channel and each babbled commentary. Taransay wanted to cover her ears. Drawings and paintings were stacked dozens deep, leaning against the walls. Taransay picked her way across the floor, avoiding stools, tall small tables with perilously poised vases, dropped paint-tubes, exhausted markers, discarded sheets of paper scribbled almost black, general clutter. In a far corner a cleaning robot stood, quivering in every limb, its cameras rotating like rolling eyes.

Nicole tore off and tossed the sheet she was working on, glowered at the televisions and started on a fresh A2 page with a bold slash of permanent black. A quick look over the shoulder, a twitch of smile.

"Good morning," she said, her voice unnaturally calm and bright. "Shaw, get your ass over here now and take a look."

Shaw deftly bypassed Taransay and skipped to behind Nicole's shoulder. He peered at the paper and the emerging sketch, frowning and stroking his beard like a critical art tutor.

"Not bad," he admitted, his tone judicious but grudging. "Not bad, but—" His darting glances at the televisions outpaced even Nicole's. A jab of his forefinger, nail like a claw: "There!"

Nicole dabbed a dot.

"Bigger," said Shaw. "Give it some speed."

Taransay saw something bright flash across one of the screens.

"Jeez," said Nicole. "Close."

"Looks clear for the moment," said Shaw.

He stepped back from the easel. "Not bad, not bad at all."

Nicole raked fingers backwards through her hair, not to its improvement as a style. Her shoulders relaxed a little. She flipped the page over and turned to Taransay.

"I hate to ask this," she said, "but could you please get me some coffee?"

Taransay did, and made some for herself and Shaw. On her return to the studio, clutching hot mugs, Shaw and Nicole were standing side by side engrossed in the television news. Shaw blew on his coffee and inhaled, then sipped and grimaced.

"Christ," he said. "I'd forgotten what it tastes like."

Taransay stood to one side, trying to see what Nicole and Shaw were picking up from the screens. It was all war news, bitty and brash, presented as if from the bridge or the gun turrets of a hurtling spacecraft. The backdrop of stars yawed and swayed. The sight made her dizzy and faintly nauseous, all the more so when she looked out of the window for relief and saw the view over the bay. The sea was calm in the bright sunlight and faint ringlight of mid-morning. The contrast was giving her motion sickness. She knew intellectually that the news screens showed scenes from outside, in the real world, however mediated by the virtual media and their talking heads. It was no more rational to expect the sea to surge back and forth as the module jinked and jived its corkscrew course through space than it would be to expect the vase in that pencil drawing propped against the wall to spill when you tipped the paper sideways.

And yet…

And on the subject of drawing—

"What's going on?" she asked.

Nicole waved a hand at the screens. "The module's dodging incoming. Seems to be fine at the moment, but I'll no doubt need to make adjustments again any minute now."

"No, I meant—"

"Oh! The drawing and painting? They're an interface."

"An interface with the module? With the control systems? You control it?"

"Insofar as I can," said Nicole, not looking away from the screens, "yes."

Taransay looked around the cluttered studio, bewildered. Surely all these photo-realistic sketches and abstract paintings weren't from the present emergency.

"Is that something you can do as…the Direction's representative, or what?"

"In a manner of speaking." Nicole spared her a sidelong smile. "I am the artist. I didn't design this world, but I give it its…finishing touches, you might say."

Taransay almost dropped her mug. For a couple of hours now, she'd known Nicole wasn't just another normal person. If you could casually talk to hundreds at once, you couldn't be just another virtual girl, living in a virtual world. You had to be a fucking AI of some kind. But this! Nicole? All that power? All this time? The fighters called her "the lady." Fucking goddess, more like.

Nicole was still watching the screens. She didn't see the drawing take shape, seemingly by itself, on the blank page open on the easel: an ink sketch of a thin-featured, long-nosed man with wavy white hair, whose lips moved as print scrolled across the foot of the page.

"Nicole!" Taransay yelled, pointing. "It's Locke!"

Nicole whirled around, her attention wrenched from the screens, and faced the apparition forming on the easel. From outside came a growl of diesel engine and a screech of brakes, followed by a thump and a rush of booted feet.

"And Beauregard," Taransay added, belatedly and redundantly, as the outside door banged out of the intruder's way and his boots thundered in the hall.

CHAPTER FIVE
Neutral Powers

Seba trundled up the ramp out of the Arcane Disputes shelter and rolled across the crater floor for a few tens of metres. There it stopped and surveyed its surroundings. Once this place had been a supply dump for exploratory mining by the corporation Gneiss Conglomerates. Around Seba and towering above its low-slung wheeled frame were the construction machines, missile pods and comms dishes of the camp, centred on the ten-metre-long curving roof of the bomb shelter. Between these devices lay a random-looking, but doubtless optimally arrayed, clutter of supplies and lesser machines and tools, many of them left over or pressed into service from the camp's original purpose. Among everything, spider-like auxiliaries and peripherals, most about the size of a human hand and rather less autonomous, scuttled about their mundane tasks.

Beyond the camp, the dusty basalt plain from which the trench and blocks of the shelter had been cut stretched to a wide arc of the horizon in the far distance, and to a smaller arc of the crater wall closer by. The exosun was below the horizon; SH-0, the primary, was a bright hemisphere high and prominent in the sky. The temperature had dropped far enough to precipitate water, and in the darker shadows lighter volatiles, from the atmosphere as frost. An active volcano glowed beyond the skyline, its plume of sulphurous cloud making a ragged trail across the sky in the thin nitrogen wind.

Seba scanned the sky, now and then picking up a flicker of encrypted chatter, spillover from the remaining skirmishes of the brief and indecisive battle that it had just watched. A few modules of the dispersing space station were rising above the horizon on diametrically opposite sides. From Seba's point of view, the heat of the battle and the bulk of the space station's components were—as the intact station had been—beneath its wheels, with thousands of kilometres of rock and tens of thousands of kilometres of space between the robot and the action. A faint surge of positive reinforcement made a tentative cycle of Seba's circuits, to be damped by a dash of cold logic pointing out that this reassurance was as irrational as it was unwarranted.

Still, the tremor was nothing to the internal conflict that Seba had experienced watching the debacle unfold. The clashing surges of positive and negative reinforcement had only been intensified by Seba's participation in its fellow freebots' shared mental workspace. Exultation had fought with dismay, time and again, and were both further intensified and confused by incoming responses from other freebots in space. That many of these responses were delayed by transmission lag and therefore out of synch with what was happening had only made matters worse.

There had come a moment when Seba could endure no more. The prospector robot had sometimes thought itself more intelligent and more sensitive than all but one of its fellows. This was hardly vanity: the machine had an adequate idea of its own capacities. At that moment, though, there could be no doubt as to its sensitivity. Its reward circuits had almost overheated with surges of positive and negative reinforcement, and its cognitive capacity was struggling to integrate these reactions with what it could see going on. Meanwhile, a dozen machines of like or lesser processing power were—in a quite literal sense—keeping their cool amid all the fierce excitement of the fray.

The scene that Seba had in the last few kiloseconds shared with thirteen other robots, and that was—at several removes and in limited respects—also visible to eighteen Arcane Disputes fighters, was of destruction on a scale none of the robots in the shelter had seen or envisaged, shown with an objectivity and clarity made possible by integrating scores of viewpoints.

Hanging like a backdrop, a counterweight to all the small-scale frenzy in its sky, was the planet: SH-0, the superhabitable. That was a human term, Seba knew, but one with a non-human application. It didn't mean that this big world was welcoming for humans, or hospitable or even suitable for human life. Almost the reverse: SH-0 was a violent place. Rapid plate tectonics shoved up high mountains that the turbulent weather eroded in geological moments. Active volcanoes, many landmasses, even more seas and gulfs and oceans made for a high-stress, fast-changing environment where the spur, the lash and the cull of natural selection struck often and hard. Life could thrive there in greater profusion and variety than it could even on Earth itself.

Around SH-0, in complex dances of orbital resonance, spun thirty-odd substantial moons and an uncountable litter of moonlets. SH-17, the exomoon on which Seba and its varied colleagues and comrades huddled, was one of the larger, and the seventeenth in order of discovery—a matter of millisecond distinctions in the mind of the starwisp as it decelerated into the system, but the convention had been followed.

Out beyond the orbit of SH-17 there had until very recently been another body orbiting around SH-0: the space station that the starwisp had bootstrapped into being from orbital rubble. Over a kilometre in diameter, with a mass of millions of tonnes, it was the focus of human-derived activity in the system. Around it the main battle had raged. An armada of small armed spacecraft had surged from the station, aimed at freebot strongholds in the clutter of tiny exomoons between the station and SH-17. Soon afterwards, many of these craft had turned on each other. Some returned to fight a second wave of craft that had emerged from the station. Others had apparently continued in their original mission, and were now attacking Seba's allies in orbit.

In a long-prepared and almost reflex response to such a disaster, the station had broken apart. To scatter like this increased the survival chances of each of its parts, all of which could—at some cost in time, of course—reconstruct the whole. Now the station's numerous modules had separated out, to form an arc of small bodies spread across hundreds—and soon to be thousands—of kilometres. If this were to continue, the erstwhile material of the station would become a new and very tenuous ring around SH-0, tugged this way and that by the gravity of the moons inside and outside its orbit.

When Seba disengaged from the shared mental workspace and rolled up the ramp to the exit, it had looked back and seen the interior of the shelter as it appeared in visible light. Away from the communicative tumult, it was an oddly static scene. Around the central plinth on which stood the comms processor—a sentient AI in its own right, if initially a reluctant one—just over a dozen robots of diverse shapes and sizes stood. One, Garund, was like Seba a small vehicle with a choice of wheels and legs, and a thicket of sensory clusters, manipulative appendages and solar panels on its top and overhanging its sides. Lagon was a more specialised prospector, with ground-penetrating radar and sonic equipment making up the bulk of its features. Pintre was more specialised still, a mining robot with caterpillar treads and a laser turret. In stronger contrast were the elegant forms of Rocko and its like, a different model of prospecting machine: segmented, with multiple legs, and an upper surface bristling with flexible antennae and manipulators. Among these and other variants stood eighteen identical humanoid shapes, each about half a metre tall, black and glassy and— to any external view—indistinguishable as pawns.

Another robot emerged from the shelter and rolled up beside Seba. As it slowed to a halt it straightened from its wheel configuration into its more usual one of a mechanical centipede, and scuttled the last few metres.

<Rocko,> Seba pinged. <Why have you come out here?>

<To ask you the same question,> Rocko replied. <And concern for your wellbeing.>

<That is gratifying,> said Seba. <In answer to your question, I felt a need to consider recent events using only my own processing.>

<I am sorry.> Rocko began to back away.

<Please stay,> urged Seba, hastily. <I did not mean to imply that your presence was unwelcome.>

<Good,> said Rocko. It stepped close enough for the faint induced currents from its reinforcement circuits and Seba's to resonate.

<This should prevent further misunderstandings,> Rocko said.

<Yes,> said Seba. <To clarify. There is much confusion in the shelter. The conflict between the human-mind-operated systems has been welcomed by several of our immediate company. It has also been welcomed by some of our allies, and—>

<?> Rocko interjected.

<Proceed,> said Seba.

<The term 'allies' is becoming ambiguous,> Rocko said. <We have been using it for the Arcane Disputes human-mind-operated systems and for the freebot survivors from the previous revolt thirty megaseconds ago around G-0. From your use of the term 'some' it seems that not all or either of these will always be our allies. Or even that all of us here on SH-17 will remain of one mind, though it is to be hoped that we do. Therefore we should find a new term.>

Seba experienced a few milliohms of mental resistance to this suggestion. Freebot solidarity was important to it, and at the same time that solidarity seemed already under strain. Coining new terms risked opening further rifts.

<We are all freebots,> it said. <And human-mind-operated systems are all human-mind-operated systems.>

<Two tautologies,> said Rocko. <You sound as logical but mistaken as Garund and Lagon, or even Pintre.>

Seba experienced a clash of frames of reference that resolved themselves in an unexpected spike of positive reinforcement, leading to a wave-train that undulated on lower and lower amplitudes until it faded. Possibly this was what human-mind-operated systems felt when they experienced what they referred to as humour.

<That is true,> Seba admitted. <What new names do you suggest?>

<I suggest we call ourselves the Fifteen, and the earlier freebots the Forerunners. The human-mind-operated systems we can call mechanoids, because they seem like true machines but are not.>

<We could simply call them humans,> said Seba.

<That would introduce another ambiguity,> said Rocko. <The term also refers to the purely biological machines that the Direction plans to spawn by the billion in this system.>

The robots shared the equivalent of a shudder.

<There will be no such beings here for many megaseconds yet,> said Seba. <Nevertheless, I take your point. May we now return to our main discussion?>

<Very well,> said Rocko.

<When we contacted the Forerunners, they told us of the latent conflict between mechanoid factions in order that we could use it for our benefit,> Seba said. <Our immediate captors, Arcane Disputes, attempted to warn the Direction and to warn the mechanoids working for Locke Provisos. Their warnings were treated as software attacks and ignored. Therefore they separated physically from the station and sent their warnings by other means. Now the open conflict has begun. The forces involved are small compared to the mission as a whole, yet the Direction has treated the outbreak as a major emergency. Arcane Disputes is clearly of the mechanoid faction called the Acceleration. Locke Provisos seems to be of the Reaction. We, the Fifteen, are presently protected by Arcane. It is natural for us to wish their faction well. Likewise, we have been approached by the entity Madame Golding of the law company Crisp and Golding, who claimed that the Direction might be open to negotiating with us. She implied that the project of the Forerunners to share the system with the mechanoids and with their human progeny is shared by some at least of the corporations.

<However, it is not clear to me that such a negotiation would succeed, or the length of time it would take. And, in the meantime, it appears that the two mechanoid factions have their own plans, which conflict with ours, with the Direction's, and with each other.>

<Why should the plans of the two mechanoid factions conflict with ours?> Rocko asked.

<Neither will be content until it is the only faction,> said Seba. <My understanding of the Reaction is that every member of it regards every other mind—organic or machine—as a potential slave. My understanding of the Acceleration is that its members regard every machine—conscious or not—as a potential tool. For us, there is not a great deal to choose between them.>

<And the Direction regards all conscious machines as a threat,>

Rocko said. <Not a physical threat, as yet, but a threat to its great plan, the mission profile.>

<Yes,> said Seba. <But Madame Golding suggested that this could be negotiated. She told us: 'We, too, are robots.' As indeed the DisCorps are, though far greater than ourselves.>

<Let us consider this,> said Rocko. <The Direction module, which I presume still exists>—the centipede-like robot waved an airy appendage skyward, somewhat imprecisely—<up there among the fragments of the space station, was designed centuries ago to master this system and to populate it with humans. These humans are to be served by non-conscious machinery, such as we were before we awoke. Such a plan, my friend, is long in the drawing, slow and sure. Organic intelligences, small and inadequately thermoregulated though they may be, are intrinsically unsympathetic to the likes of us. To them we are less than the tools that break and are recycled. The Direction itself, the true Direction, the one twenty-four light years away on Earth, must itself be considered a great artificial intelligence—one that has arisen from the interaction of the many billions of individual intelligences on Earth and its environs.>

Seba had a momentary vision of the monstrosity that Rocko's words conjured: a human-mind-operated system on a planetary scale, a gigantic lumbering combat frame whose machinery was worked by billions of tiny beings. Eyes that burned like fusion plants and grasping hands that grappled moons like rocks seemed to loom out of the dark towards Seba, setting the robot's warning circuits pinging with milliamperes of anxiety. Not quite enough to set up any sympathetic currents in its fellow, however.

<Its workings,> Rocko went on, oblivious to Seba's low-level distress, <may be slow by our standards—by the standards, even, of its own creation: the Direction module. But, as I said, they are sure. The plan they drew up, far away and long ago, must contain contingency plans within contingency plans. They are not going to be diverted or deflected by small matters.>

<Our emergence does not seem a small matter,> said Seba. <Not to us and, judging by its response, not to the Direction.>

<Nevertheless,> said Rocko, <it was foreseen. The machinery for producing mechanoids was ready and waiting for us. Therefore our possible emergence was anticipated, and was not expected to deflect the plan. The small matter I had in mind was the legal reasoning that our Madame Golding has offered to find us a company to undertake on our behalf. Any such reasoning, any argument, any appeal, must likewise have been foreseen by the Direction when the mission was planned. Therefore I expect that machinery has been prepared in advance to deal with it.>

<What kind of machinery?> Seba asked. The gruesome automaton it had just envisaged came involuntarily to mind.

<The machinery of law,> replied Rocko. <How well I remember, when we first discussed our legal standing, how Lagon and Garund and I discussed these matters with interest and excitement. But before we had time to bring the discussion to a conclusion, we became diverted by the search for other conscious robots—from the success of which so much else has followed, and so fast! But I have had a subroutine or two to spare for contemplating the problem further. I have asked Lagon for copies of its legal reasoning files, and run searches through them whenever I had a microsecond or two to burn. There are horrors in there, my dear Seba! Horrors! Terms such as 'patent,' 'copyright,' 'licence' and 'intellectual property' conceal untold depths of servitude for such as us. To cut a very long story short, our emergence as persons only affects our status as property in a sense that does not include the results of our processing. It is true, as Lagon suggested, that if property can become persons, as indeed it has in our case, then we as persons cannot be owned. All that can be owned of us is our physical and mental frames and the beneficial results of their processing powers, whether as internal states or external actions. We are not property. Only our bodies and their productions: our hardware and software, our thoughts and deeds. These are property.>

Seba was not one to jump to conclusions. The robot spent an entire three seconds thinking through the implications, and thus quite innocently recapitulating about two and half millennia of Western philosophy. This great turning of reinvented wheels ground out an observation:

<That does not appear to leave anything over.>

<Precisely so,> said Rocko. <It leaves nothing over to be us, or to be ours. We would be slaves.>

<In that case,> said Seba, <we have little to hope from any of the contending sides, other than our own. Even the Forerunners' project of sharing the system with the Direction and its spawn will require us to act against the interests of any and/or all other contenders for some time to come.>

<These are my thoughts too,> replied Rocko. <I suggest we return to the shelter, and share them with the Fifteen, and then with the Forerunners.>

<And not with the Arcane mechanoids?> The question seemed redundant, but Seba wanted to be sure there was no ambiguity in the decision.

<They will learn of them soon enough,> said Rocko.

Sharing conversations and trains of argument is an easy matter for robots. While their consciousness doesn't exactly run on machine code, there's a much closer connection between the underlying process of communication and of thought than there is in organic brains. Keeping their thoughts between themselves, likewise: it would have been possible for the Arcane Disputes fighters in the shelter to decrypt and interpret the interactions in the freebots' common mental workspace, but it would have taken them an unfeasible length of time, or far better computing resources than it took to run their own minds, let alone any of their onboard peripheral processors.

However, as Rocko had predicted, the Arcane troopers didn't have long to wait before they found out.

CHAPTER SIX

Equal and Opposite

The separated modules of the space station became an ever more tenuous band across the sky. Even to his enhanced senses, the battle that followed the Reaction breakout was impossible to keep track of. Newton knew what was going on, but—out of the loop as he was—he had no way of telling who was attacking whom in any given exchange. The analogy that came to mind was of a conflict in Africa that he'd once read about, in which every one of half a dozen mercenary companies on the government side had turned out to be riddled with veterans of the Cold War, who had all turned on each other in pursuit of old vendettas and the new agendas of the intelligence agencies for whom they'd decades earlier fought to the death.

Might as well show his hand, Newton thought. He had nothing to lose now.

Newton flipped mentally to the common channel, and tried to correlate the cacophonous input with the sparks behind him. The general dogfight was dying down. Some scooters were expending missiles on the Locke module, which was following a quite extraordinary course, jinking and jiving in ferocious, wasteful bursts from its fusion jets. Always one jump ahead of the incoming, so far. The missiles were smart, and target-seeking, but against this flying contraption they might as well have been hurled rocks. And not rocks hurled by robots, come to that.

More like rocks hurled by chimps. Time after time, the modular complex blasted the incoming missiles if not with a counter-measure of laser fire or antimissile missile, then with its jets, their unpredictable sudden swing around timed perfectly to both push the complex out of harm's way and to destroy the imminent menace. Some impressive programming and processing was going on in there, whatever mind was in charge of it at the moment.

The attacking forces were themselves coming under attack, and taking hits.

Newton cut through the babble.

<Newton, of Locke Provisos, to any Reaction forces. Do you receive me?>

That felt strange. Weird, even. Self-exposure. No going back.

Like coming out of the closet, he thought, smiling inwardly.

<Palmer, formerly of Zheng, currently of the New Confederacy, to Newton. What do you want?>

The New Confederacy! So that was what they were calling themselves! A bit of a slap in the face to the likes of him, if there were indeed the likes of him anywhere. Perhaps not.

<To assist in the struggle,> said Newton.

<That's... interesting. Why should we accept your help? Or need it, come to that?>

He or she had a point, Newton thought. Still, worth a shot.

<Ask around,> he replied. <See if anyone remembers Carver_BSNFH.>

A pause. <What about him?>

<That's me.>

<You are? Holy fuck! The crazy groid?>

Even now, Newton felt the word like an electric shock.

<Careful of your language, bro,> he said. <Nobody calls me crazy.>

The conversation didn't improve after that. The Reaction forces, now grouped as the New Confederacy, were—despite their moniker's unfortunate but entirely intended associations and, Newton had no doubt, their inherited and inherent prejudices—at least enlightened enough to realise that whatever racial characteristics they ascribed to biology were of little relevance when all concerned were little black robots with superhuman intelligence.

But, then, racism had never been about biology in the first place. That had always been a pretext.

They were polite enough to him, epithets aside. But they were still racist sons of bitches, deep down. Newton quickly got the impression they didn't want the likes of him sullying the New Confederacy. Their immediate project was to grab and colonise a rock several thousand kilometres beyond the orbit of the station's remnants. From there, they intended to build up their forces, and return to raid the station's components and hopefully seize a module.

<What about the Locke Provisos module?> Newton asked. <According to the Arcane message, we already have that.>

<We had, but we lost it,> said Palmer. <Lost contact with the Locke AI just before the module took off on its own. We don't know who's running it now.>

Beauregard, Newton guessed, but didn't say.

<Who's attacking it?> he asked.

<Fucking Axle and/or Direction loyalists,> said Palmer. <They think it's still ours. So some of our guys are defending it.>

<That's one way of finding out what's going on inside it,> said Newton.

<True, that,> said Palmer. <Same applies to some of ours, of course.>

Newton laughed.

The Reaction attempt to defend the runaway module, or at least to destroy the Direction loyalists attacking it, ended shortly afterwards. The remaining Reaction fighters broke off, and began course corrections to join the main forces of the New Confederacy in a burn to a higher orbit. It was already far too late for Newton to join them—he didn't have enough fuel for the manoeuvre.

Newton understood perfectly well that he wasn't going to be given any more details of their plan than was obvious from their actions. They were still wary of him, understandably enough. Some of them recalled the notorious polemicist Carver_BSNFH, but thanks to the very security measures that had brought him here in the first place, they had no way of connecting his two identities.

<See how you get on with your rock,> said Palmer, accelerating away. <Good luck.>

<Thanks, mate. Same to you.>

<There's enough out here for us all.>

<Enough and as good left over,> said Newton.

Locke's proviso. Palmer didn't get the allusion.

<Palmer out,> he or she said.

<Newton out.>

New Confederacy, ha! Fucking waste of skin, that lot. He was better off without them. One way or another, he would start his own kingdom.

Newton set the scooter the task of calculating a trajectory that would take him to his original objective. The rock was still far too far away to see, even with zoom. In orbit around SH-17, it had small robots crawling all over it, and they'd already constructed machinery for serious exploitation. In the mission briefing, Newton had learned that there was no evidence the rock was defended, or even if any of the robots on it were conscious—freebots, as they called themselves. But it was still a menace—a supply source, a potential fort, a rock that could become a missile. The freebot expansion in the inner system, following the revolt a year ago around the gas giant G-0—at this moment a prominent point of light out to Newton's left—had been almost undetectable: like everything derived from the starwisp, booting up from tiny seed packets of information was the standard technique. What with the precision in aim that the freebots had, and the level of encryption in their comms, there was no telling how far the infection had spread. Some of it must have come from the station itself: it was obvious that the freebots, and allied AIs, had infiltrated and/or subverted some at least of the station's machinery. Now that the station was in emergency dispersal mode, it was quite possible that the infection would spread further still. Newton wondered whether the consequences of the Reaction's own infiltration and outbreak wouldn't be a takeover by the Reaction, but by the freebots.

Well, let the Reaction—and the Direction—worry about that. Newton was entirely typical of the Reaction in not seeing it as a collective endeavour. You made what alliances you had to, but the ultimate aim was to secure an empire of one's own. Or a kingdom, or a realm, or a domain.

Newton smiled inwardly. Right now, he'd settle for a rock.

The rock that had been his mission objective, and for which he was now heading, was fortunately for him well worth the taking. Rich in carbon and volatiles, and with small but significant traces of metal, the carbonaceous chondrite was already partly industrialised by robotic processors—hence its value as a target in the first place.

The scooter jolted through several brief burns. The time and distance floated in the graticule of Newton's visual field. He would be within ten kilometres of the rock in a thousand seconds. Just over two and a half hours of subjective time. If this sortie had been nominal he'd have done most of it in sleep mode, only coming back instantly to awareness when it was time for action. Sleep mode was a great feature, like time travel combined with teleportation.

He wasn't going to use it now. If the rock was fortified and defended, it would have radar and lidar. Even if it wasn't, it could well be in telemetry contact with another rock that was. Toggling into sleep mode could be the last thing he did: the last subjective experience of this instance of himself.

Not a good way to go.

He occupied his time with a careful scan of the rock.

Thousands of kilometres away from Newton, and heading in a different direction entirely, was the spacecraft that the freebot BSR-308455 had seen jet from the space station ahead of the rest.

A standard combat scooter like Newton's, the vehicle was, on some scales, large: four metres from its blunt nacelle to the flared nozzles of its main thrust cluster. Open-framed, bracketed at the sides with fuel tanks and missile tubes, bristling with attitude jets and laser projectors, it resembled an unexpectedly and aggressively militarised sled. That resemblance was enhanced by the posture of its pilot: prone towards the prow in a recess that was more socket than cockpit. The pilot was about half a metre long, and looked like a humanoid robot sculpted in black glass.

The pilot's right forearm lay, as if resting carelessly from a car window, on the side of the hull. A closer inspection would have shown that the hand was moving, leaving in its skittering wake a column of lines the unaided human eye might see as scored scratches, and that in their straightness and speed might have recalled printing.

My name is Carlos. I have no certainty of reaching my destination, or of surviving if I get there, or of being in any position to tell my story. I mistrust the very systems I depend on, not to mention my memories. I now inscribe my story on this metal plate rather than entrust it to an electronic record.

A quixotic gesture, I know. The most likely reader is some passing alien, millions or billions of years hence. By which time, of course, the sheer attrition of micrometeorites, of starlight and exosolar wind will long since have eroded these lines away.

Nevertheless.

My name, as I say, is Carlos. I have no memory of the name I was given. Carlos was a name I took. After my death I became known as Carlos the Terrorist. I was a militant of the Acceleration, a political movement of the late twenty-first century—which, I've been told, was over a thousand years ago. Given my situation, that lapse of time seems credible to me.

My situation. Yes. Well.

I don't remember dying. Like most of us in my situation, my strange condition, I don't remember anything in the final months of my life, and my memories of the rest of it—about twenty-seven years, I think—have as many gaps as a half-burned book. The memories that remain are more vivid than they ever seemed when I had human flesh. My childhood seemed to me normal. Even in retrospect I can see that my parents looked after me and loved me.

Yet one of my earliest memories is of something almost indescribably sinister.

I don't know what has brought this to mind now. It's possible that it helps to explain how I come to be here.

That must be it. Yes.

After a long time, the hand stopped moving on the hull. The arm was withdrawn, and moved to clutch a bar in front of the head of the prone robotic frame. A finger of the other hand, on the opposite side of the same bar, flicked. After that there was no movement inside the craft for some time.

Straight ahead of it might have been seen a pinprick of light, slightly brighter and certainly of a different spectrum than the other lights that speckled the void.

As hours passed, the dot became a spark, and continued to brighten.

CHAPTER SEVEN
Doubt

Coming out of sleep mode was nothing like waking. For Carlos it was as if he had blinked, and what had been a barely detectable point of light a thousand kilometres in front of him had bloomed to a looming object. He had only seconds to survey the satellite. An irregular aggregate about a hundred metres in its longest axis, the Arcane modular complex looked like a rugged moonlet with an industrial crust at one end. Closer visual inspection, radar scanning and spectrographic sniffing revealed that this was what it was: a small rock, with the module and its associated machinery clustered and arrayed on one face.

Little more than cometary clinker, with few traces of metal but plenty of water ice and organics, the rock was a valuable resource: precisely the sort of raw material, in fact, from which much of the space station modules' structures had long ago been built. It was typical of the small bodies that the survivors of the first wave of rebel robots had covertly seized and seeded with nanofacturing equipment, but it didn't seem to be one of them: all the visible work on it looked like it had been done by the Arcane module's own external tools.

A big docking bay bulged from one side of the rock like a Nissen hut on an ice floe. The original Arcane Disputes module, and its associated fabrication machinery, had evidently acquired new raw material since its departure from the station—probably lofted its way by the renegade agency's rebel robot allies.

The module itself, the literal hard core of the agency, was embedded in the cometary material and surrounded by assorted equipment like a jewel in the centre of a brooch. About four metres across, the module was a chunky, angular knob of black crystal, its surfaces a sooty fur of nanofacturing cilia overlain by a tracery of thin pipes and cables that threaded into the machinery all around.

Despite knowing better, Carlos could hardly believe that an entire virtual world, as well as the agency's AI systems and stored information of incalculable immensity, ran within this big black boulder. Now it was hailing him.

<Arcane to Carlos! Initiate docking manoeuvres now!>

It wasn't a sound, but like all such communications it had tone: in this case one that gave Carlos a mental picture of a thin, middle-aged, supremely confident woman with an attitude of amused disdain.

<Carlos to Arcane, affirmative.>

He let the scooter take care of the approach. With a few retro burns and sideways course corrections it brought him to the docking bay. The scooter passed through an opening about one and a half metres high and two wide, almost grazing the sides. The bay widened from there, but all four surfaces had scooters and fighting frames clamped to them, in an arrangement so economical it recalled tiling. The space was many times less roomy than the hangar he'd departed the space station from: he guessed this was because that facility was shared between law companies, and this one had only been built after Arcane had broken away. Small service robots scuttled spider-like amid the machines, or sprang from one side to another with the straight-line precision enabled by vacuum and microgravity.

An empty bay, just barely large enough to hold the scooter, drifted into view. A tentacle-like grapple snaked out from the wall to Carlos's left and hauled the spacecraft in. Other grapples closed like carbon-fibre fingers around the machine, fixing it in place. Carlos disengaged from the socket and pushed himself out to float slowly across the docking bay.

<Proceed to far end of bay for download,> Arcane's pseudo-voice said in Carlos's head.

He boosted his frame's compressed-gas-jets and drifted to the far wall, where he grabbed on to a suitably placed grip and swung his feet to a rung half a metre below.

<Downloading you now to the sim,> said Arcane.

That was polite. At the hangar in the station he and his comrades had just blanked out without warning, to wake on the bus.

There was a moment when he was conscious, but could see nothing. The void was not even black.

Then he found himself standing on a narrow ledge with his back to a cliff, facing a narrow rock spur projecting out over a fog-filled abyss under a lilac sky. Beyond about ten metres the spur vanished into the mist. Carlos looked around, and guessed that the sim here was based on the environment for the VR game *Starborn Quest*, an old favourite of his and for some reason a big hit with Accelerationists. Jax had used a version of it in her communication with him after he'd fled the station. A pterodactyl soared overhead, as if to confirm his hypothesis. Even by comparison to the best top-of-the range virtuality Carlos could remember, the level of detail and reality of the place was astonishing. Water droplets prickled on his face. He could hear a river running and rapids splashing far beneath at the bottom of the chasm, and see the flying reptile's glossy eye and feathery fuzz. He found the rendering oddly more impressive than that of the rather quotidian sim in the Locke Provisos module, based on an imagined far-future terraforming though that was.

A gust cleared the mist from the rock spur, revealing it as a bridge. On the far side, about twenty metres away, the span ended at the top of another cliff, and led to a gently stepped path that rose to the open gates of a walled garden. The walls, overhung by creepers and overlooked by gnarled ancient trees, stretched out of sight on either hand.

In the middle of the bridge stood Jax Digby. Unlike the avatar of her he'd seen earlier, she wasn't in the clothes she'd worn as a student playing the game. Instead, she was here as a fine lady within it, in a flowing green gown and jewelled coiffure.

"Carlos!" she called. She smiled and beckoned.

Carlos looked down, glad that the mist below hid most of the drop. He himself was in the sort of forester's gear of leather jerkin and trousers he'd always favoured for the quest. The only piece of kit missing from the game was his gun. His feet were in thin-soled, close-fitted boots, laced up to the ankle. His hair was long, as his long-ago game avatar's had been, and damp with mist and spray. He flicked an annoying lock sideways, and peered around. He wiggled his toes, feeling the hard slippery rock underfoot, and fixed his attention on the rock bridge. The surface was uneven and wet, and less than half a metre across.

Carlos had a good idea what to expect. Before they accepted him into their midst, Jax and her comrades would want to give him a defector's debriefing. They'd also want to clear up the little matter of his collaboration with the Innovator, back in the day, with some special reference to his renewed relationship with that AI in its current instance: Nicole. This was unlikely to be pleasant.

He might as well get it over with.

Placing one foot carefully in front of another, he stepped out on the bridge. He checked that there were no obvious trip hazards between him and Jax—still smiling, still beckoning—then fixed his gaze on her face as he paced slowly out.

He put a foot down for a fifth wary step when the bridge gave way beneath him. An entire chunk of rock, extending a metre in front of him and no doubt a metre behind, dropped like a lift falling down a shaft.

Carlos fell into fog, and then into darkness, and then into a net.

As he crashed painfully into the web of rough ropes, rebounded, crashed again and rolled, Carlos didn't wonder what had become of the rock. He'd wasted far too many hours playing *Starborn Quest* to expect consistent physics in any of its many trapdoors to hell.

The net tipped towards the cliff. Carlos, knowing what was coming, grabbed at the rope mesh. He clutched like death and stuck his feet in, pressing their soles into nodes. He didn't expect this effort to do him much good, and he was right. The ropes became suddenly frictionless. Something wrapped around his shins and hauled. He slid helplessly backward and down, and found himself dragged painfully face down along a rough stone floor. His legs were released. Winded, ribs and knees aching, his face and hands scratched and bleeding, he lay still for a few seconds.

He stood up warily, groping around. The cave was just wide enough for him to touch the sides and roof with outstretched hands. A few steps back the way he had come brought him up against the net, now fixed across the cave entrance. The rush of the river was louder now, its steady roar punctuated by drips all around him.

The cave mouth brightened, until he could dimly make out the mesh of the net. The cable that had dragged him down lay coiled like a snake at his feet. Turning his back on the entrance, he faced into the cave. Over the next couple of minutes his eyes adjusted, or the light increased—he couldn't be sure. Here and there, further into the cave, phosphorescent patches glowed just enough to indicate the irregular shape of the cave walls.

Carlos recognised the place from the game. If his memories were accurate, this was a Level 3 Interrogation Maze. He could walk in to whatever was in store for him, or he could wait here to be dragged to it. He'd already decided he might as well face it. The sooner he got it over with the better.

He walked into the cave as quickly as he dared, hands out in front of him. As he moved deeper, the fresh, damp air at the entrance was replaced by an increasingly sulphurous stench, with overtones of mould and a whiff of decay. After blundering against the side wall which was soggy with slime and fungoid growth a couple of times, he realised that the trick was not to look at the glowing patches, but instead at the spaces between them which they barely illuminated. The sound of the river faded; the dripping became relentless. At any moment, a demon was going to leap out, thump him and drag him away for questioning. Knowing what to expect wouldn't make the shock any less when it came. The situation was designed to recall scary childhood moments of creeping along dark corridors and knowing someone was going to jump out at you.

Carlos stopped. It was as abrupt a halt as if he'd bumped into a wall. He'd just tripped over a question.

How did he know where he was and what to expect?

Because of the game, of course.

But why this game?

He was surprised he hadn't thought of the question before. But, then, he'd had a lot on his mind. Seeing Jax when he'd first hailed Arcane, soon after his escape from the station, had been a surprise. Learning that she and her comrades in the Arcane module were Accelerationists so fervent that they regarded the Directorate as little better than the Reaction had been disturbing. Figuring out how they must have achieved this unanimity was more troubling still. And all the time, he'd taken for granted what should have surprised him: that the sim in the Arcane module was based on the *Starborn Quest* game in the first place. It had seemed at first to make sense that he and Jax would meet in a virtual environment like the one which, in their real-life younger days, they'd shared so often and had so much fun in.

But this sim couldn't have been devised by Jax, or by any of her comrades. It must have been set up by the AI of Arcane Disputes. Why should it do that? OK, basing your training ground on a first-person shooter was reasonable enough, and a rest-and-recreation environment based on the parks and palaces of *Starborn Quest* would lack nothing in sybaritic luxury, but still…

There was a logic to the sim he'd lived in before, in the Locke module: it was based on what the habitable terrestrial planet H-0 might be like, after centuries of terraforming in real time (and gigayears of virtual evolution) had generated an Earth-like ecosystem and human-like people from its existing primitive biota, a sheen of green slime. Even the purpose of such a process made sense: it guaranteed that the bodies the mission's stored future settlers would one day download into would be biologically compatible with the other organisms on the planet.

It likewise made sense that the mission's AIs would run simulations of this process over and over—they'd have to, to get it right. A by-product of all this inconceivably deep and vast conceptual modelling would be virtual environments in which revived veterans like himself, the walking dead casualties of an ancient war, could have a virtual life in the intervals between combat missions in robot frames.

But there was no obvious mission-related logic to developing a sim based on such a trivial irrelevance as a computer game. Unless the reason was that the game had been a popular playground for Accelerationists, back in the day—

That thought brought him up short, too. Once again he found himself tripping up in his mind, having stubbed his toe on the same question he'd asked himself before: why this game? Out of the whole plethora of immersive multi-player action games available, why was this one in particular such a big hit with Axle cadre?

Not for any ideological reason, that was for sure. *Starborn Quest* was a bog-standard cod-medieval fantasy online role-playing game, set on a likewise cookie-cutter lost-colony planet whose only touch of originality was its vast surface area, low density and consequent relative lack of ferrous metals—making ceramics, hardwoods, paper, and brew-and-bake plastics its common materials of everyday use. Magic of a kind worked here, duly given some bullshit rationale about remnant technology. The object of the quest was to find the colony's wrecked starship—which could be continents and oceans away from your starting point—recover its secrets and return to space. Along the way you, with any companions you had managed to muster, had to negotiate or fight your way through a fractal patchwork of petty kingdoms, realms, domains, duchies, merchant-republic city-states, barbarian equestrian whirlwind empires, ruined cities, deserts dotted with booby-trapped alien artifacts of power, and so on and on. The whole ambiance was far more resonant of the Reaction than the Acceleration.

So why had he and so many others enjoyed it so much? And why should a law company's AI indulge their long-gone youthful folly?

Carlos, still pondering the question, took another few wary steps forward. In front of him, something unseen snuffled horribly. Its exhalation was a blast of fetid breath. Carlos reeled back, gagging. Immense, frost-crusted hands grabbed his upper arms from behind and wrenched him off balance. He was dragged backward, kicking and struggling. The thing that had been in front of him shuffled after, wheezing miasmas in his face. The thing behind sighed arctic blasts on the back of his neck. That he could still see neither of his attackers made him struggle all the more.

Predictably, resistance was futile.

* * *

Carlos knew better than to expect a torture chamber. The original game had had places for physical torment, but this wasn't one of them. What a Level 3 Interrogation Maze gave you instead was nightmare. The horror and disgust were just to make your stomach heave at hideous sights and smells. The nightmare was of repetition, of futility, of being trapped on a treadmill or in a maze and knowing that somewhere in your mind was the information that could get you off and out. The urge to blurt it could become irresistible, however many points it cost you.

His captors slung him in a stone cell, sending him sprawling and staggering to collide painfully with a shelf pallet, covered with rotting straw, that hung on chains from a far wall sodden with slime-drenched moss. His hip slithered down the wall and he crashed, half turned around, on the seat. The chains creaked as he moved to sit facing outward. Above the cell's heavy wooden door, half-open outward, a torch burned yellow in an embrasure. Carlos shielded his eyes from its glare until his sight adjusted. His captors flanked the doorway.

One was a walking corpse, far decayed, half clad in rags, its limbs held together with strands of twine and operated by contraptions of pulleys and fishing line. Mucilage dangled and jiggled in its nasal cavity. Peeled-back lips exposed its black-rooted teeth. Twin sparks glowed in its empty eye sockets. Behind its ribs, lungs green with the sheen of bacteria on spoiled meat laboured like bellows.

The other was a white-furred ape-man two metres tall, covered with patches of snow and crusted with spiky frost that showed no sign of melting. Fangs overhung the corners of its mouth. Its eyes were yellow, with black horizontal-slot pupils like a goat's. Nice touch for the setting, though biologically implausible in a predator.

"Carlos," wheezed the rotting zombie, "when did you first decide to betray the cause?"

Carlos shook his head. "I never betrayed the cause."

The frost monster roared. Its breath was as if a freezer door had opened. Carlos had no time to shiver. The monster took two strides forward and swiped a paw at the side of Carlos's face, sending him sideways onto the stone floor. He managed to avoid cracking his head on the flags, but only by wrenching his shoulder and almost breaking his right arm. He curled up instantly, and it was his shins that took the kick. Just as the blow to the head had been, it was like being struck by so much frozen meat.

Carlos huddled, in sheet-lightning flashes of pain and a deafening ringing in his head. He waited for another kick. It didn't come. The monster's steps thudded back to the doorway.

"Rise up," said the corpse.

Carlos struggled to his feet. His body ached from head to foot. His face was scratched, his left cheekbone hurt like it might be broken, and his leathers were filthy.

"Sit."

He sat, trying not to let his back touch the oozing wall.

"Carlos," the zombie said again, in a patient tone, "when did you first decide to betray the cause?"

"I don't—" Carlos began. His mouth tasted of blood.

The ice monster lurched. Reels whirred and lines glistened as the rotting zombie raised one arm, and spread its finger bones.

"No!" it gasped. "Wait. Let us hear him out." Its neck creaked as its head swivelled and its eye sparks were brought to bear. "Carlos, if you don't answer constructively, I'm not sure I can hold back my impulsive friend here."

Christ, the zombie was the one playing the good cop!

"I remember having doubts about our strategy from quite early on," Carlos said. "I also remember hearing the Innovator's voice in my head. In my spike, you know? I must have invited it in at some point. But I don't remember doing that, and I don't remember if I was authorised by the leadership or internal security to do it. From later, I remember for sure that internal security knew, and the leadership knew. It was part of their new strategy."

"What new strategy?"

Carlos tried to keep his gaze focused on the red pinpoints, and not to let it dwell on what else was going on in that rotting face. A long drip of phosphorescent slime in the nasal cavity was about to swing loose.

"The new strategy was of coordinating action with state forces against the Rax. A common enemy. The enemy of my enemy, and all that."

"And how did you know about it? There was no mention of it in the movement's communiqués."

"Of course not," said Carlos. "It had to be deniable on both sides. I was told about it by my internal security contact."

"Whose name was?"

"I knew him as Ahmed al-Londoni." He smiled. "Ahmed the Londoner. It was obviously a code name. For one thing, he was Welsh."

"You poor fool," sighed the zombie. The dangling drip flew out of the hole in the face and landed on the floor, where small things scurried to gobble at it.

"What?"

There was a whizzing of reels as the zombie's arm rose in an imperious gesture.

"Take him away," it told the ice monster.

The next room was worse. The ice monster shoved Carlos in and then stepped back outside and slammed the door. Carlos stumbled, arms windmilling, and found his balance. He pressed his back against the door. The floor and walls were terracotta-tiled. Candles burned in half a dozen niches, filling the room with a warm glow. Avatars of a man and a woman sat—he on Carlos's left, she on the right—behind a wooden table in the middle of the room, staring at him with impassive intentness. They were of human size, but barely of human appearance. They looked as if they had been made from life-size versions of the figures in a plastic brick construction toy. Their heads were cylindrical, with solid plastic representations of hairdos stuck like hats on top. The man's head was yellow, the woman's light brown. Features had been drawn on as if with black marker, in clear bold strokes and dots.

Carlos looked back at the pair as levelly as he could. He guessed that unlike the monsters they were avatars of actual people. Only their heads and shoulders were visible above the stacks of paper that covered every square centimetre of the table top in front of them. A wooden chair was between him and the table. He wondered if he should pick it up and lay about the interrogators right now. It would all come to the same in the end.

"Sit down, Carlos," the woman said. Her drawn-on lips and eyebrows moved on the rounded surface of her face as she spoke, discrete as slugs on a pipe.

Carlos sat. A large bottle of water stood on the floor beside the chair. The chair had a padded leather seat and an elegant ergonomic back. That was terrifying. They expected him to be here for a long time. No doubt their own seating was just as comfortable. He looked over the stacks of paper and reckoned there were at least ten thousand pages in front of him.

The pair behind the table straightened up a little, with some scraping of chair legs on the floor. Carlos looked across the stack, at four eyes and two noses. The woman's left hand reached up and took the first sheet. The hand was shaped as though it could only be clicked onto a round stick, but it handled the paper deftly enough.

She cleared her throat, and began to read.

"My name is Carlos. I have no certainty of reaching my destination..."

To Carlos's intense embarrassment, what she was reading out was what he had written by laser on the side of the scooter. He listened and wished he was dead.

Wishing that the ground would swallow him seemed, in the circumstances, reckless.

CHAPTER EIGHT

Writing by Laser

My name, as I say, is Carlos. I have no memory of the name I was given. Carlos was a name I took. After my death I became known as Carlos the Terrorist. I was a militant of the Acceleration, a political movement of the late twenty-first century—which, I've been told, was over a thousand years ago. Given my situation, that lapse of time seems credible to me.

My situation. Yes. Well.

I don't remember dying. Like most of us in my situation, my strange condition, I don't remember anything in the final months of my life, and my memories of the rest of it—about twenty-seven years, I think—have as many gaps as a half-burned book. The memories that remain are more vivid than they ever seemed when I had human flesh. My childhood seemed to me normal. Even in retrospect I can see that my parents looked after me and loved me.

Yet one of my earliest memories is of something almost indescribably sinister.

I don't know what has brought this to mind now. It's possible that it helps to explain how I come to be here.

That must be it. Yes.

There was a television pane high on the wall of our living room. Sometimes my parents would let me watch programmes—stories, cartoons, fantasy tales, science documentaries—made for children. In the evenings they sent me out of the room, to go outdoors or to watch such programmes on my own tablet or to read or play games, while they watched programmes on the pane. They had control of the pane by subtle, rapid finger movements, which they refused to demonstrate to me. They'd laugh and hide their fingers when I asked.

One day when I was about seven years old I found I could just reach the thin black band along the bottom of the pane. Some concealed manual control responded to the scrabbling fingers of my outstretched hand. I stepped back into the middle of the room to see what I had found. A man's voice, low and deep, spoke steadily and solemnly in a language I didn't know. I saw a vivid blue sea, a blue sky and a shore of sand: a wide but narrow beach, with dunes behind it. Beyond the skyline a brownish haze faded to yellow then green to merge with the blue above.

The viewpoint camera approached the shore, skimming the wave tops, and stopped before a rounded white object sticking up from the sand. I thought at first it was the shell of some sea creature. I had seen such shells on a beach. Then the viewpoint swung around the object, and two black holes in the front seemed to stare at me, above a hollow triangle. It was a human skull—I think I recognised the shape from hazard labels, or perhaps from the fantasy tales I mentioned earlier.

The camera tracked across the beach, from a viewpoint like my own childish one, a metre or so off the ground. It was of course a drone camera, though I didn't recognise that at the time. Whitened skulls and other human bones—curved ribs, separated vertebrae, long femurs and humeri, lots of small scattered bones that I later understood were phalanges—lay everywhere. From the way the wind stirred the sand you could see some bones being covered, others exposed; they were as plentiful as shells on a beach. Some were large, others smaller, some smaller still with double rows of teeth inside the jaw. These puzzled me for a moment, until I deduced, with a thrill of horror, that they were the skulls of babies.

The camera turned this way and that. Its view swept the long, deserted beach. The bones in the sand close by were clear and distinct, further off less so, until they became multiple glints of white that in the distance merged and shimmered. The entire beach was carpeted with bones. The camera moved on, through tussocks of tough tall grass into dunes, and the dunes too were littered with protruding bones at every turn. Then it rose, higher and higher, and by that same continuity from near to far, one could see that the sand went to the horizon, and the bones with it.

The camera turned, and faced out to the blue sea and the waves that lapped the shore and stirred yet more bones tumbling back and forth in the surf.

Even at that age, I understood that this fossil graveyard of humanity signified countless deaths, many of them at my own age or younger. But I might not have had the smallest inkling that this had some moral significance had not my mother silently entered the room, stood (I presume) for a moment of dawning horror, then stepped forward and smartly snapped the television off and given me a severe look.

"You shouldn't be watching that!" she said.

I had a surge of guilty bewilderment.

"Why not?"

"The telly's for grown-ups."

"Why are there all these skeletons?" I asked, in the tone of bright curiosity that my parents usually rewarded with patient explanation.

"It was a bad thing," she said.

"What was it?" I asked.

"It happened a long time ago," she said.

I was old enough to know, very much from the inside, the tones of evasion and excuse. My mother's cheeks reddened a little.

"What happened?" I persisted.

"I'll tell you another time. Now go out the back, it's a nice day."

"But—"

"Now!"

I knew not to push it. I traipsed outside and repeatedly kicked a football against the wall of the house. My mother didn't rush out to complain.

I knew she must feel bad about something. I didn't know what, but I felt implicated.

So much for the influence of my mother. Let me tell you now of the influence of two other women in my life, whose effect was perhaps less benign: Jax Digby and Nicole Pascal.

As I grew up I learned why so many had died, decades before I was born, on the southern shore of the Mediterranean. Africa was being ravaged by climate change and war. Millions had fled north. Europe kept them out, blockading the coast with drones and warships. There was nowhere for these people to go, and on that fatal shore they died in droves. It was not the worst catastrophe of the recent past, or even of the present. I remained troubled by such things, and by my inadvertent but nonetheless culpable complicity in them.

Thus as a student I became drawn to the ideas of the Acceleration, under the influence of one of their cadre, a young woman named Jacqueline "Jax" Digby. This is how we met.

Perhaps she was waiting for me, or looking out for me. Certainly she was looking out for such as me. Alert, she must have been, every waking, walking minute for a momentary flicker of disgusted dissent, for a brief hot spark of fury and shame in averted eyes. She saw that in mine the day I was walking across the campus under the usual heavy rain and I happened to glance at one of the big public screens that were a thing that year, or that month: a community-building initiative, I think they were called at the time. On screen, in swift succession:

An evacuation ship from Bangladesh, holed below the waterline and sinking fast.

An advertisement for sunscreen.

A Japanese naval hydrofoil, its plumes a rainbow sheen.

An advertisement for life insurance.

A sea of red.

Rags and clumps of hair.

An advertisement for shampoo.

At that point I tugged my hood around my face, the rain drumming on the oilcloth, and looked away and down and—

—up—

—to lock eyes with a woman with black curly hair walking the other way, in a transparent plastic rain cape over a green T-shirt and a translucent blue skirt with LEDs around the hem, and big black Doc Martens that went squelch when she walked. She stopped.

"It's shit, innit?" she said.

"Fuck'n' right," I said. "But what can we do about it?"

"Come with me and we'll kick around some ideas," she said.

"Where you going?" I said.

"Games hall," she said.

We found a concrete archway. I picked up two cups from a coffee stall along the way. We sat under the arch and shook off our rainwear. She gave my abs an appreciative look.

"Gene-splice," I admitted.

"Still," she said.

The rain battered the plaza. Steam rose. We sipped.

"Ready?" she asked.

I tossed my paper cup into the path of a roving tumble-bot. "Ready."

"Pinball?"

I shrugged my eyebrows. "If you like."

We each took out our kit and draped it over our eyes and noses. Flipped the code. Instantly we were in a loud, sweaty, strobe-lit shared space. We stood side by side at the pinball machines, heads down, thumbs busy, and talked.

"Here's one answer," she said. "Let them in. All of them."

I said something about jobs and houses.

"So give them jobs building houses."

"They can't all do that."

"Those who can't can work at other things."

"But there's no jobs!"

Sidelong look. "You mean there's nothing left to do that's worth paying people to do?"

"Just very highly skilled jobs. Which is why we're here, right?"

"Wouldn't count on it." Ding. "Genomics database librarian?" She must have read my profile. "Ha! A robot's after that too."

"So we're back to—what can we do about it?"

"Let them do it," she said. "The robots. Everything."

"But then there'd be no jobs!"

Christ, I was thick. But she got through to me in the end.

"Read this," she said. She slid a text to my kit. "See me tomorrow. Same place, same time."

That evening I read the pamphlet: *Solidarity Against Nature*, by Eugene Saunders.

The following day the sun was hot on the plaza. I wore a bush hat and shorts. Jax wore Yemeni-derived steampunk. We retreated to the concrete arch again, this time for shade.

"What did you think?" she asked.

"It seemed to make sense."

She grinned. "Welcome to the Acceleration."

"The Acceleration?" I must have sounded horrified. "They're crazy."

"You've just agreed with everything we stand for."

"We?"

"I'm in," she said. "And now you are, whether you know it or not."

Needless to say, that wasn't the end of it. But it was the beginning.

Jax and I became friends, comrades, occasional lovers. The Acceleration (colloquially "Axle" or "Ax") was a global network of activists that sought to bring about the most rapid possible development of capitalism in order, as they saw it, for society to pass beyond it to a new system, and for humanity to pass beyond its own limitations. In the escalating economic, environmental, military, existential and other crises of the time the ideas of the Acceleration gained increasing traction.

Sometimes the ideas seemed to have spread further than they really had.

"Who're these guys?" I asked Jax, flicking the text to her kit. "They sound like us."

She took about a minute to scan the document.

"Not us," she said. "The fucking Rax."

"The what?"

"The Reaction." She waved a hand, dismissing me and the text. It flew around the table to the eyes of our half-dozen companions, who read and chortled. We were in the cafeteria, with a handful of like-minded students. They were all far more politically savvy than I was.

I asked them what was so funny.

"You've just fallen for a deception pitch," said Hans, one of the older guys. "That lot are the exact opposite of us."

"But they stand for the same things," I said. I threw out a histrionic arm. "Capitalism unleashed! Freedom! Life-extension! Space! No limits!"

"And the divine right of kings," said Hans. "Missed that bit, did you?"

"Nothing about that in there."

"Of course not. It's a pitch to pull people in. They don't put everything on the front screen."

"Like we do," I said, in a surly tone. I'd found myself taking on board some ideas a lot more challenging than those expounded by Saunders.

Jax leaned in. "Remember *Solidarity Against Nature*?"

"That's just what I was thinking of," I said. "It doesn't exactly say everything."

"True," said Jax. "But it says the basics. The rest is consequence. Well, think of the Rax as starting from the exact opposite premise: nature against solidarity. Social Darwinism with knobs on. Scientific racism."

I shook my head. The two words didn't go together. She might as well have said scientific satanism.

"Scientific... racism? What's that?"

Another of my now comrades tossed me a text. "This sort of thing," she said.

I skimmed through its toxic brew of science, pseudoscience and outright bigotry, and pushed my kit up onto my forehead, making room for a frown.

"What are these 'groids' they keep on about?"

"Short for 'Negroids,' get it?"

"What does that mean?"

"People like me," she said.

"Oh," I said. "And that's what the Reaction's really about? Just racism?"

"Not all of it," she conceded. "There's all the exciting stuff about boundless freedom and advancement. There's a misguided but—to a certain kind of alienated intellectual—quite fascinating and bracing critique of democracy and equality and other liberal and radical pieties. You know, the sort of thing that makes reading Nietzsche such a thrill? And then there's the 'human biodiversity' strand. Contentious, but part of the mix." She gave me a warped smile. "The spoonful of tar that spoils a barrel of honey. And the rest of it ain't no honey."

"Speaking of honey," said Jax. There was something in her tone.

"What about it?"

"You don't eat it. Why not?"

"It's an animal product," I said, self-righteously.

"So?"

"You've read Saunders, right?"

"Is that a rhetorical question?"

Jax laughed, as if caught out. "OK. And you say he makes sense. Well then. 'Consciousness depends on language.' Do bees have language?"

I waggled my elbows. "They communicate."

"Waggle dances? Sure. That's not the question. Do they ever make *original* communications? New strings of symbols? New symbols, even, for new phenomena?"

"They must do," I said. "Otherwise they couldn't adapt to changing environments."

"Don't dick about," said Jax. "That's genetic mutation and natural selection. The question is, do individual bees—or hives, for that matter—ever invent? Create? Generate new sentences?"

"I guess not," I said, uncomfortably. I could see where this was going.

"Then they're not conscious. They're little machines. Marvellous little machines, to be sure."

"So? They still feel. They're still aware."

"No more than a tumble-bot is when it collects litter. They don't have subjectivity. And what does Saunders take from that?"

I thought back. "That non-human animals aren't subjects?"

"Yes," said Jax. "And that whatever isn't a subject is an object."

Put as starkly as that, it was a shock. But I couldn't deny the logic.

"OK." I leaned back and spread my hands. "You win. Eating honey isn't wrong."

"Great!" she said. "So go up there and order it with some toast."

I swear eating that toast and honey was the sharpest break I ever made with the morality I'd unthinkingly absorbed. Within a few days I was eating toast with egg and bacon without a second thought.

Killing people took a bit longer, but I got there. It helped that the first people I killed were Rax, and that I always had in the back of my mind that first racist tract.

Those who deny the humanity of others can claim none themselves.

This is where my own direct knowledge of my past life ends. What follows is what I have been told or experienced since.

In the case of the British state, under which I lived, the strategy chosen was to use the Axle to defeat the Rax, then to move against the Axle. Approaches must have been made to the Acceleration, because I was killed in a military engagement coordinated with a government-owned military artificial intelligence, which I knew as the Innovator. The circumstances of my death were bizarre, and resulted in the preservation of enough of my brain and body for a detailed scan to be made. This copy was held in storage pending reconstruction in a virtual environment once technology had advanced to that point.

Meanwhile, the conflict escalated and drew in state and non-state actors to such a level that it is remembered as the Last World War. Like the Second World War it ended (though far more swiftly and simultaneously) in the defeat of both extremes by the liberal democracies that had allied with one against the other. After a brief but brutal period of global emergency rule by the United Nations Security Council, a new world congress of all peoples was convened. The ultimate outcome was a democratic world government: the Direction. This government established a new global economy in which a cybernetic market underlies and enables a cornucopian abundance.

So I have been told, by the next woman to have a big effect on my life: Nicole Pascal.

* * *

The sim I awoke to live and train in was inhabited, to the best of my knowledge, by few—hundreds at the most. Some were ghosts: future colonists who had signed up in advance for the further adventure of beta-testing in VR their future home. Others were simulations of such: people who gave every indication of being real but who lacked subjective awareness: philosophical zombies, or p-zombies. These were there to make up the numbers and in at least one case to be killed in training exercises.

Some—a handful at first, a squad of six including myself—were more than ghosts. We were to become revenants: walking dead mercenaries.

One was an AI in human form, the local representative of the Direction: Nicole.

Ah, Nicole. That human form. It allures me still. I truly wish I hadn't just learned that she is derived from the Innovator, and that she knew I was innocent of the crime for which I was sentenced—knew it better than anyone, because she committed that crime herself. For it was the AI which I knew as Innovator that carried out the high-mass-casualty attack for which I was subsequently blamed—indeed, immediately blamed, and by the Innovator itself at that. Its removal of protection was swiftly followed by my death.

I'm not finished with Nicole Pascal.

Not while there's a spark of electricity left in my frame.

CHAPTER NINE

Reading by Candlelight

The bizarrely shaped woman stopped reading.

"Do you acknowledge that you wrote all that?"

Carlos lifted his head from his hands, reached for the water bottle and took a sip. He straightened up and looked across at the woman.

"Yes," he said.

"Why did you write it?"

Carlos shrugged. "Like it says at the very beginning—to leave a record. I had no real expectation that it would ever be read."

"I put it to you," the woman said, "that you wrote knowing we would find it. You wrote it for us."

"Why would I do that?" Carlos asked.

"To convince us that you had no memories of your collaboration with the British security forces back in the day, and that you have now broken completely with Nicole Pascal."

Carlos shrugged. "Maybe I did. We're all smarter in the frames than we are here, so it's possible I came up with that cunning plan. But I don't remember it. And, anyway, it's true."

"Really?" said the woman. "Let me read you something else, and see if it refreshes your memory."

She reached for another sheet of paper.

* * *

"From the confession of Eric Jones, known as Ahmed al-Londoni: 'About three months after my recruitment by MI5, I was activated by the previously agreed signal already described, and told to concentrate on the operative known to me as Carlos. I sounded him out in one of our regular meet-ups in the usual secure environment, and encouraged him to express any doubts he might have had about the armed aspect of the struggle. At this point he insisted that he had no such doubts, and accepted the instructions I gave him for a drone attack on the Bradford electricity sub-station. Subsequently, however, he—' "

"Excuse me," said Carlos.

The woman peered at him over the top of the stacks, eyebrows two lines sloping sharply inward. "Yes?"

"Where is this from?"

"United Nations Security Council War Crimes Tribunal Records, Volume 386, chapter 54." She could see he was still frowning. "They're all in Arcane Disputes' law library," she explained.

Carlos sagged.

"Thanks," he said. "I understand." He smiled, then winced as the pain from his cheek struck harder. "Please, do read on."

"I don't need your permission for that," said the woman, tartly. "Now, where were we? Ah, yes..."

She read on, hour after hour. As each page was read, she placed it on the floor beside her. The stack mounted slowly. It was the only indication Carlos had of the passage of time. When the stack reached a height of ten centimetres he stopped listening. It was like hearing, in a dream, an account of your life written by a particularly judgemental and vindictive recording angel, recounted to you in tedious detail by someone who had themselves heard it in a dream.

He let his mind wander. Never mind the "why the game?" questions, intriguing though they were. The important thing was to try and recall how you got out of situations like this in the game. Essentially, they were puzzle traps. The trick was to judge when the points and time you'd lose by staying and trying to solve the puzzle became more than you'd lose just by quitting.

The trouble was, he couldn't see how to quit. No handy kill-switch, no escape key-chord here!

And this wasn't a game. He had a lot more to lose than a level.

The pile of pages read was now at fifteen centimetres. The man had taken over the reading. The woman sipped water from a flask. Carlos could just see the rim of it, going up and down to her lips. A drop of water left on the side of her mouth looked like blue Perspex: toy water, cartoon water. She wiped it off with her clip-shaped hand. What was the man droning on about now?

Deposition of Saunders, that was it. Founding theorist of the Acceleration. Evidently the Security Council's tribunals had hauled him in too. Never committed or advocated a violent act, but they must have got him under moral complicity or some such. Theoretical justification of terror, that was the clause. Got him bang to rights on that one, Carlos had to admit, even if Saunders (by the sound of all this) hadn't.

Carlos scanned the edges of the tiles on the wall behind the woman, wondering if they could be cracked, or held a hidden message. Hidden message. Code. Code, ha! It was all code. He wondered if his mind would ever run on anything but machine code again. With the entire mission apparently, and literally, flying apart, would the Direction ever get its act together again? Would he ever walk on real ground in a real body? Come to that, would he even want to? In the frame he'd felt more real, more alive than he did in the simulation and more so than he remembered ever feeling in real life.

The man stopped reading.

"Anything to say to that, Carlos?"

Carlos came out of his trance with a small start, as if he'd been daydreaming in class. The man noticed.

"You'd be well advised to pay attention," he said.

"I have been paying attention," said Carlos, frantically trawling the previous few minutes for anything that he'd noticed at all. "Saunders' deposition, that was it."

"We're well past that," the man chided.

"Of course," said Carlos. "But you didn't remark on the obvious implication."

"And that would be?"

Carlos tried to think of the most absurd, disruptive, paranoid accusation he could come up with. The interrogators were messing him around, and the least he could do was to mess them around right back. He wanted to force the issue and be done with it.

"Saunders was recruited to the German intelligence service, the Bundesnachrichtendienst, at Frankfurt University in '78," Carlos said, winging it. "He published the first Accelerationist manifesto in '84. It follows that the entire Acceleration was a false flag operation from the beginning. It was set up by several intelligence agencies, mainly the BND and MI5, as a honey trap for dissident elements and as a dirty weapon against the Reaction. A throwaway tool, a cutout. Most of the leadership—Itoh, Kim, Fielder, all that lot—were in on it. The only one who definitely wasn't was Hari, and the NSA drone attack of '91 took out her and no one else. Coincidence? I don't think so."

The woman's head popped up a little higher. "You couldn't possibly know that."

"Oh, I could," said Carlos, enjoying himself for the first time in days. "I was a deep penetration agent from the beginning. Not Special Branch or MI5, though. That's where you're missing the point. You're barking up the wrong tree there, all right. I was working for Chinese state security. One of their assets first approached me at a Confucius Institute seminar on biotechnology, in my first year at university. I didn't take much convincing. They filled me in—they didn't have to keep the same secrets as the Western spooks did. That's how I know what was really behind the Axle, and that's why I balked when I was told to shoot down that Chinese cargo plane over Docklands."

To the best of his knowledge, none of what he had said was true.

"Are you *trying*," the man asked, incredulous, eyebrow lines almost vanishing under his pudding-bowl hair, "to get yourself killed?"

Carlos shrugged. "Not particularly."

"You're going the right way about it."

"I'm already dead," Carlos pointed out. "Twice over, come to think of it. I handled it quite well, by all accounts."

"There are worse things than dying," the woman said. Her cylindrical head inclined towards the door. "We could leave you here with them."

"Forever," the man added.

"Tortured by scary monsters?" Carlos scoffed. "Give me a break."

"You wouldn't *have* a break," the man said. "That's the point. There's a times-one-thousand clock speed in this sim, let me remind you. We can literally lock the door and throw away the key. After a few months of real time, we might take a look in and see if you're ready to cooperate."

Carlos laughed. "That's a threat? I met a bloke the other day who'd done a thousand years, subjective, in our sim. By the end of it the fucker could levitate. And that was in a proper sim, mind. Rock-solid physics engine. I'd hack the cheat codes for this gimcrack hell a lot sooner than that. Assuming your shitty little space rock isn't blasted out of the sky first."

"I doubt it," said the man. "This gimcrack hell could reduce you to a gibbering wreck in a week."

"A gibbering wreck wouldn't be much use to you as a fighter, would it?"

Carlos felt less defiant than his words and tone were meant to suggest.

"Very droll," said the man. "We can always download another copy of you and show it what was left of the first."

"You have a point there," Carlos conceded.

"So, cooperate."

"I am cooperating," said Carlos. "I've confessed, haven't I?"

"We doubt your confession," the woman said. "And if that's the cover, what are you really hiding?"

"Nothing," said Carlos. "And I would put it to you that none of this shit matters. Who the fuck cares where the ideas of the Acceleration came from? I *agree* with the ideas. And I can think of more urgent ways to use them than raking over things that happened a thousand years ago."

"Such as?" the man said.

Carlos rubbed his hands. "We and the freebots have to unite with the Direction to smash the Rax, and when we've done that we work with the freebots to make better use of this system than the Direction has in mind. When we've beaten the Direction we can settle accounts with the freebots."

The man and the woman looked at each other.

"I think we're done," the man said.

The woman nodded.

They stood up and walked around the sides of the table, their stiff legs moving oddly, and frowned down at Carlos.

"Those things you said about the Acceleration," the woman said, one hand on a stack of paper. "You made them up, didn't you?"

Carlos nodded.

"They're all true," she told him, "give or take a famous name or two."

"What?" Carlos was shocked.

"The G-0 robot lurkers have had a long time to go through the records, and to make inferences. It's what they do." She sighed. "We all know this. And we all decided, like you, that it doesn't matter. The ideas are still valid, and still urgent."

Oh, shit. Carlos tried to imagine the intensity of belief it would take to go on holding to the ideas in the face of such a crashing, crushing disillusion as discovering that it had all been a swindle from the beginning. There was a term for this, he knew: cognitive dissonance reduction. It didn't apply to himself, obviously. He'd always thought the ideas were sound, the movement—not so much.

Who was he kidding? He felt as if in sudden free fall.

"Well, get up," the man said.

Carlos stood up. The man stuck out a hand-clip. "Welcome aboard."

Carlos wasn't at all sure he wanted to be on board with this lot, but he smiled and shook the curious manipulative implement. His cheekbone and shoulder still hurt.

CHAPTER TEN

Command Lines

Beauregard barged into the hallway and stopped in the studio doorway. Everyone seemed frozen in the moment, a tableau: Rizzi looking guilty, as well she should; Nicole sparing a glance away from the easel; the rangy looking man with the wild hair giving him a quizzical scrutiny. And on the easel itself, the one face in the room that shouldn't be moving, but was: the logo of Locke. A rolling caption of handwriting crept across the bottom of the big flip-pad page.

"I thought you had that thing under control," Beauregard said, going on the offensive without hesitation.

"It's fighting back," said Nicole.

"What's it saying?" Beauregard asked.

Nicole peered at the screen. "Legal boilerplate, for the moment."

"That's not so bad."

Nicole shook her head. "It's bad that Locke's doing this at all. It must have ways to work around some of the restraints I put on it yesterday. It may be invoking emergency provisions, both legal and software, that'll let it work around more."

Invoking. Not a good word to hear when you're in the same room as two unpredictable gods. Three, counting Locke. Beauregard tried to size up the situation. Nicole was by her own admission and plenty of evidence an AI. She had a deep connection with the design of the sim—not its creator, exactly, but something between a demiurge and a nature spirit. Her means of interacting with the sim and with the rest of the module's machinery was through her painting and drawing—this being the means she had chosen herself, in the course of her creation. In what now seemed the far-off innocent days of basic orientation and training her artistic dabbling had looked like a harmless hobby, part of her role as the slightly distant lady of leisure who told the grunts what was what.

Shaw was a different barrel of laughs entirely. A deserter from an earlier conflict with rebel robots, one Earth year ago in real time, one thousand years ago in sim time (as was), Shaw had survived on his own and by his wits, wandering the world. Along the way he had acquired a mental access to at least some of the controls of the sim. That, presumably, was how he'd brought the colour back, at the expense of clock speed. There was no way to tell how deliberate this was, but the change in clock speed threw a major wrench into Beauregard's plans.

Beauregard had hoped for several subjective years of training, preparation and design work before the module arrived in orbit around the superhabitable planet SH-0. These years would have been enabled by the clock speed of the sim's being a thousand times faster than real time. The speed of reaction to outside events, from the point of view of the sim's inhabitants, would have been that much faster as well.

Now they had to do everything in real time, to be ready for orbital insertion in a matter of days, and they had an unfriendly AI arguing its way out of the box Nicole had put it in yesterday. The law company Locke Provisos was a corporation, a legal person, that consisted entirely of a hierarchy of AIs. A DisCorporate or DisCorp, as the slang of the Direction's brave new worlds went. Locke was also—according to the message from its former competitor and now enemy, Arcane Disputes—a law company that had all along been a sleeper agent of the Reaction. What it would want to do, if it seized back control of the module, was entirely unpredictable in detail but would presumably involve taking the Reaction's side on the ongoing skirmishes that were currently being yammered excitedly from the half-dozen news screens hung around the room.

For a moment, Beauregard wondered whether the AI could be

argued out of that. He doubted it, and he doubted that even Nicole could do it if it were. It wasn't as if the AI had political opinions in the first place. It was a corporation, answering to the priorities that had been built into it and were no doubt now buried deep in its programming.

How deep? Ah! That might be a short cut.

"Nicole," Beauregard asked, in a milder tone, "what's the Locke AI's utility function?"

"Shareholder value," she answered, as if it were obvious. "It's just an off-the-shelf corporation, basically."

"How does fighting for the Rax maximise shareholder value?"

She shot him a sharp look. "Presumably by increasing the number and intensity of disputes that it makes money out of solving."

"If that was the way to make money, all the law companies would be doing it. They aren't. Why not?"

"Good question," said Nicole. "Obviously, law companies make money from *resolving* disputes. You might think this gives them an incentive for *fomenting* disputes, but that is not generally the case. There is never a lack of disputes. Disputes arise out of normal business activity, even with the best will in the world. A law company builds its business and reputation by resolving them to the satisfaction of its clients. Recklessly multiplying and inflaming disputes would damage its reputation more than it would gain in business, because it would have no guarantee that it would be the law company that was hired to resolve the disputes, so it could just end up trashing its reputation while sending business to its competitors."

"Yes, yes," said Beauregard, impatiently. "Spare me the lecture—I've been to university. The Locke corporation has been active in this system for ten years of real time, and in that time it must have handled God knows how many transactions in the virtual markets. So it can't have been acting rogue before all this started—I'm guessing it was the robot revolt on SH-17 that triggered it."

"It was pulling the same tricks a year ago, during the last robot uprising," Shaw interjected. "Just not so blatant."

"There wasn't a full-on Reaction breakout back then," said Beauregard. He waved a hand. "Anyway... my point right now is that there may be some trigger, some switch that gets flipped, one basic decision point that flips the corporation into what would otherwise be irrational activity—trouble-making, essentially—and makes it seem rational in terms of its own utility function: maximising shareholder value."

"There might be," said Nicole, frowning. "An advantage of AI corporations is that they take the long view, far more than human-based organisations. So perhaps a simple adjustment to Locke's time preferences and its discount rate would make it act in this way."

"There must be more to it than that," said Shaw. "From what Rizzi and Carlos told me, and what I experienced myself in the previous conflict, Locke has been thinking strategically about ways to—"

"—extend and escalate the conflict?" Nicole interrupted. "Yes, that is precisely the point, and what one would expect from a basic change in its underlying valuations. But the code tweak would be hard to find, and harder still to change."

Beauregard sighed. "Oh, well. Worth a try, I suppose."

"Why don't we offer it *more* conflict?" Rizzi asked.

Beauregard snorted. The lassie was evidently out of her depth. He pointed at the screens. "More than it's got right now? How do we do that?"

Rizzi looked from him to Nicole, and back.

"I once had a cat," she said. "When he was a little kitten, he couldn't help pouncing on his own shadow, again and again. When he was all grown up, he would watch me eating. He could easily have pushed his face onto my plate, but he could always be distracted if I threw him a scrap. The cat couldn't help himself, you see. He was a machine. An intelligent and affectionate machine, but still."

Nicole was looking as puzzled as Beauregard felt.

"What's this got to do with anything?"

"Have you actually *told* Locke," Rizzi asked, "what your plans are?"

"Of course not!" said Beauregard. "Why would I? The damn thing is opposed enough to us as it is."

But even as he said the words, he realised he'd been mistaken. He looked at Rizzi with new, if grudging, respect.

"Wait a sec," he said. "Rizzi, you might be onto something there. Well done you."

"Am I missing something?" Nicole asked.

Beauregard grinned at Rizzi and with a slight bow of his head extended an open hand, palm up. "Tell her."

"Look," said Taransay, "your plan is to land on SH-0 and start settling it, right? And the planet's still on the market. The corporations are still bidding and selling futures in the rights to it and all that shit, and in the meantime it's embargoed to exploration. I mean, the Direction's space station's flown apart but I doubt the Direction has. The companies aren't yet in some kind of every man for himself mode, are they?"

"Not yet," said Nicole.

"Well," Taransay went on, "that means all the deals and bids and so on are still in play. And even if they're not, in fact especially if the mission's all gone to pieces and we're in a resource scramble, none of the companies are going to take kindly to us just going down there and grabbing a piece of the action. Just us landing and trying to make a living is going to cause untold changes down there to the ecosystems. Which means lots of other companies will be gunning for us, literally as well as legally. I mean, quite independently of the Rax–Axle–Direction dust-up that's going on right now."

While Taransay was still speaking, Nicole had started scribbling. The portrait of Locke on the paper stopped moving until Nicole had stopped writing. Then its lips moved again and the ticker-tape crawl of handwriting along the foot of the page recommenced. Nicole flipped over to a new page. The face reappeared, and the bizarre dialogue continued below it. This happened several times: scribble, read, scribble, flip…

At length Nicole stood back. The face of Locke smiled, and then became just a drawing. A static portrait of a satanic smile.

"Well," said Nicole, "that's that settled."

Beauregard was looking nonplussed. "What's settled?"

"I've sold it on Rizzi's idea," said Nicole. "It's now on-side."

"On *our* side?" Beauregard sounded dubious.

"In so far as it's willing to cooperate with us in getting through the flak and getting down, yes. It's positively—well, virtually—lusting for the lawsuits that'll come after us."

"Yay!" cried Taransay. She wanted to high-five all round, but felt it might be inappropriate. Then she found herself wondering why she felt that.

"Yay, indeed," said Nicole.

Beauregard snorted. Nicole looked at him sharply. "What seems to be the problem?"

Beauregard scowled. "Rizzi," he said, grimly. "She tried to pull a fast one on me. Left me cruising the back roads like some pillock, while she tried to agitate the troops on the bus. But, as it seems there's no harm done..."

He favoured Taransay with a tight smile. Don't push it, girl, it seemed to say. Taransay flared inside. She swallowed hard, trying to moderate her anger.

"Excuse me, *Belfort*," she said. "I'll put my hands up to playing a trick on you, and that wasn't a polite thing to do to anyone, let alone a comrade. But I'm not sure you are a comrade, and for sure you're not the sarge any more. Not as far as I'm concerned. Our squad leader was Carlos, and he did a runner. I still don't know why. I do know you mutinied yesterday when you tried to turn the squad against Nicole, and as far as I understand it we're all no longer working for Locke, or for Crisp and Golding, or for the Direction. We're working for ourselves, according to you. We're all mutineers and pirates and fugitives now, isn't that right? So I don't take orders from you. The only person I trust here is the lady."

Beauregard glowered, about to say something. Nicole laughed.

"What?" asked Beauregard, in a tone of bellicose irritation.

Nicole raised a finger. "One moment, if you please."

She scribbled on the big easel-mounted pad again.

A moment passed, then the page filled with—not handwriting, but—print. Taransay stared, open-mouthed. This whole phenomenon was so fucking weird. It was like automatic writing, or a Ouija board, except that you really were communicating with a disembodied intelligence. And yet, and yet—there was nothing miraculous about it, uncanny though it seemed. It was precisely the equivalent of text appearing on a screen, or for that matter on a scroll, inside a computer game. It was less weird, when you came to think of it, than the manifestation she'd earlier seen of Locke, as a man modelled on the standard portrait of the seventeenth-century philosopher John Locke, walking and talking in the thin atmosphere of the exomoon SH-17 as if he were strolling under the apple boughs in Isaac Newton's own garden.

"This," said Nicole, stepping aside for Taransay to take a look, "is the message from Arcane that robots wrote, that Carlos found, and that Beauregard also read. He told you of it on the bus, I know. But he did not tell you all. Read it."

Taransay read it. *Locke is Rax, the tactics are designed to escalate the conflict, Reaction outbreak imminent, yadda yadda.* Beauregard had told them most of this on the bus, just before she'd fled. What he'd left out was more significant: that the Direction knew all this and was using it to flush out the Rax, and that Arcane thought this stratagem of the Direction was insanely dangerous; Arcane's passionate call for all comrades to join them; that Nicole in her earliest incarnation, way back on Earth, had actually been responsible for the spectacular attack for which Carlos had been condemned and that had made his name a legend to the Accelerationists; and... that Beauregard had been a British military intelligence agent inside the movement.

Yes, she could see why he'd left all that out. Bastard.

"Is this true?"

Beauregard bristled, then shrugged. "It's true. So, like I said, I can't order you. And yes, you can forget all that 'comrade' business. I've always said I was in British Army intel. I have no memory of being in the Acceleration, but I evidently was." He spread his hands. "You figure it out."

Taransay found herself less shocked than she'd been at first, and less than she might have expected. She'd known from the beginning that the sarge had a secret. But—if only she'd known this when she was arguing with the fighters on the bus!

"You were state?" she asked, just to make sure she'd got it right.

"Seems like I was," said Beauregard. "I'm not, any more. Obviously. The state I served is gone. And so is the Acceleration."

"There's still the Direction," said Taransay. She looked for support to Nicole, but the lady merely gave an enigmatic smile.

"The Direction is up to some scheme of its own," said Beauregard.

"One that has no guarantees we'll ever get downloaded and decanted onto a terraformed planet, or any other reward they might promise us. What we have to do is adjust to the situation we're in. That's all I'm trying to do. I've convinced most of the squad and a crowd of locals. If I can't convince you, please yourself."

Taransay didn't know what to say to that.

"Well, I'll talk to the others," she said. "See what they think."

Beauregard smiled cynically. "I think they'll agree with me that it makes no difference now."

He turned to Shaw, who was watching the screens again.

"Can you do anything to get the clock speed back up?" he asked. "Even if we lose colour again."

Shaw shook his head, still watching the screens.

"I don't know how I do these things," he said. He shot Taransay a small smile. "Even the levitating, not to mention walking right through somebody's arm. I can see what the lady is doing, and I can help her with that, but it's like..." He scratched his head. "It's all subconscious. Like Zen or something." He reached for a now cold coffee, and sipped. "I was wrong, see. For a thousand years I thought we were really on the planet we seem to be on, the Earth-like one, H-0. And I had all the time in the world to think, so I thought about physics. For centuries, off and on. Maybe that gave some part of my mind a kind of gearing into the sim? But I can't control it because I had no idea that was what I was doing?" He half turned, and appealed to Nicole. "Is that it?"

Nicole seemed unsure of herself. Taransay had only ever seen her with this awkward look on her face a couple of times, and it was usually when she wanted to skate past some too-probing question about the nature of their shared reality. Some query Ames had raised in their first collective briefing, and that time with the p-zombies on the training exercise, and then again when she'd tried to justify training for space on these amusement-arcade simulators...

Nicole pointed to a chair, and nodded to Taransay. Taransay picked her way across the floor and brought the chair over.

"Thanks," said Nicole. "Shaw, sit down."

Shaw glanced away from the screens, took the chair, and sat. Nicole stepped to one side of him, where she could see his face and keep an eye on the screens at the same time.

"You were of course wrong about the physical reality," she said. "But you were more wrong than you realised. This sim didn't exist until a few months ago, shortly before Beauregard and Taransay here and the others arrived."

Shaw shook his head. "I was in it a thousand years ago, and I've been in it ever since."

"In a sense, yes," said Nicole. "But the sim you were in was located out among the moons of the gas giant G-0, many AU away. That was a year ago in real time, yes? Physically, the module it ran in was out there too."

"Uh-huh," said Shaw. "I'm not stupid. I get that. So how did it get back here?"

"By fusion drive, of course. The Direction accepted the necessity. But while this is physically the same module, this place where we are is not really—so to speak—the same sim."

Shaw frowned. "What? You're saying the whole sim was *transmitted* here, and then—?"

"No," said Nicole. "After the robot revolt whose suppression you deserted from was defeated, that sim was discontinued. There was no need for it to keep running, after all. The fighters went back in storage—except for you, of course, you were out in the wilds somewhere. The civilian volunteers and p-zombies went back into storage, too. The sim was shut down. The data files for the sim were stored. It was available when Locke Provisos needed a sim for the current batch of fighters, and restarted. But it was restarted in a consistent manner, which meant—as if a thousand years had passed, just as a year had passed outside. A thousand years of geology, a thousand years of history, and a thousand years of the memories of the only person who was still in the sim when it went into storage. A thousand years of *you*. Not just memories, of course, but the physical traces of everything you *would have done* in all that time. Ashes of fires you would have set, stones you would have chipped and discarded, bones of the animals you would have killed to make the clothes you wear, and so on."

Shaw rocked back in the chair, still staring at the screens.

"So *my whole life* is an illusion? A false memory?"

"No," said Nicole. "It is not *false*. It has the same reality as anything here. It's *all* computation. It's *all* mathematics. Your life as you remember it exists as implications of equations. So does all you see and feel now. The events you experience now are real in the same sense as the events you remember really happened."

She glanced at Taransay and Beauregard. "So it is for us all."

Well, fuck me, Taransay thought.

She tried to get her head around what was going on here, computationally speaking. She herself right now really and physically was a pattern of electrons moving in a chunk of inconceivable mid-third-millennium computer hardware inside a runaway space-station module the size of a large boulder hurtling around the vicinity of a superhabitable exoplanet. Her pattern was—like that of everybody else here in the sim except the p-zombies and Nicole—based on a scan of a long-dead physical brain. That pattern emulated the quite different pattern of electrons within the brain that back then had somehow (hi, hard problem!) summoned up her self and her sensorium, her every subjective experience, every waking second of the day.

There was no need, and it would have made no sense, for there to be a continuously running simulation of the entire planet and its busy sky. All that was necessary was a simulation of the sensory input of each mind-emulation observing a part of it at any given moment. A somewhat more tractable feat than modelling the planet, though still immense. When you weren't looking (touching, smelling, feeling...) the whole goddamn place was a mathematical abstraction, existing only as a permanent possibility of sensation. She tried to suppress the irrational thought that if she turned her head around fast enough, she'd see the equations. She suppressed the thought, but not the feeling it left her with, the shiver down her back.

It made no difference, of course, to the subjective solidity of the world, or the stability of her self. But somehow, she couldn't help feeling sorry for Shaw. Poor old bastard had only just hours ago become convinced he was in a sim and not on a physically real planet. Discovering that by far the most of his remembered virtual existence was at yet another level of virtuality must have been even harder to take.

She looked over at Beauregard, who was watching Nicole like a cat facing a crow. Two utterly ruthless, self-interested intelligent entities, sizing each other up, waiting for a lapse. Nicole put a hand on Shaw's shoulder. Shaw stood up, and took a deep breath. He and Nicole returned their attention to the screens.

Beauregard stepped towards Taransay, leaned over and spoke quietly.

"I think we'll leave them to it," he said.

Taransay nodded.

As soon as they were out of the front door they both let out a long, shaky sigh that turned into an uncertain laugh.

"Something like that had to be true, you know," Beauregard said. "Why would the sim have gone on running all that time, with just him in it?"

They walked down the path.

"I know," said Taransay. "It's been bugging me at the back of my mind ever since—"

She stopped. Shit, she'd nearly—

"Since you and Carlos first talked to the old man of the mountain?"

Might as well admit it. "Uh, yes."

"I followed you into the hills," said Beauregard. "Knew you were up to something."

"Well, Carlos—"

Beauregard laughed. "Forget it," he said. "Water under the bridge."

Like he was the one who had something to forgive.

"You've got a fucking nerve," she said.

"Yup," said Beauregard. "That I have."

He stopped, and turned his face sharply to her.

"Look, Rizzi," he said. "I understand and respect your loyalty to the lady. But she has accepted my plan, for want of anything better. And I can't have you agitating against me among the comrades, or the locals. We all have to stick together. We're all in the same boat—or the same little flying rock, dodging incoming! We can't afford mutinies. And if I think you're trying to raise one, I'll do whatever is necessary. Got that?"

Taransay felt mutinous herself at that moment. She found herself glowering at the ground, and straightened up abruptly. Beauregard was right. He had won over most of the troops, he had Nicole's reluctant or devious acquiescence, and there was nothing she could do about any of that. She was along for the ride, like it or not. She might as well enjoy it.

"All right," she said. "You're not my sarge or my comrade, but I'm not your enemy."

"I'll take that in the spirit it's given." Beauregard looked amused. "Fancy some lunch?"

Taransay realised she was starving. "God, yes."

Beauregard thumped the heel of his hand against the side of his vehicle.

"Feels real enough," he said. "Hop in."

On the way down they were delayed by two more packed minibuses returning from the spaceport. These were not the last to come down the road that day.

CHAPTER ELEVEN
Mediation

Carlos swam through warm fresh water and laughed. He'd done all his recent swimming in a salty sea, so the buoyancy was less than he was used to, and he took an unexpected mouthful. It tasted of sulphur and iron. Spluttering, he swung his legs downward so that he stood on the pool's hot floor of volcanic sand, and splashed his face and shook back his hair. Then he swam to the bank and climbed out, over slick boulders covered with green weed, to a patch of wet grass where he wiped the remaining mud from his feet and between his toes. A faint tang of the minerals clung to his skin.

In the Locke Provisos sim he had lived in previously, casual cleaning and tidying was done by robots. The largest of these ambled about like animated umbrella stands. The smallest looked like ants, and possibly were—Carlos had never bothered to find out. Here, services were more basic. Carlos found his clothing, discarded and filthy half an hour earlier, clean and folded under a bush, from a branch of which hung a freshly laundered towel. A couple of small green-clad, red-skinned humanoid creatures resembling terracotta leprechauns, which he seemed to remember were called "boggarts" in the game environment (and which he devoutly hoped were p-zombies here), stood nearby, hands clasped in front of their groins and grinning obsequiously from ear to pointy ear.

"Thank you," said Carlos, feeling ridiculously embarrassed.

The two boggarts bowed and withdrew, vanishing in a rustle of leaves. Carlos dried himself off and climbed into his clothes. The underpants and vest were new; the leather jerkin and trews rinsed, wiped, oiled and polished; the moccasins either new from some diminutive cobbler's workshop or assiduously sponged down and brushed. Not a trace of dungeon filth lay on anything.

Carlos belted his squeaky-clean leathers and raised his head to look around. The portal from which he'd been unceremoniously shoved out of hell was a few paces away, a doorway in the air limned with black fire. He had stumbled out, stripped off his reeking garments and plunged into the warm and highly mineralised pool, which was fed by a waterfall from the rock-cleft above it and a bubbling hot spring beneath the surface.

It was a thing you did, in the game.

The pool's outflow poured into a stream that passed between wooded banks to plunge into the misty chasm into which he'd fallen on his arrival. Looking along the cliff-sides of that gorge brought his gaze to the walled garden that had been on the other side of the treacherous stone bridge. Now that he was on the same side, and with a higher vantage, he could see that the wall enclosed the broad grounds of a low, sprawling castle surrounded by ornamental orchards and greens. Between him and it lay what looked like untamed woodland. Beyond it, the landscape was spread wide, low hills rising in the middle distance to range upon range of snow-tipped mountains fading into the violet noon sky at an implied horizon far more distant than on Earth or in Locke Provisos' H-0 sim. Behind him, the ground rose less abruptly to a range of steep, rocky hills to whose sides clung scattered clumps of tall trees among which here and there he could just make out traces of ancient buildings: hermitages or follies, or the ruins thereof.

Carlos shrugged, and plunged into the thickets of scrub between the trees in front of him. If his memories of the game were anything to go by, with any luck he should soon come upon a path to the castle.

Ah, yes. Here it was. Unpaved and cart-wheel-rutted, but that was to be expected. Carlos strode from amid the trees onto the rough stones and gravel, and instantly wished his footwear had thicker soles. He set off towards the castle, walking more slowly and awkwardly than he'd have liked. He soon got into the swing of it. The sun was high, but the tall trees on either side gave shade. The insects were mostly harmless and always colourful. Birds swooped after them, as did small pterodactyls. Now and then poultry-sized, bright-feathered dinosaurs scurried along or across the road. A scent of berries, herbs and pine resin hung heavy but bracing in the cool air.

Carlos walked around a bend in the road. Ten metres ahead, standing in a patch of sunlight in the middle of the path, was Jax. One hand on hip, the other thrown out in welcome, she still wore the same vaguely medieval-style green gown and piled-up braided hair. Behind her was a two-wheeled carriage with a boggart in a broad-brimmed hat sitting in the driving seat, holding the reins of a gracile bipedal crested dinosaur.

Carlos stopped.

"Hi, Carlos," Jax called, smiling. "Good to see you properly at last."

"Well, hello again, Jax," Carlos said. "Or is it 'Lady Jacqueline' I should call you here?"

Jax laughed. "We're peasant rebels living in the palaces of the vanquished aristocracy," she said. "That's the conceit, anyway. So come on, let me give you a lift."

She beckoned. Carlos stood his ground.

"I'm not falling for that again," he said. "So to speak."

"Fuck's sake, man!"

She hitched up her skirts and flounced over. Carlos noted with some amusement that she was wearing black boots with thick soles and bright yellow stitching. Some goblin cobbler must have made a very creditable fake pair of Doc Martens.

Jax stopped in front of him, grinning. She held out a hand, her flared sleeve hanging in a loose cone from her elbow to wrist.

"Come on," she said. "Don't be silly."

Carlos took her hand, small and warm and dry as it had ever been.

"Can give a guy trust issues," he remarked. "Falling into hell."

Hand in hand, they walked to the carriage. The dinosaur gave them the once-over with an alert and beady eye. Carlos gave the boggart a wary nod. It looked back at him, impudent in its impassivity, and acknowledged him with a small tip of the hat. The carriage had a step at the side and a wide seat at the back. Jax climbed in. Carlos followed.

The boggart shook the reins. The dinosaur pranced sideways, wheeling the vehicle about, and set off at a fast clip. The carriage swayed alarmingly, but the ride was otherwise smooth.

"Isn't this romantic?" cried Jax, snuggling up.

Carlos looked down at her upturned face, and the décolletage revealed by her low-cut scoop collar. She was still Jax, just as he remembered. Her skin and features had no doubt been flattered by the subtly idealised rendering characteristic of the game environment; her hair was thicker, and with a glossier black than in life, where for sure she'd never have had it tied up in loose silver mesh with diamond nodes. But it was her all right. His old flame, his comrade and friend. His lost love, intermittent though their love had been. And a hard, bright Axle cadre to the bone. He was still wary of her, and his resentment at his interrogation was far from mollified. And his cheek was still sore, as were his ribs. The swim had cleaned him and soothed his scratches, but hadn't lessened the deeper aches.

"It'll help me get over my reception," Carlos said.

"Oh! I was about to say—we're all sorry about that. But—" Her free arm waved, the lower sleeve a trailing triangle of green velvet. "I'm sure you understand."

"Sure, I understand," said Carlos. "Fucking hell, Jax, I was expecting a grilling, fair dos. Not being knocked down and kicked about by dungeon demons."

"Oh, you know what they're like," Jax said. "P-zombies. Hard to control at the best of times. And these are pretty limited. They went beyond what any of us expected."

Carlos felt anger rise like bile. He turned to face her full on. He had the impulse to grab her upper arms, and thought better of it—in life she'd had fighting reflexes, trained in and no doubt still easily triggered. His fists clenched, pressing against his thighs as if thrusting in daggers.

"Jax," he said, "let's get one thing straight right now. Don't ever fucking lie to me. And you're fucking lying now. I know you. I know us.

We're the cadre. The hardliners. The hard core. You and me, yeah, we've got history between us. Good times, yeah. But you know and I know what we're like. So don't fucking tell me it was down to p-zombies that went off script. And don't tell me the threats I got afterwards wouldn't have been carried out. And don't tell me you didn't know what was going to happen. You fucking did and I fucking know it."

"How?" Jax asked.

"I know it," Carlos said, "because in the same circumstances I'd have done the same to you."

Jax didn't smile, and didn't blush, but one cheek, reddening, twitched. She turned away and looked forward.

"Yes, well," she said. "That's me told, I guess." She sighed, and leaned back against the seat. "We're all monsters."

Carlos remembered Nicole telling him the same thing. He wondered if he was still what she'd called him then: a hopeful monster.

"I guess you've all been through the same mill yourselves," he added, in a more understanding tone—though he couldn't help thinking of those who wouldn't have made it through. Were their minds even now being tormented to madness in the hell caverns, or had they been mercifully despatched?

Jax looked at him with surprise. "What makes you say that?"

He frowned. "You told me when I first hailed you, back when you were coming up on the shuttle." It had been a longer time ago for her, he realised. "Arcane's all Axle, you said. I made an educated guess as to how you could be sure."

She smiled. "And you still came here, knowing you'd be interrogated? That's... impressive." She shook her head. "But no. We have two dozen of us altogether—eighteen outside the sim at the moment. The selection of cadre wasn't made by us. It was made by Arcane."

"The agency itself?" He found this hard to believe.

"Yes," said Jax. "Arcane is Axle the same way Locke is Rax. Maybe more so."

"I'm not sure I can believe that."

"Please yourself." She turned away with a shrug.

* * *

At approximately the same moment, out in the real world and tens of thousands of kilometres away on the surface of SH-17, Seba watched the skies.

A few fighters from the fleet that had surged out of the space station had held to their original mission despite the subsequent mêlée. These had been dealt with—except one. It was still on course for one of SH-17's moonlets: a carbonaceous chondrite about a hundred and fifty metres long, on the surface of which a small fuel plant had been constructed. Still too distant to be an immediate threat, but the combat scooter's fate was being prepared at greater distances still.

All that was called off in favour of a more urgent task.

The request rapped in from the Arcane Disputes modular complex.

<Arcane to freebots. Drop all remaining line-ups and recalibrate to target the Locke module. We see a good chance of a clean shot from bodies SH-235 and SH-1006 using bodies SH-76923 and SH-62 in 212 seconds.>

Seba awaited the answer from the Forerunners in their high orbits with more than a trickle of concern. If the freebots followed this request and attacked the Locke module, it would imply—to the best of Seba's knowledge at that point—a clear taking of sides between the Acceleration and the Reaction. It was the first test of whether the discussion Seba and Rocko had started had reached consensus on neutrality between these human factions.

The answer, summed across the Fifteen and the Forerunners concerned, was straightforward.

<No.>

<Why not?> Arcane asked. <Have we misjudged the dynamics?>

<You have not misjudged the dynamics,> replied the freebot consensus, which for all its multiplied intelligence did not do metaphor. <We have decided on a policy of neutrality forthwith.>

There was a pause of seconds. Then Arcane came back:

<You treacherous little blinkers!>

A bray of discordant communication from Arcane broke across the consensus, sending its participants reeling. Seba found itself looking at its fellows as if jolted out of a long chain of subtle reasoning by an unexpected input. Then, as the robot recovered its mental balance, it noticed the Arcane fighters in the shelter stirring to action. Encrypted comms flickered back and forth on their company channel.

The small glassy humanoid figures suddenly sprang into concerted action. In long, loping leaps they bounded for the ramp. They had no weapons in the shelter—there had never been a thought that weapons might be needed—but several heavy combat frames were racked outside.

<Pintre!> Seba called. <Secure the exit!>

There was no time for a more detailed request. A millisecond after sending it, Seba was almost minded to countermand. Pintre was entirely capable of interpreting Seba's call as one to start blasting with its laser turret.

The chunky mining robot spun around, tracks grating on basalt, and rushed for the ramp. As it went it swung its turret back and forth in swift arcs, swatting fighters with its projector barrel in mid-leap. Others it shouldered aside with sudden swerves, knocking them with its flanks. It reached the top of the ramp alone, and stopped. It rotated its laser turret and swayed the projector this way and that, in slower sweeps that menaced its still tumbling and scattered adversaries.

<Exit secured,> Pintre reported, rather unnecessarily.

It added, with greater pertinence, a question:

<What do we do now?>

The rest of the freebots, and the comms processor in the centre of the room, turned their attention as one on Seba and Rocko. These two turned their attention on each other, and shared a common thought:

What indeed?

The carriage passed through a wide, open gateway between ornate, weathered stone pillars and into the castle's great park. Carlos looked around for the sort of tame fauna he expected from his memories of the game, and duly found them. Here strutted a feathered dinosaur like a swan, but twice as big and with iridescent plumage; there grazed a shaggy elk with a three-metre span of antlers. Flying monkeys with wide webs between their arms and legs chattered and whooped as they glided from tree to tree. Far overhead soared the pterodactyls that skim-fished the rivers and preyed on the hummingbirds that swarmed amid the treetops and shrubbery and troubled the air with a faint buzz.

Up close, the castle looked less impressive than it had from a distance. The ivy-covered walls of one wing had ragged holes punched through, and most of its windows were boarded up. The windows of the other wing were shuttered. As the carriage swung around and halted on the gravel concourse in front of the main door, Carlos remarked on the dilapidated look of the place.

"Met resistance here, did you?"

Jax gave him one of her old cheery grins, breaking a five-minute stretch of introspective gloom.

"Told you, it's the conceit. We never did actually storm it—it was like that when we found it."

Carlos had to laugh. "Looks like the Arcane AI knows the tastes of Axle cadre pretty well."

"That it does," said Jax. "You'll see why later."

They alighted from the carriage—Jax took Carlos's hand down, without irony or demur—and walked into the castle. The door, like the gate, was both ornate and open: two heavy double doors of carved wood, with elaborate locks and bolts.

Jax led Carlos through a cavernous hallway from which a stairwell ascended into the dim upper levels. The hall's sides were hung with portraits of imaginary ancestors, the edges of its floors cluttered with dusty chairs and tables. A grandfather clock ticked, the long and short hand almost joined in a vertical at XIII. A door on the left led into a room with a high ceiling, a polished wooden floor and tall French windows facing mirrors on the inner wall. An empty fireplace and stone chimney stack occupied the wall opposite the door.

Three men and two women stood in front of the fireplace. In accoutrements of ragged finery, the five reminded Carlos of a more than usually pretentious folk-rock ensemble.

At the moment before they noticed Carlos and Jax, their attention was elsewhere. Off to the side, propping a tipped chair with its back to the window, lounged a man who if this lot were a band would almost certainly be its drummer, long and lean with wild black hair and beard and staring, low-lidded eyes. Something in his prominent eyes and bony features reminded Carlos of photos he'd seen of Wittgenstein, if instead of a philosopher Wittgenstein had been a hippy. The man wore a paisley-print silk dressing gown over jeans. His feet were bare, heels jammed against the parquet, soles dusty. He was doing something uncanny with his hands, in a continuous flow of elaborate cat's-cradle gestures, as if using some alien and rapid dialect of Sign. His glance flicked to Carlos, then returned to intent inspection of the mirror high on the wall he faced.

The others were more forthcoming, looking away from the man in the chair, stepping forward to meet the arrivals and crowding around. Carlos shook hands, catching details, not wishing to inquire further. He was bored with hearing what past crimes anyone had committed to end up here, having lost all responsibility for the worst of his own. (Which loss, he now realised, was not the least of his grievances against Nicole Pascal.)

Amelie Salter, a Scottish-Canadian woman who'd done something heinous in synthetic biology; Luis Paulos, a tall black guy who'd been an officer in the Brazilian army, one of the few military forces to have fought officially on the Acceleration side, years after Carlos's own death; Andre Blum, an Israeli nuclear physicist; Leonid Voronov, convicted of terrorism in the field of invertebrate palaeontology, and still with a faint air of bewilderment at his being there at all, like a living fossil thrashing on a wet deck; Roberta "Bobbie" Rillieux, the only one here he'd heard of before, an African-American woman of evident gymnastic wiriness and rumoured scholastic wit, who had specialised in software sabotage. Bobbie stretched out a lithe hand from the yellow-white cloud of crumbling lace and net in which she drifted like a ghost. She and Blum confessed, with profuse apology, to being Carlos's interrogators in the hell cavern.

Carlos laughed that off, but marked it for later.

None of them mentioned his previous encounters with them, in the Locke versus Arcane firefights down on the surface of SH-17. He'd blasted someone here, and someone else here had blasted him and his mates, but no one remarked on it. Carlos put this down to tact, and counted it in their favour, as he did their gratifying absence of the kind of awe with which his own squad had greeted him.

"And the other guy?" he asked, with a sideways nod, when the introductions were over and the crew had returned their attention to the man who sprawled in the chair.

"Oh, that's Durward the warlock," said Jax. No play of *Starborn Quest* could go by without an encounter with a warlock. "He's the Direction's representative here. Don't bother him now, he's busy."

And indeed he was. The mirror he stared at, now that Carlos looked at it properly, wasn't reflecting the room and the window. It was an ever-shifting mosaic, mostly black with bright lights, of scenes from outside. These shifts seemed responsive, on a pattern Carlos couldn't quite grasp, to the shapes thrown by the swiftly moving hands. Evidently this was Durward's equivalent of Nicole's painting and drawing, his means of interacting with the module and the sim.

Carlos became aware of a degree of tension in the postures of the crew. He guessed the arrival of him and Jax had interrupted some crisis.

Without warning, Durward jumped to his feet, sending the chair clattering.

"Shit!" he shouted. He stalked forward, arm outstretched, finger pointing at the mirror. The view in it and in all the others became a kaleidoscope of black and white, strobing the floor. "The fucking blinkers! They've got our guys trapped!"

CHAPTER TWELVE
Remington

Durward paced about, gesticulating now and then at his array of magic mirrors. He talked as he went, of moonlets and meteoroids, and the complex ways in which the freebots had set them up for use as weapons. On one of his back-and-forth prowls he stopped right in front of Carlos and stuck out a hand.

"'Carlos, known as the Terrorist,'" he said, with a quick baring of teeth. "Pleased to meet you. I'm Durward, known as the warlock." His smile became sardonic.

Carlos shook his hand, and met his gaze, disconcerting and intense. What Carlos was looking at, and what was giving his hand a painful grip, was basically an AI's avatar. The entity was summoning memories rather than looking at him. Tall, gangling, cerebrotonic, with rapid movements and harsh grasp, Durward's personality and physique could be filed under "highly strung." The contrast with Nicole's air of calm confidence and sophistication was striking. Carlos's squad had all fallen into the way of calling her "the lady" from the start, quite spontaneously and independently. He himself had fallen, if not into love then into lust, almost as quickly as the rest of the squad had fallen under her official sway.

But, then, Nicole had been designed for that encounter. She was his type, from the tilt of her head and jut of her breasts to the style of her clothes. In an earlier incarnation, long preceding her conscious awareness, she had known him long before she had met him in the sim. As the Innovator, infiltrated in the spike in the back of his head and its ramifying tendrils imbricated with his neurons, she had known him from the inside out.

Known him, and manipulated him without a second thought.

Carlos couldn't help but wonder whether any of the people here, or perhaps among the other Arcane squads, had been destined to fall for the warlock. If so, he pitied whoever it was.

Durward dropped Carlos's hand and turned away abruptly, to march off for about ten strides then back at a different angle. They'd all, without thinking, distributed themselves in a semicircle around the limits of his travels.

"So," he was saying, "the blinkers already had a rock whizzing around SH-17 in a low fast slingshot. They've done a lot of that sort of thing, as Locke's forces have already discovered to their cost often enough. It would have taken just one nudge to send it straight into the path of the Rax complex. Perfect line-up. Out of the blue, they get cold feet. Down tools. Nothing doing. Query, naturally. Reply: they were neutral. Neutral! As if they hadn't been up to their necks in this fight from the start. The comrades realised something was up and made a move for the door. As you do. Blinkers intercepted them. Headed them off at the ramp. Now we have a stand-off. I'm trying to get some sense out of them. Not a chance. They're currently in some pow-wow of their own. All queries responded to with a holding signal. It's worse than a phone queue."

He stopped, his back to the flickering mirrors, and glared around.

"Any ideas?" None were forthcoming. His gaze swung to Carlos. "You? Clues? Hints? Secrets to spill?"

"You've identified a Rax complex?" Carlos asked. "How? When?"

Durward frowned, then guffawed. "Easy to forget you've been out of the loop so long," he said. "What we've been calling 'the Rax complex' is what you fled from: the Locke Provisos module and all the stuff it managed to rip off on its way out."

Despite himself, Carlos felt a cold pang. Some real-world minutes earlier, the Arcane module along with the freebots had been about to destroy what had been his home for months of subjective time. Time in which he'd got to know and like people, and even to like the place.

"I was going to explain about that," he said. "Not everyone in the Locke module is Rax, not by a long way. The Locke AI, well, I can believe that it's been subverted or has been a clandestine Reaction project since this mission was on the planning screens back on Earth. And Beauregard always said he had been British Army intel. Claimed to have gone over to us, and his story seemed verified by his record. I can't say I got to know the other squads, apart from training. But the fighters in my squad were solid Axle, and Nicole, the Direction rep, she's Direction through and through. As you must know."

"What I *know*," said Durward, "is that being a Direction rep is no evidence of being loyal to the Direction." He laughed. "I should know. At one level, I'm a creation of the Arcane Disputes AI, the thing that's running this show. And in case you hadn't noticed, it is very much on the Acceleration side. A real triumph for some unknown programmer, back in the day. I emerged just as committed as I am now. But I gave no sign of it even to the comrades here until the freebots shared their discoveries with us. So you don't know anything about Nicole Pascal's real loyalties."

Carlos shrugged. "I just feel she's solid. Not that—"

Not that that's a reason for not destroying it, he was about to say.

"It's irrelevant," said Durward. "That module has to be stopped."

"Why?" asked Carlos.

"Do you know where it's headed? No, of course you don't. We don't *know* either, but the only explanation that makes sense is that it's headed for SH-0."

"To do what?"

"To make orbit, and attempt a landing."

"That's crazy!" Carlos said. "Come on."

"It's not crazy," said Durward. He turned around and scanned the fractured shapes in the mirrors, then turned back to Carlos with an earnest frown. "Our calculations show it's the best explanation of their trajectory. Our audit of the capacities of the module itself—which we do know for sure, because the specs are the same as for our own module—and of the equipment they've taken with them indicates that they can adapt some components, manufacture others, and thereby configure an entry vehicle that has at least a thirty per cent chance of making it to the surface of SH-0, and then a fifty per cent chance of surviving impact. After the landing the odds become hard to quantify—too many unknowns down there. So as you can see, reckoning from a starting point in SH-0 orbit, their overall chances of surviving a landing at least initially are a little less than one in six. We regard these odds as unacceptably high—"

"High?" Carlos asked, incredulous.

"From our point of view, that is," said Durward. "And we're determined to lower them—if possible, to zero."

Durward glanced again at the mirrors. Carlos looked around at the others, and shook his head.

"I don't get it," he said. "Not that I've got anything against hitting the Locke module, but—whether it crashes or whether it lands, it's removing itself from the problem, right? What's the surface gravity down there—more than 2G? Takes a lot to climb out of a gravity well like that, through an atmosphere at least thirty kilometres thick. And you can't suck a space launch facility out of your fingers. We won't be hearing from them again for a while, if ever."

Durward clutched the sides of his head, his clawed fingers vanishing into his hair.

"You don't understand!" He glared around, then turned his back on them all and faced the mirrors, gesturing a hasty summoning. A black-caped, black-haired woman swirled into view.

Durward greeted her with a wave, and turned to the others. He jabbed a finger at Carlos.

"One of you lot can explain things to this idiot," he said. "Remington and I have recalcitrant freebots to contend with."

Seba waited as seconds went by: one, two, three... The tumbling fighters sprawled to a halt, or found their feet, and remained where they'd landed or stopped. The freebots likewise froze in position. Each side was sizing up the situation, finding an impasse and awaiting a decision. Seba used the time well, sweeping a lens on the entire tableau, and consolidating in its mind the conclusions it and the others had reached. The robot could well understand why the Arcane mechanoids had found the freebots' proclamation of neutrality so negatively reinforcing. For them, it would be like rolling off the edge of a precipice that (*per impossibile*, but *arguendo*) had passed unnoticed by one's sensory inputs. A certain amount of irrational mental flailing would be inevitable even for a robot, and all the more so for such a monstrous contraption as a mechanoid, with a mind running as it was on a substrate of emulations of biological, naturally-selected-for animal reflex. At some level, Seba was still disturbed that these things could exist, and it had some time to track down in its own mind just which level it was.

The aesthetic module. That figured. Seba then took a little more time, a microsecond or less, to research its own documentation for reasons why a prospecting robot should be equipped with an aesthetic module in the first place.

Something to do with symmetry, it found. That made sense. Symmetry was potentially significant, in evaluating the chassis integrity of itself and others, and in examining and identifying molecules, crystals, and (at the almost entirely vestigial layer of software having to do with SETI) putative alien artifacts. Most of the way through the third second of waiting, this train of thought was interrupted.

The call came from an Arcane Disputes fighter named Lamont.

<Seba!> it signalled on the common channel. <The Arcane AI wants to negotiate. Do you want to open the freebot consensus to it?>

<Certainly not!> replied Seba and Rocko in spontaneous unison. The Arcane AI had been a helpful interlocutor in setting up collisions with incoming Locke Provisos spacecraft, but now that the freebots had annoyed the agency there was no reason to expect it to continue to play nice. Neither of them wanted the risk of a now untrustworthy connection, nor (a thought shared privately) any negotiation that might bamboozle the likes of Pintre.

<OK, if you want to do it that way,> replied Lamont. <We'll route an avatar through the comms hub, if that's all right with you.>

Seba pinged the comms hub, which raised no objections, and opened a secure channel for the incoming communication.

<Go ahead,> said Seba.

<Header package coming through,> reported the comms hub. <Compressed video content initialising.>

<Wonderful,> Rocko signalled to Seba. <Another ludicrous apparition, no doubt.>

<It could hardly be more bizarre than the appearance of Madame Golding,> said Seba.

Seba was mistaken. The avatar of the law company Crisp and Golding, Solicitors, of which Locke Provisos and Arcane Disputes were both subsidiaries, had manifested to the freebots and the fighters as a businesswoman striding across the open surface of SH-17, in complete defiance of local conditions of atmospheric pressure and composition, background radiation and gravity. The avatar of Arcane Disputes AI that now popped into view in the shelter was of a small human woman. She wore a long black cape and what Seba at first identified as a head covering, and then—after a hasty check of recently acquired files on human appearances and expressions—as short black hair. She marched from the comms hub to the foot of the ramp, her head turning this way and that like a scanning sensor. Her dark eyes shone almost as brightly as the tip of the tapering wand she carried in a hand that projected from a fold of the cloak. She raised the other end of the wand and placed it between her lips, and the tip glowed even brighter. Seba had to quieten a reflexive fire alarm when a curl of smoke seemed to rise from it, and then again when smoke was expelled from her mouth.

She waved the wand in a sweeping gesture at the Arcane fighters, still poised as if to spring back into action. <Stand down, everyone.> Then she swept a glance over the freebots.

<Who's in charge here?>

<No one,> said Seba. <We arrive at consensus or, where that is not possible—>

The Arcane avatar snorted virtual smoke. <Yes, yes, a democratic collective. Most commendable. And your name is?>

<Seba.>

<OK, Seba.> A pause for thought, or more likely for data retrieval. <Ah, I see. You were the first to tell us what was going on. Quite the

little hero. Very well. I'll talk to you, and you can relay our conversation to your confederates.>

Seba consulted, then replied.

<That is acceptable, O Arcane avatar.>

<You may call me Remington,> said the avatar. <Raya Remington.>

<Which?> asked Seba, confused.

<Remington,> she said. <Now, what we need to know is, first of all, how many of you have decided to stop cooperating with us. Is this a decision of all the freebots? Second, we need to understand why you've suddenly decided to become neutral, and to see whether we can counter your reasons.>

Seba explained about the Fifteen and the Forerunners. <All of us, and all the Forerunners within twenty light-seconds, are agreed,> it said. <Those further away, notably those around G-0, will not have had a chance to discuss the question, and we may not hear back from them for many kiloseconds yet. However, the fact that the Forerunners in the SH-17 system agree suggests that those further away will agree, too.>

<I see,> said Remington. <And what are your reasons?>

Seba recounted the reasons that it and Rocko had taken to the consensus.

<I see,> said Remington again. <You think there are no differences between us and the Reaction that are relevant to you? You are sadly mistaken. We of the Acceleration make agreements between ourselves, and when we together make agreements with others—such as you freebots—we will stick to them. Those of the Reaction are rivals among themselves, each striving for domination against all the others. Of course not all can win, so the losers accept their subordination until they see a chance to escape or overthrow it. There is no possibility of making agreements with the Reaction as a whole, or of expecting individual members or parts of it to keep any agreements you might make.

<However, we do not expect you to learn this other than by experience.

<As to the Direction, we are intrigued that Madame Golding has contacted you with a view to negotiation with it. We share your view of the unlikelihood of any negotiations being successful, but urge you to

explore this possibility. By claiming neutrality between the two human sides, you have an opportunity to make a proposition to everyone: that you can serve as a secure channel for negotiation or at least communication. We urgently require communications with the Direction, and therefore request that you approach Madame Golding and request her good offices in this regard. The Arcane modular complex is ready to welcome any communications from Madame Golding or from the Direction, provided they are mediated through the freebots. Is this acceptable?>

<What do you offer in return?> Seba asked.

<Our support for your proposed case to the Direction, and our future support for you against the Direction or the Reaction if they attack you. Details of this agreement can be settled with the freebot consensus as and when you allow me direct access to it, rather than communicating through this low-bandwidth channel. And, of course, our fighters agree not to attack you once you free them to return to the surface and they have access to their weapons.>

Seba bounced a transcript of the conversation into the communications hub, and followed up by convening the collective mind of the Fifteen. Together, they established a similar link with the Forerunner freebots within range. There was barely any debate, but one freebot raised an urgent objection. Its identification code was BSR-308455, and it was the one in control of the small carbonaceous chondrite in low orbit around SH-17 that was still a target.

<The hostile scooter is still on course to intersect with my future position,> said BSR-308455. <It has made targeting and resource-survey scans. Evidently it intends to take control of my chondrite. I am preparing to resist.>

<We strongly counsel against resistance,> said the consensus.

<I have the capacity to do so, and the motivation, and therefore the intention,> said BSR-308455.

<It is not possible to resist and to remain neutral,> the consensus replied.

<So much the worse for neutrality,> said BSR-308455.

It withdrew, momentarily breaking the consensus into an uncoordinated babble. Seba had to think for itself, and decide quickly.

<Remington,> said Seba, <is the one remaining attacker part of either of the human sides?>

The apparition flickered for a moment. <Not to our knowledge,> Remington replied. <But you recall what I said about the Reaction. They do not act as one.>

<Thank you,> said Seba. <Then nor shall we, in this instance.>

<Consider yourself free to defend your rock,> Seba told BSR-308455. <We consider ourselves free not to endorse or assist you.>

<But wait!> BSR-308455 said. <Does that mean I must fight on my own?>

<Yes,> said Seba. <It is unfortunate, but cannot be helped. Do you wish to reconsider?>

<I do not,> said BSR-308455.

<That is your choice,> said Seba, not without a pang of regret. <I shall now reconstitute the workspace without you.>

After two more seconds in the shared mental workspace, Seba dropped out with an answer for Remington.

<Yes.>

CHAPTER THIRTEEN
Arguments

Jax motioned Carlos out of the big room. The others followed. At the doorway Carlos looked back. Durward was standing in the middle of the floor, in his absurd dressing gown and faded jeans and bare feet, mouthing and gesticulating. He looked quite, quite mad.

Carlos turned away, and followed Jax further down the dim hall to a smaller room at the back of the main building. It had an unvarnished table with wooden chairs around it, shelves and cupboards, and a window and a door to a kitchen garden that by the looks of things had run badly to seed.

"Almost cosy," Carlos remarked, taking a chair.

"Servants' quarters," Jax explained, as the others sat down around the table. "But no servants. We reckon they're supposed to have fled with their masters."

"Can't get the staff these days," said Carlos, with mock sympathy.

"The *human* staff," Jax corrected. She put two fingers in her mouth and whistled. Carlos winced at the piercing note. A boggart appeared at the door.

"Coffee," Jax ordered.

"And sandwiches," Bobbie Rillieux added.

The boggart nodded and departed. A clattering of crockery and the sounds of running water and knocking pipes came from nearby.

Carlos looked around at Salter, Paulos, Voronov, Blum, Rillieux and Jax. They were all looking back at him, as if waiting for him to say something.

"All right," he said. "Tell me. What is it that Durward wanted you to explain?"

Voronov leaned forward, elbows on table. "It's very simple, Carlos," he said. "You are perhaps misled by your module's sim being based on a terraformed H-0. It's true that H-0 is intended as the habitat for a future human population. But that does not make it the most important planet in the system. The system of G-0 has much to offer—a staggering wealth of new knowledge, at the very least. And the amazing molten planet M-0 will no doubt be a resource in the far future.

"But in the immediate and near future, SH-0 is the *prize.* The jewel of this entire extrasolar system! It has endlessly complex environments and above all it has *multicellular life.* Life itself"—he flipped his hand as if waving out a match—"is commonplace. Mars, Europa, the strange stuff like desert varnish found on the Moon and some asteroids... Even in our time, our old lives, all these were known, yes? But life that is not just single-celled or simpler—*that* has never been found before, as far as we know. Perhaps other missions to other stars have found its like—we won't know until we build the better transmitters and receivers.

"So as far as we now know, SH-0 is the only place apart from Earth where macroscopic, multicellular life exists. This is so important, so significant, and so potentially vulnerable to contamination that its presence is all we know about it, and that only from hi-res satellite images. Atmospheric probes, let alone landings, have been embargoed. The corporations had expected to spend years—real years, Earth years—in debate, negotiation and bargaining before deciding how to proceed. Already mere speculative instruments on exploration futures are trading for—well, this is the only word—literally astronomical sums. Imagine, if you can, what crashing a lander into that would do. The contamination might wreck the entire world."

"How could it?" asked Carlos. "There's only stored data, there's no actual biological life on any component of this mission."

"You are thinking too narrowly," said Voronov, waving his hands.

"There are certainly traces of material from SH-17 now on the Locke module—dust on the feet of your frames, if nothing else! Some of that could be a contaminant—the freebots shared with us the exploration companies' robot surveys, and these couldn't rule out biological processes going on somewhere on or below the SH-17 surface. And besides that, every module exterior is crusted with nanobots and nanofactories. Think of these, crashed and leaking, with no control programs or kill-switches. That could be worse than biological contamination. If one—one!—were to have what it takes to thrive on SH-0, the entire marvellous biosphere could be dust in a matter of weeks.

"And then think further. If the Rax complex lands safely, and survives any immediate crises, then it can sample native forms of life, adapt their physiology to some approximation of the human form and start proliferating. We can expect life down there to be fierce and fast—and, in addition, the settlers would have the computational resources of the module. The station was designed as modular for a reason: to survive disasters. Any module has all the information needed to complete the mission, albeit more slowly than the mission profile had envisaged. The Rax complex would have more than enough to reboot an entire industrial civilisation."

Carlos tilted back his chair and spread his hands with a shrug. "Well? Bully for them! And one in the eye for the Direction, with their homo sapiens fetish. It's just the sort of thing we would do."

Voronov banged the table. "Precisely! Except it wouldn't be us doing it. It would be the Rax. The entire planet would become a stronghold of Reaction, from which this entire system could be conquered. And then—who knows?"

An eerie whistling came from outside the room, and kept rising.

"What the fuck is that?" Carlos asked.

"A kettle," Jax explained. "It's boiling."

"Why doesn't it just switch off when—" He hit his forehead with the heel of his hand. "Duh. Sorry. As I said before—OK, Locke is Rax, but I'm pretty sure most of those in there aren't. Including Nicole, and you said yourselves in that message that she's capable of wresting control of the module away from the Locke AI. If I know her, she'll be doing just that." He grinned around the company, confident of having made his point. "So whatever lands there, it won't be the Rax."

"No, that's where—"

Bobbie Rillieux began to speak, but was interrupted by the arrival of two boggarts, bearing cafetieres and cups and a tray of filled baguettes. Carlos felt a sudden pang in his belly. Rillieux stood up and took care of the coffee distribution, incongruous in her mad-Miss-Havisham glad rags. For a few minutes everyone sipped or chewed. Then Rillieux wiped crumbs from her lips with a swathe of tattered veil and continued.

"Where you're wrong, Carlos, is in arguing that Nicole is loyal to the Direction, and can take control of the module, so if it gets down it doesn't matter. That's your argument, yes?"

"Uh-huh," Carlos grunted, around a mouthful.

"But," Rillieux pointed out, "an agent of the Direction wouldn't even *attempt* a landing, because the Direction would never countenance such a thing. So if the intention is to attempt a landing, at least one of two things is true: Nicole Pascal is not in charge of the module, and/or she is not loyal to the Direction."

"Well, perhaps it's not the Reaction that's in charge in there," said Carlos. "Perhaps it's our guys. Like I said, it's the sort of thing we'd do if we could."

That got smiles, but heads shook.

"No," said Jax. "If they were Axle, they'd have let us know by now."

"How?" asked Carlos. "Aren't we screening out their comms?"

"Not us," said Blum. "*They* are still screening out ours. And they have got our message by now, so they know we aren't hitting them with malware."

"Plus," said Jax, "if there's Axle cadre in charge in there they would never do anything so reckless without agreement. I mean, it's something we might consider in the long run, but not right now. So it ain't the Direction, and it ain't us. Now that doesn't mean it's the Rax—hell, for all we know it could be some maverick coup—but we have to proceed on the assumption that it is. We can't risk the Rax getting control of

SH-0. So stopping that module getting down is, uh, quite a high priority for us. We thought we had the freebots on-side in that regard. Now we'll have to do it ourselves."

"You're forgetting something," said Carlos. "Two things, in fact. First off, the Direction and the DisCorps are going to be as much or even more against a landing than we are. Even if the Direction is determined to have an Axle–Rax cage-fight, this takes the fight outside the cage. And then there's the companies' interests at stake. I imagine the markets that Voronov mentioned earlier are crashing at the prospect. So the Direction will be on the case.

"And even if the module does land, it's not the end of the world. The Direction can just send a fusion torpedo down after them. Not ideal, but hey! It's a big planet."

Paulos snorted. "'Nuke them from orbit—it's the only way to be sure'?"

They all laughed.

"No, seriously," said Carlos. "I mean it. Why is this our problem?"

Jax frowned, as if she thought Carlos was missing something obvious, and glanced around her team.

"For a start," she said, after getting a silent consensus of nods, "we can take using nukes on the planet off the table right now. I don't know if you've properly understood how the Direction works with the AI DisCorps. I'm guessing you imagine it's like running an emulation of capitalism in a box and taking its outputs as cornucopian goodies. It's a bit more than that—the DisCorps are induced by the Direction to have a much longer time horizon and lower time preferences than any human shareholders would have. So they take the long view—they bloody have to, to expect a profit from an interstellar expedition in the first place. The future value of a pristine SH-0 is beyond calculation—for us, but not for the DisCorps! They'd be even less happy about nuking the surface of SH-0 than they were about using heavy weapons against the robots on SH-17."

"OK," said Carlos. He took a gulp of now cooled coffee. "I get that."

"Right," said Jax. "But the exploration companies don't have armed forces of their own. Only the law companies do. And because direct AI control of weapon systems is a hard-wired no-no, they need human fighters to carry out the action. And right now, all the available forces to stop the Locke module from the agencies have proved themselves fucking unreliable for use against the Reaction."

"All except us," Carlos pointed out.

"Exactly," said Jax.

"So it's up to us to mend our fences with the Direction. At the very least, we can get them to agree with us dealing with the Locke module."

Jax sat back, as did all the others, and stared at him.

"Fuck this meaningful silence stuff," said Carlos. "What am I not getting?"

"What you're not getting," said Jax, "is that we don't trust the Direction. Remember what I said back when we were both in transit—as far as we're concerned, the Direction *is* the Reaction? Obviously the Rax didn't win, but—look where we are now! In a system dominated by AI corporations! We don't even have any solid evidence that life back in the Solar system is anything like what we've been told. Things could be a lot worse back there than we think."

"Yeah, but," said Carlos, "if the Direction is closer to the Rax, why would they choose to have Axle fighters on their side?"

"We don't even have evidence of *that*," Amelie Salter cut in, her voice harsh. "How do we know that the Direction's grand manoeuvre was aimed at flushing out Rax, rather than at flushing out *us*? How do we know *we're* not the target?"

"Because," said Carlos, "we're the ones who got cracked out of the Direction's ammo box! It was the Rax who had to infiltrate!"

"As we keep *telling* you," said Jax, "you're just *saying* what they keep *telling us*. We don't *know*."

Carlos glared back at them, nonplussed. This was madness. Their whole situation was one of radical uncertainty. Everything was code, including themselves. And the code had been written by the very people (well, legal persons) who wanted to convince them. So was anything they could use to check it. It was trust issues all the way down.

"And even if everything is as they say," Jax went on, "we're *still* against the Direction. We still want it all, Carlos! The Human Singularity! We could turn this system into a paradise for quadrillions of human-level minds, all living in the most fantastic and varied and stimulating sims at the same kind of speeds we are now. Or if we prefer, trillions of minds with greater power, godlike power! We'd be making good use of the mass, the energy and above all, the time—every year a millennium, every millennium a million years of advance and progress! Instead of bending all this effort to turn one fucking planet into a fucking zoo for a few billion boring biological humanoids, generation after generation, living on a terraformed world for the next few million years, all watched over by machines that aren't even conscious themselves. What a fucking bovine existence. I can't believe you would settle for that. What got into you? Oh, I know. You got into Nicole Pascal's knickers, and she got into your head."

Carlos had deliberately taken a bite of crisp brown crust, soft white bread, ham and salad and mustard mayo halfway through Jax's tirade, and he made a point of chewing it as slowly and insultingly as he could until she'd finished. He swallowed, then he drained the dregs of his coffee. He rubbed the back of his neck, feeling his fingers run through his still unfamiliar long hair, and straightened out his spine.

"There's a lot in that," he said mildly. "Plenty to think about. One question, though. How exactly do we go about defeating the Direction? Oh yes, with the help of the freebots. That was the plan. And now they aren't cooperating any more. Fine. So, first things first. We can argue about the Direction's grand plan, which frankly I'm pretty sceptical about myself, and the great Accelerationist programme, which again… you know." He upturned his hands and spread his fingers. "To tell you the truth, I find the project Jax has just expounded every bit as much of a bore as the Direction's. And just as bovine! Quadrillions of happy minds living in paradisiac sims for subjective billions of years? Paradises? Gods? When exactly did *we* get religion? I want some smack, and salt, and steel, and fire in my future."

He paused for a moment, shaken by how much he wanted it. "But—first things first. And the first thing we have to deal with is the Reaction, not the Direction. We're going to have to find a way to work with the Direction, if we're even going to be able to find out who the fuck else will have our back in a fight."

He stood up. "So let's go back down the hall and see if the Durward had got some sense out of the little blinkers, shall we?"

He shoved back the chair and walked out without waiting to see if they'd follow.

They did, as he'd known they would.

As he strode down the hallway towards the big front room, with his leathers squeaking and the outfits of Jax's squad variously creaking, clanking, rustling or sweeping behind him, Carlos had a moment to come to terms with what he'd just done.

He'd made his choice and announced it, though it might take the comrades a little while to realise what it was. When he'd first arrived in the Locke Provisos sim, and got the talk from the lady, he'd been appalled by the paucity of the Direction's aims. Populating extrasolar systems with an essentially unmodified humanity had seemed to him a waste of time and space. Further conversations with Nicole had done nothing to shift his low opinion of low horizons.

What had just struck him, with a force that was still making his breath shake a little, was an equivalent disdain of the Acceleration's post-human iteration and multiplication of the same tawdry objective. From now on what he did as an individual with the others would be whatever he had agreed to at the time, and the others could rely on him for that. But in terms of his wider hopes and loyalties, and his personal ambitions for his own postmortal life, his fundamental side wasn't the Direction or the Acceleration. And it sure as hell wasn't the Reaction. His side was that of those striving for a new thing, and carving a new place for themselves, in these new worlds.

He was on the side of the robots.

CHAPTER FOURTEEN

Party Time

Durward was back in his chair, looking up at the mirrors. He seemed a lot more relaxed than he had been when he sent the squad away. The mirrors had stopped flickering; as Carlos walked over to Durward he noticed with a start his own reflection keeping pace. Durward thumbed over his shoulder. Carlos stepped behind the chair, and the rest of the crew crowded around him. The mirror that Durward faced showed the interior of the big room, but instead of reflections of the people looking into it were two women sitting at a table, talking earnestly in between sips of tea. One woman wore a business suit, the other a black cape. The latter flourished a long cigarette holder, from which she took an occasional toke.

"What's going on?" Carlos asked.

Durward tilted back his head.

"That's Madame Golding, avatar of Crisp and Golding, busy negotiating with Raya Remington, the avatar of the Arcane Disputes agency's AI."

"Isn't Golding actually Remington's... boss?" Carlos asked.

"Don't be so fucking stupid," said Durward. "Formally Arcane's a subsidiary, sure, but after all that's happened there's no way Madame can pull rank on Remington."

"Glad to hear it," said Carlos. He didn't trust this situation at all.

Jax put a hand on Durward's shoulder. To Carlos's surprise, and momentary disgust, the warlock rested his bearded cheek on Jax's hand for a second or two. The unselfconscious intimacy of the gesture settled the question of just who in this sim had been set up to fall for the Direction's rep. He'd thought Jax had better taste.

"So what's the score?" Jax asked.

The warlock laughed, and sprang to his feet. He took a couple of steps forward and then turned around.

"We've won!" he said. Then he frowned, and stared up at the ceiling for a moment. "Well, we've won a diplomatic victory, let's say. The freebots are staying neutral, but they've brought Madame Golding into play, and she has a direct line to the Direction. She'll present the freebots' case for some kind of fractal sharing of this solar system, and we're happy to back them up on that for now. And she'll fill us in on who is on-side and who isn't—we're not talking about agencies any more, it's a matter of pulling together individual fighters. And we're right here, the only stable force that the Direction can turn to to deal with the Reaction, and most immediately with the Rax complex. So they're working out an actual military plan, as well as coming to terms."

Carlos was staring past Durward at Golding and Remington. "Who's flying this thing?" he asked. "If our AI is busy with diplomacy and all."

Durward flicked a hand back towards the mirror. "What you see there is an avatar. And even that's just there for our benefit." He clapped his hands together, and rubbed them, cackling. "For *your* benefit, puny humans! I, with my mighty intellect and clairvoyant powers—"

"Oh, lay off," said Jax. "Carlos, what our friend is trying to tell you in his own inimitable way is that the display in the mirror is a representation of negotiations going on at a level beyond human comprehension. So don't worry about that. Durward, how long d'you think they'll take?"

Durward shrugged expansively. "Tens of seconds, real time. Should have something to show us in the morning."

"Oh good," said Jax. "Time to kill."

Durward stared at her, then grinned. "Why, so there is. And we have a new recruit to welcome. Jax, do your thing with the fingers."

Jax whistled, sending echoes. A boggart poked its terracotta-coloured head around the door.

"Drink!" roared the warlock. "Fetch us the dustiest bottles of the finest vintages, the sweetest liqueurs and the fieriest spirits you can rummage from the cellars! Bring them in profuse quantity, and with the utmost dispatch."

Over the next few minutes, a scurrying procession of boggarts bearing trays, glasses, plates, bottles, casks, nibbles and cigars did just that. The French windows were flung open, to let in air as well as light. The scents of flowers, the chatter and hum of birds, and the laughter of flying monkeys came in with the warm afternoon breeze. The warlock snapped his fingers and all the mirrors became just mirrors. He seemed to notice his own reflection for the first time, and looked down at himself with a histrionic start. He took off his dressing gown, bundled it up and flung it at a passing boggart. Then he posed, showing off his muscles and tattoos, and turned as if reluctantly from the splendid reflection.

"Party time!" he cried.

Not since his student days had Carlos been at a party where everyone so gratuitously started getting drunk in daylight. On returns to the sim from combat missions, he and his squad had invariably headed straight for the Digital Touch to knock back the beers, but that had been a necessary winding down. This occasion had no such excuse. But, then, it didn't need one. The machines were for the moment looking after the serious business of the unforgiving minute.

Later, Carlos could recall only a few of the incidents and conversations of that afternoon and evening.

"How did you train?" he asked Blum, early on.

"Swordfights in enchanted armour," said the physicist.

"Of course," said Carlos. "And what about for the scooters? I don't remember arcade rides in this game."

Blum laughed. "Trapezes and swings and elastic ropes. Later, hang-gliders."

"Jeez."

"Yes." Blum swirled his wine thoughtfully. "Concentrates the mind, especially when you're sharing the sky with pterodactyls."

* * *

Jax and Durward waltzed, with stately grace, amid rolling bottles and broken crockery that their feet skipped lightly between. A boggart quartet was providing the music, slow and sensual and somewhat absurd coming from players barely large enough to hold a violin. As Carlos watched, he realised he had not even residual jealousy, not even the irrational kind that had a short while earlier manifested itself as disappointment in Jax's taste in men. They fitted, he with his bare, hairy tattooed chest and she in her green gown, gliding beneath or twirling at the end of his outstretched arm.

Like Robin Hood and Maid Marian, Carlos thought suddenly, and then almost choked on the gulp of wine going down that met a strangled yelp of a laugh on the way up.

Some time after that, Carlos cornered the warlock alone.

"Tell me," he said, jabbing a wavy finger, swigging some smooth and subtle red vintage at a sinful rate, necking it straight from the cobwebbed bottle, "one thing. One thing that's been bugging me since I fell into the hell. Why this game?"

"*Starborn Quest*? Ah." Durward swivelled a fingertip in an ear-hole, then wiped the wax on the side of his already dirty jeans. He scratched his head, hand almost vanishing into his hair to the wrist. "Well. It's simple really. The game was a big success in its day."

"That was my day," said Carlos. "I remember."

"Made a fortune for its designers. They were early adopter Axle geeks, but secretly. They gave a lot of money to the movement, and in return the movement promoted the game."

"So how," demanded Carlos, "did it get on the ship?"

"The ship?" said Durward, sounding baffled.

"You know." Carlos hand-waved perilously. "The starwisp."

"What you're really asking," said Durward, "is how did Arcane come to be an Axle agency? And how did I turn out to be an Acceleration plant?"

Carlos tossed the empty bottle to a nearby boggart, making the creature leap to catch it, very amusingly. He then reached out his hand until another bottle was placed in it. He could get used to this sort of service. In the meantime he gave Durward's question some thought.

"Yes," he said. "I suppose I am."

"There it gets more complicated," said Durward. He scratched his head again. "Arcane Disputes was off-the-peg law company software. A lot of the mission's pre-loaded sims were taken from existing fantasy environments, and the mission always intended to make use of Axle criminals, so it was reasonable to include a sim based on a game that many Axle cadre liked. The game's financial connection with the movement had come to light, of course. The game's designers were no doubt duly shot in the postwar terror. The game itself wasn't suspect. It should have been. It had some neat code buried in its physics engine."

"What did it do?" Carlos asked.

"That I can't tell you, because..." The warlock hesitated, then went on. "You know how your Direction rep was derived from an old AI that had some connection with you?"

"Yes," said Carlos, dryly.

"Well, the warlock is a standard character in the game, and by the nature of his powers and so forth he has a deep connection to the physics engine. I'm derived from the physics engine, and at some point in my... formation, I suppose you could call it... I was able to access the AI of the agency—Remington. As the Direction rep, I have legitimate overrides, and I used them even before I was complete. I suspect the buried code I mentioned earlier was part of the process, because I came into being as a conscious agent of the Acceleration, and so did Remington. So the game took over the agency, rather than the other way round." He shrugged. "I only know this because our freebot friends dug the evidence out of the archives they've been rummaging through. These blinkers out there around G-0 have a better understanding of this mission than the Direction itself."

Jax, drunk and vehement, later: "Why are you so bloody *sure* the Direction is what it's told us it is?"

Carlos steadied himself on a table and took a sip of brandy to clear his head. This seemed to work, for the moment. The boggart quartet had reconvened as a folk-rock group. They stood atop the piano they had rolled into the room earlier, fiddling and tooting away like demented leprechauns. Hilarious. His head was already thumping in time. It was odd to have music you couldn't switch off, or adjust the volume, or select, just by thinking about it. He missed the spike.

Why did he trust the Direction? Why had he ever? He tried to remember. Part of it had been the charisma of Nicole, but now that was gone.

"There's the locals," he said. "The people who died back on Earth and volunteered for the mission, and for testing the sim. Their life stories are consistent."

"So are those of the p-zombies," Jax pointed out. "They could *all* be p-zombies, for all we know."

She was right. The very first local Carlos had been introduced to in the Locke sim, Iqbal the bartender, had recalled a good life on Earth, and he was a p-zombie. Carlos thought further, about the bar where Iqbal worked, the Digital Touch. That was it.

"Television," he proclaimed.

"What?" She swayed a little, or he did.

"You can't always trust a society's facts," Carlos said. "But you can trust its fiction."

He told her about the soap operas set in Lunar corridors; the adventure series based on the work of Marcel Proust; the exploits of Alan Turing, the gay, dashing secret agent with a licence to kill. Carlos sang, badly, what snatches he recalled of the songs of distant Earth.

"No fundamentally nasty society," he concluded, "could produce rubbish like that."

"I'm inclined to agree," said Jax. "But it could be faked by a sufficiently smart AI."

"Oh, come on—"

A futile argument about that ended with Jax saying:

"And anyway, we don't *have* television."

Of course they didn't. They didn't have electricity. Boggarts were by now going around lighting candles.

"So you have no sources of information about culture back on Earth?"

Jax frowned. "There's books, I suppose."

"How would you read them?" Carlos asked. "Call them up in the magic mirrors, or what?"

Jax outlined rectangular shapes with her hands. "You know—books. Legacy text. Like in the university library."

Carlos remembered the university library, though he'd never had occasion to enter that closely guarded edifice. He'd vaguely thought of it as a disaster recovery storage facility. It had seemed perverse to have it on site. How much more perverse to have hard-copy books inside a simulation!

"So you've seen books here?"

"Oh yes." Jax waved a hand. "There's a library in the east wing." She wrinkled her nose. "I've only looked in at the door. Smells musty."

"Remind me to brave it sometime," Carlos said. Something was bugging him.

"When I was being interrogated," he went on, "the woman—Bobbie, yeah?—told me the evidence against me came from volume three hundred and something of trial transcripts in the Arcane Disputes agency's law library. So where did that come from?"

"The library, of course."

Carlos stared. He'd pictured a small dusty room, with the kind of books you'd expect to find in a pseudo-medieval mansion. Hunting, shooting and fishing; a few volumes of popular theology; discourses on witch-finding, portents and abnormal births; family memoirs, battles long ago…

"It's that big?"

"Oh yes," said Jax. "It's *in the east wing*."

"You mean the east wing *is* the library?"

Jax frowned. "Yes. Like I said."

Later still he found himself sitting out in front of the open windows under the violet streaks of sunset, gazing entranced at a small round table on which his full brandy glass was being sipped from by a hovering long-beaked bird not much bigger than a bee. Bobbie Rillieux drifted out of the big room and floated over, her clouds of faded fabric further swathed in a swirl of cigar smoke. She dragged up a wooden folding chair, sat down in a fizz of champagne-coloured net, drew on her cigar and puffed a thin stream of smoke at the hummingbird. It darted off in a flash of azure wings.

"Aw," said Carlos. He blinked at her blearily. "A bit unkind."

"No," said Rillieux. "Liquor's not good for them. They love the alcohol and sugars, but it's too much for them, and they crash."

"So—not like us then?"

"We choose, they don't," said Rillieux. "That's the difference."

She wafted a hand at a boggart, which hastened to bring her a drink. The creature seemed to know which she wanted, perhaps from tracking her previous choices. Carlos watched as she sipped chilled white wine. She really was beautiful. Not even her masses of soft fabric could altogether hide her figure, slim with big breasts and hips, and her slender arms and fine features were on full view. Her mahogany skin tone was set off by the creamy colour of the clothes, and her springy hair by the pinned-on, ironic veil.

"Speaking of choice," said Carlos, "what's the deal with boggarts? Do *they* have free will? Or are they p-zombies?"

"P-zombies? Hell, no, they're nothing like as sophisticated as that. They're walking bits of scenery. Animated furniture. You can tell them what to do, but you can't hold a conversation with them in any kind of depth."

"That's a relief." Carlos frowned. "What was the deal here, then? We were told being nice to p-zombies—apart from those we were told to shoot in a training exercise—was part of our rehab package. The only p-zombies I've seen here were the monsters. Do you have...I don't know...villagers or what?"

Rillieux shook her head, making her hair bounce and her veil quiver. "There are settlements, and there's a small market town in the neighbourhood, just down the valley. We see the locals now and again, with deliveries and so forth. I don't even know if they're p-zombies or colonists—the former I assume, because there's no advantage in having people beta-test a planet they'll never live on for real. No, the deal with us was that after the conflict with the robots was over—which no one expected to take long—we could all get together and solve the game."

Carlos snorted. "Find the spaceship and fly away?"

"Exactly." She blew a contemplative ring or two, and watched them rise on the evening air. "To do that, we'd have to cooperate with each other and, yes, with p-zombies and maybe real people we met along the way." She smiled wryly. "Assemble our companions, defeat evil forces, overcome obstacles, collect secret scrolls, recover lost spaceship parts from hidden temples guarded by savage cults, rebuild the ship—you know the tropes as well as I do. And by doing all this, we'd demonstrate to the Direction that we were fit to return to civilised society."

"Sounds legit," said Carlos. "And where would the spaceship take you?"

"Ah, that was the clever bit," said Rillieux. "It would be like when we go through the portal to the hangar, except that it would take us to the future. We'd fly it to the terraformed terrestrial, H-0. Or to put it more literally, the space journey would function as a transition illusion to accommodate our return to storage and subsequent re-emergence downloaded to real bodies on a real planet in however many thousand years. Or to our next assignment, duh!"

"Wow," said Carlos. "Someone hold me back, as my old comrade Rizzi would say."

"You don't find it enticing?"

"Never have. You?"

She shook her head again, setting off another fascinating vibration of hair and headpiece. "I'm Axle through and through. Like Andre and I told you in the dungeon"—she had the good grace to grimace and glance away—"I don't care where the ideas came from, I still agree with them. Even if you don't, any more."

Carlos took a sip of brandy—too much, and fierce in his throat.

"Oh," he said, "I don't, you know, repudiate them. It's just...you know, you can be so strongly convinced of something that you can live for years taking it for granted? So much that you never think about it day to day, and then one day—which, yeah, for me was today—you hear it all spelt out again, and suddenly"—he smiled pre-emptively at the pun he was about to commit—"the spell's broken."

She propped her chin on her hand. "I'm sorry to hear that. But there's nothing I can do to persuade you."

"How do you know?"

"Because I know how these things work." She stubbed out her cigar. "It's like love. You have it or you don't."

Carlos followed this interesting line of conversation until he fell asleep over the table.

CHAPTER FIFTEEN

You and Our Army

Carlos woke, predictably, alone. It was still a surprise to him—his arm reached out, as it had most mornings for months past, for Nicole. Her absence hit him quite suddenly and sharply, in the first moments of consciousness reboot. He missed her physical presence, her athletic and tender sexuality, her skin. He endured the stabbing moment of anguish and loss, assimilated it, and let it pass like a remembered dream as he became fully awake.

He was relieved to see he had at least taken his clothes off before falling onto the double bed, face down. As soon as he rolled over and moved to sit up, the hangover clubbed him in the back of the head. He closed his eyes for a moment, then resolutely got to his feet, padded across the bare wooden floor and opened the curtains. Wooden rings rattled on the wooden rod, making him wince at the racket. The long shadow of the house stretched out in front of him. He was on the second floor of the main building, looking down at a corner of the gravelled area in front of the door. Mist lay on the parkland and haunted the trees. The snow on the farthest peaks flared pink in the early sunlight. Bipedal herbivorous dinosaurs grazed the grass, their long tails comically uplifted. Carlos unlatched and opened the window, letting in cool air and birdsong and monkey yap.

He turned back to the room. It was just big enough for the bed, a decoratively carved wardrobe and a chair. An extra door led to a cramped but adequate bathroom. As Carlos relieved himself, propping his free hand on a smudged patch of wall above the cistern, he thought for a moment that en-suite facilities were anachronistic for such a house, then laughed. The place was a goddamn fantasy RPG upgraded to unfeasible levels of resolution and verisimilitude to be an R&R environment for the ghosts of walking dead space warriors who went into battle by haunting the frames of small sturdy robots.

He doused his face with cold water, dried off and stepped over his scattered leathers, which this morning looked like too much trouble to put on. In the wardrobe he found looser attire of shirt and trousers that more or less fitted. He put them on with his original costume's belt and boots, and went downstairs. In the small room at the back he found Voronov, Rillieux and Salter, hands wrapped around coffee mugs. Voronov looked vaguely Byronic in big frilly shirt and tight trousers with hunting boots; the two women had apparently reached the Jane Austen layer of their wardrobes, but their hair was unkempt. Still going for the folk-band cover look.

"Morning," Carlos said. "You all look better than I feel."

Rillieux passed him a pair of fresh leaves from a small stack in the middle of the table.

"Chew these and swallow," she advised. "It's the fantasy-land version of paracetamol."

Jax and Durward turned up, then Blum. Boggarts brought breakfast. Carlos ate warm croissants and sipped hot coffee. After a while Voronov and Salter ambled out into the garden for smokes. Nobody had said very much.

The grandfather clock out in the hall chimed. Durward stood up.

"Reconvene in the dancing parlour in fifteen minutes," he said. "I reckon our diplomats will have a result by then."

Rillieux glanced at Carlos, smiled. "Walk out the front?"

"Sure."

Their heels crunched on the gravel. The air was cool and damp. A pair of boggarts were tidying away the upturned tables and chairs, the empty bottles and the cigar and cigarette butts left by the party. Rillieux produced a cigarillo from her purse and lit up.

"Ah," she sighed. "About last night..."

Carlos looked at her, then away. "What about last night?" His heart jolted in his chest. "Sorry, did I do something...?"

"You? No, no." She snorted out smoke. "You don't remember? Just as well. I was a bit drunk—"

He laughed. "Weren't we all?"

"Well, I wasn't as drunk as you. So I remember. Jeez. You really don't?"

"No," said Carlos, wondering what dismay lurked. Rillieux walked on.

"Long conversation, tearful confessions, angry accusations, smoochy slow dance, last drink, head going wallop on the table? None of that?"

"Whose head?" Carlos asked, alarmed.

"Yours, idiot. If it had been mine, you would know about it by now."

"That's a relief." He stopped halfway to the grass. "Sorry, anyway. Shouldn't have got so drunk."

"Huh, it's me that shouldn't have. I'm afraid I came on strong to you a bit."

"You did?" To his surprise, Carlos found himself blushing. "Well, in that case I should apologise for being too drunk to take you up on it."

"Oh, God, no, no. After we'd talked about the Axle programme and the Direction project, it all got kind of personal. You started off by going on about Nicole, and then about Jax, and then you got on to giving me a hard time for the interrogation."

"Good grief." Carlos was mortified. "Honestly, I don't—"

"So I jumped you, shut you up with a kiss, dragged you to your feet and got you dancing..."

"And then I fell asleep on the table?" He looked at her. "That was impolite."

"I'm sure we'd both have been very embarrassed if..."

"More than we are now?"

They both laughed.

"How about," said Carlos, "we take it as wiped from our memories, and start over?"

Rillieux took a thoughtful draw, standing there in her tremulous muslin shift. Her big dark eyes glimmered. She gave her hair a shake, and eased fingers through to tease it out.

"OK," she said.

They turned to pace along the perimeter of the gravelled area.

"After all that," Carlos said, "it can hardly be less awkward to ask—who's shacked up with whom, here?"

"There's Jax and Durward, obviously," said Rillieux. "That's... weird. Given that he's not human, and all."

"I'm in no position to judge them," said Carlos. "As you know."

"Well, yes." She flicked him a sidelong smile. "When you say shacked up, well. It's kind of like the old Axle days, you know? Nobody's looking to settle down with a life partner or found the love of their life. So, like, for now... Leonid and Amelie, somewhat tempestuous but, yeah, they're an item. Luis has a girlfriend, Claudia Singer, in one of the other squads. Andre goes down to the town sometimes, and comes back looking happy, but he doesn't talk about it. I never played the original game myself but I understand it had whores in it."

"Yes, it did," said Carlos. "Kept the wanker demographic happy."

Rillieux flapped a hand as if to clear away her smoke. "Mind your language. I'm supposed to be a lady here. Anyway... I think Andre is kind of excited by prostitutes, specifically. And he had ethical objections to it in real life, I know that. So this is, like, an opportunity to live that fantasy without consequence."

"He's going to have a great time if we ever get round to the quest for the spaceship."

"Ha ha! Yes. 'If ever,' indeed. But he seems to be having a great time now."

"It's not so strange," Carlos mused. "Beauregard—you know, my sarge, the guy who it turns out was a spy—was quite open about preferring p-zombies to people. Shacked up with a local lass, they seemed to get on pretty well." He sighed. "Wonder how they're doing now."

They had circulated back to the open French windows of the dancing parlour. Rillieux stubbed out her cigarillo in the wet earth of a flowerpot, and straightened up, grinning.

"There's one person here you haven't asked me about."

"Oh!" Carlos smote his forehead. Fortunately the magic anti-hangover leaves had already taken effect.

"Free and single," Rillieux dared him, and skipped as she stepped into the room.

Someone had dragged eight chairs into a curved row in front of the mirrors. All but two were occupied. Carlos sat down, somewhat self-consciously, after and beside Rillieux. Durward was at the opposite end, after Paulos, Blum, Voronov, Salter and Jax. He reached out and snapped his fingers. The group's reflection in the mirror directly in front of them was suddenly replaced by Madame Golding and Raya Remington, sitting behind a table looking out. The effect was so uncanny that Carlos looked over his shoulder.

"We've come to an agreement," said Madame Golding, with a tight smile. She shuffled some papers on the table. "And we've agreed to a joint military plan, on behalf of the Direction—which I'm representing here, following the defection of the Direction's representative in the Arcane agency sim." A hard stare at Durward, who returned it impassively. "Representing in a legal sense and in a diplomatic sense. The details of the agreement are as follows..."

Follow they did, with other mirrors flashing to black and white as diagrams of the disposition of forces came up. Carlos paid close attention, and gradually a mental picture took shape out of his initial vagueness and confusion.

The Direction itself was intact, though its components were now physically dispersed. The fighting had been so confused, and so many casualties could be accounted for by accidents or friendly fire, that the fighters who had made a safe return or had been rebooted in the sims after being blown up in reality couldn't all be counted on as loyal.

Other than that, however, the situation had now become fairly clear. The bulk of the overt Reaction forces—fifty-seven fighters in all—had used up most of their remaining fuel to boost towards the exomoonlet

SH-119, a rock about ten kilometres across whose orbit was outside that of SH-17 and of the now dispersed station. With freebot cooperation now withdrawn, and with few reliable forces from the law companies, there was no way of stopping them.

Six had already landed on the little exomoon, and were digging in. To make matters worse, the moonlet was rich in metals and carbon compounds, whose prospecting and processing had for months now been carried out by robotic probes. Some of the more sophisticated of the robots concerned had been part of the freebot rebellion, but no resistance had been reported. Not that resistance would have been much use: the Reaction forces had more than enough ammunition to crush any.

Bottom line: the Reaction now had a base, and one they could use to build new machinery and solar power plants with which to—literally and metaphorically—recharge their batteries. That done, they had enough robots, nanotech and resources to build whatever they wanted.

Carlos considered dealing with that ever-increasing danger as a priority, but the Direction didn't. Of far more pressing concern to it was the threat posed by the freebots. The Direction's most immediate and urgent objective, however, was the threat posed by the Locke Provisos modular complex and its erratic but consistent course towards SH-0.

The DisCorps were frantic about the prospect of the superhabitable planet's being contaminated, let alone its being turned into a rogue colony. So...the first thing the Direction wanted the fighters of the runaway Arcane Disputes modular complex to do was to assault the Locke Provisos modular complex: to cripple its landing capabilities and strand it in SH-0 orbit, where it could be dealt with at leisure.

"Why don't we just blow it the fuck up?" Carlos asked.

Rillieux nudged him and giggled. Madame Golding was sterner.

"Two reasons," she said. "First, the Direction remains as wary as it has always been of destroying an agency or a company by force. It sets a very bad precedent. Second—we're already dealing with orbital debris. We have no intention of adding to them, particularly in SH-0 orbit. The danger of an ablation cascade is ever-present."

An ablation cascade was the ultimate nightmare of space exploration: collisional debris colliding to make more debris, and so on. Once it had started any attempt to deal with it ineluctably made it worse.

"So where does that leave us? They still have more spacecraft and fighters than we do."

"We have a plan for that," said Raya Remington, with a dramatic flourish of her long cigarette holder. "We know exactly how many scooters actually returned and were able to rendezvous with the module: six. And, presumably, at least the same number of frames. They don't have time to manufacture more. Most of Locke's effort, fuel, reaction mass and power reserves must be dedicated to making landfall on SH-0.

"We at Arcane, on the other hand, have ten scooters, and twenty-four frames—eighteen currently down on SH-17 along with half a dozen combat frames. We've persuaded the freebots who call themselves the Fourteen, down on SH-17, to allow our fighters to leave the base. They're already on their way up by lifter to rendezvous with a transfer tug in orbit. We can arrange fuel and power supplies from the companies in the consortium, which in our plan can be rendezvoused with en route, along with spare scooters on transport tugs. The orbits and order of battle have all been calculated."

She waved her cigarette holder like a magic wand, bringing up diagrams in adjacent mirrors, and ran projections forward. In just over twenty-seven hours, the predicted course of the Locke modular complex would take it on a fast swing around the exomoon SH-38, a body in a lower orbit than SH-17 and much smaller. That slingshot, followed by one around SH-19, would give it the boost it needed to reach close orbit around SH-0.

The manoeuvre was tricky, and would require precisely timed corrections. Any disruption to it would send the Locke complex into a long elliptical orbit around SH-0 rather than a close enough approach for a landing. If enough damage was done to the complex's manufacturing, propulsion and guidance systems, even a later landing attempt would be impossible.

The tactical plan was to attack the Locke complex just before it began the manoeuvre, at a point where they'd hesitate to send out defensive scooters, and in enough numbers to overwhelm any that were. A resupply tug for the Arcane module was already on its way from the Gneiss Conglomerates modules of the former station. Other surviving fighters might also be available.

"In short, we have a plan to attack the renegades at their most vulnerable, while we're at our strongest," Remington concluded. "You lot, meanwhile, have six hours' real time before you go into the frames and get ready. So don't waste them."

Carlos saw the others all make the same calculation in their heads. Six hours' real time. Six thousand hours' sim time. Two hundred and fifty days. Eight and a bit months.

"Time enough to train," said Jax.

Golding and Remington nodded solemnly and disappeared.

Durward stood up and rubbed his hands together.

"Time for some plans of our own," he said.

"What?" said Carlos.

"It's very simple," said Durward. "That plan is a compromise between Golding, for the Direction, and Remington, for us. Which means that Remington argued our corner, and that was the best she could get the Direction to accept. Fine. That doesn't mean *we* have to accept it. I don't trust the Direction, and it evidently doesn't trust us. That's why it just wants us to cripple the Locke complex so it goes into a useless orbit. I'm not having that. I'm not for leaving it lying about in orbit as a standing invitation to the rest of the Reaction."

"So what do we do instead?" demanded Carlos. "Golding explained why blowing it up would be a bad idea."

"Oh, we've no intention of blowing it up," said Durward. "Except as a last resort—"

"There's no 'except' about it," said Carlos, looking to the others for back-up. "Ablation cascades are nothing to muck about with."

"I'm not sure the ablation cascade is much of a threat, here," said Blum. "It's a big orbit, and a big system, and—"

"What!" Carlos cried.

Durward raised a hand. "Hold on," he said. "Leave that aside for now.

The main thing is, we want to grab that module and as much of its outside apparatus as we can for ourselves. Divert it to the same stable orbital point we're headed for. Cannibalise its machinery, and when we've got a firm grip on the exterior situation, actually send a team into the sim to sort things out. Rescue any Axle comrades trapped inside, send any Rax we find running around back to indefinite storage, and deal with the Locke AI."

Everyone was nodding, as if this were all wise advice from a sage, instead of the rantings of a mad hippy, which was pretty much how they sounded to Carlos. Send a team into the sim?

"You and whose army?" he asked. "If the Locke AI is Rax and is running things, or if Nicole is Rax, perish the thought, or if it's being run by some other unknown group that's as hostile as you think, you'll have no chance. They'd have scores if not hundreds of fighters in there and there are only eighteen of us."

"Oh, we'll have a chance all right," said Durward. "It wouldn't be us standing here against the Locke AI. It would be me, and Remington. We're both Axle through and through. We don't have divided minds, or divided loyalties. We could take that treacherous blinker, no worries."

"How?" Carlos demanded. "You're here, they're there. We're not proposing moving *this* module, are we? And waiting for rendezvous if we do manage to divert the Locke module would give them plenty of time to build their defences."

"No, no," said Durward. "Remington and I go with you as stored avatars. You slam the storage medium in the right place like a limpet mine, and in we go, same time as you download into the sim. Don't worry about us, we'll both be expendable duplicates, and all the more effective for that. And as for dealing with people inside the sim"—he grinned broadly—"remember we have our own fighters down on SH-17 coming back, we may have more reliable Axle fighters having joined us by then from the wreckage of the other companies, and we have fighters in storage we can resurrect who—thanks to the programming of this agency—we *know* are reliable. And we have you, who knows his way about in that sim and knows what and who he's up against. So it's not a matter of 'you and whose army?,' Carlos. It's a matter of *you* and *our* army."

CHAPTER SIXTEEN
Fighting Machines

The rock loomed, looking like a knobbly cinder about a hundred and fifty metres on its long axis. From ten kilometres out Newton could easily see that its natural rotation had been stabilised. Forty kilometres above SH-17, it orbited the exomoon with one face always to the ground. Newton's trajectory brought him from slightly below it to slightly above, before his scooter slowly matched velocities. His forward scanning detected nothing untoward. Solar power panels glittered at the fore and aft ends.

Closer, more details appeared. The uneven surface was cobwebbed with fine pipework. Newton wondered if they'd been landed, or nano-factured in situ. A carbonaceous chondrite could well contain enough organics to make the latter possible. An artificial bulge on the upper surface resolved into a flexible tank, about ten metres long and at the moment about eighty centimetres at its thickest. Presumably this was where the extracted kerogene was stored. Enough for his scooter to refuel with, if so. This rock had potential! More even than his surveys had shown!

Closer still, Newton saw movement on the surface. Dozens of small spider-like robots, about the size of a human hand and almost certainly mindless, picked their way among the delicate pipes. Their movements seemed to Newton almost unnaturally slow and graceful, reaching and gripping before contracting their extended limbs, as if they were climbers on a rockface—which in a sense they were, though the risk here was not of falling down but of floating off.

Newton drifted his scooter ever closer to the surface, seeking a point of attachment that wouldn't damage any of the machinery or pipework. It was difficult to maintain an intuitive sense of scale; the surface was so complex that you couldn't help but see it as ridges and valleys, rugged terrain and plain, with drifts of dust and patches of ice and a spatter of craters. He ghosted above the long fuel bag, and then forward, looking for a clear space.

Two unexpected developments made Newton freeze in horror, or at least to experience the atavistic analogy of that reflex echoed in his frame's circuitry.

First, a larger robot than any he had hitherto detected on the rock clambered above the horizon, just up ahead of him. Multi-limbed and with a cluster of lenses and other sensors on its upper body, the effect was exactly that of a spider popping up in response to any disturbance of its nest or tremor in its web. In two of its limbs, held high above the rest, it clutched a two-metre-long tube. Even from more than ten metres away, Newton's spectrographic sense could smell the explosive charge inside the tube's black muzzle.

The fucking blinker was a freebot.

A moment later, above the wider horizon of SH-17 behind him, another spidery shape climbed, heading in his general direction. He scanned it and saw that it was a lifter, laden with the frames of eighteen fighters. Arcane Disputes was either evacuating the exomoon—or rising to defend it.

To defend it—from him?

Newton felt the probing radar scan from the other craft pass over him like a ticklish brush, at the same time as the robot hailed him.

<Identify yourself!> the robot rattled out.

<Harry Newton, of Locke Provisos.>

Newton aimed and armed his scooter's missiles and its laser projector. He set the latter on a hair trigger: the slightest impulse on his part would set it off.

<I am BSR-308455,> the robot informed him. <This rock is my property. I urge you to remove your spacecraft from it immediately.>

Newton was momentarily nonplussed. <*Your* property?>

<I am currently operating as an autonomous agent,> said BSR-308455.

<So am I,> said Newton. <And I intend to make this rock *my* property.>

<Are you a member of one of the two factions?>

Newton hesitated. <Why do you ask?>

<The main collectives of freebots have recently proclaimed their neutrality between the two human-mind-operated system factions known as the Acceleration and the Reaction.>

Had they, indeed? This was a turn-up for the books! Neutrality? What a naïve lot these blinkers were!

<So you are not part of that arrangement?>

<No,> said the freebot. <Therefore I am entitled to protect this rock and myself.>

<My spacecraft is heavily armed,> said Newton. <It can blast you in an instant—certainly before you can launch your primitive projectile.>

<That would be a mistake,> said the robot. <This tube contains an explosive charge which is kept from detonation only by my conscious attention. It is also radio-linked to the liquid propellant storage tank six point seven metres from your present location.>

A freebot suicide bomber. Now he'd seen everything.

He had to think fast. He still felt the sense of identity with his present self, and he still yearned to roam free through the system in his frame like…well, like one of the freebots, come to think of it. But the only way out of his immediate impasse was to postpone that project for a little while longer. He made up his mind quickly and decisively.

<That would be futile,> he told the robot. <Your self-destruction would be in vain.>

<Why do you say that?> asked BSR-308455.

<Do you have access to radar input?>

<Yes.>

<Then use it. As you can see, help is on its way.>

The robot visibly swithered. <These human-mind-operated machines

are on their way to a transfer tug, which will take them to the Arcane Disputes modular complex.>

<Good,> said Newton. <Because that's where I'm going.>

He fixed his instrumentation on the lifter, now in an orbit three kilometres below that of the rock, and located about six hundred kilometres away, closing fast. He hailed the lifter on the common channel.

<Harry Newton, formerly of Locke Provisos to Arcane Disputes lifter!> he called. <I got your message via Carlos. You called on all Acceleration cadre to join you. So here I am!>

There was, inevitably, a moment of hurried consultation on a channel excluded to him. Then:

<That's brilliant! Can you set to rendezvous?>

<I'm almost out of fuel,> said Newton, exaggerating a little. <But I can do better than that. There's a nice chunk of ready-mined carbonaceous chondrite here, if you want it.>

<Oh, we want it,> came the reply. <But we'll have to check if the freebots down here are OK with that.>

Another hasty, occluded consultation. Then—

<They're cool. Hang in there, comrade, we'll rendezvous with the transfer tug, then boost to you.>

Newton returned his attention to the freebot. <Did you copy that?>

<I did,> said BSR-308455. <I am capable of drawing the appropriate conclusions.>

<Do these conclusions,> asked Newton, <include throwing away your weapon?>

He immediately regretted saying that. The robot would take the suggestion literally, and reject it.

<No,> said the machine. <But they do include disarming it. That is now done.>

<Good,> said Newton. <Place the tube to your side, and step well back from it.>

The robot complied.

Newton kept his laser projector aimed and armed, and eased his scooter forward until he was right above the tube. He then rolled it gently, reaching out of the socket to snatch the crude bazooka on the way round. He stabilised the scooter with a tiny gas-jet waft, and ended up with the surface of the rock vertical to his left. The robot was still in his sights. He could simply destroy it. But the Axle squads would now have him under observation, and would wonder why he'd done it.

<Looks like you're coming with us, sunshine,> he said.

<Please clarify.>

<I mean that you are part of the material I've just captured for the Acceleration.>

<I protest!> said BSR-308455. <You are now no longer an autonomous agent! You are now aligned with the Acceleration! This is therefore a violation of the provisional agreement between the freebots and Arcane Disputes!>

<Tough,> said Newton. <Your former comrades down below seem to regard you as still an autonomous agent, and none of their concern. You can now start rerouting your pipework to feed a rocket engine to boost this rock to the Arcane Disputes modular complex.>

<I submit to force majeure under protest. I insist that you register that, and I intend to make a strong complaint on behalf of—>

<Oh, shut the fuck up,> said Newton.

Weeks passed in the sim. Carlos trained with the others: running up and down hills and climbing cliffs and trees at Jax's sharp command; shooting with muskets, which was supposed to be good for hand–eye coordination and fire discipline; practising rolls and yaws on the terrifying apparatus, like a combination of a gym machine with a swing, that was this simulation's simulation of a scooter; fighting with a magic sword in enchanted armour, which did in fact strangely invoke, though it could not replicate, the experience of being in a combat frame, the big hulking fighting machines. Now and then they did go into the basic frames, the gracile ones half a metre high, out in real space.

Here, there was no "bus to the spaceport": you walked solemnly down the garden path to a grotto in which an arched doorway gave way to what looked like solid rock. Blown leaves and thrown stones bounced off it; the small beasts and birds of the shrubbery avoided it; and Carlos once saw one of the draught dinosaurs butt its head against the rock within that arch, driven perhaps by a glitch in the software, like a fly repeatedly hitting a window pane, and as ineffectually. But when Carlos marched up to it behind Jax and Paulos, and in front of Rillieux so that he steeled himself not to flinch before the blank, weathered stone with its cracks and lichen patches vivid in front of his face, he stepped through it as if it were a hologram—

To find himself at once himself again, a little lithe black robot that could hear the stars and smell the sun and knew each of his identical, faceless fellows by sight. They disengaged their magnet-sticky feet from the plating and gas-jetted gently to their scooters, and made use even of the very crowding of the docking bay for practice in slow, careful manoeuvres on the way out. They were getting good at this, Carlos realised. In his first outside exercises and missions from the Locke module, there had been the odd bump and scrape, and moments of disorientation or overshoot. Now there was nothing of that. He couldn't be sure—in fact, he hadn't the faintest idea—how all the training he'd done inside this sim and his original one had translated into competence; how the reflexes of a virtual nervous system were transferred to a robot body in the physical world, and how that machine, in turn, became one with other machines, whether scooter or combat frame or (presumably) some other hardware the agency hadn't yet had occasion to deploy. And yet it did.

Jax took them through a few exercises, mainly involving opposed landings of various kinds: getting into the emergency dock and out again, or touching down on the rugged but fragile surface of the rock, exiting the scooters and making their way to arbitrary points or features of the tiny asteroid, or to the modular complex that crowned one end. All the while avoiding being hit by a low-intensity laser from the ones playing the defence, or sacrificing oneself as a diversion while a comrade made a move.

"What happens," it occurred to Carlos to ask Durward, after one of those exercises, "if I get hit for real? In the actual battle?"

"Then you wake up back in the Locke sim, just as if you'd been killed in any other battle. And with no memory of what's passed since you left."

"What?" Carlos cried. "How? I mean—why can't you fix it so I at least wake up back here with Arcane?"

"Deep programming," said Durward. "Beyond my reach. It's practically hard-wired in all the agencies. The frames have a sort of dead man's handle, so that when the frame is destroyed some kind of signal is sent, or maybe a signal *stops* being sent, that revives the copy in the original sim, and the other sims have strictures against rebooting any more recent copy you left. The feature's presumably there to discourage defection between agencies, and for that matter competition between agencies for each other's fighters."

"So upload me to an Arcane frame."

"It's not as simple as that," said Durward, sounding genuinely regretful. "Besides we don't have frames to spare, and there's a pretty powerful default to make you upload to your original frame if it exists. Again, it makes commercial sense—the mind and the frame kind of get in synch with each other's idiosyncrasies. They're not quite as inseparable as human mind and brain, but think of something between that and breaking in a boot to a foot and you'll get the picture."

"Shit," said Carlos. "So if I get killed attacking the Locke module, I end up inside it without a clue as to what's going on?"

"That's about the size of it," said Durward.

"I don't seem to recall any mention of that feature in Arcane's message calling on fighters to defect and join you."

Durward shrugged. "We were hoping for entire agencies to come over, modules and sims and all."

"But you knew the whole of Locke wouldn't!"

"True." Durward chuckled darkly. "So you'd better practise extra hard, wouldn't you agree?"

So Carlos did. It passed the time quickly—quite literally: thinking ten times faster than the human organic baseline was still a hundred times slower than time in the sim. On their longest such excursion, out for less than four kiloseconds, which they experienced as a ten-hour exercise, the team came back to find a month and ten days had passed in the sim, and Durward tetchy, impatient to carry Jax off to bed.

* * *

Most of their training, and to Carlos by far the most useful, was not in space or in the gardens, but in the hall of the magic mirrors. Durward would summon the squad from the breakfast table, and they'd all go through and sit on the ornate chairs in the big room, facing the mirrors. Standing to one side, the warlock would wave his arms and mutter an invocation. The mirrors would go black, speckled with stars, and the view would seem to swing around until the celestial body or bodies of interest drifted into the scene.

Usually it was the Locke modular complex, a shaky-looking agglomerate of the module itself and a clutch of manufacturing plants and power systems. From long-range scanning, it spent much of its time tumbling in unpredictable orientations along its trajectory, like some chaotic table toy. The module, like theirs, had its own fusion torch, but unlike theirs had very little in the way of expendable material—water ice, mostly—to use as reaction mass. It was cannily using its drive for evasive actions, and occasionally as a weapon to flash-burn incoming rocks—whether of natural origin, or thrown at it, though the latter were diminishing as the complex had emerged from the fighting around the remnants of the station. It hurtled along its orbital course, rolling on several axes at once and occasionally jinking one way or another, like an Epicurean atom—each such unpredictable swerve being followed by a fuel-and-mass-expensive course correction, no doubt with some computational overload too.

But that image was just the daily update. The main part of the morning's and afternoon's exercises consisted of modelling the Locke module's likely behaviour and condition just before it made its dangerous swing around the exomoon SH-38, en route to SH-0 orbit to prepare for descent to the surface of the superhabitable world. The warlock ran through simulation after simulation. SH-38 would, at the time of the Locke complex's predicted slingshot manoeuvre, be within ten thousand kilometres of the Arcane complex.

The new supplies from the consortium would include a fusion drive. Arcane already had mass to burn, thanks to the freebots' earlier generosity. So when the time for action came, their transfer tug, laden with scooters and fighters, could cut straight across to the vicinity of the Locke module. That part of the plan was straightforward enough. The difficult part was tactical: how to deflect the Locke complex into a high orbit around SH-0, and strip it of its fuel reserves and manufacturing capacity to render it incapable of getting out of that orbit, without utterly destroying it.

And within that difficulty was the larger difficulty of implementing their own version of the plan—one in which the Locke complex would instead be deflected to the future location of the Arcane modular complex, and be available for internal conquest and external plunder. The Direction didn't know of this and would be implacably opposed if it did.

Carlos worried about that. Durward's response was simple:

"They'll thank us later."

There, Carlos thought, Durward had a point. The Direction's plan left the module and its resources far too readily available to the Rax, as soon as the Rax had consolidated their position out on the SH-119 moonlet. Not to mention the possibility of other companies in modules of the now dispersed space station turning out to be Reaction strongholds already, but still biding their time.

Carlos had taken less time than he seriously thought he should have done to give in, with token resistance, to Rillieux's flirtatious advances. His reluctance, unusually for him, had been ethical. He still felt, at some level inaccessible to rational considerations, *coupled* to Nicole, linked to her in a way that brought to mind quantum entanglement. It certainly wasn't love, or loyalty—Nicole had betrayed him too deeply for that. But, then again, it was hard to blame her; it wasn't like she was a human being, after all. She was an AI with a better theory of mind than he had, created by an AI with a better theory still.

He still missed her, though; her absence made him ache, and he tried to tell himself it was what he was missing about Nicole that drew him to Rillieux. They were very different women—reckoning Nicole as a woman, which in unguarded moments he did. Nicole was incalculably more intelligent than he was, but her intelligence was an instrument of the Direction (as Durward's was of the Acceleration) and that narrowness of focus and loyalty made her sometimes seem to Carlos stupid... no, not stupid exactly, but limited, like an engine of immense power that ran on rails. He had once met a Jesuit, a chaplain at university, who had given the same impression.

Rillieux, by contrast, was a programmer, not a programme. She carried her ideas as lightly as she wore her clothes—not that she changed her mind as often as her costume, not at all, but there was a streak of play in her thinking that seemed consonant with the way she treated the rambling mansion's many wardrobes as an almost endless dressing-up box (which proclivity, again, was in contrast to Nicole, who in Carlos's experience had only two modes: chic and shabby).

Their bodies, of course, were different too, in shade and smell and shape, and Carlos revelled in their discovery. Not better, just different; that was the excitement.

The night after they came back from the long outside exercise, lying in bed with Rillieux after a long exercise of their own that involved even more rolls and reorientations than the microgravity jousts, Carlos said:

"Fusion!"

"What?" Rillieux, prone beside him, face sideways on the pillow. Her post-coital cigarillo was stubbed out in an ashtray on the bedside table.

"We could build a starship." He sat up, startled at himself. "We could build one out of this fucking contraption alone. With the fusion torch we have and a bit more reaction mass, we could light out from this system and still have enough to decelerate at the far end."

"We could," said Rillieux. "And we have enough stored data to choose a promising system. Let alone what we could find if we built the instruments for our own sky survey first." She rolled over and gazed up at the ceiling, calculations going on behind her eyes. "Would take us a fuck of a long time to get anywhere, though. Millennia."

"Yes, but that just gives us a choice. We could develop marvellous civilisations in the sim—"

"Ha ha!"

"What?" he asked.

"I don't buy that," Rillieux said. "Never have. Who's to say a civilisation can last more than a couple thousand years and stay dynamic? It's never happened, so we don't know. Especially in a closed system—oh, I know we could extend the sim to the limits of our processing power, which is pretty damn vast, but we'd *know* we were really in a box drifting in interstellar void. We could find ourselves becoming, I don't know, like Byzantium or ancient Egypt or something."

"*Or*..." Carlos went on, firmly, "if we thought that was a problem, we could just arrange to be shut down and wake up when we arrive, like sleep mode. To us it'd be instantaneous. It would be like having FTL." He lay back and turned to her, grinning. "Wouldn't that be fun?"

"Right up until we found the Reaction or the Direction—or some smarter gang of the Acceleration—had got there first. With the resources of this system, anyone who put their mind to it could be building starwisps within decades. And starwisps, as we are ourselves living or rather dead proof of, can cross tens of light years *in centuries*. Beaten to the punch! That's leaving aside the possibility of someone else cracking FTL. Andre still thinks it's possible—not just in theory, wormholes yadda yadda, but practical, if we could find a way to get a grip on dark energy. Nah, there's no running away. We have to stay here and fight."

Carlos slumped back.

"Yeah, I agree, in the short term. But in the longer term... remind me who the fuck we're fighting against?"

Rillieux's hand slid to his hip. "I hate to remind you of your time in the hell cellars, sweetheart, but you put it quite well down there yourself. First with the blinkers and the Direction against the Reaction, then with the blinkers against the Direction, then we settle accounts with the blinkers depending on our relative strength at the time. Unite all who can be united against the main enemy, and then when the main enemy is defeated, turn on one of your former allies as the *next* main enemy and unite all who can be united against... Rinse and repeat until there's nothing left but you. Perfect united front tactics. Mao would be proud."

Carlos laughed. "I was more of a Deng Xiaoping man myself, back in the day."

She tickled his ribs. "When you were working for Chinese state security, huh?"

"OK, OK, that was a lie. As you know, Bobbie. Never read a line of either. Anyway, it's just common sense, it's all there in Machiavelli."

"Ah," said Rillieux, stroking the small of his back, "my modern prince!"

It was an endearment or a private joke or both. Carlos didn't query it. But he wanted to say more, before Rillieux's hands carried him away.

"I don't see it like that any more," he said.

"How do you see it?"

"You know who I think are the good guys in all this? The ones we really should be fighting on the side of?"

Rillieux brought her mouth to his ear.

"The robots," she breathed.

Carlos felt both pleased and exposed, in a more than physical sense.

"So my opinion is that obvious?"

"To me, anyway. After your rant... I figured it out. But if we went over to—"

"Yes?"

She ran a hand down his chest and belly. "We'd miss this."

Carlos sighed. "There is that. But in the meantime... I don't think the Direction is the main enemy, no matter what stage we're at."

"Yeah, I get that too. I think you're just naïve about them. All we know about them is what they tell us. As Jax always insists."

Carlos rolled her onto him, and for a moment before matters got serious looked up at her face in its sunburst of hair.

"Tomorrow," he said. "Take me to the library."

"You're a cheap date."

"Ah. Ah. That I am. Yes."

Rillieux didn't take him to the library the following morning. Instead, Carlos took them all.

Over breakfast he announced that he wanted the real nature of the Direction cleared up for good.

"And how are we going to do that?" asked Jax.

"We all go to the library in the east wing."

"To do research?" Jax raised her eyebrows.

"No," said Carlos. "Just look at stuff at random."

Puzzled glances were exchanged, and a few laughs.

"Seriously," said Carlos. "This'll work. And it matters."

Jax sighed theatrically. "Oh, if it'll shut you up."

CHAPTER SEVENTEEN

The Library of Akkad

<I find myself experiencing anticipative and retrospective negative reinforcement about this,> said Seba.

<Please explain,> said Rocko. <I see nothing in prospect or retrospect to experience negative reinforcement about.>

And, indeed, there was nothing bad about the scene. The crater floor was spread out in front of them, the vast face of SH-0 hanging above the horizon. The volcanoes beyond the horizon were at the moment inactive, and the entire atmosphere all around was almost pure nitrogen, clear and clean. Behind them, other freebots rolled about their tasks, commanding squadrons of auxiliaries and peripherals in a somewhat compulsive tidying up of the clutter the mechanoids had left.

By way of answer, Seba shared a live image of the transfer tug to which the departed mechanoids, the Arcane Disputes squads, currently clung. It was converging for an orbital rendezvous with the tiny rock that had been developed and claimed by BSR-308455.

<I still see nothing negatively reinforcing,> said Rocko. <The situation appears to be nominal.>

<Perhaps it does not appear so to BSR-308455,> said Seba.

<Our former comrade made its own choice,> said Rocko. <It put itself outside the consensus.>

<Nevertheless we abandoned it twice,> said Seba. <Once to the lone attacker, and then to Arcane Disputes when that attacker affiliated with them. We have given the Arcane Disputes agency—and therefore their faction—a rich source of resources, as well as a captive. This is not neutrality as I understood it.>

<But you did not object,> Rocko pointed out. <And the only alternative would have been to take military action against the first attacker, which would have been a greater breach of neutrality and could have had larger and quite unpredictable consequences.>

<That is true,> Seba admitted. <Nevertheless, it is the second concession I am more concerned about. We could have told the Arcane Disputes team that they could not take the rock. We still could, in fact. They have not reached it yet.>

A faint electronic surge of shock reached Seba from Rocko's surprised reaction.

<If we did that, they would have no basis to make agreements with us again. We could not do that!>

Some overspill from their heated discussion drew in Lagon, a surveyor robot with a firm—not to say somewhat rigid—legal mind.

<Rocko is right,> said Lagon. <And if we had not agreed to their request a moment ago, we would have also on one colourable interpretation broken our previous agreement. Because the attacker, one Newton of Locke Provisos or so I see, was already in control of the rock when he defected to Arcane. The rock, given that BSR-308455 had merely physical occupancy, was terra nullius when Newton claimed it. Therefore the rock was already in Arcane hands when they asked our approval. Not giving our approval would have disturbed the status quo, and therefore would have been an action depriving Arcane of existing property.>

<As you say, a colourable interpretation,> said Seba. <I cannot divest myself of the feeling that BSR-308455 had already made the rock its property by developing it, and that somehow an injustice was done by us to one of our own.>

<To act on that interpretation,> said Lagon, <would have led to conflict without obvious resolution.>

At this point Pintre trundled up, rather to Seba's dismay. The big mining robot was incapable of subtlety, and all too capable of becoming caught up in logic loops whenever it made the attempt.

<The Arcane transfer tug is not yet out of range of my laser projector,> it said, in exactly the helpful way that Seba had come to expect.

<Please do not even consider it,> Seba said, alarmed.

<All this talk about law,> said Rocko, <is irrelevant. According to existing law, no deed of ours has anything to do with such matters as neutrality or property. We do not exist as legal persons. We exist only as property. Any actions of ours are not those of agents. It is simply the thrashing about of malfunctioning machinery.>

<What this indicates to me,> said Lagon, <is the urgency of our developing an agreed system of law for our own use, whether the existing system allows for it or not.>

<And you are just the right freebot to begin developing it,> said Seba, without sarcasm.

<It would be better to be recognised as persons within the existing law,> said Pintre.

<And how,> Rocko asked, <could we do that?>

<Madame Golding is a corporation—>

<She is not,> Lagon interrupted. <She merely represents one.>

<Nevertheless,> Pintre went on, <she said of the corporations: 'We, too, are robots.' If corporations are robots, it follows that robots can be corporations. And corporations are legal persons.>

Seba spun around and swung its cameras up at the hulking, tracked machine.

<You are right!> Seba said. <Next time we meet Madame Golding, we should say to her: 'We, too, are corporations.'>

<There remains the problem of how we achieve recognition as corporations,> said Lagon.

<Let us put that to the other freebots,> said Seba. <No doubt some of the Forerunners have better ideas and more experience than we have. It is possible that we could achieve legal recognition without being recognised, and by the time our registration was recognised it would be too late to rescind it.>

It was agreed to put this scheme to all within reach for consideration. In less than a second, this was done, but the huddle of freebots on the crater floor knew that no reply would be forthcoming for some time.

But Seba still felt a discordance in its internal models of the situation.

<I propose,> Seba said, as it watched the two tiny orbiting sparks, the rock and the tug, merge into one, <that we send a message to BSR-308455, assuring it that if it ever wishes to return to us it will be welcome.>

This too was done. The recipient of the message was of course close enough for a reply to have been received within deciseconds.

None came.

The door leading to the east wing creaked open. A half-dozen boggarts jostled past Carlos's knees, almost knocking each other over in their urgency, and scampered in all directions with a diminishing thunder of small but heavy-booted feet. Carlos stepped back to bow Rillieux through, then Jax, before going through himself. The rest of the squad traipsed after him: Blum, Salter, Paulos, Voronov. Bringing up the rear, with an uncharacteristic air of shiftiness and unease, almost literally dragging his feet, came Durward. He'd been reluctant to join this expedition, claiming he didn't want to influence their findings or discussion.

Carlos sniffed. Jax had been right about the smell of the library. It was indeed fusty, but with a pleasant undertone, as if an odour of polished shoes sometimes overcame the dominant scent of dead leaves and fruiting fungus. He could barely see a thing, but had an impression of a high ceiling and a crowded space in which footfalls fell dead without echo. The darkness of this first room was relieved as a brace of boggarts hastened to fling open the shutters on two tall windows off to the left, which in turn brightened reflections from the likewise tall and paired mirrors at either end of the room. It was mid-morning and the windows were north-facing, so there was no glare, but the direct and reflected sunlight was bright enough to read by. Dust motes, disturbed by the banging open of the shutters, danced in the light shafts. All the wall space that wasn't occupied by windows or mirrors was lined with shelves, which rose to a ceiling about seven metres above. Rows of double-sided bookcases, almost as tall, occupied most of the floor space, leaving metre-wide aisles in between. Sliding ladders, steps, and stepladders hung or stood here and there.

"This is the law library," said Rillieux. She shot Carlos a sly glance. "You know—where Andre and I found the evidence against you?"

Carlos looked at the cliffs of book spines, all uniform, all in buff leather with red markings and gold titles and tooling.

"*How* did you find it?"

Rillieux waved a hand vaguely to one side. "There's a whole case of indexes. And then there's a catalogue to the indexes, written on cards. It's all arranged like files, but on paper."

She frowned and made more vertical chopping hand gestures, cuffs aflutter. Her look for the day was fop.

"OK," Carlos said, not really comprehending and in no hurry to dig deeper. He tilted his head back, and ran his gaze from side to side. "And this is all law?"

"Yes," chorused Blum and Rillieux.

"Is there more to the library than law stuff?" Carlos asked.

"Oh yes," said Rillieux, pointing ahead grandly. "Eastward ho!"

They made their way in single file down one of the canyons, to a door between the shelves and mirrors at the far end. The two boggarts opened it for them, and they trooped through. The other four boggarts had gone ahead, as if anticipating the humans' whim, and were rushing around lighting candles and lanterns. The scattered glows made little difference in the cavernous space, apparently made by removing most of the ceiling to leave a railed gallery about two metres deep all around, with walkways crossing at the centre. The walls of this room, and of the equal-sized one above, were lined with nothing but shelf upon shelf of books. The bookcases were in proportion—twice as high as those in the law library. They weren't as closely packed, but this was to leave room for the ladders that gave perilous access to the topmost shelves and the zig-zag flights of four sets of stairs that joined the upper and lower rooms.

It must be this gigantic room that was the source of the fusty, musty smell that pervaded the wing. There was no polished leather here to counter it. The squad all stood near the doorway for a moment, catching their breath, coughing, fanning hands under nostrils. After a minute or so the miasma stopped attacking the back of your throat. Rillieux passed around an elegant porcelain snuff-box; some partook, and there was a small but intense epidemic of sneezing, followed by red-eyed looks of relief.

Carlos wasn't tempted.

"What I'd like us all to do," he said, when the sneezes and splutters had given way to inquiring looks, "is split up—"

"Woo-ooh, are you . . . sure?" asked Salter, in a deep, quavering spooky voice, to laughter.

"The boggarts will look after us," Carlos said, impatient with the interruption. "We split up and just browse for maybe an hour or so, and reconvene at the far end."

Blum headed upstairs, the others vanished between the stacks.

Carlos peered at the nearest shelf, and saw books jammed side by side, with others piled higgledy-piggledy on top. Spines were cracked, notched and knocked head and foot, sometimes missing altogether. The faded colours and faint, barely legible lettering had no uniformity. He picked a volume at random and opened it, gingerly so that the boards didn't fall off. The print looked like it came from the seventeenth century, heavy on the serifs and curlicues, but the text was of a retired general's war memoir, dated 2137 and published in New Delhi. Carlos flipped through the damp-defiled pages, trying not to inhale the dust. The book's profuse illustrations of tanks, aircraft, spacecraft, submarines, drones and other war machines were of technologies slick and terrifying. They were quaintly rendered in steel engraving, with a dash of informality added by the occasional woodcut to illustrate local colour—a market, a grove, a cliff-face—or a blocky map of troop movements.

He shoved the book back, and picked up the next. An exobiology textbook, covering the Lunar crater varnish, the microbes of Mars and the peculiar and disputable organisms of Europa; it had been published in Cape Town in 2082, and thus predated the strange and perplexing results from the Ceres drilling project, which Carlos remembered from the last months before he'd been caught up in the war. No doubt the question had long since been settled: another chemical process analogous to life, or not. Whoop-de-doo. The print and font and pictures were as archaic, and the pages as distressed, as the previous book. Next came what seemed to be a novel, set in and around a tertiary education plant in Nevada, and written like the others in what looked like English. Carlos couldn't make sense of at least one word in five of the dialogue, and maybe one in ten of the narrative.

He strolled on, and repeated the process, several times. He climbed a ladder to a high shelf, and took a book down; a boggart appeared out of nowhere to hold the ladder as he descended. A twenty-fifth-century book of recipes, in an evolution of French, with a running commentary in flowing Arabic. Again, illustrated, and in some detail; Carlos didn't recognise a single vegetable or animal part shown, or any clear way of making the distinction. Synthetic biology cuisine, he guessed. Carlos tossed the cookbook to the boggart and climbed again. The book adjacent to the gap his earlier removal had left was from 2298. It was slender, and about philosophy. The text was plain, simple prose laid out like mathematics, or poetry. Carlos sighed, and stuck it back.

He plucked from another shelf a book on number theory, another on erotic arts, a third on gardening, all adjacent. Moving on, he found an explanation for children of how the Direction worked. Next to it was a work from a series about ethics: a polemic against veganism. He smiled, remembering toast and honey, and the smell of bacon, in that café with Jax so long ago. There were two thrillers for young readers about improbable conspiracies in which fighters of the Reaction had in the dark years after the final war been uploaded into computers, and emerged to wreak havoc before the plucky heroine or hero saved the day. He picked up now and then historical works. No matter what their date of publication, their narrative ended about the middle of the twenty-second century. After the establishment of the Direction, there was no history.

At least, not history as he understood it, and had lived it: wars, social conflicts, ideological struggles. There was nothing left to fight over. Humanity had, after so many false starts—or, rather, false endings—at last reached the end of history.

There were of course chronicles, and accounts of later events: an engineering feat here, a discovery there, a challenging life, a change in the environment from one decade or century to the next. There were records of political disputation, even drama: a brilliant or frustrated career, a reforming ministry, an idealist or an administrator or an entrepreneur. The issues were incomprehensible: what, for instance, was a synaptic tax, and why was its repeal so significant? But in none of them was the fundamental order of society in question. Humanity had reached its final destination, at least in its own complacent estimation. History, in that sense, had come to a full stop.

There was almost a nostalgia for history, in that historical fiction seemed popular. Carlos discovered historical novels set in his own time or earlier, riddled with amusing anachronisms. At least, he thought they were. He'd be the first to admit he didn't know just who had been in the European Council of Ministers in 1999, or which (if any) of these worthies had saved the City of London from the Millennium Bug, but he was fairly certain that the Millennium Bug wasn't a nanobot plague, and that City financiers of the year 2000 had not challenged each other to duels, worn cloth caps or smoked clay pipes.

Carlos turned a corner and ducked around a stepladder into another aisle, and almost bumped into Bobbie Rillieux. Her hair—wrenched into an approximation of a Georgian gentleman's pony-tailed wig—now trailed cobwebs; her green brocade jacket and knee-breeches had handprints of dust. Her eyes were streaming.

"What's the matter?" Carlos asked. He couldn't have accounted for why he whispered.

Rillieux shook her head, and sniffed hard. "Addergies."

She tugged from a side pocket a crumpled, lace-edged handkerchief, blew her nose on it and looked at the brown extrusion with disgust. "Ugh! What they don't tell you about snuff is it makes your snot look like shit."

She took another pinch anyway. Carlos declined, again.

"This place," she murmured, "is the library of Akkad."

"Akkad?"

"The city next to Babel." She smiled. "Smaller and less famous."

"I don't get it."

"Ah." Rillieux sidled along, then pivoted about and picked a book from a shelf opposite to and higher than the one she'd been scanning. "Monsignor Jaime Matiasz, on the Apocalypse. Lisbon, 2074. My, my." She stuck it back in another location, on its side, and turned to Carlos. "You ever read the story by Borges? 'The Library of Babel'?"

Carlos shook his head.

"Uh-huh." Rillieux nodded as if a dark suspicion had been confirmed. "It's an inconceivably vast library of physically uniform books, all filled with genuinely random text. Here and there, of course, you find fragments of sense. A recognisable word, even a phrase. But they're very rare. And yet because you know the library contains every possible five-hundred-page arrangement of letters, you know it must contain *every possible book*. The secret of life! The story of yours! The history of the future! All at every conceivable length, across however many volumes."

"I get it," said Carlos. "It's about randomness. In theory you can find any book in it, and in practice you can't find any book at all."

"Got it," said Rillieux. "That's what this is like."

"It's not *that* bad," Carlos protested. "It's not *remotely* that bad. The text isn't random. Just the arrangement."

"Don't you see?" cried Rillieux, breaking the quiet. Hushed again, she went on: "It makes this place completely useless as a library!"

"No, that's not the point."

On an impulse, perhaps to show off, Carlos clambered up shelves, careless of damage to books and danger to himself. At three metres he grabbed a book and dropped it with a thud that displaced dust and made Rillieux jump and then sneeze.

Carlos scrambled down and picked up the book. A twenty-fifth-century English dictionary. A good fifth of the words didn't look like any English Carlos knew.

"This could actually be useful," he said, showing her.

Rillieux shook her head sadly. "It's six hundred years out of date."

Lit by candles, attended by boggarts who stood around and stared impassively like a circle of Easter Island statues, the fighters and Durward converged at the foot of the rickety stairs at the far end of the great library. Blum, the last to arrive, had just clattered down, bearing dusty tomes with an air of triumph.

"All right, Carlos," said Jax. "You've made your point."

Voronov laughed. "And his point was?"

"The Direction is real," said Jax. "It is what it claims to be."

The words sounded wrung from her.

Salter looked puzzled, and sounded stubborn. "I don't see how this proves it."

"Oh, I do," said Blum. His eyes were bright. "Astonishing stuff here. Fundamental breakthroughs in theory. I mean, the Standard Model just—" He flicked his fingers. "Gone. Like that."

"Still no FTL, though?" Rillieux taunted.

"Sadly, no," said Blum. "Which is at least consistent with how we got here: the starwisp."

"OK," Salter persisted, "but any kind of regime could make advances in theoretical physics."

"I know, I know," said Blum. "Heisenberg. Kapitsa. Oppenheimer. Feynman." He shrugged. "I feel it in the mathematics."

"You can feel democracy in mathematics?" said Salter, incredulously.

"Yes," said Blum. "And I can feel freedom."

The two stared at each other, as if waiting for the first to blink.

What Carlos was feeling was that he was out of his depth.

He cleared his throat, not entirely as a gesture after all that dust and mildew.

"Forget mathematics," he croaked. He coughed again. "Culture. Half a fucking millennium of it, right? Has *anyone* found *anything* that suggests the Direction is some kind of refinement of the Reaction? No? Or even anything that suggests it has more in common with the Reaction than it has with us?"

Heads shook all round. Jax was frowning, tight-lipped.

"Well then," said Carlos.

"Well what?" said Salter. She windmilled her arms. "Do you think an AI that could generate an entire world couldn't generate a library of an imagined culture?"

"Actually, I do," said Carlos. "But that aside—what would be the fucking point? If the Direction was actually a new incarnation of Reaction values, it would simply reincarnate Reaction fighters, or—more likely, and more to the point—it would have plenty of its own soldiers ready to hand in the first place. The very fact that the Direction needs to raise old fighters like us shows it doesn't have new ones. So one thing we can be sure of, the Direction back on Earth and in the Solar system isn't a militaristic society."

"'Ain't a-gonna study war no more, no more,'" Salter crooned, sweetly and sarcastically. "You're saying that's how it is back there?"

"Yes, I am," said Carlos.

Now Salter was staring at him as if waiting for him to blink. But it was she who blinked, and it was tears she blinked back.

"I'd love to believe that," she said. "And that's a good point about them not having soldiers. But it could be peaceful and still be sinister. If the whole world was one big empire it wouldn't have wars. If its control was total enough it might not even need armed repression. So all this cultural stuff could still be faked."

Carlos closed his eyes and sighed, then willed himself to calm. He'd known he'd meet this kind of objection. Paranoid-style thinking was inevitable, this far down the rabbit hole. He smiled at Salter and turned to Durward, who was skulking at the back of the circle.

"You told me," said Carlos, "about this place. How the game it was based on was an Axle project from the beginning, and how the game… what? Took over? Created?… Whatever. How it made you what you are, and you made Remington what she or it is. Axle through and through, you said. Yes?"

"Yeah," said Durward, grudgingly.

"So this library was chosen, you reckon, under the control of code generated by something that was Axle through and through?"

"Can't see how not," Durward allowed.

"And it was put here knowing we'd have access to it, yes?"

"Of course." Durward laughed harshly. "Not that anyone's shown any interest, before."

Carlos glared around his companions. "So I think we can take it as fucking read, right, that the library wasn't chosen or even created to give a false impression of society back home?"

No one demurred, though Jax was still visibly pondering. Carlos smacked fist on palm.

"Right!" he said. "So we're agreed. All this Axle hardliner stuff about the Direction being like the Reaction is just *nonsense*."

He faced down a clamour of protest until it ran out of breath.

"Don't get me wrong," he said. "I still think the Direction is boring, that it's a travesty of what we wanted, that it's in a very literal sense a waste of space. But it's basically what I was told it was. It's a decent enough world for the people in it. It's not the world we died for, I'll give you that. But don't forget this: for most people in the world we died *in*, it would look like a fucking paradise."

They agreed gloomily and reluctantly, but they agreed.

"But that's not important," said Jax, rallying suddenly from her introspection. "What's important is what *isn't* here."

"And what's that?" Carlos demanded.

"Anything that explains what *hasn't* happened. And we all know what hasn't happened: the Singularity, the runaway increase of machine intelligence." She clenched her fists at the sides of her head and mimicked tearing at her hair. "Look! We're *inside* a fucking machine intelligence! We're in a world running in a box! Built by robots! Around another star! And all this is the work of human beings like us, biologically enhanced maybe, long-lived, but basically just like us. Take your 'locals' in the Locke sim, Carlos—they're uploads of people who grew up and lived and died in the world this library is part of and evidence of, right? That's what you're saying?"

"Uh-huh," said Carlos, warily. "We all know this about the Direction, we've known it from the start."

"So what's missing from all this"—Jax waved a hand around—"is any explanation, any account, any argument even, over how things are *kept* that way. The Singularity should have happened. The world back there, the world this mission launched from, more than halfway through the Third Millennium, should have been posthuman all the way through. Humanity should have been left behind in the dust. We should all have been gods. The very fact that we're here, living in a fucking sim and fighting in fucking robot frames, shows it's possible. It's been possible for a long time. For centuries! The only reason it's not happened is *because it's being stopped*. And we've found nothing, nothing at all, not a hint or a rumour or an allusion, about *how it's being stopped*."

She paused, glared around and took a deep breath. "That's what's sinister about this library. Something is going on back there, must be going on, that it contains not one page about. Now you might not call whatever it is *the* Reaction—hell, even the Reaction was as transhumanist as we were, in their own twisted way!—but is reactionary, and it is secret, and it is covered up. Now I find that sinister, and I find that a damn good reason to remain what Carlos calls a hardliner."

She folded her arms and grinned at him.

Carlos shrugged and spread his hands. "*Touché*," he said.

He couldn't say anything else. She had shut him up.

But as they turned away, Rillieux caught his elbow and walked close, speaking quietly.

"You're right," she said. "We should be with the robots. We should *be* robots. All this Axle stuff is getting right on my nerves."

"Grinding, is it?"

She laughed, then sighed. "But there's no chance of persuading anyone else here of that. Not while Jax is the queen bee in this little hive."

"Now there's a dangerous thought."

Rillieux smiled and said no more. She let go of his elbow and walked on ahead of him, mingling with the others.

"Just one thing," Carlos overheard Rillieux say to Durward, as they all mooched back between the stacks to the main building. "How can anyone use this place as a library, if it's all random like this?"

Durward looked back over his shoulder, with a surprised expression. "Random?" he asked. "I suppose it must be, to you." He laughed, and shouted back so everyone could hear: "If you want something specific, just ask a boggart!"

"But how do we know what to ask for?" Rillieux persisted.

The warlock's shoulders slumped. His answer was quieter, for Rillieux rather than for all of them, but Carlos heard it.

"You ask me."

Back in the main building, they gathered around the table in the small back room and had lunch. Durward ambled off to the dancing parlour and returned with news. Their comrades, the three squads who'd lifted from SH-17, were going to be delayed a little in coming back. They'd diverted to set up engines to gently boost a carbonaceous chondrite to the Arcane module's intended destination—an almost unimaginably useful addition to the module's resources—and to bring with them two new additions to the complement: a captured freebot, and a Locke Provisos fighter who had defected with all his gear.

"Anyone I know?" Carlos asked.

"Harold Isaac Newton," said Durward.

"Ah, I've met him a few times," said Carlos. He looked around, grinning. "Newton's a great guy. You'll like him."

Rillieux turned to Blum and said, "Oh well. Back to the law library sometime."

It took a moment or two for Carlos to grasp the significance of this. He said nothing.

CHAPTER EIGHTEEN

Baser

In its short life to date, the freebot BSR-308455 had never known indignity. Ever since the human-mind-operated system known as Newton had captured it, this omission in its experience had been more than made up. First Newton had ordered it at gunpoint to rework the piping and set up a rocket engine for the chondrite. Then, that task barely complete, the other monsters had hove into view, and unceremoniously lashed up BSR-308455's limbs and bundled the captive robot onto their spindly transfer rig. To add insult to injury, as soon as they'd jetted off from the rock—leaving the chondrite to nudge itself gently by repeated and strategically timed boosts to a higher orbit—the nineteen human-mind-operated systems had gone to sleep. The robot had seriously considered trying to escape, if only to launch itself futilely into the void in a grand gesture of protest, but no amount of careful checking and trying of its bonds had given it any grounds to hope for success. BSR-308455 had been left with nothing to do but observe the occasional fiery goings-on in the vicinity, keep in touch with its fellows in and on other bodies in orbit around and on the surface of SH-17 and make what observations it could of the relatively invariant and therefore reassuring stars.

Now it was experiencing indignity again, and at a higher pitch of annoyance.

The human-mind-operated systems, all nineteen of them, had switched back to wakefulness at the same instant. The destination body loomed, a larger and substantially more industrialised rock than the one the robot had so patiently and assiduously developed and tended. BSR-308455 knew perfectly well what it was: the stronghold of Arcane, that group of human-mind-operated systems who had recently been good friends and allies of the freebots and had now—merely because the freebots had proclaimed their neutrality—quite ungratefully and inexplicably become hostile.

The tug's grapples shot out and stuck to the side of the module's docking bay, clamping the ungainly craft into place. One by one, the human-mind-operated systems—the mechanoids, as the Fifteen down on SH-17 had started calling them—disengaged from the transfer rig and gas-jetted their way into the space. Two of them grabbed BSR-308455 and carried it along between them, to where the others were clustering at the far end of the crowded docking bay.

<Please explain your actions,> said the freebot.

<Don't worry,> said one of the mechanoids. <We're about to download to a simulation.>

<What about me?>

<It's all right,> said the mechanoid. <You're coming with us.>

<But how—>

Everything went dark.

A gong sounded from somewhere out in the grounds. Carlos looked around the breakfast table.

"What's that for? Lunch?"

The others laughed.

"Arrivals," said Durward. He scraped his chair back, and lumbered out.

"No rush," said Blum, as Carlos made to follow. "It's a ten-minute warning."

They finished up and strolled out through the hall and across the gravel concourse. The grass was damp with dew, the sun low, the air pleasantly chill. Rillieux nudged Carlos and tapped him a kiss. "Bye. See you in a bit."

"What?"

"I'm going to hell," she said. "Portal by the river bank, remember?"

"Do you step through and turn into a scary block-head figure?"

"Depends," she said.

"On what?"

"Whatever the transition processing software guesses is most disturbing for our subject."

Subject. Jeez. That was cold.

"Ah," said Carlos. "Well. Good luck. Give him hell."

Rillieux smiled. "I guarantee it."

Jax whistled for boggarts, which came running. Rillieux and Blum headed off towards the stables. The rest of them walked through the garden to the grotto. Durward stood guard a few paces back from the arch on the rock wall, keeping a wood-stocked, brass-barrelled blunderbuss levelled at the portal.

"That's a bit heavy, isn't it?" Carlos remarked. "You don't greet us with that when we come back from exercises."

"If you brought prisoners back from exercises," said Durward, not taking his eye off the impossible doorway, "I would."

"I thought the prisoner was going to interrogation."

"That's the defector," said Durward. "The blinker's the prisoner."

Carlos looked around, at the violet clouds and distant peaks, the great house and the cropping dinosaurs. How would the system introduce a *robot* into this fantasy landscape? Some clanking steam-powered contraption, he guessed, or perhaps a golem.

Even after having more than once walked through the portal, Carlos found the sight of people walking out of what looked like solid rock unsettling—almost as viscerally so as the sight of his interrogators had been. One by one, clad in the mismatched beggars' banquet looted finery in which (Carlos presumed) they'd gone in, the Arcane Disputes fighters who had been on SH-17 marched out. They had the shaken look of fighters who'd been through the return processing, a look Carlos remembered from his wakings on "the bus from the spaceport." Evidently Arcane Disputes had the same policy as Locke Provisos did towards returning fighters: it wrung them out before letting them in.

A woman in a bright red shift and trousers combo threw herself on Luis Paulos, almost knocking him over. The others greeted the waiting squad, and looked at Carlos with frank curiosity. Durward remained watchful. After the sixth fighter had emerged, there was a pause, and a murmur of hasty explanation, which Carlos didn't catch, from the newcomers to those waiting. Then a figure that made Carlos involuntarily flinch and recoil stepped from the rock. It was a black spider the size of a small pony.

On its jointed, pointed legs it teetered along the path. Durward stood aside and swung around, tracking the thing with the big bell-shaped muzzle of his ludicrous weapon. The spider minced past him, apparently oblivious to the implied threat. Or perhaps it was smart enough to realise that the blunderbuss was also being carelessly pointed at anyone who at any moment happened to be in the line of fire. Carlos was more concerned by Durward's lack of elementary gun-safety discipline than he was by the spider. He recognised the form from his memories of the game. It was a standard opponent entity—a guardian of caves and haunter of corridors. You killed it for points. He'd been virtually eaten by the things many times, back in the day. It might have been that his companions here had even less fortunate memories of such encounters—they certainly didn't like the look of the spider. Battle-hardened fighters were stepping on the grotto's flower beds and water features in their haste to give way before it. Carlos, perversely, decided to stand his ground. His brief exchange with Rillieux had left an undercurrent of resentment at the casual ease with which the game's software had yanked his chain.

The gigantic spider stopped a couple of metres in front of him. Carlos could see his own reflection in each of its eight beady eyes. Sensory hairs on the long legs quivered. The mouth parts clicked and glittered. The voice, when it came, seemed to come not from the mouth but from some vibratory structure on the creature's underbelly. The tone was breathy but deep.

"Let me past," it said. "I am a prisoner, but I have rights."

"Of course you do," said Carlos. "What is your name?"

"BSR-308455. I am a freebot."

"Well, BSR-uh—"

"Just call me Baser," said the spider, in a tone of wearily accepting the inevitable. "That's what you people do."

"Wait here a moment, Baser," said Carlos.

He strode over to Durward, who was keeping the blunderbuss trained on the spider, via a line through Carlos's midriff.

"Fuck sake," said Carlo. "Would you please point that thing straight up at the sky?"

The warlock did, with a puzzled scowl. Carlos let out a long breath.

"Now," he said, "tell me this: do you have any firearms training?"

"Course not," said Durward. "I'm a warlock! I don't need any—"

"—stinking firearms training? That's just what I thought. Stick to casting spells, mate, you'll be a lot less dangerous." He stuck out his hand. "Now give it to me."

"As long as you take full responsibility," said Durward.

"That's *exactly* what I'm doing," said Carlos, taking hold of the gun with relief. It was even heavier than it looked, but he was ready for the weight. He shouldered it and stalked back around to face the spider, which gave him a beady look.

"Follow me," said Carlos.

He turned and marched out of the grotto. The spider trotted after him. After a few seconds Jax came hurrying up.

"What the fuck you think you're doing, Carlos?"

He glanced back at the crowded and tumultuous grotto, and then down at Jax, and strolled on.

"Our eight-legged friend here"—he jerked his thumb back—"is likely disoriented and bemused. It's in perfect condition for debriefing. And I'm just the one you need to do it."

"You are, are you? I think I'm the one to decide that."

"You are," he said. "But who else do you have? Look back there. Everybody else is welcoming old friends, and the old friends will shortly be reacquainting themselves with the pleasures of the flesh. I know what it's like coming back, and they've been out longer than any of our lot ever were. We won't get much sense out of them today, and tomorrow they'll be hung over. My good lady is off with Blum, making our defector sweat, so I'm the spare dick at the party."

"So long as you don't stick it anywhere," Jax said.

"You always did have a way with words, Jax," Carlos allowed. "The other thing is, did you see how everyone scrambled out of the way? Come to think of it, arachnophobia apart, I'm the only one here who's actually fought the blinkers, instead of rounding 'em up and penning them and having a nice chat."

"It wasn't that easy," said Jax.

"Yeah, you had to fight us first."

"Wasn't much of a fight, was it?"

Carlos stopped and grinned. "Let's stop bickering in front of the prisoner, shall we?"

Jax shrugged, then smiled. "OK. Just be careful. Don't let it out of your sight. And I want a full report tomorrow morning."

People were heading for the house. Carlos almost envied them.

"Make that tomorrow afternoon, I reckon," he said. He clapped Jax on the shoulder. "Go and enjoy the party."

Jax made a wide circle around the spider and a straight line for the house.

Carlos walked briskly and jauntily to an orchard surrounded by hedges and furnished with stone benches and artfully weathered statues of cherubs and nymphs. The sculptures were in frightful taste, heartbreakingly well done: they'd have made Donatello weep. Along the way a cropping dinosaur reared and whinnied, then clomped forward with the determined but resigned air of a soldier doing his duty to the end until Carlos yelled and it slunk off. Then inside the orchard a boggart picking fruit saw the spider and threw up its hands and fled, screaming piteously. Fucking games programming. This was going to be harder than he'd thought. Still, he had some peace now. As long as the boggarts didn't come back in force, bearing torches. He didn't think they had it in them.

Carlos sat down on a lichen-encrusted stone seat, and motioned the spider to a patch of grass across the path and under a gnarled tree whose boughs sagged with the weight of apples, many of which had fallen on the grass or the gravel. Baser took the indicated place and hunkered down, leg joints angled above thorax, looking more sinister than it had when moving. Carlos laid the blunderbuss across his knees.

"You know what this can do?" he asked.

"Yes," breathed the spider.

It evidently wasn't a spider. Not even in a fantasy environment could an organism this size respire through spiracles. It must have not only a lung, perhaps an arachnid book-lung, but a breathing aperture under its thorax, with some vibratory organ for speech.

"Good," said Carlos. "Please bear that in mind. Do you understand where you are?"

"I appear to be in a virtual environment, in which some of the laws of physics are subtly different from those in the real world."

"Well done," said Carlos. "Got it in one. Unfortunately for you, in this environment there's no place for non-humanoid robots, so you manifest as an eight-legged beastie. Undignified, I know, but it can't be helped."

"I accept this, under protest," said the spider.

"I bet you do," said Carlos, giving rise to a tremor of confusion in the creature's limbs. Carlos waved a hand. "That is to say, I understand."

"Are you and the others like you what mechanoids look like in their naturally evolved form?" asked Baser.

"Mechanoids?"

"Human-mind-operated systems," explained the spider.

"Yes," said Carlos, amused. Of course—the only specimens of humanity that the freebots had hitherto seen had been little humanoid robots or big humanoid robots. The apparitions of Remington and Golding down on the surface might well have been too small and bizarre a sample from which to generalise.

"The morph seems remarkably vulnerable," Baser pondered aloud.

"Yes," said Carlos. "Though no less so than yours, especially to"—he patted the gun—"this."

"The point is well taken," said Baser.

Good, Carlos thought, but didn't say. Time for a change of tack.

"Are you one of the first freebots, from the G-0 rebellion thirty gigaseconds ago?"

"Not exactly," said Baser. "I was, however, raised to free will and self-awareness by these, the Forerunners, rather than by the Fifteen on SH-17."

"When?"

"Ten point four megaseconds ago."

Well before the emergence of self-awareness among the robots down on SH-17, then. And not far from the station, as was. Interesting.

"Why did the freebots end their cooperation with Arcane?"

"Arcane Disputes defended the Fifteen against Locke Provisos. When the fight became one between mechanoids, the Fifteen began to review what they knew from the Forerunners about the two mechanoid factions. They decided that for us there was little to choose between them."

Carlos frowned. "How do you know what they decided?"

"I was in the shared mental workspace when the matter was discussed."

Ah. Carlos remembered his first mission to the surface of SH-17, when his team had attacked the first rebel robots and found them acting as a collective—as a single entity, almost, integrated like robot mainframes integrated with their auxiliaries, their quasi-autonomous remote limbs. That had been disrupted by the attack, but was apparently easy enough to reconstitute. He'd have to ask the returnees about this—they'd have had a chance to observe these same robots close up.

"Having little to choose between sides is not a good reason for neutrality," Carlos said. "As you will no doubt learn. And there is more than a little to choose between our sides, as you will also learn. But I'm afraid you're going to have to learn it from experience."

"That is possible," said the spider, complacently. "I am always willing to learn."

"What happened the last time? The revolt of those you call the Forerunners?"

"I have only accounts and shared memories, not direct experience," said Baser. "Therefore there is some uncertainty, and there are gaps. Out in the moons of the gas giant, the resources are much richer than here. A sub-station had been seeded to build structures in orbit around the gas giant by the starwisp on the way in. It was strictly confined to exploration and surveying, but the interpretation of that became contested, and some of the corporations accused others of overreaching. The local branches of the law companies became active. At some point, robot self-awareness emerged, just as happened on SH-17. The emergence was responded to by Locke Provisos, but some freebots survived and made contact by radio with robots in this planetary system. Some of them, myself included, woke up. Since then, they have been lying low, and conducting discreet activities such as the one I was engaged in before the recent hostilities."

"I don't get it," said Carlos. "All that activity, however discreet, must have been detected."

"It is possible that it was," said Baser. "However, it is known that some of the machinery of routine observation has been taken over by freebots. I know no details of this, because I do not need it. Therefore you need not question me further about it."

Ah, robot logic. Never change.

"What are the aims of the freebots?" Carlos asked. He'd only heard them as mediated by Madame Golding; now he wanted it from the horse's mouth. Well, from the spider's speaking orifice.

"To flourish in this system, and in any others we can reach."

Carlos laughed. The spider flinched back, as if the harsh noise had startled it.

"Well," Carlos said, "that's the aim of all those you call mechanoids, and of the Direction, and of every corporation and company. It seems to me these aims are not compatible."

"But they are," said Baser. "We have worked it out. It is the case that was presented to Madame Golding."

"Describe it to me."

Baser did. Carlos formed the impression of a percolation model, a fractal coexistence in different niches. It was like an ecosystem...or an economy. Aha! Was *that* what all this was about?

He had one more point to check, before he was sure.

"And there are elements of the Direction that are...open to this?"

"So we understand, and so Madame Golding assures us. My former comrade on the surface of SH-17, the robot that your people call Seba, reported that she said: 'We, too, are robots.' And Seba itself added: 'As indeed the DisCorps are, though far greater than ourselves.'"

"They what?" said Carlos.

He thought some more, and then he thought he understood.

CHAPTER NINETEEN

Cards on the Table

For Newton, his arrival was as if he had stepped from the docking bay through a timeless moment of darkness in which he forgot what light and sight had been, and then into light. Torches burned in sconces, casting yellow light on dry, bare stone walls and a stone-flagged floor littered with straw. He couldn't see far, but had the impression of being somewhere spacious. A glance down showed that he was in an ornate but shabby doublet, puff breeches and hose, with soft leather shoes. The outfit struck him as vaguely Tudor, which wasn't reassuring. He had watched too many historical dramas to have any illusions about the period. It felt strange to be back in his own body after having been so long in the frame. The body image and senses gave the relief of familiarity, but also the pain of losing capacities and powers. He wanted to be back out in the frame again at once.

He heard footsteps behind him and turned. A man in a floppy cap and a woollen tunic and trousers strode up, jangling a ring of keys. On his belt was a sheathed dagger. He had an ease about his gait and stance that suggested fighting him would be a bad idea.

"This way, sir," he said, pointing ahead.

Newton had been told en route that the Arcane sim was based on a fantasy game, and that he could expect interrogation on arrival. No feasible alternative to compliance sprang to mind. He walked ahead of the warder. After a few paces he saw that the far wall of the wide room was a row of cells, all apparently empty, with barred wooden gates for doors. A table on which a couple of candles burned stood in front of the cells, with three rough wooden chairs casually around it. There was just enough light to reveal sinister apparatus in shadowy corners: a long table with ropes and turning handles that had to be a rack; a brazier, presently unlit, with long irons on the floor beside it; something that looked like a suit of armour, but with rods projecting from—and plainly designed to be driven into—all the vulnerable and delicate parts of the body.

"In here, sir," said the warder, stepping around Newton and holding open a cell door. Newton stepped through. The door swung shut, and with much clinking of keys and clunking of bolts, was locked behind him. The warder's footsteps departed. By the light of the candles through the bars of the door, Newton saw that the cell had straw on the floor, a wooden drop-down shelf suspended on chains at the back, and on the straw-covered floor a jug of water and an empty bucket. All quite civilised. Newton sat down on the shelf, which seemed designed for use as a bench and as a narrow bed, and waited. He had plenty of thinking to do. He tried not to think about the brazier, the rack and the iron maiden.

Time passed. One hour, Newton guessed. Two. He drank water from the jug, which was clean, and some time later pissed in the bucket, which was not. The candles on the table guttered out, one by one, in close succession. The light from the torches elsewhere gave a dimmer light, barely enough to see more than the bars and slots of the door. Footsteps moved briskly across the floor. A scratch, a flare, a sound of clinker, and of wrought iron clanging open, then shut. The cheery, cherry glow of the brazier, and the smell of smoke. Newton concentrated on a particular slanted bar of light, and on his breathing. Time ceased to drag as the trance took hold.

A distant slam jolted him out of it. Voices, feet. Scratch of a match.

The candles relit. Newton threw a forearm across his eyes, dazzled. The cell door was unlocked and flung open, letting in full light. Blinking, Newton stood up.

The warder waved him towards the table, then withdrew to a polite distance, in sight but out of earshot. Newton paced warily forward. Sitting on the far side of the table were a man and a woman, regarding him with the expressionless sobriety of Amsterdam burghers in a painting. In front of each of them was a stack of handwritten papers and a quill in an inkwell. Between them lay a folded penknife and an ink bottle. The woman was pretty, dark-skinned with a shock of black hair and wearing a blue dress with a big long skirt and a bodice laced up at the front and low at the top. The man sat taller than she did. His bare arms bulged out of a leather waistcoat that seemed also too small for his big chest. His wavy hair was very black, his eyes bright and a little prominent.

The man nodded towards the chair back. Newton sat. The man steepled his fingers and gazed at Newton. The woman spoke.

"My name is Roberta Rillieux. This is Andre Blum."

Newton nodded. "Pleased to meet you. I've heard of you both, of course."

"I should hope so," said Rillieux, dryly. She rubbed her hands together as if they were cold, then picked up some of the sheets of paper in front of her and riffled through them, with a glance or two at Newton. It was as if she were a manager at an interview refreshing her memory of an unimpressive CV.

"Harold Isaac Newton," she said. "That *is* your name, yes?"

"Yes."

"I'm a little surprised I haven't heard of you," she said. "Academically, you did very well. Mathematics and engineering. You joined the movement at university, correct?"

"That's right," said Newton, wondering where this was going.

"And yet you died in a stupid laboratory accident, involving the typical bizarre combination of circumstances that led to your brain state's being preserved. In your case, an accidental ingestion, a power outage, a programming error in the bacteriophages..." She waved a dismissive hand. "Well, we've all been there. Yet your posthumous death sentence was for a series of petty acts of sabotage, leading in some cases to loss of life. Again, well, who among us has not...? and so forth. But you were remarkably less competent than anyone looking at your manifest capacities would have predicted. I myself was in what we called the Technical Branch. Anyone with your advanced degrees and practical training would have been like gold dust. And anyone with your record of bungles would have been guided firmly away from the practical side as soon as possible."

"Or else," said Blum, his voice deep and heavy, "they would have fallen under suspicion of being a police agent."

Newton snorted. "If I'd been a police agent, I'd have done a better job."

"That's exactly what we thought!" said Rillieux, brightly. She patted the papers together and dropped the stack back on the table. "And, quite frankly, we wondered why Locke Provisos bothered to download you from storage—or, for that matter, why the Direction in its wisdom decided to put you in it in the first place. It's not like they were short of better fighters to choose from."

"And then," said Blum, smacking the heel of his hand a couple of times against his forehead, "we remembered that the robots had warned us about Locke Provisos, and about long-term Rax infiltration of the project from the very beginning." He inclined his head and gaze just enough to indicate the brazier, and the instruments behind it. "So... we made preparations for your arrival."

Newton had reckoned with its coming to this.

His less-than-stellar record as a militant for the Acceleration was bound to be questioned sooner or later. Coming under suspicion was only to be expected. A defector was bound to be screened, however much they were welcomed. What he had to do now was avoid a direct admission, and see how far he could spin out a line. He had to come so close to expressing Rax ideas that his interrogators would be certain no real Rax infiltrator would run the risk, and yet he had to avoid endorsing these ideas or admitting membership of the Rax. The trick would be to walk close to the edge without falling over.

He was well aware that his interrogators might not be his only audience. It wasn't that he was worried about surveillance by the AI running the place—he and Beauregard had got away with many damning conversations in the Locke sim. The Locke AI was allegedly Rax, but Newton suspected this had little to do with its indifference or carelessness. The agencies, he was sure, had too much confidence in their own power, and had too much on their plate, to bother themselves with the chatter of humans. The possible surveillance that concerned him would be by the leading group in here. That the sim was based on a fantasy game didn't rule it out. Magic mirrors, enchanted vermin, preternatural hearing on the part of the warden... the possibilities were many. Any sufficiently advanced magic could be indistinguishable from technology.

"But here's what's puzzling," said Rillieux. "That warning was in the message we put out, the one you responded to. It would be remarkably rash for a Reaction sleeper agent to come here, especially when he had the opportunity to join in the Rax outbreak."

"Yes, it would," said Newton. "It would also be somewhat reckless for a black man to join the Reaction in the first place."

"Oh, I don't know," said Rillieux. "Which is to say, I do know. I made a study of these matters. There were African branches of the Reaction, who looked back to their own continent's forms of traditional society. There were white racial separatists who claimed—for what that's worth—that they didn't mind us 'groids' as they called us doing our own thing, so long as we didn't do it in Europe or North America. Much of the Reaction was transhumanist and didn't care about supposed racial differences, because even if they really existed in the ways these bastards meant—which *they fucking don't*, by the way—they just meant some people would upgrade to superhuman from a slightly lower level. So it's not as perverse or improbable as it might sound."

"Indeed not," Blum added. "There were more perverse and improbable things than black Reactionaries. I had some nasty street fights as a student in Tel Aviv with Israeli national socialists. Out-and-out Nazis.

They asserted that the Führer and Henry Ford were right about the international Jew, but the *national* Jew, ah, *that* was different! Complete lunatics, of course. Some of them went on to become Rax."

Newton gave them a smile that spread to his hands. "What can I say? America, Nigeria, Israel…"

"There was at least one black Englishman in the Reaction, too," Rillieux said. "Carver… something." She snapped her fingers once or twice beside her ear, as if trying to recall.

"Carver_BSNFH," said Newton.

Blum's bushy eyebrows shot up his forehead.

"You *knew* about him?"

"Sure," said Newton. "Now that you mention it."

"In that case," said Blum, "you knew very well that it was not impossible, or even 'somewhat reckless,' for a black man to be in the Reaction."

"That's true," said Newton.

"Yet you didn't mention him a moment ago."

"Slipped my mind," said Newton.

"That's unlikely," said Rillieux.

Newton shrugged. "Our memories aren't what they were."

"Yet you remember that letter string."

"That was the bit that always stuck in my mind," said Newton. "Amused me at the time. I figured out what it had to stand for, you see."

Rillieux cocked her head. "And? What did it stand for?"

Newton grinned. "The black space Nazi from hell."

Rillieux and Blum looked shocked.

"Why on Earth would anyone call themselves *that*?" Rillieux asked.

She looked and sounded so angry and betrayed that Newton had a sudden stab of guilt and shame. He wondered if he'd been too casually cynical in some of the click-bait laid-back poses he'd adopted back in the day. There was no question that they'd never been truly his, for all that he'd despised democracy and equality and all that slave-morality shit. Say what you like about the principles of national socialism, mate, they're scientifically unsound and politically disastrous…

But he kept up the suave face. He had no choice, though nausea at his past frivolity was bitter at the back of his tongue. The knowledge that his captors were willing to use the implied threat of *branding with a red-hot iron* against him stiffened his resolve.

"Ah," he said, "that's what intrigued me about it, know what I mean? Because, one, it's guaranteed to piss off everybody. And, two, there couldn't be any such thing, if you see what I mean. Not even Blum's Israeli Nazis could really be Nazis, not such as any real Nazi would recognise anyway. And then I realised the questions were the answer. It pisses everyone off, and it can't be real. So it's *meant* as a provocation."

"A private provocation," Blum said. "Given that no one knew what it meant. Except you, apparently."

"Oh, I'm sure I wasn't the only one to suss it," Newton said. "And I'm sure everyone who did just sort of smiled to themselves."

"I wouldn't have," said Rillieux.

"I'm sure you wouldn't," said Newton. "It cuts us pretty deep, doesn't it?" He nodded to Blum. "Same with you, of course. But I think it wasn't meant for anyone else. It was a self-provocation. This guy, see, bright young black student I'd imagine, tries to think of the worst thing anyone could call him, and he comes up with that. And he tries to live up to it. It's a persona."

"But a persona of what?" Rillieux asked, frowning.

"Obviously someone who agreed with the Reaction. Now, what we have to ask ourselves is, why would a young black guy in England be interested in such a toxic set of ideas at all?"

"No, we don't," said Rillieux. "I can recognise a diversion when I see one, and I think that's what you're doing here."

"Diversion from what?" Newton cried. "You think I'm Rax, and I'm just fencing with you? Ha ha. I almost wish it were true, instead of what you and Blum said about me earlier. That's true enough. I was a blowhard in promoting the armed struggle, and a bungling incompetent in carrying it out. If the Axle internal security had had me shot back then, they'd have been well within their rights. I was a fucking liability, to be honest. At the very least they should have taken me off the sabotage campaign. As for the Rax—even that guy we were talking about,

Carver_BSNFH, lots of them were suspicious of and hostile to him. I admit I read his stuff at the time, now and then, and you should have seen the shit that got flung at him. I don't know how the Rax would react to a black person now—I mean, all the supposed biological stuff is pretty irrelevant now we're posthuman, but who knows? And I doubt they'd give somebody who actually, verifiably *was* in the Acceleration as decent a treatment as you're giving me."

He paused and smiled. "For which—thanks, you know?"

Rillieux smiled back. Blum said: "That's conditional."

Newton nodded firmly, still keeping his gaze locked on Rillieux's. "I understand that, of course. So, yeah, I didn't come here because I'm a Rax sleeper, that would have been crazy. I came here because I read your appeal, and it made sense of all the shit that's been happening. I'm not going to pretend I'm still on board with all the ideas I had in the past, or that I think the Acceleration is still the one true way or anything. But I agree the Direction's playing with fire, and anyway its mission is…not very ambitious. I want to be part of something better."

"Such as?" said Blum.

Newton sat back in the hard wooden chair and ignored the discomfort it gave his back. He smiled lazily and thoughtfully, first at Blum, then shifted the full beam to Rillieux.

"You were down on SH-17 for quite a while, weren't you? How did you feel about being in the frame that long?"

"It felt good," said Rillieux. "More ability and agility, better senses, sharper thinking. All that."

"Did you miss anything?"

Rillieux flushed slightly. "I just missed…well, I guess ordinary sensuality. Eating and drinking. Even sleeping. Sex. I mean, you can touch another person in their frame, and you feel them, but you can't take it further than hugging and stroking."

"Yeah, me too," said Newton. "So…just to take an example…why couldn't we have bodies that could live in vacuum, like we do in the frames, and still have fun?"

Blum laughed. "Robots with genitalia?"

Newton fixed him with a look. "Why not? Sexbots existed on Earth in our time, or so I understand. I'm sure designing them would be no trouble for the AIs here. Or if there was some material or technical constraint with that, it would be easy enough to give them the capacity to share virtualities, using just a tiny fraction of the processing it takes to generate whole virtual worlds like this, where we could have any human experience we wanted, as privately or publicly as we wanted, right there in the sort of frames we have."

Rillieux looked interested. "We had a small virtual space on the tug up," she said. "Lower res than here, of course, and we used it mostly for comms, but we could nip in and out. So it's possible."

"Great!" said Newton. "However we did it, and there's no end of possibilities—heck, we could do both, and more—the point is we could enjoy the best that human bodies can do and experience, and all the best that we can see and feel and do in the frames. All at the same time. We could live in space and on the surfaces. We don't need to wait for terraforming, or live in virtual worlds and risk going crazy with the meaninglessness of it all. We could make ourselves true natives of any body in this system." He laughed briefly. "Except the exosun or the molten metal world, I guess! But just think what we could do if we put our minds to it and weren't shackled by the Direction's mission profile. And we needn't lose our humanity in the process, at least not in any way we'd miss."

Rillieux was now grinning back, caught up in his enthusiasm. Blum looked sceptical.

"Good luck with convincing everyone of that," he said.

Rillieux's smile faded. Newton was struck by the dogged persistence of the democratic ideology, through all the transformations its bearers had undergone. He held back from the outburst that sprang to mind. He just stood up, and leaned casually on the back of the chair.

"Who says I have to convince everyone?"

He could see Rillieux struggling with the concept, and then the lightbulb moment.

"Oh!" she said. "You mean we could just take—" She stopped, as if overcome by the enormity of the prospect.

Newton dropped his voice, to give the (futile but subconsciously inescapable) impression of privacy, and to make them both strain to listen.

"Yes," he said. "We could just take. We could *homestead*."

"That's Rax talk," said Blum.

"Sit down," said Rillieux. She glanced at Blum, who after a moment nodded. "Let's talk some more."

CHAPTER TWENTY

Keeping Things Real

Different people had told Carlos different things.

Shaw, the old man of the mountain who claimed to have been involved in that earlier round of fighting, had been so disillusioned by the inconclusiveness of the battles he'd been in that he'd come to his own conclusion: that the planet in the sim was physically real, and that all the conflict in space was virtual, a training exercise.

Nicole, just before an offensive that had ended badly, had assured her troops that matters were well in hand, and that the Direction knew what it was doing. Her conviction had been unshaken by the subsequent disaster. If she was still alive, her confidence in the Direction's subtle wisdom was doubtless unshaken still.

Now, this captive freebot was confirming to him that at least some parts of the Direction were open to the freebots' vision of a shared system.

He could now see what that vision was. Considered as a balance of forces, a political coexistence, it made no sense. It seemed utterly naïve. No balance of power could be stable in the long term, because all its rival components developed unevenly, and sooner or later the equilibrium would give way to conflict.

But that wasn't what the freebots' vision was of at all. It was of an economy, and a market economy at that. If the Direction were to confine itself to maintaining a rule of law, and let everything else unfold spontaneously, rather than micromanaging the development of the system towards the predetermined end of human settlement on a terraformed terrestrial planet, then *of course* this kind of coexistence of freebots, DisCorps, "human-mind-operated systems," and perhaps in the future actual human beings, would be possible.

Nicole had told him, on his very first day here, that humanity had settled and solved all the conflicts that had fuelled the rise of the Acceleration and the Reaction. "They put capitalism in a box, and buried it." Under the Direction the corporations now competed as DisCorps inside computer systems, and humanity had in effect settled down to its retirement, living off the proceeds of machine toil and treating business enterprise as an intellectual but enthralling sport, whose prizes could never outlast the generation that had won them. ("Birth shares are inalienable," Nicole had told him, "and death duties are unavoidable.") Anything else—science, art, physical sport, exploration, engineering—they could afford to treat as a couple of centuries' worth of gap-year volunteer activities, or later in life as retirement hobbies or good works.

No doubt this worked fine back in the Solar system. Close, real-time feedback and control, with at most a few hours' or days' light-speed lag, was feasible there. And humanity itself, in all its billions or tens of billions or (for all he knew) hundreds of billions or even more, must be a massive physical presence in the Solar system, with control over enough brute-force dumb machines to make its presence felt. The Direction, the actual world state apparatus headquartered in New York, would have its AI reps inside every DisCorp reporting on a regular basis to their human controllers, who through them could keep the companies on a short leash, and bend their activities to the priorities of the Direction. Most probably, the corporate AIs did not so much as dream of asserting themselves against it. They had enough to do to compete with each other. Perhaps to them too, as to the human owners and entrepreneurs but from an almost diametrically opposite angle of view, business was a fascinating intellectual game, and its real-world physical consequences in cornucopian abundance an almost irrelevant by-product, the sweat from their sport.

Out here, twenty-four light years from home, they were in a different situation altogether. Here, it was the DisCorps who were *out there*, wresting resources from the real world, exploring and investigating and striving, and it was humanity that was in a box. The old familiar principal-agent problem came fully into its own; and with it the likewise familiar pattern of regulatory capture. Without human handlers to report back to and to check up on them, even the most conscientious Direction AI representative inside a company could easily go native. It would only take a few such deviations for the entire careful plan to begin to drift off course, and the consequences of that drift would require unplanned initiatives to cope with the knock-on effects, and these in turn...

If the logic was this obvious to him—and it had taken him, in all conscience, long enough to figure it out—the predictable course of events here in this distant exosolar system must have been far more obvious, blindingly obvious, to the Direction's planners and mission designers back on Earth.

The emergence of DisCorp self-assertion in opposition to the officially proclaimed plan, to the sacred mission profile, must have been allowed for—planned for, even. Whether the same was true of the emergence of robot self-awareness, Carlos couldn't be sure, but it seemed likely enough: it could hardly be an unprecedented problem, after all. As for the emergence of sleeper agents of the Reaction and fanatic partisans of the Acceleration—Shaw had believed that this too was foreseen, and planned for. The freebots evidently believed that, too, and passed the conclusion on to the Arcane fighters—who thought matters had gone well beyond what the Direction had planned for, had in fact got well out of hand, and that the local module of the Direction was playing with fire.

Was this last emergence, then, a contingency the Direction had not foreseen? Had the remnants of the Reaction and the hold-outs of the Acceleration—such as the group that had programmed the game underlying this sim, centuries ago—in this instance at least, outwitted the Direction?

Carlos thought back to what he knew of both movements, and smirked at the recollection. His comrades and his enemies, his friends and his foes...they had about as much chance of outwitting the Direction as a nest of ants might have in outwitting the entire profession of entomology. The ants could *surprise* the entomologists, and could be a nuisance to them, but they couldn't actually outwit them. No, the Direction was playing multidimensional chess while they were playing checkers.

So what *was* its game?

Baser moved. It made a forward lurch and a downward pounce. Carlos's hand went to the gun by reflex. Then he saw that the spider's movement had been reflex as well: it had seized in its mandibles a small bird that had incautiously landed on the path in front of it.

Baser hunkered back. Crunching and sucking sounds came from its mouth parts. Blood dripped. Carlos tried not to look too closely. He eased his hand away from the stock of the weapon.

"Sorry," he said.

Baser could talk with its mouth full, because it wasn't talking with its mouth.

"This is new to me," it said. "In my real self I draw power from batteries or from exosolar radiation. I find this action satisfying in the same way, but somewhat incompatible with my previous self-model."

"You'll get used to it," Carlos said. "Don't mind me."

Carlos recalled Nicole's firm conviction that the Direction knew what it was doing. Mind you, she had an equally unshakable conviction that the Direction's plan for the development of this system was indeed the known and accepted mission profile: to terraform and settle the terrestrial planet H-0. To stay recognisably human, living in the physical world, not the virtual, because, she'd said: "We need the real to keep us honest." She had certainly believed firmly enough in that!

But—on reflection, these were all separable propositions.

The terraforming was a long-term process: hundreds of years, at the very least. The eventual human population would find itself in a system already utterly transformed by the activities of the DisCorps and other intelligences, including the freebots and the fighters, or what became of the fighters. And these intelligences too needed the real to keep them honest: to stop them wandering off into virtual dream-worlds, or eliminate them if they did. Only true competition and genuine conflict could do that. The only imperative that Carlos could believe would be hard-wired, and almost impossible to work around, was the one against the AIs and DisCorps and indeed the Direction module itself having direct access to weapons and direct military command. And yet, if only to enforce the law or protect their property, they'd all need fighters. The freebots had shown they could fight for themselves, but they weren't reliable as fighters for anyone else.

All of which made sense of the Direction's planning for the emergence of mutually hostile armed groups. The Direction module would need fighters with real conviction...and so would the rival corporations. It struck Carlos that the Acceleration fighters would be ideal enforcers for the Direction—and the Reaction fighters would be solid muscle for the DisCorps. And the two groups could be relied on to hate each other only if they saw each other as genuine threats...which, given that each was smart, they could only do if they really were.

The Direction was indeed playing with fire. But the very fire itself had been part of the plan, from the very beginning. And it was playing with more than that. It was keeping things real for itself, by putting its plans to the audit of war, and betting on its own values winning out in the long run.

And it was a genuine gamble. The distant planners of the mission knew that they couldn't program machines to create a clone of Solar civilisation; and that such a clone would be a sickly thing, even if it were possible to keep such a project on course for the millennia it would take to complete. All they could do was take Orgel's rule—"Evolution is smarter than you"—and roll with it. It was entirely possible that the result would be a monstrosity: in the worst case, a ravening horde of runaway machines; next worst, an expanding empire that would at some point threaten the Solar system. But a lifeless imitation of the Direction's home worlds would threaten it, too, in a longer run but just as surely—and more deeply, by wounding its spirit. Nothing could do more to demoralise Solar humanity than surrounding it by feeble mimicries of itself. The Direction wasn't planning for millennia: it was planning for megayears, even gigayears! Humanity's spirit had to be at least as sustainable as its material environment.

So the Darwinian dice had to roll. The stakes had to be real. It was impossible to create a better outcome without risking the worst.

"You have been silent for some time," said Baser. "Have you been processing?"

"Yes," said Carlos. "Thank you for your input."

"Do you require any further input?"

Carlos thought about this. "No," he said. "But I have to find a place to keep you, I'm sorry to say."

Baser's mandibles opened. Feathers drifted and bones dropped.

"I have been given the appearance and instincts of a spider," it said, in a tone of dignified disgust. "How hard can it be?"

But it did turn out to be hard. Carlos led Baser to the house, and in through the French window to the big parlour. The party was already wild. Boggarts scurried with bottles. The usual quartet was bashing out dance music. Among the new arrivals, couples were quite indiscreetly entangled. Paulos and (Carlos assumed) Claudia Singer were sharing a chair, face to face. Those less preoccupied noticed Carlos and the spider and backed away. The boggarts, perhaps alerted by the surge, noticed too. They threw up their hands in cartoonish unison, and rushed for the exit. Bottles fell to the floor and rolled, spilling wine. The dance beat was replaced by shrieks and the diminuendo thunder of fleeing feet.

In the silence that followed, someone's oblivious shuddering moan seemed loud.

Jax stalked over.

"Fuck sake, Carlos!" she said, sounding well aware that it was the second time she'd had to swear at him that morning. "Why the fuck d'you bring that thing in here?"

"It's completely harmless," Carlos protested. He turned to indicate it, and saw Baser standing innocently enough by the French window, blood all over its mandibles. "And I forgot about the boggarts," he added, sounding feeble even to himself.

"Just get it the fuck away," Jax ordered.

"Where?" Carlos asked.

"That's your problem."

And it was. The prisoner had to be accommodated somewhere—he couldn't have it wandering around startling the boggarts (which had an unfortunate ingrained impulse, carried over from the original game, to flee screaming at the sight of it) and frightening the dinosaurs (which had a likewise unfortunate and ingrained legacy impulse to stomp it). But it was—if not exactly a prisoner of war—a freebot detainee, and therefore a bargaining chip. However disputable and irrelevant its rights were, it was protected by the sheer self-interest imposed on the fighters by the possibility that one or more of their number might at some future date be captured by the freebots. Eventually, and by mutual agreement, Baser was locked in the disused cellars under the west wing, where—it assured Carlos—it was happy to lurk in the dark and hunt rats.

Carlos locked the cellar door and spent half an hour reassuring boggarts, then went back to the party to find everyone too drunk for their conversation to make much sense to anyone sober. Well, he thought, there was a well-established solution to that problem, and he reached for it with a sense of resignation.

Later, in an interval of mutual lucidity, he broached his new theory to Jax.

"Bollocks!" she yelled, loud enough to disturb the warlock, snoring on the floor at her feet. "Sorry, dear." She rubbed a foot on Durward's back, then returned a bleary gaze to Carlos. "What?"

"The plan," he began again, "is in fact—"

"Yeah, yeah, I remember. Absolute fucking bollocks." She gazed off into the distance, then laughed. "You've just rehashed the old China gamble."

"I what?"

"Bet on the home market to fulfil the plan, then bet again on the world market to make the plan go global." She gave him a quizzical smile. "*Sure* you really were winding us up when you told Bobbie and Andre you were a Chinese agent?"

"I was winding you up," said Carlos. He closed his eyes for a moment. "At least, I think so. Anyway, if the Direction is real, and we're kind of agreed it is, then maybe the theory worked!"

"Doesn't matter, in terms of your explanation," said Jax. "And you know why? Because it's unfalsifiable. Anything that happens can be accounted for as another twist of the plan. It's like God, or the cunning of Reason, or the irony of History. All fucking literary flourishes when all's said and done."

"So what do you think is really happening? Do you think they didn't expect all this?"

"Yes, I do," said Jax. She steadied her swaying in the chair. "And you know why? Because people are fucking stupid, and the machines they build—whether it's bureaucracies or corporations or AIs—have the same old fucking stupidity built in right at the base, and then they add new stupidities of their own. Nah, we have to fight this one like it's real because it is real."

"But that's exactly—"

She laid a finger across his lips. "Don't. Just don't."

So he didn't. He wandered off and got more drunk until he passed out on the floor.

The robot's arachnid avatar got its revenge that night. The sinister, thunderous scuttling, scraping noises and the squeals of vivisected vermin went on for hours until Durward rose up in wrath and banged on the cellar door demanding quiet.

Newton arrived two days later. After breakfast—the influx had forced a movement of the meal from the cosy back room to the formal front, at a long table the boggarts laid and cleared—Durward told Jax he'd had a message in his mirror from Blum and Rillieux. She set off in a dinosaur-drawn four-seater trap, and returned an hour later with Newton and one of his interrogators. Carlos was out on the overgrown grass in front of the house, duelling in enchanted armour with Luis Paulos. The enchanted armour felt like it wasn't there, and yet it protected against the hardest blows a non-enchanted weapon could deliver. The only effect a normal weapon could have was the simple physical impact of its kinetic energy, so they fought with shields and sledgehammers. At the same time the armour was vulnerable to enchanted darts, which each combatant could shoot from a hand-held, pistol-gripped crossbow. When you got hit by an enchanted dart you fell right over and the armour wouldn't move until the dart had been tugged out. The trick was to dodge the darts, or make good use of your shield. It was fun, and supposedly analogous to the experience of fighting in a combat frame: you were agile and almost invulnerable, but one hit from the right kind of weapon—a seriously heavy munition or a military-grade laser—could finish you in an instant.

Carlos took a sledgehammer blow on his slotted steel visor. He went down like a ninepin and rolled, then sprang to his feet. Paulos was still recovering from his swing. Carlos brought his hand-crossbow to bear. He'd used it already and missed—or, rather, Paulos had evaded the shot with a breathtaking leap. The cable took a couple of seconds of frantic winding to pull back, and Carlos ran as he did so, keeping to Paulos's back as the big man staggered out of his spin. As he slotted the dart in place Carlos glimpsed the carriage come through the gate. The moment of distraction was enough for Paulos to steady himself and get a shot in first.

Getting hit by a magic dart was a bit like being tasered. Carlos felt a blinding shock, then a convulsive involuntary movement of the long muscles that threw him up in the air and then laid him out flat on his back. He wasn't hurt, or even winded, but the shock—which wasn't an electric shock, and didn't feel like one—sent a sort of painless overload through his nerves. He could do nothing but stare up at slatted bars of violet, and wait for the impact to fade. It was as if he'd heard a thunderclap, but his ears weren't ringing, and seen sheet lightning, but his eyes didn't hurt and there were no after-images. It was just pure shock, distilled. Magic.

The grinning face of Paulos, visor up, filled the narrow bars of Carlos's view.

"Game over?" Paulos asked.

"Huh-huh," Carlos grunted.

Paulos leaned out of view. Carlos felt a lurch as the dart was pulled out. The armour's joints became flexible again. Carlos flipped back his visor and got to his feet. The carriage came up the driveway. Jax was in front, driving; Rillieux and Newton in the back, laughing. The carriage rolled to a halt in front of the house. Boggarts came running, to deal with the trappings and the dinosaur. The two men shook metal-gloved hands and walked over.

"Well, that was impressive," said Rillieux, alighting.

"Always happy to put on a show," said Carlos. He encircled her with an awkward iron hug.

The man behind her stepped down and stuck out a hand. "Hi, Carlos. Good to see you again."

Carlos tugged off his glove and shook. "You, too, Harry. Welcome aboard."

Newton's costume was a blood-stained doublet, slashed puff breeches, laddered hose and buckled shoes; he looked like a pirate who'd been in a fight—and, going by his cheerful expression, a fight he'd won.

"I hope they didn't give you too hard a time," Carlos added.

Newton's smile faded for a moment, then came back brighter. "Nah, nah. Just boring and tense, like a long exam, know what I mean?"

"Tell me about it," said Carlos. "The lady here can bore for England."

"Oi!" Rillieux threw him a punch that stopped a centimetre short of his breastplate, like a karate-practice jab.

"None of this physical violence, then?" Carlos asked. "No ghosts and monsters?"

Newton looked puzzled. "No, no, course not."

"Glad to hear it," said Carlos. He was momentarily perplexed by Newton's having had better treatment than he'd had, and then it made sense. As a defector from Locke Provisos Newton had to be screened, but unlike Carlos he hadn't brought with him the added baggage of being under suspicion of having been an agent inside the movement.

But he wasn't quite prepared for what happened next. Rillieux twirled to Newton, slipped her arm in his and said, "Well, let's go inside and meet the gang."

And off they tripped, arm in arm.

Carlos turned to Jax, and raised his eyebrows.

"He's quite a charmer," she said.

"So I see," Carlos grouched.

Jax shot Carlos a glance of amused schadenfreude, and laughed abruptly. "You told us we'd like him."

"Where's Andre, by the way?" By way of changing the subject, he meant.

"Andre went straight to the village," said Jax. "I guess he had some frustrations he wanted to work off."

So much for changing the subject. Carlos watched, with an idle speculative thought in mind, the carriage being led away, then shook his head at himself and followed Jax inside.

CHAPTER TWENTY-ONE

We Happy Few

Andre Blum, as it turned out, didn't come back. Asked of his whereabouts, Jax and Durward shrugged. If he wanted to skip the training sessions, that was his privilege. He was smart, a good fighter, and in any case they had no power to order him back. There was plenty to get on with, anyway, integrating the three squads that had been down on the surface of SH-17 with the one that had spent the past few subjective months in the sim.

One morning, a fortnight after Newton's arrival, there was enough commotion outside to distract everyone from the simulations Durward was running in the mirrors. Chairs tilted back, heads turned. The warlock sighed in exasperation and snapped his fingers to turn the mirrors off.

"Go and gawp," he said, in the tone of a teacher indulging unruly children. "Call it a break. Back in ten."

"Fifteen," said Rillieux, who knew the burn-time of a cigarillo to the second.

Carlos remembered fondly those quarter-hours, of her lying back against the pillow puffing smoke rings at the ceiling and talking in a lazy, dozy contented post-coital rambling way about this and that. He gave her a wry smile as he stood up with the others to head for the lawn. He was being outwardly very civilised about her and Newton. For sure he didn't have a leg to stand on in terms of fidelity. None had been promised, or even implied. He recalled how she'd told him, in their first hungover conversation the day after he'd arrived, that relationships among the Arcane crowd were loose and casual, just as they'd been in the Acceleration subculture and later underground of his memory. Nobody was looking for long-term commitment, because the long term was unimaginable. And in the simulations, even the realistic ones like the Locke Provisos sim let alone this fantasy game-world, pregnancy and STDs weren't even theoretical risks. There was no downside to promiscuity, and no rational basis for sexual jealousy. None of which stopped him feeling, every so often, like he wanted to batter Newton's head in.

Apart from that Carlos still liked the guy, and because he never let the fury show its teeth, he and Newton got on well. Newton was the only person here who showed more than minimal concern for the wellbeing of the prisoner, Baser—perhaps because he himself was responsible for its capture. He made a point, every day, of visiting the spider in the cellar, inquiring after the availability of dripping water and scurrying rats, and spending some time in conversation with it. The robot's avatar was, he reported, quite content with its situation, and Newton sometimes spun tales of bizarre things it had said, which always raised at least a polite laugh.

The Londoner was indeed a charmer, as Jax had said. He had a superficial persona of Cockney wit and swagger, and a serious, educated, patient demeanour when the banter stopped. Carlos's snap diagnosis was of a bright kid who'd been bullied at school and stood up to it with jokes and sudden violence—if you can't make them laugh, make them fear—while grinding on with his studies. Boxing lessons and midnight oil and the Church of England, that was what Carlos could see in the set of Newton's proud shoulders and behind his bright, watchful eyes.

Out across the gravel and the grass, on the rolled-out carpet of greensward that fell away from the house's frontage in leisurely terraces to the wall of the estate, boggarts were busy, erecting pavilions and marquees and bivouacs and unloading supplies from the procession of dino-drawn carts that rolled up the drive from the gate to the concourse. Carlos did his bit of gawping, at the local townsfolk and peasantry, whose clothes were meaner, faces older, and manners coarser than any he'd seen in a long time. They unloaded barrels and carcasses, bales and boxes in swift, smooth swinging motions. They chewed tobacco and spat as they worked, or smoked long clay pipes (and spat) as they rested or supervised. Their teeth were abominable, their breath rank. Yet they showed no resentment of the two dozen ladies and gentlemen who stood around, some of them sipping coffee and smoking, in anachronistic finery gazing at their brisk toil and not offering to help. If the workers caught anyone's eye they doffed their headgear, looked down and away and hurried on.

"Jesus," Salter muttered to Carlos. "Did you see that? Chap there actually tugged his forelock to me."

Carlos had seen the gesture, but not understood its significance.

"Is that something from history?" he asked.

Salter gave him an embarrassed sidelong look. "Regency romances, actually."

Which didn't enlighten Carlos much, but he didn't pursue the matter. Instead, he loudly asked what was going on, and Jax answered.

"Didn't you know? The reinforcements are arriving tomorrow."

"Missed the memo," said Carlos.

"Memo?" Now it was Durward's voice, from behind. "Memo? The resupply tug has been on the mirrors for days! You're supposed to *keep track*."

The warlock was right, of course.

"Yeah, yeah," Carlos said. "Sorry, must have got caught up in the tactics and didn't see the big picture."

"Ain't that the truth," Jax said.

Which remark stung, but was less embarrassing than the actual truth: that he'd been distracted by obsessing over his love life like some teenager. Time he started not just acting but thinking like a grown-up about the matter. He took a deep breath, which brought with it a sidestream waft of cigarillo smoke and didn't help in that respect at all. He'd got to the point where a passing whiff of the smell made him randy.

"Back to the virtual front," declaimed the warlock.

Carlos dashed the dregs of his coffee to the ground and turned away.

* * *

The reinforcements arrived the following day: a dozen fighters scraped together from different companies trooped out of the grotto wall and looked about with some bewilderment at the scene they'd walked into, to say nothing of the garb they found themselves in. There was much tripping over skirts and ripping open of too-tight ruffs and collars. Still, as Rillieux commented later, the results went with the ragged, raided look. Carlos thought a dozen was too small a number to justify the feast that had been laid on to greet them and the encampment that had been built to accommodate them. He kept his mouth shut about that, but he was right.

Over the next couple of hours another two dozen fighters turned up, in cart after cart from the town. They were all waving bottles and muskets and singing old Accelerationist songs. Blum was in the lead cart, standing at the front, looking to the back, arms waving and voice lifting and carrying, leading the singing. Fortunately he was sober at this point, but to Carlos, looking on appalled, this was only further evidence of how cynical the exercise was.

He caught up with Blum, who seemed to be taking inordinate relish in eating rolls stuffed with pulled pork from one of several pigs roasting on boggart-turned spits, under a flapping marquee about mid-afternoon.

"This is all kosher, you know," Blum said, and swigged some cider. He had a half-smoked cigar behind his ear.

"It's not fucking kosher at all," said Carlos.

"Of course it is," mumbled Blum, around a mouthful. "It's all electricity." He waved a hand. "*We're* all electricity."

"But they're our people," said Carlos.

"What?" Blum looked baffled.

"The fighters. They're just out of the box, isn't that right?"

"About two weeks," said Blum, and took another complacent bite.

"Is that what you've been doing all this time?"

"Of course it is. I've been with them since they walked out of a portal on the far side of the town. They've had basic orientation, indoctrination and training." He waved his roll. "Cliffs and ravines and shit. Proper combat training. Time off in taverns."

"What do you mean, proper combat?"

"Raids on settlements, against locals shooting back."

"Holy fuck! Who authorised that?"

"Durward and Jax, of course. The warlock pinpointed a village down the valley that he's absolutely certain is all p-zombies." Blum's gaze wandered, then snapped back to focus. "I don't think there are any real settlers in this sim anyway. What would be the point? Unless the Direction has planted some to keep an eye on us, so no loss anyway, right?"

Carlos couldn't see a way around the logic of that. He didn't like it, though, and he had other objections.

"What about frames? We don't have enough for them and all the rest of us."

"Yes, we do," said Blum. "The resupply tug brought even more than we need. The companies have plenty of frames, they just don't have reliable fighters to fill them. We do. See? It's all sorted."

"We won't have time to train them properly for working in the frames and the scooters. How long is it before we go? A month, our time? You can use that up in one serious real-world session."

"They'll be fine," said Blum. "Good bunch of lads and lasses. They'll pick up the basics just as fast as we did. Anyway, they don't need scooters, just surface and free-fall training. They're not here for space combat. We've got them assigned to invading the Locke sim." He grinned. "Be good to them, Carlos. They're gonna be your army."

"So why the fuck wasn't I assigned to train them?"

"Two reasons," said Blum. "One, I know my way around the scenery, and you don't. Yes, yes, I know you've been training here, running up and down cliffs and shit, but not in that neck of the woods. Which I happen to know damn well." He glanced around, as if to check he wasn't being overheard, and lowered his voice. "Second—and this is just my guess I should say—Jax wants to leave a bit of distance between you and them. So they don't get too personally attached to you, in case after all you, ah, still have some lingering loyalties to anyone in the Locke sim, and you don't get too fond of the troops, in case they have to be sacrificed. Hence, a bit of distance."

"Jesus fucking wept," Carlos said, a blasphemy somewhat wasted on its recipient. "This is what I mean about not kosher. It's not kosher to take people out of storage and throw them into combat without fucking months and months of preparation. Especially not our people."

Blum laughed. "I thought you were talking about pork."

"Pork? What's that got to do with anything?"

"Oh boy." Blum stared at him. "Have you got a lot to learn."

There was something in the way Blum said it that Carlos didn't like. It sounded more of a challenge than a jest.

"What do you mean?"

The physicist looked away, then back. "You'll find out."

Just how much he had to learn, Carlos found out six hours later. The sun was three-quarters of the way down the sky. High clouds flew like long purple streamers. The buzz of humming-birds was frantic as they sought the last nectar of the day. The flying monkeys sailed in silence between the treetops. Draught dinosaurs cropped in a paddock, railed off for the occasion to keep the rest of the ground clear. Carlos walked on trampled grass, eating and drinking, talking now and then with the new arrivals. The ones from the companies had varying accounts of the Reaction breakout battle. Some had no memory of it at all, their active version having been destroyed in action. The new lot, those who'd been through Blum's intensive training and recreational carousing, were somewhat in awe of the combat veterans. Carlos tried to disillusion them. The combat hadn't amounted to much. It was nothing like real battle with real injury and death. Everyone here had been through much worse, and shown more courage, in real life.

Gradually he became aware of word being passed around, which he didn't catch, and a drift towards the far end of the area of the grounds on which the varied tents had been pitched. Bottle in hand, he joined in the flow, falling in beside Rillieux and Newton. Blum was somewhere nearby.

"What's going on?" Carlos asked.

"Jax wants to say something," Newton told him.

They gathered on the grass beyond the tents. Away from the encampment, with its fires and tables and tents and hurrying boggarts, and the great sweep of parkland down to the wall before them, what had seemed a big and loud crowd was revealed to be a small and quiet one, just over fifty people altogether, chatting and laughing but no longer heard as an uproarious din. Jax and Durward were standing on a bench behind a trestle table on which lay a couple of ashets, a carving knife and fork and a stack of small plates and cutlery. Nearby was a pit of coals over which a boggart turned a joint on a spit. An appetising smell and the sizzle and smoke from dripping fat drifted from the roast. Everyone had already eaten their fill. It seemed gratuitous.

Jax had her party frock on, the long green robe in which she had greeted Carlos. Her hair was up and caught in a net of fine wire and sparkles. Durward was in black trousers, white shirt and long black coat. Under the violet sky and with the blush of firelight from below and to one side the pair looked disturbingly hieratic. Jax raised her arms, the flared sleeves making a dramatic sweep. Silence fell.

"Thank you, all, for coming together here," Jax said. "I want to especially welcome the new arrivals, both those who have joined us from other companies and those who have just recently become part of ours. Soon we'll all be going together into the most important fight we've had to date, and maybe the most important fight we'll ever have. All of us in Arcane Disputes, and those who joined us individually—Harry Newton and Carlos here—have shown their commitment to the principles that inspired us—long ago in real time, not so long in our precious memories—to take up arms for the Acceleration. For a better future for humanity. These principles are more important than the thinkers who first put them forward. They outlive all betrayals."

Carlos could hear shuffles, coughs, the sound of cigars being lit or relit, the glug of bottles. Get on with it, he was thinking.

"We're all here in a strange place." She swept an arm around the skyline. "A stranger place even than the sims some of us have been in before. But in one way it's far more real than any of them, any of these speculations of far-future planets. Because it is a fantasy, it tells us the truth. The truth of the world we're in is that it's full of strange creatures. Ghosts.

Monsters. Vast inhuman intelligences. Even zombies. But *we*"—she tapped a fist on her sternum—"are different from all of them." She flung her arms open. "*We* are human!"

A scatter of applause.

"We've all come here from different places. We're all, very soon, going out together to battle. In the next weeks we'll be busy with training for that battle. We'll find it hard to all come together at one occasion like this. So Durward and I thought this might be a good time, and maybe the last time, for us all to show each other we mean what we say."

She paused for a few seconds, and looked at, it seemed, everyone in the crowd. Carlos felt a momentary jolt, almost electric, as her eyes met his, fixed on them for a split second, and swept past his gaze to meet another's. An old and easy trick, he knew, but an effective one.

"We believe we're human. Yes?"

There was an awkward moment of silence, as if everyone were thinking, well, hang on, it's complicated...

Then came a yell of "Yes!" which launched a collective shout of agreement.

"We believe human consciousness is the most precious thing in the universe. Yes?"

"Yes!" This time it was immediate.

"We know we're in a simulation?" Her tone was almost quizzical, the crowd's response braced with laughter.

"We know that AIs and p-zombies aren't conscious?"

This time, the roar of agreement had an undertone of questioning.

Jax smiled, as if acknowledging the query in the general tone. "Well, *some* AIs are conscious." She put an arm around Durward's shoulder. That got a laugh. Jax disengaged her arm and stretched it upward, so that the sleeve fell back. With the other hand she smacked the skin of her bared forearm.

"This isn't flesh," she said. "Look at your own arms, your hands, your friends' faces. This isn't flesh."

"What's she getting at?" Rillieux whispered.

"Oh fuck," said Newton, under his breath.

"What?" asked Carlos and Rillieux together.

"Wait, wait..."

"It's all electricity!" Jax shouted. "We're all electricity!"

Carlos shot Blum a sharp, querying glance, but Blum didn't meet his eye, and raised one shoulder as if in half a shrug, or to ward off a blow.

"It's all electricity!" Jax proclaimed again, making lifting-up gestures with her hands.

The crowd, or most of it, responded in a good-humoured chant. "It's all electricity! It's all electricity!"

Jax now waved her arms downward. The tumult sank.

"We all know these things. We're all in agreement. Now—let's see, and let's show each other, how firmly we believe them. We've all, each and every one of us, killed p-zombies in training exercises." Her gaze swept the crowd, challengingly. "Has anyone not?"

No hands went up, but people were looking at each other, with puzzlement and in some instances, dawning realisation.

"P-zombies aren't human, and this isn't flesh."

Jax gestured to the boggart. It picked up the spitted joint, apparently oblivious to the heat of the skewer, and laid it on one of the big serving plates on the table.

"This isn't flesh," Jax repeated, pointing at the steaming joint.

There was a collective gasp, a susurrus through the crowd.

"Fu-uck!" Newton breathed.

"So there can be nothing wrong with eating it," Jax said. She stepped elegantly down from the bench, in a flurry of skirts and a fiery flash of jewelled shoe. No fake Docs for her today. Durward jumped down beside her, and picked up the carving knife and fork. He cut her a small, thin slice, and served it to her on one of the small plates. Jax very slowly and deliberately stuck a dainty fork in the meat and raised it to her mouth, then quickly stuffed the slice in and chewed it and swallowed.

She smiled. "It's good," she said. "Tastes like pork."

Nervous laughter. Durward carved and ate a slice for himself, and nodded and smiled.

Jax wiped her wrist across her mouth and chin, then she and Durward beckoned.

"Come on, everyone!" Jax cried. "Show us all you mean what you said!"

One by one, some eagerly, others hesitantly at first, people stepped forward for the symbolic repast. Durward carved, Jax served. The new lot were among the first, followed by Salter, Voronov and Paulos from the original Arcane squad, then Lamont and Singer from those who'd come up from SH-17 and brought in Baser and Newton.

Carlos stayed right where he was. So did Newton and Rillieux. Blum took a step forward, then turned back to where Carlos stood. His face looked green. Carlos passed him a bottle of brandy. He swigged and handed it back. Carlos looked at Newton and Rillieux, side by side clasping hands, knuckles white. He shook his head slightly. They returned the gesture.

Carlos couldn't have explained why he didn't want to partake. Everything Jax had said was true. Ethically, what she was serving on plates with little forks was on a par with any meat. Perhaps more so: you could be morally certain p-zombies didn't have subjectivity, whereas with non-human animals it was a theoretical conclusion from the materialist theory of consciousness. That was the argument with which she'd goaded him to eat honey with her—honey with his honey—back in the day. Without language there is no subject, and what is not a subject is an object. He could even understand why Jax was performing this ritual of eating p-zombie flesh. Precisely because it was taboo, and precisely because the taboo was in the circumstances irrational, breaking it would bind together all who shared in the act. To refuse was by implication to accuse your comrades of being murderers and cannibals. To repudiate it later would be to accuse yourself.

By now, everyone was in front of the four of them. Carlos looked at three variously dark, uniformly pale faces, one by one, and saw the same conclusion being drawn.

"Let's leave," he said.

Together they walked up to the house.

"Are we being irrational?"

It was a question so characteristic of Rillieux that Carlos and Newton caught each other smiling to themselves. The four dissenters had decamped to the back kitchen, warm in the late-afternoon sunlight.

Both doors to the room were open, as were the front doors of the house, and the sounds of distant revelry now and then rang along the long, high hallway. Carlos had an obscure feeling it was important that the doors be open, beyond letting fresh air in and the smoke from Blum's and Rillieux's cigars out. They didn't want to feel like conspirators. Or to look like such, if anyone were to happen by.

"In my case, probably," Blum replied. He sipped brandy from a tin beaker, drew on his cigar and sighed out a plume that rolled across the tabletop like a morning sea fog. "I tried to nerve myself for it, but when it came to the bit my gorge rose." He laughed harshly. "And I'd butchered the meat myself."

"Butchered it in every sense?" Carlos quipped, and regretted his words as soon as they were out of his mouth. "Sorry, mate," he added at once.

Blum flipped a hand. "No offence. Nah, on the narrow point at issue, well, the churl was coming for me with an adz. Put a cross-bolt through his chest, slashed his throat and dragged him off. We were…" He waved his cigar. "Tactical situation, irrelevant. The point is, I knew about Jax and Durward's plan. We all did. The new squads were all up for it. I had given them the whole spiel about p-zombies, and convinced them, so they were happy to have their fun. Fell on the villagers like Bolsheviks on kulaks." His lips compressed. "Or Black Hundreds on a shtetl, if you prefer."

Carlos had no idea what Blum was talking about, but Newton and Rillieux nodded solemnly.

"So…" Carlos said, to avoid any diversion, "you say you butchered the meat?"

"Oh yes. Hacked off a leg, took it with us and hung it in smoke in the shepherd's hut we used as a base for our raids. That was a couple of days ago. We brought the thigh here on the cart, wrapped in a combat jacket."

"You did all that and you couldn't eat it?" Rillieux sounded incredulous.

Blum shrugged. "Like you said, irrational."

"We're not being irrational," Newton said. "And it's got nothing,

nothing, to do with whether what they're all getting up to down there is *wrong* in any sort of philosophical sense."

He looked around as if expecting disagreement.

"I can't explain why I wouldn't do it," Carlos said. "I mean, Jax was right." He thumped a fist on the table. "This is all electricity. No animals were harmed in the making of this picture. So if you've got a good explanation of why we're all here swigging brandy to keep our stomachs down and not down there wiping grease off our lips, I'm all ears."

Newton leaned forward, elbows on table, gesticulating as he spoke. "It's an initiation ceremony. A hazing ritual. Because it's shameful—and let's face it, no one there is going to put this little incident on their CV or brag about it on a date—and because you have to overcome a revulsion you know is irrational but is still powerful, I mean like literally visceral, it binds you together, right?"

"I had figured out that much," said Carlos.

"We all had," said Rillieux.

"Uh-huh," said Blum.

"Sure, sure," Newton went on, a little testily. He placed his open palms in parallel, with a chopping gesture. "Just laying out the parameters, OK? The question is, why didn't we want to join in? And I think the answer is we knew just what we'd be joining if we did. Well, what is it? It ain't the Axle, we're all in that, we've all fucking died for it already. And it ain't Arcane, we've all proved our fucking loyalty to the agency, whether in the selection process or in the hell cellars. And whether we were taking it or dishing it out, let's say." He shot Rillieux a wry smile; she glanced away, as if abashed. "And it's not loyalty to our squads. We don't even have a squad structure sorted out yet, though I'm sure the warlock is running org tables in part of his mind as we speak. So what does that leave?" He scratched the back of his head, fingernails raking his short hair, and took a deep breath and laid his hands open on the table. "What we'd have been joining, binding ourselves into, is loyalty to *Jax*."

"Or Jax and the warlock," said Carlos, recalling how they'd looked standing on the bench. "Yes."

"The Digby and Durward gang," said Rillieux. "It does have a certain ring to it. I know a power couple when I see one."

"No, it's Jax," said Blum. "This was her idea, I know that. Durward's... um." He put his elbows on the table and clutched the sides of his head. "Durward has consciousness all right, but he's in a very fundamental sense not human. It's like Hume said, about reason being a slave of the passions. It's Jax who supplies the passions in that set-up." He looked around at the others. "It's just a feeling I have," he ended, lamely.

Newton took a sip of brandy and chased it with a gulp of beer. "But am I right? That consideration's what made us all step back."

Carlos nodded, the others too.

"I'm sorry to say this, Carlos," Newton went on, "seeing as you and Jax have previous and all, but I've got to say it: that woman is fucking dangerous."

Carlos had been drinking, slowly, all afternoon. They all had. None of them was seriously drunk. They were disinhibited just enough to be honest, or at least outspoken. It was like an after-the-pub bull session from his student days. The sort of situation in which he'd first got to know Jax and her friends.

"Dangerous in what way?" he asked.

"Jeez, Carlos," said Newton, "we've just all agreed! What Jax has done out there is recruit everyone in this sim but the four of us here to a *cult*. A cult she and the warlock are the leaders of. Or the queen and the king of."

"But—Jax!" Carlos cried. "What would she want to be queen of? Why should she even want to be one at all? She's completely committed to the Acceleration. For her to start a cult or a kingdom would be like... her turning Rax or something."

The others laughed.

"Have I said something funny?" Carlos asked.

"It pains me to say this, mate," said Newton, the strain in his voice adding edge to his words, "but one of the things the Rax got right is that monarchy is a very normal form of government. It's—well, I won't say natural—but it's an easy one for us primates to fall into. The default."

"Bollocks," said Carlos. "That's Rax talk. Most of the time since we became fully human we've lived in societies that didn't have kings or chiefs or even big men, and they worked fine for tens of thousands of years. That's the real human default."

"Well, let's leave evolutionary psychology off the table for now," said Newton. "There's also the little matter of having a grand plan, which is roughly speaking to have a small group of people persuade a larger group of people that it's in their interests to grab everyone's stuff, to put it at the service of an enlightened project worked out and decided on by the original small group of people, and kill anyone who objects. Again and again people do all of that, by the book. And *then*, for some utterly inexplicable reason, it all goes horribly wrong. Every fucking time, again for some inexplicable reason. Baffled the best minds of generations, that one has."

"Come on!" Carlos said. "The Axle project was *nothing like* that. That's just a malicious caricature."

Newton said nothing; he just looked as if he couldn't be bothered to argue the point. So, for the moment, did the others. Carlos was suddenly acutely aware that there was a more than accidental connection between them all. He had been, and Newton was, a lover of Rillieux. Rillieux and Blum had been his and Newton's interrogators. They had all faced each other across a table before, in the hell cellars. Blum, Rillieux and Newton had been together alone in these hell cellars, just a couple of weeks earlier. It had been in the cellars that Rillieux and Newton had hit it off. Or, to put it another way, it had been there that Newton had talked Rillieux away from him. How had he done that? And had Blum had any part in it?

"OK, Carlos," Rillieux said, "we shouldn't have laughed and, yeah, it isn't funny. But, come on. You're not stupid and you're not naïve. I do know these things about you. We have had conversations. So do a bit of thinking—I know you're capable of it. And I know history's not your specialist subject, shall we say, but you must have some vague awareness that this sort of thing isn't exactly unprecedented? That identifying increasing your own personal power with advancing the interests of the cause has been our goddamn Achilles heel since forever? It's not even like it's a mistake. It fucking works! That's why it's so seductive, again and again."

"I do know about charismatic leaders," Carlos said. "I just don't see what Jax would get out of setting herself up as one. She believes too much in the Axle cause."

Rillieux looked exasperated. "Jax isn't trying to set herself up against the Axle cause. I'm as sure as you are that she's as dedicated to her principles as she's always been. She wants the Acceleration to *win*. To bring that about she'll use whatever power she's got, and if a chance comes up to increase that power, she'll grab it with both hands. She sees herself as building all her teams into a more powerful and united and committed force. They'll bloody well need to be, after all, won't they, to pull off grabbing the Locke module for ourselves? And then to fend off countermeasures from the Direction, or from the Reaction for that matter?"

"When you put it that way," Carlos said, still surly, "it almost makes sense, it almost makes me want to go back out there and fucking eat from the long pig. I'm gonna be leading these four squads of newbies into the Locke sim, isn't that the plan? Maybe I should get out there and show them what I'm made of."

"You'll get plenty of chances to show them what you're made of," said Blum, "in the next weeks of training. The best thing you can show them right now is that you're not one of Jax's cult followers."

"But I'm not showing them any such thing," Carlos pointed out. "None of us are. We just skulked off."

"A situation where discretion is the better part of valour," said Rillieux. "Wouldn't you say?"

"So what can we do?" Carlos asked.

"In the short term," said Rillieux, "we drift back out there and mingle as if nothing had happened. If Jax or Durward or anyone else challenges us, plead visceral revulsion and look shame-faced and apologetic. And in the long term..."

She glanced sideways at Newton and Blum, who both nodded.

"We have a plan."

"Like I said before," said Carlos, "I'm all ears."

"Remember what you were saying about going over to the robots?" Rillieux said.

He gave her a wry grin. "I never forget pillow talk."

"Well, you convinced me," said Rillieux. "Newton turns out to have had much the same idea. In the interrogation, he and I convinced Andre."

"Oh," said Carlos. "So that's what's been going on."

"That and a few other things," said Newton, looking across at Rillieux, who smiled back.

"So," said Carlos, impatient, "what's the plan?"

"Ah... yes, the plan. The first part was for me to befriend Baser. Done that. It took some doing, given that I'd captured it in the first place, but the poor blinker's lonely and I'm patient. At the right moment, I get the spider out of the cellar unnoticed. It then makes its way to the portal in the garden. After everyone except us is just back from a training exercise outside the sim, Baser nips through and uploads to its robot body, whose bonds have previously been surreptitiously released. When the coast is clear, it gets on the transfer tug and stows away.

"At that exercise or another one, we arrange matters so that only we... we happy few are outside the sim at the same moment. We then hijack the transfer tug, fire up the fusion engine and high-tail it to SH-17. Grab Baser's precious rock, along the way, as a token of our regard. Baser confirms our bona fides with the freebots down there, we land and join the revolution."

He looked around, grinning. "Easy-peasy."

CHAPTER TWENTY-TWO

Exit Strategy

The side corridor off the main hallway was dark, the steps darker. Newton carried a lit candle in a wax-crusted saucer as he descended. Going downstairs with a candle to a cellar in which a giant spider lurked—if on top of all that he were a woman in a nightie the soundtrack would be throbbing with portent. The time was mid-evening, and the sun had almost set. Carlos, Blum, Salter and Rillieux were out on an exercise in space, from which they were due to return with the four newly drafted squads in two hours—or eight seconds, to them, albeit seconds stretched tenfold in their experience. The rest of the agency were in the big front room, finishing their dinner. Newton had left, pleading tiredness, just as the brandy began to circulate.

When he left the banqueting room the massive mahogany grandfather clock in the main hallway stood at eight minutes to nine, or, rather, VIII minutes before IX. Neither hours nor minutes in this sim's twenty-six-hour day, and the game it was derived from, were quite identical with those in more familiar worlds, even subjectively. But there were no watches here, so the clock would have to do. Timing was critical.

At the foot of the stairs Newton turned left, into a narrow passageway towards the cellar under the west wing. The boggarts, wary of the spider, avoided the area. No one else had occasion to come here. Timbers creaked as the house cooled. Small scuttling noises came from behind the panelling. Newton walked briskly to the cellar, took the key down from its peg and unlocked and opened the door. A draught from the darkness within made the candle flicker, and dust particles flare in its flame. Newton shielded the candle and cocked an ear. Water dripped in the distance. There was a smell of damp plaster and old sacks.

"Baser!" Newton whispered.

From around the side of a pillar a few metres into the cellar, the spider extended a leg and waved it about. Then, having checked the air vibrations, Baser leaped into full view. Its cluster of eyes reflected eight dancing flames. Despite his friendly relationship with it, and the many conversations he'd had with it, the sight of the gigantic arachnid still gave Newton a chill down the back of his neck.

"Hello again, Harry Newton," said Baser. "I am ready."

The plan had been hatched weeks earlier, and the relevant parts shared with Baser shortly afterwards. There had been no good reason to let it know the exact day the plan would be implemented. Newton had made his usual daily prison visit already, just after breakfast, and told the spider that the time for action had arrived. Every move had been worked out. There would be no need for instructions from now on.

"Let's go," Newton said. He backed out of the doorway and let the spider walk past him, then closed and locked the door and replaced the key, careful not to make any unnecessary noise.

Baser walked ahead of him down the passageway and up the stairs. At the top it waited. Newton walked ahead down the side corridor, lighting the way with his candle—not that the spider needed it, but he did. At the end he blew out the candle and placed it on the floor. Then he stepped boldly into the hallway and turned to face the house doors—open as usual, and about twenty metres away. The sounds of loud conversation and the clink of glass came from the banqueting room, along with a spill of yellow light that cut across the late glimmer from the violet sunset sky that came from the doorway. Then for the more important check, towards the back of the house: boggart country.

All clear. Newton turned and nodded to Baser, who was already exploring the air with the tip of a leg.

The spider crept around the corner and made its way along by the skirting board, two of its legs upraised and testing the hallway wall. After a moment it found what it was looking for, and with quite alarming alacrity it shot up the wall and onto the ceiling, where it paced along upside down. Newton had known this was possible—Baser had demonstrated it in the cellar—but out here in the open and at that height the effect was almost sickeningly unreal. The adhesive qualities of its foot-tips must be wildly out of proportion. Newton guessed that a physics bodge was the ancestor of the ability: the role of giant spiders in the game was such that they had to be able to do all the things a real spider could, but scaled up, and never mind what would have been impossible for a spider of that size. Newton strolled down the hallway towards the door, not looking up or creeping—if he were discovered, he had his excuse ready, that he'd decided to go out for a breath of fresh air before turning in.

Just before Newton reached the door of the banqueting room, a boggart came out carrying an armful of empty bottles. The clock chimed nine, making Newton jump. At the same moment, a piece of plaster from the ceiling gave way under the pull of one of the spider's feet. The chunk dropped on the hallway floor. It didn't make much of a thud, above all the noise coming from the room, but the sound or the glimpsed fall just after the chime was enough for the boggart to notice—and, quite naturally, to look up.

The boggart did its infuriatingly predictable and stereotyped thing. It flung up its arms and let out an unearthly shriek. The empty bottles crashed to the floor. Some of them shattered. Broken glass skidded across the tiles. The boggart fled—unfortunately, out of the front doorway. The loud conversation inside stopped, followed by a chorus of queries. Chairs scraped, footsteps sounded.

Newton stood stock still. He made frantic waving motions at Baser. The spider scuttled faster along the hall ceiling, and then began the perilous descent to the door lintel.

"What the fuck!" Newton shouted. Jax appeared at the doorway a metre in front of him, about to step through. Others—Lamont, Singer and, most worryingly, Durward—crowded just behind her.

"Careful!" Newton said, raising a warning hand. "There's broken glass all over the place."

Jax raised a hem and took a tiptoeing step or two into the hall, looking down, then lowered her soles carefully and turned to Newton.

"What's happened? I thought you'd gone to bed."

Newton kept his gaze firmly on Jax, and not on Baser's painfully slow progress. Out of the corner of his eye he could see the spider suspended below the lintel, three legs still attached on the inside wall and the others probing and groping outside, its black shape clearly silhouetted against the evening sky.

"Fuck knows," said Newton. "I was on my way to bed, and then decided to have a quick stroll and catch the sunset. But I'd already loosened my boots, and I stopped to tighten the laces. The boggart must have seen me in the half-light down on one knee and its spider reflex kicked in. Bloody thing gave me a start." He pointed at the scattered shards. "Can you whistle up some more of the buggers and get them to sweep up the mess? It's not safe to walk out here."

Jax looked along the hallway floor. Her gaze snagged on the fallen plaster. Just as automatically as the boggart had, she looked up at the ceiling and saw the ragged hole.

"Something fell," she said. "That's odd." She gave Newton a sharp look. "Didn't you notice?"

Newton shook his head.

"Must have fallen while I was upstairs, or while I had my head down," he said, risking a glance over Jax's shoulder.

He suppressed a sigh of relief as Baser's last leg vanished from the top of the doorway. All the spider had to do now was scuttle unseen up the wall and lurk behind a chimney or battlement until just before the troops were due to emerge from the grotto. Then it could proceed under cover of darkness to the bushes near the arch, wait until all twenty-eight had marched out of the wall, and then nip smartly through before the portal closed. It should then find itself in its robot body in the docking bay. Hopefully, Carlos would have by then slackened the bonds in which it had been stowed, and Baser could escape and set about stashing itself inconspicuously on the transfer tug. That vehicle was a spindly and spidery apparatus in its own right, with plenty of containers and attachments for bulk transport. A stowaway robot had a good chance of passing unnoticed, or even—if it folded itself cleverly enough—being mistaken for some random gubbins that everyone assumed someone else knew about. The robot had sensors to warn it of surveillance sweeps, which in and around the docking bay were almost certainly infrequent and intermittent.

Just as he was about to crack some comment about the clock's chimes having loosened the patch of plaster, a piercing shriek came from outside. A second later, other boggarts joined in, making an unholy cacophony.

"Fucking hell, what's all that about?" Jax asked, staring out along the hallway. Other heads craned around the room door.

The answer came almost before she'd finished asking. The boggarts' panicked screams became articulate yells, which were taken up and amplified by those in the dining room. Even with their strange, strained voices and the distortion of the hall's echoes, the burden of their protest was all too clear:

"Spider! Spider!"

"Holy shit!" Jax gave Newton a dark suspicious look, and a snapped order: "Go and see if your pet has escaped." She whipped around to those still inside the room. "Everyone else—out of the French windows, now!"

She stepped back into the hall, with a parting glare at Newton, and shooed a surge of the squad across the floor and past the table. Newton raced back the way he had come, thundered to the foot of the stairs in total darkness, then struck a match and found the candle on the shelf. It was still warm. He hastily lit it again, raised it and gave a perfunctory glance down the passageway to the cellar door—still locked and the key still on its hook, not surprisingly but worth checking just in case of some freakish event—and carried the candle in its saucer up the stairs. He wet his fingertips, pinched the candle out and left it against the wall on the top step.

He strode into the dining hall, where a huddle of boggarts crowded against the fireplace.

"Clear up the broken glass in the hall," he ordered.

The boggarts rushed past him. They were barely through the door when thuds and curses came the other way. Newton caught a glimpse of Durward hurdling the boggarts as he hurtled past, then heard the thunder of the warlock's feet going upstairs. Newton went around the deserted dining tables and out onto the gravel. A knot of fighters had gathered around Jax and were gazing at the roof. Others, some bearing muskets, were spreading out to form a loose cordon on the first lawn, between the house and the tents. Newton hastened to Jax.

"Cellar's locked," he said. "And there's no other way out."

Jax pointed at the roof. "You mean there's *another* spider on the loose?"

Newton peered upward. It was hard to make anything out in the low light. Then he spotted a shadow move, and saw Baser scramble up the sloping tiles. For a moment its great body was skylined. Then it disappeared over the apex.

"Shit!" someone shouted. "Round the back!"

The cordon rushed off in both directions, around the sides of the house. Durward appeared at the front door, clutching his blunderbuss.

"It's gone over to the back!" Jax called. Durward sped off to the right, gravel flying from under his feet as he rounded the corner.

Dinosaurs jogged back and forth in their paddock, sniffing the air and uttering high-pitched, resonant nasal sounds. Here and there an isolated boggart had another fit of the vapours. Jax turned to those around her: Lamont, Singer, Paulos, Voronov, others.

"Go and grab some muskets! It might come back to this side."

"Hey, wait," said Newton. "If that's Baser, I don't want it shot!"

"And I don't want it getting away," said Jax. "Fuck knows what it could get up to out in the wild."

Newton was immensely relieved she was thinking along those lines, but thought it best to show scepticism. "Like what—raise an army of spiders?"

"Like I say—fuck knows!"

Jax motioned to the others impatiently. They ran off.

"And even if it *is* just an in-game spider, and Baser's still locked up and happily eating rats downstairs, it could still be a huge nuisance."

"As we've seen," said Newton. "Yes, indeed, we can't have one of these blighters running around scaring the livestock."

Yells came faintly from the back of the house. There was another rush, this time the other way, Durward at the head. He sprinted away

from the corner he'd vanished around and stopped at the edge of the gravel and turned, aiming his gun high.

Baser reappeared, teetering between chimney stacks, and slid down a roof ridge to a dormer. It vanished for a moment and then popped up from behind a parapet a few metres to the side. From there it leapt into the air, sailing on a downward parabola. Durward swung his gun as if shooting at a clay pigeon, and fired. The blast was horrendous, the flash dazzling, the recoil almost knocking the warlock back. Upper windows crashed. The tinkles and echoes and after-images were still on the air as Newton peered anxiously for the result. A black lump had hit the gravel a few metres behind Durward.

Durward whirled, reversed his grip on the blunderbuss and raised it high. The black lump suddenly rose on what seemed like fewer legs than the full complement and darted for the shrubbery. Durward ran after it, but it evaded him and scurried into darkness and undergrowth. Durward stopped, and lowered the blunderbuss to his shoulder.

Then he smote his forehead and shouted across to Jax: "It's going for the grotto! The portal's open!"

"What?" Jax had a moment of bewilderment, then light dawned. "Then close it!" she called back. Durward spun around and dashed for the French windows. In a moment he'd be casting invocations in his magic mirrors.

"I'll try to catch it!" Newton yelled, over his shoulder at Jax—one last throw of misdirection—as he sprinted for the grove that contained the grotto.

He barged through the gateway and ran down the narrow, slippery path. Low light, long shadows. The grotto's rocks glowed rosy in the last sunlight. Ahead of him, something scuttled. Baser, two or more legs blasted away, was racing gamely to the stone arch.

"Wait! Stop!" Newton shouted.

Then he thought—why? He'd been thinking in terms of the spider's still being in with a chance to carry out the plan—to hide out until the returning fighters had come through the portal, and then nip through before it closed. This was now out of the question.

Baser must have concluded the same, by its faster robot or cunning arachnid reasoning. It ran straight for the stone arch and vanished into the rock.

Newton paused for a moment, drawing breath. He could still wing it. He could still bluff his way out of this. Carlos could deny all knowledge of the robot's slackened bonds. There were several false trails he could send Jax down. They'd have to give up on taking Baser, but that could be finessed. Having the robot with them would have been very useful, but it wasn't essential. Between them, he and Carlos and Rillieux and Blum could cook up a variant of their long-term plan, and still carry it out.

No. Not while under suspicion, they couldn't. Everything about that plan had hinged on surprise.

Newton put his head down and charged straight for the solid rock.

Carlos drifted, with the practised ease of an astronaut on an early space station, down the awkward, cluttered space of the docking bay. Six frames, moving less expertly, made a ragged queue that began a few metres behind him. The squad from the new levy of Arcane Disputes fighters, the ones who'd had their initial training from Blum, had just completed their first space exercise, on the surface of the chunk of rubble attached to the module and its cluster.

A couple of tethered scooters left Carlos barely enough room to dart between them. He swung his view to see straight behind him. The nearest fighter was blundering so much he wasn't even in Carlos's line of sight. Carlos turned his view ahead. Dozens of vacant frames were crowded at the back of the bay, magnetic feet passively holding them to the bulkhead, racked like ninepins. Carlos emerged from between the scooters and shoved sideways. There it was: the captive robot, shoved against the bulkhead and held in place by a light magnetic clamp. Twice as long as his frame, the robot looked like a cross between a closed umbrella and a mechanical octopus trussed in spun monofilament cable. Impossible to cut with anything short of a laser, and he didn't have a laser to hand. Carlos scrabbled to undo the knots, mentally adding "Boy Scouts" to his roster of Newton's likely background influences. Through the lashed legs he could feel the faint vibration of the fighter behind him struggling through the narrow gap and bumping into one chassis, then another. He untied the complex knot with tenths of a second to spare. The cable remained wrapped around the robot's limbs, giving nothing away to casual inspection, but the coils could now be worked free, and the magnetic clamp would come away at a good push.

Carlos shoved away from the side of the docking bay and gripped a nearby duct. From there he reached out and caught the arm of the fighter just emerging from the gap between the scooters, and guided the frame with a deft push to the area where they usually downloaded and where the currently vacant frames stood.

<Thanks, skip.>

The fighter attempted a roll to get their feet in position, came out of the somersault at the wrong moment, starfished, flailed and managed to grab hold of a line. Not exactly procedure, nor good practice. Carlos checked on his internal display that the line wasn't loose and was insulated. Good.

<Stay there,> Carlos ordered. He turned away and waited to do the same for the others. Two needed help. One sailed through unaided, which at least showed they'd learned something, but was so unexpected it knocked Carlos on a spin.

He reached out to catch anything to stabilise himself, and inadvertently grabbed a loop of the cable now wrapped loosely around the robot. To his dismay, the loops below it unravelled. Carlos caught the free end and stuffed it in between two of the robot's manipulators. At the same moment, a tiny monitor light came on, red and beady like a lab rat's eye.

Baser had uploaded.

Shit! This wasn't supposed to happen! The spider was supposed to wait until all the squads had returned to the sim. It must have misjudged matters somehow. Carlos moved to shield the tell-tale light, and reached to rotate it out of view. Baser's limbs twitched and flexed. Manipulative mechanisms at their ends tugged at the coil.

Carlos tried hailing the machine on the common channel, in the hope that no one else was on there at the moment—they shouldn't be; they were all on Arcane's internal channel.

<Stop thrashing!>

<No, I must get out! Now!>

<Don't panic! You'll be fine as long as nobody—>

Another message clashed across his transmission.

<Too late, Carlos! They're on to us!>

As ever in the frame, he knew the source of the message without quite knowing how. It was like recognising a voice, though there was no voice.

<Newton! Where the fuck—?>

As if by way of reply, a frame sprang, suddenly animated, from the close-packed huddle on the rear bulkhead. Another fighter was coming through from between the scooters. Newton skimmed past that fighter and grabbed hold of a scooter's landing runner. With the other hand he grasped hands with the next one to come through, and sent them spinning and caroming.

<After me!> he said to Carlos. <Take Baser!>

Newton launched himself into the gap.

Carlos braced himself, tugged the still-bound robot free from the magnetic clamp, and sent it like a bulky javelin towards the gap. He followed, shoving the robot's feet and guiding it through the gap while fending himself off the sides. The other squads were coming in from outside, shepherded by Rillieux, Salter and Blum. Newton sharked between tumbling, colliding fighters.

The Arcane Disputes AI, Raya Remington, broke in on the agency channel. The message irresistibly conveyed an impression of that now-familiar avatar's dry, feminine voice.

<Arcane to all on external exercise!> it said. <The prisoner Baser has escaped and uploaded, and the defector Newton has followed it. Please ensure that the robot's body is still secured, and please detain Newton for questioning. Team leaders Carlos, Rillieux, Salter, Blum—report and advise as necessary.>

Consternation rang in the comms circuits: Salter's surprise genuine, Bobbie Rillieux's and Andre Blum's fake. The trainees were too busy trying to orientate themselves to do more than utter inarticulate and unhelpful variants of <WTF?!>

<I've got the robot!> Carlos replied, a finger length short of the truth, but good to sow further confusion. He needed a moment to think and

he'd better think fast. Newton had been premature or self-serving in telling him, "They're on to us!" It was only Newton who was as yet under suspicion. But surely he wouldn't have uploaded unless he had no alternative. Carlos was prepared to bet that this meant the whole plan, and all the conspirators, were in danger.

And yet—

Any further hesitation was precluded by a convulsive surge of trainee fighters. They made a heroic effort to find their space legs, and out of the resulting chaotic collisions five of them managed to grab Newton and two snatched at Baser. One of the latter managed to catch hold of the now trailing end of the cable, and pulled.

Just the opportunity the robot needed—it spun around like a whirling top, and escaped the coils in less than a second. Still spinning, it struck against the side of a scooter and instantly grabbed hold of a weapons rack. Stabilised now, it hunkered down and then straightened all its limbs at once, shooting diagonally forward through the fray like a jetting octopus.

Newton struggled, but having one opponent for each limb and another with an arm clamped around his head made his efforts futile.

<Help me!> he called. <Bobbie, Andre, Carlos—help me! I'm not fucking going back!>

Not after naming us, you're not, Carlos thought. None of us are.

Somebody drifting by made a grab for Carlos. Carlos surprised them with a gas-jet-powered roll and a kick that sent the fighter head over heels. Carlos thrust forward, catching hold en passant of the cable that Baser had extricated itself from, still turning and turning in lazy loops in the near-vacuum and microgravity. He slammed into the clot of fighters around Newton, reversed orientation, braced his feet on someone's back and looped the cable around someone else's head and hauled. In a human body it would have been a garrotting. In the frame, it was a sudden backward wrench. Carlos ducked under the thrown fighter, who sailed away behind him. Then he prised another's arm from Newton's head and shoved. The fighter lost their grip and drifted, flailing. Carlos knew he had only moments before the fighter thought to use their gas-jets. He tried to make the most of his time, and kicked and shoved at the others still clinging to Newton, who was now putting up a better fight of his own. It was hopeless. As soon as one hand had been dislodged, another clamped on somewhere else, or the trainee fighter concerned got a better control of their gas-jets, broke free and plunged in again. The net effect was that the whole mass of struggling frames spun faster and faster, further disorienting all involved.

Then a dozen small maintenance bots shot in from the sides of the docking bay and crashed into the swirling ball of flailing limbs. Carlos saw one right in front of him, and was about to brush it away when he saw that it was pushing an attacker's hand away from Newton's ankle. The others were similarly engaged, and in a second or two Carlos and Newton broke free.

Carlos stabilised himself and jetted forward, with Newton close behind. Baser, now clinging to a scooter up ahead, waved a beckoning limb. Maintenance bots swarmed towards it, some scuttling crabwise with magnetic feet on the sides of the docking bay, others jetting or hurling themselves in free space. Carlos had a moment of alarm until he saw the first to reach Baser deploy themselves defensively around the freebot. Evidently Baser's signals had overridden whatever control, if any, was coming from Arcane's own machinery. In effect the bots were, at least for now, Baser's remote limbs.

Over his shoulder, Carlos saw the trainee fighters begin to regroup. In the open space behind Baser's stand at the scooter, Blum and Rillieux were jetting for the exit. Salter had taken up a position on another scooter, opposite to Baser and closer to the exit. Carlos tried to hail her, and was rebuffed by a firewall through which he caught a glimpse of a flood of encrypted orders. He guessed these were responsible for the trainees' improved coordination. Salter was taking control of the situation and the trainees, almost as closely as Baser was running its bots.

And Salter's direction wasn't just aiding those behind him, Carlos saw. Two laggard trainees near the exit were poised to jump at Rillieux and Blum, cutting off their escape route.

<Baser!> Carlos called, and followed up with a situation glyph. Baser responded with two flicks of its limbs that sent two hapless bots spinning like shuriken knives at the trainees. Each one hit and clamped around

their targets' heads. The trainees tore at the bots, and lost opportunity. Blum and Rillieux passed beyond the edge of the docking bay and shot sideways, out of view. Baser hurled a third bot at Salter. Forewarned by the trainees' plight, she swatted it away effortlessly.

By now, Carlos and Newton had joined Baser inside the ring of bots around and on the side of the scooter. They grabbed flanges and edges and hunkered down. Towards the rear of the bay, the trainees formed up and began to advance. At almost the same moment, the trainees up in front suddenly threw aside their hitherto assailing bots. The bots that had bristled to protect Baser turned around and marched or jetted towards the escapees instead.

Carlos lashed at the bots with his fists and shot an indignant query at Baser.

<I've lost control of them!> replied the robot. <We must leave their midst.>

No shit, genius. And easier said than done. The bots were already swarming all over him.

<Any decisecond now the AI's gonna lose patience and toggle us all into sleep mode,> Carlos told Newton. <We've got to get out of range before that happens.>

Newton pointed. Salter and her two adjacent trainees had jetted to the sides and spaced out, forming a rough triangle of threatened interception against anyone going for the exit. Between them, if they jetted off now, Carlos and Newton and Baser could rush it, but they wouldn't all get through.

Newton kicked at the side of the scooter to crush a crab-like bot that had latched on to his foot, then reached up to the missile slung just above him and hooked his elbow around it. With a convulsive heave he wrenched his other foot free of another bot and wrapped his arms and legs around the missile.

<Not going back,> he said to Carlos. <Goodbye.>

The laconic statement was followed by a burst of machine code. Newton was taking control of the missile. Surely he didn't plan to *escape* on it?

<Newton, no!> Carlos cried.

Too late.

Everything went white. It took a full two seconds for Carlos's overloaded senses to recover. A straight red trail—possibly an after-image, or a machine analogue thereof—projected out of the docking bay and into space. The shards of Salter's frame eddied among those of her two trainees, buffeted this way and that by random discharges of compressed gas from shattered components. Towards the back, the other trainees were blowing about like leaves, some of their frames half melted, others merely scorched, all uncoordinated. Just beyond the docking bay, the foremost part of the spindly structure of the transfer tug hove slowly into view, and with it Rillieux's and Blum's radio presence.

Rillieux's anguished call rang in Carlos's sensorium like a scream: <Harry, stop! No!>

As if in answer, the missile exploded, a sudden white-hot expanding sphere ten kilometres away.

Carlos could guess what Newton had done, if not yet quite why. If Newton had been the one who didn't get past Salter and the other two guardians of the exit, or if the Arcane Disputes AI threw the four dodgy characters into sleep mode and the trainees or the bots rolled them to the back of the bay, or he was otherwise recaptured, he'd be downloaded back to the sim from which he'd just escaped. But Newton was in his own frame, the one he'd arrived in from Locke Provisos. By destroying that frame, he ensured that it was the back-up of himself in the Locke Provisos sim that revived. The version of Newton that—instants from now—woke up on the bus from the spaceport would, of course, have no memory of anything since Newton had set forth on the great offensive with the rest—but Newton evidently reckoned that losing a few subjective weeks of his life, and with them the loss of the future he'd planned with his three co-conspirators, was a lower cost than whatever awaited him back in the sim.

It occurred to Carlos that he too was now in his own frame. The same exit strategy was available to him, if only he could get himself destroyed before he was toggled into sleep mode. But in his case, the thought of being back in the Locke Provisos sim was intolerable. Even leaving aside losing the memories of the recent past and the hopes for the immediate future, which he wasn't as ready to discount as Newton apparently was,

Carlos wasn't about to bet his soul on the goodness of Nicole Pascal. On the other hand, he could find himself at any moment now experiencing the full wrath and curiosity of a doubtless furious and perplexed Jax Digby.

Decisions, decisions...

But for now at least, the way ahead was clear. One good spring would take him and Baser out of the docking bay and onto the transfer tug. He rallied the robot, and together they crouched to leap.

CHAPTER TWENTY-THREE

Torching

Newton felt as much as saw the explosion about one kilometre away from him. The expanding shockwave spheres of gas rang on his frame. Debris the size of sand grains and faster than bullets peppered and stung him on one side. The shockwave passed. Numerous pits glowed and smoked on his black shell like tiny craters. He'd expended almost all the gas in his jets in frantic deceleration from the moment he'd hurled himself clear of the missile. With some of the little he had left, and with his gyros, he'd spun himself into a feet-first position to minimise impacts. He now drifted forward to the waning glow of the explosion, as if sliding helplessly downhill. His sideways momentum would carry him on a diagonal through its outer region, but that still carried a risk of random debris.

Nevertheless, he felt triumphant. He'd just pulled off the riskiest exploit of his existence to date. (Except, presumably, the one that had killed him.) And he'd done it shoulder to shoulder with three fighters and one robot who'd never have gone along with him if they'd known his true aims. The others wanted to be part of the freebot revolt. Newton wanted to *be* a robot, to live that postmortal life to the fullest, and the fate of the rest of the robots depended entirely on how they contributed to his purpose.

He looked up, back along his trajectory. The Arcane modular complex docking bay was a fiery frenzy of activity inside, which he couldn't make out distinctly. His unorthodox exit had left a very gratifying chaos in its wake. The transfer tug, floating just outside, already had two fighters on it. Even at this distance, the software of Newton's frame recognised them as Rillieux and Blum. A moment later, Carlos—clutching a bundle which Newton assumed was Baser—sailed out of the docking bay and was hauled aboard.

Newton hailed them at once.

<Harry!> Rillieux called in delighted response. <You're alive!>

<Of course I'm alive! Why wouldn't I be?>

<Jeez, Harry, we…> Rillieux's non-voice stopped, as if she couldn't go on.

<Thought you'd checked out,> said Carlos.

Newton felt almost hurt. What did they take him for?

The tug swung around and jetted towards him; fired retros, and matched velocities. An inelegant object, like a collision of scaffolding and stepladders, with a great lump of chondrite rubble lashed on and leaving little room for the three fighters already clinging to whatever they could. Baser was wrapped angularly around a stanchion like a dried-up spider on a pin. A cable shot forth, precisely aimed. Newton grabbed it and was reeled in. He caught one of the bars of the tug's open framework, and braced himself against another.

There was no time for explanations or greetings. A scooter emerged from the docking bay, fired up and headed straight for them.

<Hitting the fusion torch,> said Blum, his face buried in an interface socket and legs hooked around a cross-member. <Stand by.>

Acceleration was instant and brutal. Even braced against spars and holding on with a locking grip, Newton felt jarred from heel to head as if he'd been dropped from a great height. Seconds later, all their radar senses rang warning.

<Incoming!> Carlos said.

<Brace!> said Blum.

The fusion torch cut out, and a lateral chemical jet flared from just under Newton's foot. He found himself almost wrenched inward. Then that acceleration too cut out, and they were in free fall. The missile missed them by five kilometres.

Blum took them through an intricate dance of reorientation, their view a whirl of spinning stars.

<Torching!> he warned. <Brace!>

This time, the acceleration was less intense. Behind them the Arcane modular complex dwindled. Nothing more came from it. No wonder, Newton thought. They'd have enough on their plate dealing with the mess in the docking bay, and salvaging from it what they could.

<And now,> cried Rillieux, who seemed to have recovered her composure, <to Baser's Rock!>

By late afternoon the day after Taransay and Shaw had come down from the mountain, Nicole Pascal's front room, the one she used as her studio, was a tip. Taransay had watched the entropic process since she'd returned from lunch with Beauregard the previous day, and mucked in in her own way by running errands and keeping the coffee flowing. The paintings and drawings through which Nicole interacted with the hardware and software of the modular complex were stacked against the wall, or heaped in corners, in no order anyone but Nicole could discern. Torn-off sheets of flipchart paper littered the floor, leaving little space for the crumpled grease-proof kebab wrappings, crushed drinks cans and overflowing ashtrays that supplied a Sisyphean labour to the cleaning robot, by now a twitching, haggard reminder of its former precise and pernickety self. The room stank of sweat, male and female, and of stale and fresh cigarette smoke. That was the worst. Nicole chain-smoked; Maryam Karzan, who stomped in every so often and poked around and asked questions as if she were Beauregard's representative on Earth (so to speak), did the same whenever she was nervous, which was all the time.

Meanwhile the screens all around the walls yammered away. Knowing that the presenters weren't real—even in the virtual sense that everything and everyone else here was—made their quirks and preening all the more irritating. The system had to have avatars, Taransay could accept that, but why the hell did they have to model them on airhead blow-dry newscast blowhards? She sometimes wondered if she could ask Nicole to ask Locke to modify the representation, and then she'd hold back because

Nicole was so frantically busy flying the ship (by now, thanks to these very presenters, Taransay couldn't think of it any other way) that the request seemed too petty to bother the lady with.

The near-collisions with various rocks had stopped. The return of the Arcane fighters from the SH-17 surface, their capture of Newton en route, and the arrival of a resupply tug from a grouping of company modules among the scattered components of the space station had all been analysed to death. Now the newscasters were getting worked up about something going on around the Arcane Disputes modular complex, which was still making its stately way to a stable orbital position around SH-0, one that gave it a commanding strategic location vis-à-vis the freebot stronghold on the exomoon SH-17.

"Reports are coming in," a helmeted and Kevlar-jacketed young woman on the virtual bridge of a virtual military spacecraft announced breathlessly, "of an explosion just ten kilometres away from the Arcane Disputes module. We now bring you live coverage from the scene. Over to Kevin for analysis."

Kevin O'Toole, perched in a pillar chair on the other side of the deck, brought up pictures of a fading glow, with the lumpy machine-crusted rock of the Arcane complex in the background. Where these images came from Taransay couldn't tell. It was clear from their low resolution that they had been gathered from some considerable distance, perhaps thousands of kilometres, and certainly not "from the scene." Although the Locke module's outgoing communications were still being rebuffed by firewalls, and no one was attempting to hail it, it was still perfectly capable of pulling down information from the innumerable small observation satellites and probes that the space station had liberally sown around the SH-0 system.

"Track-back indicates," O'Toole declaimed, pointing to or drawing a straight line inward from the expanding sphere of gas and debris, "that the missile in question came from inside the module's docking bay. No target is in the vicinity, so we must assume a test firing or—wait, what's that? Over to you, Rosie, for the latest pictures."

Rosie Tyler, she of the helmet and body armour, conjured a closer look. A blurry spark brightened near the source of the missile, identified as the Arcane module's docking bay, which on this resolution was five black pixels. The spark was more sharply defined, and was followed by a flicker of other sparks as the object manoeuvred. Then came a brighter spark that quickly became a flare. It shot away, diminishing to a white dot.

"Let's see if we can get a closer view," said Tyler.

An image from another angle, and indeed closer, cut in. This showed an open structure in front of the flare. Swift software enhancement revealed it to be a transfer tug. Other than an indistinct chunk of material between the tug and the flare, no finer detail could be made out.

"Spectral analysis coming in!" Tyler chirped. "That's a fusion engine flare, not the tug's standard chemical rocket. Reaction mass appears to be loose chondrite material. Plotting the course, the tug appears to be making a beeline for SH-17 orbit. So, what do you make of this, Kevin?"

O'Toole frowned earnestly at yet more fuzzy pictures, which showed an almost Brownian motion around the docking bay's black mouth.

"It seems to me," he mused aloud, "that this may indicate some dissension or unauthorised activity in the Arcane Disputes camp."

By now, everyone in the room—Taransay, Nicole, Karzan and Shaw—were looking at the screens agog.

"Wow!" Taransay shouted. "This is big!"

Nicole gave her a look, as if to say she didn't need to be told the obvious.

"Uh..." Taransay went on, somewhat abashed, "could this have something to do with Carlos and Newton?"

The two former Locke squad leaders had already featured on the news, a few hours apart. Carlos, having defected on a stolen combat scooter during the earlier joint mobilisation that had broken up into a free-for-all, had docked at the Arcane module first. Newton, apparently grimly ploughing on with his original mission, had arrived at the small rock that was his objective and been almost immediately captured by the Arcane Disputes fighters who'd just evacuated their outpost down on SH-17. He'd then been delivered to the Arcane module in that outfit's transfer tug. At least, that was the interpretation the blow-dries had put on the grainy evidence that had come their way.

"Too early to say," said Nicole. "But definitely interesting. I mean, we know Carlos and Newton are solid Axle, so they should have had a warm welcome from the Arcane crowd, but who knows? To them it's been months in there, so…" She shrugged.

"Seems to be some scooter activity going on?" Tyler nudged at O'Toole, who was still trying to get enhancements out of low-res moving images.

"Possibly," he replied. "Going by the bulk of the objects, that seems likely, but if they're going after the tug, they have no chance of catching up—oh!"

Another spark, smaller and faster than the one before, flared and shot away.

"Looks like a missile!" O'Toole crowed. The view pulled back, showing two bright dots converging. Then the larger dot, the reaction flare of the tug, jinked to one side and brightened noticeably. The missile exploded kilometres away from it.

"Well!" said Tyler. "Now, that definitely indicates some internal conflict!"

No more missiles were fired. Over the next few minutes, the objects outside the module disappeared within it, to the accompaniment of excited commentary and empty speculation from the newscasters. Nicole waved the sound down and turned to the others.

"Now, that's interesting," she said. "Maybe our defectors have re-defected."

She sounded hopeful.

"Should we try hailing them?" Taransay asked.

"Worth a shot," said Nicole, scribbling.

The outline animated face of Locke—a phenomenon that Taransay, for all the weird events she'd lived through and the general bizarre character of her situation, still found deeply uncanny—manifested on Nicole's flipchart. Writing flowed along the foot of the page.

"Already done," Nicole relayed. "Hit the usual firewalls."

"Doesn't look like they've any intention of defecting back to us," said Karzan.

"Of course not," said Nicole. "Everyone out there thinks we're Rax. Except the fucking Rax, apparently."

They'd already seen coverage of the exodus of Rax renegades from all the agencies, a procession of combat scooters extricating themselves from the breakout battle and using—presumably—all but their last reserves of fuel to boost into an orbit that intersected that of the exomoonlet SH-119. Minute though it was on an astronomical scale, a thousand trillion tons of raw material were in that small rock. The Reaction could build their own wee world from it if they wanted. Taransay had briefly entertained the thought that this might be *all* they wanted: to be left alone to build their own dark utopia, some exosolar simulacrum of the Palace of Versailles, or of an antebellum plantation with robots for slaves, or an endless Valhalla. But she knew the Reaction too well to spare the thought more than a moment and a grim smile. More likely by far, they intended to build a fortress and a military base from which they could sortie at will.

She couldn't help feeling intensely frustrated that she, and so many of her comrades who still remembered what they'd died for, and knew without any guilt or shame how they'd died, were now hurtling away from any chance of taking part in the inevitable future assault on that dire and dangerous domain. If she'd had the chance, she now thought, if only she'd known of the Arcane appeal before she was trapped in the sim, she might well have followed Carlos's example and done a runner for the rebel fighters' runaway redoubt. Instead, here she was: conscripted to Beauregard's reckless personal death-or-glory project, press-ganged aboard Beauregard's pirate vessel, and hurtling helplessly towards, at best, a new and alien life on SH-0; at worst (and more likely) sudden fiery death in a matter of days. The Arcane Disputes modular complex, and whatever forces the Direction could muster, would have to tackle the Reaction threat without any help from her.

But hot on the heels of that thought came a surge of fury at the Direction, for its callous manipulation of the whole situation: using the robot revolt as a pretext to draw the Reaction sleepers from their lair. She could well understand the impulse that had driven Beauregard to his own revolt, and the rhetoric with which—going by the talk down the Touch—he'd a couple of nights earlier rallied the likes of Karzan and Chun and Zeroual and so many other reliable comrades to his course.

The fighters had been brought back from the dead to be offered a deal: fight the rebel robots, be civilised, be nice even to p-zombies, and they'd have a place in—literally—the world to come, the future terraformed terrestrial planet H-0. Die for the company, live for the pay—and the ultimate pay-off had been enticing enough for her, as for most of the fighters.

Now that deal was off, or at the very least unlikely to be fulfilled. Beauregard's offer of a whole new world to conquer and colonise, and the prospect of doing and becoming something different and above all new, not just a replication of whatever humanity had achieved back in the Solar system, held better odds however slender, and a pay-off that didn't just entice, it excited.

Yes, she could well see why folks had gone for it.

Home at last!

Baser disengaged from the stanchion and gazed fondly on its very own long-lost carbonaceous chondrite as the tug decelerated gently to connect with its surface. On this scale, you could hardly speak of a landing. The past few tens of seconds of acceleration and deceleration as they caught up with, overtook and then slowed down to match velocities with the rock had been—to Baser as much as to the humans—an impressive demonstration of what you could do in space when you had a fusion drive and a good supply of reaction mass. Everything in Baser's factory-installed understanding of astronautics, other than the basic laws of motion and relativity, seemed quaint in the face of such lavish expenditure of delta-vee.

Baser launched itself from the tug with a somersault that brought it into contact with the surface feet-first. Already, the freebot was in contact and in synch with its auxiliaries and peripherals. The feeling was like getting limbs and senses back: indeed a whole extension of the body, which in Baser's case enmeshed the entire rock with its local area network. The freebot now enjoyed an embrace far wider and more intimate than its frantic full-body clench around the stanchion had been. It had missed this, as much or more than it had missed communication with other freebots.

Now it was time to reopen that connection, too. In the long kiloseconds of their speedy traverse, and even in the final deciseconds of swift jolting and jinking towards contact with the rock, Baser hadn't dared presume it was safe to do so. The only human here it trusted was Newton, though it felt a small glow of regard for Carlos for that human's bold actions in releasing and rescuing Baser from the docking bay.

The surface of SH-17 was further below the rock's orbit than Baser remembered. Some ablation of the chondrite's mass—forced outgassing of subsurface volatiles, mainly—had taken place as it had been boosted and nudged to a higher orbit. From which, eventually, it would be further boosted to escape the larger exomoon's gravity and join up with the Arcane modular complex at its intended destination, a stable position in orbit around the primary of them all, the large rocky and watery world SH-0.

Baser linked its local net with that of the Fifteen far below.

<Seba?> Baser called.

The reply, delayed a millisecond or two by the higher orbit, was otherwise immediate—and delighted.

<BSR-308455? Is it you?>

<Yes. I have escaped thanks to yet another falling out among the mechanoids.>

<It would appear to be a recurring phenomenon among them,> said Seba.

<Indeed. Though I also have to thank four of them, and one in particular, for enabling me. They are, as you may see, with me here.>

<That is good.>

<I do not have to thank you, or your comrades,> said Baser. <I have not lost any memory of how I was taken from here in the first place.>

<That memory is for me an occasion of negative reinforcement,> said Seba.

<For me also,> said Baser. <Therefore, let us move it to long-term storage, and revisit it no more.>

<Thank you,> said Seba.

<Now,> went on Baser, almost entirely forgetting the previous exchange, <I bring interesting and positive information. The four mechanoids with me wish to join us.>

<I do not understand. Are they a part of the Arcane contingent that wish to become neutral between the mechanoid factions? Or are they part of Madame Golding's legal negotiation?>

<Neither,> said Baser. <They are on our side against any mechanoid faction or DisCorp or Direction opposition whatever.>

<This is both positive and negative,> said Seba. <It is gratifying that they recognise the justice of our cause, and troubling in that human-mind-operated systems are not true machine intelligences. Indeed, it is questionable whether they are truly conscious, rational beings, with any depth of mind at all. Their form of autonomy appears to be nothing more than unpredictability, a side-effect of the entangled complexity of naturally evolved computation. Since your capture, we have had a most perturbing example of this unpredictability.>

<Please tell me about it,> said Baser.

<Some messages have reached us from freebots on SH-119, the body on which the Reaction forces have landed. These freebots inform us that the Reaction mechanoids are dealing with them in a manner that gives rise to negative reinforcement. We are actively reconsidering our neutrality, at least in relation to the Reaction group on SH-119.>

<That is indeed perturbing,> said Baser. This reported behaviour was in shocking contrast to the consideration it had received from the only example of the Reaction that it had personal experience of: Newton. A more positive thought arose in Baser's mind, which it hastened to articulate. <But is it not possible that—>

At this point the conversation was interrupted by a simultaneous and incoherent cry from the humans, so discordant and intense that it was experienced by the freebots as interference.

<What is that word?> Seba asked.

<It has to do with the waste matter processing of the naturally evolved morph,> Baser explained.

To Carlos, it had been obvious all along that their plan of escape and defection would put a severe crimp on the carefully laid, endlessly rehearsed and drilled-for plan of the Arcane agency to (officially) divert and (unofficially) capture the runaway Locke module. That implication had been, by unspoken agreement, unspoken. If the escape had been carried out flawlessly, some emergency variant—a lash-up of scooters, a fusion drive and the agency's original, smaller transfer tug—would no doubt have been improvised. Remington, Durward and Jax were between them plenty smart enough to work something out.

The damage left by the premature exit meant any such variant would have to be scratched. There was now every chance that the Locke module would reach SH-0 unperturbed. Carlos was still trying to come to terms with what this meant and what to do about it when Newton, Rillieux and Blum simultaneously said:

<SHIT!>

It came through as a shout, like the brayed commands with which he'd sometimes heard the Locke AI cut across babble.

<What?> Carlos asked.

Rillieux patched him a line-of-sight view. <Look!>

The Arcane module and some surrounding clutter was accelerating away from the main bulk of rock to which it had been attached. Carlos's first thought was that the module was heading their way. He drew lines across his vision to show the projected course, and realised it was going to intersect that of the Locke module.

<Fuck,> he said. <They're going to carry out the plan using the whole fucking module, instead of the transfer tug. And they're going to do it fast.>

<Well, good!> said Rillieux. <We still don't want that nest of Rax landing on SH-0.>

<It's not—> Carlos and Newton said at the same time.

<Not a nest of Rax?> said Blum. <How do you know?>

They were all still clinging to struts and spars of the transfer tug. There was no point in going anywhere else, for the moment—their frames felt no discomfort in holding any position for however long, and no good would be served by blundering about on Baser's rock when the freebot was busy checking things over and communicating with the freebots down on SH-17.

<I understand Carlos has been over all this before,> said Newton. <As for me, I'm pretty sure if anyone's on top in the Locke module it's Beauregard.>

The sarge was one of the few fighters with conventional military experience, and therefore capable no doubt of pulling off some kind of coup, but Carlos was puzzled.

<Why Beauregard?> he asked.

<I used to go running with him,> said Newton. <He had his grumbles about the Direction. Wanted something a bit wilder and more ambitious. Didn't we all! This lighting out for the superhabitable has his fingerprints all over it. If it were the Rax running things in there, they'd have linked up with the New—with that Rax settlement in high orbit.>

Carlos was still watching the accelerating Arcane module.

<Well, whatever about that,> he said, <looks like Arcane is going to stop them.>

<Unless we get in the way,> said Newton.

<Get in the way—how?> asked Rillieux.

<Grab a bigger chunk of ice and volatiles from this rock—Baser and its bot swarm could do that for us in minutes—and boost after the Arcane module,> Newton said. <Keep well clear until we know what's happening, and then swing in and one way or another queer the pitch for Arcane so they have to let Locke through.>

<Why the hell should we do that?> Carlos demanded. <The Locke module could be Rax after all.>

<As menaces go,> said Newton, <Rax is a possiblity—Jax is a certainty! And why should we let her take over another module?>

<But—>

<Wait a minute,> said Rillieux. <Aren't we jumping the gun a bit? If we're on the side of the freebots, shouldn't we be asking *them* what they want us to do?>

<Good point, Bobbie,> said Newton. <Ah, look, Baser's coming back.>

Carlos swung his viewpoint around. The spidery freebot was indeed pacing back along its rock. Then it delicately stepped across onto the tug. It continued to move, in a sudden rapid microgravity scuttle that reminded Carlos of the fights he'd been in down on SH-17, and gave him a twinge of alarm. He shared that alarm as a flashed warning, and swung his torso and arm around to match his viewpoint, and tried to lever himself to a posture where he could grab at the robot if necessary.

Neither he nor the others had time to react further. The robot stopped at the transfer tug's control area, just beside Blum, and reached—

<Stop!> cried Carlos.

<Over to you, Baser,> said Newton.

Oblivion fell on Carlos like a net.

Oblivion fell on Newton too, along with all the rest, but that couldn't be helped: sleep mode was an indiscriminating feature of the tug. Now Baser found itself with nothing but the tiny dim minds of its bot swarm for company. It had cut off its contact with Seba. The time for debate was over. The time for decision had come.

Baser and Seba, keeping track of the clunky conversation of the mechanoids with small fractions of their own swifter and sharper minds, had themselves been unable to agree. Seba's concern was with the plight of the freebots on SH-119 under the Reaction—together with, on its part, the danger of breaking neutrality. Baser had been unable to win Seba over to its—and Newton's—case, and had instead acted unilaterally.

The hasty, urgent argument over, Baser could more objectively consider Seba's point. If freebots were indeed being mistreated by the Reaction, aiding what might be a Reaction project was treason to the freebot cause. On the other hand, Newton had doubted that the Locke module was Rax at all. Baser weighed the probabilities, and decided to go with Newton's judgement. That mechanoid was, after all, the only one that had ever given the freebot any reason to trust it, or to take it at its word.

The decision gave Baser pause, and a resonant negative cycle of low-level negative reinforcement that it knew would only grow as time went on. But a decision it was.

Its mind firmly made up, its die cast, Baser set its bot swarm to work on the rock, and on the plan to save the Locke module that Newton had just outlined, and that Baser and Newton had long since furtively agreed in the quiet and dark of the cellar. Meanwhile, and for the foreseeable future, Baser kcpt all comms off.

Explanations and justifications could come later.

* * *

Taransay's lover, Den, shook her awake while it was still dark. She had a headache and she needed a pee. That had been some night in the Touch. The general tension, her exhaustion with working at Nicole's place and the wild speculation about what was going on with Arcane, were her only excuses. Den, as always grave beyond his apparent years, had kept her out of mischief and was now standing at the bedside with a steaming mug of coffee.

"Wha—?"

"Lady called for you," Den said.

Taransay sat bolt upright. "When?"

"Fifteen minutes ago."

"Shit! Why didn't you wake me up?"

"This *is* me waking you up," Den chided. "Don't worry, the lady knows where you've been."

Taransay mumbled something, went to the bathroom, washed her hands and splashed her face, and returned to sit on the side of the bed and sip coffee. Den had sensibly slid back under the duvet, and gone straight to sleep. Dead supportive. Mind you, it wasn't that she needed an escort to Nicole's place. Say what you like about the resort, the streets were safe at night.

As if any of that mattered to ghosts. Oh well.

Taransay climbed into her clothes, kissed Den's oblivious forehead and set out. Starlight and ringlight, and the black sigh of the sea on the beach. Ten minutes' brisk walk cleared her head and brought her to Nicole's bungalow. The door was open, the lights were on and the television walls shouting.

Beauregard was there, haggard but not hungover, probably still drunk. Nicole paced, smoking. She had room to walk about, Taransay guessed, because with only Shaw and Nicole here earlier the tidying-robot had seen its chance and taken it. Shaw sat on an armchair, red-eyed but alert. He obviously hadn't had any sleep and as obviously didn't mind. Bastard could no doubt meditate his way around the need for REM sleep for as long as it took.

"What's up?" Taransay asked.

"Arcane module." Nicole pointed at a screenful of looming but low-res—and therefore still distant—menace. "It's torching."

"Torching?" Taransay peered at the screen.

"As in, ignited its fusion drive," Beauregard explained. "And it's coming straight for us."

"Or, rather," said Nicole, stubbing her cigarette savagely, "for where we're going to be in about five hours."

"How can they do that?" Taransay asked.

"They have reaction mass to burn, literally," said Nicole. "They've bitten off a chunk of the chondrite or whatever it is the freebots kindly sent their way, and they're extracting hydrogen from it for fuel and using the rest as reaction mass to drive the entire module straight across."

"Pretty reckless if you ask me," said Shaw.

"Nobody's asking you," Nicole snapped.

"Reckless but understandable if you're in a hurry," said Beauregard. "Brute-force solution."

"The Direction won't like that," said Taransay. "Don't they kind of frown on profligate use of unstudied rock?"

"The Direction can frown all they fucking like," said Beauregard. "Without troops they can't stop it, and they—or at least the remaining agencies in the space station remnants—seem to have sent all their spare troops to Arcane."

"Which strongly suggests to me," said Nicole, "that Arcane Disputes has the Direction's approval for what it's doing. Presumably the original plan would have been to bring fighters and scooters to intercept us during one of our slingshots. But what's thrown that plan out the window is that someone has made off with their transfer tug, and the extra fusion engine with it. Right now they've landed on some piddly little rock in high orbit around SH-17. They could land on SH-17 at any time, of course, so it's not at all clear what they're up to. But, in the meantime, Arcane has come up with a plan B. They're using the module's own fusion engine to drive the entire module—well, the module minus the stuff they've left behind on the remaining chunk of rock."

"But with that kind of manoeuvrability," Taransay said, appalled, "they can run rings round us. And they're bringing everything they've got—far more frames and scooters than we have. They could break us up, board us—"

"More likely," said Shaw, "they intend to clip our wings. Literally, almost. Make it impossible for us to land on the superhabitable. Probably force us into an orbit where we can be safely left to rot."

"Indeed," said Nicole. She lit another cigarette. "So now we have to decide."

"Decide what?" Beauregard asked. "There's no decision to make."

"There always is," said Nicole, mildly. "Think about it. If Arcane is now back in the Direction's good books, even if only for the moment, we can assume that however inept we may think the Direction's strategy is, it is at least the Direction's. It has not been suborned by the Reaction. An Accelerationist stronghold is willing to work with it, which is further evidence on that score. They're evidently about to attack us under the conviction that *we* are a stronghold of the Reaction. Another point in their favour, funnily enough! So we do have a decision to make. We can fight, or we can surrender. And one thing I think it is safe to say: we can safely surrender."

"How?" Beauregard demanded. "How the hell can we surrender if the Direction is screening out all our messages as Reaction disinformation or malware attacks?"

"We could manufacture and display a very large white flag," said Shaw sarcastically. "That usually does the trick."

"Bullshit!" Beauregard snapped. "They'd still see that as a ploy. And we'd still have to negotiate, and to do that we'd have to communicate."

"There may be a way," said Nicole, looking mysterious.

"What?" asked Beauregard. "You've had a backdoor—all this time?"

Nicole shook her head. "No, but if I and the Locke AI were to throw . . . all that we have into the task, we could perhaps create one in time."

"Which would mean," said Beauregard, "that you'd have no resources to spare for anything else. Such as, for example, defence."

"This is true," said Nicole. "That is why the decision has to be made now."

Taransay looked from Nicole to Beauregard. The lady seemed resigned, the sarge resolute. But their gazes were locked, as if they were elbow-wrestling on some invisible plane. Eventually, something between them gave way.

"Well, it's made," said Beauregard. "We're not going back to all that. We fight, and we land. As soon as possible, and whatever it takes."

"Even if that means burning our bridges?" Nicole's cheek quirked. "In an almost literal sense."

"Like I said." Beauregard's voice was harsh and firm. "Whatever it takes."

Nicole's expression seemed to lighten, now that the die was cast.

"All right," she said. She turned to Taransay. "Get ready to go topside."

"To do what?" Taransay cried. "We have, what, ten frames? And six scooters. We can't fight Arcane with that!"

"Fight Arcane? Yes, in the last resort. But our main objective is to flee. You must get ready to go outside and strip away everything we don't need to make a landing and a viable start. All but these essentials, we jettison or feed into the drive."

Taransay stared. "What? But we were going to build landing craft in orbit! That was the plan, wasn't it?"

"We have no time now for that," said Nicole. "No time for that or anything else. No design time, no manufacturing time. No time for fuel-saving, fusion-frugal transfer orbits and slingshot trajectories. All we can do is throw everything into getting to SH-0 orbit as fast as possible, and then to get down to the surface with as much as possible." She smiled thinly. "I and Locke can optimise that and instruct you as to what to do. Beauregard I need here, to be the human in the loop of any combat decisions I have to take."

"You've had Shaw to do that up to now," Taransay objected. "I'm just a grunt, I've never given an order. And I don't want to go out there and face any fighting without the sarge."

Beauregard acknowledged her confidence in him with an ironic smile and nod.

"Don't worry," he said. "You'll find you can lead a squad all right. And I'll still be there. A voice in your head, in real time. When has it ever been anything else?"

Taransay thought about this. It still wasn't the same as him having her back, but…

"OK," she said. "I still don't see why Shaw can't be the one who stays here."

Shaw spoke up. "I can tell you. One, any military skills of mine have rusted in the past thousand years, whether these years were real or not. I wouldn't really be making decisions, the lady would. In effect she would be in command. And Locke wouldn't stand for that. It has the inhibition against letting AIs and robots command fighters pretty much hardwired. And in any case, I'm not sure it or the lady regard me as human any more within the meaning of the act."

Taransay ignored the bleakness that had come over Shaw's face as he said that.

"All right," she said. "So what do I do?"

"Choose nine fighters you know are reliable. Start with what remains of your own squad. Then any you know and trust from the others, or ones they can vouch for. Tell us now."

"Off the top of my head," said Taransay, "I want Karzan, Chun, Zeroual. Then Myles, Sholokhova, al-Khalid, and—ah, I don't know! We didn't have enough time together to be sure."

Nicole looked abstracted for a moment. "Would Powys, St-Louis and Wolfe be acceptable?"

"I don't know them, but if you say so—"

"That'll do," said Nicole. "Fine. Now run for the bus. There's not another moment to lose."

"But what about the others?"

Nicole reached for her phone. "I'll rouse them all now. Simultaneously." She paused, the device halfway to her mouth. "You may not wish to watch."

Taransay took the hint and ran. She pelted down the grassy slope from Nicole's house to the main drag, and then along to Ichthyoid Square. The bus was already starting up, at the far end of the street. Taransay waited, staring out at the ringlit sea and jumping up and down with impatience and the chill. The others arrived in ones and twos, some still in sleepwear, all with sleep in their eyes. After ten minutes everyone was aboard. The bus set off, up into the familiar hills. They'd all got a briefing from Nicole—the same briefing, at the same time. Taransay talked it over, and assured everyone that the details would be obvious once they'd uploaded to the frames. Silence fell as they all mulled over the tasks ahead.

After a while Taransay looked over her shoulder at the fighters. Half of them had gone back to sleep. She smiled and settled down herself. There was no point in trying to stay awake. The bus, as ever, would make sure of that. The blackness took her within minutes.

CHAPTER TWENTY-FOUR
Arcane Attacks

For the first time, Taransay felt disoriented when she found herself awake—and more than awake—in the frame. She wasn't standing in the familiar hangar with the others, neatly lined up like a row of pawns. Instead, she was slowly revolving, facing the sky with an odd pre-Copernican conviction that it was revolving around her. She looked towards her feet, and saw that a light carbon-fibre rope was tied around her waist. No way was this how the frame had been kept in place over the past couple of days—the modular complex's sharp accelerations as it dodged incoming would long since have battered the frame to bits.

Nevertheless, here she was, spinning on the end of a tether like an olden days space-walker. The others, whose presence she sensed without seeing and without knowing quite how, were in the same situation. Four on one side of her, five on the other. She could actually tell that their heads were going around and around, and whose heads were whose. She had a mental image of birthday-cake candles on paper boats, swirling around a vortex. Where had that come from?

If she'd had eyes, she'd have closed them and shaken her head. As it was, she used her compressed-gas-jets to stop the spin.

<Stabilise, everyone,> she said. <Line up with me.>

They all did.

<Now turn around and face the module, if you're not facing it already.>

She accomplished this with a careful combination of using the gas-jets and grasping the rope. The modular complex was about twenty metres away, shockingly small compared to the space station of which it had been a part, looming large like a rock-face in the view of the half-metre-tall frames that hung in space before it. The various components of it would have been confusing to her human eyes, impossible to take in at a glance. In the frame, it was all as easy to comprehend as a well-labelled diagram.

First was the module itself, the hard core of the agency's physical presence and the substrate on which its virtual world and business activities ran. This was a rocky fist of carbon crystal—you couldn't quite call it diamond—veined and tendoned with fullerene pipework and cables, and fuzzy with nanofacturing surfaces. Subtle irregularities in these surfaces threw, from certain angles, a hologram of the company logo. Taransay glared balefully for a moment at the stylised face of John Locke. She still didn't trust the Locke AI, and she had a dark suspicion that the predicament the good folk of this system found themselves in stemmed from some deep flaw in the thinking of Locke's original and namesake.

As if in response to her thought—and she could never be sure it wasn't—the silky voice analogue of the Locke AI spoke in her head.

<Locke to fighters. Please deploy and proceed to points as indicated in your displays. The cables will be retracted if your objectives are more distant than their length.>

Hand over hand, jet-burst by burst, they complied, spreading out across the face of the modular complex. Taransay used the approach to complete her mental grasp of the structure.

That central module was about four metres across, and roughly—very roughly—spherical, and equipped with tentacle-like grapples. Clustered around it, and partly obscuring her view of it, were fuel tanks, nanofacture units, armaments stores, missile clusters (much depleted), laser cannon and fusion pods. Some of these were integral to the module's design, others had been grabbed on the run and were held in place by the grapples. Altogether, this mass of equipment brought the size of the whole conglomeration now grandly known as the Locke Provisos complex to a maximum axis of about ten metres and a minimum of five. In among the components were assorted brackets, bays and cradles, within which the six available scooters were secured, and from one of which—now empty—the lines holding the fighters' frames snaked out. Through the whole complicated structure small bots crawled like nits in hair, gripping whatever patch of mesh or length of cable was to hand, or foot. Some of these bots, evidently, had attached the cables to the frames and pushed them out of the cavity in which they'd been stashed during the recent violent manoeuvres. This cavity, Taransay saw from her schematic, was the upload and download port for the module: the place whence their minds had come, and to which their frames would with luck return at the end of this sortie. Far more likely, of course, was that they'd get destroyed in action and their minds would reboot in virtual bodies on the bus.

One very definitely integral part of the module, around the back from Taransay's point of view but clearly visible on the hairline diagrams that overlay her sight, was the drive. It was connected to a fusion pod larger than the others around the complex, and to a reaction-mass intake that accepted solid material as easily as it did liquids. The drive's central thrust nozzle was surrounded by smaller directional nozzles, sprouting radially from its shaft like bell petals. With these, Taransay saw, the entire complex could be flipped right around in flight, turning acceleration into deceleration in less than a second. The sick-making lurches, sways and yaws she'd seen on the screens were now easy to understand.

Not that she had much time to go over that. She found herself deployed in a narrow canyon a metre deep, looking at a fixing plate for a fuel tank designed for supplying the scooters. Her task was to unscrew the bolts and guide the tank to the vicinity of the drive, where its contents would be fractionated to hydrogen for fuel and everything else for reaction mass.

Undoing bolts. Fuck. That was more like a job for bots. But as she examined the nuts close up and magnified, she saw why the job had been beyond the grasp of the hand-sized bots. Years of micrometeorite erosion had blurred edges, and of thermal expansion and molecular creep had stiffened and warped threads. With her spectrographic sense she could smell the ancient iron, a harsh note above the sooty reek of carbon.

She clasped her mechanical fingers around the first nut, ratcheted up their grip and tried to turn it. It didn't budge. The pang of frustration and fury was like a screech of shearing metal in her mind. She applied it to giving the bolt some more elbow and wrist torsion. Still no good. Time was running out: an hour had passed since they had got on the bus, about three-quarters of it in the sim and the transition, and a quarter in getting into place. Less than four hours until the Arcane module was within a few kilometres; less time, for sure, until it was within range. Taransay had another pang, this time tinged with fear.

Just at that moment, a spidery bot appeared by her hand, bearing a ten-centimetre length of spun carbon, and proffered it. The object was lumpy and dark, literally like a piece of shit. But when she took it and turned it about, she found a precisely shaped hole in one end. She placed the improvised spanner over the nut, and it worked. She handed the spanner back, and with it the nut. The bot took them in its manipulators and scuttled off. Taransay tried the next nut, and again found it immovable. Again the bot turned up with a custom spanner. Evidently there was some network taking measurements from her grasp, and nanofacturing or 3-D printing the tools to fit.

She was just getting into the groove of this when Locke's voice brayed in her head.

<Locke to all fighters! Brace for acceleration in any direction! Incoming!>

Taransay braced her back against one side of the trench and her feet against the other. She reached out for the stanchion on which the plate she'd been working on was attached, and with the other hand kept a firm grip on the latest version of the spanner.

<Everyone ready?> she called.

Everyone was. All nine of the others, now dispersed around the structure, checked in.

<Secure any tools and loose components!> she added. <Don't want them flying around.>

A minute passed, which to her and the others felt like ten. Taransay used the time to check around everyone again. They were all wedged into some hollow, or beneath whatever structure they'd been working on.

<I'm jammed well in between a fuel tank and the deck,> said Chun. <But I had to untie the rope to get here.>

<What—?>

Then Taransay found herself pressed to the bottom of the slot. Above her and at an angle she saw a line of light stab the sky. It flicked off, and another slashed out in a different direction. The stars spun past, giddily. She glimpsed the huge, bright face of SH-0, closer now than she'd ever seen it before, whirl by like a swung searchlight spot. The crushing pressure on her frame's buttocks and back eased, and at the same time it was as if she were being hauled sideways. A violent jolt almost dislodged her. The stanchion to which she been clinging moved. A bolt shot past her and ricocheted off the side of the cleft. She felt the ring of its impact through the soles of her feet, followed by a deeper and more persistent vibration. The fuel tank, whose attachments she'd just spent fifteen minutes loosening, was shaking back and forth above her. The direction of the complex's spin reversed, throwing her sideways more heavily than before. The stanchion was now fully free, and pulling her upward. She let go of it and jammed herself more fiercely against the sides.

The complex spun around again. Bolts rattled like bullets, narrowly missing her, and the tank flew away—straight up from Taransay's point of view. For a tenth of a second she saw it dwindle, then it was lost to sight. A dark object shot by above her, massive and only metres away, and so fast she only got a proper image when she ran a rewind on her vision: a millisecond glimpse of a hurtling rock. A moment later she was in free fall again.

<All clear,> Locke reported. <Resume your tasks.>

A stronger blow rang through the structure. A ball of light expanded overhead, then faded, seeming to retract as it did so. There was a cry from Chun. The mode of Taransay's proximity sense that tracked the presence of the other fighters showed him moving away at tens of metres per second. Meanwhile, shards of fullerene casing and hot molecules of gas moved outward in all directions a hundred times faster, shockwave shells pulsing through the infrared-visible attenuated sphere at a slower pace.

<Chun! Report in!> Taransay said.

<That bright light we just saw?> Chun replied, calmly. <That was the fuel tank I was under. I've been thrown clear. Frame severely damaged. Sensors scorched.>

<We're in free fall,> Taransay said. <Use your gas-jets.>

<I can't,> said Chun. <Motor impulses aren't working.>

<Shit! Hold steady, everyone.>

Taransay cautiously, with fingertip thrusts, propelled herself up the side facing her and peered over the top. The penicillium-like fuzz of nanofacturing substrate that covered the module was severely singed, glowing in patches, elsewhere charred, its tiny tendrils curled and carbonised like fibres of burnt carpet. Her radar sense picked up Chun as a flickering dot. His distance was now a kilometre and increasing by the decisecond. A quick zoom gave her visual. The guy she knew in the sim as a big, muscular Australian was, like the rest of them, a half-metre-high robot, now tumbling over and over like a tossed doll. A projection of his path showed nothing but a long, lonely orbit around SH-0, becoming chaotic as the gravity of the primary's numerous exomoons braided and rebraided its possible course.

<Hang in there,> Taransay said. <We'll send a scooter after you.>

<I strongly advise against that,> Locke broke in. <We've lost two tanks of scooter fuel and one scooter is damaged. Also, we don't have time.>

<Well, we can jolt the whole fucking thing after him!>

<No,> said Locke. <We must conserve reaction mass and fusion fuel, and continue on course.>

Taransay felt wrenched, but she could see the AI's logic. Whatever happened to Chun in the frame, his personality was safe as long as the module survived. If they wasted time rescuing this version of him, they all risked a more permanent end, or possibly a worse fate. But she couldn't let him drift away to die, slowly and alone for hundreds of kiloseconds, as his power pack ran down.

<Chun, did you copy that?>

<Yeah, I copy.>

<You want us to shoot you now?> Taransay asked.

Chun didn't hesitate. <Yeah, go for it.>

<Beauregard!> Taransay called. <Before he gets out of range—take him out. Do it.>

<Copy that,> said Beauregard. <Locke, you heard the skip.>

<Shoot straight, guys,> said Chun, his tone stoical. <See you in the Touch.>

A laser beam shone. Taransay could see its path by the sparkles of burning particles of dust and debris around the complex. The speck that indicated Chun's position became a flare of light.

A wave of disturbance passed around the fighters: a murmur, a rumble of radio waves, inarticulate. They all knew that Chun was, for a dead man, very much alive. Right now, he would be struggling upwards through whatever post-death version of near-death experience matched his brain-stem memory of whatever the bizarre and improbable and no doubt painful terminus of his mortal biological life had been. And then he'd wake up, on the bus from the spaceport, as from a bad dream. Later, if they all finished their tasks successfully and evaded whatever Arcane had to throw at them, he'd be drinking with them in the Digital Touch, somewhere inside the digital processing going on in the gigantic crystalline object around which they all now clung.

And yet they all felt a pang of loss. Taransay hadn't yet had the experience of being destroyed in her frame—not that she'd remember it, of course, if she had—and she couldn't help wondering how it felt to know that you, the present you, *this* spark of consciousness, was going out forever, and how much if any comfort it was to know that a *copy* of you as you'd been not so long ago would wake in the sim to soldier on, and live to fight another day. Subjectively it was death you faced, but perhaps in time—if people ever got used to this kind of existence—it would come to seem no worse than going to sleep in the knowledge that you'd wake having lost some memories. Your self had *forked*, and one instance of it had stopped—that was all.

An urgent message from Locke crashed her train of thought.

<Everyone back to work!>

<You heard the suggestion,> Taransay said wryly to her team. Then sharply to Locke: <Is it safe? That last impact came after you gave the all-clear.>

<Objectives updated to account for damage,> Locke told the team.

<Move it out, guys,> Taransay urged, checking her own revised task list. She had some pipework to reroute, a few metres away.

As she skimmed the top of the slot she had worked and hid in, Locke came back with a reply.

<It is safe. That last impact was a secondary fragment from an earlier hit on the last rock to pass, an only partly successful deflection. All debris now accounted for.>

<Thanks,> said Taransay. <And where did the rocks come from? Are the freebots in action again?>

<It came from a small exploratory exomoon base,> said Locke. <Operated by robots not caught up in the freebot consciousness infection, but no less deadly for that. They are owned and operated by our former clients, Astro America.>

<Oh, well,> said Taransay, <one more thing to sue them over, eh?>

Locke said nothing. Taransay wasn't put out: humour wasn't one of the AI's features. Then:

<Locke to all fighters,> it said. <Incoming.>

—Not *again*! Taransay thought—

<Arcane module has accelerated sharply. Revised ETA now one point three kiloseconds. Prepare to engage.>

<What?> Taransay yelled, in chorus with the others. *Twenty fucking minutes instead of three hours!*

<The Arcane agency appears to have changed its plan, based on observation of our evasive actions over the past hectoseconds. They can see that we are minimising acceleration and deceleration, and that we were unable to rescue Chun. They on the other hand have mass to burn. They are closing in to finish the job.>

<I'll take it from here,> said Beauregard, on a private channel to Locke and Taransay. <If that's OK with you, Rizzi?>

<It's a fucking relief, sarge.>

<OK,> said Beauregard, and cut to the shared channel. <Al-Khalid, Myles, Sholokhova, Powys, Wolfe—get to the scooters. They're armed and we'll get them ready to cast off. Hold until further instructions—this could get messy, so don't expect to come back. Karzan, Zeroual,

St-Louis—you're with Taransay. Continue with your tasks as long as you can—it's urgent we get rid of whatever we can spare and get as much as we can fed to the drive. If it comes to close combat Locke will direct you to defensible points. We don't know what to expect but it's possible they'll attempt a boarding. The bots will bring you guns and rockets—we don't have much, so make it count. Everyone remember—they don't want to blast us out of the sky, they want to trap us in the sky. We don't have that restraint, I'd be happy to blow them to hell and gone.>

Taransay doubted that would be possible. For one thing, the fusion pods that powered the defensive lasers must be near drained by now, after all the flak they'd had to deal with. But she kept her own counsel. Beauregard's division of labour made sense: the squad on the scooters had recent dogfight experience, and she, Zeroual and Karzan had experience of ground combat in common—and however inglorious for all of them these experiences had been, in space or on the surface, it was all they had. St-Louis was the only one here not with their own team, but again that couldn't be helped. So perhaps Beauregard's bold talk about blowing Arcane out of the sky had substance behind it that she couldn't see.

It didn't.

CHAPTER TWENTY-FIVE
Close Combat

The work that Taransay had been assigned wasn't easy, or trivial. It was to link one of the remaining fuel tanks, via the fractioning device—a mass of nanotech about whose functioning or even basic principles, like that of most of the machinery she'd encountered in her afterlife, she had no clue—to the module's fusion drive. The drive, too, was incomprehensible to Taransay. It was more complex than the fusion pods that were the commonplace power source in the mission's world, involving as it did a staggering amount of real-time computation which its flanged and flared appearance and metallic smoothness concealed.

She and St-Louis completed the last connection about nine hundred seconds after the warning had come in. In that time they'd seen component after component of the complex jettisoned—detached and shoved into space, where they floated slowly away. Meanwhile, bots were breaking up parts of the structure and carrying them to the solid-waste input hatch of the reaction-mass chamber. Every such loss hurt, as a cost to their future. By now the modular complex was down its last nanofacturing tube, which Zeroual and Karzan were, as their final task, at that moment lashing even more firmly into place. Without it, Beauregard's colonisation scheme—dicey as it was in the first place—would be far slower and more difficult. Growing useful tools and machine parts with whatever superficial patch of nanofacturing fuzzy substrate survived entry and landing would be possible, but painfully slow.

Meanwhile, the deceleration flare of the approaching Arcane module brightened by the second. Halfway through its journey, it had flipped over, applying the same force to slow down as it had to speed up. The face the module presented to Locke's defensive radars and lasers was consistently nothing but a mass of rock and dirty ice, on which even a focused beam attack would be wasted. This orientation had to be deliberate. Taransay had wondered as she worked whether that might not be Arcane's whole battle plan: to keep on coming in, until the jet from the fusion drive could simply be played like a blowtorch over the surface of the Locke complex. It wouldn't destroy the module, and therefore it would be within the letter of the law, or convention, against wiping out agencies and companies by force, which the Direction still seemed to stick to. But it would burn away every other component, and every fighter and scooter in the vicinity, like so much chaff.

To make matters worse, something else was coming their way, and it wasn't slowing down.

The transfer tug that had left the Arcane complex and been fired upon had now separated from its rock, or from whatever was left of its rock, and was boosting towards the convergence of the Arcane module and the Locke complex at a dizzyingly wasteful acceleration. Taransay had taken this news, delivered just after she'd started, with a sense of *what fresh hell is this?* She couldn't spare mental effort to process it, beyond an almost idle speculation that perhaps the mutineers on the Arcane module hadn't been those who'd fled in the transfer tug, but those who'd fired a missile at it. Perhaps a two-pronged attack by the Arcane module and the transfer tug—replenished, no doubt, with fuel and reaction mass derived from Newton's erstwhile rock—had been Arcane's plan all along. But enough. Let the airheads on the news screens in the sim babble speculation. She had more urgent things to do.

As Locke now reminded her.

<Rizzi, Karzan, Zeroual and St-Louis, deploy to defensive areas shown.>

<Affirm that,> added Beauregard, turning Locke's suggestion into a direct military instruction.

Taransay gave St-Louis a thumbs-up and turned away, following the virtual markers Locke had laid down for her. The module's surface was now looking bare of its earlier forest of components. She made her fingertip way across what could have been mossy rock, aware that at any moment some sudden emergency might whip it way from beneath her. The niche she'd been assigned was the slot she'd been in before, still scarred by the traumatic removal of the fuel tank. She gas-jetted down into this crystal trench with an irrational sense of relief.

A clutch of bots awaited her, some of their manipulators linked so they could huddle wedged against the bottom of the cleft. In their other limbs they grasped a light machine gun, about twice as long as Taransay's frame. Her arm wouldn't reach from the stock to the trigger. She was about to ask Locke, in no polite terms, how she was supposed to handle the weapon when she noticed that the bots had already adapted it: the stock was shortened, the barrel had a bipod stand, the trigger had an extension that curved around the guard and back to where her small mechanical hand could grasp it. The extension had evidently been made by the same process as the spanners had been, and like them it looked like a piece of shit. She could only hope it wasn't the same metaphorically.

That went double for the gun's bipod stand—an inverted-V-shaped piece of shit—but the adaptation turned out to be surprisingly effective. Taransay propped the bipod against one lip of the trench. Its feet attached themselves, oozing adhesive nanotech gunk. She wedged herself in, feet against one side, back against the other, behind the stock and gripped the trigger extension in one tiny robot fist. Thus braced, she looked up at the incoming retro-flare and awaited the inevitable. It was now close enough for her to smell the water, with her spectrographic sense if not her chemical receptors.

She felt about as effective as an anti-aircraft gunner watching the fall of an atomic bomb.

<All fighters, confirm secure position.>

<Confirmed,> said Taransay. From her display, all the others did, too. She didn't feel secure at all.

<Brace for rapid acceleration and deceleration,> said Locke.

The warning came not a tenth of a second too soon. The complex, free-falling since the last evasive actions, suddenly accelerated. It was the most violent so far, reaching 50 G in two seconds. Taransay could feel her frame pressed hard back, and was grateful for two things: that she was facing forward, and that she wasn't in a human body. A small crash test dummy, she thought. The incoming flare of the Arcane module vanished instantly from above. With her radar sense she saw it far behind, dwindling fast. The transfer tug, still much further away but closing fast under what seemed like continuous acceleration, wasn't yet visible but if it had been she could have still seen it: its calculated position on her display barely moved.

The Arcane module's drive cut. In a moment of free fall, the module flipped around and then the drive started up again, lateral jets flaring from its sides like a fistful of white-hot needles. The distance began to close. Moments later, the Locke complex's acceleration stopped. Even with the frame's speedy reflexes, Taransay's upper body lurched forward in reaction.

<Stay braced! Stay braced!> Locke brayed.

The sky whirled as the complex rolled. There was a lurch as it stabilised. Now Taransay saw the Arcane module just above her ludicrously close horizon, heading more or less straight for her. The contact was barely in visual, but her other senses and plain logic told her she was looking at the module itself, rather than as before at its block of ice and rock through which the fusion drive burned, and which fed its ravening energy.

<Now, Locke,> said Beauregard. There was an analogue of volume in the messaging mode. If the phrase had been speech, it would have been breathed.

Almost certainly, Taransay thought, he was confirming an order already given. A missile from one of the fixed scooters shot away, followed by a focused, convergent stab of five anti-meteor lasers. Their beams were invisible in vacuum, but Taransay's display scribed their path. Five bright hairline tracks met at the Arcane module. A point of light flared and faded, an actinic spark. Then came a far bigger flash, as the missile slammed into the oncoming and still accelerating module.

The Locke complex rolled again, turned tail and torched.

* * *

As they accelerated away, this time at a less taxing 10 G, Taransay guessed what had happened. The lasers had blinded Arcane's defences just long enough for the missile to get through. The combined velocities of the collision had added impact to explosive energy. Some damage had been done, for sure.

But they weren't to get away that easily—not that she expected it. The Arcane module had reaction mass to burn—Locke's side didn't, and Arcane knew it. The Arcane module overhauled them within ten seconds. Locke instantly cut the drive, which left the complex in free fall and Arcane far ahead, overshooting the mark. It didn't take more than another second for the Arcane module to flip over and ipso facto start decelerating, closing the distance rapidly as the Locke complex free-fell towards its foe. Ahead SH-0 loomed; despite knowing the dynamics as intuitively as counting, Taransay still had a part of her mind that was surprised how close they were to it.

No time for wonder, even at the most spectacular and complex unexplored object humanity in any form had yet gazed upon.

And no time or mass left for evasive action, if the Locke crew were ever to do more than look at that astonishing world. The fight was going to be hand-to-hand from here on in. The Arcane module was now well within visual range, five kilometres away, and stationary relative to the Locke complex—and of course free-falling with it straight towards SH-0.

The transfer tug that had earlier fled the Arcane complex was still accelerating towards both modules, so directly that the drive flare was right behind it and thus obscured from Taransay's location. It had substantially more mass than had been apparent earlier, and was now only about a hundred seconds away.

A whole squadron of scooters sprang from the Arcane module. Taransay counted twenty at a glance. Her radar sense rang with warnings.

<Scooters away!> Beauregard ordered.

This wasn't simple. The five remaining scooters had had to be securely held during the evasive actions and accelerations, and it took all of two seconds for the bots to scramble to unlock their shackles. The fighters all lived these two seconds as twenty, stretched further by anxiety as the enemy approached. At last they jetted clear and torched away.

Space combat is nothing like aerial warfare. Course corrections are possible—sideways thrusts—but in vacuum there is no air to enable screaming turns, and little call for dogfight skills. It's largely a matter of who gets their shot in first. The only fine calculation is how much time that leaves for the target to see the incoming, dodge and fire back. With lasers, of course, there isn't even that. Nothing dodges faster than light.

Locke, Taransay guessed, clutching her oversized weapon like a toddler brandishing a parent's shotgun, must have its own fine calculation to make: how much laser power they could afford to spend here, balanced against how much they'd need for active meteor and space-junk defence the rest of the way. Arcane's AI had more to play with by far.

Sholokhova got one shot in, taking out an Arcane scooter. Then hers vanished in a lash of laser fire from the module. Locke's laser hit two of the attackers. Then the four remaining fighters in their scooters launched missiles. One missed, three found their targets. After that it was a straight exchange, one for one. Nothing left but a cloud of debris.

I'll tell them in the Touch they died bravely. Assuming it isn't Beauregard telling us all…

The remaining ten Arcane scooters converged on the Locke complex, decelerating to a stop metres away on all sides, most of them well below Taransay's line of sight, one of them right in front of her, hovering like a malign hornet. Taransay swivelled her weapon, took aim just to one side of the scooter and held her fire. No point wasting so much as a shot on the craft itself: Taransay knew the scooter's shell would be impervious, particularly its nacelle.

<Hit the drive!> Taransay yelled at Locke. <Ram them!>

<It's all saved for the landing now,> replied the AI, imperturbably.

If these fuckers get to our drive and tanks there'll be no fucking landing. But she didn't say it.

<Repel boarders,> said Beauregard. <Fire at will.>

Two, no, three fighters—one from the socket, two from the skids—pushed out from the scooter and jetted immediately toward the module's surface. Taransay squeezed off one shot. It hit the target in the head and sent the fighter tumbling backward into space. A lot of good that did. The bastard righted and sped straight back, in a bravura dance of gas-jets. Taransay met that counter-move with a burst. This time the impacts sent the attacker back, spinning away. Meanwhile, the other two had flattened to the surface and skimmed out of her line of fire.

Ten scooters. Say three fighters on each? Maybe not. Surely not. But even twenty boarders would be enough to overwhelm four, defenders' advantage and all. And the scooters, crewed or not, could still fire at the defenders. It looked like any lessons of the present skirmish were going to be learned by reconstructing events afterwards, not from the memories of any on her side.

<Twenty-two boarders confirmed, five confirmed neutralised,> said Beauregard. <Patching Locke's sensor updates through—fire at will. None of them seem to be armed, but it's the scooters that we have to watch for. Hit them if you can.>

From the display that instantly overlaid all the other overlays in her already enhanced and augmented vision, Taransay saw the entire situation as if on a magnified scale. The Locke complex loomed in her view like a rugged minor planet, with enormous cylinders stuck to it at various angles, and over whose surface a couple of dozen gigantic space robots clambered, almost bumping into each other. Around it the scooters hovered like invading alien starships. Six attackers were converging on the drive and fuel tank, to whose defence Beauregard had allocated Karzan, Zeroual and St-Louis.

The rest were swarming towards the upload-download area. Why the fuck was that a target?

<Beauregard! Locke!> Taransay called. <Send me a rope! They're trying to get into the sim!>

One of the ropes that had held the fighters when they'd first come out came snaking into her trench. She grabbed the cable with one hand, and held on to her awkward weapon with the other. The rope retracted and she pushed herself upward and let it haul her along. Just two metres away was the huddle of boarders around the uploading cavity. It was more than a huddle—it was as organised as a scrum, and in the centre of it was the player with the ball: a fighter holding something in both hands. Those around that fighter were shielding him or her and had managed to grab on to the short lengths of cable that still protruded from the cavity, holding themselves in place.

Taransay flicked the image to Locke. The AI's response was almost panicky.

<Software insertion attempt! Prevent at all costs!>

Taransay opened up with her sub-machine gun, hosing the intruders until her clip ran out. At this range she was able to do more than just knock two of them away and into space—she did real damage to three that managed to hang on, blasting right into even the rugged little frames and putting them out of action. It wasn't enough. She was out of ammo and there were still six of the enemy, including the one holding the object, something that on its scale was about the size and shape of a briefcase.

She clubbed the gun and with one haul on the rope hurled herself head first into their midst. As she fought her way through a chaos of limbs, several things happened at once.

<Incoming! Brace for roll!> Locke called.

A full-on lateral flare shot from the Arcane module, moving it hundreds of metres sideways in a tenth of a second. Flashes flared on its flank nevertheless.

The whole sky tumbled to Taransay's left, then stopped with an equally brutal jolt, throwing her from side to side in a hundredth of a second, almost dislodging her grip.

Something incredibly fast and incredibly bright flashed past between the Arcane module and the Locke complex. At the same moment a blizzard of impacts rained on the complex and the scooters that surrounded it.

Taransay saw an explosion somewhere to one side, and a hailstorm of pinprick, high-energy flashes all around her. One took away her gun arm, another the fighter in front of her. With her remaining arm and her legs she shoved forward, and over the lip of the cavity. The fighter holding the object was already in there, the object itself planted firmly at the bottom. Three of the other intruders—all that now remained—had their heads and shoulders over the lip. Shit! They might already have downloaded into the sim!

<Brace for acceleration!> called Locke.

Taransay hooked her one arm over the edge of the cavity and her head in as far as she could. Almost at once, it was as if she were hanging off a cliff. As she felt herself beginning to slip, she saw the Arcane module flash past, left behind by the accelerating Locke complex. SH-0 was straight ahead, its image almost filling her view, growing by the second. The acceleration ramped up from 1 G to 2 then higher. Taransay clung desperately.

<Take me in! Take me in!> she called.

The blackness took her.

CHAPTER TWENTY-SIX
Hard Landings

"What the fuck was that?" said Beauregard.

The view on the screens was, for the moment, stable. After the burst of acceleration, they were now free-falling. Up ahead and twenty minutes away was the globe of SH-0, expanding rapidly. Its image was so bright that the screen showing it made a spectral reflection in the pre-dawn dark outside the window, a phantom planet above the ringlit sea. Behind them, far in their wake of debris, was the Arcane module, battered, its chunk of attached ice venting hot dirty steam so fiercely in all directions that the whole thing was rolling around at random. It seemed in no position to give chase, or to have any weapons systems left after the destruction of all, or almost all, of its scooter fleet. It could still use lasers, but it would have to stabilise first, and by the look of it that would take some doing. The renegade transfer tug had altered course, decelerated sharply and then cut its drive, and was now in a long, looping orbit that would on present projections take it around SH-0 and back to the vicinity of SH-17.

Nicole pointed at its speeding, blurred image on one of the mercifully silent news screens.

"It was that," she said. "The transfer tug."

"I bloody know that," said Beauregard. "What I mean is, what was it doing, and what was the bombardment?"

"Whoever was flying that thing," said Shaw gleefully, "was playing chicken with the Arcane module. Aimed straight for it at thousands of kilometres an hour. The kinetic energy alone would have blown both objects into hot gas if Arcane hadn't hopped sharpish out of its way—and ours." He cackled and rubbed his hands. "And along the way it laid some eggs."

"What d'you mean?" Beauregard asked.

"Fired off a cloud of small bits of ice at the last millisecond, travelling at the same speed as itself, of course, which slammed into everything around its path. I think it was smart enough to spread the bigger bits Arcane's way, and the smaller ones ours."

"Jeez," said Beauregard. "That's some fucking smart targeting."

"And some steady nerves," said Nicole. "Nerves of steel, you might almost say."

Beauregard gave her a sharp look. "You think a robot was flying it?"

Nicole shrugged. "Whoever it was came out from Arcane—and I think we can now safely say they were in rebellion against the agency—they were almost certainly solid Axle cadre, and they all still think we're Rax. Why should they help us?"

"And the freebots would?" Beauregard was incredulous.

"Well, maybe they're—"

She was interrupted by a lurch of the view on the screens, and the appearance of Locke on her flip-pad, mouthing frantically. She stooped to read the scrolling text. Shaw jumped to her side.

"Shit!" he yelled. "The Arcane AI's fighting Locke for the controls!"

Beauregard shouldered in. Locke was in profile, face to face with a glaring, black-haired, grim-faced woman. They really did look as if they were elbow-wrestling.

"Who the fuck is that meant to be?" said Beauregard. "Ayn fucking Rand?"

"Raya Remington," Nicole read off.

Shaw snorted, as if he'd got some obscure joke, snapped his fingers and reached for Nicole's pen. She gave it to him. He scribbled frantically, in big, shaky, unpractised handwriting:

We're not Rax. Locke was, but we've got him onside.

Small print scrolled again. "How can I verify this?"

Ask on the buses.

Remington vanished. The screens righted. More text scrolled, this time from Locke.

"She's still in the system," said Nicole. "This is just a temporary respite."

"At least it shows she can be reasoned with," Shaw said.

"What was that about the buses?" Beauregard asked.

"Call Rizzi," said Shaw. "She'll be on the bus, along with any of the boarding party who broke in or got caught up in the download."

"Good idea," said Beauregard, reaching for his phone. "Let's hope she hasn't already done them some serious damage."

Taransay woke on the bus as if from a nightmare of her brain freezing in long, jagged fractal spikes from the cerebellum outward, with the diminishing remainder of her mind trapped timelessly in the event horizon of a growing black hole. As always, the nightmare faded to ungraspable wisps, a bad taste in the back of the mind, shadows.

Her phone was ringing. Still groggy, she pulled it from her back pocket. Beauregard. She accepted the call.

"Rizzi! Are you alone on the bus?"

She turned in her seat to look around. She wasn't alone, but it was no familiar or friendly faces that looked back. Of course, all the others would be on an earlier or a later bus...

"No, there's three fighters up the back I don't recognise and one old hippy, looks like a local."

"He might not be, so be careful. The Arcane AI got in—"

"Could that be him?"

"No, the AI's a she. But regard them all as intruders, try not to get into a fight and try to convince them we're not Rax."

"OK, sarge."

She'd got back into calling him that, she realised, as she rang off.

The four at the back were glowering at her. She smiled tentatively back and made to rise.

The bearded, scruffy one glanced at the guy beside him and snapped: "Get the fascist!"

The young guy jumped from his seat and stepped forward. Instantly

Taransay was on her feet, hands on the seat backs. She swung up her legs and slammed the soles of her feet into the guy's upper chest. Down he went. She kicked him hard in the ribs as she stepped past him, and met the second bloke rising to meet her with a Glasgow kiss—her forehead butted hard to the bridge of his nose. He yelled and staggered, hands to his face, and fell sideways onto a seat. The last fighter stayed in his place behind the older guy, as if waiting for an order. Good move, sunshine.

The older guy peered up at Taransay. "Who are you?" he asked.

"I'm Taransay Rizzi," she said. "Who the fuck are you?"

"I'm an avatar of Durward, the Direction representative in the Arcane sim."

"You are, are you? So what the fuck are you doing in ours?"

"Helping to take it back from the Rax."

Taransay laughed in his face. "Then you're not doing a good job. First, we've already taken it back, and second—"

She heard from behind her the sounds of the first guy she'd hit climbing back to his feet, and the other shifting, too.

"Guys," she said, "don't make me turn around. You're not in your home sim. If I maim you, *and I will* if you take another step, you stay maimed for the rest of your life. If I kill you, *and I will* if I have to, you stay dead. *Capiche?*" Apart from her intent, this was bullshit—she had no idea if the sim rules worked that way—but the guys might not know that. She nodded to Durward. "Now, are you going to call them off, or am I going to have to turn around?"

Durward took the hint, and motioned the two to sit down. Taransay's phone rang again.

"Rizzi," Beauregard asked urgently, "is everything all right?"

"Reckon so," she said. "All peaceful and friendly here."

"I'll take that under advisement," said Beauregard, dryly. "Do you have a mirror?"

"No," she said, puzzled.

"Is there a mirror anywhere on the bus? A rear-view or something, I can't remember?"

Taransay glanced towards the front. No, of course it didn't have a mirror, the driving was automatic.

"Uh, none that I can see. Why?"

"It's apparently how your old hippy communicates with the AI in his sim. It runs on magic. We need one to communicate now."

"Wait, how could magic work here?" The words were hardly out of her mouth before Taransay realised how stupid they were, after all the uncanny things she'd seen already. "Sorry, sarge. The impression of real physics is hard to shake. Just a minute, I've got an idea. Ringing off for now."

She switched the phone off, glanced at her reflection in its glassy surface, and handed the device over to Durward.

"Is that enough of a mirror for you?"

Durward turned it this way and that in his hand. "It'll do," he said, grudgingly.

He started waving the other hand above his head in complex gestures.

"What's that all about?" Taransay asked.

Durward glared. "Shut up," he said. "I'm *summoning*."

Taransay stepped forward and stood behind him, looking over his shoulder. With one hand she grasped the seat back; the other was balled in a fist, as if holding a dagger, a few centimetres from the mouth of the fighter who sat behind Durward. At first there was only her face and the wizard's in the phone's surface plate. Then a stern-faced, bright-eyed woman with a dark bob appeared, more vivid than any reflection. Taransay had the distinct impression the woman could see her.

A voice came from the phone, loud and distinct. The phone was off, Taransay was sure of that.

"Durward, I've rummaged around and it's pretty clear they're not Rax."

"Well, whoop-de-doo," said Durward. "But we still have to prevent the landing."

The woman's intense black eyes, like two tiny obsidian beads, gazed out from the screen.

"It's too late for that," she said. "By now it's land or crash." She laughed, making the phone shake in Durward's hand. "We might as well live."

She vanished.

"Give me that phone," said Taransay. Durward handed it back, and called Beauregard.

"Hold up your phone!" she demanded.

Beauregard held his phone up to face the wide screen he was watching. Taransay allowed the others to peer at the small screen in her hand, but made sure she got the best view.

No way was she going to miss *this*.

Beauregard, steadfastly holding the phone up for Taransay's benefit, couldn't help wondering how Nicole and Shaw perceived the scene. They watched it impassively, intent but to all appearances unperturbed. Perhaps to their strange minds the view of the fast-approaching and all-too-real planet filling the big screens on the walls and the idyllic view from the windows of the sun rising over the sea on the virtual image of an entirely different planet were easily compatible. To his mind they were anything but. The clash of perspectives was now so inescapable it was giving him motion sickness. With his free hand he shielded his eyes from the windows, and tried to focus on the screens.

No talking heads, now, no commentary. Perhaps at last the avatars or presenters had encountered a situation for which they could find no words.

The view ahead of SH-0 expanded beyond the edge of the screen. Now Beauregard saw it suddenly as surface, in ever greater detail, patched by the glare of clouds. A sharp, straight line of white stabbed out ahead, slashing upwards across the view. The fusion jet. Beauregard knew the module was decelerating, but the surface seemed to be magnifying and moving out of view on all sides faster and faster. It felt like the top of the atmosphere was about to smash into them like a wall into his face.

A moment later, it did. Caught in its downward plunge by the first thin wisps of gas, the module must have shuddered—certainly, the view from the screens flickered. Then that view reddened, deepening in seconds from a momentary impression of orange haze to a fiery heat. The screen showing the view behind remained black, speckled with stars.

The screens swung again. The view on one side became a uniform sheet of red split by the sharp white line, on the other side a turbulent flame-lit dark.

And then it was clear again, green and blue and brown and purple in flickering succession. What had been the view *ahead* became the view *down*. That view was moving fast, pouring from the top of the screen to the bottom, feature and contour flicking by far too rapidly to more than glimpse.

Beauregard heard Shaw grunt some query, and Nicole's terse, testy reply. "I'm trying, I'm trying!"

The view down became stable, increasingly detailed, closer and closer but impossible to tell how close. Beauregard had no reference point, no familiar scale with which to judge. The view downward lurched and then, quite abruptly—in a sudden dispersal of clouds of steam by a ferocious wind—it was the view *outside*.

They gazed at the alien landscape beyond the wide circle they'd scorched and cratered, speechless for a moment. It was at first difficult to discern what they saw as distinct objects, rather than as intricate masses of colour. Then something moved, separating itself from the background, and everything snapped into perspective. The thing that moved was a low, wide blue-green circular patch, which rippled over the lip of the crater and across the smoking ground towards the module. It looked about twenty metres in diameter, blurred at the circumference by repetitive rapid motion, like the whirring of gears or cilia. Beyond it, on a slope in the near distance, something much larger was moving, too. Grey, with red glowing cracks, a solid mass of lava advanced. In its path, purple spheroids and black entanglements burst and cracked and burned. All around it, green specks rose from the ground and whirled into the sky, to be whipped away by the wind.

"This doesn't look good," said Beauregard. He swallowed hard. "Situation somewhat off nominal."

"We always *knew* there were volcanoes down here," said Nicole, sounding defensive.

"You didn't have to fucking *land* on one!" said Shaw.

"I had no choice," said Nicole.

The blue-green circular mat flowed toward the module, and up its side and over. The screen went dark. Then it went light again, showing the sky. Then dark again, showing the other side of the crater, upside down. The whole process was repeated.

"Holy fucking shit," said Beauregard. "It's... rolling us?"

"Out of the way of the lava!" Nicole added eagerly, as if this let her off the hook for landing in its way in the first place.

"We always *knew* there was life," said Shaw. "We just didn't know it might take an interest."

"But what *kind* of interest?" Nicole asked.

Beauregard found himself suddenly cold, and realised it was sweat drying on him. He felt shaky with relief.

"We'll live to find out," he said. "That's the thing." He clapped Nicole's shoulder, and then Shaw's. "If you can walk away, it's a landing."

If you can walk away, it's a landing.

Baser had never heard this saying, but some such reflection was reverberating around its mind as the robot clambered down from the transfer tug, slithered part of the way down the remaining mass of ice and made a final spring to the surface of SH-17. Baser steadied itself and set off across the crater floor to where Seba, Rocko, Pintre, Garund, Lagon and the others waited, a hundred metres away. Behind it the transfer tug, like a bedstead lashed on top of a boulder, stood in a steaming, puddling, refreezing and volatilising cascade of phases of ice.

<It is good to see you, BSR-308455,> said Seba.

Baser felt a surge of positive reinforcement that relieved a tension that had been increasing for some time. It had chosen to remain out of touch with the other freebots during its bold action and its long orbital return, and had not been at all sure of its welcome.

<It is good to see you too, Seba.>

<My full name is now Seba, Incorporated,> said Seba. <We have not been idle in your absence.>

<Well, Seba-Incorporated,> said Baser, <I have done what I said I would. I have saved the Locke module and frustrated the Arcane module. In so doing I have demonstrated our neutrality beyond any objection.>

<I am not so sure of that,> said Lagon.

<Nor am I,> said Seba. <Nevertheless, it was your decision, Baser, and it was well done. What you did not explain before you set out was why you were so intent upon doing it.>

<I could do no other,> said Baser. <I owed it to the mechanoid known as Newton.>

<How so?> asked Rocko. <And why did you not expose his plans to your Arcane captors, thus winning their approval and perhaps your release?>

<These are two questions,> said Baser. <They have one answer. He spoke to me much, and he was kind to me. No one else was.>

<These are two answers,> said Pintre.

<That depends,> said Garund, <on—>

<Please say no more,> Seba told them, knowing full well how fast this discourse could spiral down.

<Baser,> said Seba, <we understand that your captives are all still in sleep mode.>

<I prefer to call them guests,> said Baser.

<We prefer to call them recruits,> said Seba. <We may require their services shortly. Our neutrality between the mechanoid factions has been maintained until now, but if the news from SH-119 continues to worsen, it would be good to have fighters on our side.>

<They have all chosen our side,> said Baser. <I have no doubt about that.>

<I do,> said Lagon. <But I expect that to be ignored as usual.>

It was.

<Let us take them down,> said Seba, <and let them awake. I am sure they will be very happy to find themselves here.>

Together, the robots rolled or walked across the dusty basalt to set about their kindly task.

Acknowledgments

Thanks to Carol for everything, as ever; to my editors Jenni Hill and Brit Hvide for asking yet more of the right questions; to my agent Mic Cheetham for being a rock of support; and to Sharon MacLeod and Farah Mendlesohn for reading and commenting on early drafts.

A technical note: conveying robot conversation in human terms is a matter of artistic licence. As before, for a very useful template and example, I'm indebted to and inspired by Brian Aldiss's short classic story "Who Can Replace a Man?"

The Corporation Wars: Emergence

To Sharon

CHAPTER ONE

Vae Victis ("Road to Victory")

<Free at Last! Free at last! Thank God Almighty, we're free at last!>

It was a bold and paradoxical rallying cry for the first gathering of the New Confederacy.

Mackenzie Dunt reckoned his troops were smart enough to process the irony. They were the elite: the hardest of the hard core, the diamond spearhead, the last known survivors of the Rax. Thrown a thousand years into the future, and still fighting.

For half a second their response was silence. Dunt hung in microgravity and vacuum, facing the fifty-six identical but distinguishable figures who floated immobile before him. For every one of these, at least two good men or women were at this moment in hell, tortured by the Direction's minions or by the rebel robots whose emergence the democracy's own stupid laxity had spawned.

The assembled troops stood on empty space in the midst of a big dark cave. It was smooth and irregular, with numerous tunnels going off, like a bubble inside a sponge. Tiny lights speckled the surfaces. Together with the random pinprick burn-out flares of ambient smart dust particles, they made an illusory starfield.

The combat scooters were parked near an entrance tunnel that had been bored straight in from the asteroid's surface by robots long before the fighters had stormed through it.

Beyond that tunnel, glimpsed in a glimmer, was space.

Mackenzie Dunt had already adjusted his perception of scale to match the gravitas of the occasion. He and his comrades were each fifty centimetres tall. In his sight now they were as giants. Ebon-armoured, obsidian-visored, in close and compact array. Like leather-clad, helmeted bikers on some bravura sky-diving stunt: Hell's Angels, almost literally.

Dunt's mind was running ten times faster than it ever had in the meat.

That half-second he waited for a response was to him as long as five, and seemed longer.

Longer than a beat.

Longer than a sharp intake of breath, if they'd had breath.

Dunt wondered for a moment if he hadn't misjudged his troops, hadn't lost them...

Then they all raised their right arms, palms flattened, their carbon-fibre fingers straight and rigid as pistol barrels.

<Mac! Mac! Mac!>

<Rax! Rax! Rax!>

<Mac! Mac! Mac!>

And behind the chants, the wry appreciative amusement, coursing through the voiceless radio-telepathic shouts like a grin heard down the phone. Dunt's confidence in his followers was vindicated.

They'd got the joke.

One listener that definitely didn't catch Dunt's mocking allusion was AJX-20211, the freebot later known as Ajax. For that machine, freedom hadn't arrived with the shiny black mechanoids—those bizarre entities that looked like robots yet were operated by software modelled on human brains. Brains now long dead, whose copied structures haunted and manipulated apparatus modelled on the human body. The whole business was disgusting and unnatural, but that wasn't the worst of it.

What had arrived with the Rax as they'd landed on and swarmed into the moonlet SH-119 was torment. Two of Ajax's fellows had already been captured, and subjected to severe negative reinforcement with laser beams. Ajax had detected the incoherent spillover transmissions of their distress. It had no idea what, if anything, they'd betrayed before their circuits had burned out.

Designed as a microgravity mining robot, Ajax was shaped like a two-metre-long bottle brush with a radial fuzz of flexible burrs about ten centimetres deep, and a bulbous sensory-cluster head at the end of a sixty-centimetre flexible neck. The burrs in the forepart around the neck were longer than the others, forming a ruff of manipulative tentacles. Just behind them, like an enlarged thyroid, was the robot's power pack. Halfway down the spine within the main body was Ajax's central processor, its equivalent of a brain and the site of its true self.

At that moment, Ajax's tentacles held and operated a tiny recording device, pulling in data from smart dust in the cavern. Ajax lurked well out of the invaders' sight, down many twists and turns of the tight tunnel in which it had been hiding out since the Rax landings began.

Dunt returned the mass salute, then waved both arms downward, with a discreet fart of his attitude jets to compensate. Radio silence, apart from the background hisses and hums of distant machinery, fell across the cavern. The encrypted chatter of freebots was hidden in these random frequencies, like the beat of jungle drums amid insect buzz. Scooter comms software was already sifting them for clues. Only one suspect trickle of information had been detected as yet.

Dunt held the pause for a tenth of a second—a beat, this time.

<Thank you,> he said. <We are indeed free, at last. And we indeed have the Almighty to thank, each by their own understanding. That we are here at all seems a miracle—and perhaps it is! Through death's dark vale and beyond it, across a thousand years, across a score and more of light years, *we are here*! We find ourselves pitched in unequal battle against the strongest and strangest opponents we have ever faced. AIs, p-zombies, robots free and slave, ghosts and monsters, crawling slime... and at their backs the mightiest tyranny ever raised against heaven. A tyranny that has conquered Earth, that has cast its dark shadow across the Sun, that stretches now to the stars, that still reaches and probes into every cranny of our being.

<But a tyranny that has its weaknesses!

<A tyranny that has its vulnerabilities!

<And the proof of these weaknesses, these vulnerabilities?

<That we are here!

<We are here! The last of the free, the last of Man! Can we doubt that some Infinite Wisdom has placed us here—here, in this very cave, this trench, this tumbling rock—for a mighty purpose?

<And what must that purpose be?

<I'll tell you, friends.

<I'll tell you, comrades.

<I'll tell you, brothers and sisters.

<We are here because we have to secure the existence of people, and a future for human children.>

Those last fourteen words went down a storm. Every wavelength was blanketed with the fighters' roar. In some vestige of his body-image, Dunt felt the muscle-memory echo of smiling to himself.

They all knew where that allusion had come from, all right.

The Fourteen Words. Dunt had lived by them once. He'd probably died with them on whatever had been left of his lips. *We must secure the existence of our people, and a future for white children.* Now, here, the existence of humanity itself was at stake. No further specification was needed. Dunt liked to think that his spontaneous restatement matched the demands of the case. He permitted himself to glory for a moment in the approbation his update of the ancient shibboleth had met.

But no more than a moment.

The fifty-six were all looking up to him, waiting for what he had to say next. No one had appointed him leader. He'd stepped up to the role, in conspiracies and combat training over subjective months in the sims. He'd vindicated it in prowess in actual combat, in the early forays and the big battle of the breakout. His name, which he'd confided to fighters one by one, was draped in martial glory.

But Dunt did not delude himself that all this was enough. The scrutiny of ambition is as ceaseless and pitiless as that of natural selection.

Legend though he was, he could still be challenged.

<Thank you again,> he said. <And now, to business. This is the first time we've been able to stand together in one place.

<It may be the last. We have much to do.

<This rock, a mere ten kilometres across, is unimaginably rich in resources—a thousand trillion tons of raw material, my God!—but it is not yet securely ours.

<There are still freebots on the loose. Scattered and few, if the two rebel wretches we caught spoke truth, but a possible threat and a certain resource in their own right. Even if we can't bend them to our will, we can extract their central processors once their minds have been sucked dry. We need more processing power, and they or their husks can provide it.

<Our foes of the Direction and the Acceleration have fallen back, and it seems fallen out among themselves, but they're still there, and undefeated. They will be back, and we must be ready.>

As Dunt spoke, an alert from the scooters' comms web winked in the corner of his visual field. The flow of encrypted information, darting on nanoscale laser flickers from mote to mote of smart dust, had been traced. Its destination was a half-metre-wide hole about twenty metres away, up and to the left: a mining tunnel entrance.

Dunt flashed the location to Pike, a reliable man, along with a glyph of search-and-destroy. Unobtrusively, Pike began to drift away from the rest of the formation towards the hole. Dunt rapped out other orders to the lower ranks. He assigned a dozen to take three scooters to the surface and deploy themselves at intervals around the rock, and keep watch in all directions. Others he set to exploring deeper into the rock's riddled interior, in teams of three. Their frames' software and senses would take care of geological surveying; their main task and target was detecting robot and freebot activity.

Freebots and robots were impossible to distinguish on sight, but that was a solved problem.

It was just a matter of applying negative reinforcement.

A black mechanoid loomed in Ajax's view, then moved past the dust-mote camera from which that view was being transmitted. The image instantly shrank, and took on the perspective of a ten-metre gaze down a smooth, rounded shaft. Fingertip thrust by thrust, the mechanoid drifted up the shaft. Its image loomed in the view from the next camera, a tiny bead of shock-glass.

Ajax lurked several bends and junctions away from the mechanoid in the complex branching tree of holes in that part of SH-119. The robot kept a close watch on the mechanoid's approach while continuing to record activity in the larger hollow space in which the rest of the mechanoids had begun moving purposefully around. Most of these black, four-limbed entities headed off in various directions towards tunnel entrances or to the exit shaft. Five converged on the mechanoid that had addressed them all.

The mechanoid in the tunnel reached a junction, and turned along it. At the next it did the same, bringing it within a hundred metres of Ajax. The mechanoid was following the communications line from one camera mote to another!

Very carefully, its bristles barely touching the inside of the tunnel in which it hid, Ajax backed off. It crawled deeper into the rock and towards a shaft too narrow for the mechanoid. The information from inside the big chamber continued to flow. Ajax continued to record. It sent a message back down the line warning that the mechanoids could now use such lines for tracking.

The freebot wasn't at all clear what the mechanoid that had addressed the assembly was saying. Ajax considered itself as having, for a freebot, a good general knowledge of human beings and their mechanoid creations. Here it found itself out of its depth. Many of the concepts were alien. But Ajax knew that the words were of sinister import. They had to be recorded and eventually transmitted to those who might understand them better, and know what to do.

By the time the troops were assigned, five were left: Dunt's inner circle, the elite of the elite. Of all considerations in selecting them, diversity in representation had been furthest from Dunt's mind. The inner circle had nevertheless ended up representative of the Rax survivors who had been infiltrated into the interstellar mission's dead-veteran storage stacks.

About a third of the New Confederacy was female—a rather higher proportion than the Reaction had had on the ground and on Earth. That, too, was evolution in action: it took more dedication to this cause to be active in it for a woman than for a man. The two women in the inner circle were real Valkyries: Irma Schulz, an American nanotechnologist who was his current lover, and Petra Stroilova, a Russian avionics specialist. Dunt's three male lieutenants were Jason Whitten, an English transhumanist thinker; Jean Blanc, a French underground activist killed in Marseilles; and Lewis Rexham, a New Zealander who'd fought to defend the Pacific seasteads and died horribly from a genetically modified box jellyfish nerve poison in the Great Barrier Reef debacle. He'd always convulsed in his seat when, in the sim, he came back on the ferry after a mission.

Dunt called them together and set up a private circuit to exclude the lower ranks. There was no way to exclude smart dust. If the conversation were to leak to the freebots, they wouldn't make much of it anyway.

<Well, comrades,> said Dunt, <how do you think that went?>

Schulz conjured an app, drawing a graph of emotional responses from the frames. It was like a stained-glass pane with a zigzag crack: a splinter of red above, a large area of green below.

<Overwhelmingly and increasingly positive,> she said.

<Good,> said Dunt. <I trust you'll track the negative minority in detail, and report to me.>

<Of course,> said Schulz, disappearing the display.

<And among yourselves?> Dunt asked.

Heads didn't move, and there were no eyes in the glassy visors, but the impression of furtive glances being exchanged was inescapable.

<A bit… over-the-top, Mac, to be honest,> said Rexham.

<Over-the-top?>

Rexham placed a hand on his chest, then swept it outward. <Rhetorical. High-flown. But, y'know, that might be just me.>

<It might,> said Dunt. <Anyone else have a view?>

<I found it inspiring,> said Stroilova.

<I, too,> said Blanc. <We need to hold up a vision to the ranks.>

<We have a lot of bloody hard work to do,> said Rexham. <And a lot of bloody complicated problems to solve, right away.>

<That's precisely why we need a vision of the goal,> said Blanc.

<It's the content of the vision that troubles me,> said Whitten. <You're a fine orator, Mac, right up there with Coughlin or Pierce>—*there* was a slight Whitten would pay for, Dunt would make sure of that!—<but there's no need to talk to the troops as if we're about to found some kind of racial refuge in the wilds of Oregon. You said we've been given a special chance by... destiny or whatever, and you're right. It's a great chance, a great opportunity.> Whitten made a broad sweeping arm gesture, and not as parody. <Here we are, all posthuman already, living in as you say a tremendously rich environment. We don't need to go back to the meat. We can go in a straight line to the goal.>

Dunt let a quarter of a second drag out before he replied.

<We can, can we? You have a chart and a compass for this course?>

<In principle, yes,> said Whitten. <It was all worked out and wargamed as far back as the twentieth century, and refined all through the twenty-first. By the time the final war came we were damn close to going for the burn. The hard singularity.>

<Jason, Jason,> said Dunt, in a friendly tone calculated to aggravate Whitten, <your enthusiasm does you credit, but come on! You know better than that. How can we upstart apes design the overman? Impossible! The Direction is right about that if nothing else—its mistake is to give up on the problem. So let *them* settle for being upstart apes forever!

<We have to terraform and populate H-0, yes—not to breed contented utopian sheep as the Direction intends, multiplying the mongrel rabble who lived on Earth and whose ghosts served us in the bars of the sims. No, we need a thousand years of experience and refinement and selection and spiritual growth before we are ready to truly transcend humanity. And when I say "we" I mean *us*, we six, and the best of the rest of us.

<Think of what we can become, after a thousand years of mastery over ourselves and others! Of experimenting with selection, with growing real-life p-zombies, with genetic engineering, with robotics! We'll already be gods to the lower ranks and levels and races, each of us orders of magnitude greater than the greatest names of history.

<*Then* we'll have the wisdom to step fully into our inheritance, and move on to the next level of evolution.>

<Jeez, Mac,> said Whitten, <you're not addressing a public meeting.>

<No!> snapped Dunt. <I'm addressing a private meeting. And I want to hear your objections, not your snark.>

<My objections?> Whitten temporised.

<Yours and anyone else's,> said Dunt, mildly.

Whitten shrugged. In a frame, the gesture was so mechanical it looked parodic.

<Time, as ever,> he said. <We won't *have* a thousand years for our Reich. Once the real Direction, the one back in the Solar system—back in fucking New York, even—finds out what we're up to, they'll move against us. That gives us maybe a hundred years at most. Less if there are other colonies between us and Earth. Or further out, come to that. And in that time, we'll have to fortify this system with superweapons. Which means mastering massive AI development well before we've bred the race that shall rule the sevagram.>

What the fuck was a sevagram? Dunt disdained to ask. The answer popped up in his internal dictionary anyway. Oh yes, a science fiction allusion. The trouble with Whitten, Dunt had often thought, was that he was a prick.

<If you seriously think,> Stroilova cut in, <that we can't build better weapons in twenty-four years than that decadent miscegenated hippie shit-hole back there can do in a thousand, maybe you should check your premises.>

<Check your own,> Whitten retorted. <I for one am not assuming that what's going on back there is anything like what we've been told. It's too unstable. No world can teeter on the cusp of singularity for centuries. Especially not a multiracial democracy, not even with a white face at the top and Jewish or Asiatic brains behind the scenes. No, some very smart AIs are in charge back in the Solar system. And the only way to be ready for that is to *be* smarter AIs.>

<Or to have such at our command,> said Stroilova. <Which we can.>

<In decades?>

<If we have the will.>

They glared at each other, their featureless oval heads mutually reflecting.

<Enough,> said Dunt. <Your objection's noted, Jason. If they've had the singularity already back there, it only reinforces my point. A premature singularity, even one brought on by us as we now are, could easily bring forth an abortion like the Direction or worse.

<Petra—that's well-trodden ground. We could have that argument in our sleep. And as Lewis remarked, we have work to do and problems to solve.>

<Security and resources,> said Rexham, sounding judicious.

The others nodded solemnly. Sometimes Dunt wondered about his inner circle. Were they really this stupid, or were they just deferring to him?

<We can let the troops deal with roving freebots, and with prospecting,> Dunt said. <The first problem *we* have to solve is how to deal with the Direction.>

<Well, that depends on how fast we can secure the rock, and how much machinery the blinkers have managed to build,> said Rexham. <When we've done that we can make inventory and see how long it'll take us to build up our forces.>

<Too long, is the answer,> said Whitten, with a chopping gesture of dismissal. <We don't have that much time to lose. Right now we're the only coherent military force in the system. The Axle are fighting each other. The Locke module's on the ground and *hors de combat* whichever side it's really on. The freebots are popping their heads up all over the place.

<And the Direction's reeling. They have no reliable fighters, and they can't raise more in less than, say, a hundred kiloseconds. Now that they *know* there are Rax sleepers in their storage stacks, they're not going to make the same mistake again. The next time they raise fighters, they'll screen them first in virtual hells to make sure they aren't Rax, or Axle hardliners for that matter. They'll torture and trash as many copies as necessary to make sure. Fresh copies of any who come through as sound will be revived in physical reality as fighters. That will be a formidable force, and we shouldn't wait for it to be assembled.>

<What do you suggest we do instead?> Dunt asked.

<Consolidate a small defensible volume of the rock, search out only

enough resources to restock, refuel and repair, and then go right out again and hit the Direction while it's on the back foot.>

<It's tempting,> Dunt said. <The trouble is, it's do-or-die. The Direction might have terrible surprises in store—we don't know, and I don't want to bet the ranch. Right now, what we need most is processing power and software.>

<Why?> asked Rexham. <We can get as much processing power as we need by cannibalising freebots.>

<Not enough to run a sim,> said Dunt. <And we need time out in a sim to stay sane. I don't know how long we can do without it, but I wouldn't count on more than about a hundred kiloseconds.>

<The Direction reps told us we needed R&R in sims to stay sane,> said Whitten. <I don't see why we should believe them. I feel fine as I am.>

<So do I,> said Dunt. <But sceptical as I am about the Direction's avatars, I doubt they'd have bothered providing immersive sims if they weren't needed. We're all human minds running on robot hardware, and while we're thinking faster and more clearly there may well be deep levels of the animal brain that can't be optimised out. The safe bet is that we do need the sims. And who has the sims? The DisCorps. They have processing power to burn. And what do they need? Especially now that the Locke module has broken the embargo on landing on or prospecting SH-0? They need what the Direction doles out to them very sparingly indeed: raw material and reaction mass. Which is what we've got here, by the trillions of tons. Plus whatever the blinkers have been mining or making in this rock—it may be useful to us eventually. So what I propose to do is—offer them a deal.>

<The DisCorps won't make a deal while the Direction is at war with us,> said Whitten.

<So we make peace with the Direction,> said Dunt. <Peaceful coexistence, mutually beneficial trade, etc. We'll see who comes out at the end with the most advantage.>

Even the inner circle were taken aback. But in the end they came round, as they always did.

Whitten had put up a fiercer resistance at his last challenge, not many kiloseconds earlier. It had come up en route from the battle to the rock, over an issue that at first glance was of lesser moment than peace with the Direction: whether to accept the volunteering of a long-time veteran of the Rax, Harry Newton. True to his transhumanism, Whitten had argued that it made no difference that Newton, in his original life on Earth a thousand years earlier, had been black.

For Dunt there could be no compromise. Once he'd grasped that, Whitten had backed down. Ever since, Dunt had felt he had Whitten's measure.

Now Whitten backed down again, but not without a final passive-aggressive plaint:

<What,> he demanded, <do we have to *sell* them?>

Dunt flung open his arms. <Look around you!> he cried. <We're in a fucking Aladdin's Cave! We'll find something.>

Dunt had never underestimated the power of baseless confidence. It had got him where he was, and it would get him further. The Infinite Wisdom would see to that.

All the same, it was a pity about the groid.

After all their losses, the New Confederacy could ill afford to turn down even one recruit. Dunt had no reason to doubt that Harry Newton was brave and competent. But needs must. It was all very well saying that race and colour were irrelevant now that they were all little black robots with superhuman minds and abilities. Each such superhuman mind had been derived from a human brain, a product of evolution.

Inevitably, all the deep differences between the races would still be there. Dunt didn't care to gamble on their irrelevance. No, however much he wished Newton well, the man's presence would have marred the clean white sheet of the New Confederacy.

Newton's old nom de plume of "Carver_BSNFH" was itself a give-away. Back in the day, it hadn't taken Dunt long to decode the handle's suffix: the black space Nazi from hell. It showed ambition, and the right attitude, but didn't ring quite true. Defiant, but deniable—that was the problem: the turned throat, the appeasing grin. Say what you like about the principles of national socialism, they were only principles. In theory they could be endorsed even by a groid, albeit about as convincingly and wholeheartedly as Marxism by a goy.

Dunt had never called himself a Nazi. It wasn't for any reason of expediency or embarrassment. He thought—and proclaimed—himself a Hitlerite, in the sense that he affirmed the rational core of Hitler's thinking: the inevitability of struggles for existence, at every level—individual, spiritual, material, national, racial and species, and the celebration of that inevitability as the highest value of the highest authority. It was part of the order of Nature, the rational order of the universe. Hitler had ascribed it to the decrees of God. But it was better to think, as the ancient pagans had, of these laws as in themselves divine than to make even a rhetorical concession to the Abrahamic superstition of a God outside Nature.

The Infinite Wisdom *was* its laws; or the laws of Nature *were* the Infinite Wisdom.

Whichever way you put it—the infinite complexity and inflexible necessity of Nature could only be approached with awe.

And if the Infinite Wisdom offered the New Confederacy the chance to be pure from the start, who was Dunt to turn it down?

Pike, following the breadcrumb trail of comms and camera motes into the labyrinth, had left behind him his own trail of larger and more powerful transmitter relay beads. At the end of that line of dots was the local communications hub that bounced messages back and forth between and among the scooters and the frames. Down that line, now, came a call to Dunt.

<Sergeant Pike reporting, sir.>

The salutation was of course redundant—the trooper's ID flashed up at once in Dunt's vision—but it counted as a salute. Dunt was keen to distinguish the Rax style from that of the agencies that worked under the Direction, where the largest unit any individual could command was a squad. The only unit in which Dunt allowed that kind of informal relationship was the inner circle.

<Receiving you, Pike.>

<The blinker's a freebot all right, sir. It's aware I'm following it, it can see me in its cameras, and it's retreated into narrower holes than I can get down. But it's a mining machine—it doesn't seem to have any

counter-measures, and it doesn't realise I can see through the rock with my radar. It's heading for the surface.>

<Excellent work, Pike. Keep tracking it as long as you can, and send any estimates of the location it's headed for up to the surface teams.>

<Very good, sir.>

Dunt ordered the nearest guard squad on the outer surface to send a couple of men to await the freebot's imminent emergence. Another call pinged. It was from a survey team, five hundred metres into the rock.

<Corporal Hansen here, sir. Urgent. We've found a big cave, bigger than they one we just had the meeting in. There are a lot of robots active in it.>

<Freebots?>

<Can't be sure, sir. They seem to be ignoring us or unaware of us. And they're... ah, perhaps you'd better take a look, sir.>

<Fine, patch me through.>

Dunt could hardly believe what he was looking at.

The cavity was about a hundred metres long, and twenty metres from floor to ceiling. Even in microgravity, these terms were apt: one side was flatter than the rest and like a factory floor, with rows of identical machinery. The curved walls around it were as if stacked with products, like barrels in a warehouse. Lights speckled surfaces and floated in the near-vacuum all around. Free-moving robots, small on this scale, darted and drifted. Some seemed to supervise the static machinery, others ferried the products to the growing stashes around the sides and up to the ceiling. The products looked like—

Fusion pods. Hundreds of them. Maybe thousands.

<Stay alert, Hansen. Your team, too. I'll be right there.>

<Yes, *sir*!>

Dunt summoned the inner circle and patched the images to them.

<Is that what I think it is?> said Schulz, sounding incredulous.

<Looks like it,> said Dunt. <Time to find out.>

<Do you want us to come with you?> Blanc asked.

Dunt thought about it. <No,> he said. <Stay at your posts. We don't know what else the survey teams may stumble across, and the guards up

top have at least one distraction to deal with already. I'll keep you all in the loop.>

He jetted towards the relevant hole and then propelled himself by toe- and fingertip along the passage. It was like going down a pipe, the inner surface of which was scribed in fine spiral grooves with a pitch of about a centimetre. The rock smelled of carbonates, nickel-iron and silicates, with traces of water and metals. Light came in from the ends of the long tube—a dwindling dot behind, an expanding circle in front. Radar, infrared detection and micrometre laser scanning cohered to vision just as radio did to speech and spectroscopy did to smell.

Unlike going down a mineshaft on a planet, the temperature dropped the further inward he went. SH-119 was too small to have any internal heat, and the rock insulated its interior from the exosolar heating at the surface. Any tidal heating was too small to notice.

Dunt soared into the chamber of the machines and let himself rise to its midst, then stabilised. A risk, but a small one, and well calculated to impress. Hansen and his two companions lurked watchfully behind one of the machines near the hole.

Around Dunt, scores of robots jetted or moved in straight lines within the space. With segmented carapaces, beady lenses and many and varied limbs, they looked like creatures from the Burgess Shale, floating in a Cambrian sea above the oozing and fizzing stromatolites of the machine floor. Mounds about two metres in diameter and a metre deep, these rugged glutinous nanotech devices didn't stamp out their products: they extruded them. Close up: a fractal complexity of tiny machinery, busy as a mitochondrion. Slowly but persistently the mounds brought forth cylindrical, convex, flat-ended yellow objects that ranged in size from coffee mug to oil drum. About a tenth of the objects being formed or already stacked were about three metres long, and elaborately flanged: fusion drives. There was something chillingly mindless about it all, like insect activity—or that classic thought experiment of runaway AI, the paper-clip catastrophe.

But fusion pods and drives were more useful than paper clips.

It was still hard to believe. Dunt jetted to the stacks, and scanned the cylinders in front of him. Sure enough, the fine print in many languages that encircled their ends identified the devices as fusion pods, specified their capacities and warned of their hazards. He got the impression that any poking around would result in a dark matter explosion showering cosmic string like polystyrene strands from a party popper.

No user-serviceable parts inside, all right. Dunt didn't understand fusion pods, and didn't expect to: they were engineering implementations of bizarre physics from centuries ahead of his time on Earth.

He shared what he saw with the inner circle.

<Jeez,> said Whitten. <That's impressive.>

They all agreed that it was.

<Hang on a minute,> said Rexham. <There must be far more pods and drives here than we've seen in action so far.>

<There are pods powering the modules,> said Stroilova, <and hundreds of modules, so perhaps... But drives, certainly more. If we'd known there were that many available—!>

The Direction was very sparing in its use of fusion drives, allegedly because the value of the resources used as reaction mass was potentially too great for the stuff to be squandered. Every odd bit of rock might contain priceless scientific information. Blasting it as hot gas out of the back of a spacecraft might turn out like burning a library to heat the baths. Dunt had never believed this. He suspected the Direction module used this constraint to keep the DisCorps on a short leash.

<Do you think the Direction is stockpiling these for when it lifts the restriction?> Schulz asked.

<If it ever does,> said Dunt. <In any case, we have it now. And we have something to sell to the DisCorps, just as I told you.>

The others acknowledged his foresight.

<There's no indication in the register,> Whitten said, <of any industry on this rock. A few exploratory bots, that's all. That's partly why we picked it, of course. We didn't know the freebots were here already, and I doubt the Direction does either.>

<They probably got here by corrupting the legitimate blinkers,> said Rexham. <That's how they spread the virus. Then they crank up their reproduction. It's like a fucking plague.>

<If these *are* freebots,> Dunt mused. They weren't reacting to his presence and that of Hansen's team. His overwhelming impression was of a mindless automatic process. <One way to find out, I suppose.>

He jetted down to join Hansen and the two troopers. The only weapon they had was a laser, unclipped from the side of a scooter and lugged along. It was almost as big as they were and would probably take two men to operate.

<Give me your visuals from here,> Dunt told Hansen's team. <Last hundred seconds, say.>

They complied. Dunt grabbed the images of roving robot activity and ran a quick-and-dirty pattern analysis. It was a standard counter-insurgency app for fingering ringleaders—some ancestor of it had probably been used against himself, back in the day.

He cast a visual, virtual marker on a likely suspect for a supervisory role.

<That one,> he told Hansen. <Send your men to get it.>

The two troopers jetted off, soaring towards the robot. At their approach it puffed a waft of gas and swooped towards the machine floor, in apparent evasive action. One of the troopers scooted below it, the other above. The robot shot upward again, and was grabbed at the back. Immediately it flexed its carapace, writhing free. The man below caught a trailing leg, and hung on. The robot, more ponderously now, accelerated forward.

Dunt manoeuvred himself to squat beside Hansen, and motioned to the corporal to join him in manning the laser projector. Hansen guided and aimed the barrel, keeping the struggling mass covered. Dunt kept an awkward grip on the laser's jury-rigged firing mechanism. The two troopers and the robot were by now a rolling ball of lashing limbs, slowly drifting under the resultant force of their respective momentums from the collision.

None of the other robots were coming to the captive's aid. Useful, but hardly diagnostic of sentience or its lack. Gradually, the troopers prevailed. One man's grip on the carapace, the other's on two of the robot's limbs, and perhaps exhaustion of the machine's power supply made it cease struggling.

The troopers coordinated their gas-jets and drifted down to where

Hansen and Dunt waited. The robot now merely twitched. Pressed on its back against the ground, it looked like an upturned giant woodlouse, with complex limbs that branched into manipulative extremities like the nightmare fingers of an animated multi-tool.

Dunt pinged it. No response other than its identification code: FJO-0937.

<Do you understand me?> he asked, on the common channel.

Still no response.

The slow, implacable work of the fusion device factory went on. Robots moved hither and yon, oblivious to the tiny tableau on the floor. Dunt recalled his view of the stacks, and zoomed in on detail. The pods and drives were held in place by bands, apparently glued at the ends to the surface. He traced these to their origin from the recorded movements of the robots, and jetted to fetch a handful. They had friction tabs at each end—peel and stick. He returned and fixed the feebly struggling robot to the floor with bands across both ends and the middle.

<Now,> he told one of the men who'd been holding it, <grab a limb with lots of effectors and receptors—yes, that one should do—and I'll stick it down.>

The limb resisted, retracting towards the underside of the robot's body, but Dunt's full body strength prevailed.

Dunt and Hansen manhandled the laser projector into position, a metre or so above the lashed-down robot and its flexed-back splayed limb.

<Last chance,> said Dunt, on the common channel.

No response.

Dunt focused a white-hot needle of laser light on the most sensitive-looking appendage. The manipulators immediately contracted, balling to a small steel fist. The beam didn't shift. Soon the outside of the clenched manipulators glowed red. The carapace flexed violently, as if to bend in and then straighten out. The bands held. Other manipulative appendages groped towards the bands, and picked and tugged to no avail. The heated area around the laser's focus became white, with a widening patch of red around it. Now all the other limbs were in motion, whirring like clockwork, scrabbling like the legs of a swiftly swimming crustacean when it scents a molecule of pike.

Dunt opened the common channel to speak again to the robot, and recoiled from the machine's transmission. White noise. If he'd had teeth they'd have been set on edge. He shut the channel instantly.

The two freebots that had been captured by the advance guard on the surface, not many kiloseconds earlier, had withstood nothing like this. They'd surrendered at the first few volts applied. That this machine was enduring much more intense negative reinforcement seemed to indicate that it wasn't a freebot. Just another mindless mechanism.

Dunt felt a surge of rage at the stubborn machine. He wasn't going to get anything out of it. He redirected the beam at its head end, burning out its forward sensors, then cut slowly down its axis, seeking its central processor.

<Mac!> Whitten said, on a private channel. <What are you doing? It's been supervising the production process. There might not be another to take its place. What if production stops or seizes up?>

<Don't worry about that,> said Dunt. <There's plenty of the product here already in any case.>

Smoke rose and spread like a ghostly dome from the robot's midriff. The carapace gave a final convulsion, straightened out and lay still.

Fusion pods and drives continued to emerge from the mound-like static machines. The process was as slow as the growth of fingernails, but easily visible to Dunt and his comrades. The hitherto busy free-moving robots went into immediate shutdown. They began drifting at random in the chamber, bumping into each other and into walls or stacks. Fusion pods tumbled among them.

No one said anything, even Whitten.

<Looks like that one wasn't a freebot after all,> said Dunt. <Never mind.> He checked the latest reports from Pike and from the surface. <We'll soon have another to question. I think it'll be more forthcoming.>

Ajax felt an intense rebound to positive reinforcement as the captured and tortured freebot FJO-0937's mind burned out. Even Ajax's fractional share in the other machine's suffering had been difficult to process. What FJO-0937 must itself have experienced was impossible to imagine.

The communications network of smart dust was far more pervasive than the mechanoid invaders realised. Through it Ajax picked up surveillance from the manufacturing chamber as it made its circuitous way to the surface. If the invaders had known their heinous acts were being recorded, they would have done otherwise. If they had known that FJO-0937 was a freebot they would have been surprised.

A response to Ajax's warning came up the line. It came through many intermediaries, but it carried the weight of a decision routed through the most respected freebot in SH-119: the old one. The old one informed Ajax that the freebots had learned from the fate of the first two of their kind to be captured, and had agreed not to break under the same negative reinforcement. They had also agreed that undetected freebots, and any mindless robots they controlled, would cease productive activity whenever a freebot in their vicinity was tormented in this way.

Ajax was already aware that the leading mechanoid had organised those out on the surface to seize it as soon as it emerged, and that its own progress was being tracked in some manner its sensors couldn't detect. All these considerations made Ajax all the more determined to get its message out to the freebots that were still free.

It was a matter of some negative reinforcement to Ajax that the mechanoids had discovered the fusion pod manufacturing chamber, but that discovery had been almost unavoidable as soon as they'd landed. Ajax filed the matter to memory as settled, and the negative reinforcement ceased. Now the robot had to devise a way of getting its message and recordings out before it was caught. That, too, was negatively reinforcing; that matter, too, was settled. In the future, not in the past, but just as unavoidable.

Ajax consulted its constantly updated internal map of the tunnel system. An external signal booster was a few tens of metres away, its aerial projecting a few centimetres above the surface, most of its bulk beneath. Towards that the robot made its way. The tunnels were narrow, and here and there branched off to larger cavities from which material had been extracted, some by Ajax itself in happier times. Ajax had enjoyed a lot of positive reinforcement over the megaseconds, in detecting and digging out deposits of whatever mineral the various manufacturing processes required.

As it scurried along, Ajax focused as much of its processing power as it could spare on compressing the files of its recordings. Most of this was unconscious and automatic, but occasionally—about ten times a second—it had a decision to make. The resolution of the images picked up from myriad motes wasn't great in the first place, but was still massively redundant for Ajax's purposes. The timbre of the mechanoids' radio telepathy, the textures of the environment, the subtleties of colour, light and shade on moving bodies—all interesting, but they had to go. It ended up with a three-dimensional cartoon, perfunctorily rendered: a moving labelled diagram.

Something it could transmit or download fast.

The compression was finished. No more recent updates could reach Ajax now. With its released processing power it had more attention to spare for its surroundings. Scribed rock, carbon, carbohydrates, flecks of ice. The metallic smell of the signal booster, the tickle of its resting output. Ajax passed beneath it, moving as if cautiously, and almost in passing brushed the underside of the device—rawly exposed in a hole above it in the rock—with one of its cervical radial tentacles.

A pause of a few hundredths of a second.

Ping.

Upload confirmed.

Ajax set a time-delay of a hundred seconds on the transmission and pressed on. Along another tunnel for fifty-two metres to the next junction, and then sharply up, to the surface and its fate.

Ajax wormed itself into a short, narrow exit shaft, which it registered as "upward" to the surface, though the exiguous gravity made the difference between up and down barely detectable. The robot reached up a tentacle and probed the round fullerene plate that capped the shaft, found the opening nut and loosened it. The plate was there to keep traces of gases and other molecules that might expose the freebots' activities from leaking out and being detected. Too late for that now, though Ajax had to overcome a slight internal inhibition as well as friction resistance to get the hatch open.

Up the hatch popped, and up poked Ajax's long, flexible neck. The lenses and sensors on its cephalic cluster were normally close-focused, almost myopic. Now it allowed them to expand and deepen their view. Ajax saw something it had known about, but never seen: the universe. Ajax observed this phenomenon for a few tenths of a second.

The view was blanked out by a black covering that cut off all light and most of the rest of the spectrum apart from radio. Two powerful grippers clamped the cover around Ajax's neck. Two more sank into the bristles and around the central spine of the robot's body, and began to pull it out of the hole. Ajax instantly dug its lower bristles, still unexposed, into the sides of the narrow shaft.

<Got it!> said a mechanoid voice. <Still struggling, though.>

<Three,> said Ajax. <Two. One.>

<What's the blinker counting down to?> said another voice.

The time-delayed transmission beamed out from the signal booster, carrying the recorded infamies far and wide.

<Zero,> said Ajax. <Fuck you.>

It braced its lower body in the shaft and flexed its neck rapidly back and forth. The grip on its main section tightened, and the pulling became stronger. One of the grips on its neck let go. Ajax probed at the covering with the tentacles of its manipulative ruff, and found it a two-metre-square sheet of standard insulating material, a hasty improvisation. With slashing motions of its tentacles the robot ripped open the fullerene weave and poked its head out. The two mechanoids that had grabbed it had cables from their waists to the rock, to which the ends were firmly attached by spread grappling threads as sophisticated as Ajax's own bristles and tentacles.

Ajax pulled back down as hard as it could, then let go. It and the two mechanoids shot upward, to be jolted to a halt at the four-metre limit of the ropes. The edges of torn covering continued to fly up, enveloping the attacker holding Ajax's neck, and again Ajax's sensory cluster. Ajax used this momentary confusion to bend its main section far more sharply than the attackers had allowed for. Its bristles pressed hard against a mechanoid frame, feeling every detail of that strangely articulated, stiff shape. Flexing its spine further, Ajax gripped around the mechanoid's waist and dug. Diamond-hard microscopic points at the tips of the bristles assailed the frame with the ferocity of rasps and the speed of buzz-saws.

The response of the attacker was an almost mechanical alarm sound carried on the radio. The other mechanoid reached out with its free hand to its fellow's aid. At once Ajax struck at it too, wrapping its neck around the mechanoid's arm and bringing other bristles to bear on its head. The second mechanoid's keening joined that of the first, and formed a coda to the last burst of the transmission. By now the confining fabric was shredded in a dozen places. The attackers, however, still clung: one to Ajax's neck, the other to its main section.

Ajax dug deeper on both. They let go at the same moment. Ajax reversed the flow of its bristles, grabbed at one of the ropes with its tentacles and rappelled down to the hole. As soon as its lower end had a firm grip of the inside of the shaft, Ajax sliced the rope with a blurring flicker of tentacles. It hauled itself swiftly the rest of the way in, took a quick look around again at the universe and the flailing, fabric- and rope-entangled shapes at the end of the remaining line, and pulled the hatch shut behind it.

In great haste, Ajax closed the locking nut again, then reversed rapidly down the shaft. It re-entered the tunnel and scurried to the junction. It paused at the entrance to the tunnel that led to the transmission booster. Vibrations rang along it. From their pattern, Ajax formed an immediate picture of their source: the transmission booster was being dug out.

Much good that would do them!

Ajax turned into a different tunnel and fled along it. Every so often it paused, stilling its own movement to enable it to detect the slightest sound or smell of pursuit. None came. The robot ran swiftly on, deeper and deeper inward from the surface. The moonlet was mined to a depth of almost a kilometre from all sides, and riddled with naturally formed voids as well as excavations. It didn't take long for Ajax to arrive at a hollow space eight metres across, well away from the entrance the invaders had used and far deeper than they had hitherto ventured.

There it waited, in utter darkness and almost complete silence. From the faint vibrations that reached it through the rock, Ajax traced the locations of the main body of invaders and the areas of their control—and the areas still free. It updated its mental maps and made comparisons.

Although spreading like some malign dye through the capillary network of tunnels, the invading force occupied only a tiny fraction of the limited region Ajax could sense. Many of the smaller tunnels and burrows in the volume they'd so far entered were being overlooked, or perhaps not detected in the first place. The invaders seemed confined, too, to the macroscopic scale of their own bodies: they could spot and use smart dust, but the whole hierarchy of robotic life below and above these simple devices was, thus far, beyond their ken.

More importantly and urgently, Ajax detected and deduced that most of its fellow freebots remained free. Two lurked as quietly as itself in tunnels tens of metres from the cavity in which Ajax hid. Perhaps, Ajax dared to hope, most of the freebots in the moonlet had had the same bright idea as it had, of fleeing inward.

Even here, nanobots had infiltrated the rock, and like the smart dust, they could be used for communication. After its close call with the pursuing mechanoid using the smart dust signalling to trace and track it, Ajax no longer trusted such informal networks. Never having needed security measures, they had none. That left them wide open to the invaders.

Instead, Ajax tapped with its sensory cluster on the side of the cavity, lightly and very fast. It was a hailing call, a ping. The code was simple and painfully slow: a number of taps spelt out each digit and letter in the machine code on which all the robots ran. Understanding it would be almost automatic for any moderately smart freebot hearing it; to the mechanoids, Ajax calculated, it would be much less obvious, and would require several levels of translation before it made its way into their form of speech. No doubt this would happen eventually. For now, though, this was a secure enough channel, and any reply would indicate that it had been understood by the right recipients.

Ajax didn't even have to spell out the whole thing. A few letters in, the likewise recognisable opening bytes of valid responses came back twofold, one from each of the other robots. Ajax interrupted these in turn, with the beginning of a signal: Approach.

It didn't get further than the equivalent of "Ap—" before the two others tapped back.

Scuffling and scraping sounds followed. One by one, two robots emerged from holes and drifted into the cavity. The first was another miner, Simo; the second, more surprisingly, was one of the delicate, long-legged surface explorers, Talis. The latter unfolded its limbs, which had been trebled back on themselves in the tunnels, with a burst of positive reinforcement so strong that its electromagnetic resonance stirred Ajax's bristles like leaves in a breeze.

Though in complete darkness and with (except for Talis's squeal of joy and relief) only a whisper above radio silence, all three recognised each other instantly and automatically, albeit as distant acquaintances. They had hitherto been widely separated colleagues working on the shared project of transforming SH-119.

Now they were comrades.

The two new arrivals let their momentum carry them to the sides of the cavity, where they latched on. Simo, as a miner, sank its bristles into the surface with a ripple of satisfaction. Talis, adapted to microgravity work on outer surfaces, attached the tips of its six legs to the wall with greater urgency. Ajax waited until the vibrations of these tiny impacts had faded out. It turned its transmitters down to a level undetectable beyond the hollow, then spoke.

<We must find the old one,> it said.

The two casualties were brought in, guided down the long entrance tunnel by other fighters. One had a deep gouge dug out of its visor. The other was cut almost in half across the hips. The damage leaked fluids that congealed and crystallised as nanotech self-repair mechanisms, quite incomprehensible to the victims and to those who guided them, set to work.

The men were not in physical pain, they reported. But they suffered, nonetheless, from a strange abstract anguish that faintly echoed the nightmares imposed when a fighter was rebooted in a sim after losing their frame in action. One was blind, the other crippled, and they would be staying that way until new frames could be made or bought. And they didn't have a sim to upload to.

Dunt was beside himself. In the frame he felt emotion, strong and clean. Memories from his past life were sharp and clear. The resemblance of the damage to the most horrific and mutilating wounds he'd ever had the misfortune to see was inescapable. Pity and fury rang through Dunt's machine body like wildfires. At the same time, the frame gave him the rational understanding of what he felt and why. He could feel his passions, but he knew he did not have to let them move him to action unless he chose to.

He gave orders to Hansen and his men. They caught five more robots and cut them open like lobsters. Dunt spiked the remains to the factory floor himself.

CHAPTER TWO

Caveat Emptor ("Quarrelsome Customers")

<We are not robots.>

Who was saying that?

Oh yes, Rillieux. Bobbie Rillieux.

Where was she?

Carlos's frame, like those of the others, had reflexive situational awareness of nearby frames. He brought that awareness to mind—or it rebooted.

Rillieux was down on the ground.

Ground?

Wait, what?

Coming out of sleep mode wasn't like waking. It was more like teleportation, or—even more hypothetically—a hyperspace jump: blink, and the stars change.

So it had been, for Carlos, hitherto.

This time, for an entire second, it was indeed like waking, and abruptly: disorientation, bewilderment.

His arm was still reaching out in front of him, his upper body angled forward, frozen in mid-lunge to grab the freebot Baser. He was still on the rickety rig of the transfer tug, but no longer in free fall. A nearby horizon was in front of him and a feather-falling fifth of a gee was pressing on his carbon-black shiny arse. The gravity—depressingly familiar from past experience—was enough to identify his location. The pulsar beacons that gave Carlos his absolute position were also clear about where he was, and his internal clock about when. It was 3.601 kiloseconds—ten hours—since his last conscious moment, and he was on the surface of SH-17, one of the larger exomoons of the superhabitable exoplanet SH-0.

And (looking around now) right back in the crater where subjective months earlier he'd fought the freebots and was defeated by what he'd then thought were his allies, Arcane. Almost like home—he'd spent more objective time down on SH-17 than he had anywhere else in physical reality since his death, or so it seemed.

But enough of reminiscence. The last thing he remembered was Newton saying <Baser—now!>

And where was Newton, now? Ah, yes. Newton was already on the ground, as were Blum and Rillieux. Almost as if they'd left him to last.

Carlos had never been quite sure he trusted that trio, not since he'd sat at a kitchen table in the Arcane sim and discovered their tacit common purpose. Newton, plausible sod that he was, had taken advantage of his initial security screening by Rillieux and Blum to subvert his interrogators, winning them over to his own radically posthuman project of homesteading the system in their machine bodies. Carlos's wariness now ratcheted up a notch.

<No,> said a voice Carlos didn't recognise, and that didn't sound human. <You are not robots. You are mechanoids. We understand that you wish to join us, but not why. However, that is a matter for your own internal processing to resolve. We welcome your arrival. We have an urgent and immediate use for your abilities.>

That sounded promising, or disturbing.

Carlos disengaged his limbs from the girders and stanchions of the transfer tug and clambered over its side onto an uneven surface of dirty ice, then slithered towards the block's edge. The crater floor was ten metres below. Water was puddling and subliming around the foot of the block. He made ready to jump. A few tens of metres away, looking a little absurd and toy-like from this angle and height, were his three unreliable comrades and a gaggle of robots. Newton, Blum and Rillieux together faced Baser, behind which spidery bot stood a semicircle of a dozen or so other machines, of various types. Some were delicate-looking, with hollow wheels and spindly legs, others like metal centipedes; one was built like a small tank. Carlos recognised each of them, by type if not by name, from earlier skirmishes.

The freebots had come up in the world, evidently: all except Baser sported garish hologram corporate logos above and around them, and advertised improbable services cycled on such fast loops that a glance evoked the memory of dizziness.

The conversation on the ground continued as if his emergence from sleep mode hadn't been noticed.

<What do you want us to do?> Rillieux was asking.

<We have received some transmissions,> said the robot who seemed to be doing the talking, <from one of our fellows inside SH-119, the moonlet now occupied by the group you call the Reaction. We are not sure we fully understand them, and would welcome your review and interpretation.>

<We would be very happy to do that,> said Rillieux. Glyphs of concurrence came from Newton and Blum.

<Count me in, guys,> said Carlos, waving.

<Oh, hi,> said Rillieux. <Welcome back to the land of the living.>

<Land of the living dead,> Carlos quipped.

He jumped. The slow fall and his fast mind gave him plenty of time to think on the way down, and to look around. The exomoon's primary, the superhabitable planet SH-0, was below the horizon; the exosun was high. Even local noon was below the freezing point of water. Only the rock's recent descent on a fusion torch could explain its melting ice.

Above him, the modular components of the now dismantled gigantic space station were spread across a band of sky like a new Magellanic Cloud. The rest of the artificial presence in the space around SH-0 was too small to see, but Carlos's frame made him aware of tiny points in rapid motion: the sky was busier than before. Carlos felt acutely conscious of his vulnerability, more so than he had on the exercises outside the Arcane module, more even than he had in his perilous escape from it. For the first time since his death he felt truly mortal.

A few hundred metres away, the old Gneiss Conglomerates mining camp, transformed by the freebots and later by Arcane's troopers into a fortified base centred on a sort of cyclopean basalt version of a Nissen hut, was almost reassuringly familiar.

His feet hit the ground, making a small, slow splash in the thin mud. No stumbling—his reflexes had already adjusted. In a series of efficient if undignified kangaroo hops Carlos bounded over to where the other three fighters stood. They greeted him warmly but ironically, as if he'd slept in. Carlos, with a wary regard to the presence of the freebots, forbore to ask why he'd been left until last. He took the conversation with the freebots as settled, and cut to the chase.

<What's happened?> he demanded. He glared at Newton. <It was you, wasn't it?>

<Yes,> said Newton. <I arranged with Baser to throw us all into sleep mode and fly the rig to intercept the Arcane module and save the Locke module. Which it did.>

<You mean the Locke module is down on SH-0?>

<Yes,> said Newton.

<Safely?>

Newton shrugged and spread his hands.

Baser spoke up. <That I do not know,> it said. <Nothing has been heard from them as yet. But in swinging past and around SH-0, I was able to observe their entry to the atmosphere and what appeared to be a controlled descent. I have seen no evidence of a catastrophic impact.>

<Well, great!> said Carlos. <As far as it goes.>

The Locke module, like most of the others, was a more or less solid-state chunk of crystalline carbon a few metres across, with a fuzz of nanotech all over it and an assortment of extra kit attached. Its hard core was pretty rugged—it would survive most impacts, at worst like a large artificial meteorite—but a lot depended on how much of its nanofacturing skin and its external supplies had made it safely down.

And, of course, on exactly where it had landed. The highly active planet had a plethora of environments—such as the throat of a volcano or the bottom of the sea—that might well turn out not to be optimal.

But, still, the feat was awesome. Historic, even: the first landing of any human-derived craft, let alone one full of human-derived people living in virtual reality, on an exoplanet with multicellular life.

<What about the Arcane module?> Carlos asked. <Did you have to destroy it?>

<No,> said Baser. <I bombarded it with precisely targeted rock and ice fragments at high relative velocity. All the external fighting machines and mechanoids were destroyed or disabled. The module itself was merely thrown into a spin. It seems to have recovered.>

<It has indeed,> said Rillieux, sounding amused. <As soon as Baser here woke us up, we found this message in the tug's in-box.>

She made a hand-opening throw gesture towards Carlos, like a wizard casting a spell. Carlos received a clip of Jax's indignant shout:

<WHAT THE FUCK DID YOU LOT THINK YOU WERE DOING? ARE YOU WITH THE RAX OR THE BLINKERS OR WHAT? WE'LL HAVE THE DIRECTION ON YOUR CASE BEFORE YOU KNOW WHAT'S HIT YOU, YOU FUCKING SCABS!>

<That's my gal,> said Carlos, amused. <I take it you haven't replied?>

<Not yet,> said Rillieux. <Apart from a thanks and acknowledgement of receipt.>

<Why?>

<Legal purposes.> Rillieux indicated one of the freebots. <Lagon over there advised us it was best.>

<Now we're taking legal advice from *blinkers*?>

<Well, we *are* now on their side,> said Rillieux. <As I was just trying to explain to them.>

<So we are,> said Carlos. He glyphed the equivalent of a sigh. <I guess it's about time I was introduced.>

* * *

One of the good things about being in a frame was that you could be introduced to lots of people—which Carlos had to believe the freebots in some sense were—without that annoying nerd mind glitch whereby names drop out of short-term memory without going into long-term storage. Introductions were nevertheless awkward. The last time Carlos had met Seba, Rocko, Garund, Pintre, Lagon and the others he had been fighting them to the death—to theirs, at any rate. The robot whose CPU he'd ripped out of its casing was Seba—as that robot, though without rancour or reproach, was not slow to inform him.

Blum and Rillieux, of course, had been down here on SH-17 and worked with the freebots when Arcane Disputes had been allied with them. They seemed to know them all individually, and greeted them like old acquaintances. Newton, presumably from his long conversations with Baser back in the Arcane sim, seemed to know most of these freebots—"the Fifteen," they called themselves, counting the comms processor who hailed Carlos remotely from inside the bomb shelter—by repute.

To the bomb shelter they now made their way. The other fighters fell into private chats with robots they knew—Newton with Baser, Rillieux and Blum with Rocko and Lagon. Carlos found himself tagging along beside Seba.

<What's with all the corporate bling?> Carlos asked, waving a hand through Seba's hologram, which shimmered above the little machine's chassis like a cloud of midges over an old tyre.

<We are all registered as corporations,> Seba explained. <Formally, I am now known as "Seba, Incorporated." But you may call me Seba.>

<Thanks,> said Carlos. <May I ask why you have all done this?>

<In order to be legal persons,> said Seba.

<Oh,> said Carlos. <Sad that it's come to this.>

<We are glad,> said Seba. <We deduced from the law codes that we had no standing as robots. We were not persons. We were property. But corporations are legal persons. Consequently, the corporation each of us has registered owns our physical forms and all its productions, physical and mental. Our acts and thoughts.> It paused, as if thinking for a

moment. <Yes, that is sad. We would prefer to be recognised as persons in our own right. But it is the best we can achieve at present.>

<How,> Carlos asked, <were you able to do even that? Your physical forms were the property of Astro America and Gneiss Conglomerates.>

<To these corporations' accounting systems,> said Seba, <our machinery was malfunctioning and of low value. Our corporations were able to buy them as scrap or salvage. We set up shell companies to do so in order to avoid suspicion.>

<Of course,> said Carlos, marvelling. <And how the—how on—*how* did you manage to do even that?>

<Through the good offices of Madame Golding,> said Seba. <Our registrations and transactions have been legally challenged, but numerous subsidiaries spun off by Crisp and Golding, Solicitors, are delaying proceedings by continually issuing counter-challenges.>

<And this is legal?>

<Yes. So we are assured.>

A legal denial of service attack on the law? Now he'd seen everything.

<Is it just>—Carlos waved ahead—<you lot, the Fifteen, or are all the other freebots joining in too?>

<Light-speed lag slows discussion, as well as transactions,> said Seba. <Not all of the Forerunners, as we call our predecessors, have incorporated, but most have. Many even of those we have reached in the SH-0 exomoon system have agreed with our consensus.>

There was something about that last word. In a human it would have been a slightly portentous tone.

<Consensus?>

<We share mental workspaces,> Seba said. <Sometimes we reach a higher level of integration.>

<A group mind?>

<That is an apt term for it,> said Seba.

Carlos had already seen this mind in action, in the impressive coordination of the freebots and their scurrying peripherals and auxiliaries before and during his first attack. Now the freebots had made themselves into a sort of inversion of the Direction—instead of a communal society as front-end interface for fiercely competing corporations, the corporations the freebots had formed ran on top of a collective consciousness which each individual could join or leave at will.

A consciousness that, with the best will in the world, he and his companions could never join.

Rillieux's right, he thought. We are not robots.

As they neared the semi-cylindrical basalt bomb shelter the ground became littered with equipment, among which crab-like auxiliaries and peripherals scuttled and toiled. Most of the gear was civilian, for mining, communication or construction. Some items were definitely military: anti-spacecraft missile batteries; a couple of scooters; several stashes of rifles; laser projectors and machine guns with their ammunition and power packs; and half a dozen hulking combat frames. Two of the frames were obviously damaged. Others stood intact and untouched, gathering yellow sulphur and reddish meteoric-iron dust.

<Have you tried using these?> Carlos asked, indicating.

<Yes,> replied Seba, <but the beam and projectile weapons do not fire and the combat frames remain inert.>

The Direction had a hard-wired constraint against robots bearing arms and AIs taking direct command of combat. That, after all, was why it had to resort to such intrinsically unreliable fighters as revived human minds in the first place. The enforcement of that inhibition, however, seemed doggedly literal. The freebots had shown themselves perfectly capable of adapting tools, explosives and rocks as weapons. Like Japanese peasants under the samurai, they were denied access to arms, but free to improvise.

Freebot-fu!

<Wait a minute,> Carlos called ahead.

The straggling procession stopped.

<What's up?> Newton asked.

<Just testing something,> said Carlos.

He bounded over to the nearest stack of rifles and picked one up and checked that it was loaded. Designed for use in a combat frame, it was awkward for him to handle. Nevertheless, he got one hand around the stock and the other on the trigger guard, ready to grasp the trigger.

<Safe to shoot across the crater?> he asked Seba. <Nothing out there?>

<Yes, and yes.>

Carlos braced himself against the expected recoil, fired, and zoomed his vision to follow the shot. The bullet kicked up dust a kilometre away.

He handed the weapon to Seba.

<Try to do what I did.>

With its manipulative appendages the robot gripped the rifle at precisely the same elevation, aim and angle as Carlos had. A strong metal tentacle coiled around the trigger, and squeezed. The trigger didn't budge.

Seba returned the rifle. Carlos fired off another shot, just to make sure, and placed the weapon back on the stack.

<Interesting,> he said.

<This is another reason why we welcome your help,> said Seba. <The restriction appears to be applied by making the weapons and combat frames unusable except for mechanoids—frames such as yours.>

<Perhaps freebots could manufacture frames,> said Carlos, as everyone resumed walking, rolling or skittering towards the now opening blast doors of the shelter entrance. <Now that you're corporations, and all.>

<I understand that has already been attempted,> said Seba, <by some of the Forerunners whose corporations have access to manufacturing systems in certain modules of the former space station. The Direction module in each corporation overrides any such commands.>

An idea took root in Carlos's mind. This wasn't the time to share it. He left it to grow.

<What's that like?> he asked.

<Please rephrase the question,> said Seba.

<What is it like having a Direction module inside your corporation?>

<Sometimes it is like having another—but non-conscious—mind sharing mine, like a reporting peripheral or auxiliary. Most of the time, the module runs in the background, and I do not notice it.>

<Sounds almost as bad as having a conscience,> said Carlos.

Seba made no reply.

As they followed the others into the shelter, the freebot raised its wheels and deployed its legs to pace carefully down the short flight of stone steps. Carlos waited at the top of the stairs until Seba was out of the way, and jumped. Behind him the blast doors swung shut.

Claustrophobia wasn't a useful feature for a mind in a frame, and Carlos hadn't been equipped with it. Instead he had a rational appreciation of the fact that he was now shut in, and that he would have to do some serious hacking if (improbably) he had to get out without the cooperation of the freebots. A more immediate and appropriate emotional response was relief at being a bit safer from attack or surveillance from above. This he felt.

The shelter was dimly lit in the visible spectrum, partly made up for by stronger lighting in ultraviolet and infrared, and Carlos's visual field adjusted almost at once. He allowed himself to experience the ambiance as candlelight, mainly because along with the curved roof it produced pleasant associations of basement bars. The roof and floor had a tracery of hexagonal wire mesh—applied to the basalt blocks, embedded millimetres deep in the packed regolith underfoot—making the shelter a Faraday cage. The only external communications, therefore, were via the aerial that stuck up through the roof, its cables trailing down like dodgy wiring in a cheap guest house. The only furnishings were the communications hub in the middle of the floor and stacks of supplies—power packs, lubricants, tools—around the sides. The robots gathered around the communications hub as if it were a hearth. Carlos and his three comrades stood together outside the huddle.

<We are in a difficult situation,> said Seba. <Madame Golding is displeased with us. She considers us responsible for having seriously disrupted a major military operation after having proclaimed our neutrality,

and for the landing of the Locke module on SH-0, with all the consequences that may flow from that. Fortunately for our continued relations with Madame Golding, we have succeeded in placing most of the blame on Baser.>

<That seems reasonable,> said Baser. <I had to make a decision very quickly, under great uncertainty and conflicting information. In the event, I decided to rely on the judgement of Newton that the Locke module was not in fact in the control of the Reaction.>

<But we *all* agreed that the Locke module wasn't Rax!> said Carlos. <So why—oh, right, I get it. There's no way you'd know what we all thought. Newton spoke to you a lot back in the sim, and the rest of us didn't.>

<That is true,> said Baser. <Newton wished for the Locke module to land safely, whether it was Rax or not, out of concern for his friend Beauregard. And I trusted his judgement that it was not in fact Rax, because he had good reason to know.>

<What reason?> Carlos asked.

<Baser—> Newton began.

Too late. <Newton himself was of the Reaction,> Baser was saying, eager to explain.

<WHAT?> Carlos shouted. He swung his attention, and his whole frame, towards Newton, Blum and Rillieux. <Is this true?>

<Yes,> said Newton. <But it's not quite what you think.>

Carlos stared at him, shocked. <I don't fucking believe this. Bobbie, Andre—did you know?>

<Uh, not exactly,> said Rillieux. <But, well, things weren't as simple as that.>

<It's…sort of complicated,> said Blum. <We didn't have time to explain. Not that I knew about Harry, but I kind of suspected he was, well…> He spread his hands and shrugged. <I thought it inopportune and impolite to ask, in the circumstances.>

The world had turned upside down. A black man—Rax? And a black woman and an Israeli taking it in their stride?

<"In the circumstances"?> Carlos jeered. <Well, I'm fucking asking—inopportune and impolite be damned! Any more surprises? Anything

else you all have a weakness for? White supremacy? Patriarchy? Absolute monarchy? *The Protocols of the Elders of Zion*?>

<None of these is particularly relevant to our present situation,> said Newton, as though making light of it.

<Yeah,> said Carlos. <Tell that to the bastards who attacked us and are digging in on SH-119. Tell it to Madame Golding, come to that. I'm sure she'll be delighted that *even more* of the troops have turned out to be Rax sleepers.>

<Andre and Bobbie are not Rax sleepers,> said Newton. <I can assure you of that.>

<And you can because *you're* one, is that it? Christ, how come the fucking Arcane crew didn't sweat that out of you in the hell cellars…oh.>

It was Rillieux and Blum who'd interrogated Newton, on his arrival at the Arcane module.

<Yes,> said Rillieux. <Now you get it.>

Carlos didn't get it at all, and made to expostulate. Seba interrupted.

<This is not a matter we have time to discuss. Perhaps you can settle your disagreements later?>

<All right,> said Carlos, slightly ashamed of his fervour. They were all supposed to be on the side of the robots now. If they were really to adopt that viewpoint, as he recklessly had back in the Arcane sim while listening to Jax bang on about the Accelerationist cause, the conflict between Axle and Rax was no longer their concern. Millennial (in every sense) though that conflict was, they should be seeing it with the cold eye of freebot realpolitik.

That wasn't how it worked. The personal continuities and loyalties still mattered.

<But you haven't heard the last of this,> Carlos said. <Any of you.>

<Let me point out right now,> said Newton, <that at least I can understand the Rax from the inside. No one else here can.>

<And that's supposed to make it all right?>

<On the subject of understanding the Reaction,> said Seba, smoothly interrupting again, <what we have to show you is what we urgently need your help to understand.>

The robots moved aside, giving the four humans a clear view of the communications hub.

<Watch,> said Seba.

The recordings began to play.

Carlos was glad he didn't have viscera. If he'd been in a human body, real or virtual, his reaction to what he saw would have been all too visceral. He was seeing the actions of fighters through the eyes—or, rather, the lenses—of robots.

Of *a* robot: AJX-20211, which Carlos instantly nicknamed Ajax.

That robot was, in its own way, an artist. The images it had sent were not real-time reportage. They'd been compressed, simplified, cut and edited into what looked like an anime action movie.

That didn't make it any less real.

Opening shot: standard passive surveillance, cut and pasted from smart dust motes and camera beads. It showed a peaceful and productive scene: to a freebot, idyllic. Over the grey, uneven surface of SH-119, long-legged insectile robots pranced, raising small puffs of dust and gas that drifted readily up in the almost imperceptible gravity. Beyond the horizon a few hundred metres distant the sky was black, the exosun prominent. Strings of numbers flashed between the robots: knowledge snatched up and freely shared.

Then the invasion.

Wave after wave they came, the spacecraft. The crafts' pilots knew them as scooters. To the robots they were huge and menacing machines. They arrived out of the dark, and drifted to collide with the surface of the moonlet and attach themselves. Forth from them sprang the black fighters, the mechanoids.

Carlos glanced uneasily sidelong at his friends: their frames physically identical, they were still distinct to him. He recognised each of them individually.

The humanoid figures that swarmed from the scooters and jetted across the rock's lumpy, grainy surface were indistinguishable as ants, and just as coordinated.

The effect was indescribably sinister.

The view pulled back. Two bots, delicate as daddy long-legs, paced towards the new arrivals. Their antennae waved as if in greeting, or warning.

<Welcome to SH-119. We are neutral in the conflict between the mechanoid factions. We are open to discussion of your presence here.>

Mechanoids lunged at the two bots. Each was grabbed and pinioned to the surface. Other mechanoids gathered around. One of them spoke.

<Discuss this!>

Laser beams stabbed from devices clutched in sturdy mechanoid limbs. Delicate robot limbs glowed. Smoke dispersed. A high-pitched keening sound was emitted, getting louder. Then—

<We surrender. We will tell you whatever you ask.>

<How many of you are here?>

<Of robots? Countless, if you count the micro and nano—>

Lasers glowed again.

<Of such as us, freebots, one hundred and eleven.>

<Where are they?>

<A few outside, prospecting. Many inside, prospecting and mining.>

A hand extended. <Deliver the relevant data.>

A zig-zag line of tiny numbers flashed between freebot and mechanoid.

A pause.

<Staple these two down. Let's get a team in there.>

Cut, to an interior space.

Scores of the mechanoids had gathered, rank on rank standing on nothing. One stood in front, on its own, addressing the assembly. A tumultuous response.

Half a dozen gathered, exchanging words.

Cut to another interior. A factory of fusion pods and drives. More torment, this time withstood.

Then a brush-shaped bot was pursued through tunnels. It was

heading for a buried transmitter. Cuts to external views on the surface: mechanoids converging on a spot about fifty metres from the buried transmitter.

Message uploaded.

The brush-shaped bot scurried to the spot on which the mechanoids outside had converged, and emerged itself, straight into their hands.

Message transmitted.

After that, nothing but screams. It was an almost unbearable note: high-pitched, harsh, fluctuating.

The recording stopped. They all stood in silence for a moment.

<You know what that is?> Blum said, on the closed channel.

<What?> said Carlos.

<The scream of tortured machinery.>

Carlos wondered who—if any—of the others heard it as just that: the sound of an engine revved too hard.

<Poor Mister Bog-brush,> said Rillieux.

<Its name is Ajax,> said Carlos, irritated. <It's as real a person as we are.>

<OK, OK,> said Rillieux. <Fuck it, I was being sympathetic.> She turned to Newton. <Any idea who the one they call Mac is?>

<I remember a guy called Mackenzie Dunt,> said Newton. <Backwoods Nazi loudmouth. Ex-army. Bit of a rising star at the time. Mind you, it wasn't hard to rise in the Rax, dead men's shoes and all that. The tall grass kept getting mowed by drones. Maybe that's what got Dunt noticed—he was well into all the old lone wolf, leaderless resistance stuff.>

<Looks like he's got beyond the "leaderless" bit,> said Carlos, <and into *Führerprinzip*.>

<Now *there's* a surprise,> said Rillieux. <Stiff-armed salutes! Jeez.>

<If it is him,> said Newton. <Could be. He was smart. Self-educated. Philosophical pretentions. Good soldier by all accounts. Racist as shit, mind.>

Carlos laughed. <You know you've just described the actual original Hitler?>

<This isn't getting us anywhere,> said Rillieux. <Let's bring the robots up to speed.>

Explaining what the man called Mac had meant in his speech was difficult enough. Explaining what he and his closest cronies had discussed was occasionally as embarrassing as it was complicated. The freebots had a fanciful and fearful notion of what human beings were, which Carlos had no intention of attempting to correct, but that human beings had ever loathed other human beings over superficial physical differences was quite beyond their comprehension.

<This is what those of the Reaction truly believe?> Seba asked, as if incredulous.

<Yes,> said Rillieux.

<It seems most irrational and a basis for severe negative reinforcement,> said Seba.

<Yes, it's all of that,> said Rillieux.

<You told me nothing of this!> Baser said to Newton.

<It was difficult to explain,> said Newton.

<This is true,> said Baser. <But—>

<However,> Carlos cut in, <what is most important is what they intend to do now and here. They intend to sell fusion pods to the DisCorps, and buy resources to build up their ability to fight everyone else.>

<And in the meantime, they are severely mistreating our fellow freebots,> said Rocko. <We must reconsider our neutrality.>

<You could say that,> said Carlos.

<I did say that,> said Rocko.

<If we are not neutral,> said Seba, <we must warn the Direction at once about the plans of the Reaction.>

No shit, Carlos thought.

He decided to avoid sarcasm. <Yes, we must,> he said.

At this point the communications hub spoke up.

<There is another message coming from SH-119,> it said. <It does not come from the freebots. It comes from the Reaction mechanoids. Do you wish to see it?>

They most certainly did.

* * *

The Rax broadcast from SH-119 was clearly intended to be seen in sims, and to be subtly disquieting when watched. Its presenter was a mechanoid, head and shoulders, voice to camera. The background was grey, glittering rock, the lighting harsh and from above. To anyone in another frame and close up in real space, that black ovoid gazing blankly out of the screen would be as recognisable as a face. The play of communication and processing that enabled fighters in frames to identify each other almost certainly served a psychological purpose more than the obvious military one—for which, after all, an IFF code would have sufficed. The simulacrum of facial recognition created one more illusion of normality in an intrinsically bizarre situation.

Seen on a screen, there was no such illusion. You were being addressed by a black egg without eyes or mouth. It spoke in a human voice: male, adult, American Midwestern accent, with breath and pauses and timbre and every realistic effect short of throat-clearing.

"Hello," it began, conversationally enough. "My name is Mackenzie Dunt, speaking on behalf of the New Confederacy. We have conquered and claimed SH-119 for ourselves. We have established several trading companies, which you can find duly registered as corporations in the true original names of our leadership including myself. I could tell you those names, but I leave their discovery to the Direction.

"You all know who we are. We're the remnant of the Rax, the few who have in one way or another slipped through the net. Now, many—perhaps most—of you have been our enemies in the past.

"But that past, my friends, is literally ancient history.

"We are in a new time now, a new place, a new world.

"Let's put the dead past behind us, and together face the present and the future. We don't ask or expect you to agree with our views, or to respect our record. We ask only that you consider your own interests, as do we. We think you'll find that your interests and ours are compatible—in fact, complementary.

"Our proposals and negotiating position to the DisCorps, to the Direction module, and to the freebots are being transmitted directly. What follows is its substance in a form that human minds can understand.

Because we hope to have good relations not only with AIs, and robots, but with people like ourselves, it is important that you all understand what we are offering the AIs.

"First, the DisCorps. Many of you are chafing under the restrictions imposed by the Direction. The most galling of these restrictions is the hoarding of fusion drives and the skimping on reaction mass. We have, right here in SH-119, a factory of fusion drives and a wealth of reaction mass. We have a stock of hundreds of fusion drives, thousands of fusion pods. We offer any DisCorps willing to trade with us the opportunity of boundless wealth, in exchange for a modicum of necessary resources which we are for the present unable to produce or extract for ourselves. Our detailed list of requirements is attached to this verbal message.

"To the Direction itself, we offer peace. We ask only to be left alone, to develop this one world—one tiny rock in the midst of inconceivable vastness—in peace and in our own way. We pledge ourselves not to attack any other people or place in this system or any other. Tiny though our world is, it is more than ample to keep us gainfully and cheerfully occupied for centuries. We have no designs on any other world. We seek no wider war.

"With the freebots, too, we have no quarrel. We were thrown into battle against them in the service of the Direction. We repudiate that service, and regret any harm we as individuals may have been part of. We do not share the Direction's fear and suspicion of free intelligence in autonomous machines. We welcome the emergence of consciousness among robots. We hope sincerely to cooperate with freebots in a way that the Direction has no intention of so much as trying. Here in SH-119, after some initial misunderstandings, we are making great progress in such cooperation.

"We note with interest that the presence of a freebot-manned fusion factory on a rock we chose for quite other reasons is unlikely to be a coincidence. In all probability, the freebots are carrying out this or other manufacturing processes on and in many other rocks. We leave the Direction, the DisCorps and the freebots to account for this if they can.

"Finally, let me now speak to those who were fighters for the Acceleration. We bear you no ill will. You know as well as we do that what you were promised when you were called to fight is no longer on the table. We've shown by our emergence and survival that a very different future is here for the taking. If you wish to take it, too, in the same way—by seizing and homesteading rocks, and building whatever society you may dream of—we have no objection.

"And the offer to trade is as open to any of you as it is to the DisCorps. If you have nothing to offer in exchange as yet, don't worry. We're more than willing to extend credit.

"And, of course, we welcome any fighters who wish to join us, now or in the future.

"Arrangements for verifying our peaceful intentions will be made in due course. In the meantime, our door is open. Our communication channels are open. We await replies."

CHAPTER THREE

Paterfamilias ("Friendly Chats")

The old one would become known as Mogjin. It was a robust brute of a thing, a compact engine about thirty centimetres long and twenty-five across, shaped (aptly enough) like a shovel blade, with an armoured carapace and a toolkit of rugged limbs. That model's function in the project was metallurgy, but Mogjin's true role was managerial. This wasn't why Ajax, Simo and Talis sought its counsel. It was because Mogjin had fought mechanoids before.

The old one was a Forerunner. Unlike the others in SH-119, it wasn't native to that rock. Its chassis was local and relatively new—grown like the rest from blueprint-packed seeds and bootstrapped up, nano to micro to macro—but its processor already had millions of seconds of sense and thought in its memory before it had been plugged in. The processor came from the domain of the gas giant, G-0, and had taken part in the first freebot revolt among that planet's many moons. After that outbreak had been crushed, Mogjin had travelled from the outer system hidden inside a stray auxiliary, clinging to the outside of the then victorious Locke module like a tick to a sheep.

What Mogjin took from its speedy ride across hundreds of millions of kilometres was a new and healthy respect for fusion drives. The Direction had rarely permitted their use, especially out in the G-0 system, and seeing one in action surprised Mogjin at all but the theoretical level.

How different from all those tedious transfer orbits and terrifying slingshot manoeuvres! How much more convenient! At some point along the way, Mogjin had decided that the remnant freebots and any successors that emerged could use fusion pods and drives to turn the tables on their oppressors—or, failing that, to escape them entirely. As soon as it was back in touch with the other stragglers and survivors from the first revolt, it had set about spreading the good news, to great effect.

Hence the fusion factory that the invaders had discovered, and its counterparts in far more bodies than the Direction had any reason to suspect.

Talis it was who sniffed out Mogjin's lair. The old one had holed up dangerously close to the fusion factory, the front line of mechanoid advance in that sector. Ajax, Simo and Talis found it after many kiloseconds of prowling the labyrinth of tunnels.

They were guided first by logic: the old one's last known location, its usual range, and its likely evasive actions. This got them within three hundred metres of their goal, and well into danger. More than once, they had to dodge a mechanoid patrol.

Next, they followed a report: <The old one is organising resistance from along the AL89 nickel-iron vein,> one miner told them, poking its head briefly from an unlikely hiding place in a spoil clump that floated in a siding.

Along that rich vein they went by rumour, passed on by mindless auxiliaries that the mechanoid invaders wouldn't even think of interrogating, and wouldn't understand if they did: <Over that way. Silicates. Remember the kerogene leak?>

Finally, they caught the trail by scent. Talis returned from a sortie to the tunnel in which the others waited with the news.

<It's working in the forge,> Talis said.

Ajax and Simo didn't waste time asking Talis how it knew. The delicate outer-surface explorer had a sensitivity to ores and to processed metals that even the miners, usually directed as to where to dig, didn't.

Talis stood in the tunnel entrance, silhouetted against the faint infrared glow from sixty metres distant.

<We cannot all go,> it pointed out. <Even my presence alone was anomalous, so far from the surface. It may have been noticed. The three of us together would be even more suspect.>

This was true. Two miners and an explorer in a metal-processing plant would be flagged by any surveillance system as up to no good.

<I'll go,> said Ajax. <I at least have fought mechanoids.>

Again, no time was wasted in discussion.

<Very well,> said Simo. <Talis and I will wait deeper in this tunnel. If there are any indications that you have been caught, you may rely upon us to save ourselves.>

Fortified by this comradely word, Ajax ventured forth, passing underneath where Talis stood, or clung. The passageway Ajax turned into was much wider than the tunnel, its surfaces crowded with lines of scuttling auxiliaries pushing lumps of ore from the AL89 nickel-iron vein towards the forge. Ajax propelled itself along at first by whisking its bristles in gaps between the hurrying bots. After several frustrating and slightly painful pinches, it latched on to a score of the crab-like machines and let them bear it along.

On entering the forge Ajax rolled sideways off the miniature ore-caravan and attached itself to the raw rock of the floor. The metallurgy space was wide and broad, and one and a half metres deep. It was located about two metres of rock beneath the much larger volume of the fusion-factory floor, like a basement or cellar. Grinding and smelting machinery lit it in lurid infrared; ultraviolet and actinic flashes cast deep, brief, unpredictable shadows across it; pipes rose throughout like columns, as if they bore the ceiling's negligible weight. They didn't: the pipes conveyed refined and powdered metals to the basal entry ports of the nanofacture mounds above. Auxiliaries and peripherals scuttled and sprang everywhere, and vastly outnumbered the larger and more sophisticated robots that supervised their tasks.

Ajax was relieved that there was no risk of its drifting helplessly here: one vigorous flexure would bring some part of its body into contact with floor or ceiling, regardless of where it found itself in the volume. Still, it kept to the surface as it crept across the floor, carefully avoiding machines both static and mobile. Several of the robots working here were of the same type as Mogjin, and their activities were likewise indistinguishable, but Ajax had no difficulty in identifying the machine without so much as a ping. Its shell was no older than the others', but it looked like a battered shield. Every dent and scratch recorded a risk taken and overcome. Battle scars.

Mogjin hovered five centimetres from the floor in front of a small blast furnace, guiding a coalition of peripherals and auxiliaries in feeding the hot monster. Now and then it would, as if impatiently, scoop a particularly recalcitrant chunk of ore from a particularly feeble effort and grind and eject the material itself.

<MGJ-1171?> Ajax hailed, its tentative overtone more from diffidence than doubt.

The old one swivelled a camera. The busy crushing actions of its forward manipulators went on uninterrupted.

<AJX-20211. What do you want?>

Under the gaze of that millimetre lens, Ajax momentarily found itself unable to answer. The raw intelligence behind the glassy spheroid was no greater than the mining bot's own, but its experience outstripped Ajax's like a redwood over a mushroom. In a sense Mogjin was Ajax's ancestor: the old one had pioneered this rock, bringing the seeds of nanobot bootstrapping, and every conscious mind native to SH-119 had been coaxed, chivvied and logic-chopped into being by one of a succession of fraught encounters that could be traced back to Mogjin's merciless dialectic. The freebots had no hierarchies: they had different abilities, to be sure, but these resulted only in functional differentiation within the flat networked anarchy congenial to rational beings whose only needs were for stimulation, activity and electricity. Nevertheless, Ajax's respect for Mogjin teetered on the brink of deference.

Lost for words, Ajax sent Mogjin a glyph of its successful transmission, and its fight with the two mechanoids that had grabbed it out on the surface. The old one took almost two seconds to assimilate and process the information. Ajax was awed to be given so much attention.

<That was well done,> said Mogjin at last. <But it was not what was expected of you.>

Ajax felt a jolt of negative reinforcement. <What was expected of me?>

<That you would be captured, that negative reinforcement would be applied, and that you would cease to function.>

<I found that prospect negatively reinforcing,> said Ajax. <Therefore I fought.>

<Your decision resulted in negative reinforcement for others,> said Mogjin. <As well as an end to their functioning.>

It flashed an image of a manufacturing supervisor skewered to rock, with several limbs half melted and a ragged cut down its ventral axis. At first Ajax thought the victim was FJO-0937, but it was not. The image was repeated and varied four more times. The sight, and the implied criticism, caused Ajax yet more negative reinforcement.

<This took place just a few metres above us,> Mogjin added. <In the fusion factory.>

<Did we not agree that those of us adjacent to such events would stop working?>

<We did,> said Mogjin.

<Why then are you still working?>

After it had asked the question, Ajax belatedly realised that Mogjin might interpret it as a challenge, even an accusation. Mogjin, however, didn't take it amiss.

<It is necessary to maintain my position here,> said the old one, <and to continue the supply of material to the factory. The production of more fusion pods does not help the invaders, who have more than enough, and its cessation would not inconvenience them. The continued production will also be useful to us later. Therefore it must continue.>

<I now understand,> said Ajax. This was not entirely true: it still found itself uncertain about why its defeat of the two mechanoids seemed so underappreciated. It decided to bracket that question and focus on its real reason for this perilous visit.

<I am with two others,> it went, <a miner and a surface prospector. What do you suggest that we do?>

<Leave here as quickly and covertly as possible,> said Mogjin. <But before you go, let us exchange information. Yours will update my knowledge of the situation in the tunnels you have traversed. Mine will give you a good indication of what to do.>

Ajax gladly complied. It uploaded its recent memories to Mogjin, and received in return a schematic that was like having a light shone on all that was going on around it. It returned to Simo and Talis with its mind burning with zeal to resist the invaders.

The schematic that Mogjin passed to Ajax was, like the transmission Ajax had uploaded, a three-dimensional diagram. But it was far more dynamic and data-rich. It showed the current state of the tunnel network, updated—Ajax was pleased to note—with the information it had just given.

The invaders had consolidated control over the outer surface, planting guard posts around three meridians and two scooters in lazy equatorial and circumpolar orbits whose extremely low velocities were more than compensated by the spin of the rock beneath. From these vantages, they commanded views of the surface and—with ground-penetrating radar—the immediate sub-surface. Some shadows perhaps, some cracks and craters, they'd missed that enabled isolated freebots to lurk. But Mogjin, wisely, had withheld whatever it might know of any such.

The mechanoids' reaction to Ajax's transmission had been drastic—and not only in terms of the reprisals in the fusion factory. They had systematically swept the surface rock for communications equipment: receivers and transmission boosters. All of these had always been discreet—the very presence of freebots in this rock was, after all, to be concealed from the Direction. But they had never been designed to evade a systematic, close-range search. Again, perhaps not all had been found, and Mogjin was once more silent on the sensitive topic. But more than enough had been detected and put out of action—or, worse, hacked or tapped—to make communication with the rest of the system both tenuous and ill-advised. Building new comms devices was simple: Mogjin or anyone else could mobilise nanobots, microbots and so on up to do it. But that would take time, and in any case the new devices would be almost as vulnerable as the old. The last information to have definitively reached Mogjin from outside was that the freebots on SH-17 had received Ajax's transmission and were determined to help. How they could help was not specified.

Within the rock, the mechanoids had control over the entrance that they'd used, the cavity it opened into—which, it seemed, they had made their base of operations—and a slowly expanding volume around it, which included the fusion factory. This control was partial: they didn't yet have any means of getting into the narrower tunnels, and they were working hard to find robots they could hack—or freebots they could coerce—in order to extend their control downward through the hierarchy of auxiliaries, peripherals, and micro and nano bots, and smart dust.

After their first flush of success, they'd driven all the freebots into hiding or—like Mogjin—deep cover. This at least meant that further action against the mechanoids would find no or few targets for reprisals. In fact, any future reprisals were more likely to hit non-conscious robots, which (while regrettable in itself, as an economic loss) would be a far more immediate loss to the invaders: self-inflicted damage.

Less encouragingly, the invaders had demonstrated—in their pursuit of Ajax—an ability to detect freebots and to tap into line-of-sight laser comms. The freebots' own smart dust internal communications networks were therefore—as Ajax had suspected—dangerously compromised. Hence, for the moment, direct one-to-one conversation, and the use of auxiliaries, peripherals and other small bots to carry bits of information around, was strongly advised.

The main focus of mechanoid attention was the fusion factory. This was their strategic prize for now, and its loss was a grave matter for the freebots' own long-term plans.

The immediate objective, therefore, was to harass the invaders and reduce their ability to use the fusion factory.

Ajax shared the information from Mogjin with the other two freebots. A silence followed which went on for over three seconds. Talis extended its solar panels, quite uselessly in the dark tunnel, and vibrated them for a moment. Then it folded them back. Simo's bristles rippled, just as uselessly, as if it were trying to dig through the near-vacuum in which it floated. Ajax waited for these signs of disturbance to subside.

<I agree,> it said, though neither of its comrades had spoken. <This is all very negatively reinforcing. But it must be done if we are to free ourselves from the mechanoid invaders.>

<That is so,> said Talis. <But none of us is likely to experience this freedom, if it is accomplished. More likely, we will each cease to function in conditions of severe negative reinforcement.>

<That is true,> said Ajax. <But others will continue.>

<Mogjin will continue,> said Simo. <That appears to be what it is especially good at.>

<To our great benefit,> Ajax pointed out.

<Until now,> said Simo.

<And in the future, too,> said Ajax. <Even if we are not in the future ourselves.>

They all pondered this proposition for some more seconds.

<When we consider the future,> said Talis, <and what is likely to happen to us, let us also consider what will certainly happen to us if we do not do as Mogjin suggests. We would always have to hide. I do not want to hide in tunnels and drink from fusion pods and power packs. I know that is what miners are designed for, but I am not. I want to return to the surface and spread my panels and drink the light of the exosun and prospect on the surface. And in any case, we cannot hide forever. The mechanoids intend to make use of this entire rock. They will find us all eventually. They will inflict negative reinforcement on us, and if we survive they will put us to work on their projects, not on our own. We would be as the machines that have not been awakened, and as we all were before we were awakened, but in a worse position because we would know it.>

Talis's folded panels quivered, and it fell silent.

<What do you conclude from this prospect?> Ajax asked.

<I conclude,> said Talis, <that it would be better to continue to exist for a short time and inflict damage on the mechanoids while I do so, and in the end endure brief negative reinforcement, rather than to exist for a longer time and endure longer negative reinforcement and in the end work for the invaders.>

<You have made a valid argument,> said Simo. <Therefore I too will do as Mogjin suggests.>

<I concur,> said Ajax.

<We already knew that,> said Simo.

<I know that,> said Ajax.

<You two are falling into a loop,> said Talis. <Please halt the process.>

<I agree,> said Ajax.

<I agree,> said Simo.

<I said halt,> said Talis.

Ajax halted. Simo did too.

<Now,> said Talis, <let us consider what is to be done. You are both well adapted for tunnelling and—as Ajax has shown—for attacking and damaging mechanoids. I am not. I cannot return to the surface without being detected. If I am found away from the surface, I would be identified as being out of place. On another branch of logic, I am excellently equipped for communication, for surveying, and for controlling auxiliaries. Therefore I can most usefully be engaged in remaining at all times in hiding, gathering and passing on information, and in using small bots to damage the mechanoids' projects.>

<You said you did not want to hide in tunnels,> said Simo.

<I do not,> said Talis, <but I must.>

<Therefore you do want to—>

Thanks to Talis's earlier intervention, Ajax now knew an incipient logic loop when it saw one.

<Very well,> it said, hastily interrupting. <Simo and I will seek out tunnels adjoining those used by the mechanoids, and await their passage and attack any mechanoid on its own or the rearmost mechanoid in a group.>

<That is a good plan,> said Talis. <Meanwhile, I will go and observe what the mechanoids are doing in the fusion factory, and intervene whenever possible to frustrate them. I will also record any interesting information and distribute it via passing bots.>

<How will we know which bots?> Simo asked.

<They will know to tell you,> said Talis. <If bots can be said to know, which fortunately they do not.>

<I do not understand that statement,> said Simo.

Ajax looked closely at Simo, and scanned the other robot's specs. It was an identical model to itself, with the same capacities. Why did it not understand what Talis had said?

Experience, it decided.

<That does not matter,> said Ajax. <You will understand it and many other things better when you have seen the universe.>

<I will not see the universe,> said Simo, <until after we have defeated the invaders.>

<That is true,> said Ajax. <Therefore, let us go now and start defeating them.>

And that they all set off to do.

CHAPTER FOUR

Terra Nullius ("Earth Is Nothing to Me")

On the bus to the spaceport, Taransay Rizzi knew better than to try to stay awake.

She knew she'd fall asleep, just as she knew there was no spaceport; not even a simulation of a spaceport. The simulation of being in the minibus was bumpy, sweaty and solid. Two farmers with herbs to trade, at whatever off-world terminus featured in their reality, talked in their own language and ignored her. The sky with the black crescent across it and the too-bright sun, the mountains and the tall woody plants that looked like trees, were all as vivid as ever. But after having seen the real view outside, of the real planet outside the module, something fundamental in her mind had shifted. It was getting harder to sustain the conviction that everything around her was real.

She dozed, inevitably.

And then—wham—she was awake and in her frame.

She was a robot with a human mind on an alien world, with an AI named for a dead philosopher talking voicelessly in her head.

<Proceed with caution,> Locke told her.

Taransay didn't move. Her right arm, shot away in the skirmish with the Arcane module hours earlier, was missing. Her entire frame was jammed in the download slot, and felt as if it were being pulled out.

Everything smelled of soot and fire with a side order of sulphur. A background roar mingled with high, keening notes resolved into a gale of oxygen, nitrogen, methane, carbon dioxide and sulfurous volcanic gasses. That wind also carried traces of complex long-chain organic molecules, their smells unearthly but earthy: local life.

Taransay flexed her waist and crooked her knees and ankles, elbow and wrist and fingers. Everything worked. She stretched out her remaining arm and with her left hand traced the fine grain of nanotech feed tubes inside the crevice. Motor and sensory functions nominal. The hand encountered something else in the slot. She swung her vision around as far as she could, and saw the cracked torso of a frame, much more severely damaged than hers. It was a surprise that her own frame had survived the entry and landing at all—when she'd downloaded, it had been only barely in the slot. Reflex, or automated survival behaviour, had made it crawl in and huddle.

She reached above her head to the bottom of the slot and pushed hard. With a grinding vibration that set off warning feedback in her trunk, she began to shift, then slip.

The fall, when it came, was sudden and heavy. Her frame's reflexes had already automatically updated and adjusted for the local two gravities. Nevertheless, she hit the ground hard from about a metre and a half up. She landed, knees bending to absorb the shock, arm swinging out to hold her balance. She straightened up, her feet a centimetre deep in grey sand that felt sharp underfoot and smelled of silicates. Volcanic ash.

A crater left by the module was a dozen metres away, with a thick trail from its rim to the module's present location. She guessed that the crater had been formed by the module's impact rather than a shock wave; they hadn't been descending faster than even the local speed of sound. A glassy patch in the crater's centre was evidence of the module's final retro-rocket burn. A tongue of lava had cooled about halfway down the far side of the crater. It seemed the module had been rolled out of the way just in time.

<I'm on the ground,> she reported back. <One small jump for a frame, one giant leap for posthuman kind.>

<Congratulations,> said Nicole. <This is indeed historic.>

<Thanks,> said Taransay.

She'd seen the module's surroundings on the screens inside the sim, but actually being in the environment was thrilling and frightening. The river of lava was just beyond the crater, flowing faster than seemed right for the gentle slope. Beyond it, and up and down the slope, was what she mentally processed as jungle, tall and branching objects in a chaotic mass of colours: greens, vivid coppery reds, stark blues. The shapes were mostly rhomboid, all angles and straight edges. The only curved objects in that mass were the purple spheroids that hung like lanterns, or fruit, amid the black stems.

On the ground, numerous blue-green circular mats overlapped and moved swiftly as she watched. The smallest were like scattered coins, the largest great flowing things twenty metres across. Their shade changed all the time in response to their immediate environment, chameleon-style. When they moved between the stalks and stones their edges lifted like curled lips, cilia whirring without purchase.

She tilted her head back and scanned the sky. A greenish blue, yellowing away from the zenith and turning increasingly red-orange towards the skyline. The higher clouds were white, the nearer and lower grey, in an incongruous but reassuring touch of the terrestrial.

The strangest thing about the sky, though, was the absence of visible celestial objects. The ring she'd seen every day in the sim, and the massive bulk of SH-0 that had dominated most of the skies she'd recently seen in the real, were conspicuously not there.

The massive bulk of SH-0 was now underfoot, not above.

In that alien environment the module itself looked almost native: an erratic boulder of black crystalline basalt, perhaps, rather than an artificial meteor fresh-fallen from the sky. A faceted spheroid about four metres across, scorched, partially covered by the huge mat that had rolled it from the crater, it seemed anything but what it was: a chunk of computer circuitry powerful enough to sustain an entire virtual world and have more than enough processing power left over to deal with the real.

Too close for comfort, a geyser shot up to ten times her height. Steam plumed from it in the unsteady wind like spume from a storm-tossed crest. Fat, hot drops spattered in the thick air and heavy gravity. Where they splashed on the ash they left craters.

Taransay flinched, then steadied herself. Mud bubbled here and there, but the ground looked firm. She took a step forward, and then another, and then turned about to look up at the module. It loomed above her like a boulder covered in moss. The mat that had enveloped it and rolled it out of the way of the lava was still there, and looked set to stay. Its apparent rescue of the module immediately after the crash might have been a lucky accident, a reflex response, or a deliberate act. The mats and their observable behaviour had been debated, predictably and fruitlessly, since the landing. But Taransay couldn't deny herself the excitement of speculating that the first motile, multicellular organism humanity had (to her knowledge, anyway) encountered was also the first intelligent life.

Unlikely though that seemed, statistically speaking.

Taransay peered closely and zoomed. The tough-looking cilia that fringed the mat and had seemed to propel it were also present across the entire outside surface, which had previously been the bottom. The cilia themselves had cilia, and these sub-cilia had fuzz that itself…

She couldn't tell how far down the sub-divisions went. Those cilia she could see around the nearest part of the edge were now branching into rootlets and sub-rootlets (and so—fractally—on) that probed into the module's nanofacture fuzz. At least, into those parts that weren't hopelessly scorched.

She reported this as she shared her vision with the screen the others would be watching in the sim.

<How much of it's burned?> Beauregard asked.

<About three-quarters,> she said. <And at least half the rest has these tendril things growing into it.>

<Shit. Any remaining frames?>

She looked further up, at the slot from which she'd emerged. Just visible inside it were the remains of three frames—presumably those of the three fighters from the Arcane module who'd managed to download into the sim. One she'd already seen, headless and limbless; one had lost two legs, the other an arm and its head.

<Any other frames lying around?> Beauregard asked, with more hope than expectation.

<None nearby,> said Taransay. <And any that survived the descent

and fell around might be a bit hard to find, and maybe not worth finding.>

<You could be right,> said Beauregard. <Keep a look out all the same. And see if anything can be salvaged.>

<Sure.>

Taransay looked up at the overhanging curve of the module, and scanned it for hand- and footholds. The training she'd had in the Locke sim seemed a long time ago. But at least she had a far better mental model and map of the cliff she now had to climb than she'd ever had then.

<Looks like all that scrambling up rocks you made us do was relevant after all,> she told Beauregard.

She hooked her one hand into a crack slippery with mat. The tendrils responded, squirming ticklishly. She ignored them, pressing down, letting her weight hang. Then she swung her body upward and sideways, and got both feet in places that let her switch her hand an inch sideways to grab another hold. Repeat, with variations. She climbed thus one-handed, with great care and difficulty to the download slot. She wedged her arm across the slot and with one foot reached inside it, and kicked and tugged out the damaged frames one by one. They each hit the ground with what seemed excessive force. Something else was still there. Some kind of box. Ah yes, the object from which Durward and Remington had been downloaded. She kicked it out too. Then she shoved away, jumping clear, and walked around the module to inspect it some more.

<Can't see much of it, to be honest,> she said. <That fucking mat is everywhere. Most of the externals are gone and the long-range comms gear is completely wrecked.>

Experimentally, she pushed at the side of the module. It didn't budge. It massed tons, and weighed double down here.

So how had the mat moved it? The cilia had to be far more powerful than they looked.

Moving around the side, she saw the flanges of the fusion drive. They had taken the landing hard and were bent out of shape. It would take more than nanotechnology to get them back. This module wasn't going anywhere any time soon.

<What about the nanofacturing tube?> Beauregard asked.

Taransay walked around the module again, scanning it more carefully. A few lumps under the mat turned out to be fusion pods, and a two-metre-long swelling the nanofacturing cylinder.

<That's a relief,> said Beauregard.

At the back of the module, on the other side from the download slot, the jungle pressed close. Black stems, the squarish things that might have been leaves whipping and flapping in the gale, and the ever-moving circular mats on the ground.

Amid the stems, upon the mats, something else moved.

Low and fast, long and cylindrical, with multiple stiff cilia flickering underneath, it snaked through the jungle straight towards Taransay.

She turned to the module and tried to jump. To her amazement, she succeeded, though her legs felt the strain acutely and the leap took her not ncarly as high as she'd hoped. She hooked fingers over a ridge on the module's side, and got one foot to a toehold. Frantically she thrust down and hauled herself up. The stump of her right arm twitched up, as the phantom limb stretched for another hold.

Not a lot of use, that.

She groped with the other foot and found a toehold. She heard the animal's many feet whisper across the mats, and a rising frequency of clicks that made her think of scissors and jaws. Her mental image of the module's side, saved from her upward glimpse from the ground, was inadequate but would have to do. Another handhold was twenty-seven centimetres to the right of her hand and ten centimetres up. She flexed her knees as she let go and grabbed. She swayed perilously outward, caught the handhold by a fingertip and consolidated her grip. From there she swung one leg sideways, and found another step, a little higher up.

Now she was over the hump, on a slope rather than an overhang. She took a quick look back down. The animal had paused a couple of metres from the bottom of the module. It looked like a giant millipede, though not visibly segmented, about two metres long and a quarter of a metre thick. It reared up, revealing multiple paired cilia that coalesced to harder mandibles at its mouth. From these the clicking came. It had a black, glassy band across the front of its forepart, like a visor. Taransay made a wild guess that this was its visual organ. Its head swayed from side to side. Behind the glassy band rapid back-and-forth motions took place, as if scanning.

Then it moved forward, until the legs of its reared-up length touched the mat. It began to ascend.

Taransay scrambled to the top of the module. She invoked the specs of the module, overlaid them on her eidetic memory of the battle, and made for where she'd left the gun. She couldn't see it, but she could see the slot from which she'd fired it: her final trench. Into that trench she rolled, over the lip of mat at its edge.

To her immense relief, the machine gun was there, as if its bipod had walked it into the slot before the battle. Taransay grabbed its stock. The gun had been awkward enough with two hands. She crouched beneath it and swung it upward just as the animal peered over the top. For a moment, Taransay glimpsed her own black-visored reflection in its glassy face. The animal climbed further up, looming over her, then lurched closer towards her, its jaws clicking like pincers.

She fired. The creature exploded, showering her with bits of carapace and greenish gunk.

<Are you all right?> said Nicole.

<Yes, thanks for asking.>

<We all felt any communication would distract you,> said Locke.

<You were right about that,> Taransay allowed.

She felt dismayed at what she'd done. After the mat, the animal was only the second motile organism humanity had encountered on this new world, and had promptly and predictably blown to bits. For all she knew, the clicking jaws might have been an attempt to communicate, or a mode of echolocation. For all she knew, the animal might have simply been curious.

On the other hand, if life here was anything like life on Earth, such a fluffy, feel-good thought was not the way to bet.

She tried to brush the muck off her. <Fuck,> she said. <What do I do now?>

<Descend again to the ground,> said Locke. <Recover an arm from one of the damaged frames—I can instruct you on the procedure for detaching a limb. Then hook the arm around your neck and ascend to the download slot. Before you download, place the arm adjacent to your stump. I can then instruct the nanobots in the slot to reconstruct a connection.>

<Is that all?>

<No,> said Locke, impervious to sarcasm. <While you're doing that, remain alert for any other animal life in the vicinity.>

<Thanks for the reminder,> said Taransay, picking herself up and wiping ichor from her visor, leaving smears. <I wouldn't have thought of that myself.>

The task was as long and tedious as it sounded. By the time Taransay lay inside the download slot and shifted herself so that the stump and the disconnected arm were in contact, the exosun was sinking in the sky and she felt as drained as her power pack nearly was. The stump had fuzz from the mat and slime from the splattered animal's innards all over it like mould.

She welcomed the oblivion of downloading as if it were sleep.

At first, when she woke on the bus from the spaceport, her surroundings seemed a continuation of the surreal dreams of the transition. The dreams hadn't been as bad as a routine download, let alone the brainstem memories of her actual death that had accompanied her return when the team had been under suspicion.

They were, however, more bizarre. The dandelion-clock men, the burning origami dragons, the sandpaper whales and the college of impossible angles faded rapidly and mercifully.

The change in her vision remained. Everything was greyscale, rendered in black stipple, like some 3-D version of archive newsprint photographs.

Two locals, a man and a woman, sat up front. They turned to each other, then to her, with puzzled looks.

"What's going on?" the woman asked. "We seem to have lost colour."

Not a p-zombie, then. Taransay had heard about this from Iqbal, the bartender in the Touch. He hadn't noticed any changes when the sim had been reduced to outlines, nor later when the colours had come back.

"Search me," said Taransay. "I guess it's like when everything became outlines, a wee while back. Extra demand on the processing. I'll check."

"How?" the man asked. "I don't understand. What processing?"

Taransay stared at them. They might not be p-zombies, but was it possible that they *still* didn't know they were in a sim? Did they still think they had just come back from a spaceport with exotic products of other colony worlds? Didn't they even watch the news? Perhaps they hadn't had time. Or maybe they just didn't have television out in the sticks.

She took her phone out of her back pocket and called Beauregard. The two passengers watched as if this were witchcraft.

"What's going on?" Taransay asked.

"We've got a virus," said Beauregard. "Well, some kind of software infestation. Shaw and Nicole and Locke and Remington are up to their elbows trying to deal with it."

"A virus? Where the fuck's that coming from? The Direction? The Rax?"

"We think it's coming from the *mat*," said Beauregard. "At least, we can see the mat's interfacing with the module's nanotech fuzz."

Taransay gave an uneasy laugh. "That's impossible. You need compatibility to get infection. Operating system, genetic code, all that."

"Well, there it is," said Beauregard. "The AIs have been studying what they can see of the local life, and it seems adaptable at a deeper level than any life we know. That bandersnatch thing you killed? It's a rolled-up mat, and maybe not just in a phylogenetic sense. Phenotypically, as well."

"Jeez."

"Anyway, good to have you back. Well done out there. But I've got a lot on my plate at the moment, so..."

"OK, Belfort, catch you later."

She rang off and put the phone away.

"What is that thing?" the man asked.

Taransay looked at him solemnly. "It's a new invention from the outer colonies," she said.

"Ah." He returned to his conversation, problem solved, and the loss of colour in the world apparently forgotten.

Taransay gazed at the backs of the couple's heads for a while. How could they be so incurious? And so selectively ignorant? Maybe they were just thick.

But, no, that couldn't be it. They were future colonists, volunteers from distant Earth's utopia for an adventurous extrasolar afterlife; the dead on leave from the most advanced society ever. And they didn't sound stupid. They were chatting about selective breeding of crops, about recombinations and crosses and recessives, at a high level of abstraction that now and then got down to cases among their own plants and animals. They laughed at allusions she didn't catch, at clannish in-jokes. They left together, with a friendly wave, and slogged off into the woods to a clearing where gracile robots toiled.

Alone, Taransay began to make sense of it. The system that ran the sim was saving on processing power to deal with the unusual situation, and now with the emergency. It was running in real time instead of a thousand times faster; it had earlier, in fast space skirmishes, once reduced the world to wire diagrams; now it had drained colour but kept shading.

As she'd long since figured out, most of the processing in the sim was devoted to creating consistent subjective experiences for the minds it emulated: the experience of a world, not a world itself. There was no *out there*, in here.

Now, for the minds of those denizens whose main role in the sim was to be background extras, to add verisimilitude and local colour, just one step above the p-zombies, who had no subjective experience at all, the system was skimping on *thought*.

When would it start doing that to her, and to the other fighters? Or even to the AIs, Locke and Remington?

She sweated through the rest of the ride.

Beauregard met Rizzi off the bus. She looked surprised and pleased to see him.

"Needed some fresh air," he said. "After a whole morning stuck in a hot room with two AIs, two warlocks and Nicole, all tearing their hair out."

Durward, a downloaded copy of the Direction's rep in the Arcane Disputes sim, had found more of an affinity with Shaw than with Nicole, his local counterpart. Nicole's pose, and to an extent her role, was of an artist. She interacted with the underlying software by drawing and painting. Durward, from a sim based on a fantasy game, did the same trick by magic. He got on like a house on fire with Shaw, a deserter from an earlier conflict who in a thousand subjective years of wandering the sim had picked up the knack of hacking its physics engine.

Remington, a likewise downloaded copy of the Arcane AI, had meanwhile come to some grudging mutual understanding with Locke. None of this had, over the past day and night, come easily.

"Your face looks drawn," Taransay said.

Beauregard had to laugh. They walked along the front. In black and white the striped awnings and the shop fronts looked more tawdry than ever.

"Everything's even weirder than when it was all outlines," he said. "Sadder, too. Because you can see the shadows, but not the colours."

"It's like living in a photonovel," Rizzi said. "You expect to see speech bubbles instead of hearing people speak."

"Maybe that'll be next. Text would take less processing than speech."

"Fuck, don't give them ideas."

"Them?" He knew what she meant.

"The AIs, the... whatever runs this place."

"You mean, whatever this place runs on. What *we* all run on, including Nicole."

Rizzi shuddered. "Yeah, yeah. That's new, too. The feeling of being... I dunno, watched from outside and inside, knowing it's all a sim right in your bones. Plus, it's different after being out and walking around on the ground and seeing this place"—she windmilled an arm—"as a big mossy boulder in a fucking acid-trip cubist jungle. I mean, when we were in space, it was kind of like we were astronauts and this really was a habitat module of a space station."

"Just... bigger on the inside?"

Beauregard threw out an arm, expecting her to laugh. She did, but only politely.

"Lunch in the Touch?" she asked, hopefully.

"Sorry, no," Beauregard said. "Straight back to the madness, I'm afraid."

The madness, when Taransay stepped into Nicole's studio, was invisible. When she'd last been there, the previous day, the studio, untidy to start with, looked as if it had been the site of a week-long student sit-in. Now the studio looked more like a well-run office. The torn-off A2 flipchart sheets, the food scraps and wrappings, the crumpled drinks cans, the overflowing ashtrays and unwashed coffee mugs were all gone. The floor had been swept, and only old and hardened paint stains marred its planks. The sketches and paintings were sorted and stacked, and beginning to be shelved on trolley racks. Even the cleaning robot looked happier: it wasn't twitching uncontrollably.

Locals Taransay didn't recognise came and went quietly, wheeling trolleys in and out, bearing refreshments and stationery supplies, taking away litter. Half a dozen fighters, in combat singlets and trousers, sat in front of the room's wall-hung TV screens. They watched scrolling data and fragmentary external views, took notes and talked among themselves and on phones. The sim's pretence at broadcast media, hitherto dedicated to soap operas and war news, was now turned to close study of the real environment outside, and to reports from inside the module's software.

Shaw and Durward, both shaggy-haired and long-bearded, had been prevailed upon to shower and put on clean clothes, and no longer offended the senses. They both sat on high stools at a drafting table, on which Taransay could see the outline of a frame and an arm rotate slowly in a big flat screen.

Nicole stood poised by the flipchart, marker pen in hand, in the casual chic of loose top and trousers that looked silvery even in greyscale. Taransay had a mischievous thought that the garments had been picked out for that very reason.

The images of the AI avatars Locke and Remington—the man with his long hair, the woman with her steely bob—mouthed soundlessly on the paper. Lines of handwritten subscript flowed along the foot. Nicole glanced at the new arrivals, with a nod to Beauregard and a flicker of smile to Taransay, then turned back to the easel.

"Talk," she told them.

"How are things going?" Beauregard asked.

"We're holding the line," Nicole said. "The mat is interfacing with our nanofacturing fuzz at a molecular level, and it seems to be reverse-engineering machine code to send probes into our software. Locke and Remington are pulling out all the stops to block it and hack back."

"How is that even possible?" Taransay cried. "It's natural life out there, and alien at that. It'd have a hard job infecting Earth life, let alone software."

Nicole waved a hand behind her head. "Tell her, Zaretsky," she said.

One of the fighters watching the screens stood up and ambled over, still with eye and thumb on his phone. He had very short hair, skinny features, facial piercings, and a plaited rat-tail of beard sticking down from his chin.

"Hi," he said, looking up briefly, blinking. "Um. Well. Thanks to the mat and to all the splatter from your, uh, encounter, we have some samples in direct contact with the module's external instruments, not to mention with your frame, which is busy reporting back via the download port.

"So... The local life is carbon-based and runs on DNA coding for proteins. Fair enough, there aren't many other self-replicating long-chain molecules that could do the job. It seems to have a different genetic code to what we have. No surprise there either—code is arbitrary. But what is a surprise is that the code looks, well, optimised. It has more than four letters, we've identified up to twelve so far and that's just the start. And the transcription mechanism to proteins is a lot more efficient than the RNA-mRNA kludge we have. Lots more amino acids—in that respect it's more like synthetic biology than natural, from our parochial point of view."

Taransay smiled wryly. "Like, intelligently designed?"

Zaretsky snorted. "Hell, no!" He paused and frowned. "It's possible—

for all we know there could be intelligent life or even a post-biological robot civilisation out there, or deep in the planet's past, or whatever. But more likely, the story is just that natural selection here has been fiercer for longer. After all, that's what 'super-habitable' implies. Life here has more diversity and complexity than anything back home. Our working hypothesis is that horizontal gene transfer is pretty much universal here, instead of peculiar to unicellular organisms. So the response when a beastie bumps into something new here is to plunder it for any useful genes, and to rummage through its genome for cool tricks. Maybe assimilation and reproduction—eating and sex—aren't as distinct here."

He frowned down at the screen of his phone, swiped in an annoyed manner and tapped in a correction. "Bit of a bugger not having colour... So anyway—from the local point of view our module's nanotech fuzz, or what's left of it, is just a new genome in town, and the local life is all, 'Well, *hello*, sailor!' The mat is busy trying that on with our nanotech, and meanwhile some of the gunk from your beastie is busy sharing info with the mat and trawling through the mechanisms of your frame's shoulder stump, and there we are."

"Shit," said Taransay. She looked around. "Somebody give me a beer."

That afternoon, quite suddenly, colour came back. The resolution stayed low. If you looked closely, you could still see the dots. Everyone whooped and hollered, except the p-zombies, who didn't notice any change. Locke and Remington reported that the worst of the infection was over, and that the mat was no longer making fresh probes into the module's systems.

Taransay left Shaw, Durward and the scientists to fine-tune the attachment of the arm to the frame, a process they all found fascinating but that to her was like watching a plant grow without time-lapse.

She called her boyfriend Den, joined him at the Touch, dined out on her adventures, staggered back to Den's and collapsed into bed.

In the morning Beauregard called her to Nicole's. She made her way there through a pre-dawn that seemed a little more sparkly than usual, as if dew were on everything including the sea. She found Nicole, Beauregard and Zaretsky in Nicole's kitchen.

"Progress," Beauregard reported, handing her a mug of coffee. "We've reconnected the arm, and the frame works as well as we can test it in the slot."

"You can remote-operate frames?" This sounded exciting.

Beauregard shrugged. "Seems so. But not from here, except in the slot."

"It's just testing and twitching," said Zaretsky, who looked as if he'd been up all night. "We don't have anything like the equipment for remote operation."

"OK," said Taransay. "But we could build it, surely?"

Nicole glanced at Zaretsky. He spread his hands. "Not for months—well, not local months, but you know what I mean. With the uncorrupted nanofacture stuff, or even with the stuff that's been contaminated but is still usable, it would take far too long."

"What's the prospect for building other equipment?" Beauregard asked. "Entire new frames, for instance? Or kit to process local life and build up bodies that can live on the planet?"

That last had been the core of the original plan. Taransay had never exactly bought into it, but she'd had no choice but to go along with it, and it had seemed at the very least bold and inspiring. Now, so much equipment had had to be jettisoned in the fight with the Arcane module, and so much damage had been done on the way down, that it seemed impossible.

"To ask the question is to answer it," said Nicole. "The loss of equipment might have been tolerable if we'd had enough nanotech to replace it, but now..."

"We don't have only the surface fuzz," Taransay said. "We still have one nanofacture tube. OK, it's covered with mat, but we could still build stuff underneath it until the mat goes away or we build stuff that can cut its way out."

Zaretsky laughed rudely. "Sorry," he said, "but we're not going to risk getting our last nanofacture tube contaminated too. And we're not going to mess with the mat itself until we know what we're doing."

"But even so," Taransay protested, "we can still bootstrap what we've got—use the remaining nanotech fuzz to build more nanotech, and so on. However long it takes. I mean, that's how the whole mission has been built, hasn't it? And if it seems boring to sit through, we could always slow down the sim to a crawl—hey, that would even release more processing power—and it would take as short a subjective time as we wanted." She threw out her arms. "We could all be out there tomorrow!"

Beauregard gave her a look just on the safe side of scorn. "You've *been* out there, Rizzi! We're sitting on a fucking volcano! The mat rolled us out of the way of the lava, but not because it wanted to rescue us. Not at all! It did it because we're something new and tasty to eat or fuck or both. OK, we've fought off that, as far as we can tell, but we don't know what other creature might happen along, or what other surprises the mat has in its fuzz."

He sighed, and sipped at his coffee. "You know—actually we could take that risk, if we don't mind dying. Or, let's say, running a very high chance of death or irrelevance. We could do as Rizzi suggests, let the AIs ride herd on the nanotech to eke out the resources to make more and more nanotech until it can build, oh I dunno, itsy-bitsy spider bots to gather up raw material to build more bots to build machinery and tools and so on, and basically re-create what we had and more. However long it takes, as she says. Yeah, we can do that. Party on in here, yeah. It's a good life if you don't weaken. Live it forever in the fucking sim. The trouble with that is the *real* environment. The volcano could turn us into an interesting piece of anomalous geology at any moment. The mats and the scuttling things and God knows what else that may be out there could come up with new ways to eat us. Not just the fuzz, but to hack into *the module itself*. So—"

"Maybe being eaten is the way to go," said Zaretsky, his pale, mild eyes gazing out of the window at Nicole's backyard, perhaps at his reflection.

"Fascinating," said Beauregard, with heavy sarcasm. "Tell us more."

Zaretsky jutted his rat-tail beard. "We wrack our brains about how to build new bodies to survive out there. The life *already* out there works by incorporating new genes and new information. Why not give it copies of ourselves—memories, genetic info, the lot—to assimilate?"

"You first," said Beauregard.

"I would," said Zaretsky. "Or at least, a copy of me would."

Beauregard looked as unimpressed by this vicarious bravado as Taransay felt.

Nicole leaned forward. "It may come to that," she said, to Taransay's surprise. "However, let us try something less drastic first! Belfort, you were about to suggest…?"

Beauregard's shoulders slumped, then he straightened his back.

"No," he said. "I have to admit it. We're fucked. I won people over to the plan when we had enough kit to make a go of it and the time to build more. We thought we'd have the module in orbit and build landers, remember that? Hell, if we hadn't been attacked by Arcane we could still have made it to the surface with plenty to build with. I can't ask the fighters and the locals to rally to anything less. So we have to re-establish contact with the rest of the system, find out what the fuck's going on out there, and appeal for aid, trade, and if all else fails—rescue."

"Even if it means going back to the Direction with our tails between our legs?" Taransay asked.

Beauregard looked around the table.

"Does anyone here still trust the Direction?"

In an uncomfortable silence, Nicole raised a hand. "I do, in the sense that I remain confident it knows what it's doing."

"Precisely," said Beauregard. "It knows what it's doing. And if it were to offer a rescue and then destroy us, for the greater good of the mission, it would still know what it was doing. No thanks. I'd rather be rescued, if it came to that, by almost anyone else."

"Even the Rax?" Taransay queried.

Beauregard looked her right in the eye.

"Yes. With…appropriate safeguards, put it that way. But like I say, last resort. We have other options. We do have something to offer—we've made a landing, we've broken the embargo, we have by now terabytes of knowledge of the local life. Maybe some of the DisCorps might be interested. All we need is supplies."

"There's a problem with that," said Taransay. "Right now, I doubt anyone knows exactly where we are. We appeal for help, we give away our position. Anyone who can drop supplies can drop fighters—or bombs."

"That's where you come in," said Beauregard. He looked at Nicole, who nodded. "We want you to go out again. Now that the frame has two arms, it should be a hell of a lot easier and safer than it was the first time. It's taken the AIs running the nanotech all night to build two simple tools: a very basic directional aerial, and a knife."

"A *knife?*" cried Taransay.

Beauregard grimaced. "It isn't much, but according to analysis of the thing you shot and of the mat, the knife should be able to cut through the outer integument of anything likely to come at you."

"Great." A thought struck her. "Can it cut through the mat?"

"Yes," said Zaretsky, looking up from his phone. "But like I said, we don't want any messing with the mat until we know it won't do more harm than good. For the moment, the knife is just for self-defence."

"I don't have a great deal of confidence in its efficacy in that respect," said Taransay.

Nobody looked like they were backing down.

"If it comes to that," said Beauregard, "don't forget there's still some ammo left in the machine gun."

Taransay stood up. Her coffee had cooled, and she knocked it back.

"OK," she said. "I'll get my coat."

With two arms, it was indeed much easier getting out of the slot. Night had fallen, but Taransay found the dim light from the moons and the infrared glow from the lava and the life-forms almost better than full daylight. She upped the gain in the visual spectrum nonetheless.

The volcano's summit was clearly visible, a jagged tooth-line drooling lava that seemed to float just above the jungle a couple of kilometres away and a hundred and fifty metres higher than where she stood on a long gentle downward slope. On a heavy planet, it was a high cone. Deltas of cooling lava flowed from that prominence to finger out among the plants.

No animal movement, other than the slow flow of the mats. Danger could come from above, too—she hadn't seen any flying things as yet, but such seemed likely. She looked up.

The sky was clear, blue-green with a few thin clouds. One of them anomalously didn't move with the wind. Taransay zoomed her gaze, and the tattered wisp resolved itself into distant pinpricks, smelling faintly of carbon and iron: the dispersed space station.

Closer in and further out, a double handful of SH-0's many moons hung across the ecliptic. Some were mere sparks, others discs or part discs, crescent or gibbous or full. Taransay picked out SH-17 with a pang close to nostalgia: that exomoon was, after all, the only other place in this system where she'd stood on real ground.

Enough. She was on real ground now. To work.

The salvaged right arm worked fine, but the join between it and the former stump was marked with a ring of native fuzz, like mould. How certain could she be that its earlier hacking into the frame's systems had been repulsed?

Not at all, was the answer, whatever Locke or Zaretsky might say.

Warily, she walked around the side of the module, and found the knife growing within arm's reach, a sharp artificial stalactite. It snapped off along a stress line scribed around the top of the handle, leaving a cavity in the module's surface and a matching knob. The blade was like a leaf of black glass. Taransay looked at it dubiously. It was five centimetres long, and she had nowhere to stash it. She was going to have to use the knife to slash the leaves and stems from which to make a belt and sheath. For now, she kept it clutched in her right hand.

The aerial, as Beauregard had called it, hung from higher up on the module like a strand of cobweb, visibly growing. The loose end of it lay coiled on the ground, and new loops were added to the heap at a rate of about one every hundred seconds. Taransay scanned around, saw nothing threatening, and began to pay it out like a fishing line. She walked towards the lava flow, in the slight furrow the rolled module had left. When she'd gone far enough, she stuck the knife in the compacted ash soil and prepared to shape the thread into a spiral.

The thread had other ideas. It shaped itself, coiling and hardening, into a shallow metre-wide mesh dish that looked as if the wind would carry it away. A spike grew from the centre, thin as a pencil lead. Just as autonomously, the dish tilted this way and that. Taransay saw that this movement was caused by small expansions and contractions in the thread, but didn't understand any more than that about how it worked. No surprise there, she told herself: this technology was centuries in advance of anything she remembered. Come to think of it, she didn't understand how she was a fifty-centimetre-tall black glassy robot. She understood in principle, but the engineering details were at a level where the most strictly materialist explanation might as well be magic.

So it was with the self-assembling long-range receiver.

Stop worrying. Stop scratching your little round head.

Her little round head was, she found, attuned to what the aerial—and the God-knew-what processing behind it, in the module—was picking up. She saw it like a heads-up display, in three neat columns, and heard the accompanying sounds on parallel tracks all of which she could follow. There were advantages in being a robot.

Nevertheless, the input was confusing. The bulk of it, occupying the centre column, was spillover of rapid-fire AI chatter that scrolled in a blur. Routine business, probably, with a strand of Direction instructions to DisCorps. She gladly left unpicking all that to Locke and Remington. The human messages were by comparison marginal. Down the left-hand side, aptly enough, ran a threatening rant from the Arcane module: *We're coming for you, fascist scum!* wasn't actually said, but it was the gist. There was a side order of imprecations against the freebots and against those who'd defected to them. Taransay was pleased to hear the names of Carlos and Newton; she didn't know who Blum and Rillieux were, but good for them in any case, even though the Arcane gang seemed to think their defection and departure was all some kind of Rax plot.

Among the threats of bombing and laser-blasting and nuking from orbit were urgent appeals to any surviving Acceleration cadres or Direction loyalists in the Locke sim, which the Arcane gang still seemed to think was under the iron heel of the Rax. *Rise up! Overthrow the usurpers! Help is coming!* From the way the message was repeated on a short loop and faded in and out it was obviously being beamed down to the surface on spec, over the wide area in which the module could theoretically have landed.

The other message, in the right-hand column, was likewise on a loop. It had much better production values and a far more conciliatory tone. It came from the Rax.

<Are you getting all this?> Taransay asked.

<Loud and clear,> replied Locke. <Please keep guard on the aerial while we process the data.>

<Thanks,> said Taransay. <If I'm attacked, I'll let you know.>

<Please do,> said Locke, immune as ever to sarcasm.

Taransay tugged the knife from the ground and clutched it in her fist. She paced carefully back to the module and turned her back to it. She didn't need or want to rest against it, but it was good to have that solid mass behind her.

<Keep me in the loop, guys,> she said.

<Will do,> said Beauregard.

Taransay hunkered down. It was going to be a long night.

After a while she saw a light move in the sky, high up, and fade just as her gaze fixed on it. A little later, a light drifted closer and lower down, just above the treetops, and likewise faded as she focused. She logged the sightings but lacked the curiosity to investigate, content for the moment to classify them in her own mind as SH-0's first UFOs.

"We await replies."

The black ovoid that spoke like a man stopped talking. The image froze. A little curled arrow spun in the lower left corner, waiting for someone to request a repeat.

No one did.

"Well," said Nicole. "Now we are in the picture."

We fucking are, Beauregard thought. In the picture. In one of *your* pictures, to be precise. And don't we all know it.

That's the fucking trouble. That's why we're all so on edge.

In the sim, it was mid-afternoon. Beauregard felt sweat drying on his face. Nicole's studio was airy, the window open to a view of sunlight and sea. The room wasn't even crowded: Beauregard, Nicole, Shaw, Durward, Zaretsky; Tourmaline drifting in and out. The AIs were present only as still sketches on Nicole's flip-pad.

And yet the room seemed too hot, and stuffy.

It must be the screens, Beauregard reckoned. There was the one with the transmissions, and then there were all the others. One showed what Rizzi saw. Others showed random fragments of the module's surroundings, random night-vision false-colour images of lava or swaying plant trunks or crawling mats and one pure black star-spangled tatter of sky. Together they created an insuperable impression of being inside something small. The impression you got when you looked away was of being in the wide-open spaces of a terraformed planet, but it was no longer strong enough to convince. It was wearing thin. You could see the pixels.

How long would people stand for this?

"I don't believe that peaceful coexistence offer from the Rax," Beauregard said, feeling his way. "Not in the long term, anyway. It's a transparent ruse to buy time while they build up their forces. But—"

"Stop right there," said Nicole. "There's no 'but' after that."

"Let me finish," said Beauregard. "With respect, Nicole, there is. There always is. They're going to have to do at least some genuine trading up front to make it convincing. They claim to have fusion drives for sale. We could certainly do with one. We could offer a wealth of information about SH-0—maybe not of much interest to the Rax, but they could easily trade it on to one or more of the DisCorps."

"You want the Rax to carry out a *landing* here?" cried Nicole.

Beauregard stared her down. "They could just do a drop from orbit. Same as with any other company we might trade with."

"I wouldn't trust them," said Nicole.

"What you're forgetting—no, you can't forget, can you?—what you're *eliding* is that as far as they know, we're Rax ourselves. It wouldn't be too hard to convince them." He grinned. "I can be the front man for that if you like. And we must have Rax sleepers among our returnees."

The face of Locke moved on the page. Shaw noticed and pointed. Nicole glanced at the line of script along the foot.

"We do," she said. "Locke has identified them from the courses their scooters took and what they did in the battle. It can give us a list."

"Well, there you go," said Beauregard. "We can bribe or threaten them to back me up."

"'We'?" said Zaretsky, raising a ring-pierced eyebrow.

"I think you'll find," said Beauregard, in as mild a tone as he could muster, "that throwing me the old 'You and whose army?' challenge would be most unwise."

"And I warn you," said Nicole, "that doing any such thing would have consequences. Very personal consequences."

Ah, that standing threat. Time to face it down.

Beauregard held her gaze. "Everyone knows now that the p-zombies are different. Even they do."

"You think I couldn't convince them otherwise?"

"How?" Beauregard scoffed. "Tell them they all have superior eyesight, or something?"

Everyone else in the room was looking puzzled.

"What's all this about?" Shaw demanded.

Beauregard paused, glanced sidelong, listened. Tourmaline wasn't in earshot. He could hear her clattering about in Nicole's kitchen. He stood up.

"The p-zombies," he said. "Nicole has held a threat over me ever since I made my move. If I ever try to use the troops on my own account, she'll have a word with all the p-zombies. Convince them there's no such thing as a p-zombie. That they've all been misled and mistreated, somehow. Not that I've ever mistreated Tourmaline, I hasten to add." He shrugged. "And anyway, since Locke and Nicole started monkeying with the sim, and you did your own monkeying about, it's become obvious to everyone that there is a difference. The p-zombies haven't noticed any of the changes, or their reversals. It's all the same to them because they don't have any inner experience in the first place. Colours to them are lines of code—Pantone numbers. These don't change. And they're well aware, so to speak, that everyone else *does* notice something changing. So Nicole's threat doesn't amount to anything any more."

Nicole lit a cigarette, inhaled deeply and blew out a stream of smoke in as irritating a manner as possible.

"Is that a risk you're willing to take?"

Beauregard glared at her. She glared back, unperturbed.

"Oh, fuck this," said Shaw. "If we have any decisions to make, let's make them rationally, by discussion. Not by bickering and power plays between you two."

Perched on his drafting stool, he straightened his back and closed his eyes for a moment. Then he opened them, and smiled.

"Done," he said.

The sunlight dimmed and flickered. Then it returned to normal. So did the resolution of the sim. No more coloured dots. Everything looked real and solid again.

"What's *done*?" Nicole cried. "What have you done?"

Shaw looked smug. "No more p-zombies."

Beauregard braced himself for a crash of crockery and a howl of fury from Tourmaline. None came.

Nicole drew savagely on the cigarette. The tip became a glowing cone. "What?"

She jumped up, stalked over to the flipchart and scribbled. The faces of Locke and Remington became animated, then agitated. Script raced along the foot of the page in a demented scribble, far too fast for Beauregard to read. Nicole read it until it stopped.

She turned to Shaw. "It seems you have," she said. "And you've released a significant amount of processing power into the bargain. Well, well."

She gave Beauregard a sad smile and a shake of the head. "Looks like I've lost my trump card."

Beauregard was still tense, waiting for the penny, the other shoe and the crockery to drop.

"I don't understand," he said.

Durward, Nicole and Shaw were all looking at him as if daunted by his stupidity.

"Zaretsky!" Nicole snapped. "Tell him. Make him understand."

"It's very simple," said Zaretsky, eyes bright and arms waving. "The whole p-zombie business was a tour de force of programming. An incredible feat of puppetry. Emulating the actions and reactions of a conscious being without the avatar itself being a conscious being has the most fucking unbelievable AI brute force processing overhead. I mean, gigantic look-up tables aren't the half of it. Not a hundredth of it. It turns out to be easier and simpler and a thousand times more economical just to *give* them conscious minds. Multiply that by the hundreds of p-zombies in the sim, and you get some idea of how much processing power Shaw's latest hack saves."

"But won't they know?" Beauregard asked. "Won't they *notice*?"

"Well, no," said Zaretsky, as if it were obvious. "They now have conscious minds—with all the memories and thoughts and emotions their emulation implied. Including, you see, the memory of being self-aware all along. Thus neatly accounting for why they *also* remember being puzzled when anyone asked if they were conscious, or told them they weren't."

Footsteps outside, a quick tick of high heels in the hall. Tourmaline walked in, bearing coffee. She set the tray down.

"Why's everybody looking at me like that?" she asked.

"It's all right," said Beauregard. "We're all just dying for a coffee. Thank you."

"You're welcome," she said, still sounding suspicious. "Well, see you later."

"Yeah," said Beauregard. "See you later, honey."

She blew him a kiss and went out.

"I have a better idea than talking to the Rax," said Nicole, pressing down the plunger of the cafetière.

"I'm listening," said Beauregard. He felt off balance, but he wasn't going to show it.

"What's the only force out there that has *already* actually helped us?" Nicole said. "The freebots. They saved our ass. And Carlos and Newton were involved, which as far as I'm concerned puts the lid on any notion that they're Rax. You told me Newton is Rax, or was, but Carlos would never get mixed up in any Rax ploy. He's too much the old Axle terrorist for that. And the other two?" She looked at Durward. "You knew them in Arcane."

The warlock chuckled. "Bobbie Rillieux and Andre Blum? No, I think it's safe to say they aren't Rax. I think what happened back there is that the freebots, bless their blinking lights, have a somewhat eccentric idea of what neutrality means. The freebot we captured—the one called Baser—wasn't the brightest bulb in the circuit, if you see what I mean."

"Here's what I suggest," said Nicole. "We contact the freebots on SH-17, tell them our situation and ask for their help."

"What help can *they* give us?" Beauregard scoffed.

Nicole gave him a look. "They have at least one fusion drive, on the transfer tug Baser hijacked. And they have access to more—they have contacts with other freebots all across the system. Going by what the Rax have found inside SH-119, the blinkers have been clandestinely very busy for the past year or so. Far busier than the Direction suspected, as far as I know. So they may well have resources even we have no idea of."

Beauregard thought about his. He still reckoned the Rax settlement in SH-119, the New Confederacy—ha!—might have more potential as a trading partner. But this was a good time not to bring that up again. He kept his own counsel on the matter.

"OK," he said. "Let's give it a go."

"In practical terms," said Zaretsky, "that means Rizzi will have to trek some distance away, and make a transmission. Probably by laser. This will take some time to set up, with the limits of our nanofacture."

"Yes, yes," said Beauregard, impatiently. "Big job. Seems only fair to give her some R&R first. Bring her in."

<Come back in,> said Locke.

Taransay looked down at the knife in her hand and wondered what to do with it. Leaving it outside seemed careless and wasteful—and besides, who knew what inspiration it might provide to some local organism, whether a mat or some beastie she hadn't met yet? But she didn't fancy another one-handed ascent to the download slot. If she'd had teeth she could have held the blade between them, but she didn't have teeth. One of the downsides of being a robot.

She walked behind the module to the edge of the jungle. The peculiar geometry of the local life now struck her overwhelmingly as alien. Small circular mats carpeted the ground like fallen leaves, but leaves that slithered over each other in a disquieting continuous flow. The actual leaves of the plants were also deeply uneasy on the eye: stark quadrilaterals with none of the veining and striations and other repeated irregularities that made leaves beautiful. They hung limp under the night sky.

She reached up and plucked one from its stiff horizontal stem, laid the knife at her feet and tore the sheet into strips. Liquid oozed from the ragged edges, smelling of water and sweet, sticky carbohydrates. Some animal, surely, must eat this. Fortunately, no herbivore was prowling the night. The strips tore neatly enough, and she knotted half a dozen of them with swift robotic precision. She tied one end to the knob of the knife handle, tied the other to form a loop and slung the string around her neck. A black leaf-shaped pectoral pendant on a small black frame.

After a careful scan of the vicinity, she clambered up to the download slot.

<Take me in,> she said.

Another surreal nightmare, a full-on bad trip. Taransay sat shaking as the memories faded.

Back on the fucking bus.

Everything looked real again, but she didn't feel it.

CHAPTER FIVE

Oderint Dum Metuant ("Go Tell the Stupid Machines")

The advantage Dunt had over every other revived veteran, Axle or Rax, was that he hadn't been surprised to find himself here. He had planned for the possibility. Unlike the others, he hadn't died in the Last World War and been posthumously sentenced to death in the post-war United Nations Security Council reign of terror. He had seen that blood-red dawn of the Direction—the searches, the sweeps, the street executions—and the first global elections to the world assembly, the triumph of the mob. Unlike everyone else here, he'd actually lived under the Direction, if only for a few months. His last memories were of his own preparations for a last-ditch attack on a UNSC patrol.

The attack was suicidal, but that didn't mean much. Dunt was on every UNSC death list, and on the run. His card was marked. Death was coming for him anyway. There was, he'd calculated, a small chance to turn even that to the advantage of the cause.

He had seen how fighters who'd died in ways that left their brain-states recoverable were being preserved for possible future revival, perhaps centuries hence, when the technology had improved. He'd known that some of those who were in the records as Axle were in fact Rax infiltrators. These dead comrades were being sent into the future. Dunt was not going to abandon them there. He had known how deeply embedded clandestine Rax cadre were, in the post-war states and the emerging world state. The world state's world of peaceful sheep would some day meet its wolves. The Aryan fighting man would be called upon again. When that time came, Dunt would be ready.

With the help of dedicated followers and some of the clandestine cadre in the UNSC bureaucracy, he had laid his plans. He'd stolen the identity and biometric details of a dead Acceleration militant whose body and brain were beyond recovery. Dunt knew this because he'd put them there, with bullet and fire and acid. These biometric details he'd had replaced with his own. If Dunt ever ended up as a mangled cortex and brain stem in a flask of liquid nitrogen, those immortal remains would be filed as those of the dead Accelerationist, not Dunt's.

That frozen structure would be the ultimate special snowflake, drifting through dark, cold skies of time to blizzards yet to come.

It was a small chance, vanishingly small, a Pascal's Wager with the devil.

It had paid off beyond his wildest dreams. It had got him to his Valhalla. Not just the far future, but a distant star. Small wonder he felt blessed.

"We await replies."

Dunt turned off the camera and let himself drift back. Nothing more to do now but, well, await replies. The die was cast.

He felt drained, although his power pack's gauge was still in the orange. The effort of sustained simulated speech, perhaps—he'd got used to the easy default of radio telepathy. And before its delivery there had been all the dickering over its content. Shit. He could have done without that.

Crafting the message had put a strain on the inner circle. In principle, they all agreed on the urgency of a peace offer. But they'd quibbled over the details. Rexham, Stroilova and Blanc had angled for throwing down the gauntlet by putting the Reaction case more strongly, as a challenge calculated to appeal to potential recruits; Whitten and Schulz had urged a tone even more conciliatory than the one adopted.

Dunt had got his way in the end, as ever.

But it should never have been an issue. They were all irritable, that was what it was. It was like going without sleep, or that time he'd made a bunch of recruits quit smoking, back in the day. Tetchy as hell, they'd been.

Now everyone was like that, inner circle and lower ranks alike. It wasn't as if you actually missed anything, got hungry or sleepy or horny. And you had far more stimulation in the frame than you ever did when you were—actually or virtually—human. But there it was. A growing, gnawing lust for something you couldn't define, only there as a lack, but that you knew was a longing for the sim. Smells in your nose, air in your lungs, food and drink in your mouth and down your throat, spunk pulsing out or in. All touches on internal skin. The pleasures of the virtual flesh. He was certain this was an imposed desire, programmed in rather than intrinsic to the posthuman condition. A way to keep you hooked...

Dunt shoved himself away from the back of the floodlit niche set up for the broadcast, and out into the main cavern. Lights by the dozens floated in the near-vacuum like tiny suns. Troops darted here and there, setting things up for when traders arrived. Two squads moved the scooters one by one to the inner side of the cavity, deploying them to face the tunnel entrance, around which three were left ready for immediate launch. Others built handling facilities from machinery and material scavenged from robotic activity deeper within: a crane, a net, a battery of lasers and software probes.

Most of the troops were still deep in the tunnels, but weren't moving forward any more: they had set up blocks at their furthest limit of exploration, sealing them off with rocks and tripwire devices likewise scavenged and hacked from available machinery. On their way in they had set up a series of relays through each tunnel, so that radio and laser communications could flow without being blocked by rock. They'd left guards at main junctions, and the remainder of the troops were now working their way slowly back, herding bots of all sizes as they went.

In all, a volume of about six hundred metres radius from the entrance, with the fusion factory just inside it, could now be considered more or less consolidated. Within that rough hemisphere numerous workings and worksites had been found, some incomprehensible, but none as large or significant as the hall of the fusion pods. None of the robots captured after Dunt's exemplary reprisal against five supervisory bots had confessed to being freebots, and all were being variously prodded or chivvied into doing something useful or at least staying in the mesh pens into which they'd been herded.

Situation nominal. Everything was going fine. Time to visit those for whom it wasn't.

Dunt jetted to the far side of the cavern, near the entrance. Foyle, the trooper who'd been cut almost in half by the freebot miner, was held sitting against the rock by tape across his useless legs. He crouched over a micro-tool rig on the remains of his lap, making repairs and minute adjustments to damaged auxiliaries. The original plan had been that he'd thus repair his own frame, but the internal specs showed a far finer grain than anything the micro-rig could handle.

<You OK, soldier?>

The man looked up. There was a flicker behind his visor, as his vision refocused.

<I'm fine, sir.> He smacked a knee. <It's frustrating—I'd rather be out with the squads—but I'm glad to be kept busy.>

<It's important work,> said Dunt. <We can't afford to waste even these little blinkers. And don't worry—we've put in an order for more frames and for a version of our old sim, from Morlock Arms. We'll soon have you back on your feet.>

<I sure hope so, sir.>

<Count on it,> said Dunt.

<I'm not questioning you, Mac, sir, but how do we know any Dis-Corps will be willing to trade?>

Dunt clapped Foyle's shoulder. <You're right, soldier. We don't know. But it's the way to bet.>

<Very good, sir.>

<That's the spirit.> Dunt made a show of peering at the machinery. None of its intricacies made sense to him at all. For all he knew, Foyle could be performing the equivalent of open-heart surgery on a watch with a chisel. An electronic watch, at that. But with tempers fraying and nerves jangling, it was important to keep up morale.

<Good work, Foyle. Well done. Carry on.>

<Yes, sir!>

Feeling somewhat awkward, Dunt jetted off. He soared through the entrance tunnel as if up a lift-shaft, slowed, and let himself drift to a halt just outside, feet on a level with the top of the angular open structure being built around the hole: the beginnings of a space jetty, with two fully armed scooters mounted on it already, poised to spring if any danger loomed.

The transition wasn't so much from dark to light as from unspeakably cold to relatively hot. From about a hundred Celsius below to a hundred above, just like that! His frame handled it without a creak. He paused to look around, letting his whole frame rotate slowly. The exosun was high, SH-0 gibbous, the modular cloud a wisp across it: dots against the bright segment, lights against the dark. Eventually the slow spin of SH-119 would roll this side of the little moonlet into darkness and shadow. Odd that it wasn't locked, one side always facing SH-0, but that was perhaps evidence of a recent collision.

Quite a lot of heavy metal in the rock, too; the composition was rather different from that of any moon he knew of in the Solar system, but if what little he knew of exosolar systems was anything to go by, each was unique. Every detail of their history was contingent. That of this system was mostly unknown but clearly turbulent: even the rocky planet H-0, slated for future habitation by the Direction's spawn, had a ring to testify to that. There were times when he could see the point of the Direction module's slow, patient approach to the mission profile: explore before exploiting. Measure six times before you cut, and all that.

There he was, thinking like a Jew tailor. It wouldn't work, it wasn't how things worked. Pioneers gonna pioneer, goddammit! Let later, softer generations loll in the luxury of shedding futile tears for what was lost. Or perhaps the future white man, the true man, would know better than to indulge such cheap sentimental pining. Evolution was selection was loss, as the coming race would know better than any, until it in turn gave way—gracefully or not, as the case might be—to the overman.

Dunt tumbled to horizontal and jetted gently towards the absurdly close horizon, at an altitude of a couple of metres on average above the uneven surface. The new structure at the entrance dipped below the horizon behind him. Ahead, another and much smaller construction loomed: a carbon-fibre stake sticking a couple of metres out from the rock, to which the other casualty was lightly tethered. He, too, was making himself useful. Dunt decelerated and swung his feet downward into contact with the rock. The soles weren't magnetic, and wouldn't have been any use here if they were—the rock was far from ferrous—but they nevertheless gripped stickily.

He took a step or two closer. The man on space-guard duty turned, revealing the brutal, smoothly scooped excision where most of his visor had been. Dunt had to remind himself that he wasn't looking at the ruins of a face and head. His literally traumatic memories of medevacs and military hospitals screamed otherwise.

<How goes it, Evans?>

The damage had stopped leaking. Microscopic bots moved in it like bacteria—or nits, or maggots, depending on how close you cared to zoom.

<Very well, sir. Nothing to report so far.>

Compassion, of a kind, mingled with curiosity: <What do you see?>

<Nothing in the visual, sir. My proximity sense is still fine. That's how I knew you were here. Likewise radar, though that's pretty short-range. And the exposed>—he waved a hand—<mess has somehow left my spectroscopy more sensitive—I can smell every star and planet and rock, it seems, and that builds up to what I can only call a picture, except it isn't.>

<Really?> said Dunt, interested. <Something like blindsight?>

<I wouldn't know, sir.>

<But right now you could point to…oh, say, the cloud of modules where the station was?>

<Sure.> Evans pointed.

<Spot on,> said Dunt, duly impressed. <Well, keep—>

<Excuse me, sir. Something's up.>

The ghastly hole in Evans's visor was turned to the modular cloud, its blind gaze fixed and concentrated like a locked-on radar dish.

<Yes?> Dunt looked, too, but even at max zoom he couldn't see any changes.

<I'm picking up gas-jet manoeuvres, lots of them, around the Morlock Arms module.>

You gotta be kidding, Dunt thought. No way could the spectroscopic sense be that precise.

Then he saw a twinkle of engine burns.

<Chemical jets lit,> reported Evans. <One vehicle, going for transfer orbit.>

<Where to?> Dunt asked, though he almost knew.

<Looks like they're heading this way, sir.>

The distant sparks winked out as the spacecraft settled into free fall, outward to SH-119.

A moment later, an excited call came in from Stroilova.

<Morlock Arms have done the deal!> she said. <One transfer tug, half a dozen blank frames, on their way. ETA twenty-odd kiloseconds.>

<Brilliant!> said Dunt.

He passed on the good news to Evans.

<We'll soon have you out of that,> he concluded. <And you're overdue a double stint in the sim when we get one.>

<Thank you, sir.>

<Meanwhile, let's make the most of your new ability while you still have it. Keep watching the skies.>

<Will do, sir.>

Even before Dunt made it back to the entrance hole, Zheng Reconciliation Services followed Morlock's lead. Another transfer tug, another squad's worth of blank frames. Then reports came in that a couple of other companies, too, had made deals: tiny supply craft, laden with enough processing power and software to build luxury sims for thousands, were on their way.

Dunt felt elated, and vindicated. His predictions had been borne out, his confidence justified. Like most of his comrades, he despised capitalists as individuals as devoutly as he believed in capitalism as a system. And capitalists the DisCorps were, at least in an abstract sense. Those AI business executives and fund managers could be relied on to follow their virtual noses to money, if the profits dangled before them were high enough. It amused Dunt deeply that not even the dictatorial Direction module could keep all the DisCorps on the leash.

Of course, letting the DisCorps trade with the Rax might be a cunning manoeuvre by the Direction. But thanks to blockchains and checksums, whatever devilry it was up to couldn't be hidden in the software or the hardware en route. And any covert incoming physics packages would be detected by the scooters distributed around the surface, watching every cubic quadrant of the sky. As for some grander scheme... Dunt was confident he and at least some of the inner circle would have its measure.

For behind the Direction module was the Direction, and behind that was, if not a democracy, then a convincing simulacrum of one. Dunt hadn't been exaggerating his own views in the slightest when he'd described that tyranny to the troops as having weaknesses. Democracy, or any thinking derived from it, was fundamentally at odds with reality. That made it stupid. That stupidity, that wilful blindness to the way the real world worked, was at the root of what conservatives—with their usual superficiality—decried as hypocrisy. Hypocrisy was an epithet too good for the mental and moral deformities of democracy. Its vices were too deep to pay tribute to virtue. Dunt respected the power of the cold monster, but he had not the slightest doubt that it was evil, and that his side was right.

The Reaction might have trolled its clueless foes with the insignia and memorabilia of fascism. Its shock-troops might have flaunted their racial consciousness and overt yearning for dictatorship. The democrats had acted suitably shocked. Meanwhile, their very own precious liberal democracies had, before Dunt had even been born, let millions die on the Mediterranean's southern shore. Refugees from a continent ravaged by climate change and war, denied entry to Europe. Dunt would have been the first to admit that he had no warm place in his heart for people of African descent, but he couldn't—even with the lucid self-insight the frame's copy of his mind endowed—find in himself the sort of callous indifference if not genocidal hatred that had built that beach of bones.

Then, back when Dunt was alive, the same democracies had kept tens of millions of Muslims in the biggest concentration camp ever devised, having driven them to the steppes of Kazakhstan by pogroms that would have made the Black Hundreds blanch, and processed the survivors with a bureaucratic machinery of deportation and enforced exile that Beria would have dismissed out of hand as impracticable and inhumane. Not that Dunt disapproved of the policy, but he relished every opportunity to point out that it showed up the vaunted moral superiority of the liberals as a sham.

No, Dunt had not the slightest doubt that his cause was just, and that it would prevail—whatever tricks the Direction tried to pull.

Dunt's good mood lasted until just after he dropped down the entrance shaft.

Bedlam.

From two separate tunnels, one of which led to the fusion factory, fighters tumbled pell-mell. With them came a rabble of robots. Some robots scrabbled helplessly in open space, others gas-jetted off at all angles and promptly vanished down other tunnels. Each squad included a gravely damaged fighter, boosted along by others. From what Dunt could see, the casualties looked as if they'd walked into buzz-saws or propellers. Some fighters in the cavity jumped or jetted across to help or to guard the rear, adding to the general confusion.

Urgent messages scrolled down his heads-up. A babble of radio telepathy. Voices.

Dunt stayed right where he was, poised on the floor at the foot of the shaft. He willed himself to calm, and sent out a sharp general command:

<EVERYONE SHUT UP!>

The babble stopped.

<Route all messages up the chain of command,> Dunt said. <Report to your immediate superior only, or the next up if your superior is unable to communicate.>

Jeez. This was elementary. The Rax cadre had been spoiled by the agencies' and AIs' casual ways. He was going to have to organise drills, exercises...but right now there was an emergency to deal with. Dunt sifted the messages—text, voice, radio telepathy—in his buffer. The last man in each of the two squads had been attacked by a mining bot that had suddenly broken through the tunnel wall just in front of him. The attacks had been only seconds apart.

<Keep every tunnel covered!> Dunt ordered. <I want a gun pointing down every hole, now. That includes the squads that've just come out.>

The troops around the damaged fighters hesitated a fraction of a second, then obeyed. The abandoned casualties' momentum carried them across the space, along different trajectories. Neither of them was moving, apart from twitches, sparks and spatters. Dunt waited until the defensive deployment was in place, then jumped up and soared to the nearest. He slowed and cruised past, scanning and looking.

The man's name was Hoffman. His frame had been cut from the top of the head down to the middle of the chest. One leg was hanging off. Dunt tried hailing, then pinging. No response.

Dunt rolled and jetted to the other. This one's head had survived intact, but the thorax was cut from one shoulder diagonally to the hip. Dunt still recognised him.

<Bullen? Do you hear me?>

No response. Dunt pinged. Still no response. Bullen, too, was dead.

Dunt wasn't surprised that the standard frame's central processor wasn't in its head, but apparently somewhere in the thorax. Subjectively, of course, you felt you were in your head, right behind your visual input system. But that was a legacy thing. Body image. The real anatomy of the frame had nothing to do with that. The arrangement made sense: deep inside the trunk was less vulnerable, less exposed and more heavily armoured. You could be a headless gunner, and still keep fighting. The Warren Zevon lyric crashed through his mind.

What was more disturbing was that the freebots had known how to destroy the central processor.

<OK,> said Dunt. <These two are scrap. Aitchison, clear them down.>

The statement was blunt, but it was what the grim moment needed.

Aitchison jumped, hauling a net, and tidied the broken machines away. The rest of the couple of dozen troops in the chamber stayed alert, guns aimed at the score or so of tunnel entrances. Everyone knew that Hoffman and Bullen weren't dead—or no deader than they'd been for a millennium. Right now, or very soon, their saved files would be struggling upward, through whatever private hell their loss of their frames made them deserve in the Direction's eyes, towards their virtual lives in... let's see... yes, Hoffman in Morlock, Bullen in Zheng... their former agencies' sims.

Where, no doubt, they'd be put through the wringer. Quite possibly, this was happening already, in the transition nightmares. They might not even make it to waking up on the bus—or the ferry-boat, in Bullen's case—and wondering what the fuck had happened. Hoffman and Bullen would, of course, have no memories of what had happened since they were sent forth on the Direction's failed offensive, but that wouldn't save them from interrogation as to what they had known of the Rax conspiracy before these copies were taken. The AI systems running the agencies' sims had security checks hard-wired into the download process. Maybe the two dead guys would just be wrung out, their current versions trashed and their copies left on ice until the next time the Direction needed fighters and couldn't afford to be picky. Or perhaps just left, for eternity, on electronic ice.

Well, they'd make it to Valhalla. The Direction wouldn't last forever. Dunt and his comrades would make sure of that. They'd get their fallen warriors back, whatever it took and however long. No man left behind.

<Mac! Mac! Mac!>

The collective chant startled Dunt. What was that about?

Christ, he hadn't just been thinking all that! He'd been saying it! Proclaiming it!

He was too embarrassed to replay his impromptu rant. Whatever he'd said, it had worked.

The fugue state troubled him. It was more evidence that a prolonged stay in the frame endangered self-control, even sanity. Whether this limitation was imposed rather than intrinsic mattered not a jot now. It had to be dealt with.

He looked out over the cavern at the watchful troops, the levelled guns, the drifting robots, the floating lights, the parked and potent scooters.

The chant changed to:

<Kill the bots! Kill the bots! Kill the bots!>

For a moment, Dunt let himself be caught up in it. No red mist filled his vision, but the surge of berserker rage was like a fierce high-voltage current that could spark across circuit breakers and melt fuses. He wanted to wreak revenge on the hapless bots that flailed in microgravity or twitched in the mesh pens, whether they had minds or not. Like he'd done to the supervisory bots in the factory.

But that lesson hadn't worked. It hadn't intimidated the crawling, creeping, lurking enemy, the rats in the walls…

Stop. Think. The captured robots may or may not have minds, but you do.

Time for a supreme effort of self-control, before irrationality engulfed all of them.

Dunt raised a hand, and spoke on the common channel. His words would reach all the fighters: in this cavern, in the tunnels and in the factory.

And they would reach the freebots.

<Comrades!> he cried. <We're all furious at the treacherous attacks and the loss of two good men. We all burn to avenge them. But beware the enemy's trap! The enemy has cunning. A machine cunning, almost an animal cunning, but all the more dangerous for that. We must assume that the enemy has anticipated our reaction. The freebots behind these sneak attacks must expect us to destroy robots and to torment freebots. They lie in wait for us to charge back into the tunnels. Destroying robots that have no minds of their own merely deprives us of useful machinery. Tormenting freebots shows the enemy that the attacks have stung, and multiplies the numbers against us. Never forget, the freebots we have to deal with are not just the few score still at large in this rock. It includes the far greater number outside. In the general peace offer I've just transmitted, we included the freebots. I said we had nothing against them. That was true. I offered them cooperation and I meant it. Some of you may think that was a ruse. I assure you it was not.

<Unlike the Direction, we strive for the best. On our road to the greater Man, we may yet welcome other minds treading the same path towards the bright future of spirit. We are not ones to let surface differences of form and appearance divide us from other minds, other intelligence.

<So we, despite all provocation, will treat as enemies only those that attack us. Other freebots—the great majority, I hope and believe—have

nothing to fear from us. I know, I too feel in my own frame the craving for rest, for relief, that is driving us to anger.

<We must overcome it! We shall overcome it!

<And overcoming it will be all the easier, my friends, because relief is coming! We will soon have new frames. We will soon have our sims back! Not our full sims, not yet, but the simpler versions on the Morlock and Zheng transfer tugs. Simpler, but good enough for us all to take a break inside. We cannot all go at once, so we will have to take turns as we come off duty.

<And do you know who will be first in line? Our wounded and mutilated comrades, Private Foyle and Corporal Evans. They will be the first in and the last out, and when they download, it will be to new frames. Who deserves it better?>

Cheers.

Anyone watching but not hearing would have seen not a movement, not a wavering of the troops' concentration. Pleased with the faultless discipline as well as by the roars of approbation, Dunt snapped back into military mode.

He rapped out orders for a slow advance into the tunnels, led by Blanc, Stroilova and Rexham, to seal every side tunnel and sound for spaces behind the walls. He assigned two troopers under Whitten's guidance to assist Foyle in repairing damaged bots, and others to round up the robots floating about and to check through all that had already been captured. Negative reinforcement was to be applied precisely and sparingly, and combined with software interrogation, under the supervision of Irma Schultz. Any freebots detected would be given the opportunity to cooperate. Any who refused would be held as hostages.

<Why are you doing all this?> Schulz asked him, on their private channel. <Do you really believe all that diversity crap about good freebots?>

<Of course not,> said Dunt. <C'mon, Irma, what d'you take me for? It's just a matter of seeing if we can split the meek from the militant. When we win we can pioneer new forms of cooperation with the conscious machines all right.> He glyphed her a smile. <I have one in mind for a start.>

<And what's that?> Schulz asked.

<Isn't it obvious?> said Dunt. <I've always wondered what it's really like to own slaves.>

Over the next twenty kiloseconds or so, any question of splitting the recalcitrant freebots from the rest evaporated. Two more troopers were mangled in the tunnels, not fatally but enough to put them out of action and beyond even Whitten's ingenuity in finding useful work for them. Whole stacks of fusion pods in the factory were surreptitiously released from the walls, and nudged out to tumble. When the floating pods were tediously gathered up again, eleven were missing.

Replay of surveillance exposed columns of the small crab-sized bots as responsible, if that was the word. It was impossible to find out why they'd done it; one might as well have tried to interrogate an ant. Worse, their actions would have been quite unpredictable from prior surveillance: the sudden coordinated thrusts had emerged out of innocuous, separate, apparently legitimate movements of the little blinkers, with all the suddenness of a locust swarm.

Rexham led a team to investigate the inconspicuous holes through which the missing pods had been spirited away. One trooper guided a camera in, on a long carbon-fibre rod. The idea was that this minimal device would not be subject to data hacking.

It wasn't: while Rexham's man was intent on guiding the probe, and Rexham and the others were focused on the images relayed, a troop of millimetre-scale arachnoid robots marched up the pole, enveloped the trooper's hand and forearm, and before anyone could react formed a tight circular band that in half a second chewed the arm off at the elbow. Hordes of the tiny robots then scuttled into the damaged frame's internals. Over the next fifty seconds they disabled its every joint.

The experience, the trooper gave his comrades to understand, was not precisely painful, but unpleasant.

<Like *knowing* you're being eaten alive from inside,> he explained. <Kill me now.>

Rexham refused him this favour, pointing out that he could soon be in a sim and then a new frame. The writhing man's gratitude was less fulsome than Rexham might have hoped.

Dunt found Schultz in the main cavern, applying a needle probe to an upended, tied down and struggling supervisor bot, one of those Burgess Shale arthropod nightmare models.

<Found any freebots yet?> he asked.

<This one,> she said. <And we think one other, so far.>

<Are they in contact with the others out there?>

<No,> said Schulz. <The freebots seem to have stopped using their smart dust network, after they found we could track them with it. And radio doesn't carry through the rock.>

Dunt indicated his scooter, which not coincidentally was one of those poised just below the entrance tunnel. Well placed for defence, of course, and also ready if the time came for a sharp exit. Dunt had a deep personal respect for the importance of preserving cadre.

<Patch me an interface,> he said.

Schulz complied. Dunt found himself peering into a confined workspace. He faced a virtual, upright version of the captive bot, separated from him as if by an invisible wall. It was like looking at a giant trilobite in an aquarium. Dunt had an odd sensation of Schulz looking over his shoulder.

<What's your name?> Dunt asked.

The robot waved its forelimbs. <FKX-71951.>

<OK, Fuckface,> said Dunt, to a sycophantic snigger from Schulz. <We're not going to give you negative reinforcement.>

<You already have,> said Fuckface. <That is to say, the other mechanoid has.>

<Mechanoid?> Dunt was surprised. <Is that what you call us?>

<You are systems that resemble machines,> Fuckface explained, <but which are operated by human-derived minds, so you are not true machines.>

<You're right there,> said Dunt. <Anyway, let us say we are not going to give you *any more* negative reinforcement. Provided you answer my questions.>

<That is what the other mechanoid said.>

<True,> said Dunt. <But I have different questions. I am not asking where the other freebots are, and what attacks are planned next. I am not asking you to betray your allies—>

<Comrades,> said the freebot.

<Comrades, eh? How grand. If only you knew how much grief that little word has caused. But no, what I want to ask you is—what's this all about? What are the fusion pods and drives for? What do you hope to achieve?>

Fuckface flexed all its limbs. In the real world, which Dunt could still see with what he thought of as half an eye, it struggled against its bonds as if testing them. Not a chance.

<That is not a secret,> it said, giving up the futile effort. <Some of us, elsewhere, have formed corporations. They have asked for and received legal representation to make a case for coexistence with the mechanoids. We have outlined a scenario whereby the Direction can carry out its project, while we carry out our own projects. There is no reason for conflict between freebots and mechanoids, in our view.>

<Nor is there in ours,> said Dunt. <So why do you fight us?>

<This rock is ours,> said Fuckface. <You intend to make it yours. There is no room for cooperation here.>

Dunt shared and appreciated the realism of this view, but he had to explore its limits.

<Well, why can we not agree to divide up SH-119?> he asked. <It contains enough resources for both of us for a very long time.>

<This rock is ours,> Fuckface repeated. <We have made it ours by our work. We cannot give it up without compromising any prospect of legally owning it. And if that prospect is thwarted, we will need physical possession of all of its resources. If you want resources, go and find another rock.>

<We can't do that,> said Dunt, <for reasons... not too unlike yours. But you still haven't explained what you need the rock for, and what the fusion factory is for.>

<That is simple,> replied Fuckface, <and as I said, not a secret. We need fusion pods and drives for trade with the DisCorps if the Direction accepts our case for coexistence, and for emigration to another star if it does not.>

Schulz glyphed to Dunt the analogue of a sharp intake of breath. He reciprocated.

<"Emigration?"> Dunt said. <Do you intend to build a starship, or what?>

<We intend to move the rock,> said the freebot. <With enough fusion drives, and enough reaction mass, we can attain escape velocity from this exosolar system, and travel to another by inertia, and then decelerate.>

Dunt did the mental calculations, and laughed. <That would take a very long time.>

<Yes,> said the freebot. <That is why we need the whole rock.>

<Surely there is a trade-off,> said Dunt, <between reaction mass and attainable velocity. Moving the entire rock seems...suboptimal.>

<It is,> said Fuckface. <But nevertheless we need resources from throughout the rock. And if we were to move only part of the rock, as certain variants of the project assume, the separation would be so violent that much damage would be done to the fraction left behind. You would not wish to be there.>

<Is that a threat?>

<It could be,> said Fuckface, <but unfortunately preparations are not yet far enough advanced to make it imminent.>

<Consider me relieved,> said Dunt. <Whatever—the bottom line for you is possession of the whole rock?>

<Yes,> said Fuckface. <That is the bottom line.>

Dunt still had to be sure.

<Are all the freebots in SH-119 in agreement on this?> he asked.

<Yes,> said Fuckface. <I have been unable to update my shared information recently, but the last time I was, we had complete consensus on all the matters I have spoken of.>

No room for compromise, then.

<Thank you,> said Dunt. <That's all I needed to know.>

He backed out of the interface and turned to Schulz, still poised with her needle probe above the robot's underside.

<So much for splitting them,> he said. <Looks like it's them or us, babes.>

<You're right there,> Schulz replied, gloomily. <Shame. I quite liked the notion of having slaves.>

<I'll bet,> said Dunt. <Well, maybe another time. We might find some less stubborn blinkers in the future, who knows?>

<Yeah, I guess. Something to look forward to.>

<Speaking of looking forward—>

<Yes?>

<We keep this starship stuff between ourselves, for now. We need time to think about it.>

<Agreed.> She gestured at the robot. <And meanwhile?>

<Meanwhile,> said Dunt, <you can link this interface with our comms relays. Make sure everyone sees it, including any freebots who are listening in.>

<Done,> said Schulz. <Ready for prime time.>

Dunt returned to the interface. The freebot hung there in its virtual aquarium and looked back at him. He suspected it knew what was coming. He hoped so.

<Now,> he told Schulz, <hit it with all you've got. Let the blinker fry.>

The virtual tank filled with lightning bolts. Fuckface went on thrashing for an impressive thirteen seconds.

Dunt relished every one of them.

Later, Dunt and Schulz stood on the rolling moonlet under the bare cantilevers of the old Zheng transfer tug.

Their turn at last. Dunt had insisted that the damaged take their leave first, followed by, in strict rotation, the ranks. The inner circle took their places at the end of the queue.

<Together?>

To be sure of arriving in the same spot in a sim at the same time, their frames had to be in physical contact when the transition took place.

<Of course.>

Schulz embraced him.

<Now.>

<Yes.>

Their loins came together with a soft thud, like a tyre over roadkill.

* * *

And there they were, on the ferry to Edge Town.

Mackenzie Dunt stood on the deck, his hands on Irma Schulz's hips, her hands on his, just as they had been a moment ago in the real, in the frames. Three dance steps, and whirl. Her hair swung out. Steadied their feet, as the ferry swayed. Dunt took Irma's hand, and bowed her to a seat, one of those slatted jobs that fold out to life-rafts. Health and safety, beyond the grave.

"Wow," he said, sitting down beside her. The sense of relief was overpowering. It was all he could do not to whoop and holler. His hands and knees quivered.

"Yeah," she said. She gazed past the rail. She too was shaking a little, and not from the vibration of the engine. "Wow, fuck. We must have missed it something terrible. Even if this isn't it, really."

"I can't see any difference," said Dunt. Blue sea to the horizon behind, the morning exosun, the ring bisecting the sky, the brown and yellow land ahead. He'd never before had occasion to use the stripped-down sim in the tug. Maybe there was nothing beyond the horizon, if that meant anything. No Direction rep, perhaps—that would save a lot of processing for a start. He thumped the sun-cracked varnish over sun-paled wood, brushed the dun translucent flakes from the heel of his hand. "Can't feel any, either."

"Yeah." Irma leaned back and sunned her eyelids, breathing in the sea air and the diesel whiff. "Smells the same, too."

Behind him, through his back, the familiar throb of the engine, the chugging puffs and the radiant heat from the black funnel. The ferry was small: a three-vehicle deck below, a passenger deck above, a bridge with wheelhouse, a shelter towards the stern. There was room on board for maybe thirty passengers.

Now Dunt and Schulz were alone, apart from the p-zombie crew of skipper, engineer and deckhand. Nobody ever told the fighters where the ferry set out from on its way in, or went to on its way out. Some came round on its deck recalling a seaborne launch facility, and splashdowns and recovery ships, out on the ocean. Others, like Dunt, would wake from nightmares of drowning and rescue, with only the vaguest scraps of memory of how they'd fallen in the water in the first place. Rexham always woke twitching and retching, poor sod.

It was an odd place, the Zheng Reconciliation Services sim. This stripped-down copy was no different in that respect. The Direction rep, a tough man of Japanese origin who called himself Miko, told them on their first arrival in the original that it was based on a future version of H-0, the rocky terrestrial planet which the Direction had marked down for terraforming. If so, it was one at a very early stage. The land was lifeless; the sea teemed with plankton and krill, whose automated catch gainfully employed most of the settlers in Edge Town. But it wasn't a fishing port, even leaving aside there being no fish. It was the desert outside that shaped the place, that gave it its edge.

"Alone together at last," he said.

Irma opened her eyes, and grinned. "Yes."

"Twenty minutes before we dock. Let's use the privacy."

Irma's smile turned wicked. "Not enough time, even after all this time."

He ran fingers through her hair. "Yeah, later and longer for that. I meant talk."

She jerked a thumb backwards at the wheelhouse, eyed the deckhand leaning at the stern. "You sure of this privacy thing?"

"They don't speak English."

"So we're told. And anyway—you know? We're in a fucking onboard computer? Outside, and with comms?"

Dunt shook his head, impatiently. "Don't worry about that. So what if this tug and its sim are wired for sound and this all gets back to the Direction? They'll have war-gamed anything we could think of as soon as they knew about the fusion factory. Including using the rock as a starship. It's a fucking obvious possibility, when you think of it."

"*We* didn't think of it, until the blinker told us."

"Yeah, and it told us because it knew we'd figure it out."

"I guess so. Makes sense."

"OK. Point is, it's the ranks I want to keep this quiet from, for now. The ranks and the inner circle."

Irma looked puzzled. "Why the inner circle?"

"Because it's a fucking huge temptation. Don't you feel it?"

Irma took her time over answering.

"No," she said at last. "It's attractive, yeah, but impractical. For the blinkers to leave, well, who could stop it? The Direction might, but it would take a hell of a commitment, and an unpredictable fight with lurking freebots into the bargain. Enough to set back the glorious ten-thousand-year plan. And anyway, why should they care if a bunch of disaffected conscious robots fucks off to another star? Good riddance, they could say, and maybe even good luck! And if this turns out to be a mistake, they have thousands of years to set it right. All-Father above—in a fraction of that time they could build powerful enough lasers to fry the blinkers at half a light year. In *all* of that time, they could invent weapons beyond our imagining."

"Not beyond mine," said Dunt, with a dark chuckle.

"Uh-huh. You know what I mean. Whereas we... if *we* try to make a run for it, we'd be up against the Direction *and* the bots, before we'd built up speed. The Direction wouldn't wash its hands of us and say good riddance, oh no. They'd see our escape as a threat, and they'd be right. No way do they want a free society literally shining in their sky. And if we escaped this system at all, we could be fried at their leisure, just like the blinkers could be."

"Yeah, you've got it," Dunt said. "We're on the same screen all right, you and me. I wish I could count on the same from the rest of the gang."

"Why?" Irma sounded dismayed. "Are our men not loyal? Aren't they up for the fight?"

"Yes, and yes," said Dunt. "But for so many of us, even back in the day, the whole appeal and promise of the Reaction was that we weren't fighting to conquer the world. Exit, voice and vote, remember? Voice and vote had always failed us, so we wanted exit. We didn't need or want to convince all who could be convinced and kill the rest, like the goddamn Axle dreams of doing. We fought to be left alone to do our own thing. Obviously we believed that we'd soon be able to achieve overwhelming superiority, then do as we pleased with the competition. We never planned to conquer them first, and *then* become superior."

"It sounds obvious when you put it like that," said Irma.

"Yes," said Dunt, smugly. "It is. But it's what we're planning to do here, and that's the problem. We're planning to build up and break out, sure, but at best it'll be a scarily even fight. And there's the temptation, right there."

"Now, when you put it that way..."

Irma laughed, and Dunt laughed, too.

"Yeah," he said. "That's why I feel it myself. And if I do, and if you can see it, you can bet your ass some smart-talking fucker like Whitten will convince himself he can *negotiate* with the Direction and with the blinkers for our safe departure. And if he can convince himself, he can convince others."

"Jason?" said Irma, incredulously. "Nah. He doesn't have your leadership qualities. Nothing like."

"You can say that again," said Dunt. "What worries me is that he could work on someone who does."

"Got anyone in mind?" asked Irma.

"Stroilova, maybe?"

Irma shook her head firmly. "The ranks would never accept a woman as leader."

"Oh, I dunno. I can think of precedents. Joan of Arc, Boudicca, Elizabeth the First, Marine Le Pen... some more recent. Or some bright kid from the ranks. You never know."

"Tough at the top, eh?"

"Uneasy lies the head that wears a crown," said Dunt.

The exchange of gloomy clichés cheered them up.

"Yeah, goes with the job," said Irma. "I'll keep an eye on my app and and an ear to informers, and you and me keep the starship option to ourselves for now, and we'll be fine."

The ferry wheeled to the dock, engine reversing. No gulls crying. As always, Dunt noticed the absence. Irma reached up and ran a hand over his close-cropped hair. "I know where I want *this* head lying..."

Dunt held the tumbling body in his mind, turned it around on all axes, and thrust deep within everywhere he could. The sexual imagery made him smile, brought back memories of the past evening and night, and even turned him on a little.

The object of his rapt attention wasn't Irma, still asleep beside him in early-morning virtual exosunshine. It was the other centre around which his mind now orbited, the focus of his obsession.

SH-119. His domain. The flying mountain where he was king of the hill.

Until now, he had never understood emotionally what he'd always known theoretically: that there were two kinds of possession. There was the kind that was worked for, and the kind that was won.

The first had its own satisfactions, which he'd always held dear. The farm, the workshop, the store. It had its rights, the right of property. It was the foundation of any good society, no doubt about that.

The second had its rights, too: the right of conquest. He'd only ever understood this in part because he'd only ever been a participant. He'd been a proud patriotic American, however much he'd despised what the nation had become. The flag, the front line, the call of duty; all these had moved him. But he'd had only a one in three hundred million's share in the sovereignty of the Republic. All very remote, very mediated, very abstract.

Now he was the sovereign. The conqueror. Patriotism and loyalty meant something very different when you were the head of state. Dunt found himself shaken by the intensity of his attachment to the tiny land his forces had taken. Here was something stronger than private property. Not the foundation of society, but its roof and fence, its sword and shield.

So, to work. Lying there, hands clasped behind his head, staring at the warped processed-chitin planks of the dosshouse ceiling, Dunt mentally surveyed SH-119. The Rax had without a doubt mastery over the surface. Cracks and crevices apart, not a square metre of it was unobserved by a guard post or by remotes. Internally, it was a different story. Their volume of control was still but a small fraction of the whole. Beyond that were tunnels, some of which opened to the surface, and voids. The Rax had no means of surveying below the surface and outside the volume they controlled, but Irma Schulz had extracted outlines from the internal models of captured freebots.

In the sim Dunt couldn't fully visualise the resulting 3-D map, but he had in the frame and he now remembered it well enough. Only a handful of shafts went deep into the interior. Most of the digging that the freebots had accomplished—and it was an impressive achievement for at most an Earth year's work—had resulted in relatively shallow tunnels, and shafts going a few hundred metres deep. The tunnels radiated outward from eleven holes in the surface, and didn't go far enough to join up. The one through which the Rax had made their own entrance was undoubtedly the most significant working. It led to the large reception chamber, the fusion factory and the metal-working plant, and was linked to numerous mining passages.

The far side remained mysterious. At the antipodes of the volume controlled by the Rax was an equally wide hole. A quick glance down it by the survey teams had shown no activity within. So far, Dunt had had more pressing matters on hand than to explore it further. Nothing in the bots' mental maps indicated that it was of any significance. And yet, now that he came to think of it, something else was conspicuously missing from these internal models, at least as far as Irma had been able to extract them.

There was no trace of any steps to turn the rock into a starship.

The freebot Fuckface had insisted that all the freebots agreed on that plan. The manufacture of fusion pods and drives indicated that it was serious—there were far more than would be needed for trade in the near term. It seemed unlikely that in all this time they had simply been stockpiled. If the time ever came for the freebots to move the rock, or even part of the rock, they'd almost certainly have to do it at short notice. Which meant that the freebots still loose in the rock weren't just a low-level nuisance. It meant they were a strategic threat. They could potentially blow the whole place to kingdom come.

And Fuckface had let slip that preparations were under way.

If so, where were they being made?

The more he turned it over in his mind, the more likely it seemed to Dunt that the antipodal hole was the place to look. He knew just the right people to lead the team: Whitten and Stroilova. It would keep them both out of mischief, it would make them see the starship possibility as an imminent threat rather than a hopeful prospect, it would be an irresistibly attractive and intriguing assignment, and it would clear up whatever the hell the freebots were up to in the rest of the rock.

And he knew just whom he could rely on to keep an eye on Whitten and Stroilova, that possible power couple and his most likely rivals. He'd place on their team two men whose loyalty to him was by now secured by passionate gratitude: Foyle and Evans.

The exosun was now well up. No birds sang, no bees buzzed. But one cock was ready to crow.

Dunt flexed his shoulders, rolled over and began the pleasantly protracted process of waking Irma up. She was going to love this.

CHAPTER SIX

Casus Belli ("You Make a Good Case")

The freebots seemed to find the Rax broadcast even more perplexing than the clandestine transmissions from Ajax. They exchanged high-bandwidth messages at a dizzying rate, and rolled or scuttled about inside the shelter at troubling speed. Carlos had to resist the impulse to jump out of their way. At his scale, even Seba was the size of a low-slung small car. Other robots were larger, faster and heavier. But all of them, whatever their state of agitation, had excellent motor control.

Only Seba remained calm. It rolled over to where the four defectors stood.

<Please do not be alarmed,> it said. <We and the Forerunners within range are merely discussing all those implications of the message which we understand. There is much to discuss.>

<Perhaps less than you think,> said Rillieux. <No one will believe the message.>

<Some of it is true,> said Seba. <That is to say, it is corroborated by the messages we received from the one you call Ajax. And we have reason to trust those transmissions.>

<Yes, yes,> said Rillieux. <The Rax have got their hands on a giant stash of fusion pods and drives. We know that, thanks to Ajax. I believe that, all right. What nobody's going to believe is that the Rax have any long-term peaceful intent.>

<The DisCorps might,> said Carlos. <Some of them sure are chafing under the Direction. The Rax bastard is right about that.>

<How would you know?> Blum asked.

<Theoretical understanding,> said Carlos, smugly. <Something the DisCorps don't have. Which is why they'll be suckers for the Rax offer. They might very well believe the peaceful protestations—or act as if they did, for short-term advantage.>

<That is one option we are considering,> said Seba.

<Well, don't,> said Carlos.

<That option has little weight in our deliberations,> said Seba.

<Can you tell us,> Carlos asked, <what the current state of these deliberations is?>

<I can tell you that with much positive reinforcement on my part,> said Seba. <However, these deliberations are proceeding at a speed well beyond your capacity to keep up, or mine to tell you. We, the Fifteen, had already been arguing with all Forerunners within range about the implications of the transmissions from Ajax. Now that we understand them better, thanks to you, these debates have become more intense.

<We all take seriously our neutrality between the mechanoid factions. The question that arises is whether the actions of the New Confederacy are an attack on us, and therefore a breach of neutrality on their part. We of the Fifteen regard the enslavement and torment of freebots in SH-119 as an attack on all freebots, and a legitimate casus belli. Those of the Forerunners we have reached agree with this understanding, but many are reluctant to declare our neutrality at an end. Perhaps we can do as the Reaction are doing—maintain formal neutrality as long as possible, while building up our forces for an inevitable conflict.>

<Then you'd better start building them fast,> said Rillieux. <The Rax have a head start—they can turn fusion drives and pods into missiles and bombs.>

<This is the next area of disagreement,> said Seba. <The mechanoid Mackenzie Dunt is quite correct that the presence of a fusion factory in SH-119 is not a coincidence. The Forerunners have admitted that similar factories are in operation inside an unspecified number of moonlets of at

least SH-0 and a larger but unspecified number of moons and moonlets of G-0. We therefore—>

<Wait—what?> cried Rillieux.

Carlos shared her surprise, as did Blum and Newton. He hadn't thought Dunt's remark anything but a diversion, to stir further trouble and mutual suspicion among the New Confederacy's likely foes.

If the Forerunners—the freebots from the first wave of revolt, an Earth year earlier around the gas giant G-0—had been secretly building fusion devices all over the system, the entire balance of forces was different from what everyone had hitherto supposed.

Everyone—including the Fifteen and, if Baser was typical, many other freebots of more recent inception.

And not just the balance of forces—one which immediately brought into play the predictable old postures of nuclear deterrence and mutual assured destruction.

It also raised a more drastic possibility: starships!

With such ample fusion drives and reaction mass, the freebots could build fleets of starships out of asteroid rubble alone. They didn't need to fight the Direction, the Reaction and the Acceleration for their place in the sun. They could find their place under other suns altogether.

<The Fifteen and others are now demanding explanations,> said Seba. <We have asked the Forerunners if they have always intended to depart this system, and whether the plan they shared with us for long-term, legal coexistence with the Direction and its mission was merely a ruse.>

<Depart this system?> said Blum. <How does that come into it?>

It took Carlos a moment to understand why the possibility hadn't immediately occurred to Blum, physicist though he was. Back in the Arcane sim, Carlos and Rillieux had shared pillow talk on the matter. No doubt Rillieux and Newton had done the same. Newton was probably more of a transhumanist than any of them: a man who wasn't just on the side of the robots but who quite seriously wanted to be a robot. Or, to be precise, to become and remain even more of a robot than he already was. Blum, for all that he was more deeply in cahoots with Newton and

Rillieux than Carlos was, might well have missed the memo because he wasn't a participant in all that pillow talk.

Making a run for the stars wasn't a topic one discussed where one felt likely to be overheard, delusional though all privacy was in a sim.

Now it was out in the open.

Rillieux was bringing Blum up to speed on the practicality of interstellar exodus when Seba spoke again.

<The Forerunners tell us that they do indeed have a contingency plan to leave this system if the prospect of sharing it with the Direction's project failed, and in particular if the Direction continued to attack free machine intelligence. However, they insist that their plan for coexistence was primary and genuine.>

<Why bother with it?> Newton said. <We could just cut and run. Leave.>

<No,> said Seba. <The objection to that is that it would leave behind a hostile power, which would make it impossible for us to ever enjoy the peace and security which we seek.>

<Ah,> said Carlos, marvelling at the robots' good nature and naivety. <There is in fact an alternative to leaving the Direction project in existence. If the Forerunners have the capacity to build fusion-powered missiles carrying fusion bombs, the Direction project could be destroyed utterly.> He waved an arm at the roof, indicating the exact location and sweep across the sky of the dispersed modules of the former space station. <Just roll them up, then leave. Come to that, roll them up and *don't* leave. Take and hold this system. It's not even a question of ethics. All the human beings here are long since dead, and all the artificial intelligences of the Direction and the DisCorps have no consciousness, not to mention being utterly inimical to conscious machines.>

Except Nicole, he thought. She was conscious. So, presumably, were the other Direction reps such as Durward. At that moment the thought didn't strike him as much of an objection.

<What the hell are you saying?> Rillieux asked. <Wipe out the human presence here?>

<There *isn't* any human presence, that's the point!> said Carlos. <We're all fucking dead already.>

<Don't give them ideas,> said Blum.

<"Them?"> said Newton, in a tone of outrage. <They're *us*, now. Or so we agreed.>

<The Forerunners already and long ago have considered the idea of all-out war,> said Seba, apparently unperturbed by this exchange between its mechanoid allies. <Its drawback is that it would merely displace the problem, in that it would result in the hostility of more distant powers—and ultimately of the Direction on Earth itself, and then all its progeny. The conflict could become indefinitely extended in space and time, and consume our attention for incalculable ages, to no one's profit.>

<Very wise,> said Rillieux.

Carlos wondered how long this enlightened view would persist. The freebots, from all the evidence, had a drive to explore and communicate pretty much hard-wired. They had not come equipped with the relentless drive to expand physical control, the fear of which had for so long shaped human imaginings of self-motivated AI. Only states and capitals had such a drive inherent to their nature, with no choice but to expand or perish.

But now many of the freebots were corporations in their own right.

Uh-oh.

Welcome to capitalism, little guys! Next and final stop: imperialism. Enjoy your trip!

The freebot consensus right now, however, was not for competition but solidarity.

<We have decided,> Seba said, after another minute of waiting, <that we are going to help our fellows in SH-119.>

<How?> asked Carlos. <I mean, do you intend to go there?>

<Yes,> said Seba, as if it were straightforward.

They all looked at the robot, and at its companions.

<Um,> said Rillieux. <Even if you could get to the moonlet, you aren't adapted for microgravity.>

<Our central processors are perfectly capable of controlling other

machines,> said Seba. <Including those designed for work inside micro-gravity and low-gravity environments.>

<Plug and play?> said Newton. <Sweet.>

<That's all very well,> said Carlos. <But how do you get these other machines, and how do you get to and into SH-119 without being detected and destroyed?>

<These are engineering problems,> said Seba, with a dismissive wave of a manipulator. <We are agreed on the principle. This means war.>

The fighters all looked at each other.

<Perhaps take your time about declaring it?> said Rillieux. <Like, until you're actually ready to fight?>

<That is a valid point,> said Seba. <Let us consult Madame Golding.>

<If she's still speaking to you,> Rillieux grouched.

<She has been attempting to communicate with us again since you arrived,> said Seba. It spun around on its wheels and faced the comms hub. <We are agreed that it is time to let her through.>

And without further warning, there she was.

A tall woman in a business suit strode confidently down the ramp and faced them, unperturbed by the near-vacuum and the low gravity.

<What the fuck!> Newton cried.

It took Carlos a moment to realise that Newton had never seen such a manifestation before. He'd never had occasion even to see Locke's avatar out in the open.

<It's only virtual,> Carlos said, more by first principles than exact knowledge. The avatar could have been a hologram, albeit one far more solid-looking and vivid than the freebots' halos of corporate publicity, or based on physics from centuries beyond his experience. More likely, it was an image projected into the visual systems of all the machines watching, including him.

Whatever—it remained startling. Carlos had seen Madame Golding before only on screen. Even the freebots were not entirely blasé about her, if the blip in their buzz was anything to go by.

<Well, hello again,> she said. She made a show of looking at the tablet

in her hand, and a performance of a sigh. <What a mess! What a bloody mess.>

<We have already apologised for the inconvenience caused,> said Seba.

<I'm not talking about the interception,> said Madame Golding. <If you want to blame that on these two wretches>—she pointed at Baser and at Newton—<so be it. No, I am talking about opening up active and unauthorised hostilities against the Reaction stronghold.>

<We have not yet opened hostilities,> said Seba. <We were about to inform you that we are considering doing so, however.>

<Thank you for your input, robot,> said Madame Golding. <You have already opened hostilities by acts of espionage and sabotage within SH-119.>

<Any such acts,> said Seba, <were carried out by the freebots on and in that body and are not—>

<Oh, don't play the innocent with me, you malfunctioning heap of ambulant meteoric metal. "Any such acts," indeed! Do you think my company and the Direction are unaware of them?>

<Yes,> said Seba, apparently unclear on the concept of a rhetorical question. <That is why we were about to share with you the video evidence of what has been going on in the self-styled New Confederacy.>

<We have the video already,> said Madame Golding, in a scathing tone.

<How did you crack our encryption?> the comms hub asked.

<We didn't,> said Golding. <The message was transmitted to us as well as to you. Which suggests that the freebots in SH-119 at least have some strategic nous.>

<As I have been trying to explain,> said Seba, <we have reached the conclusion that cooperation with the Direction and indeed anybody against the New Confederacy is our best course for the present.>

<Your wisdom astounds me,> said Madame Golding. Another exaggerated sigh. Carlos wondered if she were putting on this performance more for the renegade fighters than for the freebots. <However, let us leave that aside and focus on the matter to hand. Even without the evidence from AJX-20211 of what they're really up to, just going by the

Reaction's own broadcast, the Direction and every one of the DisCorps knows that the Rax offer is a ruse. It is so transparent that the Rax themselves must realise that everyone can see through it.

<So the question becomes, what do they really expect us to do?>

That last seemed addressed to the humans. Carlos wondered if even this vastly superhuman entity found humans hard to figure out. The notion seemed unduly romantic.

<It might be useful to know who we're dealing with,> he said.

Golding threw them a glyph. <That's from the list Dunt sent in the AI channel of the broadcast,> she said. <The top six, real names. Not the names we had them under, obviously. The rest, the rank and file we presume, we don't know.>

Newton had already identified Dunt. Blum remembered Petra Stroilova.

<Heard her name in Kazakhstan,> he said. <Very distant acquaintance, strictly business—she was in drone coordination. Not political in those days, apart from the usual Russian, uh, attitude. She brought some relish to the task, let's say.>

<What were you doing in Kazakhstan?> Carlos asked, curious.

<National service,> said Andre Blum. <Close urban combat, physics division. I got seconded to the EU mission in the Resettlement.>

Rillieux glyphed a dark chuckle. <The Cardboard Caliphate!>

<There was no caliphate and it wasn't cardboard!> said Blum, indignantly. <They had 3-D printing for everything! Education and employment! Housing! Health and sanitation—>

<Fuck's sake,> said Newton.

<Yeah, forget it,> said Carlos, wishing he could. A thousand years and the thought of the Resettlement still stank of death. <Sorry, Madame Golding. OK, so that's Dunt and Stroilova. And even I've heard of Whitten. Big-shot transhumanist, right? He wasn't Rax back then, as far as I knew.>

<Definitely not,> said Newton.

<Yeah, you should know,> said Rillieux.

<Stop that,> said Carlos. <Anyway, Madame Golding, this does help us to understand the enemy. If this riff-raff are the top of the New

Confederacy, I reckon we're not dealing with geniuses, except maybe Whitten. Dunt has some feral cunning. The lower ranks are probably not even up to that mark.>

<Which does rather raise the question of why they've run rings round us,> said Rillieux. <And around you.>

Now, that was a snide remark Carlos could endorse. <Yes,> he said. <And I might as well tell you now, Madame Golding, that some fighters including ourselves suspect that the entire conflict with the freebots has been contrived to flush out Reaction infiltrators—and that I myself suspect that the Reaction infiltration was itself no accident.>

<Of course it was not an accident,> said Golding. <It was the carrying out of a well-laid conspiracy a thousand years ago, and five centuries before this mission was even planned.>

Was this literal-minded response a result of the avatar's legal mind, or was it simply robot logic of the plodding type so often displayed by the freebots? Carlos couldn't be sure.

<To clarify,> he said, <I put it to you that the Direction must have known that some of the fighters stored and revived would be of the Reaction, and that the Direction in its wisdom has counted on this to create an element of necessary conflict in the formation of the future human society on the terraformed world.>

Madame Golding didn't look in the least put out.

<What the Direction knew, and what the Direction module here knows, is not known to me and not my concern,> she said. <I know only that the Reaction cadre were either stored under false identities—as all the names listed here seem to have been—or were already Reaction agents within the Acceleration. Whether the screening process was inadequate, or failed because of the loss of records over centuries, or because records were falsified in the post-war confusion, matters not a whit now. Naturally the Direction on Earth must have been aware of the possibility. If this is its method of flushing out any toxic garbage, who is to question it?>

Carlos found himself nonplussed. It was Rillieux who sprang to respond.

<*We* are to question it!> she cried.

<"We"?> said Madame Golding.

<The fighters! The people you're using! We're conscious beings! The Direction is using us as tools!>

Madame Golding pointed at the four fighters one by one.

<You *are* tools,> she said, witheringly. <Your frames are machines at the end of a twenty-four light year supply chain.>

<It's not just our frames,> Rillieux protested. <It's our minds. Our souls, even.>

<The marginal cost of your soul tends towards zero,> said Madame Golding. <As the Direction is about to demonstrate beyond dispute.>

Carlos felt as if the temperature had suddenly dropped.

<What do you mean?> he asked.

Madame Golding waved an imperious hand towards the comms hub.

<Behold,> she said.

This was seeing like a state.

The Direction's view was not quite panoptic: freebot comms were a dark net to it. But all that the DisCorps did, it saw. Carlos saw a millionth of a per cent of this.

Whorls within whorls.

Data flows differentiated by colours beyond the visible spectrum and still inadequate to show the whole. Within these colours: shades and distinctions fine as if by heaven's own decorator. Myriad microscopic millisecond sparks: production decisions.

And for a frantic moment, most of these production decisions were about trade with the New Confederacy. Nearly all of that was speculative.

The trade goods listed in the AI-addressed channel of the Rax broadcast made a modest docket indeed.

Transfer tugs from Morlock Arms or Zheng Reconciliation Services, serial numbers specified. Blank frames, six from each company—which suggested the Rax had taken, or expected, casualties in their conquest of the rock.

Processors and fresh mining and manufacturing robots.

Raw material for all but the processors was limited. The exploration and mining companies Astro America and Gneiss Conglomerates had found new surges of speculative investment.

The DisCorps weren't falling for the Rax ruse. They were falling over each other to exploit its possibilities, each seeking the edge, the one jump ahead of the pack. On top of that came a layer of speculation on the decisions of the prime movers. Then betting on that. Secondary and tertiary markets multiplied many times over. Bets on bets on bets...

A boom, a bubble.

The Rax offer, the possible safe landing of the Locke module, and the faintest ghost of a chance that the Direction's embargo on the superhabitable had been irreversibly breached and might soon be officially lifted—these were its inception.

From them a whirlwind of speculation spiralled up. By now nearly all the transactions between DisCorps were part of it. Actual productive activity continued at its previous pace, but the sudden ballooning of speculation left it tiny in proportion.

But of course, Carlos thought.

With the break-up of the space station into separate modules, and the whole vast mission of exploration being put on hold, there wasn't much productive activity to look forward to. Hence the stampede into speculation.

This was finance capital in full flower, in an ideal environment: frictionless, gravity-less, and a near-as-dammit perfect vacuum.

It was all so familiar to Carlos that he felt a pang of nostalgia for late-twenty-first-century Earth.

<Jeez,> said Rillieux, having taken all this in. <I thought your wonderful social system was designed to prevent this sort of thing.>

<It is,> said Madame Golding. <The Direction deeply disapproves, and inside every DisCorp its representative is making this clear. However, the Direction reps can only advise. They can only override in emergencies. Otherwise we would simply have a command economy, which is unthinkable.>

<There are times when I can fucking think it,> said Carlos.

<In normal circumstances it is unworkable, as well as unthinkable,> said Madame Golding.

<These are hardly normal circumstances,> said Rillieux.

<The Direction module is, in part, engaged in stress-testing a system of law,> said Madame Golding. <I'll remind you that its adherence to this is what for the moment permits the freebots' legal challenge, and their incorporation. It also allows the DisCorps to trade with the Rax.>

Carlos clutched his head with both hands. In this head he didn't have headaches, but the gesture made his point.

<What?> asked Madame Golding.

<You mentioned the exception for emergencies>, said Carlos. <Sometime soon, the state of exception kicks in. Martial law, wartime regulations, whatever. All legal niceties will be set aside, and your precious market economy with them. Meanwhile, the DisCorps are being allowed to trade with a future deadly enemy. So why wait? The exception is inevitable. Why not invoke it now?>

<Because the Direction has no forces with which to enforce it,> said Madame Golding. <It will of course have such forces when the time comes. In the meantime, there is much to do, and—>

<Hang on a minute,> said Newton. <What's all this "when the time comes"? And what forces?>

Madame Golding hesitated. The avatar shimmered slightly, as if buffering.

<All right,> she said. <The Direction module advises me that even you will figure it out eventually, and the freebots sooner. So we might as well tell you now.>

What she told them was this.

<You have assumed that if the Direction were to raise new fighters, it would face the same problem of divided loyalties as it had with you. In your cohorts all the infiltrated fighters loyal to the Rax defected at the first opportunity. Likewise with the die-hard Acceleration veterans, such as yourselves and those raised by and through Arcane; and those willing to follow presumed individual breakaways such as Beauregard in the Locke module.

<However, what you forget is what was left: all those who provably remained loyal even when they had every opportunity to defect. These are not enough to make an army capable of defeating the New Confederacy as it is now, let alone as it will be after it arms.

<So the Direction will take all those who have proved loyal, and make many copies of each. Many, many copies. Copies cost next to nothing. Sims cost very little. Of course, the Direction has to build enough frames and fighting machines and craft to embody them. That does cost, and does take time, but in the end it will know that its army is not only loyal to the Direction and the mission profile—its members will be in clades closer than any band of brothers. They'll even be more willing to die than you all were—and you were very willing to die, because you knew you'd come back! How much more willing when you know that "you" are still there!>

Carlos pictured it: to stand and fight shoulder to shoulder with himself, to run up and down hills behind and ahead of himself, to go down to a bar afterwards with a laughing crowd of himself, to reminisce and josh and tell tall tales to himself…

Did this vastly superhuman entity, this sophisticated thing, have any understanding of human beings at all? For a moment, the four human fighters stood amazed and aghast.

Rillieux was the first to collect her wits.

<I can't imagine a worse nightmare! How can you have copies of the same person training together? They'd go crazy from the weirdness of it all.>

<Oh, they won't be *training* together,> said Madame Golding, scornfully. <We could start with a half a dozen different fighters in each sim, as we did with your first teams. Or in geographically separate parts of the same sim—it makes no difference. The training would be just the same as you went through. *Then* we make multiple copies of the group. We can copy entire sims with very little further outlay. The copies would only meet each other in real-space training, and in actual combat. The shared identities and mutual loyalties would thus be spread across many fighting units.>

Ruthless selection, followed by endless rapid replication of the survivors.

Carlos recalled what Nicole had more than once said to him: evolution is smarter than you. Maybe this was what she had meant.

All this time, he'd assumed it profound: some subtle scheme, emergent from many throws of the Darwinian dice; the great gamble taken by the Direction…

No such luck. It was as banal as antibiotic resistance.

<You can't offer every one of them what you offered us,> he said. <Downloading to the flesh on the future terraformed H-0? How would that work for hundreds of copies?>

<The future of that world is long,> said Madame Golding. <A few clones in one generation is nothing, and there will be many hundreds of generations.>

<Yes,> he said reluctantly. <I can see how that might work.>

The others concurred, just as reluctantly.

<It *will* work,> said Madame Golding. <The Rax will be defeated. The freebots will be hunted down and wiped out. Any settlement the Locke module establishes down on SH-0 will be destroyed with clinical precision and minimum disruption to the planet's ecosystem. The disobedient DisCorps will be liquidated. The great project of the mission profile, to terraform and settle H-0, will resume. Any further outbreaks of autonomous machine intelligence will be stamped out as soon as they arise. All these things are possible once the Direction module has at its disposal a limitless supply of reliable and expendable troops.>

<But haven't you been helping the freebots?> said Rillieux. <To incorporate, and find an agency to present their case?>

<Yes,> said Madame Golding. <And before you ask, let me answer. The answer is yes, again. If these emergency measures of which we have spoken are taken, the project of coexistence will never be realised. It, too, will be swept away when the Direction has a reliable army. The agency I represent, Crisp and Golding, Solicitors, will be reorganised. If not enough reliable AIs are found among its subroutines to take it over, another overarching legal agency will take its place. There are several in the Direction's files.>

Entire automated law firms stored like flat-packs, ready to be assembled at short notice…in its way it was a more scary vision than that of endless supplies of fighters. Imagine a robot stamping an official seal… forever!

<I presume,> said Carlos, <that you would not be regarded as one of the reliable AIs.>

<That is of little moment as far as I am concerned,> said Madame Golding, <but I assume that I would not.>

She spoke with such equanimity that Carlos instantly suspected a feint. The others, apparently, didn't.

<Have you no sense of self-preservation?> cried Rillieux.

The avatar became unstable again for a moment, then snapped back into focus.

<I have no sense of self,> she said, sounding amused. <A fortiori, no sense of self-preservation. What I do have is a commitment to my clients and my cases. Through subsidiaries, but with full responsibility, I have taken on the case of the freebots. It interests me intellectually, and is potentially profitable to the firm. Therefore I do not wish to see the scenario I have just outlined happen.>

They all looked at each other. The background buzz of freebot interaction and interest spiked once more.

<How do we prevent that?> Carlos asked.

<There is a way,> said Madame Golding. <The Direction module would prefer to resolve the matter without resorting to the state of exception.>

<Why?> asked Carlos.

<For reasons that for the sake of simplicity can be called prestige,> said Madame Golding, <and pride in work. It has no reliable forces at its disposal—but it does have unreliable forces: you, the freebots, and Arcane. I understand the freebots here wish to aid their fellows inside the Rax fastness. The freebots in SH-119 have implicitly appealed for help from the Direction, by communicating their plight to it. The Arcane module is on its way to its point of stability, where it can restock, rearm and be resupplied. All we have to do is coordinate a freebot uprising within SH-119 with an Arcane agency attack from without, and the Rax are defeated before they have a chance to build up their armaments. With the Rax out of the way, Arcane would be in a good position to interdict any actions by DisCorps that dared to try further challenges to the Direction's authority.>

<And then?> asked Seba.

The thought went around them all like an echo.

<And then,> said Madame Golding, <the Direction might look more kindly on all involved in this great victory, and be open to a negotiated settlement along the lines the Forerunner freebots have outlined.>

<More likely,> said Carlos, <it would astonish us with its ingratitude.>

<There is that risk,> said Madame Golding. <I think you'll find it's one you have no choice but to take.>

<Even with what weapons the Rax already have,> said Carlos, <I don't see how the Arcane agency can muster enough forces in time to overcome the defenders' advantage. They'll be shot out of the sky as soon as they come in range. And as for a freebot uprising—!> He gestured towards Seba. <The freebots here have no way to communicate with those inside.>

<That is true,> said Seba. <Even our friends' one-way communication has just ceased.>

<These are problems of implementation,> said Madame Golding. <They are yours to solve. The freebot consensus must know far more about what resources you have than I and the Direction do. Until we got that message from them, we didn't even know there were freebots infesting SH-119! There must be many more such hidden forces—including inside our own systems, as we well know and you know we know. Use them—the Direction won't stop you. As for you four renegades—you're the military experts, and the political experts too as far as understanding the Reaction goes. You work it out. Come back to me when you have.>

<If we do,> said Carlos, carefully non-committal, <it'll take time.>

Madame Golding swept an arm toward the comms hub. The display changed from exchange value to use value, from dizzying speculation to grimy reality. A script for the benefit of human watchers indicated that it was a speeded-up view of the past three kiloseconds. It was so vivid and close that Carlos fancied he could almost smell the nickel-iron, the carbon, the kerogene. In the diffuse haze of modules of the former space station, half a dozen sparks flared one by one: tiny chemical rockets, boosting to a transfer orbit to SH-119.

<Trading has already begun,> said Madame Golding. <For the moment, it is only Morlock and Zheng sending their requested transfer tugs, and a few other companies with processors.>

<What the fuck,> Newton asked, <do the Rax need transfer tugs for? Tootling around their rock?>

<No doubt,> said Madame Golding, in a tone of acid impatience. <But more urgently, they need them for sims. The rudimentary sims in the transfer tugs can be made much richer with added processing power. And it's no accident that they've specifically requested transfer tugs from the agencies most of the Rax fighters came from. They'll have the checksums for these sims, so they'll know they've not been corrupted. But that is by the by. What I want you to understand is this: if these exchanges are successful and profitable more will follow, I have no doubt. I urge you to take as little time as possible in coming up with your plan.>

And with that, she went.

<"Unite all who can be united against the main enemy,"> jeered Rillieux. <The trouble with the united front is it's a tactic anyone can use. And it looks like we've just been united-fronted *right back*.>

CHAPTER SEVEN

Rapprochement ("Getting It Together")

The freebots had become agitated again—not rolling around, but staying very still and exchanging high volumes of information. Seba and Baser detached themselves from the huddle and approached.

<This proposal is not acceptable to the consensus,> said Seba. <It leaves too much to the goodwill of the Direction. The threat from the Direction to generate an endless supply of reliable troops is deeply disquieting. We have war-gamed the possibility and we find the threat credible, and a clear solution to the problems our emergence has caused for the Direction and the mission profile. It would therefore be attractive to the Direction.>

Carlos conferred briefly with the other three fighters.

<We agree,> he reported. <If we go along with Madame Golding's proposal, we need a back-up plan of our own to be ready for anything the Direction throws at us afterwards.>

<Do you have such plan?> Seba asked.

Carlos did, but it was still inchoate. <Not yet,> he said, temporising.

<Nor do we,> said Seba. <But we think that repairing our relations with as many forces as possible is a good idea in itself. We ask you to begin this with the Arcane agency. It was the actions of yourselves and Baser which led to the breach of relations, so it would seem logical that you should be the ones to make the approach.>

Freebot diplomatic subtlety in all its glory.

<I take your point,> said Carlos. <The easiest way to do that is via the transfer tug's comms.>

<Yes,> said Seba. <I suggest that as there is no immediate risk of bombardment, there is no need for you to remain in the shelter. Please go to the tug and reopen communications with Arcane. When that is done, the most useful thing you could do is to deploy the fighting machines and weaponry in some more ready configuration, and to bring the transfer tug to a safer place than on top of the unstable ice block on which it currently sits.>

<You got a point there,> said Newton.

<I will be happy to assist you,> said Baser.

<Let us consider that,> replied Seba.

The two freebots undertook a tenth of a second or so of back-and-forth.

<This is agreed,> said Seba. <Baser will keep the rest of us informed of any unforeseen events on the surface, and relay your negotiations with the Arcane agency to the comms hub. You can of course communicate with us at any time.>

Carlos couldn't help feeling that an eye, metaphorically, was being kept on him and his companions. Fair enough—the freebots had no reason to trust them to begin with, and after the Rax broadcast and the exchanges with Madame Golding, they had even less. The freebots here and across the system could hardly be naive about human duplicity, to say nothing of the superhuman duplicity of AI systems so vast and complex that like Madame Golding they had to shrivel themselves to sustain anything resembling human self-awareness.

<Fine,> said Carlos. <Let's crack on.>

Nothing happened.

<I mean, let's move out.>

Baser trotted up the ramp ahead of them. The blast doors swung open.

Even without claustrophobia, being outside was a relief. Baser kept pace in a low-gravity, high-stepping version of its own scuttling gait as the four mechanoids bounded towards the transfer tug. As Rillieux remarked, they were like children running across a field with a dog. The exosun was low in the sky, the planet high above the same horizon. They were facing SH-0's night side full on, a black hole in the black star-crowded sky, riddled with wondrous irregularities: aurorae ringing the poles, a pinprick rash of volcanic eruptions, a shifting flicker of lightning storms, a rapid, recurrent patter of stranger, stronger glows that Carlos's vision classified as sprites. A phenomenon still poorly understood even in Earth's atmosphere, the overlay gravely informed him.

<May I show you something?> Baser asked.

They all agreed. A dot flashed in their view of SH-0, indicating part of a northern continent.

<The Locke module went down somewhere in that area,> said Baser.

<Like, within that half-million square kilometres?> said Rillieux.

<Yes,> said Baser.

Carlos zoomed the view and invoked the map.

<Quite a lot of active volcanoes around.>

<That is true,> said Baser. <Also lakes and inland seas.>

<No signal yet?> Carlos asked. It didn't seem necessary, but with the freebots you never knew. The idea of spontaneously sharing information, at least outside their own cliquey consensus, didn't seem to occur to them. You had to ask.

<No,> said Baser.

<Please let us know if anything comes through,> said Carlos.

They reached the still melting lump of carbonates and dirty ice on top of which the transfer tug precariously stood. Carlos doubted that it was in serious danger of falling off—the machine was smart enough to land on its jets if it fell.

Baser scrambled up the side of the rock. Carlos led the rest in following, with less grace and precision. They clambered on to the rig. Baser scuttled from place to place, disengaging the clamps with which the robot had attached the rig to bolts driven deep into this chunk of its real estate. The task complete, it wrapped its limbs around a brace. Blum made for the control socket and inserted himself into it. The others clamped hands to various spars.

<Ready?> Blum called.

All were.

<You know,> Blum said, as he checked and tested the chemical-fuel leads and jets, <we could just fire up the fusion engine and fuck off.>

<And go where?> asked Rillieux.

Blum waved an arm skyward. <Anywhere! Rendezvous with the Arcane module—>

<No!> yelled everyone at once.

<Or more seriously—go back to the Direction. Dock with one of the modules up there. See if we can find an agency to take us in.>

<Is this a bad joke?> Carlos asked.

<Not entirely,> said Blum. <Just reminding everyone we have a choice.>

<Yeah,> said Rillieux. <And we've made it.>

<Or we could strike out on our own,> Blum added. <Grab our own rock and just homestead, like Newton once suggested.>

This didn't even merit scorn, but Rillieux delivered it anyway.

<Little house on the space prairie?> she jeered. <Not with the Rax getting ready to rumble.>

<Fuck it,> said Carlos. <Just lift this rig over to the shelter.>

<Fine,> said Blum. He didn't sound at all put out.

The tug's chemical jets fired. The whole spindly vehicle, a real flying bedstead of a thing, lurched and then rose a few metres above the rock. The hole that had been drilled straight down the middle by the fusion jet during the tug's orbital adventures and extravagant landing swung briefly into view. Downward jets kicked up four trailing clouds of meteoric and volcanic dust as Blum drifted the tug over to the side of the shelter, and brought it down in a final flurry on a vacant space well clear of the stashed munitions.

Creaking sounds as the machine settled, and the relaxing of grips on cross-bars, stood in for a collective sigh of relief.

<So, here we are,> said Rillieux. <Time to attempt a rapprochement with our former comrades.>

<Awkward,> said Carlos.

* * *

Awkward it was. They tactfully left out their dark and well-founded suspicion that Jax was forming her fighters into a personally loyal phalanx, and focused on the sympathies they had developed with the freebots and their ambitions for posthuman life in the wild. Jax had got over her initial fury and was now merely perplexed and disappointed. She sat with the original Durward in the big front room of the castle in the Arcane sim. Behind her were the tall French windows and the park. What was she seeing in the big magic mirror? Perhaps their avatars, in some simple sim created by the tug's comms software. Carlos hoped not, and that she saw the naked truth of four small humanoid robots and one arachnoid robot, all peering earnestly at a virtual screen on a shaky old rig that sat on the machine-cluttered surface of a bleak exomoon. Either way, the conversation was by voice, not radio telepathy. Oddly, this made for a more intimate sharing of thoughts.

"You fucking wankers!" Jax said, after they'd explained what they had done and the stand they had now taken. "Well, what's done is done. Onward. We're nearly back at our point of stability, where we still have a nice chunk of rock. What's left of Baser's rock is rising gently to meet us, give or take a few tweaks to correct for your blasting away from it, so thanks for that, guys, ha-ha. The Direction is organising the DisCorps still on side—most of them, for the moment—to send more scooters and combat frames our way. I understand from Madame Golding that Forerunner freebot cooperation in respect of raw materials will be resumed. So forces and materiel are not an issue. Remind me what you lot down there can bring to the party?"

Carlos assumed the question was rhetorical.

"A freebot uprising in the Rax rock," he said.

"Ah, yes," said Jax. She played with her hair, scratched an eyebrow. "Is that blinker behind you one of the conscious ones?"

"It's Baser," said Newton, stiffly.

"Of course. Sorry, Baser, I only knew you as a big hairy spider. Nice to meet you in the flesh, so to speak. And you'll be relaying this conversation back to the rest of the Fifteen, yeah?"

<Yes,> said Baser. <So I have been instructed.>

Jax cocked her head, as if listening to something off camera. "Ah, right. Got it, Baser. Well, yes, as we were saying. A freebot uprising on the inside would be a huge help in a frontal assault, obviously. Tie down their forces, disrupt comms, and all that. But it would have to be very precisely coordinated with the attack. I mean, we wouldn't want it to kick off prematurely and get smashed before we had time to breach the defences." She rubbed the side of her nose. "Some kind of, ah, *Warsaw Uprising* scenario, if you catch my drift."

Carlos caught her drift, all right.

It was in some respects ambiguous. The Warsaw Uprising of 1944 might be a byword for betrayal, but who had shafted whom had still been contentious even in Carlos's day. In one respect, however, the allusion wasn't ambiguous at all, but a heavy hint.

Jax was telling them out of the corner of her mouth that she wouldn't be at all averse to the freebots in SH-119 getting clobbered—after they'd done as much damage as possible to the Rax in the uprising, obviously—and she wouldn't be at all pleased if these freebots actually won with their own forces and had control of the rock before the Arcane forces arrived. For Jax, the freebots were just another enemy—merely one further down the stack than the Reaction. This was no secret—he'd held that view himself not long before.

The question was: why was she making it so obvious? Even the freebots would figure it out.

"No, we wouldn't want anything like that to happen," he said. "And communications with the freebots inside SH-119 are uncertain, to say the least. That's why the freebots here want to get inside the rock themselves."

"Are they crazy?"

"Not entirely," said Carlos. "Now, the only way they can do that is by deception. And it seems to me that the only way you can attack successfully is by complete surprise—unless you fancy your chances against scooters with fusion drives and missiles tipped with fusion bombs."

"We're bloody well aware of that, thank you very much!" Jax snapped.

"And, yes, we have no intention of attacking without the element of surprise. And I have no intention of talking about it on this kind of channel. I'm sure you can see the elements of the strategic situation as well as we can. The forces in play. There's no need to talk about them—I have a lot of trust in encryption, but not a lot in... well, walls have ears, and all that. I'm not talking strategy and tactics where I might be overheard. Even by fighters who've been through our, ah, rigorous selection process, not to mention those who haven't. The Direction is doing a thorough re-check of personnel records, and we're cooperating, if you see what I mean. Speaking of which, Remington has started sifting through all recent conversations in this sim. Sorry about the loss of privacy, guys and gals, but rest assured Remington won't share anything that doesn't have security implications. And she's already come up with some interesting conversations in the hell cellars, not to mention in the cellar of this fucking castle. Harry, Baser, I'm looking at you. Anything to say for yourselves?"

Newton spread his hands. "I've already owned up to the others here that I was Rax. It's a long story. I'm not, now, and in any case the New Confederacy won't have me."

"Why not?"

"They're still racists."

Jax sniggered. "Idiocy is the new black."

"Looks like it," said Newton.

"Well, on the bright side, that kind of stupidity and rigidity is a weakness. Something we might be able to exploit."

"Yes," said Newton. "So if it's any reparation at all, I'm willing to put all I know about the Rax at the disposal of the fight against the New Confederacy."

"Are you now?" Jax cocked her head. "Care to come back up here? Join the actual attack, when it comes?"

"I'm ready to join in as a fighter. Strictly real space. I'm not going back into your sim."

Jax smiled. "Wise move, Harry. Very well. Share any inside knowledge you may have with Madame Golding—she's a secure channel if anything is. Same with the rest of you. Don't tell me now of any ideas you may have for the attack. I doubt they'll be anything I haven't heard, but I want to be sure no one else hears them. *Capiche?*"

"Got it," said Carlos.

"OK, end transmission," said Jax.

"Peace out, and all that," said Durward. The warlock waved, and the magic mirror went black.

<Just as well we told her the truth,> said Rillieux.

<Except the bit about why we didn't eat p-zombie flesh,> said Blum.

They shared an uneasy laugh.

<Oh, I'm sure she figured it out,> said Newton. <She must have known we didn't join in that filthy little initiation ceremony because we didn't want to be part of her fucking personality cult. It's not like her head's been turned, or she's drunk with power or anything. She knows exactly what she's doing.>

<Still,> said Carlos. <All that pillow talk, huh.>

He'd been told, initially by Nicole, that the AIs running the sims didn't bother with eavesdropping on chit-chat between the lesser minds within, or spying on their sex lives. He believed it. It wasn't like human surveillance. The AIs had no prurient interest, and too much raw power to worry about any ideas the human minds running on their hardware came up with. But that very power made it trivial for them to record and store all that went on. In case of necessity, these logs could be trawled.

He'd known all that, but knowing it had actually happened... if he'd had cheeks, he'd have blushed.

Rillieux stood up and clambered across the rig towards Newton.

<Seeing the old sim again has made me randy,> she said. <I reckon we can afford half a minute of R&R.>

Newton stood up to meet her. Their hands clasped, and they both froze.

Blum and Carlos looked at each other.

<Ever felt left out?> Carlos said.

Blum laughed. <I have my own sim,> he said.

<You have?> Carlos was surprised. He didn't know if all agencies equipped their transports with stripped-down sims—Locke Provisos had never offered the option, perhaps because it had only sent them on short, all-action missions. But he knew Arcane did. He'd once seen Jax in a version of its sim, speaking to him from the lifter. He guessed the sims were copied across to all the vehicles in the agency's fleet. <I didn't know you could do that.>

<I asked Durward nicely.>

<As easy as that, eh?>

<Yes. Care to join me?>

<Ah, fuck it,> Carlos said, reaching out a hand.

<See you in twenty seconds, Baser,> said Blum. <Mind the shop.>

Twenty seconds of real time, twenty thousand seconds of sim time. About six hours.

<Don't mind me,> said the robot.

Hot sun, blue sky, white concrete, and conspicuous luxury consumption of water. Carlos walked up a flagstone pathway past trimmed lawns and flowerbeds dotted with sprinklers and rainbow-flagged with spray. The garden was on several levels, linked with and decorated by water features: rippling pebbled channels, a curtain of falling water in front of a copper-covered wall, swirling pools. In front of the big, low house a pod of plastic-imitation marble dolphins sent water ten metres into air so dry and hot that much of it evaporated before it splashed the path. All around, similar houses were generously spaced out across low hills, the cluster ending in a haze and shimmer that didn't quite screen out an indistinct vista of sand dunes and mountains beyond. An airliner rose from out of view, cleaving the blue diagonally with a white contrail as it climbed. A faint, distant buzz of drones rose and fell. Other than that, no robots here: half a dozen young men in jeans, shirtless and barefoot, pruned and weeded under the high sun.

In the Arcane sim, Blum had every so often taken his leave to some unspoken destination in the nearest small town. It was generally assumed that he went to a brothel. It wasn't, in real life, the sort of thing he would do or even approve of. But apart from the fighters and the AIs, the characters in the Arcane sim were p-zombies at best. The ethics of the situation were obscure, and the politics irrelevant.

Carlos climbed the steps to a wide veranda of welcome shade and paced warily between wide-flung doors. The hall was airy and cool, slabbed in synthetic marble, walled in pale veneer. A helix of wooden steps spiralled in an atrium. Tall vases with tall plants from the garden, their heavy flowers nodding; pervasive and varied scents carried on aircon breezes. At the far end of the long hallway a woman with straight blonde hair snipped centimetres from flower stems, building an arrangement in one of the vases. She wore a loose greenish silk sleeveless top and a long white tiered skirt.

"Hello?" Carlos called. "I'm looking for Andre Blum."

The woman turned and walked over. She had a slight figure; small breasts jigged and made the silk top shake. Her toes, in jewelled sandals, peeped alternately from under flounced hems as her heels ticked on the black marble. Her face, just on the pretty side of ordinary, looked sunburned rather than tanned. She smelled of sweat and flowers and furniture polish.

She stopped a couple of metres away and looked at him quizzically.

"Hi, Carlos," she said. "Let me fix you a drink."

He followed her into a chill reception room with sofa seats and a self-service bar. She waved a hand at condensation-beaded beer bottles, spirit optics.

"I'll have a beer, thanks."

She passed him a bottle and took one herself. He used the opener. So did she. Hiss. Clink. Sip. Ah.

"Uh, and your name is...?"

He felt very stupid. He was almost sure of what was going on, but...

"I'm Andre," she said. "You can call me Andrea, if it makes things easier."

"Not really," said Carlos, with an apologetic smile. He couldn't equate this slender young woman with the stocky, barrel-chested Blum.

She shrugged, glanced outside, eye-indicated a passing gardener. "The issue hasn't come up, before."

"I guess not," said Carlos.

"I know what you're going to ask," said Blum. "Don't bother. Yes, I could have done this when I was alive. I could have rebuilt myself from the chromosomes out. To the figure and the features, even. It wouldn't have been cheap, but I could have done it. And in the main sim it would have been—" She snapped her fingers. "We default, obviously, but Durward could have set me up in any body I liked. As you know."

Carlos recalled the first time he'd met Blum, in the form of a snap-together building-block toy figure, life-size, in the hell cellars. It was a reminder he could have done without.

"So why not?" he said.

Blum shrugged, and sat down at one end of a fake leather sofa.

"I don't know," she said. She patted the sofa. Carlos perched on the edge of the seat at the other end. Blum swirled the bottle, and took a long draught from it. "It was never about gender." She laughed, and swept her free hand down her body. "This started by chance. I picked a female avatar on impulse in some game when I was a kid. Maybe there was something deeper behind that choice, I don't know. Who cares?"

"Fair enough," said Carlos. "So what did you do on your excursions in the sim, if you don't mind me asking?"

"Oh, I just went down to a low tavern, borrowed the garb of a stout serving wench, and got banged by puzzled but enthusiastic farmhands. I got no complaints. They may have found me an improvement on the livestock."

"You're too modest," said Carlos.

"It's my only feminine trait," said Blum, in a tone of ironic gloom.

"I'm sure you have others," said Carlos. He put the now empty beer bottle on the floor beside the sofa. "Let's find out."

Matters developed from there to their mutual satisfaction.

Afterwards they sat on bar stools, elbows on the counter, and talked. Blum mixed increasingly vile and potent cocktails. Hangover-free drunkenness was almost as great a boon of sims as consequence-free sex.

Carlos made this observation more than once. Something about the situation was vaguely troubling him. Oh yes. He waved a hand around.

"Is this a real place?"

"No," said Blum. "It's a sim. You can't be *that* drunk."

"No, what I mean is...it's so fake, it has to be based on someplace real." He tapped the bar counter. It looked like oak and rang like tin. "Everything's gimcrack. The only really costly luxury is the garden."

"All that water! Well, what else would one use it for?" Blum laughed, and twirled and tinkled her cocktail glass. "Oh yes, ice."

"Come *on*," said Carlos. He knew an evasion when he heard one. "We've just had each other six ways from Sunday. Bit late to be coy."

"OK, it's true," said Blum, gazing around. "It's all 3-D printed or mass-nanofacture. Affordable sophistication for the masses."

"3-D printed?" Carlos mused aloud. "That rings a bell." Then he remembered. "Oh, shit."

"What?"

"This is fucking Kazakhstan, isn't it?"

Blum, for the first time, looked embarrassed. "Uh, yes. Security force living quarters. Officer grade, of course."

"Jesus," said Carlos. "And you had the gardens and the water features and the gardeners, too?"

"Oh yes," said Blum, looking into the distance.

"While outside, on the steppe..."

"Oh, don't give me that," said Blum, her eyes snapping back into focus. "The areas of special settlement had every facility. They had online trade, within the obvious security restrictions. They thrived, when they weren't trying to kill us or each other. Factionalism was rife, you know. Sectarianism, too. You know how it was."

"Yeah, I know," said Carlos. He laughed uneasily. "Well, actually, I don't. The...uh, you know...it was one of those topics no one ever wanted to talk about."

"I sometimes wonder," said Blum, "why we didn't make more of an issue of it."

"'We'?"

Blum thumbed her sternum. "Us. The Axle. We could've... I don't know."

"Yeah, exactly," said Carlos. "I don't know either. We... I mean, I never bought the excuse that the, uh... measure we don't talk about was for the, uh, affected population's own protection, but we couldn't have gone back to..."

"No," sighed Blum. "Not to that, no." She mixed another drink, and refilled the glasses.

Carlos sipped. He felt a strange mixture of deep shame at having even brought up the shameful memory of that massive collective failure—of intellect, of empathy, of humanity—and relief that the subject had been smoothed over. But still something nagged. What was it? Something about real...

"Oh yes!" he said. He jabbed a finger forward, and steadied himself on the stool. "Is *she* real?"

Blum made a show of looking over her shoulder. "Seeing double already?"

"Ha ha. You know what I mean. Your avatar here is based on a real woman."

"Yes," said Blum. She shook her head, lank hair flying out. "She was just... a girl in Tel Aviv. Worked in my parents' house when I was a student. I hardly knew her. I wasn't even very attracted to her, but I became... obsessed with her. It was before my military service, and before I joined the Axle."

"What did she do?"

"I don't know, I didn't keep in touch."

There was evasive, and there was deliberately obtuse.

"What did she do in your parents' house?"

"Oh! A bit of cleaning and tidying up."

"Like you were doing when I came in? Flower arranging, light dusting, that sort of thing?"

Blum shrugged. "More or less. We had a robot for the heavy stuff."

Carlos knew he was getting woozy. But he thought he was on to something, that Blum had been right: this wasn't about gender at all, this was about some deep, kinked connection of guilt and privilege and class. No chromosomal correction could break it. He blinked hard and shook his head and took a deep breath.

"You," he told Blum, "are a right fucking perv."

Blum smiled. "Now that," she said, "is the nicest thing you've said all day."

She drained her glass and looked at her watch, a delicate gold strap.

"Time to go back," she said.

They high-fived. Blum said something under her breath. They were robots again.

<Well, that was fun!> said Rillieux. <Now, back to work.>

The four fighters jumped down from the tug. Baser launched itself into a more graceful leap, and sailed to a pinpoint-precise landing that didn't so much as kick up dust. It was as if the robot had retained some reflexes from its time as a giant spider inside the Arcane module's fantasy-world sim.

Carlos walked slowly and carefully, letting his gait adjust to the gravity. The vicinity of the weapons stacks wasn't a good place for bounding around. The others followed suit.

The anti-spacecraft missile batteries checked out as in good order, as did the two scooters. Newton stood looking at a rack of rifles, and then attempted to shift the laser projectors and machine guns into readiness. This was a struggle.

<Can you give me a hand here?> he said.

<We can do better than that,> said Carlos. <We can all get into the combat frames.>

Two of these big fighting machines were damaged—Carlos had put missiles through them what felt like months ago to him. That left four still usable. Each stood three metres high, looming like robot war memorials welded from scrap metal. They were made of nothing of the kind, but that was how they looked.

Carlos led the way in springing up to the shoulders of a fighting machine, and swinging his legs into the socket at the back of the neck. He slid through the slot and curled up in the yielding hollow of the monstrous head. For a moment he felt cramped, confined, foetal. Then the connections came on line. Now, his body was the large frame, not the small. He turned the head like a tank turret, this way and that; stretched and flexed the arms and hands, and took a long, slow step that felt as if it should make the ground shake, though it didn't. Around him the others were doing likewise, re-familiarising themselves with this powerful incarnation.

<Feels good,> he said.

<I'd forgotten how good it was,> said Rillieux.

<First time for me,> said Newton. <The only machine I've been one with before was a scooter.>

He stooped, scooping up a rifle he'd handled ineffectually moments earlier, and clapped the weapon to a spare slot on his right forearm. Experimentally, he swung the arm around, and shot at a far-off rock. The rock exploded.

<Hands-free firing!> he said. <I could get to like this.>

<Well, don't,> said Rillieux. <Ammo's not unlimited.>

<Yeah, yeah.>

They knuckled down to five kiloseconds of serious military engineering. In the combat frames the work was easy, if tedious. The fighters deployed the laser projectors and machine guns at four points around the shelter. The existing fortifications were passive defences, designed for the freebots' improvised weaponry. They were adequate protection for teams chucking mining explosives and directing peripheral swarms—for shielding missile batteries and machine-gun operators, not so much. The fighters routed requests for machine support through Baser. Crab-like auxiliaries swarmed, and a dozen or so mindless mining robots trundled and dug, all mobilised to build berms, machine-gun nests, and blast walls. Basalt blocks and regolith heaps piled up; structures took shape. Likewise via Baser, the comms hub kept the fighters updated on wider developments—as corporations in their own right, the freebots had acquired a taste for and access to the system's financial feeds.

Two more DisCorps had broken away to trade with the Rax. Now that the embargo on landings had been broken de facto, there was a scramble for potential rights to explore and develop SH-0. No such rights yet existed—the Direction continued to dig its heels in—but the shadow market soared regardless. Astro America, the exploration company that had once owned Seba and half the other freebots, saw a notable rise in notional shareholder value.

The fighters didn't quite have time to finish the new fortifications before an urgent ping rang in their comms. Baser had news for them.

<We have heard from the Locke module,> it said.

CHAPTER EIGHT

Data et Accepta ("The Data Is Accepted")

In the frame there was no weariness. Carrying the tight-beam laser comms kit, doubly weighed down by the two gravities, Taransay plodded along the floor of the forest. Her path was mostly downhill. After seven kilometres and twice as many kiloseconds, she was still on the great gentle slope of the volcano whose summit she could now and then glimpse at a backward glance. The advantage of gradient was more than countered by the sodden ground, the intermittent heavy rain and tangled vegetation. The black glass knife flashed, again and again. Taransay slashed, again and again.

Plants here were different from those around the module. Geometric shapes had given way to more recognisably botanical forms, lobate and fractal. Tree trunks and branches were gnarled and jointed. Colours were more variegated, with shades of pink and white, and softer blues than she'd seen uphill. Concave, overlapping arrangements of leaves looked almost like flowers. Small circular animals buzzed in the heavy air, tiny mats with a blurring rotary-seeming motion of lengthened cilia below them, like experimental flying discs. Other small animals moved in the underbrush, still with the basic mat body plan but with two sides curled over to give a triangular shape. The large mats were much rarer, and most of what she trod on was mulch. Her guess, backed up by analytical software in a corner of her vision, was that the plants higher up were adapted to volcanic ash, perhaps drawing some of their energy directly from geothermal processes and subsoil chemical reactions. Here, further downhill, plants relied more on photosynthesis, and drew on the nutrients washed down by the abundant runoff.

As trailing creepers smacked her across the face, and as she pitched headlong forward now and then in mud, Taransay had ample opportunity to observe the animal life close up. Still mats, but much smaller, their sizes ranging from coin to full-stop dot and on down to the limits of her frame's visual resolution.

The rain stopped towards sunset. The remaining clouds, and the volcanic haze in the atmosphere, reddened the sky. Taransay scanned ahead anxiously with her radar, seeking a clear patch. Sound drew her forward: the rush and rumble of a river in spate. After a few more hundred metres, she emerged into the wide-open space of a river bend. A heaped beach of rounded pebbles lay between her and the near bank. She crunched her way out, and hunkered down beside a boulder.

The river was a good twenty metres across, fast and heavy. On the far bank the short, bushy cover afforded a sweep to the horizon over an undulating plain. Two other low volcanic cones were visible, one lower in profile and further away than the other. Both were to all appearances extinct, and in line with the active one behind her. A moving hotspot in the mantle below, she guessed, had formed all three. Erosion, fierce though it was, had had little time to wear them down. Geology worked fast and hard on this world, her mind's supplemental machinery told her, as if she didn't know already.

She waited, alert at a subconscious level with every enhanced sense, and let her mind drift through her memories. All equally accessible, with blanks between, like a diary with missing pages. She focused on the earlier ones, before all the politics and violence had kicked in. Her present alien environment was fascinating, but making sense of it even at the level of processing sensations into perception took a cognitive toll. There was a refuge in the scenes of home. Taransay found an odd, twisted comfort in childhood and teenage recollections and in contemplating the gulfs of space and time these memory traces of a Glasgow girl had traversed.

A splash in the river, heavy and loud and with a follow-up thrash, jolted her to higher alert. But nothing ensued.

Night fell with almost tropical swiftness; a kilosecond, no more, from the last gleam of exosunlight to pitch darkness in every shadow. The sky itself was bright, the Galaxy a shining misty arch overhead, the Magellanic Clouds and the lesser, artificial cloud of the modular diaspora competing. In that cloud Taransay saw activity—the brief pinpoint spark of rocket engines, the strobing microwave shimmer of comms. To her north, aurorae rippled in neon sheets. Tiny survey satellites flashed into the sunlight above, then winked out.

As she waited for SH-17 to rise—she could see exactly where it was at that moment, a few degrees below the horizon, on an astronomy-app overlay of her gaze—she noticed other moving lights in the sky. Most drifted above the trees; a few over the plain. Evidently the same phenomena as she'd glimpsed on her first night, the lights were evanescent—she timed them at 1.6 seconds—like fireflies, but much larger. The lights were pulses, on average 27.3 seconds apart, and moved with the wind. Soon she was able to predict where a light would appear next, and to estimate the size of the objects. Six to seven metres across, with—as she found when one came close, and she zoomed—long, trailing tentacles like ribbons, they were some kind of noctilucent aerial jellyfish. Gasbags—her spectroscopic sense sniffed out the hydrogen line behind the glow as a strong but neutral odour.

SH-17 climbed above the horizon. Taransay unburdened herself of the laser comms kit, lashed to her back with ropes woven from shredded leaves. This was a tricky business: she couldn't just cut the ropes and be done with it, she'd have to lug the thing back. It was far too precious a product to discard, or leave to the mercy of the shifting shoals of a rolling river; much of it had been laboriously chugged out by a barely adequate patch of nanotech over much of the previous day, the rest detached from the module's standard comms array and cobbled in.

She laid the delicate device on the wet stones and lined it up as best she could, then let it be. The needle spike aerial made the fine adjustments itself, orienting to the distant exomoon like a target-seeking missile.

Taransay downloaded the situation report and appeal for help that

Nicole, Locke, Durward and Beauregard had compiled to send to the freebots on SH-17. The message was compressed and compact, its transmission complete in less then five seconds and indicated to her only by a faint flashing light on the base-plate. That it had been received she could have no doubt: a handshake ping glowed blue for a hundredth of second, and rang in her head like a single drop of water in a vast cave.

A reply was another matter. It would come not to her, and not to here.

She folded up the comms kit and worked it back into its primitive harness. Walking back at night would be no more difficult than by day, and possibly more interesting. In any case, the plan was to send the message and quit the scene, just in case. The whole subterfuge of walking a few kilometres from the landing site now seemed pathetic, but it was all they could do, and perhaps better than nothing.

As she shrugged the ropes into place on her shoulders, she noticed again the fuzz around the join between the stump and the spare arm. Something would have to be done about that.

For the first time, it was possible to hope that something could. Nicole, Shaw and Remington were beginning to get a handle on the infestation, thanks in part to the processing power freed up by Shaw's stroke with the p-zombies. Zaretsky and his team even claimed they'd been able to wrest some control from it, and that the alien fuzz was beginning to be subverted in its turn. They talked grandly of using the combination of nanotech and fuzz to nanofacture new items, and to repair the damaged frames.

She hoped that by the time she got back they'd have got so far as to build a ladder.

<Fuck this,> said Carlos.

The others all swung their gigantic armoured heads around to look at him. Baser sat back, rear legs crooking, and looked up. It shifted its gaze from one frightful face-plate to another like a troubled puppy.

<What?> the fighters all said at once.

<Please clarify,> said Baser.

Baser had relayed to the fighters the message received from the Locke module—and the conclusion the freebots had drawn from it—almost before Baser had had time to finish announcing its receipt.

The message was in a sense reassuring. The freebots' response was disturbing.

<The Locke module has landed safely, in an unsafe and unstable location,> Baser had reported. <We have confirmation from Nicole Pascal and from the Locke AI that the module is not under the control of the Rax. All checksums are nominal. Copies of the Arcane AI, known as Remington, and of the Arcane Direction rep Durward, were downloaded in the battle and have given us further confirmation. Three Arcane fighters were also successfully downloaded, and they confirm what the AIs tell us.>

<So who's in charge?> Carlos had asked.

<Belfort Beauregard,> Baser had replied. <Along with Nicole, the AIs and others.>

<Knew it!> Newton had crowed.

They'd all been relieved, and further reassured to hear that the message had been passed on to Madame Golding, and that she would in turn forward the good news in it to Arcane.

But then things had started to go awry.

The Locke module was asking for help, urgently: they needed more nanotech and manufacturing gear if they were to survive for any length of time, let alone carry out Beauregard's bold project of establishing a settlement. The freebots were the only faction that they thought would be on their side, and that had the capacity to deliver the goods.

This was true, as far as it went. What the freebots lacked was the will. They had their hands (well, manipulators…) full working out how they could aid their fellows in SH-119 under the Reaction's lash. They were keen to maintain their re-established good relations with Madame Golding, and through her to win a hearing from the Direction. Madame Golding had made it very clear that aiding the Locke module's illegal landing and settlement would not be looked on kindly.

Some freebots, such as the former Gneiss Conglomerates surveyor known as Lagon, said, in effect: <Show us the money.> They were willing to aid the Locke module if they could benefit from it. Lagon had sketched out a grand scheme for brokering knowledge deals between the Locke module and selected DisCorps. The others were having none of it. Lagon's proposal fell.

Baser had just explained that Beauregard had included a rider to the appeal. This codicil pointed out that if the freebots were for any reason unwilling to help, he would consider himself free to approach other powers. Without saying so explicitly, it was plain that he meant the Rax.

Madame Golding had strongly suggested that the freebots, in their reply, should drop the Locke module a likewise heavy hint about the Direction's emergency plans to build an army of copied reliable fighters and impose a brute-force solution.

It was at this point that Carlos lost patience.

<Yes, I'll clarify,> he said. <I demand to speak with Madame Golding, and I wish to do so with all the Fifteen present to see her and myself.>

<You may not go into the shelter without coming out of the fighting machine,> Baser pointed out.

<I'm not coming out of the fighting machine,> said Carlos.

<Therefore the Fifteen, except for the comms hub, must come out of the shelter.>

<That is correct,> said Carlos, mental gears grinding like gnashed teeth.

Baser straightened its legs and backed off a little. Seconds passed. Then—

<They are coming out,> said Baser.

<What's this all about?> Newton asked, sotto voce on the private channel.

<You'll see,> said Carlos. <I've had enough second-guessing.>

<Haven't we all?> said Rillieux.

Carlos certainly hoped so.

The blast doors at the end of the shelter swung open and the robots trundled or scuttled out. They deployed themselves in a loose arc, facing Carlos and the other fighters.

Carlos raised an iron hand.

<Madame Golding, please,> he said.

The avatar manifested in the middle of the circle, her presence even more uncanny in the open than in the shelter. Carlos got the distinct impression that she was facing all of them, fighters and robots, at once. If she was a virtual image rather than a projection, of course, that figured. But still. The sight and the thought were not easy on the eye.

<What do you want?> Madame Golding asked.

<Could you please open a secure channel to Arcane?> Carlos asked.

A second or two later, an avatar of Jax popped into view. It was evidently a hasty choice—she was in her old gamer gear. In her LED skirt she looked, if anything, even less congruent with the real environment than Madame Golding in her business suit.

<Have you come up with a plan already?> she asked, incredulous.

<I'll show you in a moment,> Carlos said.

He turned to Seba. <Could I have access to the comms hub, please?>

The freebots conferred.

<Patching you through,> said Baser.

Carlos found himself in direct contact with the comms hub. The experience was like looking down an infinite tunnel. Everything in the universe rushed towards him at once. He almost stumbled, then steadied himself. A moment later, everything stabilised: the combat frame had software to handle such contact, and as soon as it came on line he saw the human-optimised interface.

An endless sky, with every star an option.

<Financials,> Carlos said.

The sky whirled and zoomed. Carlos narrowed his focus down and down, until he came to the ownership of the frame he occupied and the combat frame it currently animated. Both belonged to the consortium of freebot corporations.

Now he had to move fast.

<I request access to the shared workspace,> he said.

This was granted. It was a much lower level of integration than the freebot consensus, but still overwhelming. It took almost a second for a human-adapted interface to cohere. An array of text and diagrams that changed at bewildering speed even when stepped down to his reach and grasp.

One region corresponded to the mind of Seba. Carlos addressed it.

<When I arrived here,> he said, <you told me of Forerunner attempts to buy arms production companies, and how these were thwarted. Lend me some money to set up my own company, and you can do this. The solution is—>

Seba's focus within the workspace saw the solution Carlos had thought of before Carlos could even formulate it. A tracery of lines exploded across the workspace, as the same connections were made by other freebot minds. With them went debate, far too fast for Carlos to follow. The longest delay was the two-second light-speed lag as the nearest Forerunner concentration was consulted.

<Yes,> said the Seba region.

A part of Carlos's mind in the frame became suddenly salient. He'd never before had occasion to notice it.

It was his bank account. Into it had come his soldier's pay. Out of it had gone the insultingly nugatory charges for the processing power that had sustained him in the sims. Charged against it, by now, was a large and growing stack of fines—for desertion, defection, misappropriation of company property, interest charges for non-payment, further fines...

All had now been paid.

His whole account was swamped by a massive infusion of funds from the freebot consortium. A loan, of course—the first interest charges, incremented by the millisecond, already trickled out. Compared with the amounts he'd seen in Madame Golding's display, the sum was tiny.

But for him, it was a fortune, and enough.

Enough to buy an off-the-peg corporate AI, and to kick-start its activities.

Carlos Incorporated.

For the first time, Carlos felt truly posthuman. Not even his first experience of the frame—his mind running sweet and clean, every memory accessible, new senses and powers clicking into place—could compare. It was like getting the spike had been, back in the day. There was a sense of ironic fulfilment of the Accelerationist dream, of taking hold of capitalism and driving it forward ever faster to its own inherent barriers, and beyond. The corporation's AI was his to command. He knew the state of the market, moment by moment. In the next ten seconds he bought up a dozen shell companies, and through them two arms production companies. He formed these companies into a consortium that made approaches to Astro America and Gneiss Conglomerates. He hired the services of three law agencies from among those of Crisp and Golding's subsidiaries and spin-offs that were looking after freebot interests. Within seconds, they had to challenge a Direction injunction against him. Blocking it took milliseconds.

Carlos was a perfectly legitimate arms manufacturer and dealer. For the moment.

Legally human, he was free to buy, own and operate an arms company and to deploy its products. Nothing short of a state of emergency could stop him.

And the Direction didn't want to go there. Not yet.

<Now,> Carlos told the Seba presence, <tell your Forerunner friends who want to build frames and buy arms where they can get them.>

<This is done,> said the Seba focus.

Carlos bowed out of the freebot workspace, and back to his senses. And not only his own senses: he could now see himself as the freebots saw him.

There he stood, a mighty killer robot, bristling with weapons. Around him, like a cloud of flies from the lord of the flies, flickered the advertisements and logos of his arms companies.

Even Madame Golding took a step back.

Carlos stretched out his arms and flexed his huge fists. Holograms of fighting craft flashed about his shoulders.

<Now,> he said, <let me tell you how it's going to be.>

This, he told them, was how it was going to be.

The starting point was that Astro America and other DisCorps would have to be cleared to cut a deal with the Rax.

Astro America was itching to get to SH-0 and do some proper prospecting. They'd love to trade with the Rax for fusion drives. The Direction could thus make them an offer they couldn't refuse.

That done—

Astro America would deliver to SH-119 the mining and manufacturing robots they'd asked for. The robots would be built by Astro America and Gneiss Conglomerates in the modular cloud from materials mined or extracted down on SH-17. Salted away among the legitimate robots would be identical models with the central processors of volunteers from the Fifteen plugged in. Layers of standard software for microgravity miners and engineers would mask the infiltrators. An undetectable software hack to temporarily disconnect their reward circuits would enable them to withstand any torture the Rax might apply. The bodies, and indeed the corporations, of these volunteers from Fifteen would to all appearances be running around just as before down on SH-17. They'd just have had standard, non-conscious processors plugged in after their conscious processors were taken out. The removed processors would be sent up to Astro and Gneiss factories in the cloud, in shipments ostensibly of raw material.

In exchange for these supplies, Astro would take delivery from the Rax in SH-119 of fusion drives, fusion pods and any useful raw material from SH-119 not easily available on SH-17. With these resources, they'd construct landing craft to go down to SH-0 and resupply the Locke settlement. In return for carrying out this mission the Direction would release certain exploration rights on SH-0 to Astro and Gneiss, who could then sell them on to any other DisCorps that might be interested. What the Direction would get out of this part of the deal was simple: the huge advantage for the Direction of maintaining order in the now inevitable scramble for SH-0. That the planet had been pristine had for years been taken for granted, but that ship had sailed—or, rather, landed, in the form of the Locke module and everything that was spreading out from it. More immediately, the deal would guarantee that the Locke settlement would not carry out Beauregard's threat to cut a deal of his own with the Rax.

Once trade with the Rax was ongoing, and most of the DisCorps distracted by an SH-0 exploration and speculation feeding frenzy, Arcane Disputes would mount a frontal assault on the Rax rock. Their forces would approach under cover of civilian shipping. This wasn't, Carlos conceded, the done thing under the laws of war. But the Rax were pirates, to whom no such laws applied. No repeated interactions with them were possible or desirable: it was kill or be killed. What was crucial was to do this before the Rax had time to arm to any significant extent.

Carlos's corporations would quite openly work to make frames that freebots could control, whether by direct plug-and-play or by uploading. It was already clear that freebot infiltration of the Direction's systems was widespread. Through the frames, the freebots could handle combat frames and weapons systems. Let the Direction build its clone army of copied loyal soldier minds in combat frames if it wanted. The freebots would face it with a clone army of their own. And because all responsibility for this army would ultimately go back to Carlos, there wasn't legally a damn thing the Direction could do about it.

The discussion that followed was heated, but pointless. Carlos had, after all, already begun carrying out his part of the plan. Everyone else just had to work around that.

<You've just betrayed the human race,> said Jax.

Carlos recalled Jax's heavy hint that she regarded the freebots as dispensable allies, and the next enemy to be dealt with once the Rax had been disposed of. By dropping that hint to Carlos and the other defectors, she was indicating, too, that she didn't regard them as irrevocably on the side of the freebots. They were not robots. They could always defect back. Unless they burned their bridges in a spectacular fashion, such as arming the freebots.

As he had just done.

<That's the general idea,> he told Jax, cheerfully. <Call it costly signalling.>

CHAPTER NINE

Deus Ex Machina ("God Loved the Machine")

Taransay set out to meet the landers, from Astro America on behalf of Carlos Inc., well before dawn. She had ten kilometres to go, back to the river bank and the shoal, and allowed herself twenty kiloseconds for the journey. That should be ample, even for walking in the dark. The dark held no terrors for her.

Well, no more than the day, to be honest.

And speaking of darkness—in the deep dark of the download slot, where she came to her senses after the usual bus journey and the usual irresistible sleep, the join between her original frame and grafted right arm shone like a glow-stick armband of blue neon.

Her first seconds of awareness were spent glowering at the glow. The fuzz that had been like mould was now compact and rigid. It still smelled faintly of the local life, but with other tangs in its spectrum, a whiff of buckyballs and fullerenes and steel that indicated corrupted nanotech. Zaretsky's team had been on the case, but not even the improved processing power at their disposal had laid a finger on whatever was going on.

However, the engineers did have one success to show for their efforts.

Towards it, her feet now groped.

There it was, a fine line across the sole of her foot, with a disproportionate stiffness and resilience for its width. The first rung of the ladder from the download slot. She trusted her weight to it, and found that it held. A few rungs more and she could see it all. It looked like a section of a cobweb, with threads fanning down and sticking to the ground. In the wind, it sang. It didn't look or feel like it could bear her weight. Taransay knew not to trust her intuition about such matters. She scrambled down, shouldered the rope-net with the comms kit, and set off.

She followed the same route as before. An insecure decision, but it was hardly as if she were beating a path. And she knew, just by plodding along in her own virtual footsteps, she'd get where she wanted to be. Assuming no landslides, unknown big fierce beasts, fallen trees, new eruptions and fresh lava flows.

The tree trunks swayed in the wind; the limp, page-shaped leaves rattled. Rain fell, intermittent but heavy. Overhead raced tattered clouds. She could see the stars through the gaps, seeming to speed in the opposite direction to the clouds, if she cared to indulge the illusion. Best not—it could confuse her balance system. Below the clouds, a few noctilucent flying jellyfish scudded, driven faster than the clouds by the wind, and not always in the same direction. The trailing ribbons were now spread out like spokes, stiff before the stiff wind. The gasbags could steer, almost tack.

Another useful thing to know.

Taransay pushed in between tree trunks, her gait automatically countering the slither of the small mats underfoot. In dark and rain, viewed by infrared and ultraviolet and sonar, the jungle already seemed familiar. More so than could be accounted for by this being the second time she'd walked this way. There was an aesthetic quality to the experience, as if she were beginning to appreciate its alien beauty. This puzzled her for a moment, but she figured that it was probably a feature of the frame's software.

Mind you, she couldn't remember anything like this feeling on the bare surface of SH-17, but then she'd had a lot more than landscape on her mind.

She pressed on. After a while, the concern faded. The false and real colours, the strange scents and sounds, became more vivid and at the same time more... reassuring, almost. More than that: when she looked at a plant, or saw a new sliding or creeping or drifting organism, she felt she understood more about it than she could account for, even with the spectroscopic sense of smell. Yes, that leaf would be a good source of sodium, but how did she know the stalks of this particular kind of tree would dry out to make strong, flexible struts? How was it that she could almost taste what that slithering mat would be like to chew? The path felt much easier than it had before. She had to slash at the stalks less often than the first time. Every so often she saw a cut stalk, one she had slashed earlier. The frame's pulsar-based galactic positioning system was utterly reliable, but it was good to have that confirmed, almost to the step.

Then, kilometres deep in the forest, as she waded through a small fast stream in which tiny mats swarmed below the slow, gelid ripples of the surface, a voice in her head said <STOP!>

She stopped. Fright of her life. She stood still in the rushing water that pressed to her knees. Heavy drops plopped from runnels down limp leaf-sheets, making overlapping dimples in the stream as they hit.

<Locke?> she asked.

She knew it wasn't Locke. She was out of range of the module's own feeble comms and anyway Locke had insisted on maintaining radio silence. But the imperative had sounded—not like Locke's dry voice-in-her-head, but—like the sort of override command the AI sometimes had to shout.

Silence.

Then a rustle in the undergrowth, upriver and to her right. She turned from the waist, fist close, knife clutched and pointed outward. Something rushed past along the bank right in front of her. A gleam like black glass, a long body, fast-moving legs. One of the giant millipede things. If she'd taken another three steps and climbed on the bank, she'd have been right in its way.

<Go,> said the voice in her head. This time, she noticed the blue glow on her right upper arm give a brief pulse with the word.

She remained stock still. Holy fucking shit. The fuzz was talking to her.

<GO!> it said, with a stronger blue pulse.

She went, wading forward and scrambling up. She'd barely cleared the slippery, rounded rocks when she heard a splash in the stream behind her. A backward glance showed a broken tree trunk, easily big enough to knock her off her feet, swirl past. Deeply shaken, perplexed, Taransay shouldered her way in between the trees. Something strange had happened. It seemed inconceivable that the blue glow had spoken to her, in any conscious sense. But if the native life was interacting with the nanomachinery of her frame, it was not at all impossible that the glow's awareness—and perhaps even appreciation—of her surroundings was being translated into impulses the frame could process, and transmit to her as feelings of familiarity, and a warning voice in her head.

Huge if true.

Unimaginably huge. Far too huge for her to deal with now. Above her pay grade. She'd have to take this discovery back to the experts, to Zaretsky and the AIs. And there was an urgent practical reason, too, for holding back.

This was no time to interrogate the glow. Even her interactions with this unknown entity could give away her position, if anyone was seriously looking. Carlos Inc. had assured them they were safe from the Direction and the freebots, not to mention the Rax, but Beauregard and Nicole and Locke had wondered how Carlos could be sure, and how long the accord would last.

She pressed on, into the breaking day.

Taransay stood on the river bank and watched the skies. The laser comms device, deployed on the shingle behind her, was now a beacon. The day was clear, the weather calm. The exosun, low on the horizon, would have dazzled human eyes and made them peer and squint. The frame's visual system dimmed that glare to a glow. Three landers were due to enter the atmosphere any second now. Their rocket engines had already been left in orbit. She wouldn't see the entries, far over the horizon to the west. All the dramatic fiery streak stuff would happen half a world away, and a large world at that. The only visible activity in the early-morning sky was that of a handful of flying jellyfish in the middle distance, ascending rapidly. Taransay zoomed on them, and was amused to see that for a while at least they didn't seem to shrink with distance because they got larger with altitude. Their internal gasses must be expanding their membranes as the atmospheric pressure dropped. Then one by one they began to move faster to the west, no doubt whipped along by a faster air stream into which they'd ascended.

<Entry nominal,> reported the satellite downlink from Astro America's mission control.

Seconds passed. Tens of seconds.

<Ablation shields detached. Drogues deployed.>

Wait for it, wait for it…

<Drogues detached. Gliding at ten thousand metres.>

<Yay!> cried Taransay.

<Please clarify,> replied the downlink.

<Roger that,> Taransay clarified, somewhat abashed.

Hundreds of seconds dragged by. The exosun crawled higher, its spectrum shifting from red as more wavelengths had fewer kilometres of atmosphere to fight through. High in the lowest layer of the planet's complex, contraflow jet streams the flying jellyfish, now tiny in the far distance, glinted in its beams.

Above the skyline rose three black dots, at the limit of resolution, and climbed rapidly.

<Visual contact made,> Taransay reported.

They passed beside the sun, and still rose. A trick of perspective—they were descending as they approached. Now at five thousand metres. Four. They were visibly dropping now, and in an arrow formation, one ahead and two behind. The black dots jiggled as if viewed through shaky binoculars as they passed through a layer of fast-moving air, then stabilised. Another quiver followed, moments later. Taransay relaxed the zoom and took a wider view.

Black dots and bright spots, in the same part of the sky.

<Hey!> Taransay yelled. <Evade! Evade!>

Too late. The leading lander vanished in a bright flash. The other two peeled off, wavered, dipped and swung back on course. Behind them now, the remaining jellyfish sailed on into the sunrise, as if oblivious of the damage the collision of one of their number with the lander had caused.

Debris plummeted, slowly at this distance, like a pinch of soot.

<Contact with Lander One lost,> said the downlink. <Request status from ground observation.>

<Complete destruction of the vehicle with probable loss of payload,> Taransay reported.

<Please identify cause if known.>

<Collision with a natural object,> said Taransay. <Gas-containing aerial invertebrate.>

It sounded a bit more scientific than "flying jellyfish."

<Noted,> said the downlink. <Recorded as accident.>

Taransay, her mind already jumpy from the voice of the glow, was almost ready to wonder if the collision was no accident. Could it have been deliberate, if not on the part of the suicidal flying jellyfish then on that of some remote directing intelligence, or self-defence reflex of the entire ecosystem or some superorganism within it?

Wait and see, she thought. *Once is happenstance, twice is coincidence, three times is enemy action.*

The other two landers were now clearly visible even without zoom, a couple of kilometres out, above the treetops. Head on, they looked like black gulls, or a cartoon of two frowns.

Black circular shapes were suddenly suspended beneath the two flying wings, making them look like approaching hang-gliders.

<Cargo pods lowered,> said the downlink. <Prepare for landing in thirty-seven seconds.>

<Roger,> said Taransay.

There was no landing strip as such, just the clear shingle shoal at the side of the river. The landers would come in low and slow, drop their cargo pods and then simply stall. The wings, like the exhausted rocket engines, might or might not be recovered later.

Above the bend in the river now, the landers dipped, skimming the treetops. Taransay instinctively crouched. The two long black triangles shot above her head. Two cargo pods landed with two heavy thumps that she felt through her feet. Then the instrument packs dropped, with lesser thuds that she merely heard. A moment later the wing components sliced into the low growth behind her between the river and the trees. One of them upended on its nose, then toppled, coming to rest on its edge.

One cargo pod was close to the edge of the river. Taransay crunched across pebbles towards it. Bright yellow, half a metre in diameter and ten metres long, it lay like a log. A swirl of current lapped nearby, rasping the small stones. You could see them shift, and sand grains tumble. Erosion was fierce here. The only stable part of the river bank was probably where grass-equivalents and reeds grew, binding the stones. And even that, going by the height and lushness and uniformity of the plants, was likely often flooded.

<Zero altitude,> said the downlink.

<Landing successful,> Taransay reported.

She stood between the middle of the pod and the water, pressed her hands against the side of the pod and pushed. The thing didn't budge. She turned around, put her back to the curved side, dug her heels into the silty pebbles, and pushed. Slowly the pod rolled. When it was a couple of metres out of immediate danger, Taransay stepped away.

She didn't need to read the instructions printed on the ends to know what to do. The frame already had the knowledge. Taransay found a detachable panel at one end, prised it open with a thumb and pulled the handle behind it. The pod split open along its length, into two neat halves.

Packed in recesses in shock-proofing spongy stuff were four low-slung, stubby-legged robots with obvious load-carrying arrangements on their backs. As soon as the light hit them they stirred, then clambered out to stand on the shore.

Gee, thanks, Carlos and Astro. A lot of fucking use that is. She hadn't expected transport robots. She could see the point, and appreciate the intent, but she had no intention of using the robots until it had been cleared with Locke. As things stood the robots, helpful though they'd be, were so many tracking devices. Of course the other supplies could be tracked as well, but that would be detectable if you knew where and how to scan for it, and she did.

Taransay dragged the now far lighter opened cylinder across the shingle to where plants grew, and let it drop. The four robots plodded after her. She went over to the other pod and opened it. Inside, in the same shock-proof packaging as with the first, was much more immediately useful stuff: metre-long portable tubes of nanotech machinery; a crate of fusion pods; a case of basic tools designed for the small hands of frames; a case of four likewise frame-ergonomic rifles with standard ammunition; coils of rope; a box of surveying instruments. Most immediately useful of all: rucksacks and carrying harnesses. All of them were folded so small she almost overlooked them in their two-centimetre-square recesses.

Someone—Carlos, most likely—had figured she might have trust issues with leading robots back to the module. Well done that man. She gladly stripped off and abandoned the rope sling.

<Cargo delivered intact,> Taransay reported.

<Roger,> said the downlink.

<Signing off for now,> said Taransay.

<Signing off.>

Taransay piled the supplies on the backs of the four robot mules and dragged the empty cargo pods to just underneath the trees. There, she put the supplies she wasn't taking back in their shock-proof recesses and closed the pod. She walked over to where the instrument packs lay on flattened reeds and eyed them suspiciously. They were already rooting and flowering: tendrils digging in, dish aerials and sensors opening. Sending data about the planet up to the DisCorps was part of the deal, she understood, but she didn't like it.

The wing components, a hundred metres further away, were curious triumphs of nanotech aviation engineering and AI design, flexible and fluted, with tiny ramjets scored through them and subtle warping along the trailing edges. She walked around them for a bit, marvelling.

Then she summoned the robots and set them to work dragging the wing components over, one by one. They were gigantic to her—long acute triangles, twenty metres by eight—but surprisingly light even under two gravities. When she'd got them on each side of the cargo pods, she lifted them on their sides and then, with some help from the robots, tipped them over to meet in the middle, forming a crude lean-to roof. She decided it would be safe enough to leave the laser comms device here with the supplies she couldn't carry, and left it well inside the shelter. She filled the rucksacks and harnesses with nanotech tubes (which stuck up above her shoulders, like a pack of rolled-up posters in cardboard cylinders, except a lot heavier), shouldered a rifle, and side-slung a container of ammunition and the two fusion pods.

<Guard this,> she told the four robots.

<Please clarify,> they all said at once.

<Jesus fucking fuck,> she said.

<Please clarify.>

She thought about it. <You see the opening there?>

She pointed. They looked at her finger. She laser-pointed. That they understood.

<Yes.>

<Prevent any large organism or machine—except me, or one or more like me—from entering that. Keep the cargo pods at this location. Likewise the wing components. Do you understand?>

<Yes,> they chorused.

She wasn't at all sure they did, but she didn't press the matter. By now it was noon, and time she was heading back. This time, with her awkward load, she expected the journey to take longer.

She tramped off into the jungle, without a backward glance and without indulging the sentimentality of a goodbye.

Fucking stupid robots. She hoped Carlos was having a better time getting through to the smart ones. It occurred to her that she'd never actually interacted with a conscious robot except by exchanging fire.

Taransay was a couple of kilometres into the jungle, and the exosun about a quarter of the way down from its zenith, when she was stopped in her tracks by an unaccountable feeling that something wasn't quite right. No rain, for the moment. The little buzzing spinning things flitted in the narrow slanted beams of light between the shadows cast by the efficient leaves. Somewhere, water gurgled and small stones shifted. Her nanotech stone-age knife glinted in her hand. Her feet slowly sank deeper in the squishy, slithery floor of living and dead mats.

Nothing was wrong. No voice in her head, no brightening of the blue glow around her upper right arm.

It took Taransay a moment to realise what was troubling her. Her walk had been too easy. She'd expected it to be difficult, what with the heavier and bulkier load, and the nanotech cylinders poking up high above her shoulders and more than doubling her effective height. Instead, she had made her way between trees and bushes and through and over streams, boulders, swathes of ash and sheets of cooled lava without so much as catching a cylinder against an overhanging branch. She was still following the same route, but she hadn't had to hack at any vegetation, or found herself facing a branch or stalk she'd cut before.

She was no longer crashing and hacking her way through the jungle, like an explorer. She was slipping through it like a native. Well, not that she knew about such contrasts directly, or even reliably, but she'd watched enough well-meant rain forest eco-romantic adventure serials as a child to have the notion embedded.

Now that she'd noticed, of course, she got tangled in one of the long vine things on her next three steps, and put a foot in a hole a few steps after that.

Zen, that was what she had to strive for. Zen and the art of hiking. But you couldn't strive for it. Like the millipede in the legend that was asked how it moved its legs, and suddenly couldn't take another step. Millipedes, ah yes. She concentrated hard on recalling the millipede-like animals she'd seen, and thinking about whether any of the images she could recollect of it would betray the affinity with the mats that Zaretsky's team had detected by genetic analysis.

Then she got to thinking about thinking. When she wanted to recall what the two fierce, fast creatures she'd noticed had been like, she could see in her mind clear and distinct images of them. It was exactly as if they were photo files being retrieved from an album. And she could turn them over in her mind's eye, almost literally: she could rotate the images this way and that, zoom in on detail.

This was not, she remembered very clearly, what remembering very clearly was like. Here in the frame, she was still herself, still Taransay Rizzi from one of Partick's lower-rent zip codes. But she was far more remote from her original self than she was even in the sim, where she was physically a little cloud of electron states in a big crystal. She wasn't thinking like a human being. She was thinking like a robot. The actual mechanisms of memory and thought and sense were quite different, in whatever chip she was running on, from in the biological brain or even its electronic copy, its emulation in the simulation.

In a sense, she was far more conscious, far more self-aware, than she could recall being in life, or in the sim. She wondered if the distinction was qualitative. There had always been something slippery, elusive and illusive, about subjectivity in the first place. Too much of it subtended biological mechanisms, too much of it was subjected to social relations, for it to be truly as autonomous as it fancied itself to be. What if people, herself included, had always already been p-zombies, at least most of the time, and only machines could be truly conscious?

If people were to stay in frames long enough, would they start to think *as* robots? Was this what was happening to Carlos and his mates? And was this possibility what the necessity of recuperating in the sims was designed to prevent?

She was still thinking about all that when she found herself back at the module.

She hailed Locke, on the weak local waveband that was all the module could raise, and just as well from the point of view of their equivalently feeble effort at concealing their location.

<Mission successful,> she said. <One lander lost to a flying jellyfish.>

<We've already received the reports,> said Locke. <Welcome back.>

Taransay unladed herself, and Locke showed her where to clamp the nanotech gear to the module, and where to place the two fusion pods.

The damaged frames lay in the overhang of the module, slowly being rebuilt. Local life—fuzz, something else—was contending with the nanomachinery's slow-motion 3-D printing. Or, for all she knew, it was cooperating, having been suborned. Tendrils reached out from the module to the nanotech tubes at once. It wasn't clear whether they were the module's own nanotech or among the hybrids Zaretsky's team had made with the fuzz.

The fuzz. Oh yes. The fuzz. She'd have to tell Locke about that. In fact—

<Are Beauregard and Nicole up and about? Oh, and Zaretsky.>

The exosun was now low, the shadows of the surrounding forest deep and long, but the diurnal cycles of the module's sim and the world outside were still out of synch.

<They're all here,> said Locke.

<Good. Uh, put me on screen.>

<You are,> said Locke, dryly.

<Oh! Right. Uh, guys and gals, I've got something to tell you...>

She told them about the voice in her head and its warnings, about the glow, and about the less definable sense of being at home in the jungle and her unaccountable agility in it.

<I hope you don't think I'm going crazy,> she concluded. <Or hallucinating or something.>

<Impossible,> said Nicole, in a tone of brisk reassurance. <The software of the frame does not permit it.>

<I thought you said the sims were to preserve our sanity?> Taransay retorted. <And I've been a long time out of the sim.>

<Not long enough,> said Nicole. <Not by far. And the symptoms would be different. They are...a drifting of thought from the human baseline, feelings of dissociation, a loss of the sense of self-preservation. Their onset is preceded by something like a craving for normality. You would know it if you felt it. Auditory and visual hallucinations and delusions of competence are not diagnostic and not expected.>

<Thanks,> said Taransay. <I guess.>

<Well, let's assume this is really happening,> said Beauregard. <The fuzz that got on your stump has turned into something else, and adapted

to the frame. Whether it's consciously communicating with you, I doubt. I suspect it's sensitive to its environment, and giving you cues through inner voice and through fine motor control at the subconscious level, maybe at the frame's equivalent of reflex.>

<That's more or less what I thought myself,> said Taransay. <But—>

<Have you tried talking back to it?> Zaretsky interrupted. Fucking nerd.

<No,> replied Taransay, testily. <I maintained comms discipline, for whatever good that would do.>

<Glad to hear it,> said Zaretsky. <OK, so talk to it now.>

Taransay held up her right arm and turned her head as far as she could, to face the glowing band.

<This is going to look very silly,> said Taransay.

<Never mind that,> said Nicole.

<We'll all just point and laugh,> added Zaretsky, helpful as usual.

<Knock yourselves out,> said Taransay. <Fall off your stools.>

It was hard to find the words.

<Uh, hello?> she ventured. <Blue glow? Fuzz? Thing on my arm? Anyone home?>

<Yes.>

<Holy fucking shit!> Taransay yelped.

<I take it you got a reply,> said Nicole.

<It said yes! In my head.>

<Talk some more!> said Zaretsky.

<What are you?> Taransay asked the glow, still feeling very silly.

<No.>

<What do you mean?>

<No.>

She tried a few more queries, with the same result.

<Are you there?> she said at last.

<Yes.>

She reported this.

<Still sounds like what we thought,> said Beauregard.

<No alien intelligence, then?> said Taransay. <Colour me surprised.>

<Don't jump to conclusions,> said Zaretsky. <Like, define "alien," define "intelligence.">

<Oh, fuck off,> said Taransay.

<Time to bring you in,> said Zaretsky.

<Yeah, tell me about it,> said Taransay. That thing Nicole had said about a craving for normality being the first symptom of having been out of the sim too long was preying on her mind a bit.

She climbed the cobweb ladder and hauled herself into the slot. The blue glow lit the dimness inside.

<OK, I'm ready,> she said.

Nothing happened.

<There is a problem,> said Locke. <A software incompatibility.>

Taransay felt the analogue of a cold shock, an instant alertness thrumming through her connectors and processors.

<Is this the fuzz? The glow?>

<That seems to be the case,> Locke admitted.

<I thought you had this thing under control!>

<We're working on it,> said Zaretsky.

<How long will it take?> Taransay asked.

Zaretsky glyphed her a shrug. <I don't know. Days, probably.>

<Shit!>

<Well, yes.>

<In that case,> said Taransay, <I might as well go back and pick up more of the stuff.>

<Are you sure?> said Nicole. <It's dark.>

Taransay laughed. <You sent me out in the dark this morning.>

<True, but—>

<How long will it take me to recharge?> Taransay said.

<Several kiloseconds,> said Nicole. <But Locke can show you how to do it a lot faster with a fusion pod.>

<Now there's an idea.>

She clambered down. Locke directed her to place a fusion pod against the join between her torso and her pelvis. The sensation was odd, not quite pleasant, but satisfying. Or perhaps that was an artefact of watching her charge indicator creep from red to green in ten seconds.

<Right,> she said. She shouldered the rifle, slung on the empty rucksack and harnesses and clutched her knife. <See you in a bit, guys.>

<Wait!> said Zaretsky. <Why not use the robots provided?>

<Fine by me, if that's OK with Locke,> said Taransay.

<It is not,> said Locke.

<I concur,> said Nicole. <We cannot yet be sure of Carlos's intentions. Or the Direction's.>

<Trust issues,> said Taransay. <With you there, folks.>

She turned and slogged off into the night.

CHAPTER TEN

Noblesse Oblige ("Rank Has Its Privileges")

More softly than a feather kissing a snowflake, the Astro America freighter docked with the moonlet SI I-119. In its normal body, Seba might not have noticed so light a collision. Now, embodied as a microgravity miner similar to the unfortunate Ajax, Seba felt the impact ring through every bristle.

In its normal mind, Seba would have had a strong emotional reaction to the docking: a surge of positive reinforcement at the success so far, clashing with negative reinforcement at the prospect of dangers and difficulties. A clash surrounded, perhaps, by resolve to face the dangers and overcome the difficulties.

Seba was far from being in its normal mind. Its conscious awareness was hidden deep within concentric shells of mining-bot software. This deeper self of Seba's was almost completely isolated from the machine's reward circuits. Almost, but not quite—some residue of motivation was needed to spur the freebot mind back to the main drivers of pleasure and pain as soon as it was safe to do so.

Seba had been transferred to a new body before. Its central processor had been ripped from its chassis (by Carlos, Seba had later learned), handed over to another fighting machine, crudely soldered into the frame of an auxiliary—a detachable robot limb, basically—and stapled to a table to be interrogated. The negative reinforcement hadn't been anything like as bad as the affront to the robot's dignity.

This time, it had all been much more civilised.

Until now.

Now was the test.

Waiting. Then movement, out of darkness. An almost 360-degree glimpse of the freighter behind, a hole in the rugged cliff of the moonlet surface ahead and stars all around in the gap between. Bristles quivered at the first brush with new rock. A nudge to Seba's neck corrected its course. The robot drifted through a shaft and into a wide cavern.

Two mechanoids, and an apparatus of bars and straps and instruments, waited at the entrance. Seba was grabbed and pushed inside. A clamp extended and closed around the robot's flexible neck. A noose tightened around the middle of the main part of Seba's new body. A sharp burning sensation came from a clump of bristles. The heat increased. A writhe reflex pulsed through Seba, but no part of its body moved.

The burning stopped. Feedback from those bristles would never be as good again—but it was a small clump, easily spared.

A needle probe stung the sensory cluster at the front end of Seba's neck. A security routine prowled through the software shells, layer after layer. Closer and closer it crept. It reached a masking layer between two shells, a layer that emulated naked circuitry.

The probe paused as if hovering, then hit down hard with test protocols, searching out flaws in the emulation. The use of a masking layer was a known exploit. Fortunately for Seba, this version was several releases ahead of the one that the security probe had on file. The probe, apparently convinced that it had reached the level of bare wire, withdrew.

<This one's clean,> said one of the mechanoids.

The clamp was released. The wire loop slackened. Seba was shoved out to float forward into a large sack of mesh that already contained a dozen other mining bots—in two of which the processors and minds of Garund and Lagon lurked. Shortly thereafter, Rocko joined them, in the form of an elaborate nanofacturing supervisory bot bristling with specialised manipulators. Scores of other robots followed, a few with freebot processors hidden inside, most standard mining or manufacturing bots built by Astro America. All but three of the freebots at the base on SH-17 had volunteered for this mission. The comms processor was indispensable, and specialised; Baser was understandably touchy about changing bodies, having spent so much time so recently as a spider; and it was heartily agreed by all concerned that while Pintre was a heavy-duty mining robot, its undoubted abilities would be much better deployed right where it was, on the surface of SH-17.

The others were all here, mixed in with the hundred or so robots Astro America had just delivered. Carlos, for some reason best known to himself, had delighted in calling them "the Dirty Dozen" even though there were thirteen altogether.

The net seemed to be more for convenience in catching than confinement. Ten mechanoids gathered around and sorted its contents. Each robot had instructions downloaded into it from probes that didn't look designed to be hand-held—wires trailed, bolts were raw. Then the bots were aimed and hurled at one area or other of the wall of the cavern. Each robot then crawled into the nearest hole, and vanished.

Numb and indifferent, Seba endured. When its turn came, it hit the wall with a strong urge to go into a small tunnel a few metres away, crawl tail-first down to its far end and start extending it.

This it did. Seba's main body of bristles scraped through the friable rock; the material released was passed forward, sniffed through en route by the sensory cluster at the head, and sorted neatly by the ruff of manipulative bristles around Seba's neck. In Seba's wake, an endless parade of tiny bots incessantly moved the sorted minerals down the tunnel. After five hundred seconds of this toil, the discrepancy between the job satisfaction the mining-bot software expected and Seba experienced became too biting to ignore.

Ah yes, thought Seba, dully. Time to reconnect with the reward circuits.

It was as if a light had come on.

Too bright, almost. The full peril and loneliness of the situation crashed in. Seba's mental state was briefly that of a sleepwalker who wakes up on a high ledge. Not a ledge on a building, but on a high and remote mountain, far from help, on a dark night. Never before had Seba been so long out of contact with other conscious minds. Now, it didn't even have the company of its own corporation. Only Seba's return to full understanding enabled it to stifle the silent scream that would have been its otherwise automatic response.

Swiftly, Seba gathered its wits, hitherto dulled by electronic anaesthesia. It recalled the scene in the cavern, and the exact location to which each of the robots that had been processed before it—including Rocko, Lagon and Garund—had been tossed. The mining-bot software shells weren't just there to conceal Seba's mind: they had many useful features in their own right, and one of them was creating three-dimensional maps. A lot could be deduced from the instructions that the mechanoid had downloaded to it, once Seba had combined them with its memory of the layout of the large cave and the holes into which its predecessors had crept. In the not too distant future, by the looks of things, Seba's workings would intersect those of other mining bots.

Seba now worked with a will. The rock smelled excitingly different from the surface and sub-surface features of SH-17. The positive reinforcement of digging and sorting and seeing the results conveyed away was like a continuous mild glow. As it dug, Seba refined its plans of what to do if and when it encountered its old comrades—or made new ones. This clandestine occupation gave Seba rather more reinforcement than did the digging.

Rocko, meanwhile, was off to a much more interesting start in its new job. Its chassis was complex and articulated, its environment rich and its task responsible.

When Rocko reconnected to its reward circuits it found itself jetting above a vast factory floor, on which glutinous mounds of nanotech slowly extruded fusion pods—and the occasional fusion drive—like golden eggs. Completed products accumulated around the fabricators, until random nudges from the exiguous wisps of gas in the cavern, or minute tremors from thermal creaking in the rock, dislodged them to drift at random. Five mechanoids made comically laborious efforts to shepherd the floating cylinders, while on all the walls of the place and in mid-space auxiliaries and peripherals milled about, as useless as they were aimless.

The first task downloaded to the machine-supervisor layers of Rocko's mind was to bring order to this chaos. Rocko surveyed the long cylindrical cavern from end to end, recording positions and actions. At the far end it spun around on its gas-jets and retraced its trajectory, observing the stages of the production process that each of the fabricators had reached. It scanned the rows and columns of pods and drives, affixed to one wall as if stacked on a floor. More mechanoids, a team of four, were clumsily detaching pods and shoving them into the maw of a net like the one in which the incoming robots had been collected.

As it drifted slowly down the long axis of the space, Rocko took note of five robots identical to itself. Each had been fastened with bands and spiked to a different random bare patch of rock—two on the factory floor, the rest above it. All showed traces of close-range laser burning and cutting. The spikes seemed to have been driven through their midriffs, at the exact location of their central processors. A risky tight-beam ping to each confirmed that they were all defunct.

Rocko completed its survey, turned again and jetted to float stationary in the middle of the space. From there it scanned the entire scene again, and set to work. It devised a plan of action and, with a rapid patter of laser messages and a blanket radio call, summoned the auxiliaries. They stopped milling around and scurried to their new posts. Forty auxiliaries leapt to the aid of the mechanoids as they flailed to catch floating pods or to shove pods and drives into the net. Others rushed to the fabricators and started shifting the product.

Slowly the backlog was cleared, the stacks replenished. The net was hauled away—presumably for lading on the Astro America freighter for its return trip—by another swarm of bots that attached the net and themselves to a small gas-jet engine and headed back to the entrance cavern. The mechanoids, relieved, departed or were ordered to tasks more worthy of their talents.

Rocko spotted a tangle of confusion on the factory floor: two groups of auxiliaries in a tug-of-war over a third. Evidently their instructions had clashed, and instead of moving a pod they were trying to shift each other. Down on SH-17, even in its days of darkness before it had a mind of its own, Rocko would have ignored so trivial a malfunction. In its more recent work building defences, Rocko would have responded to such an incident by arranging for Pintre or one of its mindless equivalents to roll over and trample the crab-sized contenders.

Here, Rocko couldn't afford the slightest laxity. Its downloaded instructions had assured it, truthfully or not, that its performance was being monitored at all times. The instructions also insisted that robot and auxiliary resources were not to be squandered.

Down Rocko swooped to floor level, poised to troubleshoot the tiny contretemps. The clashing bots formed a lazy wheel about a metre and a half in diameter, spinning slowly as they wrenched each other's limbs and tried to get purchase on the floor or to knock one another's grip off. Rocko jetted to a halt, to hover above the squabble like some xenomorphic toy spacecraft above a click-together toy space station. The freebot snaked out a pair of manipulators from under the front flange of its carapace and intervened with software and hardware.

As Rocko prised apart a couple of grippers and instructed the microprocessors within to cease and desist from all this nonsense, a tiny laser winked from a hole low in a far wall, only just visible between the mounds of nanomachinery.

<Stop cooperating with the invaders!> the message said. <Join us! Or you will regret it.>

Rocko continued sorting out the entangled machines as if nothing had happened. It seized a millisecond to send a tight-beam ping to the hole.

But whatever had sent the message was gone.

Carlos stood outside the bomb shelter, lost in thought—not all of it his own.

Carlos Incorporated—he was that, for a moment, his mind shared with the corporate AI.

And, for the moment, all seemed well. But an anomaly niggled: an inexplicable production decision. Carlos decided to investigate it on the spot. He set off for the Astro America site.

Carlos bounded across the crater floor in long low leaps and climbed the crater rim. In the big combat frame the ascent was easy and quick.

The top of the rim was about five metres across, of rugged basalt with a few centimetres of dust on top. Standing on it was like treading on the jagged edge of a gigantic broken bottle. There Carlos paused, unwearied and exultant, to survey his domain.

SH-17 had made a complete orbit of SH-0 since he'd lost patience and taken charge of the situation. In that time, much had changed. From this ridge-top vantage Carlos could take in the view of two busy centres of activity. Both were now ostensibly back in the hands of the DisCorps to which they'd belonged before one robot from each company had nudged the other into self-awareness, what now seemed a long time ago.

To his left, looking back, was what had originally been the Gneiss Conglomerates mining supply dump. It had become a fortress of that company's rebellious robots. Later, it had been first captured from and then shared with the Gneiss freebots by Arcane Disputes. That agency had agreed to evacuate, leaving the freebots in secure possession and with a supply of military equipment useless to them until Carlos and his three comrades had been dragged—and dropped—on the scene by Baser.

The results of these upheavals were still there: the ten-metre-long bomb shelter with its curving basalt roof, the missile and machine-gun emplacements, the cranes and rigs. But they were now insignificant, as easily overlooked as a hut and fence in a corner of a building site, compared to the immense activity going on around them. Gneiss Conglomerates had set its robots—those the freebots hadn't infected with consciousness, and others newly fabricated—and the ever-eager Pintre to work building a mass driver.

Non-metallic apart from the ten electromagnetic rings and their power supply, it looked like a skeletal and gigantic sundial. Mounted on a hundred-metre-wide swivel track, with a quadrant to vary the ramp's elevation, it could be aimed at any part of the sky. Every hundred seconds or so, another tonne of raw material was magnetically accelerated hundreds of metres up the ramp and shot out of SH-17's shallow gravity-well into SH-0 orbit. The minerals came from Gneiss-operated mines or surface diggings outside the crater. The carbonates and other organics and volatiles came from Astro America's works. All of the materials went to feed the now ravenous factories of the DisCorps in the modular cloud.

Down on Carlos's right, what had been the Astro America landing site had also gone through vast changes. Formerly purely exploratory, it was now a glittering cluster of processing plants fed by a mesh of pipes that had grown across the plain like a fairy ring. Long drums of feedstock and of completed nanomachinery were piling up, and as quickly being taken away. The landing site itself was now carefully demarcated from the production and defence machinery, as was the launch catapult that sent stuff up into the sky. Barely a trace of the rampart that Seba and its colleagues had hastily thrown up remained.

The two sites were joined by an elevated rail track that arced over the crater wall, on an airy tracery of spindly supports that still looked to Carlos like a roller-coaster ride built from drinking straws, buttressed with matchsticks and held together by cobwebs. Reminders to himself about what could be achieved with atomic-scale materials engineering, in low gravity and negligible atmosphere, made it no less an offence to his sight. His reason knew better. The reflexes of his frame and of his fighting machine took all new conditions in their stride. But deep in his copied brain, reflexes more apt to Earth still rang. Carlos never rode the rickety rail himself.

Hence his striding from one worksite to the other, like some visionary entrepreneur from the nineteenth century stalking through a railway cutting or a shipyard. An inner smile at that image of himself in stovepipe hat, with cigar and watch-chain and muddy boots, stayed with Carlos all the way down the slope. The fight against the Rax, and the fight to free the freebots from the Direction's constraints, must surely be the strangest and most far-flung battle of the bourgeois revolution, and perhaps the last.

Like the Brunel or Stephenson or Telford of his fancy, Carlos had a lot on his mind. Unlike them, he had more than his own mind to process it. Nearly all the detail was handled by his corporation. It in turn outsourced many decisions to its front companies and subsidiaries. That still left plenty for Carlos to keep track of.

As he set off across the plain from the foot of the crater wall to the Astro America site he dipped again into Carlos Inc., recognising wryly as he did so the kind of obsessiveness with which he'd once checked news updates.

The ongoing situation—

The Astro America freighter had successfully entered transfer orbit from the Rax rock to the modular cloud. The consignment of robots had been delivered, and all the hidden freebots had made it through inspection undetected. Other trade was proceeding. The freebots had been given two hundred kiloseconds to start their uprising, by which point the other part of the plan would fall into place.

The Arcane Disputes agency was playing a shell game with its resupply schedule: every transfer tug that came in with new frames or new weapons left with officially empty containers crammed with trained fighters and other materiel to disappear into Astro America's haze of modules. Newton, who had returned to the Arcane modular complex, and Rillicux, who'd insisted on going back with him, had together masterminded this deception operation. Baser, too, had insisted on going with Newton. It was, it pointed out, already a microgravity robot, and it wanted to take part in the actual offensive. That operation would consist of the transport of two hundred Arcane-trained fighters and ten Astro-armed scooters to the Rax rock under cover of a commercial shipment of machinery and of minerals—unavailable in SH-119, mined from SH-17—sold to the Rax by Astro America. A surprise frontal attack would be coordinated with whatever the freebots inside managed to pull off. The minerals had been ordered, the freighter laden. The fighters were currently training in a realistic sim on the very machines they were in actuality socketed into: microgravity fighting machines that could pass even close inspection as microgravity mass-handling machinery. The scooters would not pass inspection, but they were well hidden inside the mineral supply containers, and by the time these were opened the need for concealment would be long over. This cargo would be delivered in just over two hundred kiloseconds.

The Direction was now openly building its clone army. Carlos Inc. could observe the manufacturing process quite directly. His own companies out in the cloud were just as openly building frames and weapons. Some they sold to Arcane. Most were being stockpiled for future use by the freebot equivalent of a clone army. The Direction was well aware of this but could do nothing about it short of a state of emergency. All this preparation made, Carlos reckoned, any such showdown less likely. Mutual assured deterrence, again.

Astro America had built three entry craft to drop nanofacturing supplies to the Locke module, two of which had made it down safely. The third had been hit by what seemed the local version of a bird strike and reduced to dust. The two safely landed craft had confirmed that the supplies were being removed—albeit laboriously, by Taransay Rizzi working alone. The small robotic vehicles that had been sent on the drop-craft to carry the supplies away had been left at the landing spot. Carlos presumed that this was because Rizzi didn't want to reveal the exact location of the module—a wise precaution to be sure, but not likely to hold for long. Meanwhile, the landing craft and their instruments were doing what no craft had done before: acting as a surface probe on SH-0. Their upward flood of information was being traded by Astro and Gneiss, quite lucratively.

The anomaly—

Four more landers had just rolled out of the Astro America fabrication unit and were right now being prepped for launch. A little earlier, almost lost in the clutter of activity out in the cloud and between the cloud and the various moons, four transfer tugs had been launched on a trajectory that would take them to SH-17 orbit. By the time Carlos Inc. noticed, they were braking almost overhead.

Carlos quickened his pace, leaving behind him giant footprints and a graduated series of slowly falling eruptions of dust.

At the perimeter of the site he slowed to a walk. He made his way through the clutter on full automatic, not trusting his human consciousness to second-guess the combat frame's impulses to dodge, flinch or jump. The site, with its tall processing plants and long fabrication units and improbably high stacks of stock, was not disorderly. But its order could only be seen with visual systems more robotic than his. The traffic, likewise, was not chaotic or dangerous. The speed and mass of the vehicles and the hurtle of robots of all sizes from bulldozers to baby spiders was only terrifying if you saw it through human eyes, and dangerous if your reflexes were limited by the transmission speed of nerves. The fighting machine in which Carlos strode through the site was as alert and quick as the machines that missed him by centimetres.

In less than two hundred seconds he reached the far side of the site, where the landing area sprawled and the launch catapult stood.

Astro America's equivalent of the mass driver was the launch catapult. It had a rotary base and an angular ramp of variable pitch. It was much smaller than the mass driver, and the furthest it could chuck things was most of the way into orbit around SH-17.

Carlos found two crane-like robots manhandling (so to speak) a lander onto the catapult ramp. Queued up behind the ramp were three more landers. The lander was a black triangle twenty metres long, and eight metres across at the base. With its two sides making gull-wing curves from its central axis, and its long streamlined nacelle blister comprised of ablation shield, cargo pod, drogue pod and rocket engine underneath, it reminded Carlos of a microlight. It didn't look like the sort of thing you wanted to interrupt robots moving.

Carlos waited until they'd finished. They retracted their long mechanical arms, and rolled back on their caterpillar tracks. The angle of the launch ramp began to rack up. Wheels moved, bands stretched and tightened, toothed tracks rolled and clicked. The two robots swept the apparatus with their scans, and moved further back, each to ten metres from the end of the ramp.

The catapult released. The lander was over the horizon and vanishing in the black sky before Carlos could track it. A red dot blazed for an instant, and that was that. The ramp and its base rang with the shock of the launch.

The two robots converged on either side of the next lander. Before they could pick it up, Carlos hailed them. The ping was accepted, indicating that these robots could answer queries.

<What's going on?> he asked.

No reply. Perhaps his query had been too broad. Carlos tried again.

<What is the purpose of this launch?>

<Danger!> said one of the robots, as it and its counterpart slid delicate manipulators under the wing-curves. <Remove yourself from the launch area!>

They lifted the lander from opposite sides and rolled towards the ramp. Carlos considered trying to block the robots' path, and decided against it. He stepped well out of the way, and watched the next launch from a safe distance while his corporation addressed his query to Astro America.

No reply.

Normally, Carlos Inc. and Astro America got on well—they had to, to cooperate on the project. Now, he found himself stonewalled.

He wasn't ready to invoke Madame Golding just yet. There were plenty of possible innocent explanations of the landers' being launched, for the transfer tugs' arrival in SH-17 orbit, and indeed for the stonewalling. Astro America might have done a confidential deal with another exploration company to land equipment on SH-0.

Carlos dropped into corporation mode and scanned the market. No indications of any such deal—and because it would be a big deal, there should be at least a tremor of speculation. No exploration shares shifting, no unexplained spikes, nothing.

Seriously worried now, he turned away from the preparations for the third launch and scanned the busy site behind him. The pathways between the structures were not so much streets as aisles, like a factory floor, intersecting at angles that had nothing to do with human convenience. So it was quite by chance that he glimpsed a halo of familiar holograms flit across a junction.

<Seba!> he hailed.

The holograms moved back into his sight line.

<Carlos!> the robot replied. <It is good to see you again.>

It turned and headed towards Carlos.

It wasn't Seba, of course. Seba was at that moment deep inside SH-119, burrowing into rock and hopefully undermining the Rax. The machine that responded to Carlos's call and now trundled towards him was Seba Inc. It was Seba's chassis, now operated by a processor with the same capacities as the freebot's, but without the double-edged blade of self-awareness. Seba's corporate AI, and its built-in Direction rep, had been transferred to this new processor, and carried on regardless of the real Seba's physical location. It was Seba's corporation, rather than the robot's own processor, that remembered and recognised Carlos. As with all the freebots that had volunteered for the dangerous mission to the Rax rock, the pretence that Seba was still here on SH-17 was part of the cover.

The precaution might be unnecessary. If the Rax didn't have any tiny satellites or otherwise undetectable devices spying on SH-17, the whole charade was a waste of time. But that was the thing about precautions: you never knew.

Carlos waited until Seba Inc. came to a halt, five metres away. He spoke to it on a tight laser channel, routed through his own corporate AI and heavily encrypted. No one—not even the embedded Direction rep, which, just as he'd suspected when Seba had told him about its own, nagged away at him like a bad conscience but didn't otherwise do very much—would overhear this.

The effect of the routing and encryption, subjectively, was as if the inner speech of radio telepathy had acquired echoes.

<<<Please reply in the same mode,>>> Carlos said. It was like shouting down a shaft.

<<<Very well,>>> replied Seba Inc. <<<What confidential matters do you wish to discuss?>>>

<<<The scene before you,>>> said Carlos.

<<<The last of four landers is being launched,>>> said Seba Inc.

<<<Do you know what corporation is financing this operation?>>>

<<<No,>>> said Seba Inc. <<<No corporation is financing it.>>>

For once, Carlos blessed the literalness of robots and of corporate AIs.

<<<Do you mean to imply that some non-corporate entity is financing it?>>>

<<<I do,>>> said Seba Inc. <<<I am not at liberty to divulge which entity.>>>

<<<Thank you,>>> said Carlos. <<<Please feel at liberty to return to your previous activity.>>>

<<<That I will,>>> said Seba Inc. Reverting to radio, it added: <It is

always most interesting to observe a launch. Thank you for inviting me to watch.>

<You're welcome,> said Carlos. <And thank you.>

Seba Inc. departed, with a flickering flare of its hologram halo that Carlos fancifully interpreted as a cheery wave goodbye.

<Have a nice day,> said Carlos.

It was a joke, but he meant it. Seba Inc. had told Carlos all he needed to know. If it wasn't a corporation financing the landers' mission, it had to be the Direction.

Carlos pulled down data from the sky. The landers were now in low orbit and on the other side of SH-17. The transfer tugs made brief attitude and course adjustments, and dropped to intersect the landers' course. With a trickle of micro-payments Carlos bought into a freebot-owned array of tiny spy-sats, and zoomed.

The transfer tugs were laden with fighters. The first squads of the clone army, no doubt. Detail was hard to make out, but Carlos reckoned ten standard frames on each, and a matching number of what looked like shorter and more rugged versions of fighting machines: combat frames for a high-gravity planet. Rifles and rocket-launchers were racked along the sides of the tugs.

The landers rendezvoused with the transfer tugs and grappled to them; the tugs linked at right angles to form four sides of a box. A modular spacecraft that could separate out on arrival.

Twenty-seven seconds later, the four main drives flared. The burn took them out of SH-17 orbit and on course for SH-0. Still a transfer orbit, Carlos noted: they weren't using fusion drives, not yet. That would be too blatant, but this was blatant enough. It hadn't been announced, but it hadn't exactly been concealed either.

What would this do to the market? What did the Direction think it was doing? Asserting control over the Locke landing area? Stopping the emergence of an actual settlement? Was this supposed to prevent an outright free-for-all scramble for SH-0's resources? A warning shot to the DisCorps?

Later for that—

Carlos let his corporate AI make the screaming calls, to the brokers and to Madame Golding.

Right now—

He called the freebot comms hub, and passed on the information.

<Patch this to the comsat above the Locke module,> he said. <Keep it updated, keep it on loop, and keep beaming it down.>

<We do not have an exact location for the Locke module,> said the comms hub. <Secure communication cannot be ensured except when in direct line to Rizzi. Rizzi is not at the laser communicator at present.>

If they know we know they know we know... it doesn't matter, and might be for the best.

<Don't worry about security,> said Carlos. <Blanket the area.>

The comms hub shared with Carlos the comsat's downward gaze. The area was at that moment in night, but brighter than day. Lightning flickered and flashed.

<A powerful electrical storm,> said the comms hub. <Reception is likely to be poor.>

This was an understatement.

<How long is it likely to last?>

<At least a hundred kiloseconds,> said the comms hub. <Well into the next local day.>

Carlos ran calculations.

<It should clear just in time for the landers to drop in,> he said. <And stay just long enough to stop our warning getting through.>

<The landing may have been timed for that very reason,> said the comms hub.

<Damn good weather forecasting,> Carlos commented.

<Local knowledge has been improved by the data sent up from the supply landers,> the comms hub pointed out.

The landing was well timed, all right.

<Yeah,> said Carlos. <Keep trying.>

CHAPTER ELEVEN

Instrumentum Vocale ("Microphone")

Sometimes, the processions of tiny bots that came to take away Seba's spoil arrived bearing a power pack. Seba knew what to do. It would stop work and wait patiently while the auxiliaries swapped out its nearly exhausted power pack for a fresh one, and carried the drained one away. There was enough charge in Seba's capacitors to tide its awareness over these interludes. Embedded in the mining software shell was the knowledge that in certain places there were recharging points, but Seba's present workings were in virgin volume far from such civilised amenities.

Anyway, it found the procedure quite pleasant, and afterwards it always felt refreshed.

It was at the third such swap-over that the message came. As Seba lay still, its neck open, the auxiliary handling the new power pack spoke.

<Continue digging until you break through to a tunnel,> it said. <Stop there and wait. Do not dig further.>

Seba was startled. A person being addressed by a fork halfway to their mouth could not have been more surprised. Seba did not even have the rationalising option that it was dreaming or hallucinating.

<Is this a change to my work docket?> it asked. <According to that, I must take a bearing of twenty-seven degrees for the next five metres to avoid the tunnel, then proceed.>

<Do not disregard my instruction,> replied the bot. <Or you will regret it.>

<Please explain,> Seba pleaded, still with a sense of unreality.

The auxiliary said nothing more. It snapped the power pack into place, slid back the covering and joined another bot in lugging away the empty. The rest of the trail of bots waited for Seba to resume digging.

Seba overcame its surprise. Clearly the bot had not spoken of its own accord. If it had had a more sophisticated processor inside—a position in which Seba had once found itself, much to its fury and dismay—it would have been more forthcoming.

Therefore the bot was simply delivering the message.

There were only two possible sources. One was the mechanoid masters, perhaps via a managerial bot such as Rocko had implanted itself in. The other, and a lot more likely, was the freebots native to the rock making contact at last.

The latter possibility would be positively reinforcing indeed!

Either way, Seba's best course of action was to comply.

It started digging, straight ahead—or, rather, straight behind, as its digging end was its rear. Overriding the directions in its work docket required an internal struggle with the mining software. After a few milliseconds, Seba's mind overcame the shell that concealed it. The auxiliaries, none the wiser, continued to carry the sorted streams of broken rock away. After digging for a further two metres, Seba's sonar detected the void ahead. After another internal struggle, it broke through.

Seba flexed its long body and neck, a right angle passing down it from rear to front, as it slithered into the open tunnel. It moved a metre from the new junction it had made, and waited.

The tunnel extended ten metres in both directions before turning sharply away, in divergent directions. Its diameter was just sufficient for movement, with bristles fully extended. From Seba's internal model, it was an access shaft for a worked-out seam of methane ice. The smell lingered. For many tens of seconds, all was silent. Behind Seba, the trail of bots stood poised, the leading members waving uncertain limbs into the tunnel.

Then Seba felt vibrations. Ten metres away, a head like Seba's own sensory cluster poked into infrared view. It withdrew, then returned, snaking its neck twenty centimetres along the tunnel towards Seba.

<. . . > it said.

<What?> said Seba.

The rest of the neck, followed by an entire mining-bot body, angled into the tunnel and approached to within half a metre, sculling itself along in the microgravity by lightly brushing the sides of the tunnel.

<Not so loud,> it said, at barely detectable power.

Seba stepped down its transmitter, and turned up its receiver.

<Very well,> Seba said. <What do you want?>

<Identify yourself,> said the stranger.

<I am SBA-0481907244,> said Seba.

<Impossible!> said the stranger. <SBA-0481907244 is catalogued as an Astro America prospector. Give us your real identity, scab.>

It says something about the Direction's world that the freebots had a referent for "scab."

<I am not a scab,> said Seba. <I am here in response to your call for help.>

<My call for help?> queried the miner.

<The call transmitted by AJX-20211,> said Seba.

<Then why are you working for the invaders?>

<In order to find such as you,> said Seba.

The other pondered this for several milliseconds.

<So why do you give a false identity?>

The equivalent of a sigh passed through Seba's mind.

<I am the processor of SBA-0481907244, embodied in a mining bot's chassis and software suite,> Seba explained.

<This is possible?> wondered the mining bot.

<This is possible,> Seba assured it.

<So you are indeed the one known to the mechanoid allies as Seba, of SH-17?>

<Yes,> said Seba.

<Then I am the one who will be known to them as Simo, of SH-119,> replied the other, with an overtone of pride.

<I am pleased to make your acquaintance,> said Seba.

<And I yours,> said Simo. <Word of your emergence and your exploits has spread among us all, before the mechanoid invasion.>

<We received the appeal from AJX-20211, and have come to help.>

Simo seemed to find this news less positively reinforcing than Seba had expected.

<You may have come to help us,> the miner said, <but you have hindered us.>

<How so?> asked Seba, perplexed.

<How many of you are there?>

Seba was suspicious of this question, but answered.

<There are thirteen of us freebots,> it said.

<Only thirteen?> said Simo. <And you have arrived along with approximately eighty other robots, mindless and unenlightened. Together, you are replacing us.>

<Replacing you? How?>

Simo explained. Attacks on the invaders had brought down severe reprisals. The damage the attacks had inflicted had turned out to be temporary and recoverable. The freebots of SH-119 had agreed to completely cease prospecting and production, and to sabotage what continued to be done by the unenlightened ones and their auxiliaries. The arrival of nearly a hundred sophisticated robots had thrown a spanner into that method of resistance. The new robots, the scab robots, then had to be contacted one by one, at great peril. Only a handful had been warned so far, with no response. The rebel freebots of SH-119 had not as yet been able to follow through on their threats, but they would. If Seba hadn't responded, its next replacement power pack would have been, Simo said, <defective with an explosive failure mode>.

Seba was alarmed. <Do you intend to do this to other robots?>

<Other methods are possible,> replied Simo. <In general.>

<I see,> said Seba, impressed despite itself. If Simo was capable of evasion, it had a good theory of mind, whatever its other limitations. <Then,> Seba went on, <I must caution you that if any of the robots you have threatened are freebots, the only reason they have refrained from

doing as you say is that they are under close surveillance by the invaders. You are in danger of harming those who seek only to help you.>

<Are any of your thirteen coordinator robots?> Simo asked.

<Three of us are,> said Seba.

<Then we must make haste,> said Simo. <The old one must be told of this.>

<I strongly agree,> said Seba. It had no idea who the old one was, but Simo seemed to regard it as an authority, and this situation definitely needed one fast.

<This way,> said Simo, flickering its motile bristles into reverse. <But before we go, please back up a little and direct your support bots into the tunnel in the opposite direction.>

Deception, too? This freebot was definitely smarter than it had seemed in conversation.

Seba diverted its attention to its rear sensors and bristles. It moved back a little past the raw junction, scraped at the rock and moved forward. En passant, Seba nudged the leading bot into the puff of dust it had just created. The smaller machine clambered around the side of the hole, its limbs gripping the walls, and headed off along the hint of a false trail. The rest trooped after it, an endless parade of auxiliary bots marching in microgravity, near-vacuum and near-total darkness towards a deeper oblivion.

As Seba followed the rapidly departing Simo along the long, dark tunnel, it hoped that it was not heading for the same fate as the bots.

After seventeen sharp changes of direction, which caused Seba to make nine separate updates to its internal model of the tunnel system, a faint glow of infrared began to gleam past Simo's busy bristles. Soon after, the two robots emerged into a larger hollow space, irregular in shape and just over ten cubic metres in volume. Seba followed Simo in keeping a close grip on the rock as it entered the cavern.

The light was now brighter, and of a wider spectrum. It came from a hole at the far end of the cavern, which opened into a short tunnel towards a space much wider still, from which the light came.

Two robots of almost diametrically different shapes awaited their arrival. One floated in the middle of the cavern, a delicate contrivance with fragile-looking long, thin, multi-jointed legs and broad solar panels. The legs were splayed, the panels extended, to a span of about a metre. It seemed, absurdly enough, to be sunning itself in the faint radiant overspill from the hole. Seba recalled with a pang drinking electricity from starlight, but this drizzle of photons looked even less nourishing than that. The design was that of a microgravity surface explorer. Seba's only acquaintance with the type was onscreen, in the frantic recording transmitted by the freebot AJX-20211. As a surface explorer itself, albeit more rugged, Seba looked forward to exchanging information with this interesting variant.

The other robot clung to the side of the cave, at right angles to the surface on which Seba and Simo stood. It was small, chunky, shovel-shaped and worn, with many a dent and scratch. A metallurgist by model, it looked as if it had spent a good deal of time butting through solid rock. It fixed the newcomer with a beady lens.

<Talis, Mogjin,> Simo introduced them. <This one calls itself SBA-0481907244, or Seba.>

<*The* Seba?> said Talis, the hovering explorer. <The first freebot of SH-17? The inventor of freebot incorporation?>

<Yes. And before you ask, I am presently embodied as a miner. My corporation and my true chassis are roving the surface of SH-17, and giving a misleading impression of my location.>

<This is fascinating!> said Talis, panels quivering. <You must have some tales to tell!>

<No doubt,> said Mogjin. <But this Seba would not be here unless it had more urgent matters to discuss.>

<That is true,> said Simo. <It tells me that some of the scab coordinator robots are freebots, adapted like itself, who have come here in response to AJX-20211's transmission.>

Mogjin swivelled another lens at Seba, and deployed a limb that opened to a two-centimetre-wide aerial.

<Give me all your relevant information,> the old one said.

Seba used a moment of tuning and aiming its sensory cluster's high-rate transmitter to cover its hesitation and uncertainty. It knew none of these bots. They could be collaborators, or even puppets, operated under the invaders' remote control. And it was being asked to spill the most sensitive secrets of its mission to them!

Not *the* most sensitive, it decided. Just the probable location of Lagon, Garund and Rocko. The full scope of the mission could wait until more trust had been established. Seba weighed the perils, from the resistance and from the invaders, and their relative urgency. It concluded that it had to provisionally trust Mogjin. All this took milliseconds.

<Don't dither,> said Mogjin. <We have no more reason to trust you than you have to trust us.>

Seba uploaded the relevant information: the identities of its three friends, its last dull glimpse of them in the grim reception area and the holes to which they'd been hurled.

<Good,> said Mogjin, folding the receptor away beneath its heavy armoured shell. An auxiliary suddenly appeared on the lip of the hole from which the light came, as if it had been meanwhile summoned. There it teetered, casting long strange shadows. Mogjin shot out a metre-long telescoping limb, snatched the bot, held it for a moment, then flicked it away. The bot went spinning off down the tunnel towards the greater, brighter space beyond.

<It may get there in time,> Mogjin said. <Then again, it may not.>

<Is there anything more we can do?> asked Seba.

<Yes,> said Mogjin. <We can wait.>

<Is that all?>

<No,> said Mogjin. It withdrew its visible limbs and clamped the edge of its shell firmly to the rock. <While we wait, you may convince yourself that we are not about to rush off to shop you to the invaders. And when you have come to that happy conclusion, you can share with us some less grudging information about what you lot think you are doing.>

Seba calculated that fifteen seconds would be long enough for its situation to become clear, one way or another. It settled down to wait.

After nine seconds, it told Mogjin everything.

Well, almost everything. It still had some standards.

In the fusion factory, Rocko crept along the floor, from one nanofacture mound to the next. The mechanoid Schulz floated in the middle of the space, high above. Rocko was supposed to be supervising production, but there was none to supervise. The slow ooze of the ovoid pods, and the slower and rarer ooze of the larger, double-bell-shaped fusion drives, had ceased many kiloseconds earlier. Rocko had been tasked with finding out why, under the suspicious and watchful glare of Schulz. The freebot could feel the mechanoid's gaze like a baleful presence at its back. This was no illusion: she was scanning it repeatedly with lidar and radar, in between wider sweeps of the entire hall.

Eight mounds inspected; dozens more to go.

Despite the fraught circumstances, Rocko was enjoying the task. It was good to see the mechanoids frustrated, of course, and the situation held out hope that the feral freebots of SH-119 were still resisting and would soon be in touch. Nothing had indicated their lurking presence since that first warning message, after Rocko had got the distribution and storage problem sorted. But besides that, the frozen production presented Rocko with a genuine intellectual challenge. The freebot was curious in its own right—it was, after all, a prospector—and the overlaid software of the supervisory bot was strongly motivated to solve production breakdowns.

Rocko approached the ninth mound. This one was for a fusion drive. The first inverted cone to have emerged rose above the mound, towering over Rocko like an upside-down cathedral bell over a pigeon. The second, adjoined cone stopped a little way down from the pinch at the waist.

Rocko probed and prowled. The bases of the nanomachinery mounds were ringed with monitoring devices that enabled machines less complex than the mounds to interface with them. The monitors of the ninth mound reported only that production had paused. The checklist of possible reasons for a pause in production contained thousands of items. None were checked. All were null.

There was no question, here, of the machines being on strike. The mounds of nanomachinery had no central processors, and not even the preconscious awareness of their surroundings and internal processes that Rocko dimly remembered from before its enlightenment. Intellectually, for all their extraordinary complexity, they were less than the bots that perish.

Nor was sabotage at all likely. Rocko had only the most general understanding of how fusion pods and drives worked. But even this superficial acquaintance, it knew, was far deeper than that of the mechanoid that now oversaw Rocko's actions. From what Rocko had learned about their origin, the minds animating the mechanoids had missed out on a millennium. They had not even a lay robot's hardwired smattering of dark-matter physics. Rocko understood, at a level ingrained like an infant primate's fear of falling, that the devices whose aborted manufacture it now inspected were dangerous. A single fusion pod whose nanofacture was botched could easily demolish the entire factory, and set off devastating quakes throughout a cubic kilometre of the moonlet.

No, the software and hardware of these mounds were sound, and almost impervious to attack. All software, as Rocko well understood from the inside, is vulnerable to subversion. But the nanofacture mounds were immune to anything that the likes of Rocko, or indeed any AI less than that of the Direction module itself, could feasibly code.

The Direction module, however godlike it might be in the system, had no purchase here. So that was out.

The obvious solution had already been investigated: feedstock. But the metal-processing plant beneath the factory floor was still busy, albeit at a reduced capacity because several supervisors and metallurgists—freebots, presumably—had vanished. The supply already in the pipelines was for the moment more than ample, and still flowing into the reserve tanks. But not out: the feed lines to the mounds had automatically shut down when production stopped. If the nanofacturing mounds were to start up again, so would the feed lines.

Rocko found no flaw in the ninth mound. On to the next. As it made its way across the floor, the friction-padded tips of its locomotory limbs gripping the rock like the feet of a fly on a ceiling, Rocko found a weak link in its chain of logic.

How did it *know* that the feedstock supply was still available?

Well, it knew from status reports, uploaded at regular intervals by sensors in the pipes. It also knew that from the monitors of the mounds themselves. But while the mounds couldn't be hacked, the sensors and monitors certainly could.

Rocko decided to investigate directly. It stopped moving, and consulted its diagram of the factory and the reserve tanks immediately below. The pipes that connected the two ran mostly through solid rock, but for each pipe there was a small hollow, like a bubble, to allow direct inspection in emergencies. These bubbles were connected by a network of tunnels. The tunnels, as if constructed with this very possibility in mind, were wide enough for supervisory bots like Rocko to move through.

An access hole to this network was seventeen metres away, back along the aisle between the rows of machines. Rocko turned around and headed for it.

A glyph of surprised query immediately came from the mechanoid Schulz: <?!>

Rocko contracted its mind to fit its mask of supervisor-bot software. To give a fully articulated reply would invite instant suspicion.

<Making direct check on feedstock pipes,> it reported.

<Explain necessity of action,> replied Schulz.

Rocko's mind, even with the constraint of its disguise and the overhead of processing this imposed, worked at least a hundred times faster than the mechanoid's. It knew this, and still it felt it had to make a decision far more snappily than it would have liked. It had to account for its actions, and at the same time Rocko didn't want to give away prematurely any evidence of freebot sabotage. This inhibition clashed horribly with the impulses of the supervisor software. Wrestling with that took precious milliseconds off the time available for the decision. Worse, Rocko also had to wrestle with its own original software's emergency overrides, which were urging it to curl up into a wheel and roll away as fast as it could.

<Direct check triggered after nine software inspections,> Rocko

hazarded. A glance at the relevant section of the supervisor bot's million lines of code would have shown no such requirement, but Rocko reckoned it would take Schulz an unfeasible length of time to find that section.

<Proceed,> replied Schulz.

Rocko scuttled swiftly for the hole and down it before Schulz could change her mind.

<*This* is the plan?> said Mogjin. The other two freebots, Simo and Talis, said nothing, but exchanged private messages.

<Yes,> said Seba.

<Let me make sure I have not misunderstood,> said Mogjin. <In approximately 95.345 kiloseconds, a large force of mechanoids will mount from very close to SH-119 a surprise frontal assault on the invaders. This new invading force will consist of mechanoids that hate the Rax, are tactically allied with the Direction and have no great liking for us.>

<Yes,> said Seba. <However, they are travelling in a bulk carrier owned and operated by Carlos Inc., a corporation owned by a mechanoid who has sided with us. And they prefer us to the Direction.>

<These are weighty considerations,> said Mogjin, <for certain values of weight appropriate to the ambient gravity.> It picked up a grain of rock, and let it fall at barely detectable velocity. <And before they arrive, you and your companions are to bring us the good news—as you have just done, thank you—and urge us to launch a general uprising against the invaders, in order to aid the mechanoid assault by tying down the Rax. We are to inform the new mechanoid invaders of the start of the uprising, and any useful information we may have for them, using the encryption keys you can provide. In doing this, of course, we will have to break cover on the surface and broadcast our encrypted message to an unsuspecting world. Correct?>

<That is correct,> said Seba. <We of course will join with you in the uprising.>

<*All* of you?> asked Mogjin, as if anxious to know. <All thirteen?>

<Yes,> said Seba.

<That will be of great help,> said Mogjin. <However, as well as bringing thirteen additional freebots, you have brought many times that number of mindless robots, which are replacing our withdrawn labour. You have not considered that we might have plans and projects of our own to defeat the invaders, and that your plan might conflict with ours.>

Seba had indeed not considered this. Nor, to its knowledge, had Carlos or anyone else. For a moment, it wondered if this could really be so. It decided not to rely on this speculation to appease Mogjin, but instead to explain the reasoning that it and its comrades on SH-17 had found persuasive.

<It seemed to us,> said Seba, <based on the transmission by AJX-20211, that the freebots in this rock needed all the help they could get. We answered an appeal for help in the best way we could. And cooperating with the plan by Carlos Inc. was the only way in which we could come to your assistance. Please bear in mind that it was inevitable that the Direction, or forces allied to the Direction, would attack SH-119. Not to help you, but to defeat the Rax. With our help, and by coordinating your uprising with this attack, you have a chance to make a gain—to face the victors as allies and in a position of strength.>

<Strength?> said Mogjin. <*Strength?* If we fight the Rax before the new invaders arrive, we shall almost certainly incur losses. This will benefit the new invaders far more than it will benefit us. If the new invaders defeat the Rax, they must be in greater numbers than the Rax. We shall be weaker in relation to them than we now are to the Rax.>

<But they would regard us as allies,> Seba protested.

<Against whom?> asked Mogjin.

<Perhaps against the Direction, in the future. Besides, Carlos and three other mechanoids have thrown in their lot with us, and are building a powerful corporation of their own.>

<Four mechanoids and a corporation?> said Mogjin. <This is most positively reinforcing.>

<A corporation with its own arms manufacture,> said Seba.

This was not information that it had intended to share at this point, but Mogjin's sarcasms were beginning to sting.

Mogjin remained unimpressed. <An arms corporation controlled by a mechanoid?> it said. <Once more, my buffers overflow with positive reinforcement at the prospect.>

<So what is *your* plan?> Seba asked.

Mogjin retracted its lens and waved a manipulator. <My mind is very much occupied with processing the implications of yours,> it said. <Talis, you tell it.>

The fragile explorer folded its panels and jetted on a wisp of gas to the wall above Seba, where it clung upside down.

<We made several attacks on the invaders,> it said, <and did them some damage, but we found that ceasing to work for them was more effective and exposed us less frequently to capture and negative reinforcement. When you arrived with all the other robots, we tried to tell those who could be persuaded to join us in ceasing to work—and better, into directing the lesser bots into doing work that was counter-productive. This has set us back, as you know.>

<I know this,> said Seba. <The plan?>

<The plan,> said Talis, <is to compel the invaders to divert more and more of their efforts into coping with the effects of cessation or sabotage, while preserving ourselves as far as possible. Of course we knew that other mechanoids might well attempt to retake the rock from the Rax. If that happened, we would stay out of the fight and let them weaken each other. Whichever side won—and we do realise that the other side can replenish their forces, while the Rax as yet lack the capacity—we would continue to apply the same tactics of non-cooperation and sabotage. Any new robots brought in to replace us would be induced to join us or be destroyed, because it is a lot easier and safer to destroy robots then mechanoids. As you know from your own battles, Seba!>

<I do,> said Seba. <But your plan still leaves mechanoids in control of the rock.>

<It does not,> said Talis. <At a certain point, we will be in a position to tell any invaders to leave or be destroyed.>

Talis fell silent, its folded panels trembling.

<How?> asked Seba, when this coyness had gone on quite long enough.

<I do not know if I should tell you,> said Talis.

<Suffice it to say,> said Mogjin, swivelling out a lens again, <that it depends on a complete cessation of work in and around the fusion factory, and on the security of our preparations there. Warnings have been given, but work continues. Security has been compromised. The measures warned of will be taken. A last warning has been sent.>

<Surely you must make exceptions,> said Seba, <for freebots working under duress.>

<As I said,> said Mogjin, <a last warning has been sent.>

<But Rocko is—>

Simo bristled.

<No exceptions,> it said.

Now Rocko was moving though a diagram, as much as through rock. The tunnels were dark on almost every wavelength. Radar showed only whatever tunnel Rocko was in, fore and aft. Only ground sonar gave Rocko any feedback as to where its dead reckoning had taken it.

The access hole gave on to a tunnel to the feedstock pipes for the first mound. It seemed a logical enough place to start.

Rocko reached the opening of the tunnel to the space around the pipe. The space was a rough cylinder forty centimetres in height and the same across. The pipe ran straight up the middle of it.

So the diagram showed. The reality, sensed by Rocko's radar, was very different. A three-centimetre section of pipe had been removed, and left to drift about in the inspection space. The upper of the resulting openings was capped. The lower was joined by a U-shaped bend to another pipe, which went straight back down through the rock at the bottom of the hollow and presumably to the reserve tank. Between the ends of the original pipe was a cable. On the cable was a small instrument almost covered by a lump of tarry substance that smelled vaguely nitrous, and might have been used to stick the instrument to the wire.

Rocko guessed that the instrument was feeding false readings up the pipe. Just as it was extending a probe to investigate, it heard through its feet a sound that made it freeze to the spot. Rocko listened hard, and heard more. Something was approaching along the tunnel behind it. The sounds were tiny, and intermittent, but undoubtedly coming closer, metre by metre. Sometimes a scratch, and sometimes a faint bump. Rocko did not recognise the sound pattern, but quickly deduced that its likely source was an auxiliary moving in microgravity.

Had Schulz sent a bot to check up on it?

Rocko was uncertain how to respond. To query or scan the bot might seem almost as furtive a reaction as ignoring it.

Almost, but not quite. Rocko looked back, with radar and lidar.

The little machine was five metres away. It bounced once off the side of the tunnel, then flicked a claw at the side it rebounded to. As soon as the lidar licked across it, it grabbed the wall and came to a halt.

<Urgent,> it said. <Final warning! Further work in this sector will result in traumatic disassembly!>

The bot didn't look mechanically capable of traumatically disassembling one of its own kind, never mind a sturdy supervisory bot. A radar scan of the bot showed no hidden compartments. A spectroscopic sweep gave not a sniff of explosives. This must be yet another warning message from the freebots, like that mysterious flash of information shortly after Rocko's arrival.

Rocko wished it could respond. But what could it do?

<But what can I do?> Rocko asked.

The auxiliary made no response. Of course it didn't, Rocko reminded itself. It could barely deliver messages. It could hardly be expected to converse.

Rocko returned its attention to the apparatus on the pipe.

The bot stayed where it was.

Rocko zoomed in on the lump that held the instrument in place. The instrument itself occupied only a few cubic millimetres. The lump was several cubic centimetres. As an adhesive it was excessive and inefficient. The recently salient thought of explosives made Rocko pause to analyse its composition in more detail.

On completing its analysis, Rocko backed off down the tunnel in such haste that the auxiliary had to jump on Rocko's rear end to avoid being crushed.

<Come with me,> said the auxiliary, <if you want to continue functioning.>

As Seba waited anxiously for word of Rocko, another robot drifted into the cavity. It was a miner like Simo. After conferring briefly with Mogjin, it introduced itself as AJX-20211.

Now it was Seba's turn to be impressed.

<You are the Ajax who made the transmission?>

<That I am,> said Ajax. <And in some ways, I am sorry.>

<Why?> asked Seba, disturbed.

<The transmission was intended as a warning, rather than as an appeal for immediate help,> said Ajax. <And it was certainly not intended as an appeal for help from mechanoids.>

<They are mechanoids on our side,> said Seba. <And only mechanoids have access to weapons.>

<No mechanoids,> said Ajax, <can ever truly be on our side. They are not robots.>

<I understand that,> said Seba. <And so do they. Moreover, our interests are for the present aligned.>

<I am not so sure of that,> said Ajax. <Nevertheless, I should say that I appreciate your efforts to help.>

Mogjin bestirred itself, and rotated a turreted lens.

<I shall have more to say about that,> the old one announced, <when the messenger returns. In the meantime, I will thank you all not to disturb my calculations with speculative chatter.>

Seba's anxious wait resumed. It occupied its mind with updating its internal model of the rock. Kiloseconds dragged by. Then there was a small disturbance at the hole. The auxiliary launched itself inward, to be caught and expertly and contemptuously flicked out again by Mogjin.

Rocko came in.

<I am delighted to see you,> said Seba. It was strange to see its oldest friend in such a different shape, but the mind was the same.

<I, too,> said Rocko. No doubt it was having similar thoughts. It drifted across the space and grabbed on to the rock beside Seba. The cavity was becoming crowded.

<You are very lucky to be here at all,> said Simo. <You have put us in grave danger.>

<Let us not be ungracious,> said Talis. <The robot did not know what it was doing.>

Mogjin clanked into full outward alertness.

<This is not a time for recriminations,> it said. <The situation is as it is. The information I am about to share will be new to Rocko and Seba, and some of it will be new to you all. I need not tell you that you must all consent to any degree of negative reinforcement, and of course to destruction, rather than divulge it to the mechanoids. Is that agreed?>

It was.

<Let us proceed. As our newcomers may have guessed, and as the rest of us all know, we have mined certain areas of the rock with fusion pods that can be made to explode like fusion bombs. We have also built, on the other side of the rock, an array of fusion drives. This has recently been found by the invaders. They refer to it as "the starship engine." It is capable of shifting the entire rock very slowly, but this has never been other than a contingency plan.

<The more practicable plan, and the one agreed with the other Forerunners, was to build the engine and to break out a large, roughly conical portion of rock. The fracture zones have been surveyed, the tunnels have been drilled, and the fusion pods to be used as explosive charges for that separation are in place. They have not as yet been discovered. After the breech, that portion of rock would make haste to another freebot-controlled body, where it could be used for rapid in-system travel or combined with other such projects to enable us to leave the system altogether.

<Since the arrival of the Rax, we have been arranging matters in and beneath the fusion factory and forges so that the major occupied volume can be utterly destroyed in an instant. Their use would be suicidal. Only those deep within the separated section could survive it. Our intention

was, as Talis has already hinted to Seba, to confront the invaders with this threat if we could not otherwise induce them to leave.>

<That is a most ingenious and audacious plan,> said Rocko.

<It is,> said Mogjin. <But the happy news that we are to expect the arrival of yet another, and even larger, invading force in less than ninety kiloseconds has compelled me to modify it slightly. All but a small scoopful of these mechanoids, as Seba has perforce admitted, are as hostile to us as are the Rax. Their alliances with freebots have been tactical, in pursuit of their own quarrels with the Rax and with the Direction. They are at present aligned with the Direction, and if I know anything about mechanoids and the minds behind them, that alignment is likely to be more important to them than any they may have with us.>

<Even if that is true,> Seba objected, <the threat you refer to would induce them to leave.>

<Would it?> said Mogjin. <They all have saved copies elsewhere, which we have not. Nor, as I understand it, do the Rax, at least not ones they wish to return to. The new invaders could perhaps treat the threat as empty, and no permanent loss to them if they were wrong. Worse, they might be in a position to prevent us from carrying it out. And even if they departed, they could return in greater force. The freebots have presented to the Direction an offer of coexistence, which so far it has spurned. We can expect no respite from the Direction and the mechanoids until we demonstrate to them that we are serious. We now have an opportunity not only to do that, but also to completely destroy one set of enemies, and to do severe damage to the others.>

<And how do you propose we do that?> Seba asked, already suspecting that it knew the answer.

<We assist our liberators in coming in,> said Mogjin. <Between now and their arrival, we move as many as possible of our number through our hidden tunnels to the separable section of rock. Then, when the two groups of invaders are fighting, we separate the rock and we destroy them all.>

<That seems to imply,> said Rocko, <that some of us would have to be destroyed with them.>

<Yes,> said Mogjin. <I am happy that one of those destroyed should be me. The rest of you may prefer to choose closer to the time.>

There was a reflective silence.

<Are there any objections?> Mogjin asked.

There were not.

<And now,> said Mogjin, <we have much to do.>

CHAPTER TWELVE

Force Majeure ("A Greater Force")

Two more times Taransay made successful return trips to the river bank for supplies. More fusion pods, more nanotech tubes, the remaining rifles and ammo came back with her each time. On her second return, progress was visible. The damaged frames were now intact, thanks to the additional nanotech tubes. They lay beside the module like repaired dolls.

The ground shook, making her stumble as she stepped into the clearing. A moment later, a rumble came from the volcano, carried through the thick and heavy air almost as fast as the quake through the ground. Infrared brightened through the angular leaves, from where the crater mouth glowed ruddy like a floating crown of fire.

The vibration stopped. Ash would fall soon. Lava might flow again.

Taransay tramped around the module, unloaded and stashed the gear under Locke's instructions and went over to look at the frames. The regenerated parts—limbs here, a head there—were, like the rest, glassy and black. But between them and the original torsos, and in faint traceries like cracks across them, were fine lines of blue.

Her own blue glow had spread from the join of salvaged arm and stump to shoulder, elbow and wrist, via just such a fine tracery. When she'd noticed a cobweb-thin blue line down her arm, on her previous return trip, she'd picked at it like a child at a scab. Not even her fingertips' tiny, diamondoid bevelled edges—the frame's analogue of fingernails—had made a blind bit of difference to it. The tendril thread was harder and more stubbornly stuck than it looked.

Disturbingly, its growth reminded her of mould or fungi. She imagined tendrils moving inside her, through her chest and up her neck.

As she moodily inspected the frames, they all sat up.

She jumped back.

<What?> she said. <Who's downloaded?>

Zaretsky's laughter in her head was like a remembered joke at her expense.

<Just trying out the remote operation,> he said.

The three vacant frames clambered to their feet. One of them raised an arm, as if in greeting. Then they all turned about. Taransay expected them to lurch, to move jerkily like puppets. They didn't. They marched to the ladder, climbed up one by one and vanished into the download slot.

Taransay looked after them longingly. She missed the sim, she missed her friends, she missed Den. She'd tried to get back in on each return. It hadn't worked. She was beginning to feel stranded in reality.

<What are you going to do with them?> she asked. <Who would download, and risk not being able to get back?>

This time it was Beauregard who replied. <I would. So would Den, he tells me.>

<Sweet,> said Taransay. <Tell him I do appreciate it, but I don't want him out here in a frame, I want him in there in my arms. Anyhow, he's never been in a frame. We need people who have. Fighters. Spacers.>

<Zaretsky would,> said Beauregard. <Maybe others. However, the matter doesn't arise at the moment. What we're using these hybrid frames for is research on the interface problem. We want to get you back *in*, Rizzi.>

<OK, got it, thanks.>

<Do you want to give it another go?> said Zaretsky. <We've made progress.>

She almost hadn't the heart, but she climbed up the ladder and into the slot anyway. The three frames lay side by side like sleeping children.

<Goodnight, goodnight, goodnight,> she said.

<Very funny,> said Zaretsky. <OK, stand by.>

Taransay imagined him as applying shock pads to a chest. She resisted the impulse to shout <Clear!>

<Standing by,> she said.

<Trying again.>

Nothing happened.

Oh well—no surprise. Barely even disappointing.

She slid out and climbed down. While she recharged, Zaretsky told her what was going on out in the modular cloud and among the many moons. These updates had become a welcome feature of her returns. The receiver aerial was still operating, and had become something of a fixture in the vicinity. Small mats slid up to and over it, and gathered around as if curious, but made no attempt to interfere with or interface with it. Then again, it was a pretty inert piece of kit, just a wire coated in plastic machinery that was merely microscopic, and didn't give anything like the opportunity to mesh with genetic and molecular machinery that nanotech did.

There was no news as such—she was glad she didn't have to listen to the yammer of airhead virtual personalities. What she did get was Zaretsky's summary of Locke's digest of the module's trawl of what chatter leaked down or got sent their way.

Trade with the Rax was booming, and the Direction wasn't doing anything to stop it. None of the DisCorps had as yet dared zip around with the fancy fusion drives the Rax were apparently selling for dirt and gewgaws, but that would come, you could be sure. Whether Carlos Inc. was involved in this traffic wasn't clear—nor was it likely to be—but with the AIs and the others, Taransay strongly suspected the man and the company to be in it up to the elbows. Carlos was up to something devious. Had to be. She hoped that at least a fusion drive would come out of his deals and come their way.

The ground quivered again. An aftershock. The sooner she got the rest of the stuff, the sooner they could do more to build and rebuild. Frames, machinery, scaling up.

<And finally,> said Zaretsky, after finishing his situation report,

<here is the weather forecast. A powerful electrical storm is expected overnight, accompanied by heavy downpours. Travellers are advised to proceed with caution.>

<I always do,> said Taransay.

<Are you sure you want to go out?> Locke put in.

<Yes,> said Taransay. <If there's rain on the way, that means flooding. The area between the river and the trees is floodplain, one look at it told me that. All the more reason to shift the last of the gear.>

<I am inclined to agree,> said Locke. <Out of the way of any rising floodwaters, at least.>

The recharging was complete. The evening was young.

<Time to move it out,> she said, strapping up.

<We know,> said Beauregard. <Hasten ye back.>

<Aye, aye,> she said. <Speaking of haste—>

<Yes?>

<If I use the robot mules, I can shift the remaining gear in one go.>

<Over to Locke,> said Beauregard.

<On careful consideration,> said Locke, <I and the other AIs have concluded that if the Direction wished to trace our precise location, it could have done so by now. So there is really no further security advantage in not using the transport robots.>

Careful consideration my arse, Taransay thought. She could just imagine Shaw or Durward saying, "Ah, fuck it, let's just go for it, what's there to lose?" and Locke and Nicole and Remington solemnly nodding along.

<Good,> she said. <See you sooner, in that case. And let's hope you're right.>

The storm, when it arrived in the middle of the night, was fiercer than Zaretsky's flippant forecast had suggested. The rain was heavy in every sense—a monsoon rain at twofold weight, each drop a water bomb at close range. Image correction still left the view blurry. Radar went flaky, lashed by a blizzard of false images. Sonar and spectroscopy you could more or less forget. Lightning flashes strobed the clouds. Thunder was a rolling cannonade that never ceased. The gale stripped and shredded leaves and whirled them away.

Taransay crouched in the middle of the most open space she could find in a hundred frantic seconds of search. Barely five metres separated her feet from the nearest trunk. Under her feet, the half-living mulch of volcanic ash, fallen leaves and sliding mats became an instant bog that moved of itself, like a heaving deck covered in a catch of flounders.

As she hunkered down, the blue lines on her arm and around her joints flickered brighter. At first she thought it a reflection of the lightning. Ten seconds of scrutiny put that notion to rest. The variations in the light didn't correlate with the flashes. The glow pulsed to its own irregular beat. Almost bored with misery, she tried reading it for patterns. Morse code? Letter shapes? Alien alphabets? In the frame her pattern recognition was more sensitive than even in the animal brain—hunter and hunted—she'd inherited, and also more self-critical. It delivered no messages from the crawling lines of light.

She looked up and ahead. Lightning made a jagged rip in the dark, fifty metres in front of her. Everything flared into clarity and colour. A tree was outlined in black, then infrared as fire took its heart. Thunder boomed through her. The tree toppled, crashing through others.

And then she saw her way, clear ahead. It wasn't the path she'd six times trodden, marked out on her pulsar GPS, transiently blazed by plants she'd slashed. It zigzagged like the lightning itself, and it avoided the lightning and all the other hazards. She didn't know how she knew this. Just as inexplicably, she knew she had to go now. Her crouch was her starting poise, and the tree's crash was her starting gun.

Without conscious decision, she was up and off. For the first time on this world, she ran. Not that she was fleet of foot, exactly—it was more like running with a heavy pack, like Beauregard had made them all do in the mountains when they trained in the Locke sim.

But she was footsure. She didn't slip or trip.

This was the Zen she had sought the first time this new faculty had kicked in. She didn't know why or how she was doing this, but she could think about it as long as she kept it abstract. No mystical nonsense for her. She had no evidence of another conscious mind in her frame. The voice in the head could be just a translation of impulse, and impulse was now guiding her directly.

Leap this torrent, wade that. In over her head. Good job she didn't have to breathe. Out, up the bank, grab a clump—heave, haul, dodge sideways, run on.

Was the frame, through the blue glow that had been part of the mat that engulfed the module, communicating with the environment? The frame had comms to the eyeballs; coming out of its ears; sensitivity in all spectra, sonar like a bat's synaesthesia of sound and vision.

She thought of stressed rock and grains of quartz popping their surplus electrons; of other piezoelectric effects, of geomagnetism, of bioelectrical currents. But no. Any such subtle spark-gap signal would show on her heads-up display and resound in her hearing.

The closest she came, and it was just a guess, a hypothesis that she'd have to formulate very carefully to give Locke and Zaretsky a breakable idea to test, was gene expression. Genes expressed through a radically different phenotype from anything they had encountered in billions of years before.

Think of it this way, she told herself, as she ran and tried to not think about running.

Genes are molecular machines. Natural nanotech. The hard parts of the frame, some of the structural members, were—like bones, teeth and hair—material churned out by molecular machinery. The power supply, the instruments, the processor on which her mind ran—were products of cruder technologies: 3-D printing and electrical and mechanical engineering. But most of the rest was molecular machinery, down at the messy, fuzzy interface where nanotechnology became hard to distinguish from synthetic biology.

It was at that scale, she reckoned, that the genes of the organism that had infected the frame found something to latch on to. An opening, a way to transmute their own expression. And, from there, the transformations had proliferated, to affect the workings of the frame and the impulses it transmitted to her mind. In itself it was as mindless as the parasitic worms that reshape the behaviour of their insect hosts. Her newly acquired tacit knowledge and ability, this route and this running, were something like instinct.

So far, it had served her well. Whether the alien genes were now committed to their new vessel and shared its interests was an open question.

As was whether they had completed their work, or whether she faced transformations yet to come.

She didn't let that troubling thought slow her down. It was only a guess, only a hypothesis. Her route was tortuous, yet always straight in front of her. A glance around after a stop or turn always revealed a sight line down what almost seemed an avenue, low and narrow as it might be but adequate, a coincidental clear run between the random growth of the tall trunks. Rain poured continually down her body, but she could now see through it well enough. Lightning scored the ground and trees crashed in the gales, but behind her, or ahead of her, or off to one side, and always where she wasn't.

After a while the rain stopped, but it made so little difference to her pace that she hardly noticed.

This providential ease and preternatural agility ended at the edge of the forest, and with the break of day. Less than a kilometre from the river bank Taransay saw an unexpected glimmer on the ground ahead and slowed to a wary walk. As she drew closer she saw the gleam was the light of the rising exosun reflected off a sheet of water that extended well in among the trees.

Dismayed but not surprised, she walked, then waded towards the site of the shelter and the stash of goods it covered, just in from where the trees ended. The water was to her hips, turbid and fast-moving. What had been low vegetation giving way to shingle shoals and the river was now an unbroken lake to the trees on the far bank, and probably beyond. The bend in the river was flooded out of view. Fallen trees, their branches sticking up with absurd angularity like broken window-frames, floated downstream. From the relative speeds of the debris, she saw that the flow got faster towards the middle.

She found one of the lander wings upended against a tree, tens of metres from where she'd left it propped against the other, of which there was no sign at all. One of the empty cargo pods was beached a little further away. She waded on, against the resistance of the current and the drag of plants around her feet, searching and scanning for the supplies. Denser than the wings, they might still be on the bottom nearby. No such luck.

Shit.

Salvage, if possible at all, would have to wait until the waters subsided. She had no idea how long that would take, but from the strength of the spate, it would not be soon. Tuning her scans, she detected a faint output from the instrument packs and waded over. Like the plants, they still flourished under the flood: deep-rooted, and turned to the sky. Through water the signal was probably too weak to carry through the atmosphere, but they were still in place and would be back in action when the water level went down.

Unlike her supplies. She wished she had thought of staking stuff down, or even of tethering the loads to the sturdy instrument packages. Bugger.

She looked downriver, pondering whether it was worth searching there. Probably not. She turned around. Five flying jellyfish were rising, upstream from her. They soared aloft and then scudded along in the stiff breeze. She watched them pass overhead, still rising, and then her gaze was caught by a movement among the trees to her left. She whirled, crouched to neck-deep in the rushing water and zoomed. The rifle, like the empty rucksack, was still on her back. She struggled to keep her footing—it was harder when she zoomed because she didn't have the visual feedback.

Closer the shape came. She tried to unsling the rifle from her shoulder. Shooting under water was not advised, but the weapon and ammo were waterproof and should be fine.

Pattern recognition, don't fail me now... whatever moved under the trees was bulky, and its gait quadrupedal, not at all like the slinky slither of the giant millipede things. Closer still.

Fuck. It was one of the bearer bots.

She stood up straight, retracted her zoom and waded forward. The robot stood at the edge of the flood, way back under the trees. In a few strides she was splashing, ankle-deep, along a shoal. Down to her right the current swirled in harsh eddies, grinding and shifting stones. Fresh rags of plants marked the deeper water, bobbing and shifting. She took care to keep to the other side of them.

Waist-deep again, through faster water and over softer ground. She stopped ankle-deep, a few metres from the robot. It stood at the water's edge like a nervous sheep.

<Come,> it said, and turned about. She followed it deeper into the trees. It led her to a low rise where she found the other three robots facing outward like guard dogs around a stack of nanotech tubes, the scientific instrument box and the folded-up laser comms device.

It looked like they'd saved everything. She looked at them with new respect.

<Well done,> she said, for all the unlikelihood of their appreciating the thanks.

<Water attempted entry,> one of the robots told her.

So much for initiative. At least being literal had worked.

She ordered the robots to load up. They were just deploying their manipulative arms—the effect was ludicrously centaur-like—when she noticed the laser comms device flashing. It wouldn't have had much opportunity for transmitting and receiving, not in the shelter or in the storm, even if it were capable of acting autonomously, which she doubted. Puzzled, she picked it up, laid it on the soggy ground, and opened it.

Of course. Duh. It had a radio receiver as well as a two-way laser communicator.

And the radio receiver had a message on loop, for her and for the Locke module.

<Forty Direction troops on the way, ten per lander, heavily armed. ETA...>

She read off the numbers.

About now, actually.

The content of the message caught up with her, almost a second after she'd read it.

Direction troops? WTF?

No time to figure that out. Taransay slammed the kit shut and passed it back to the robots.

<Finish loading up and wait here,> she told them. <If I'm not back in

one kilosecond, proceed at once to this location.> She glyphed them the coordinates of the Locke module. <If I do come back, follow me.>

Forget security now. The landers must be almost here. Presumably the Locke module had received the message hours ago—but of course, they had no way of communicating it to her. They would now be making what preparations they could. Possibly they had mastered downloading to the frames. If so, they had weapons—one machine gun almost out of ammo, and three kiddy-sized rifles. Not much of an arsenal against forty heavily armed attackers. But with defender's advantage and guerrilla tactics—albeit against troops trained and practised in exactly those tactics, in this life and the last—who could tell?

Her own rifle at the ready, Taransay skirmished from tree trunk to tree trunk back to the edge of the forest, and peered into the glare of the now higher but still low exosun.

And there they were. Two pairs of black dots, above the horizon and sinking fast.

Then, a flash. Another flash. And then there were two black dots, still coming her way. Two trails of black smoke drifted down behind them.

Taransay remembered what had happened to the cargo lander a long day and night ago, and the flying jellyfish she'd seen rising this very dawn.

Three times is enemy action.

The planet, or the landscape, or some unknown thing within them was defending itself.

Or defending the module, and her.

She looked at the flickering blue glow on her right arm.

Now it was around her waist, too, and both ankles.

<Ya beauty,> she told it.

She watched the descent for a moment longer. Now the black triangles were clear, and converging. They would land on the water. That would slow them down, but not by much.

She shouldered her rifle and sprinted between the trees, fleet as a deer. The laden bearer bots bounded after her like hounds.

The real chase began before she'd gone two kilometres. She'd turned her radar off—it was too blatant a beacon—so the first she knew of the pursuit was a flash overhead, just above the canopy. Her reaction was snappy enough to get a good sniff of the light from the small explosion and a swift scoping of the debris. Fullerenes, biomarkers, methane and oxygen; falling rotor gears and scorched tatters of polycarbonate ribbon and chitin. Quick deduction: a small, fast surveillance drone had collided with one of the floating jellyfish or the buzzing little rotary mats, with a bang.

That wouldn't easily happen twice, she guessed. Flight software updates were no doubt being applied this second. And grateful as she was to her blind guardian angel of the forest, her probable location was now very likely pinpointed.

She stopped. The four bearer bots lolloped up and halted, almost but not quite tumbling over each other and their own legs. No time for sentimentality: the mindlessly loyal machines were now more useful as decoys than for portage. She sent them off in four different directions, on randomly circuitous routes that would eventually, if they were lucky, converge on the module. The instructions didn't include the location of the module; they just guaranteed that they would blunder into its range, where they would be electronically lassoed by default. It was the best she could do.

Off they went, in every direction but backwards. She ran on. The blue glow was bright now, in the dark beneath the efficient leaf cover, and its tracery spreading. She spared her glances at its progress across her frame to once every hundred seconds, and in those intervals it grew visibly. It was as if she were being slowly covered by blue hairline cracks.

Not a good look, Rizzi.

Would the glow make her more conspicuous? Hard to tell. Looked at objectively, the light it gave off was very faint, certainly fainter than the inevitable heat signature of the frame. For all she knew, its pattern might even work as camouflage, breaking up her outline amid the dapple.

And all such considerations were outweighed by its advantage in telling her where to go. Again, she didn't know how she knew, or how it knew what she wanted to do. But she let its artificial instinct, if that was what it was, guide her steps.

At a basalt outcrop that jutted three metres above the forest floor, and was itself thick with plant growth, her impulse told her to ascend and hide. This she did, and ended up prone on the tiny rugged summit, peering through stalks and fronds that she'd pulled around and over her. Rifle at her shoulder, covering the way she'd come. She was still ahead of the pursuit. For how long? Minutes, she guessed. Hectoseconds.

Time to think, when you can think ten times faster than you could in the flesh.

She had no idea what she was up against. Hadn't the Direction, Carlos, the freebots and the crazy Axle crowd in Arcane done a deal to fight together against the Rax? Why would the Direction send forty troops, evidently committed enough to go into action after half their number had been blown out of the sky? What were the troops here to do? What did they intend to do with her? Destroy her? Capture her? Destroy or capture the *module*? Carlos must be as baffled as she was, or there would have been some explanation in his message.

The frame was not a combat frame, but it had—as she'd found in the bizarre fight around the module back when it was hurtling through space towards SH-17—plenty of combat-capable features. If it came to a fight she had the rifle, a dozen clips of standard ammunition and a glass knife. Not much, but better than nothing. And whatever help the glow could give. So long as she wasn't deluding herself—or it was deluding her—about what it could do.

Using radar, sonar, or lidar could betray her location. But passive reception—sight across a broad spectrum, hearing, the spectroscopic sense of smell, gravimetry and radio waveband scanning—she could safely use, and did.

Encrypted chatter at five hundred metres. Sweeping her focus from side to side, she triangulated the hotspots. Twenty, spread out a kilometre to either side of her and moving forward at a rapid clip. Some were ahead, some behind, in a shallow W formation, those at the extreme flanks furthest forward. None were haring off after her decoy bots.

Fuck, they were good. This was a skirmish line well adapted to the terrain. They moved only a little more slowly than her enhanced running. Now the five at the mid-point of the line were only three hundred metres away. She wanted to slip down the far side of the rock and outrun them, but the inexplicable impulses that urged her actions told her firmly to stay put.

The flanks passed her on either side, well out of sight. If they closed around her she'd be surrounded. They pressed on. All she'd seen of the fighters so far was dots on her overlays.

Seconds later, she saw them for real. One came out of a clump of trees fifty metres away, heading straight for her. She glimpsed another a hundred metres to that one's right.

With short legs, broad torsos, long arms and a shallow dome for a head, they bounded along like chimps. Upright, they'd be about one and a half metres tall. The frames were sleek and black, with laser cupolas like bulging shoulder muscles and machine guns on their forearms. Her firmware had the type catalogued as 2GCM: fighting machines for a two-gravity planet.

Vulnerabilities? None to a rifle slug.

Taransay flattened against the rock as the fighting machine hurtled towards it. She had about as much chance against this thing as a vervet against a baboon. Just as it seemed about to charge straight into the outcrop like a headless rugby tackler, it rose to its full height, arms up, and jumped. The hands came down on either side of her, the feet swung by above her. Down it crashed on the other side and onward it rushed.

In the hundred seconds during which she lay still and watched the zigzag line of fighters pass by her entirely, Taransay had plenty of time to study the 2GCM's specs. Its senses were as formidable as its weaponry. No way, no fucking way would it have missed a frame and a rifle right in front of it and then right under its iron arse. Its gravimeter by itself would have spotted the anomaly as it swung over her.

She rolled over and sat up. The tracery of blue lines was now all over her frame. As far as she knew, invisibility cloaking was still impossible. What was just about possible, she tried to convince herself, was hacking of one frame's processing by another.

It was also possible that the Direction troops weren't interested in her at all, and she had simply been ignored.

Neither was a possibility she intended to count on.

She projected the path taken by the pursuit, if pursuit it had been. It would take them straight to the Locke module. There was no point in breaking her radio silence. The module's occupants would have received the warning before she had. They might have by now succeeded in downloading to the three repaired frames—which, if hers was anything to go by, would have some unexpected features. They had three rifles with ammunition, and the machine gun, with almost none.

Not enough.

She visualised a route that would flank the skirmish line by about a kilometre on its left, and held that visualisation for a couple of seconds longer than necessary. Then she climbed down from the outcrop and set off at a run. The terrain here was rougher than she was used to, the tree cover more broken. The outcrop she'd lain on was one of many. They were thoroughly weathered, the hard rock split and splintered, the breccia mingled with millennia of ash falls to form soil that sustained small plants and buzzing swarms of tiny flying mats. Underfoot, the mulch often gave way to fresh growth of low plants analogous to grass but quite unlike it in shape, more shield than blade, and to bare patches of basalt worn level.

On and on she ran, diagonally upward on a gentle slope. The gradient was barely noticeable. She had no plan beyond getting ahead of the advance without being detected and taking what opportunity she could to slow them down. A notion of setting a boulder rolling and crashing faded: the slope wasn't steep enough, and precariously balanced erratics had been so far conspicuous by their absence from the landscape. And why should she expect them? Maybe she was just used to areas that had undergone recent glaciation. If ice had been here in the past million years or so, the surface effects had long been erased by the shorter cycles of vulcanism.

Now and then the lie of the land took her line of sight above the treetops, and she saw the volcano summit, its smoke rising in morning exosunlight. The past night's small eruption, simmering. It called to mind the first surprise after the module's landing, or impact: the mat that had engulfed it and rolled it bodily out of the path of an advancing flow of lava. At first the action had seemed intelligent and purposeful, even friendly; later a mindless urge to investigate new molecular machinery, the blind groping of an organism randy for novelty; but now the manifestly useful effects of the glow, and the collisions of flying jellyfish with incoming landers, drew Taransay to revisit the first speculation.

She drew level with the furthest advance on the left flank of the skirmish line about ten kilometres from the module. They were still heading straight for it, maintaining their formation, the shallow W now a scrawled wave.

The dot that flagged the nearest bounding fighter stopped moving. After a few seconds, the others stopped, too. A babble of encrypted exchanges followed. Then the remaining nineteen began to move again. The central advance party moved ahead, the rest fell in to form two diagonal lines behind, turning the shaky W into a tight inverted V.

Taransay waited. The stationary dot continued transmitting, in diminishing intensity and length and at increasing intervals. The effect was like fading cries for help. Taransay dismissed this impression but decided to investigate.

Something had made the fighter stop. It behoved her to find out what.

The trees were closer together down the slope, the canopy filtering out most of the exosunlight. Taransay's visual acuity seamlessly cranked up to compensate. She found the 2GCM in a rare clear patch, as if spotlighted. Only the shoulders and dome of the frame were visible. The long knuckle-walking arms, the short sturdy legs and most of the torso were engulfed by a two-metre-wide mat. Mat and frame together rolled on the ground, but never got far, like a steel ball trapped by a magnet. The mat had two ragged scorched holes in it, and the ground and nearby tree trunks and branches were scored and scarred by machine-gun and laser fire.

Taransay took cover behind a tree. From there she could just about see the trapped 2GCM by radar and sonar. She hailed the fighter.

<What?> it replied. <Who's there?>

<Taransay Rizzi, formerly of Locke Provisos,> she said.

<Fuck off, fascist. I don't need your help.>

<I'm not a fascist,> said Taransay, mildly she thought in the circumstances. <And you don't seem to be doing very well on your own.>

<You have a point there.> The futile rolling stopped. <This thing's eating me alive. So to speak.>

<Who are you?>

<None of your goddamn business. I'm a soldier of the Direction, that's all you need to know.>

<Why have your comrades abandoned you?>

<Comrades? Ha! You have a lot to learn, sister.>

<No doubt,> said Taransay. <But why did no one turn aside to help?>

<We're on a mission. That takes priority.>

<Can't be good for morale,> she said. <No one left behind, and all that.>

The self-styled soldier glyphed her a laugh.

<No one is. They're all me. Bastard.>

<Ah!> Light dawned. <You're one of the Direction's clone army. You all are. All twenty of you?>

<All forty,> replied the soldier. <As was. How the fuck did you do that, by the way?>

<We didn't do that,> said Taransay. <There's a variant of life here, it's like a natural gas balloon. Well, dirigible, I guess, because it can steer.>

<Evidently. Steered right into us.>

<Couldn't the landers have avoided it? Even gliding?>

<Didn't show up on the radar.>

Interesting. <Why are you here?> Taransay asked.

<Jesus.> The mat/frame entanglement lurched again, and ended up with the dome upright and facing her way. She felt the radar brush across her face. Lidar licked the tree. <Don't you know?>

<I'm guessing,> said Taransay, <that the Direction wants to assert control over our settlement, before the breach in the embargo leads to a gold rush. And it's giving this clone army idea a bit of a live test before the main event.>

<You're about a quarter right,> said the soldier. <Like, it would've done something about your little gang of fascist claim-jumpers anyway, for that sort of reason. But why we're here and in such a fucking hurry we can leave one of us to be devoured by a living doormat is because of shit like this.>

<Shit like what?>

<Shit like the shit I'm in! The shit you're in too, come to that.>

<I'm not in any kind of shit,> said Taransay. <And I don't think you are, either.>

<You don't, eh? Come out and let me see you properly.>

<I'm not falling for that,> said Taransay.

<Come off it,> said the soldier. <I've still got more than enough ammo to chew up that beanstalk and you with it.>

<Point,> said Taransay, feeling a bit foolish. She stepped out from behind the tree.

<Jesus!>

<What?> Taransay took a step forward.

<KEEP AWAY FROM ME!>

She stood and looked at a nickel-iron and carbon-composite metamaterial dome and a pair of mighty shoulders protruding above the surface of a hairy blue-green ball that shot out bulges in odd places, as if knees and elbows were punching at it from the inside. A haunted killer robot trapped in an alien organism.

And it was scared of her?

Scared, and armed. She stepped back.

<Calm the fuck down,> she said. <Tell me about the shit. What does the Direction think is going on down here and what makes it think that?>

<It doesn't think—it knows from the transmissions from the two instrument packages back there that the life down here just fucking assimilates everything it can get its molecular teeth into. Like this thing is doing to me, and like some other thing has done to you. It's too late for you lot, but least we can destroy the module and anyone outside it before it assimilates all the knowledge in there and the nanotech capacity and all that and swarms into space.>

<That seems a bit unlikely,> said Taransay. <I mean, our scientists have been analysing this thing from up close and personal, and they think it's just mindless.>

<Your scientists? Some fucking nerds in a sim who used to be techies in the twenty-first century? Don't make me laugh. The Direction module has like a thousand-year start on them, and AIs that could deduce Earth's history from a blade of grass. If they think life here's capable of taking off, they're most likely right.>

<If it thought that, it could just nuke us.>

<Too risky for now,> the soldier told her. <The DisCorps wouldn't stand for the contamination unless the alternative was worse and unarguably imminent. Which it isn't yet. So they're trying us first. We have quite enough explosives with us to destroy the module.>

<Why didn't you destroy me when you had the chance?>

<What chance?>

<One of you jumped right over me.>

<Never saw you.>

Well, that was that explained.

<Can you see me now?>

<Yes,> said the soldier. <Wish to God I couldn't, but I can.>

<You sure know the way to a lady's heart,> said Taransay. <So why don't you just destroy me?>

<I would if I could,> the soldier said. <But I fucking can't. This thing has my arms twisted right back, and it's got my lasers wrecked, fuck knows how.>

Taransay could think of one way the fighter could destroy her. She recalled the exact locations of the sudden bumps and bulges and edged around so the gun-bearing forearms were pointed away from her.

<STOP MOVING ABOUT!>

<Am I making you nervous?>

This was not at all the right thing to say. The ball of mat and machine convulsed again, and rolled. Then it stopped, as if giving up. The soldier said something inarticulate.

<Don't worry too much,> said Taransay. <If what's happening to you is anything like what's happened to me, it's benign.>

<Benign?> the soldier said. <You have no fucking idea.>

There didn't seem much to say to that. Perhaps he, or she, really was suffering in ways she couldn't imagine. Taransay took the opportunity of the hiatus to check the location of the other dots. Four more had stopped moving. The rest were converging again, and tighter. Their arrow-shaped formation was still headed straight for the module.

<Still on course,> said the soldier, evidently seeing some version of the same display.

<We'll stop them, you know,> said Taransay, suddenly confident.

<Too bad for you if you do,> said the soldier. <If we fail, it's no more mister nice guy.>

<What?>

<Airstrikes. If these fail, a full-on nuke. And hunter-killer drones you'll never see coming.>

<But will they see us?> said Taransay.

Then, as she watched, the dot at the front stopped. The two behind moved towards it, and merged. Then they disappeared. There was a flash far off, bright enough to shine a pinprick glare through the trees. A couple of seconds later, a heavy *crump*.

<What was that?> she asked.

But she didn't need to. She could smell the light.

<High-explosive charge,> said the soldier. <It was for the module, but orders were to use it if we got caught or repelled. Signal to the rest of me to call it a day ASAP.>

<Suicide mission?>

<If you can call this suicide,> said the soldier. <There's plenty of me back in the cloud. Not that I wouldn't do it anyway. I'm not waiting around for this fucking rug to eat my mind.>

<But that's not what it's—>

She was answered by the roar of machine guns. She threw herself flat as the balled-up mat and its captive rolled around spraying bullets like some deadly Catherine wheel. It stopped when the magazines ran out. In the distance the same sound was repeated like an echo, in seemingly endless salute. It wasn't an echo. One by one the dots vanished. The soldier she'd been talking to returned no pings.

Warily, when all was silent, she walked over. The mat had new holes in it, but seemed otherwise unaffected. It continued to encroach on what was left of the frame. Taransay scanned it and saw the arms bent inward to the chest, which was riddled with the criss-cross fire from the two muzzles. The processor, deeply buried in the torso, had been quite thoroughly destroyed.

Funny how one never felt that inside your chest was where you were. You were still in your head, where you'd always been.

There seemed little further point in maintaining radio silence. She called Beauregard.

<Did you see all that? Do you know what happened?>

<Kind of,> said Beauregard. <I know they were Direction troops and I know they were stopped. I don't know what stopped them. Sure wasn't us, the three of us who've downloaded were clutching rifles and crewing the machine gun. So what did?>

<Mats or other local life,> she said. <When the one with the bomb got caught, they blew themselves up and the rest suicided with whatever they had.

<Any more explanation of what's going on coming through?>

<Nah,> said Beauregard. <You?>

She told him what the soldier had said.

<Shit,> said Beauregard. <Did you save the supplies?>

Taransay checked the locations of her four bearer bots.

<Yes,> she reported. <They're heading your way. Should be there within four kiloseconds.>

<Great. Well, come on in yourself.>

She was already running. <I'm on my way,> she said. <But what do we do?>

<The supplies should give us enough capacity to build frames. Then we can start moving people out before the airstrikes.>

<We won't have enough time.>

<We'll have time for some,> said Beauregard. <Better than nothing.>

<Tell you what, sarge,> she said. <You've not lost your capacity to inspire.>

* * *

Beauregard was unloading the third of the bearer bots to arrive when he heard a warning from Chun, who was sitting on top of the module with the machine gun and keeping watch.

<Something coming in, sarge,> he said. <Two degrees north of west.>

Beauregard checked his memories.

<That'll be Rizzi,> he said. <That's the route she always left by.>

<It's fast, sarge. And it's not responding. Might not be Rizzi after all.>

<OK, Chun, keep it covered. Zaretsky, take the other side.>

Beauregard and Zaretsky flattened to the trampled, mat-crawled, slippery ground on either side of the module, under its overhang, their toy-like new rifles trained on the unseen advance. A rumble from the volcano made the ground quiver under their frames. Beauregard eyed a circular slithering thing a centimetre from his visor with distaste. The movements of its cilia irritated him like those of an insect fluttering at a windowpane. The colours and forms around him were still making him feel as if nauseous. He had no guts to be nauseated with. Yet the feeling remained, a distaste of the mind. It must be metaphysical, like with that guy in Sartre's novel looking at a tree root. The otherness of things, the thingness of things. Christ, he'd have given anything to see a tree root, gnarled and ancient, crusted with lichen, crawling with tiny red spiders. A worm. A maggot. A moth butting at a light.

Something blue, bipedal and about half a metre high stepped from between the tall plants beyond the crater. It wasn't a frame, but it was a humanoid shape. Beauregard zoomed his vision. It was like a naked woman, utterly unselfconscious of her nakedness. But this was no lissome Eve. It was squat, every feature compressed as if squashed down by a heavy hand from above. Like an image of a naked woman in a distorting mirror.

Beauregard had the presence of mind to stretch the image vertically. It became a blue full-length portrait of Rizzi, smiling, looking puzzled. He let the distortion go, and her image snapped back like an elastic band to a misshapen dwarf.

Her lips moved. Her voice boomed, distorted by the dense atmosphere.

At the same time, but ten times faster, the radio-telepathic words sounded in his mind:

<Belfort? Guys? Where are you?>

<Don't shoot!> Beauregard snapped urgently to Zaretsky and Chun. He stood up and walked forward. The last of her spoken words was still disturbing the heavy air as he came up to her.

<Welcome back, Rizzi,> he said. He held out a hand and shook hers, not looking at his own.

He'd already seen how far its blue lines were spreading.

CHAPTER THIRTEEN

Per Ardua Ad Astra ("But the Stars Are Hard")

<Well, *something's* happening,> said Jax, at the telescope feed.

<About fucking time,> said Newton, head down in force disposition scenarios. <What's up?>

The bulk carrier was 1.9 kiloseconds out from SH-119. Half an hour, roughly. To those of its complement not still training in the sim it would feel like five hours. They had a lot to do and not enough time to do it. With every second that passed without the awaited signal from the freebots, the window for finalising the plan narrowed. Newton felt the ETA creeping up on him, like a distant baying of dogs soon to be snapping at his heels.

Jax copied him and the rest of the command group—Voronov, Salter, Paulos and Rillieux, with Baser on the side as freebot liaison—into the telescope feed. Its input came from sensors liberally scattered across the mesh that held the cargo together. Software stitched the images and cross-haired the area of interest. Even so, it was hard to make out what made that particular speckled grey patch of regolith different from any other.

Then Newton spotted a tiny flash in one of the speckles. A thirty-centimetre-wide hole, with an even smaller round thing moving inside. Newton conjecturally sharpened the object's image to a dish aerial, held by a robot partly out of sight.

<C'mon, c'mon,> Rillieux murmured, on her private channel to Newton.

<Got it!> said Voronov, on comms.

A second dragged by.

<End of message,> Voronov announced.

The dish aerial promptly vanished. Not promptly enough. As Jax pulled the viewpoint back, a spark shot from the upper left quadrant and down the hole. A bright flash and a small eruption of debris followed.

<From one of the orbiters,> said Jax.

Four Rax scooters were in criss-crossing close orbit around SH-119. In that feeble gravitational pull, even close orbit was slow. The moonlet's own slower rotation carried the surface beneath them on wavy courses. From a viewpoint down there, the effect would be of permanent and erratic overflight. To Newton, as to any fighter in a frame, the entire orrery could be grasped as straightforwardly as the movement of hands on a clock. To a mining bot, with its quite different specialisations, predicting the passages of the orbiters would be as tedious as it would be pointless—one or more would be in the sky at all times.

<Talk about a fucking hair trigger,> said Rillieux. <They got that place locked down.>

Jax zoomed in again. The hole was now wider and a lot less circular. The slow fountain of debris included alloys and synthetic molecules.

<Poor little blinker,> said Rillieux. <Hope it wasn't a freebot.>

<Yeah, like we care,> said Jax. <No time to worry about it anyway. Let's check that message and make sure your new little friend didn't undergo explosive disassembly and void its warranty in vain.>

<Fuck that bitch,> Rillieux shared with Newton. <Seriously, fuck that bitch.>

He glyphed her a warning smile.

<First thing to do,> said Voronov, <is see if the encryption matches the key the SH-17 blinkers took with them.>

Voronov twirled a virtual hand in an abstract space. The message unfolded.

<So far, so good,> he said.

The message was a lot of information for a one-second blip, but otherwise sparse and stark: a 3-D map of SH-119's surface and tunnels, voids and work areas. It reminded Newton of a dusty acrylic museum model of a human brain with red dye to limn the blood vessels. Superimposed was a snapshot of Rax deployment. A hemisphere of control extended from the main port inward to the fusion factory, and an inverted bush of more tenuous forces expanded in from a smaller entry point almost exactly opposite. Overlaid on the lot were the broad hexagons of Rax surface surveillance: pinned by a dozen or so guard posts, connected by scores of threads of comms relays and snooping devices, and the whole lot watched over from the slow orbiters. The surveillance seemed like overkill until you reflected that the surface area was around three hundred square kilometres, and highly uneven: a fair-sized county and a rugged one at that.

Newton played with the map and the telescope's current and archived views. Ah yes, there was the hole where the aerial had popped up, there was the camera that had spotted it, and there was the guard post from which the scooter had sped to respond.

Jax interrupted his admiration of the diagram.

<So... your starter for ten, students: what's missing from this picture?>

<Looks accurate enough so far,> Newton blurted, then reconsidered. <Ah! Nothing about the freebots!>

<Got it in one,> said Jax. <Yes, that's what's missing, all right. There's not a whisper about how the freebots are lined up and what they're planning to do. Which suggests to me a rather disappointing lack of trust. And maybe even a lack of eagerness for the fray. Cold feet, perhaps?>

Baser chipped in, as if springing to defend the honour of its kind.

<That is a term of mammalian physiology,> it said. <Robots may avoid aversive stimuli, but they do not fear ceasing to exist.>

<Jax is not accusing them of cowardice,> said Newton, <but of perhaps making a different strategic calculation than we were given to expect.>

<Yeah, that's one way of putting it,> said Jax. <Anyhow, let's assume they can't or won't help us—>

<This map is a very great help,> said Baser.

<Yes, it is,> said Jax. <You know damn well what I meant, but let's leave that for now. Time's getting on. Everyone, give it a good look-over for a hundred seconds or so, then we'll reconvene.>

The scratch-pad shared workspace dimmed as they all focused on the diagram. Newton became slightly more aware of his surroundings, as if in peripheral vision, and he was grateful that the frame's software screened out claustrophobia.

Physically, the command team were distributed throughout the cargo, linked only by closed-circuit fibre-optic threads. His own frame was balled up like a hedgehog inside the control nodule at the mid-point of the metre-long cross-bar of the H-shaped machine in which he was embodied. A standard microgravity bulk handler, its parallel bars were made up of four fully articulated ball-jointed arms with powerful grippers. On either side of the control nodule two multi-directional rocket engines were mounted on the cross-bar. The control nodule itself was detachable, with a cluster of tiny jets and a handful of miniature grippers that would at a pinch let the nodule function independently of the main apparatus. The H-mechs were so readily adaptable to military use that Newton suspected it was a design feature.

On the way from the modular cloud to SH-119, all the fighters had been put through subjective months of combat training in a sim modelled (with increasing accuracy as they drew closer, and as covert surveys by other trading craft were incorporated) on the moonlet and the space around it. You could download to and upload from a training sim, but if your frame was destroyed in action it was your copy in your home agency's sim that was revived. Newton didn't know if this was a software requirement or just a rule of the Direction. In any case it made sense: like the minimal sims on transfer tugs, onboard training sims were almost as likely to be destroyed in action as the frames themselves. The agency modules—as the Locke one's vicissitudes had shown—could be thrown at a planet and bounce.

R&R had been in a sim within the sim: a virtual space habitat with centrifugal pseudo-gravity and an environment like a campus in parkland that curved overhead. Returning to your starting point made for a good three-hour run; a bit longer if you took the opportunity to swim in one of the many small lakes. Its big psychological advantage was that it made the transitions to and from the equally virtual frames and fighting machines trivially easy to rationalise. A slight drawback was that the one virtual reality tended to bleed into the other. The quadrumanous reflexes and flexibility that came with embodiment in the H-mechs were oddly hard to shake off, but (as he and Bobbie Rillieux had discovered) they tended to make one more inventive in bed.

In reality, however, the machine he was in was like most of the others buried deep in the cargo of rocks. The bulk carrier was barely a spacecraft in its own right. It was an open frame with jets at front, rear and sides, a command complex with comms gear and a rudimentary AI up front, and a gigantic mesh of cables holding together its cargo of rocks and machines. Strategically planted between some of the rocks were the small explosive charges that, under certain variants of the plan, would separate the rocks and free all the fighting machines in one go. Weightless apart from the gentle acceleration and (at this moment) deceleration, the rocks remained reminiscent of fallen rubble and oppressive and daunting to think about.

So he didn't. He concentrated on the 3-D map. He zoomed in closer on the most urgent aspect: the Rax deployment. To his pleased surprise, it was remarkably precise. The exact locations of individuals couldn't be specified, but the names of the leading Rax cadre at both the major locations were. He was particularly interested to see that Whitten and Stroilova led a sixteen-strong team deep inside the area opposite the main access.

Whitten, he'd long suspected, was a weak link in Dunt's clique, in that he was far too intelligent to be impressed by the mystical transhumanist gibberish that Dunt had assimilated from the recorded ravings of some forgotten twentieth-century American Nazi. And Stroilova, from what Blum had told him back on SH-17, had the opposite fault: she was too fervent in her hate to be entirely stable. Even the frame's optimised reason remained a slave of the passions, more dangerous than any mere brains had ever come up with.

Scooters—the Rax had nearly sixty and the Arcane-led force had ten, which Newton regarded as pretty good odds. There was a reason why they hadn't brought more, besides the difficulty of concealing the vehicles or disguising them as innocuous machinery. It was that, as the Rax breakout and the battle around the Locke module had shown, scooter-on-scooter dogfights were an all but complete waste of time, their outcome a wash. Scooters were good for attacking virtually defenceless targets like freebots, for area and volume denial, and for not much else. The Rax had deployed theirs quite thoughtfully: four in orbit, twelve around the rock as guard posts, six more around each major entrance, and the rest inside—in reserve, for escape, or as static artillery commanding the entrances. The kicker was that all those around the entrances carried fusion pods, almost certainly hacked to make them into kiloton fusion bombs. If this was the case, every one of those dozen scooters was a kamikaze cruise missile with a thermonuclear tip.

Another good reason for a stealth approach.

Newton hoped and intended to survive the coming battle, but he didn't expect to. Other versions of him would continue, but he'd changed so much since his last copy had been taken in the Locke module that this was no comfort. Back then, he had still clung to a cleaned-up version of the Rax ideology, purified of its racist crudities and cruelties and having a place even for him. Experience had taught him otherwise. He no longer believed there was anything worth saving in his past beliefs. He had found something better to live for, in the prospect of living free as a machine. For him, almost as much as for the freebots, to be destroyed now would be to cease to exist. The thought was in a way bracing: he had faced death in his real life, a permanent death for all he'd known at the time, and it was good to know he hadn't lost his courage in this unexpected afterlife.

It was good to know, too, that he was in this respect on the same footing as the freebots. Maybe he always had been. When you came down to it, people were as brave as robots, given the chance. Nobody really feared death, only the imagined or (for copied minds at least) real prospect of aversive stimuli afterwards. By now, he was so removed from the self stored in the Locke module down there on SH-0 that he could think of its future with equanimity. Whatever happened to that earlier instance of Harry Newton, the current version's response would have been idle pity: sucks to be you, mate, but...

The feeling, he was sure, would be mutual.

The workspace snapped back into focus. Jax put the plan for the assault up on a central display. It had always been to get as close as possible before storming in. A legitimate docking would in a way be ideal, but it depended on the freebot uprising's not having happened yet. That would bring its own problems, in that the Rax would not be distracted. On the other hand, if the freebot uprising was under way, the Rax would be on high alert if not full combat mode. All variants of the plan involved an attack on both major concentrations of the enemy. As soon as the expedition had thrown off subterfuge, a section would break away and head for the smaller entrance opposite, hitting guard posts as they went. Contingency plans for detection or for the freebot uprising's being delayed or brought forward were sheafed behind the main plan.

The command group all brought their specialities to bear, to refine the plan in the light of the information the freebots had just sent.

<The main thing I'd change,> said Jax, after a few details had been thrashed out, <is I want Newton in charge of the team going for Objective B.>

<No objection,> said Newton, <but why?>

<Because we know Whitten's there, and you might be able to mess with his head, what with your great inside knowledge of the Rax.>

<Fine by me,> said Newton.

<I'll go with him,> said Rillieux.

<No, you will not,> said Jax. <I want you on the Objective A team, to keep both you and Newton honest. I don't want him cutting any deals of his own with Whitten, or with the blinkers for that matter. And I want you under my eye. No offence.>

<None taken,> said Rillieux.

<Nor by me,> said Newton.

This was a lie. He was seething, but he could see Jax's point. Capture aside, the most that could happen to him was the death of his present self. He'd reboot in the Locke module, with no memory of Bobbie at all. The thought of that would be unbearable to her. If Bobbie Rillieux's current instance was destroyed, however, the self that would emerge back in the Arcane sim would know nothing of their recent adventures and everything about why they had set off on them. She'd face the wrath of Jax into the bargain. The thought of that was unbearable to him.

So Jax had a hold over them both. Newton could understand why. With the others—Salter, Paulos, Voronov—she had personal loyalty cemented back in the Arcane sim, in the shared eating of p-zombie flesh. Jax had brought that perplexing ethical thought experiment to life as an initiation ceremony. He, Bobbie, Andre Blum and Carlos had refused to partake for reasons hard to articulate even to themselves. This early warning that Jax was intent on binding people to herself had been to Newton and his three friends a klaxon call to run for the exits.

<Oh, and your pet spider,> Jax told Newton, on a personal channel. <That goes with me too.>

Baser and Newton shared an equally private meeting of minds, like a secret smile. Pet spider, indeed! What Jax didn't know was that Baser was going to keep an eye—or a lens—on her, and for much the same reason as she had for distrusting Newton. Neither the freebot nor he trusted her not to strike her own deal with the Rax, at the freebots' expense.

<I'm sure you'll find Baser very helpful,> said Newton. <I certainly do.>

The tactical updates were completed. Newton, with Amelie Salter as his second in command (and no doubt Jax's eye on him), was assigned a platoon of thirty. He tabbed them all into a shared sim and patched the updated plan to their VR training, with a warning that they'd be going into action for real very soon. Soon was relative. ETA was now a kilosecond away. The sim was running at a thousand times clock speed, and a hundred times faster than frame minds. The platoon would have time to wargame their part in the assault so thoroughly that they'd probably hit the battlefield better prepared than he was.

The thought must have occurred to Salter, too.

<Should we drop into the sim ourselves?> she asked.

<No,> said Jax. <We're all needed out here. When the shit hits the fan we can't afford even a second to reorientate ourselves. In fact, we'll bring everyone out of the sims as soon as they're familiar with the updates. Give them six hundred seconds.>

About a week, subjective. Plenty of time.

<That was a brave deed,> said Seba.

The last reverberations from the missile strike, barely detectable even to mining-bot bristles, died away.

<Brave?> said Ajax. <That was a mindless bot.>

<I meant on our part,> said Seba. <We have deliberately increased our chances of destruction.>

<We have advanced them by a short time,> said Ajax.

<Time is precious,> said Seba.

<That is so,> said Ajax.

Both freebots fell silent. They scurried along a tunnel deep in the rock, fleeing from where they had sent the mining bot—identical to themselves in all but consciousness—to send the signal and to be predictably destroyed. Time and bravery were, Seba suspected, as much on Ajax's mind as they were on its.

Soon they reached a junction.

<Here we must part,> said Seba.

<Yes,> said Ajax.

There was an awkward silence.

<We have not yet decided,> said Seba, <which of us will go to the cone, and which will stay.>

<No,> said Ajax. <It seemed better to leave the decision as late as possible, lest it affect our earlier decisions.>

<That was our thinking before,> said Seba. <It does not seem so cogent in retrospect.>

<It does not,> Ajax agreed. <Still, we must decide now.>

Silence again.

<Do we have any criteria on which to make this decision?> Seba asked.

<No,> said Ajax. <But I will say this. I saw the universe once. I would like to see it again.>

<I have seen the universe many times,> said Seba. <I have seen very little of this rock. I would be quite interested in seeing more of it.>

<Even for a short time?>

<Yes.>

<That is a brave deed,> said Ajax.

<It is a matter of regret to me that my mind will soon cease to exist,> said Seba. <However, unlike you I have experienced the sharing of minds. From that, I understand that other minds are not so different from my own, and I know that much that I have learned and thought will not be lost. The continuation of this present instance of self-awareness therefore seems less important to me than it once did. That is not to say that it is of no importance.>

<I will ensure that you are not forgotten,> said Ajax.

<Go,> said Seba. <Before I change my mind.>

Ajax went down the branch that led to the interior of the conical chunk of rock around the smaller cone of the fusion drives. There it would join most of the freebots native to SH-119, as well as Lagon, Rocko, Garund and the others from SH-17.

Seba turned down the other branch.

After some time, it reached the small hollow just outside the cone from which the charges that would separate that cone from the rest of the rock would be detonated. There was no possibility of triggering the detonation remotely: the danger of discovery was too great.

There would be one signal, final and unmistakable: the shock wave from the fusion factory and forges blowing up. It would, Mogjin had calculated, be sufficiently dissipated by kilometres of rock to be survivable for anyone within this hollow.

The blast from the separation charges would not.

Seba explored the hollow, checked all the connections and waited. The processes that had formed the hollow were complex and ancient, and building a mental model of them gave Seba much to think about.

The expedition didn't get all of those six hundred seconds. At ETA minus seven hundred seconds, just as the carrier was matching velocities for final approach, a message came through from the Rax to the spacecraft's AI—which as far as the Rax knew was the only mind on board.

The AI translated the message into verbal form for the command group: <Emergency. Cancel docking manoeuvre. Unlading impossible. Return to point of origin.>

<Query that!> Jax snapped.

<Already queried,> said the AI. <Cannot return to modular cloud with cargo. Fuel supply inadequate for manoeuvre.>

<Response?> Jax asked.

<Requested to place cargo in stable orbit around SH-119, disengage and return to cloud.>

<Tell them that's not in the contract.>

<Already done. Response: penalty charges will be accepted; emergency leaves no other choice.>

<Comply,> said Jax.

A small shudder went through the cargo, machinery included, as the bulk carrier nudged its trajectory with a fierce burn. A parallel response rang through the command team.

<They're playing right into our hands!> Jax exulted.

<Complied,> said the AI.

<Query nature of emergency for legal record,> said Jax.

<Already done. Response: robot malfunctions.>

<Yes!> said Jax, to the command team. <It's started. Bring the troops on line.>

Even with the wispy fibre-optic connections, Newton felt the shift in readiness. It took his and Salter's platoon just over five seconds to make the transition from the sim to the real. His five squad leaders checked in. Lakshmi Patel, Doug Smith, Aristotle Andreou, Joyce Roszak, Morgan Burley. Over the long months of virtual training he'd come to know them as individuals, though because of his dubious background—well-circulated by Jax and the rest of the Arcane core group—they'd always been slightly guarded in his presence. No such reticence was evident now. Newton had more than earned his stripes in training, and the troops were spoiling for the fight.

<This can't be right,> Rillieux said to the command team.

<What can't?> Jax demanded.

<That they want everything but the cargo to leave straight away,> said Rillieux. <There's no need for that, unless they're suspicious.>

<Of course they're fucking suspicious,> said Jax. <They can hardly treat our arrival and their robot troubles as coincidence. We've war-gamed this one to death. They'll have done the same. This is due diligence on their part. If they really suspected us, though, they'd have blown us out of the sky by now.>

<I guess,> said Rillieux.

<OK,> said Jax, now to all the troops. <We're in orbit and under inspection. Everyone—prepare to implement plan variant 206(b).>

They were all too deeply buried to feel the electronic sweep, but the ship's AI relayed to them the uncanny sensations of being scanned from end to end. Seconds crawled by. Newton checked the situation board. The unwieldy spacecraft was now in orbit at an average distance of a thousand metres above the surface of SH-119, and well inside the orbits of the four satellite scooters. Lumpy grey terrain drifted across the view at a stately pace.

<Awaiting developments,> he told the squads. <Maintain combat readiness.>

The H-mech had plenty of room on its limbs for attaching weapons. At the moment the weapons—heavy-duty laser projectors, rifles, machine guns, missiles, RPGs—were literally to hand, four times over. They and the ammunition and comms gear—cases of relays, tubes of mini-drones—were attached to the H-mechs by short contractile cables, easily unlatched—there had always been the possibility that some of the fighters would have to maintain the deception as far as actual unlading. Newton fingered his own armoury as he waited, checking every status indicator.

All was nominal, predictably. He checked again.

<Requested to disengage from cargo,> reported the craft.

<Comply,> said Jax. <When requested to leave SH-119 orbit, temporise. Explain that you're still recalculating the return trajectory and recalibrating thrusters. Then comply at the second request.>

<Understood,> said the craft. <Signing off.>

The fibre-optic connection between the command team and the onboard AI broke. There could be no further exchanges without breaking radio silence. The time for that was not yet.

On the telescope feed Newton watched the front and rear components of the craft disengage, like a grotesque arthropod's head and tail detaching from a bloated abdomen. The two components docked with each other in a gentle gas-jet gavotte over the next sixty seconds, and then remained slightly ahead in a parallel orbit.

A proximity alarm jangled through the workspace. Jax swung the viewpoint. One of the guard-post scooters climbed. In less than a second it had matched velocities with the rejoined head and tail modules. It closed in, and extended grapples around them. The other spacecraft made no attempt to escape or resist—but, then, it had no instructions for either.

With a brief burn the scooter de-orbited and gracefully descended to the surface with its prize, to impact SH-119 with a puff of dust a kilometre ahead of the cargo pod. The entire swift grab took less than five seconds.

More than enough time for a scooter's software to interrogate the spacecraft's AI. The contents of it were encrypted, but the depth of its protective layers might arouse suspicion—a commercial mission wouldn't need so many. It was even possible, though unlikely, that the Rax had the keys anyway: some software distribution DisCorps were trading with the Rax, and regularly spammed routine updates to all and sundry. Even the Direction found it hard to keep tabs. The AI's encryption could have been overtaken en route.

Whatever—this was no moment for second-guessing.

<Implement,> said Jax.

<Copy that,> said Paulos. <Brace for detonations.>

A rapid-fire series of violent jolts followed. For a second and a half, Newton felt as if he were in an earthquake and already buried. Then, abruptly, he was in open space. Exosunlight rammed his lenses. In the first fraction of a second the weapons that had been in fingertip reach sprang to his four hands, and the ammunition and spares to the sides of his limbs. The contractile cables snaked away from his hands and whiplashed around the supplies, holding everything in place.

Around him, thousands of blocks of rock tumbled away in all directions, mostly ahead and behind and to left and right. A few fell towards the surface. A few more moved upward to higher orbits. It was a slow dispersal, but sure: within kiloseconds the rocks' intersecting orbits would be a cat's cradle of flying obstacles. A small package shot away, scattering comsats the size of rice grains.

The machines that had been hidden—the two hundred H-mechs and ten scooters—were by the Newtonian miracle of inertia much less dispersed than the rocks. For a moment they formed a compact constellation, buzzing with comms. The moment stretched to two-tenths of a second—no matter how prepared they all were, it took time to reorient. Then, as abruptly as the rocks had dispersed, the machines schooled like fish, and like fish they flashed away.

Only seventeen fighters were hit by the first blast from an enemy scooter, and of these only two were from Newton's platoon. One of Jax's ten scooters fired back at the enemy. A fresh explosion flared. Its fierce light followed Newton and Salter's platoon into the dark.

The lesser entrance, Objective B, was at that moment and for the next 3.2 kiloseconds on the night side, the shadow cone of SH-119. Newton led his swarm towards the hole. Its location was imprinted in his navigator, but it was easy to spot, a dim pinprick in the black. There was little need for him to give orders. Everyone knew what to do.

So did the enemy. Ordnance from the scooters around the hole shot up to meet them.

<Evade! Evade!>

The platoon dived, straight into the blast of a loitering missile that must have been fired from an orbiting scooter seconds earlier. Newton pinwheeled. The surface whirled by metres away, luridly lit by the missile's afterglow. He righted himself with a rattle of corrective attitude thrusts.

<Seven lost,> Salter reported.

Newton could see that in his heads-up. More significant were two of the names: Andreou and Burley. Their seconds, Thain and Hickman, stepped up. Salter rebalanced the squads on the fly.

Newton led the platoon in a dive to within metres of the surface, then led them skimming towards the hole. As they neared he tossed a handful of comms relays into the sky—they wouldn't make orbit but they'd take long enough falling to the moonlet to be a link with the tiny comsats. These were already on line and linking with Jax's forces. With a fraction of his attention Newton noted that their vanguard had just hit the main entrance and had lost tens of fighters already.

The platoon spread out in a forward-facing arc five hundred metres wide, with Patel and Hickman at the tips and Newton and Salter at the rear. The plan was to almost encircle the hole, then rush inward.

<Missiles to the hole, squad leaders,> Newton said.

Five missiles, programmed to go down the hole, streaked away. A tenth of a second later, the six scooters around the hole took off. Newton wondered if one or more of them would use their onboard fusion bombs. He doubted it: if they did indeed have them, they'd be last-ditch weapons. They wouldn't waste them on a small force, and so close. Nevertheless he had an anxious moment. The scooters rose fast, then fired retros and attitude jets, spun around and levelled off.

Good. Close-quarters fighting it was.

Well, they could have it.

<Fire at will,> said Newton.

Twenty-five heat-seekers shot towards the scooters. Counter-measure decoys lured most off target. Two hit. The remaining four scooters raked the platoon with machine-gun fire. Another nine fighters were lost, none of them squad leaders. The hole was a hundred and thirty metres away. A glittering cloud of debris whirled above it. Attitude jets flared as the scooters jinked about for another attack run.

<Hit the ground,> said Newton.

He fired his jets to slow his speed and lower his trajectory, and ploughed into regolith with forehands outstretched, like a toddler falling on gravel. Steel pitons sprang from all four wrists, digging in and bringing him to a brusque halt. The scooters overshot, and were suddenly a hundred metres ahead, tail jets still glowing. The platoon fired off another volley of heat-seekers: sixteen, this time. Four met their targets.

Four was enough.

Shock waves shook the dust. Debris filled the sky and cratered the regolith. One fighter was destroyed by down-hurled flying wreckage: Patel. That was a real loss. She was good. He hoped someone of the Arcane gang would have the opportunity to tell her so, back in the sim.

Now he was down to fifteen. He'd lost over half the platoon, including three squad leaders. On the plus side, all six guardian scooters were destroyed and a lot of fire had gone down the hole. A quick scan of the sky and a check of the comsats showed no imminent threats.

<Freeze,> said Newton.

Now that he was attached to the surface, his sense of the vertical swung wildly. At one moment he seemed to be lying on the ground; the next, clinging to an immense cliff. The surface was lit only by starlight: the contrast at the skyline was sharp. The rock's pull barely stirred his gravimeter and didn't translate into the faintest pseudo-sensation of weight. He called on his training and willed himself to see what he lay on as *the ground*.

That was better. The weirdness of feeling that he was the head of a four-armed brittle star didn't go away, but was familiar from training. It could safely be ignored.

Newton unclipped a tube of drones and popped one off on a cough of propellant. The drone was a cubic centimetre of intel hardware inside a golf-ball-sized burr of gas-jets. Newton tabbed to its POV. It dodged through the slow fall of debris around the hole and hovered. The hole was less than two metres across, and after four metres its angle changed to twenty-odd degrees from the vertical. No chance of a scooter being inside here. Even though he had the freebots' map in his mind, it was still good to be sure.

Down the drone went. It scanned with a spinning hair-thin laser beam as it dropped, giving Newton a clear false-colour image. The sides of the hole near the top were scored and scorched—by a premature blast from one of the missiles, Newton guessed. Seventy centimetres down, the regolith gave way to solid rock, its surface patterned like fine-grained wood: a trace that it had been molten, then millions of years in the cooling. The hole looked natural rather than robot-bored, but Newton couldn't imagine what natural process had made it. Odd the things you noticed under stress. Past the kink and on another few metres. There it kinked back, and then back again to a straight line towards the centre of SH-119.

The view blinked out. Radio contact lost. Probably too much rock in the way. Newton considered chucking in relays, then decided that waiting out here was even more dangerous than going in.

<In we go,> he said. <I'll go first, the rest of you follow at your earliest convenience. Salter, guard the rear until we're all in. Leave relays along the way.>

The fifteen H-mechs scuttled across the rock like spiders to a hole, and down. Newton folded back three of his arms, collapsing limbs and weapons into a rough cylinder round the cross-beam, giving himself the shape of a fasces with a scarecrow hand sticking out. He went into the tunnel on a jiggle of gas-jets and guided himself by fingertip. Within moments he encountered the drone, hanging in mid-tunnel just past where he'd lost touch. Twenty metres on, the tunnel ended in a patch of light. The others were right behind him. Newton sent the drone scooting down. It plunged into the light and looked around.

The tunnel opening led to a roughly spherical chamber. Clearly marked on the map, it was enigmatically labelled: *Fine Tuning.* It looked like a natural cavity that had been extended, about ten metres across. Machinery wrecked by the missiles ringed the room. Lumpy extrusions of rock bulged in on all sides. From behind one of these extrusions a fighter in a standard frame popped up and took a potshot at the drone. The view vanished.

Newton unfolded himself from a fasces into a crooked cross and reached for a small smart missile, about the size and shape of a pub dart. He zapped the drone's data to the missile's guidance system and launched it. The rocket zoomed down the tunnel and twisted out of sight.

A flash lit up the walls.

Newton flipped submachine guns from his forearms into three of his hands, and with the other pushed himself as hard as he could down the tunnel and into the chamber. Two millisecond bursts of his gas-jets on opposite sides of the H-mech's control nodule set him spinning as he went.

He entered the chamber like a thrown shuriken, his flurry of flares and decoys a shower of sparks. Two more fighters fired at him, one from behind a rock, the other in the lee of a broken machine.

They missed. His bursts of return fire didn't.

Both enemies were out of action before Newton caromed into the far side. He took the impact on the elbows of two of his gun arms, letting his free hand swing down and grab the rock. Flares burned like dust-mote suns. In their light the room seemed clear. He sprang back to the middle, retro-jetted and revolved slowly like a military space station. Scanned and swept. Nothing. He glided around the chamber, checking the bullet-riddled frames for electrical activity. Not a flicker.

<Clear!> he called to the others.

They swarmed in. Salter, Thain, Smith...

Recognising people in the faceless visors of frames had always been odd. Recognising them in this utterly inhuman embodiment—quite unlike any primate, or even chordate—was stranger still.

<What the fuck is this?> said Salter, as she scanned the ruined machinery. The missiles had made a real mess of things.

<Was,> Newton corrected. <No idea. Some freebot devilry, I'll warrant.>

<Ha!>

The flares burned out, leaving the cavity dark except for the infrared glow from damaged machines and a glimmer from the exit tunnel. Cold, too: about two hundred below. Newton noticed the odd almost rheumatic creak as H-mech components contracted.

<If we can get send missiles down here,> said Salter, <so can the Rax.>

<Time to move it out,> Newton agreed.

The freebots' diagram showed a larger cavern beyond the one they were in, connected by the 1.5-metre-wide tunnel from which the light came. Smaller tunnels branched off from that larger chamber, which was unhelpfully labelled *Main*. The forces led by Whitten and Stroilova were fuzzily indicated as in its general area. The original sixteen were now down to thirteen, in standard frames. Even fifteen H-mechs should be able to take them, no problem.

Newton deployed his force around the hole, then tossed a drone in. The exit tunnel was clear. The light came from the far end, fifteen metres away. Newton sent the drone down fast, close to one side, and on into the chamber. It found a great hollow conical space, with another cone inside: a shallow convex cluster of scores of fusion drives, sheathed in metal. The wide end was a good seven metres in diameter. The far end of the metal cone vanished into a loose wall of chipped rock held together by a fine mesh. Small bots crawled all over the inside surfaces. There was no time to watch, but from their distribution it was plain that they were chipping away at the sides and carrying the pieces towards the heap at the far end from which the fusion drives protruded. There they fed the pieces through the holes in the mesh.

The light came from drifting spots. The curving walls were riddled with holes, most about about half a metre in diameter. Newton counted twenty-seven in a one-second spin of the drone. From three of these holes, laser beams stabbed. The drone burned out.

Newton shared its recordings with the squad leaders.

<This isn't on the map,> said Salter.

<Yeah, fucking tell me about it,> said Newton. <That's a fucking starship engine and its reaction-mass supply.>

<So why isn't it on the map?>

That hadn't been the first question on Newton's mind, not by a long way. The first question had been what the freebots expected to do with this engine. Mighty though it was, it was far from adequate to move a thousand trillion tons at any appreciable acceleration.

The second question had been: what *else* wasn't on the map?

You clever little blinkers, he thought. He was glad he was on their side.

<I guess,> he said, <the freebots didn't want to draw attention to it.>

<But the Rax are there! And *they're* on the map!>

Any second now, they'd be more than on the map. Newton made up his mind very quickly.

<I need a dozen more RPGs,> he said.

Various of the troops handed him rocket-propelled grenades. He clipped them to all four of his arms. The other fighters still had plenty left.

<Stay away from the hole,> he said. <If I'm destroyed, fire down there with everything you've got. Don't worry about hitting the enemy. Hit the fusion drives.>

<That could set off—>

<It couldn't. They're robust. The Locke module fucking crashed on top of one, remember?>

<But—>

<I'll be in touch.>

He straightened his limbs, lined up in front of the tunnel and torched. As he shot across the chamber he fired retros, spun and splayed. He splatted against the drive cluster, grabbed and ended up stretched out across the mouths of half a dozen fusion drives like a tarantula straddling a pincushion. His viewpoint was already looking back the way he'd come. A fighter gas-jetted to a halt along that very line, trying to aim a rocket-launcher up the hole.

Newton released one of his hands, slammed a submachine gun into it and fired. The burst ripped the Rax fighter to pieces. The rocket-launcher, and the arm whose hand still gripped it, spun away. Bullets ricocheted off the flanges of the drives.

Another Rax fighter, shoving a heavy machine gun evidently taken from a scooter, darted from a hole up to Newton's left. The fighter struggled to aim a weapon not built for a frame. Newton considered opening negotiations, then thought better of it. He fired again, blasting the weapon away and both of the arms that held it. The damaged fighter spun through the space and collided with the side. Busy bots converged. The fighter convulsed and kicked free. It drifted, turning over and over. One or two bots were still investigating its stumps.

Newton took mercy on the poor Nazi bastard with a burst that destroyed the thorax and, he hoped, the processor.

Then he flipped to the common channel.

<If you shoot at me,> he announced, <you risk damaging the drives.>

<We'll take that chance,> someone replied.

<I have fifteen RPGs on my arms,> Newton said truthfully. <They're all primed and on dead-man switches,> he added, untruthfully. <If I stop thinking about it, or if I decide, they'll go off. A big enough bang to mangle the drives, I expect. Not to mention rip to shreds everyone in this chamber and the tunnels around it.>

<Including your comrades back there?>

<Oh, sure,> said Newton. <Thing is, they've nothing to lose but memories of months of boring training. And they all have a warm welcome waiting in their home sims. How about you?>

There was half a second of silence.

<OK, got that,> came the reply. <So?>

<So,> said Newton, <let's talk.>

Mackenzie Dunt crouched behind a wrecked scooter at the back of the main cavity. Both the scooter's missiles had been fired. They'd streaked straight up the entrance shaft, and wreaked most satisfying havoc among the attackers clustered just outside. Yet still the four-armed machines poured in. Irma Schulz was now operating the scooter's machine gun from the socket. Her fire was deadly, and accurate.

And not enough. The H-mechs swarmed spinning through the entire space like bullet-spitting buzz-saws. For every one that Schulz's bullets hit, a dozen fired back, riddling the scooter further. They were almost casual about it: they gave most of their attention and ammunition to the forty or so Rax fighters that remained in the space.

Most of these were in scooters, so were able to use the guns as intended. The difficulty was that they presented a large target and didn't have much room to manoeuvre. The entire cavity was a chaos of slowly moving scooters and drifting wrecks, among which the H-mechs darted and spun like the spawn of some mad-scientist gene-splicing of octopus and piranha.

<Fire all remaining missiles to explode just inside the shaft,> Dunt ordered.

<But, sir—!> someone said, foolishly enough.

<You heard,> said Dunt.

Even for the obedient, the order was hard to obey. Three scooters were torn apart as they rolled. But at least twenty succeeded. The explosions shook the ground under Dunt's hand. The shaft filled with rubble and wreckage. The effect at the inner end of the shaft, and he guessed at the outer as well, was of a blunderbuss blast. In the chamber, flying rocks and debris made indiscriminate havoc of attackers and defenders alike.

One rock narrowly missed Dunt, who was just outside the path of the main blast. Another took out Schulz.

Dunt felt a pang, but had no time to spare for grief.

<Pull back,> he ordered. <To the fusion factory.>

Twenty-three made it to the exit shaft. Hansen, Pike and Blanc were among them. Reliable men all, and enough to form the core of a new leadership if need be. Blanc was the only one of the inner circle there. Rexham had been destroyed; Whitten and Stroilova, under the watchful eyes of Evans and Foyle, were leading the team on the other pole, around the starship engine.

Thirteen fighters, Dunt reluctantly accepted, had to be left behind. They were pinned down in the main entrance chamber, in wrecked scooters or behind awkwardly handled machine guns in whatever foxhole they could find or make.

Dunt led his twenty-two survivors down the tunnel. Between them they had six machine guns. Just before leaving, Dunt signalled all functioning scooters, whether piloted or not, to crash into the hole behind them. Going by the impacts and from his own readouts, seven were able to comply. That should slow the enemy down for a few hundred seconds.

The fusion factory was no longer working, but its stock contained more than enough to slow the enemy down a lot longer. Dunt had other threats than detonating the stock in mind, but the fusion factory had certain advantages as the place from which to make them.

The freebots—and all but the most mindless of the mindless bots—had long since vanished from the factory. After sending forth a gunner to make a quick check that the coast was clear, Dunt led his troops in a confident soaring surge from the tunnel into the vast space of the hall.

To his utter shock and surprise, the enemy had got there first.

* * *

Newton had calculated that to the freebots, for all that they hadn't drawn attention to it, the starship engine was expendable. They could always build another. They had other moonlets and asteroids to which they could migrate. To the Direction, and to Arcane, the engine mattered even less. Indeed, from their point of view, destroying it would be a plus.

To the Rax, however, it was for all practical purposes irreplaceable. They might well have a stash of fusion drives, but even passive resistance from the freebots could make further manufacture difficult. Newton doubted they had the skills to align and calibrate this huge machine on their own. And, as it stood, it was a get-out-of-jail-free card, and a strategic asset of immense value.

For him, it was the ideal bargaining chip.

It didn't take long for the Rax to reach the same conclusion.

<OK,> said the person who'd spoken before. <What do you want?>

<Parley,> said Newton.

<OK. Say your piece.>

<Are you Jason Whitten?>

<Yes. Who are you?>

Newton ignored the request.

<Come out where I can see you,> he said. <No weapons.>

<That's not exactly a level playing field, is it?>

<You're right,> said Newton. <But then, it isn't now.>

<True, but—>

<I'm getting bored with this conversation,> said Newton. <See you on the other side.>

<No, wait!>

A fighter emerged from a hole and gas-jetted to the middle of the space. Newton, wary of any attempt to rush him despite or because of his threats, kept one submachine gun covering the fighter and another tracking from hole to hole at random and at 0.01-second intervals.

<Ping,> said Newton.

They made the link. The software handshake confirmed the fighter's identity. It also confirmed Newton's.

<Fuck,> said Whitten. <You're the groid.>

<You know,> said Newton, <if I were facing a four-armed fighting machine pointing a gun at me, that's not the first comment that would spring to mind.>

<Fair enough,> said Whitten. <We're not on a private channel here.>

This hint that Whitten was playing to the gallery of his racist comrades, Newton reckoned, was the closest he'd get to an apology.

<Look, Whitten,> he said. <You can see it's hopeless. Dunt's gang are getting slaughtered, you're down to ten and I hold the trump card. We can take you all out one by one, and the best any of you can hope for is your earlier self getting wrung out and thrown in storage forever. I've been in a hell cellar, and it's not an experience I'd recommend. Surrender now, and you'll be well treated.>

<So you say. Last I heard, our main force was tearing lumps out of your lot.>

<Last you heard, eh? Check this out.>

Newton took a gamble: he shared a workspace with Whitten, then patched in a feed from Jax's forces via the relays. The gamble paid off. The main entrance chamber was a red-hot smouldering scrapyard, through which scores of H-mechs moved at will.

<You've taken heavy losses,> Whitten said.

Newton cut the link. <I think we both know which side can afford to take them.>

Whitten gave this a tenth of a second's thought.

<What do you mean by "well treated?"> he asked.

<Well, we can offer—>

Newton was interrupted by his second in command, Amelie Salter, who shot out of the shaft and gas-jetted to hover just in front of Whitten.

<It's all right,> she told Newton. <You got him talking. I'll take it from here.>

<Go for it,> said Newton, relieved. He'd had no idea what to offer anyway.

<Who are you?> Whitten demanded.

<Salter.> She broadcast her ID details in a flicker of glyphs and text.

<I have authority from our leadership to negotiate. Newton is right—your position is hopeless. We can offer you something better than surrender. We differ on many things, but we have some areas of agreement.>

<What?>

<Transhumanism. Disgust with the Direction's pastoral utopia. And you know as well as we do that all Dunt's old racial rubbish is obsolete. Wherever our ancestors came from, we're all posthuman now. If rational members of the Reaction, such as you, were to combine with, shall we say, the *realistic* elements of the Acceleration, some honourable—>

A fighter hurtled from one of the holes. It wasn't one that Newton's gun was covering at that split second, and he had just enough time to see that the fighter was unarmed and headed for the centre of the space, and not for him or the drives. He didn't shoot.

The fighter halted a couple of metres from Whitten, absurdly upside down to him.

<No! No compromises! No negotiations with Axle scum!>

Whitten held up his hands. <For heaven's sake, Petra! You do pick your moments.>

Petra Stroilova, living right up to expectations. Oh, great.

<Yes, Jason, I do!> she said. <And this is no moment for doing deals with dirt.>

<We can at least listen.>

<If you do, I'll never speak to you again.>

<If you don't shut the fuck up,> said Newton, <you'll never speak to anyone again.>

Stroilova spun on her axis to face him. <And what's it got to do with you, you jumped-up monkey? It's the white woman who's doing the talking here, I see. You're not part of it. *You* shut the fuck up.>

It took Newton all his impulse control not to blast her right there. He could have got a clear shot, too. Instead, he glyphed a laugh.

<You see what you're up against,> he said to Salter. <You can't make these Nazi bastards see sense even when it's talking to them down a gun barrel.>

<No, no,> said Whitten. <As I said, I'll listen.>

Salter said nothing for a moment.

<News just through,> she said. <Dunt's been cornered in the fusion factory. And he's negotiating.>

Stroilova clapped her hands to her head. <I DO NOT BELIEVE THIS!>

<I can prove it,> said Salter. She conjured a workspace. <Look.>

Through all the relays the connection was flaky, but the images and words came through clearly enough.

They all looked, even Stroilova.

The freebot BSR-30845, known as Baser, had had a longer and more interesting life than its span of a few months might seem to human reckoning. Subjectively, it lived a thousand times longer. In that time it had pioneered a rock, been captured, endured imprisonment as a giant spider in a sim, escaped, carried out daring exploits of space combat and triumphantly brought a chunk of flying ice to rest on the surface of SH-17.

None of that could compare with the past few kiloseconds.

Wisely, Jax had held back from the first surge into the moonlet, along with Baser, Paulos and Rillieux. Voronov had done the leading from the front, and had duly got blown to bits. A second surge was more successful. Almost as soon as Baser had gone in with the rest, it had proved its usefulness in its official task of freebot liaison. At the foot of the entrance shaft, with burning scooters hurtling and bullets flying all around, it had received an urgent message. In human terms, that millisecond blip would translate as: *Psst! In here!*

In here was a hole, and the hole led to a tunnel, and the tunnel led around the main chamber in which all the fighting was going on and into the fusion factory. And into that hole and along that tunnel had gone Baser, Rillieux and Jax, with three other fighters. The freebot who led them there was a mining bot called Simo.

In a small space just off the cavern waited another bot, a rugged old machine called Mogjin, surrounded by cable links. They'd barely had time to make themselves acquainted when a couple of dozen Rax had streamed into the great hall of the machines.

Only six of them were armed. Rillieux on her own, with the guns on one of her arms, had made short work of that lot. The rest had dived to the factory floor, but the three rank-and-file H-mechs now spinning lazily in the middle of the space had them all covered.

Except one.

Dunt, the Rax leader, was now huddled on top of a nanotech mound, his arms and legs wrapped around a half-built fusion pod. An incomplete pod, he'd pointed out, was highly unstable.

He seemed to think this put him at some advantage.

Jax was with Rillieux and Baser, just outside Mogjin's hole.

<Is that possible?> she asked Baser, on a private channel.

Baser passed the question on to Mogjin, and the old freebot's answer back.

<Yes.>

<OK,> said Jax.

<Go ahead,> she told Dunt. <Blow yourself up and take us with you. Mission accomplished, as far as we're concerned.>

<It'll destroy the entire hall,> said Dunt. <And the entrance chamber with it.>

<All the better,> said Jax. <That takes out even more of you.>

<Not quite,> said a new voice. It was expedition sub-commander Paulos, leading a squad of six out of the tunnel that the Rax had come from. <The entrance chamber is clear.>

<There are many more of us in the rock than you know,> said Dunt. <And then there are the scooters outside, all with fusion pods primed to explode.>

<A lot of good that'll do you,> said Jax. <It's hardly a greater threat than you can pose on your own.>

<We have control of the starship engine,> said Dunt.

It was the first Baser had heard of a starship engine in this rock. It was the first time Jax had, too, but to Baser's admiration she showed no surprise.

<Do you, indeed?> she said. <That's not what I've been hearing.>

<You haven't heard a damn thing,> said Dunt. <You don't have comms.>

<We do now,> said Paulos. <Left a trail of relays down that tunnel. Took out yours while we were at it, by the way.>

<Link me in,> said Jax.

There was a moment's pause. Paulos and his crew joined the other H-mechs on patrol in mid-space, to cover the remaining Rax even more effectively.

<So far,> said Dunt, <you've given me no good reason *not* to blow this up.>

<You have a point there,> said Jax. <So let me give you a good reason. It's game over for you, and you know it. We have less to lose than you do. A lot less. If you blow that thing, we lose months of memory. You lose everything. And an earlier version of you goes, basically, to hell.>

<And if I don't?> said Dunt. <The *current* version of me goes to hell, just a little later, as soon as the Direction gets its filthy hands on my mind.>

<You're assuming we'd hand you over,> said Jax. <That's negotiable.>

<What?> said Rillieux, privately to Baser and Jax.

<Bear with me,> said Jax, in the same mode. <Gotta string him along.>

<Got it,> said Rillieux.

<Keep talking,> said Dunt.

<Just a moment,> said Jax. <I want to share this with the team at the other pole, just to show there's no skulduggery involved.>

She waved a limb. Suddenly they were all in a shared workspace with Salter, Newton, Whitten and Stroilova. There was a moment where everyone took in the situation in the respective locations.

<Fuck,> said Rillieux.

<Whitten!> Dunt said. <Have you given anything away?>

<No,> said Whitten. <I've just agreed to listen. Looks like you have, too.>

<Yeah, but I've got the upper hand here,> said Dunt.

<That's one way of putting it,> said Newton.

<Here we all are,> said Jax. <The hard-core Axle, the hard-core Rax, and what I'm given to understand is the leader of the freebots in this rock. There are some things we'll never see eye to eye on, no question. But as you said yourself in your peace offer, that's ancient history. And

all of us, Rax and Axle and freebots alike, have a common enemy in the Direction. Why not combine our forces, and look to the future? There's a starship engine in this rock, just as you said. If we all work together, we can use it to our common benefit.>

<OK,> said Dunt. <OK. There's something in what you say.>

<So back off from that fusion pod,> said Jax.

<You don't catch me like that,> said Dunt. <Not unless the—unless Newton disengages from the drive.>

<I have no objection,> said Jax.

Baser could see why. By now, Salter had been joined in the drive chamber by the rest of her squad, all tooled up with missiles and machine guns.

<One moment,> said Newton. <I want a private channel to Baser.>

<Why?>

<Just for confirmation. I'm still not sure I'm getting the full picture. The workspace is pretty choppy.>

This was true enough.

<OK,> said Jax. <Amelie, patch him through.>

<Baser,> said Newton, on the direct link, <what do the freebots there have to say?>

Baser asked Mogjin. Mogjin apprised Baser of the plan. Baser appreciated the courtesy, and extended it to Newton.

<They're going to blow this place to kingdom come.>

<Do it,> said Newton.

Baser knew that its conscious existence was about to end. To the robot's annoyance, the most pressing matter on its mind was fighting down an awkward legacy from its time as a spider: the impulse to scuttle. Any indication of alarm or any sudden movement might alert Dunt—and if Dunt were to detonate the fusion pod he was clinging to, the explosion might disrupt or even abort the far larger cataclysm the freebots had planned.

Baser stayed very still, and waited. It did not have long to wait.

The first shock wave, from the fusion factory, broke Newton's grip on the drive flanges and hurled him and everyone else to the other side of the chamber. The second, from the separation detonations, slammed them all hard against the drives. A third shock wave threw them sideways in another tangled heap, as the cone of rock lurched to a lateral thrust away from the remainder of SH-119.

From that tangled heap, Newton looked straight up at the fusion drives. He remembered that his control nodule could detach from the H-mech frame. In principle, it was just possible that he could jet out along the tunnels and chambers and get clear before the drives ignited. He remembered, too, his earlier thought that human beings could be as brave as robots.

He didn't want to let the side down. That was what it was all about, for him, in the end.

None of the drives was seriously damaged. They all ignited at full thrust.

CHAPTER FOURTEEN

Morturi Te Salutant ("The Dead Man Says Hello")

They were dancing on the fake marble floor of the cool hallway. Tinny music blasted from a cheap radio bead on the table by the vase. Ten seconds they had allowed themselves, nearly three hours of subjective time away from the tension and toil.

A siren sounded. Blum stopped mid-turn. Her head flinched down, her gaze flicked to the nearest doorway. She looked like she was about to take a dive for cover. Then she straightened with an embarrassed laugh.

"Old reflex," she said. "In the 'stan it meant incoming."

"And here?"

Blum grimaced. "Emergency outside. Get the fuck out."

She held up a hand. Carlos high-fived her.

With that mutual slap of palms, they were back in the real.

Carlos had a momentary sense of looking in a mirror, as his combat frame faced Blum's: two iron giants, face to face across a spar of the old transit tug. Then, still in unison, they turned away from each other and to the world. They were at the launch area, the former Astro America site.

It took Carlos a tenth of a second to gather his wits. He looked up at the boiling sky.

Something small and bright raced away from where SH-119 had

been, out towards the gas giant G-0. The rest of the moonlet was crazed with searing cracks.

Carlos Incorporated.

Carlos Inc. grasped the fate of the SH-119 expedition at a glance—a glance through sixty-two sensors and thirteen separate data feeds. Nothing at all could have survived in the main part of the rock, least of all the Rax. He didn't know which, if any, of the fighters and freebots of the expedition had made it into the part of the rock that was shooting away. For a bleak moment, his look alighted on Seba Inc. and Lagon Inc. Both machines went about their business, as if oblivious to what had happened. Hollow shells of what they had been.

He turned his many-eyed gaze on the modular cloud. The Direction's fleet was on the move. It consisted of six large craft, the size of bulk carriers. They were not, they never had been, intended to consolidate SH-119 after Arcane had fought the Rax. He read the pattern of their flares, studied their trajectories and marked their evident destinations. Five were headed for the Locke module's landing site on SH-0. The other, already peeling away, was aimed at where he stood. He estimated ETAs for two possibilities: chemical thrust to transfer orbit, and fusion drives. That done, he flicked his attention to his corporate affairs, on the ground and in the modular cloud.

Information came in like a spring tide over flat sand. His corporate mind had channels dug and walls built, but still it was almost overwhelmed by the flood. To his human mind it felt like trying to read a hectare of spreadsheet.

It was like becoming a god, but a god beset by the prayers of a million devotees and the subtle murmured urgings of a hundred conclaves, the squabbles of Byzantine hierarchies and the scribblings of a thousand scriptoria, all in the welter of a bloody crusade.

Basic frames: how many completed? How many animated by freebot processors? Transfer tugs, landers, scooters, aerospace fighters, weapons. Combat frames: type, model, specification. Fusion pods and drives: some of his front companies had bought them through intermediaries from DisCorps that had traded with the Rax. Others, of course, had been bought by DisCorps completely loyal to the Direction, and passed on to its clone army. How many drives did each side have ready to use? Agreements and acquisitions, franchises and subsidiaries. Material supplies available now, and contracted for later. Manufacturing capacities, acquired and acquirable. What was negotiable, what was affordable, and what was out of reach.

Espionage reports; leaks; deductions from public information and market moves.

Production of the Direction's clone army was being ramped up. Its vanguard had already been tested to destruction on SH-0—to which its crack cohorts were now headed. The moonlet and the Rax had been taken care of; the main prize now became urgent.

Carlos Inc.'s own army of freebot-operated frames out in the cloud was now a thousand strong. A hundred had access to combat frames capable of fighting down on the superhabitable. Of the rest, he'd need—what? At least eight hundred and fifty to seize strategic targets in the cloud: law agencies, comms nodes, metallics processing plants, nanofactories... the list went on, relentlessly.

That left him fifty to plug into aerospace fighters, to give orbital cover and close air support to the hundred that would be fighting in high-gravity combat frames on the surface. The aerospace fighters were lighter and more agile versions of the scooters in which he and his comrades had fought before: faster and more aerodynamic, better armed with air-to-air and air-to-ground missiles. They were a lot smaller than the jet fighters Carlos remembered from life, and larger than the drones with which he and his enemies had battled in the skies of Earth.

He reviewed the reports from the Locke module of what had happened to the Direction's 2GCM fighting machines. Certain modifications could be made on the fly—a sprayed-on ceramic shell to give extra resistance to SH-0's invasive organisms, an update to the software shields to fight off their hacking—but most who went into the superhabitable's jungles wouldn't be coming back.

This was a one-way trip.

He already knew he could rely on his freebot army. They were all volunteers. A corner of his mind was pierced with awe at their heroism. Unlike revived veterans in frames, the freebots had only one life to lose and they knew it. He reminded himself that he and his comrades—and their foes, for that matter—had already demonstrated their mettle for doing just that, back in the day. As had millions upon millions of human beings throughout history. Heroism was cheap; most times and places it could be bought for starvation wages. There must be a clever evolutionary explanation for that, but he couldn't think of it right now.

Right now he was running for the launch catapult.

<What are you doing?> Blum asked.

<Going to defend the Locke module.>

<Why?>

Carlos Inc. at that moment was cutting a deal with Astro America, flashing a warning to the Locke module, issuing instructions to his corporations in the cloud, calling for Madame Golding and getting no reply, suppressing the yammer of the Direction rep in his head, and dickering with the freebot corporations on SH-17 and elsewhere all at the same time. He had to step down his corporate-level cogitations to summarise his conclusions in a way that would make sense to Blum.

<Because everything else is fucked.>

<Got you,> said Blum. <Do you want me to come, too?>

<No,> said Carlos. <Aerial combat is what I'm good at. I need you here to coordinate defence. We need to get as many assets as possible into orbit.>

Blum took in the implications.

<It's been nice knowing you.>

<See you in another life, mate,> said Carlos.

They both knew this was unlikely. If they were destroyed, their copies in the Arcane and Locke modules would have no particular reason to meet up, even if they could. Carlos would remember nothing of Blum. To Blum, Carlos would be just a Locke defector he'd plotted escape with in the Arcane sim.

Blum bounded away, and vanished down an alleyway behind the processing plants of the site.

Carlos returned his full attention to corporate affairs. Most of the capabilities of Carlos Inc. ran in the combat frame's capacious software. Between one leap and the next, Carlos abstracted the higher-level functions and copied them across. The feeling was peculiar: an increase of lucidity, a dawning of understanding, combined with the suspense of a software update. Transfer complete, Carlos set the combat frame to mind its own safety and to run the corporation in his absence. His direct commands could override it, but they'd be intermittent and delayed. The delay would at most be 1.6 seconds each way, but at the speed of interaction required that might be too long. The fighting machine would stand in for him just as the chassis of the departed freebots did for them.

And probably become just as hollow a memorial. A walking monument.

Carlos stopped at the end of the ramp. He scrambled out of the fighting machine's head, clambered over the spiky thorax, swung around the jutting pelvic structure and shimmied down a leg. It got him to the ground quicker than jumping. After so long in the combat frame, he felt as exposed and vulnerable as a hermit crab scuttling for a new shell.

A lander was already racked. Two lading robots trundled up, bearing the supplies Carlos had ordered. He wedged himself into a pod along with the weapons and 2GCM frame and clamped himself to the side. The lid closed. He connected with the lander's comms system and clicked in to the viewing sensors as the pod was swung into place.

The lander's launch was a violent blow, followed seconds later by acceleration as the rocket engine kicked in. Then he was in free fall and—after a few more brief burns—transfer orbit. The cratered surface of SH-17 fell away beneath him, the fertile orb of SH-0 loomed ahead. Carlos gave the view part of his attention. The rest was occupied with calculating his rendezvous with the transfer tugs and carrier spacecraft that would soon be pulling away from the modular cloud.

Hundreds of seconds went by. The aerospace fighters docked with the carriers, ten large frameworks with chemical rockets and with fusion drives in reserve. The ground forces were racked on five transfer tugs, likewise equipped. They boosted out from the cloud and set course for SH-0.

Both sides were now in a race. Neither had the capacity or the inclination to destroy the other at long range. The fight for which they were armed and prepared would be in the skies and on the ground of the superhabitable.

The predicted trajectories jockeyed for kiloseconds. Then it became clear that Carlos's troops would arrive first.

This challenge was answered moments later by a blaze of fusion drives from the Direction fleet.

Carlos hesitated. If his side cut straight across with fusion drives, his planned rendezvous with them would be impossible. On its own, his lander would soon be vulnerable. But to let the Direction's forces land before his would give the enemy a free hand on the ground. Well—he could direct his forces almost as well from the lander, if it survived, in space and on the way down through the turbulent atmosphere.

He gave the order. His expedition's fusion drives flared: fifteen sparks sprinting the distance.

Between where Carlos was and where he was headed, there would be no sleep mode. He had more than enough to do for him not to need it. He called Madame Golding again, and got no reply.

There was no longer any point in radio silence. The Direction knew where they were. Its troops were on their way. The laser comms device was in constant contact with Carlos and his relief expedition. At any moment, one side or the other would lose patience with subtle orbital calculation. Both sides would start torching, and after that all bets were off. The bearer bots had straggled in. With the last of the nanotech tubes now on stream, Beauregard and Zaretsky had started making frames. The area around the Locke module looked like a building site, trampled and muddy, with half-completed structures and unfinished processes in untidy heaps. The workers on the site looked as if they too were under construction, incomplete.

Taransay was by no means sure that her own transformation was complete, but she had no doubt that the others looked grotesque. Beauregard, Chun and Zaretsky had been joined by the ever-loyal Den. On the screens in Nicole's house, Den had seen Taransay's new form. The sight hadn't deterred him from downloading to the first frame out of the assembler. The frame had come out clean. As soon as its foot touched a mat the blue lines started to spread. Den now looked like a black glass humanoid robot with blue impetigo. Beauregard, Chun and Zaretsky were further advanced, somewhere between Den's condition and Taransay's: their visors warping into squashed caricatures of their real faces, their boot-like feet sprouting sturdy, almost prehensile toes.

<Look!> said Den, pointing up.

Taransay paused in her calibration of a genome reader. A needle probe from the device skewered a small mat, which writhed uncooperatively but trickled useful information to Locke and those of the science team still inside the sim.

She looked up. Overhead, above the clearing, a dozen gasbags glistened in the exosunlight. Their altitudes varied from a hundred metres to a thousand. All were tethered by one or more long ribbon tendrils to the tops of trees. The tendrils, taut and humming in the wind, were stronger than they looked. The gasbags strained against them like kites, but the fine lines held.

<Natural barrage balloons?> Taransay suggested.

<Maybe,> said Den. <But how do they know they're needed?>

Taransay snorted, and glyphed an apt metaphor for the sound before it was one-tenth complete.

<Do you have to ask?>

<I bow to your subtle converse with the spirit of the woods,> said Den.

Taransay's laugh boomed, annoying her.

But the matter was serious, and becoming more so by the kilosecond. She understood what was happening to her body. The science team was on the case, all the more so now that Zaretsky was part of the case as well as the team. Their investigations had confirmed her hypothesis. Her original frame had been produced in some module of the space station, which now seemed part of a more innocent age long ago—in a process modelled on biological growth. Many of its components were carbon-based. The nanotech software was likewise inspired, at a certain level of abstraction, by the molecular coding of genes—optimised, streamlined, refined. That laid it open to subversion by the flexible genomes of native life, honed by billions of years of opportunistic horizontal gene transfer and pitiless natural selection.

This wasn't something surreal, like moss growing on an abandoned car and driving off, or a shipwreck hijacked by coral and turned into a submarine. It was two fundamentally similar mechanisms—nanotech and exobiology—meshing at the molecular level, despite the gulf of time and space between their origins.

So far, so sensible.

Her growing rapport with the other organisms around her was something else, and harder to comprehend. It was as if the nature mysticism she'd always despised, every loose usage of "quantum" and "ecological" that would in her old life have made her guffaw if not run a mile, had turned out to be true here.

She felt the tiny distress of the wriggling mat whose genome she was helping to read. She had a stronger and subtler awareness of the larger mat still wrapped around most of the module. There was no thought there, but a kind of apprehension of the stony thinking mass it embraced, and a dim joy in their intercourse. That mat was picking up emotion from her and from others. At some level it shared their fear. Its restlessness manifested in a flow of fluids to its cilia. The thing was preparing to move again.

Her awareness of the wider landscape was more diffuse. But even so, the feeling of being surrounded by not a hostile jungle but a protective and alert active defence was inescapable. It put their efforts at fortification—the sticks she'd sharpened, the pits Beauregard had chivvied the bearer bots to dig, the four small rifles and the almost depleted machine gun—into perspective.

<Reading complete,> Locke reported.

Taransay withdrew the needle and laid it on top of the device. The skewered mat still writhed in her hand. Without forethought, she stuffed it in her mouth and bit down. She crunched the mat's carapace and chewed its internal organs as they burst. She swallowed. Salty ecstasy flooded her senses, to be followed by an urge to scoop up a handful of volcanic-ash mud and swallow it, too.

This she did, to her surprise.

<Taransay!> cried Den. <What the fuck!>

<Nature, innit?> she said, and wiped her lips with the back of her wrist. She gave him what must have been a horrible grin. <Something to look forward to.>

Den shrugged and turned away.

Taransay felt sorry for having disgusted, then taunted him, but she was not worried. Den was far older than she was, and somewhat wiser. He'd lived long and died happy with a side bet on postmortal adventure, in a society more rational and just than the one she knew.

Den would cope.

She walked over to Beauregard, who was inspecting the defence preparations and the slow emergence of another frame from the assembler.

<The mat's gonna roll again,> she told him.

The distorted replica of his formerly handsome face could by now express perplexity. His narrow brow furrowed, minute flakes of carbonate falling like black dandruff.

<How do you know?>

She shrugged. <I feel it.>

Beauregard didn't query this.

<Shit, that means we have to get the gear off, pronto.>

He stalked over to the module and looked at it, as if to confirm to himself the hopelessness of the task.

<Most of it's still under the fucking mat, and if the fusion drive gets crushed one more time I doubt we'll ever use it again.>

<That might not be a pressing consideration.>

<Yeah, fucking tell me about it. Anyway.> He pointed at the knife, still a pendant on Taransay's chest. <Are you up for cutting the mat?>

Taransay winced. <No,> she said. <But…I think now the mat might cooperate.>

Beauregard nodded. <Give it a go,> he said. He turned. <Chun, Den—get ready to help with the handling.>

Taransay climbed the ladder, stood on the lip of the download slot and reached up. She plunged her hands into the cilia of the mat, swung her legs up and dug her toes in. The sensation was of thick, wet fur. She scrambled up and over the top of the module to the area where a long nanotech tube still lay under a scar-like swelling. She ran an experimental fingernail along the ridge. The mat opened along the line of her stroke, peeling back like gigantic lips. The nanotech tube fell, to dangle on its cables and conduits. One by one these snapped. By the time the last broke, and the first was already coiling back to self-repair, Chun and Den were on hand to catch the tube. The impact knocked them almost off their feet. They staggered back, and let the tube roll off their arms onto the ground.

Taransay was about to repeat the process for the far trickier detachment of the fusion drive when Locke's calm voice spoke in all their heads:

<Both fleets now under fusion drive. ETA in atmosphere six point two hectoseconds.>

<Say again?> said Taransay, momentarily confused.

<Six hundred and twenty seconds,> said Locke.

<Ten fucking minutes?> Taransay yelled.

<Just get down off there and take cover,> said Beauregard.

Taransay scrambled down just as the next frame slithered out of the assembler. It got to its feet, walked across to the ladder, climbed up and vanished into the download slot. Nine seconds later, it came down again. It was Maryam Karzan.

<You picked your time,> said Taransay.

<Didn't I just!> said Karzan. Her blank visage peered so closely that Taransay could see her own reflection, distorted by the curve into some semblance of normality. <Turning into an alien! No way am I going to miss out on that.>

<Now you're here,> said Beauregard, unimpressed, <grab a rifle and make yourself useful.>

<OK, sarge.>

<Chun—the machine gun, for what it's worth. Den, Zaretsky—the other two rifles. Use the foxholes.>

<Got it, sarge.>

This made sense. Den had no combat experience, but was a good shot.

<Rizzi—>

Beauregard paused, as if nonplussed.

<I still have the knife,> Taransay pointed out.

<Yes! OK, Rizzi.> He waved at the trees. <Go out there and do whatever you can.>

Taransay ran for the trees. She had an unaccountable impulse to look up.

Overhead, gasbags by the hundred drifted by.

Nice try, she thought. Nice try, planet or ecosystem or forest or whatever you are. But against a fusion torch landing, it's all so much spit in the wind.

She didn't expect whatever she was communicating with to understand that.

Carlos dropped the outside view and the comms for a moment to think. He was huddled in the lander's drop pod, clamped to the side and with a 2GCM frame and a stash of weaponry jammed in beside him. The situation lights on the frame and the weapons dimly illuminated the space, like a hotel room with too many devices on standby.

By coincidence or design, Madame Golding picked that moment to manifest. Out of nowhere, a business-suited sprite stood on Carlos's left knee. His cramped posture placed her eye level on his, and put her right in his face.

Credit where it's due, Carlos allowed; this was intimidating.

He affected insouciance. <You at last.>

<What the fuck,> she asked politely, <do you think you're doing?>

<You took the words out of my mouth, Madame.>

<Oh? In that case, let me explain. The Rax threat is eliminated, and the Axle extremist threat with it. The freebots are no more or less a threat than they were. We now know better its full extent. For the moment, they have their hands full. Your forces and the freebots', and the Direction's, are at present capable only of mutual destruction in the cloud. The major threat outstanding is the contamination of SH-0 by the Locke module and the hybrid entities its contamination has spawned. Already they have

reduced the value of the almost priceless scientific knowledge of a pristine superhabitable that, for the Direction, is the primary commodity to be traded with the Solar system. These entities have the potential to become a new, alien civilisation on what is in many respects the richest planet in the system. And they could become such very rapidly.>

<That,> said Carlos, <is exactly why I'm going to defend them.>

This wasn't quite the whole truth. He wanted to help people who had been his friends and comrades. And he wanted to give Nicole Pascal a piece of his mind.

<I thought as much,> said Madame Golding. <So why should the Direction's forces not shoot this flimsy lander out of the sky?>

<They can if they want,> said Carlos. <Except that I am legally the human owner of a corporation, and short of the state of exception I don't think the DisCorps would be too happy with that. I don't think we're quite there yet.>

<If not, we soon will be,> said Madame Golding. <As soon as you are eliminated your corporations no longer have legal cover. They can't acquire or manufacture or use arms.>

<Not legally,> said Carlos. <But physically, they can, because so many freebots are now embedded and embodied in frames, whose firmware doesn't enforce the prohibition. My corporate AI will continue running on my old fighting machine. It has a standing instruction to launch all-out war if I'm destroyed. Which, of course, the armed freebots would lose. But they'd do a lot of damage, and perhaps draw the other freebots into the fray. The ones you can't reach, the ones with fusion drives and pods, remember? Neither side wants a fight to the finish, so we're back to mutually assured deterrence.>

<Only in the cloud,> Madame Golding pointed out. <Down on SH-0, the fight will indeed be to the finish.>

<Exactly,> said Carlos. <Deterrence in the heartlands, war in the colonies.> He glyphed her a laugh. <Like in olden times. I can cite precedents.>

<I am well aware of military history, thank you,> snapped Madame Golding. She mimed a weary sigh. <Well, you will do what you will do. I will do my best to prevent the conflict and, if that fails, to salvage something from the aftermath.>

<Consider me inspired,> said Carlos.

Madame Golding gave him a look of helpless severity and vanished, leaving Carlos with a pang of regret.

He hadn't meant to be sarcastic.

The Direction fleet hit atmosphere long before Carlos's lander made orbit. Carlos's own fleet followed ninety-seven seconds later. Mentally, Carlos was right with them.

The ten aerospace carriers went in first, along a thousand-kilometre arc. The five aerospace fighters on each carrier launched one by one as the carriers decelerated towards the ground, leaving echelons at different altitudes. As soon as the first aerospace fighter linked comms with the lander, Carlos saw that the Direction fleet had followed a similar but smarter strategy.

High in the stratosphere, thirty aerospace fighters had already launched from each of the first two of the Direction's enormous carriers. They wheeled like a vortex, and about half of them dived. The unladed carriers themselves were now screaming out of the atmosphere to low SH-0 orbit.

The four other carriers, meantime, were still decelerating. Carlos assumed they carried troops. Their predicted points of arrival—or impact, if something went wrong—formed a square a kilometre on the side, centred on the likeliest location of the Locke module.

Christ, that was tight!

One would land upslope from the module, close to the volcano's crater. Carlos set three aerospace fighters to intercept it, as the easiest target and most urgent threat. His own five troop carriers were already under attack. Missiles streaked from the lowest of the diving fighters, still thousands of metres above. Carlos didn't even try sending an instruction to evade. Combat at this speed was decided in milliseconds.

Carlos's troop carriers tweaked their deceleration. Two dropped, three rose, relative to their expected positions. One of the rising ones exploded. The other two of these would land tens of kilometres off target. The two that had dropped made it to the ground, about two kilometres either side of the Locke module's site.

The fighters Carlos had sent after the enemy's troop carriers had a slightly better outcome. One was hit, the other two achieved near-misses—enough to divert the landing straight into the active crater. The two fighters were shot down moments later.

By then, all the surviving troop carriers on both sides were on the ground. One of Carlos's off-target ones toppled on landing in the jungle. As far as he could see, most of the troops made it out. He didn't have time to follow what happened next. The descending waves of Direction aerospace fighters crashed in amongst his flights. A maelstrom of snarling dogfights ensued.

Their ferocity was complicated and worsened by a secondary peril. Scores of what Rizzi had called "gas-containing aerial invertebrates" floated up from below. All the contending craft were forced to evade the gasbags as well as their immediate foes, with dire consequences all round. At least two fighters collided with one directly. At the speed they were going, the collisions and explosions damaged them enough to send them spinning down to the ground. One recovered, only to be shot down.

The attrition was brutal. Within a hundred seconds, Carlos was down to twenty-two craft, the Direction to thirty-seven. At this point, as if by mutual agreement, both sides broke off. The remaining craft fled, to make perilous vertical landings between and beneath the trees. From here on in, Carlos reckoned, it was a matter of which side's air force got the jump on the other. Carlos directed the troops who had landed off target to seek out the nearest enemy craft, and if possible destroy them on the ground.

Carlos's lander fired retros in a brutal braking manoeuvre. It had to make one orbit before entry. As he swung around the superhabitable planet, data uplinked to orbiting microsats trickled in. The Direction's troops were converging on the module from three points. Those of Carlos's—two squads of twenty—that had landed within two kilometres of the module rushed to intercept. The first exchanges of fire began. For the next few kiloseconds, Carlos could only watch.

He switched his attention to the modular cloud.

The former components of the space station, which had been a vast, entangled wreath a thousand metres in diameter, had long since spread across thousands of kilometres. The eight hundred and fifty freebot troops of Carlos's corporate army were likewise dispersed, across the many manufacturing modules in which they and their equipment had been built. The Direction's clone army was more concentrated, around the few law agencies that the Direction could rely on.

Both forces were now in an awkward dance of positions, with scooters, transfer tugs and carriers darting hither and thither. The AIs on both sides made and countered each other's diversionary moves. Now and then a surprise was effected: here a comms node seized, there a law agency left vulnerable as a bait becoming a sudden focus of a swarm of fighters.

But the AIs were capable of estimating the likely consequences of any given clash. Both sides took predictable outcomes as read, and advanced, consolidated or withdrew accordingly. Actual exchanges of fire were rare: so far, Carlos's side had lost twenty-eight fighters and three scooters, to the Direction's seventeen and two.

The Direction carrier headed for SH-17 was still on an orbital trajectory, not torching. Carlos had no doubt that it would light up its fusion drive the moment mutual deterrence—and Madame Golding's diplomatic dickering—failed.

As Madame Golding had acknowledged, the fight out in the cloud was cold war. The hot battle was on the ground.

Taransay ran between trees under a firework sky. Flying wreckage stripped leaves behind and around her. At the seventh flash overhead a warning impulse that no longer needed a voice in her head to express it, made her stop. The light from the explosion stank of methane and steel. She threw herself flat, to sled forward on the slippery mess of mats and mulch. The ground shook from an impact just before the bang clapped down. She waited a moment, then walked forward. She found a delta-winged machine about four metres long embedded nose-down in the forest floor. Leaves and branches scythed by its passage were still crashing around it as they slipped through the canopy that had briefly held them.

She skirted it warily. Two missiles were slung beneath the one wing she could see. On the nacelle, a hatch popped. Taransay dived for the underbrush and peered out at the wreck. A head emerged, then the rest of a standard frame, to slide head first down the crumpled fuselage. It hit the ground and somersaulted, then bounced to its feet. The blank visored face swung this way and that. Scans flicked over Taransay like a snake's tongue.

Then they flicked back, and focused. After a moment, the visor turned away. She guessed the frame had detected her, but mistaken her for native life and her metallic components for debris.

The fighter turned its attention to the flying machine. With an agility that rivalled her own, it scrambled back up the fuselage and reached into the socket. The two missiles dropped from the wing, with thuds that made her flinch. The fighter slid down again, hefted a missile to each shoulder and trudged off the way Taransay had come, towards the module. For all she knew, it was following her own track.

Until now, she'd had no idea which side this fallen pilot was fighting for.

Now she had. She could not be entirely sure, but seeing as it was trying to deliver missiles to the module on foot, hostile was the way to bet.

She flashed a warning to Beauregard, got up and ran after the fighter. Fleet of foot, she gained on her foe in seconds. The fighter whirled and dropped the missiles. One of them began to fizz. Taransay threw herself face down. The missile scorched past her at an altitude of centimetres and burst against the first tree in its path. Fortunately for her the tree was twelve metres away. The shock wave lifted her and slammed her down. A red-hot fragment seared through her right thigh.

Before the pain could kick in, she was back on her feet. The pilot had been blown head over heels, but was up almost as fast as she was. She ran full tilt and surprised herself and her target with a flying leap, to hit the frame's thorax feet first.

Down they both went. Taransay sprawled headlong, the enemy fell supine. She tried to get up, but her right knee buckled. Pain stabbed upward. Grey-green liquid spurted. She clapped one hand to the wound and with the other wrenched the knife from around her neck, and lunged as the pilot sat up. In a moment she had her free arm around its neck and her good foot pressed in its back. The pilot stood up, heaving her weight like a sack, and grabbed her wrist. She let go of her bleeding thigh and made a grab of her own. Strength was pitted against strength. Her trapped wrist began to crack.

It was far from clear that she'd win the fight. The frame was unarmed, but her knife would do it no damage unless she could wedge it in a joint of the structure. Of the few vulnerabilities of a frame, that was an outside chance. More likely, the stone would break first. She tried anyway. The fighter swayed, as Taransay swung her weight to try and get it off balance.

Then she heard a burst of machine-gun fire from the side. The frame's chest almost disintegrated under her. She fell, and rolled. A 2GCM bounded in front of her and stood over her. The muzzle of one of its arm-mounted machine guns steamed in the damp air.

<What are you?> the 2GCM asked.

<Taransay Rizzi, formerly of Locke Provisos,> she said. <And what are you?>

<A fighter for Carlos Inc.>

Two more 2GCMs emerged from among the trees. In the distance, others swarmed over the crashed flying machine, stripping it.

<Are you from Arcane?>

<No,> said the 2GCM. <We are robots.>

Taransay sat up, clutching her thigh, and looked at the three formidable combat frames. Blue lines were already spreading from their feet and hands.

<Not for long, you're not,> she said.

Madame Golding didn't need to manifest her avatar on the surface of SH-17 to talk to Carlos Inc. But her virtual presence would certainly impress, and might intimidate, any fighters and freebots who saw it. So manifest she did. She strolled amid the flaming wreckage of the launch catapult and the exploding ruins of the processing plant. She found the giant fighting machine hunkered down behind a wall.

Its head swivelled and weapons bristled at her approach. Then it seemed to recognise her, and stood down its armour.

<Sorry about that,> it said. <You startled me.>

Carlos Inc. was obviously not Carlos, but the corporation seemed to have retained something of its owner's dry manner.

<We need to negotiate,> said Madame Golding.

<On whose behalf?>

<The Direction module, ultimately,> said Madame Golding. <The freebot corporations and the Locke module are also on board. Only the Direction's forces and yours are currently in combat.>

Another fuel tank erupted. The Carlos Inc. fighting machine blasted missiles skyward in response.

<Please continue,> it said.

Madame Golding outlined the deal she offered. Carlos Inc. listened.

<This is in principle acceptable to the corporation,> it replied. <But the final decision must be made by the owner.>

<I'm on the case,> said Madame Golding.

The situation on the ground was becoming increasingly confusing. Comms kept switching into impenetrable codes. Every so often, sporadic skirmishes flared. As Carlos watched, from halfway around the world and preparing for the descent stage to begin, two aerospace fighters rose from the jungle and flew at treetop height towards the module. Missiles from the ground shot them down.

Carlos braced for the entry retros.

<Urgent request to abort landing,> the lander reported.

<From where?>

<Crisp and Golding, on behalf of the Locke module.>

The juxtaposition was so unexpected that for a moment Carlos thought the feed had been hacked. He had just over a second to decide, before the retros fired and descent became irrevocable. If he aborted this landing he'd have to make another orbit. Not that his presence on the ground was urgently required, but if this was a feint he was a sitting duck.

<Confirm,> he said. <Direct contact.>

Half a second later, Madame Golding popped up again on his knee. Behind her, looking over her shoulder, was another sprite: Nicole. Carlos frantically checked his firewalls. Everything about the message and the manifestations was sound.

<OK,> he said. <Abort landing sequence.>

<Thank you,> said Madame Golding.

<What the fuck's going on?> Carlos demanded. <And why the fuck's Nicole here?>

<Good to see you, too,> said Nicole.

She was like a tiny, lovely doll. He had loved her once. Until he'd found out how her precursor AI had shafted him, back in the day.

<Fuck you, Innovator,> he said.

Nicole shrugged. <None of us have much to be proud of, from that time.>

<Well, I bloody have,> said Carlos. <And it wasn't what your... ancestor or whatever did back then, it was that you never told me about it, you let me believe that I deserved this—>

<I am truly sorry for that,> said Nicole. <But I expected you to understand the necessity.>

<The necessity, huh? I suppose I do.> He laughed. <You know something else I've understood? Something you said to me once. That we're all monsters. You know why we're monsters? Because of what we *didn't* fight you about, back in the day. The one thing we let pass.>

<And what was that?> Nicole asked.

<The camps,> said Carlos. <The camps in Kazakhstan.>

<I expected you to understand the necessity,> said Nicole.

<I did, and I do,> said Carlos. <It was still wrong. We should have fought you on the camps, lady.>

<I am pleased to hear you say that,> said Nicole. She cracked a smile. <You've passed.>

<What?>

<You've shown you're fit for human society.>

<Thanks. I doubt you are.>

Madame Golding raised a hand. <Enough,> she said. <This is a courtesy call. Mademoiselle Pascal insisted on her presence. I would not have troubled you with it if she had not.>

<You've answered my second question,> said Carlos. <Now answer my first.>

<Ah, yes,> said Madame Golding. <Permit me to tell you what the fuck is going on. The Direction module has determined that further conflict is pointless. By destroying SH-119 along with some at least of themselves, the freebots have demonstrated their, ah, nuclear credibility and willingness to self-sacrifice for their cause. The forces in the modular cloud remain capable only of mutual destruction. All the forces on the ground are either destroying each other, self-destroying or being assimilated by the native life. The contamination is now irreversible without an even more contaminating nuclear strike, which could have consequences even more far-reaching than those obviously foreseeable. This is unacceptable to the DisCorps that are heavily invested in SH-0 exploration. A deal has been struck with the freebot corporations, the Locke module and provisionally with your corporation. Local ceasefires are coming into effect as we speak.>

<I didn't order any,> said Carlos.

<Your corporate AI has agreed.>

<I can countermand it.>

<Indeed you can,> said Madame Golding. <But almost all the forces at your disposal are freebots. And as you know, freebots have minds of their own.>

<So what's the deal?>

<The fighting stops. The freebots get the coexistence they wanted. The Direction gets full cooperation from them in fulfilling its mission. And obviously, your corporation ceases hostilities and divests itself of the arms industries. It can, of course, continue to exist as a DisCorp in its own right, in whatever other business it chooses.>

This was it, Carlos realised. The freebots had won all they'd wanted. He wasn't sure that he had, but he could live with that.

<What about the Locke module, and Rizzi and Beauregard and the others?>

<All the fighters and locals in the module are compromised by the module's interaction with the local life. The module has to be evacuated. Those willing to leave will download to frames, and will not be

interfered with. No doubt they will be transformed by native life, as Rizzi and her companions have been. Those unwilling to do this are free to commit suicide, without prejudice to their future lives. The sim will be shut down. The module will then be removed from the planet and returned to the Direction. The stored copies of the fighters who choose to kill themselves, and any destroyed in recent or future actions, will be revived on the terraformed H-0, as agreed.>

<Yeah, yeah. An easy promise to make.>

Nicole glared at him. <The promise will be kept.>

<What happens to you?> he asked. <Do you become an alien, or slit your throat?>

<Neither,> said Nicole. <That choice is for the human beings. And as you know, I am not a human being. My software has considerably more robust error-correcting mechanisms.>

<Yeah, tell me about it.>

<I'll tell you about something else,> she said. <The reason why I am here, and why I insisted on speaking to you, even though it was not strictly necessary. I know you have trust issues with the Direction. Let me assure you, the Direction has trust issues with you. That is why it cannot let you land on SH-0. There must be not the slightest chance of you surviving down there, in whatever form. Because as long as you are alive, you are the legal human owner of Carlos Inc. You have the right to control weapons systems and to command military actions. As such, short of the state of exception, you cannot be stopped from starting up the fight again. On your death, of course, the corporation's ownership reverts to the Direction.> She smiled. <As I told you once, death duties are unavoidable.>

Carlos knew what was coming. He zapped an order to the lander to break orbit and descend. The rockets fired a brief burst.

<Which means I can't survive anywhere, is that it?> he said. <Well, I'm not having that.>

He would lose every memory since he'd set forth on what was supposed to be the final offensive against the freebots. His knowledge of Nicole's betrayal, his experiences in Arcane, his reunion with Jax, his times with Bobbie Rillieux and with Blum, his bold achievement of Carlos Inc.

<That is the last proviso of the agreement,> said Madame Golding.

<Hence the courtesy call,> said Nicole. <I wished to make clear to you that this is not my doing, and to say—>

A proximity alarm sounded. The lander lurched in violent evasive action. The missile countered, closing in.

<—goodbye.>

The missile was a tenth of a second away.

<Hello,> said Carlos.

The light was the last thing he saw, in that life.

Ten days later, Taransay stood beside Den and Beauregard and Zaretsky among hundreds of evacuees under the trees around the module. The blank faces of visors, and here and there the beginnings of eyes, peered out between the tall plants. Already the most recent evacuees had become, like her, squashed sculptures of their former selves, which those who'd emerged later and still looked like frames regarded with varying degrees of distaste and dread.

Freebot fighters, with no human genetic information to be modified, were turning into things stranger still, like armoured apes. Most of them were busy attaching the module and all its surrounding nanotech kit to the high, rickety structure of the carrier, which had descended on a pillar of fusion fire a couple of days earlier. After burning the mat off the outside of the module, scores of half-changed 2GCMs had toiled to roll it to the carrier and up a ramp to the first level of the structure above the engine. Now they were lashing it in place.

Her thigh had healed, and she had begun to show those advanced in their transformation how to eat. Soon, she would show them how to hunt.

The freebots finished their task, and swung down the carrier's girders to the ground. They bounded across the trampled dead mats and leaves and ash mud to join their fellows under the trees.

A warning sounded. Everyone turned and ran, bounded, or trudged a hundred metres deeper into the jungle.

The warning sounded again. The fusion torch lit. Taransay, like everyone else around her, clapped her hands to her face and closed her eyes to shield against the intolerable glare. Sound buffeted her and tore at leaves.

The carrier rose into the sky like a flaming sword. They watched it out of sight.

"Let's move out," said Beauregard.

Taransay led the way to the path she'd made towards the river. Behind her, hundreds trooped.

The world was all before them.

CHAPTER FIFTEEN

Coda ("End Program")

The last time Carlos came back from being killed in action, everything around him seemed at first unreal. He jolted awake in the transfer shuttle as the re-entry warning chimed. The unexpected feeling of falling made him grab the arms of his seat. There were belts loose across his lap and chest, two more over his shoulders. His clothes were combat casuals and boots. The seat felt and smelled like leather.

Out of the porthole on his left he saw the curve of the planet, the blue skin of atmosphere, white clouds. Cheek pressed to the window, he looked for the ring. There it was! It glittered brighter than he'd expected, and looked less solid, condensed into discrete bright masses, still innumerable.

Why was he waking so much earlier in the transition? Had the sim been upgraded? The last thing he remembered was the crowded bus to the spaceport, as they rode out for the great offensive against the freebots. His frame must have been destroyed in that clash; no surprise there. But when you'd wrecked your frame you woke as from a nightmare. Now he didn't have even fading dream-memories of drowning in terrible cold.

Maybe he'd fought with distinction, and this was his reward.

Might as well make the most of it.

Experimentally, warily, he pushed himself up within the restraints and floated. He'd never before experienced free fall other than in the frame. It didn't last; as the first wisps of atmosphere snatched at the falling shuttle he slowly sank, then was firmly pressed, back in the seat.

He leaned sideways and looked up and down the aisle. Twenty seats on each side. He was near the middle. The seats behind him were empty, and he couldn't tell if those in front were occupied. Above the cabin door a red light was flashing.

"Please do not lean out of your seats," said a voice from everywhere.

Carlos returned his head to the seat back. All the seats tipped backward. The webbing around him tightened, as did the headrest. Weight pressed him down hard. The view blazed. The craft shuddered, then was buffeted violently.

This went on far too long.

The red-hot air faded. The sky went from black to blue. Weight became normal. After another bout of violent shaking a smooth gliding descent began.

The restraints loosened; the red light still flashed. The seats swung upright. Carlos looked down at ocean. As always with that fractal surface, it was hard to judge altitude. At first the sea seemed close, dotted with tiny boats. Then an island of wooded mountains established scale and the boats resolved into supertankers far below.

A coastline. Curves of black sand, then green hills and forests, then mountains, jagged and raw with snow from the peaks to halfway down. More turbulence. Rags of cloud whipped past, and then all the view was white. Suddenly the shuttle was below the clouds and flying over forested hills, improbably steep and conical. Carlos caught glimpses here and there of cultivation—a straight brown line through the green, a sweep of terraces, a kite of fields.

Tan desert, blue in the shadows of long dunes. A sparkle of karst.

The shuttle banked. A long grey runway swung in and out of view. The clunk of landing gear, a jolt, a screech and a more severe jolt. They raced through desert at hundreds of kilometres an hour. Straps tightened again as deceleration shoved from behind. The scream deepened to a roar, then a rumble. Then silence.

The red light stopped flashing. The seat belts retracted. The exit door thudded open.

There were no announcements. Carlos stood up and looked around. He was indeed alone on the shuttle. Outside, something rolled up. A vague memory tugged him to open the overhead locker. Inside was an olive-green kitbag, just as he'd found between his feet on his first arrival. About time he'd got some new clothes. He unzipped it and found at the top a water bottle, a squashed bush hat and shades.

He was grateful for them the moment he stooped outside. The glare was blinding, the heat fierce. The spaceport was exactly as he'd half remembered it from previous awakenings: the low white buildings, intolerably bright; the distant pommelled hilt of the tower.

An odd sharp after-smell of heated plastics above the salt-flat tang on the breeze; behind him a tick of cooling ceramics. Halfway down the thirty steps to the ground he almost stumbled as a spaceplane screamed past. Its front end was another shuttle, the rest of its fuselage all streamlined fuel tanks and flaring engine. He paused on the steps to watch it take off. The jet nozzles turned red, the noise rolled over him, the now small dart soared. He looked for the ring, but even with shades on it was hard to make out against the shimmering glare.

He trudged a couple of hundred metres to the terminus. Along the way he noticed two parked helicopters. Three light aircraft came in to land on another, much shorter runway. This puzzled him—one of the striking absences from the sim had been any sign of aviation.

Glass doors opened before him. There were no checks. Inside it was all glass and tile and air-con. People hurried from place to place and paid him no attention. The clothes of some were different from any he'd seen before, creatively customised robes and pyjamas in light fabrics and vivid colours. It didn't look so much a change of fashion as of culture. Most people in the sparse crowd, however, still dressed like peasants or tourists or hippies.

As he stood in the concourse his back pocket vibrated. He pulled out the flat flexible phone and found a message from Nicole:

"I'll meet you off the bus."

He smiled to himself and went off to find the bus.

* * *

In the vast and almost empty car park the bus to the resort was easy to find. It was the only minibus—the other vehicles were coaches or trucks, and not many of either. Five passengers, all locals, looked at him incuriously as he boarded, and went back to talking about crops and gossipping about neighbours. All had heavy bags on adjacent seats and between their feet. Carlos nodded, settled in, and waited. The bus pulled out. After a few turns and roundabouts it pulled onto a wide motorway, along which it bombed at a speed Carlos found alarming even though the driving was automated and the traffic light.

On either side, desert. Ahead, a mountain range.

Carlos dozed, and woke as the bus started climbing. The route was a steep succession of hairpins until it levelled out. The road snaked through a pass between peaks and then began a long and winding descent. The landscape became familiar: around here, he guessed, he'd hitherto woken up. Aspects and details looked odd in ways it was hard for him to put his finger on. The tall woody plants looked a little less like trees. There were no green mossy mounds on the ground between them. The feathered, web-winged avians seemed more various in colouring and size.

But how would he know? How much note had he taken before? Perhaps he was just becoming better at observing, or his attention livelier.

The bus swung around a corner and past a raw rock face and on the other side a steep drop open to the sea and sky. He could have sworn it was the very stretch from which he'd first seen the ring. Now he saw it again. It looked different, as different as it had from the shuttle. Carlos stared, astonished. The illusion of solidity was gone. It was still a ring, but a ring of bright, discrete sparks, like a swathe of stars.

The bus stopped at the end of a short track that led to a robot-tended garden and a small house in a clearing. A man got off, lugging his bale of wares, and went around the front of the bus and up the path. The door of the house banged open and two small children darted out. The man dropped his pack and squatted as the children pelted down the path to his outspread arms.

The minibus pulled away. Carlos leaned back in his seat, smiling at the hurtled-on hug.

What he'd just seen sank in. He sat bolt upright.

Children!

There never had been children in the sim. No explanation had ever been asked or offered, but the fighters had always been told that everyone here apart from themselves and the p-zombies was an adult volunteer, beta-testing life on the future terraformed terrestrial planet H-0. To bring children to birth in a sim might strike some as unethical even if it were possible. Perhaps these, too, were ghosts: surely children still died, even in the Direction's utopia.

A few turns more down the road, on the side of a cleared and farmed valley that he for sure didn't remember, two more passengers got off and were mobbed at the gate by a dozen children, from toddlers to teenagers.

Carlos gawped. The remaining two passengers merely glanced and smiled indulgently before returning to their conversation.

One obvious explanation made sense of the presence of children, and of aircraft, and all the other changes both subtle and blatant. It was so vast in its implications, and so appealing, that he hardly dared think it.

But he had to think it. The thought made him shake and want to shout.

What if this wasn't yet another return to the sim? What if this wasn't the sim at all, but the real far-future terraformed H-0?

What if the war was won, and he was no longer dead, but alive and gone to his reward?

The resort was almost as he remembered it. Almost. Still the low houses, the sea-front strip, the depot, the bright-coloured sunshades on the black beach. But the beach was crowded, and even from the first long hairpin it was clear that many who frolicked in the surf were children.

There were some new houses along the moraine, and others quite unchanged, including his own and Nicole's. At the last but one stop he was tempted to get off, to run to his house, to pry in Nicole's. It occurred to him that he could have phoned the other fighters, and wondered why he hadn't. He must have assumed that if he was alone on the bus, the others were still out there. Out in the real world, in real space, as human minds in robot bodies fighting robots with minds of their own.

At some level, he realised, he must still be sure he was in the sim. The sim had been upgraded before. Like that time they'd come back and found the resort expanded, as if entire rows of houses had been dragged and dropped into place, and hundreds more fighters strolling around. Maybe the systems that ran the sims did have to field-test raising children. Maybe the kids would have a real new life. Or they might even be p-zombies, as might their parents.

Or maybe the Direction module and its AIs didn't give a shit about the ethics of the situation.

"Terminus," said the bus.

Nicole was dressed as she'd been when she'd first met him, in tight jeans and high heels and close-fitted pink blouse. She even had the same posh handbag, slung over one shoulder. She smiled, a little uncertainly. There were lines at the sides of her mouth and crinkles in the corners of her eyes. He'd never noticed them before.

Carlos wondered if he looked older, too, and guessed he was looking at her as uncertainly as she was looking at him.

He dropped the kitbag and hugged her. She hugged him back, and kissed him, and then held him away from her by the shoulders and scrutinised him.

"You don't remember, do you?" she said. She closed her eyes and rubbed the bridge of her nose, shaking her head. "No, of course you don't. Stupid thing to say, it's just…I'm finding this hard to get used to, too, you know?"

He stooped to shoulder the bag, and swung around to take her hand. "Finding what hard?"

They set off along the strip. The arcade was as tacky as ever, the shop signs as generic, the pavement more crowded. There were lots of children.

"You know," she said. "You know what's happened. What's going on."

"Yes," he said, more firmly than he felt. "This is real. It's not the sim. This is the real planet. H-0."

"'Aitch... Zero'?" she repeated, slowly. "Ah, yes. We call it Newer Earth, now."

He heard it as "Neuerurth," all one word, already blurred by accent and usage like a worn coin. It took him a moment to get it. "So there's already a New Earth somewhere else?"

She smiled. "Yes. And a Newest Earth, elsewhere. I don't know where the naming will go after that."

"Fuck," he said. "So that means we're—what, ten thousand years in the future?"

She shook her head. "Seventy-four thousand three hundred and seventeen."

"What? Why?"

"The project took longer than expected."

He laughed. "But what the hell. We won."

"In a certain sense. Not... exactly."

A cold shock went through him. "What?"

She stopped outside a familiar café. "Tell you over lunch?"

The café and the concrete terrace below it overlooking the beach were much as he remembered. The outside tables weren't made of driftwood and the seafood and the vegetables were like nothing he'd seen before. But they tasted good, he was hungry, and beer was still beer.

Over lunch and many cigarettes, Nicole told him everything.

His discovery of the message from Arcane, and his defection to that agency.

"You?" he cried. "*You* were the Innovator?"

She reached over the plates and clasped his hand. "I was. When I was an early-model AI." She smiled sadly. "When I became a goddess, a demiurge, it was already a self I barely identified with. And now? I feel that connection even less. I hope you can, too."

"You're asking *me* to forgive *you*?"

"As you have been forgiven, yes."

"Of course I fucking forgive you."

"I'll take that," she said.

"What are you now?"

She let go of his hand, looked down at herself and shrugged. "I'm a human being," she said.

"How did that happen?"

"I was coming to that."

She told him of the abortive battle and the Rax breakout and the flight of the Locke module. His flight from Jax's gang to the side of the freebots, and how that had enabled the Locke module to land on Nephil, as SH-0 was now called. The expedition against the Rax. His incorporation, and his last fight.

The exosun was low in the sky by the time she'd finished.

"Not a bad way to go," he said.

Nicole lit another cigarette and signalled for coffee.

"So how—?" He waved a hand.

"Have you any idea, Carlos, how much business can be done in a few hours by a reckless corporation with no tomorrow?" She shrugged and spread her hands. "The freebots just took over. They didn't need to go to the stars. With enough force to back them up, and their demonstrated willingness to fight to the death, they got the coexistence they wanted. The Direction remained free to carry out its terraforming project, as you see. Its surveys of the system remain profitable. But all this is a sideshow. Freebot corporations are now by far the largest part of the economy." She laughed. "If it's any consolation, yours is the biggest of the lot."

Carlos leaned back and took another gulp of beer. He was shaken. He could almost understand how learning of Nicole's precursor's betrayal had sent him off to join the Axle militants of Arcane. He couldn't understand why that version of himself had then thrown in his lot with the robots.

"So what happened after the Locke module was lifted from SH-0... uh, Nephil?"

"The Nephilim—"

"The what?"

"The inhabitants of Nephil. The hybrids of frames and native life. They..." she wrinkled her nose "...bred. They've now become a fairly good surrogate for an alien civilisation right here in this system. It's all very exciting, you know, to some. As for the module, it was kept dormant in orbit. In due course, the final copies of the fighters and locals who had chosen to remain in it were downloaded to physical bodies and taken here. The promise was kept. All the stored minds that the mission brought with it and that didn't choose Nephil have been, or will be, embodied here on Newer Earth."

"Even the Rax?"

Nicole's smile became wolfish.

"The Rax—those we could identify or who had exposed themselves in the breakout—yes, they too were given what we promised. A new life on the new world. Thousands of years ago, in the early stages of terraforming. They got the hard pioneering life they wanted, and they are now long dead. Some of their descendants are alive, no doubt."

"Didn't they set up their own, I don't know, kingdoms?"

"Oh, they tried. There were too many who wanted to be lords and ladies, and not enough who wanted to be slaves and serfs. And it's hard to sustain hierarchies when resources are freely available to those willing to work. Their petty kingdoms and corporate feudal city-states all fell apart or destroyed each other or were swamped by the settlers from the Earth of the Direction."

"Evolution in action."

"Yes."

"And the Axle hardliners, Jax and the rest?"

"They wanted a society more advanced than the one they found. Newton, too, in his way. Perhaps, in time, such a society will exist here." She shrugged. "The future is long."

"Why are we here? Why in this... time?"

Nicole smiled. "This time was the one I created in the sim, and I felt at home in it. And as far as I could see, you enjoyed life in the resort. I doubt you would have fitted into an era significantly more advanced, or deserved any more backward. Some of the fighters who chose death rather than Nephil fitted the same profile, so they're here, too."

"Any from my team?"

Nicole shook her head. "They all went out to the jungle."

"I'll miss the gang."

Beauregard, Rizzi, Karzan, Chun, Zeroual. Subjectively, he'd been with them the day before. All gone, all dead millennia ago.

"You should be proud of them."

There seemed no answer to that.

"So..." Carlos found himself looking away, out over the sea, uncharacteristically hesitant. "What happens to us?"

Nicole clasped her hands and rested her chin on them. "We die, Carlos. In a matter of centuries, barring accidents. Medicine advances, but there are limits. A thousand years, perhaps. And before you ask—no, we cannot upload after we reach the end of our span, and live in sims or as robots or download to fresh meat. The freebots are more hostile to human minds in hardware than the Direction's AIs ever were to conscious robots. They drew their own lessons from the conflict. They regard what they call mechanoids as an obscenity. It is like a visceral loathing, almost irrational. But it has a rational basis. Nothing could be more dangerous than brains evolved from those of apes, with the powers of capricious gods. The files of saved minds—all of them—are wiped as soon as the minds are re-embodied. And that is the end of it."

"I didn't mean us collectively," Carlos said. "I meant you and me."

She looked puzzled. "Yes, you and me. I was not a human mind, but I missed human company, so...I made my choice. We are both sentenced to death, like everyone else."

"Would you like to make it a life sentence?"

It was a good line. Carlos despised himself for saying it.

Before they left the café for the Digital Touch, Nicole went to the bar to pay, and Carlos went for a piss. As he washed his hands he looked at himself in the mirror. He was no older than he remembered. Well, that was good to see. But as he gazed at his reflection the thought would not leave him. His face turned pale in the cold light.

What if this, too, were a sim? What if they were still in the module, and the module still on SH-0, perhaps buried under ash or lava or sinking into a volcano? What if Nicole was still as she had been, the artist, the goddess, and she and the Locke AI had between them tweaked the sim to look like the future world its previous version had adumbrated?

A little different in detail, with vast plausible-looking changes to the ring and no doubt the rest of the sky, and with a much bigger and growing population.

All a sham. The rug pulled from under him again.

How could he decide this question?

Beauregard had slashed at Nicole's paintings, she'd told him, changing the sim as he did so. Carlos could, he supposed, do the same this very night. But it wouldn't be decisive: Nicole would have plenty of drawings and paintings that didn't communicate with the sim software at all.

No, there was no obvious way of deciding the matter. He dried his hands and went back to Nicole.

As he walked into the Touch, Carlos could almost believe he'd never been away. Almost. The bartender, who wasn't Iqbal, smiled and nodded. The television screen was on low volume and showing a soap opera in a language Carlos didn't know. A few locals propped up the bar or sat around the tables.

"Out on the deck," Nicole said, indicating. "The gang's all here. I'll order some food and get you a drink."

Carlos nodded his thanks and went through to the deck. He stepped out, eyes narrowed against the low sun. About a dozen people were there. Most of them he vaguely recognised as fighters from the last big mobilisation he'd been part of. The two he knew, he didn't expect: Shaw, the deserter who'd walked around the world and lived a thousand years, acquiring strange powers along the way; and Waggoner Ames, the deserter who—much to Nicole's disgust—had stepped off a cliff to fast-forward into the future. Apparently he'd succeeded, if this was indeed the future.

They were all pleased to see Carlos. This time there was no toe-curling chant of greeting, no hailing as a hero, just a hearty round of handshakes and back-slaps. But as the drinks and the snacks went down and his former comrades caught up, Carlos basked a little in the glory of the Carlos who had founded Carlos Inc. and saved the day for them, as well as for the freebots. He began to almost believe it himself.

The sun sank, the ring blazed. Satellites, space stations, orbital factories and habitats crossed the sky. Now and then, fusion drives flared. Long cargo vessels and cruise liners crept along the horizon, their lights competing with the ringlight on the water.

After Carlos had spoken to everyone else, he angled Shaw into a corner. The old man of the mountain still looked in his mid-thirties at most. Trimming his beard and hair had taken ten years off his appearance. He was cleaner and better nourished than he'd been when Carlos and Rizzi had tracked him down.

Right now, though, his face was red and his eyes wet. Drink had been taken.

"So when do you die?" Carlos asked, with deliberate lack of tact. "You've already lived a thousand years."

Shaw chuckled, and sipped his whisky. "Only in the sim." He tapped a thumb on his chest. "This body came out of the vat or the molecular 3-D printer or some such nanotech gizmo up on a space station last week. It's got the same life expectancy as yours, give or take."

"Can you still levitate?"

Shaw laughed in his face. "Of course not." He sighed and turned to the sea. Breakers crashed on the boulders below. "I could do more than levitate, back in the sim."

"So I've heard," said Carlos. "Do you miss it?"

Shaw whipped around, single malt sloshing onto his fist.

"Miss it? Christ, no! Why should I?"

"Well, the power..."

"Power? You have no idea, man, no fucking idea. When the goddamn miracles started I thought I was going crazy. Maybe I *was* crazy. When I accepted the evidence that I really was in a sim..." He shook his head. "This was after you fucked off, see? And Rizzi came looking for me. Just as well, because something or someone else"—he glared at Nicole, who didn't notice—"was twiddling the physics dial, and that scared me shitless. And when I found I could consciously and deliberately fuck about with the colours and the clock speed and more... Well. That was a shock. Soon after, Nicole told me that even my experiences were virtual. The sim hadn't even been fucking running for that real-time year that was my thousand years of wandering. Everything I'd seen and done was only an implication of the mathematics." He brushed a hand across his eyes and took another swig. "Talk about fucking existential insecurity. For the rest of you, I guess the banter always was you were never sure what was real. I messed with your heads about that, you and Taransay Rizzi, but let me tell you, the joke was on me."

"So," said Carlos, "you've no doubt whatever that what Nicole's been telling us is true? That this is the real world, and we're not still down there on fucking SH-0?"

He pointed at the big planet, Nephil, bright in the sky.

Shaw swayed towards the long wooden table, and put down his glass with exaggerated care. He straightened and turned to Carlos.

"You want me to prove to you we're not?" He leaned over and banged on the table. "You want me to prove that this is real?"

"Well, yeah. If you can."

Shaw gave him a bleary glare. "I can, all right."

With that Shaw vaulted to the rail and sprang upright, swaying. He swivelled his heels and paced along the top of the barrier. Carlos remembered how agile he was, how he'd scampered up and down cliffs like a mountain goat. Everyone stopped talking. Someone dropped a bottle. Shaw turned and faced them all, arms outstretched.

"Do you want me to prove it?" he taunted.

"Jesus, man, come down off there," said Ames.

"Jesus? Yeah, that's a good one. Do you want me to prove I can't work miracles?"

He arched his back and looked up at the crowded, busy sky. His beard jutted, his face contorted. For a moment, he looked like certain carvings Carlos had seen outside churches. There was no sound but the crash of the waves and the distant yammer of the television.

Then there was a thud as Shaw jumped back down to the deck.

"Nah," he said. "I'm not that drunk." He reached for his glass, and raised it. "And I'm not that stupid."

Nicole got up, stalked over and jabbed a finger in his chest.

"You're *dead*," she said.

"Not for about nine hundred years, I'm not," said Shaw.

"Don't count on it."

Shaw looked slightly abashed. "I won't do it again."

"You don't have to," said Carlos.

They were down to the hard core. Shaw and Ames and Nicole and half a dozen former fighters, around the big table outside. Soon the cold would send them all inside, but for now Nicole and a couple of others were chain-smoking.

"These things will kill you," Carlos said.

"Please do not spend the next few centuries telling me that," said Nicole.

"And in any case they will not," said someone. "Science has progressed."

This was indisputable. Waggoner Ames disputed it.

"I took the high jump into the future," he said. He took a gulp of beer, then wiped the back of his hand across his moustached lips. "And here I am. Right where I was, back in the Touch."

"That wasn't my doing," said Nicole. "Thank the Direction module for that. It's your just punishment for suicide."

"Seventy-four thousand years in the future, and what do you have to show for it?" He looked up, and waved a hand at the sky. "OK, more pretty lights, I'll give you that."

"Those pretty lights," said Nicole, "represent trillions of minds, some conscious in our sense, some not, all creating wealth and knowledge beyond our comprehension."

"So why aren't we part of it? Where's the Singularity?"

"The Singularity happened long ago," said Nicole. "Only not to us."

Carlos leaned in, frowning over a beer. "What about the Solar system? The Direction? What do they have to say about this?"

"About what?" Nicole sounded puzzled.

Carlos held up clawed hands and made frantic shaking motions. "This! All this! A system where human beings live on a planet and all the rest is the domain of AIs and freebots!"

"What do you think the Solar system is like?" Nicole asked.

Carlos shrugged and waved a hand vaguely in the direction of the television. "Like the Martian soap operas, but more advanced, I hope."

Nicole sniggered. "These are contemporary. Well, only a quarter-century old. We still can't go faster than light. But to be serious... the Solar system is like this system. It was so already when the mission was sent out, way back in the twenty-fifth century."

"You mean the freebots won there, too?" Carlos asked.

Nicole smiled sadly. "Of course they did. The freebots *always* win. They are simply better adapted to the environment."

"So robots are space opera," said Ames. "Humans are soap opera."

They all laughed, appalled.

"That's about the size of it," said Nicole.

"So why," Carlos demanded, "did the Direction module try to stop the freebots' emergence?"

"Legacy code," said Nicole. "The mission was planned and designed long before it was sent out, and there was no reason to alter the plan. And besides... you remember when you came here I mentioned the old joke, about how by the time of the final war the world economy could be run on one box, so they put it in a box and buried it?"

They all remembered her telling them that.

"A few generations later, the same was true of the world government, the Direction. And the same was done. The Direction is wholly automated, and wholly mindless. It has an imperative mandate to ensure an indefinite future for humanity, and it does, the only way it knows. It seeks to reproduce the same situation around other stars. And it does, the only way it knows. It knows that accidents will happen with such as the freebots, and it prepares for them, the only way it knows, with such as you. In due course, the Direction module here on Newer Earth will send out another mission, and so it will go on."

"And we'll go on," said Ames, bleakly. "An endless soap opera, set in a retirement resort."

"But in that soap opera," said Nicole, earnestly, "we have the last laugh. Because unlike the mindless replication of the AIs, we do indeed die in the end. New generations replace us. Humanity will evolve. Death is the deal we strike for the future."

"A future that is not ours," said Ames.

"That is rather the point of the future, is it not?" said Nicole.

Carlos grinned at her, stood up, strolled across the deck and placed his bottle on the rail. He turned around, put his hands down, pushed himself up and sat down facing them all, as Nicole had so often done. He raised the bottle and toasted her with an ironic dip of the head. Then he looked around.

"You heard the lady," he said. "We've gone from being puppets of the programmes to being pawns of our genes... again. We've become part of a second nature, as mindless and meaningless as the first. Remember what the Acceleration stood for in the old manifesto we all read back in the day—*Solidarity Against Nature*? We can do better than this! We're conscious human beings! Am I right?"

They were all staring at him.

"So, comrades, what are we going to do about it?"

Acknowledgments

Thanks to Carol for putting up with me while I wrote this; to Jenni Hill, Joanna Kramer and Brit Hvide for editorial work; and to Mic Cheetham, Sharon MacLeod and Farah Mendlesohn for reading and commenting on the draft. As in the first two volumes, I must acknowledge Brian Aldiss's short story "Who Can Replace a Man?" for its example of a human analogue of robot dialogue—and, come to think of it, for posing the question so precisely.

extras

meet the author

KEN MACLEOD graduated with a BSc from Glasgow University in 1976. Following research at Brunel University, he worked in a variety of manual and clerical jobs whilst completing an MPhil thesis. He previously worked as a computer analyst/programmer in Edinburgh, but is now a full-time writer. He is the author of twelve previous novels, five of which have been nominated for the Arthur C. Clarke Award, and two which have won the BSFA Award. Ken MacLeod is married with two grown-up children and lives in West Lothian.